J O H N   M I L T O N

was born in London on December 9, 1608. A brilliant scholar, he received his B.A. and M.A. from Christ's College, Cambridge, and began writing poetry. Instead of entering the ministry, he retired to his father's country house and for the next five years read day and night, devouring most of the existing written works in English, Greek, Latin, and Italian. During this period he wrote the masque *Comus* (1634) and "Lycidas" (1637), an elegy memorializing a college classmate. In 1638 he went on a tour of Europe, spending most of his time in Italy. He returned home prematurely because of the religious unrest in England and began writing tracts that branded him a radical. In 1642 he married Mary Powell, a seventeen-year-old girl. Within six weeks, she returned to her parents' home, and Milton wrote a series of angry pamphlets advocating divorce on the grounds of incompatibility. Eventually, she returned and bore him four children, three of whom survived. By 1651 Milton's poor eyesight failed completely, leaving him blind. After his wife's death, he remarried, only to have his second wife die some months after childbirth. His third marriage, to Elizabeth Minshull, was a longer and happier one. At the Restoration, Milton narrowly escaped execution because of his politics, but was left impoverished. Now he returned to writing poetry and created the masterpieces for which he will be forever remembered, beginning with *Paradise Lost* (1667). He followed this epic with *Paradise Regained* and *Samson Agonistes* (jointly published in 1671). Milton died in 1674. Along with Chaucer and Shakespeare, Milton is one of the true giants of our language.   CLASSIC

*Ask your bookseller for Bantam Classics
by these British and Irish writers:*

JANE AUSTEN

J. M. BARRIE

CHARLOTTE BRONTË

EMILY BRONTË

FRANCES HODGSON BURNETT

FANNY BURNEY

LEWIS CARROLL

GEOFFREY CHAUCER

WILKIE COLLINS

JOSEPH CONRAD

DANIEL DEFOE

CHARLES DICKENS

SIR ARTHUR CONAN DOYLE

GEORGE ELIOT

FORD MADOX FORD

E. M. FORSTER

KENNETH GRAHAME

THOMAS HARDY

JAMES JOYCE

RUDYARD KIPLING

D. H. LAWRENCE

W. SOMERSET MAUGHAM

JOHN STUART MILL

E. NESBIT

SIR WALTER SCOTT

WILLIAM SHAKESPEARE

GEORGE BERNARD SHAW

MARY SHELLEY

ROBERT LOUIS STEVENSON

BRAM STOKER

JONATHAN SWIFT

H. G. WELLS

OSCAR WILDE

VIRGINIA WOOLF

THE
ANNOTATED
MILTON

Complete English Poems with
annotations lexical, syntactic,
prosodic, and referential

edited by

BURTON RAFFEL

BANTAM BOOKS
New York   Toronto   London   Sydney   Auckland

A   B A N T A M   C L A S S I C

THE ANNOTATED MILTON

A Bantam Classic Book / September 1999

Cover painting: Martin, John (1789–1854).
The Fallen Angels entering Pandemonium from *Paradise Lost*, Book 1,
exh. 1841/Art Resource, NY

ISBN 0-553-58110-4

Published simultaneously in the United States and Canada

Bantam Books are published by Bantam Books, a division of Random House,
Inc. Its trademark, consisting of the words "Bantam Books" and the portrayal
of a rooster, is Registered in U.S. Patent and Trademark Office and in other
countries. Marca Registrada. Bantam Books, 1540 Broadway, New York, New
York 10036.

PRINTED IN THE UNITED STATES OF AMERICA

WCD   10 9 8 7 6 5 4 3 2 1

CONTENTS

CHRONOLOGY

1646	*Poems*
	29 July, daughter Anne born
1647	March, death of Milton's father
1648	25 October, daughter Mary born
1649	30 January, Charles I executed
	The Tenure of Kings and Magistrates
	March, appointed Secretary for Foreign Tongues, Council of State
1650	left eye fails
1651	*Defensio pro Populo Anglicano*
	16 March, son John, born
1652	February/March, complete blindness
	2 May, daughter Deborah born
	May, Mary Powell Milton's death
	16 June, death of son, John
1654	*Defensio Secunda*
1655	*Pro Se Defensio*
1656	November, married Katherine Woodcock
1657	19 October, daughter Katherine born
1658	February, death of Katherine Woodcock Milton
	17 March, death of daughter Katherine
	3 September, Oliver Cromwell's death
1659	*A Treatise of Civil Power in Ecclesiastical Causes*
	Likeliest Means to Remove Hirelings out of the Church
1660	*The Ready and Easy Way to Establish a Free Commonwealth*
	May, Charles II restored to the throne
	Milton arrested, released
1663	February, married Elizabeth Minshull
1665	resided at Chalfont St. Giles during plague
1667	February, ten-book edition of *Paradise Lost*
1669	*Accidence Commenced Grammar*
1670	*History of Britain*
1671	*Paradise Regained* and *Samson Agonistes*
1672	*Joannis Miltoni Angli, Artis Logicae Plenior Institutio*

PREFACE

The first version of what would become this book was written into the pages of another editor's disservedly famous edition of Milton. Principally lexical and syntactic commentary, these early annotations stemmed directly from an extremely common quandary, namely, a teacher fundamentally (though by no means completely) dissatisfied with the textbook from which, for lack of anything better suited to *his* classroom, he goes on teaching. That sort of dissatisfaction can be lived with; it can finally be put to the side; or it can lead, as mine has, to a completely new book.

I teach Milton as an English poet, one of the very greatest, most influential, important, and deeply challenging the language has ever known. Although I firmly believe, like most scholars, that the more we know about any writer the more we can understand and also appreciate the resonating excellences and profundities of his or her work, I also believe that some of the things we can know are more useful than are others. Milton's English poetry seems to me so overwhelmingly primary to both appreciation and understanding of his place in English literature that his Latin poetry shrinks to tertiary significance, and his profusely vigorous prose to secondary significance. Accordingly, this edition of Milton contains none of the Latin (or the Italian) poems, either in the original language(s) or in translation. It contains none of Milton's prose.

The text of the English poems, however, is not only complete, but has been conservatively modernized and edited for maximum accessibility. Nothing has been done to interfere in any way whatever with the prosody of these poems. The vexing problem of syllabified versus unsyllabified vowels has been preempted by (1) the use of spelling to indicate each prosodically suppressed vowel (usually by means of an apostrophe, sometimes by such spellings as "shouldst" or "didst"), and (2) the addition of an accent mark each time a vowel is syllabified ("wingèd," "blessèd"). My prosodic markings are consistent throughout this book. When, therefore, a word such as "winged" is mono- rather than bisyllabic, I have added neither an apostrophe nor an accent mark; the reader can assume that any word without one of those marks does not in my judgment require one.

Rather too much has been made of Milton's spelling, much of which is conventional and, though appropriate to his time, without significance in ours. His punctuation is in general (though not universally) a reliable guide to verse movement. I have punctuated, and capitalized, as conservatively as possible. But I have not hesitated to interpret Milton's use of semicolons and colons as requiring, in our time, a sentence-ending period. Nor have I hesitated to add reader-friendly paragraphing.

I would have been happier had my annotations been able to be placed alongside the line they refer to. The economics of publishing makes this impossible. But since I do not believe that lexical annotations consisting only of a single word are truly satisfactory, I have often given three or four or even more words in each gloss. Placing all annotations at the bottom of the page does, therefore, have at least the advantage of clearly separating annotations one from the other.

Most of my lexical annotations are to words rather than to phrases, clauses, or sentences. As a teacher, I have found that students need to know what the components mean, just as much as they need to know the meaning of the finished product. Indeed, understanding syntax becomes a good deal easier when the components are clearly understood—and many of my annotations are syntactic as well as lexical. All syntactic material is placed in square brackets: [verb]. If, as is usually the case, annotations are both lexical *and* syntactic, the lexical portion always precedes the syntactic.

I have tried to annotate everything a student—any student, all students—might need to know. Not being able to predict on which page a student might first come upon material opaque to him or her, I have annotated repeatedly, tirelessly, and for some readers surely excessively. But I would much rather be safe than sorry.

Translations of the original (and it is striking how often Milton, though writing in a form of English, requires something very like translation) are always set in quotation marks. Renderings of anything more than a single word, however, are signaled first by a repetition of the words being annotated, and second by an equal sign placed immediately after that repetition:

evil store = an abundance of evil

those in servitude: servants

When the annotation is more commentary than rendering, the colon is replaced by an equal sign:

due time = in the time that, properly, it should take

When there are multiple meanings (and Milton is enormously fond of layered meaning, as also he is far fonder of wordplay, including puns, than his reputation would suggest) that are sufficiently distinct from one another, I have grouped them under numbered headings:

(1) perilous, rash, risky, (2) enterprising

Lexical glosses involving more than one word, but not involving semantic layering, simply employ commas:

common, ordinary, uneducated

The slash is used to indicate that one of the words or phrases in a multiword annotative definition has distinct alternative possibilities:

having no material being/body

care for/prediction of the future

Note that the slash places in the alternative *only* the word immediately before it. Thus the first example above should be understood as "having no material being or body," and the second as "care for or prediction of the future." One additional example may make this clearer:

not maternal/the mother of

This should be understood, accordingly, as "not maternal, not the mother of."

Referential (informational) annotations use both the colon and, somewhat differently, the equal sign:

a Titan, daughter of Gaia (earth) by Zeus: goddess of justice

Horeb = Sinai, in Exodus and Deuteronomy

Nimrod ("hunter"): see Genesis 10:8–10

When I do not know with reasonable certainty what Milton is referring to or saying, I have said so, using a simple question mark:

not specified: the basic nature of the Godhead?

face (defiantly)? await?

Although commentary, in the usual scholarly meaning, has been almost completely avoided in these annotations, it has sometimes been unavoidable. I have kept it as brief as possible, and have usually introduced it by the signal "i.e.":

i.e., the act of building, *not* the structure being built

The pronunciation of Greek names and, on occasion, of certain other words, often requires elucidation, which I have kept as minimal as possible:

Calliope [4 syllables, 2nd and 4th accented]

Hecate [trisyllabic], ghost-world goddess

One early reader commented that users of this book might sometimes find themselves dizzy, forced constantly to look up and down the page, from text to footnotes and back, on and on and on. Depending on the opacity of Milton's vocabulary, the turgidity of his syntax, and the frequency and insistence of his allusions, these pages necessarily vary enormously in their density of annotation. Lexically confident readers are advised to ignore as many of my annotations as they can. But it would be much appreciated if lexically well informed readers, and indeed anyone who finds any of the errors, omissions, and unclarities I have struggled to eliminate, would send me corrections.

INTRODUCTION

Understanding and appreciating John Milton—Milton, that is, as an English poet—depends less on a knowledge of Christian doctrine or the rise and then the decline and fall of Puritanism as a governing force in British life, less on a wide-ranging familiarity with classical poetry and medieval and Renaissance European scholarship (including but certainly not limited to alchemy, astronomy, and astrology), and less on an awareness of the intellectual currents of seventeenth-century Europe than on the ability to understand why poetry such as the following—*not* by Milton, but written nearly a hundred years before the publication of *Paradise Lost*—maintained a continuing and sometimes worshipful readership well into the twentieth century:

Lo I the man, whose Muse whilom did mask,
> As time her taught, in lowly Shepherd's weeds,
> Am now enforced a far unfitter task,
> For trumpets stern to change mine oaten reeds,
> And sing of Knights' and Ladies' gentle deeds;
> Whose praises having slept in silence long,
> Me, all too mean, the sacred Muse areeds
> > **[advises, teaches]**
> To blazon broad amongst her learnèd throng:
Fierce wars and faithful loves shall moralize my song.

Help then, O holy Virgin, chief of nine,
> Thy weaker Novice to perform thy will,
> Lay forth out of thine everlasting scryne [chest for
> > books/documents]
> The antique rolls which there lie hidden still,
> Of Faery knights and fairest Tanaquil [wife of
> > Tarquinius; here Queen Elizabeth]

Whom that most noble Briton Prince so long
Sought through the world, and suffered so much ill,
That I must rue his undeservèd wrong:
O help thou my weak wit, and sharpen my dull tongue.

The scholarly (but not necessarily merely literate) reader will immediately recognize these lines, and their author, and will know the massive and so long beloved English epic from which they come, Edmund Spenser's *The Fairy Queen*. And any reader at all, after a quarter of an hour's exposure to *Paradise Lost* in particular, will have at least some sense of the similarities of Milton's work to that of Spenser. These include:

- insistently lofty, elevated diction, expressive of the urgent conviction that poet and reader are engaged not in some casual, friendly dialogue or in mere entertainment, but in an activity at once both serious and highly moral; note that in line 7 the Muse is called "sacred"

- constant, even fundamental reference to past persons and events, including regular allusions to past intellectual belief structures (and note, please, the use of the plural; we here meet classical Muses and shepherds along with medieval knights, Roman along with British history, pagan along with Christian religion, and so on)

- frequent reliance on archaically tinted vocabulary (I have here modernized spelling, but the attentive reader will not be fooled)

- markedly convoluted syntax, with sentences being stretched (and bent) over many lines

- what modern poets and readers might call a long breath line—rhythms that elongate and tend to roll like the waves of the sea, rather than (as in much modern poetry) poke and dart even as they loll

- reliance on more or less objectified conventions, which are the very farthest thing from "personal" to either the poet or his poem: e.g., the confession in line 3 not only of the poet's incapacity for *this* task but of his general poetic ineptitude (he is here called to "a far unfitter task"—and see also "Me, all too mean," in line 7, and the reference to his "weak wit" and "dull tongue" in the final line of the second stanza)

- a set of assumptions, apparently fixed and settled for all time, about trumpets being "stern" (line 4), knights and ladies "gentle" (line 5) and their prior praises plainly insufficient (line 6), poets and their readers being "learnèd" (line 8), what is old being always good (the "antique rolls" of line 13), royalty invariably "noble" if male and "fair" or even "fairest" if female (lines 14 and 15), and princely suffering being both romantic and unfair (lines 16 and 17)

And there is more. But this is the introduction to a book about John Milton, not Edmund Spenser, vastly influential on Milton as Spenser clearly was. All the same, to nail the point home, let me quickly carry the story of Spenser's fame and influence into the nineteenth and, just barely, the twentieth century. William Wordsworth, at age thirty-one, was reported on Monday, the sixteenth of November, 1801, to be feeling "some what weakish," but in compensation (and perhaps as a curative) "now at 7 o'clock reading Spenser" (*Journals of Dorothy Wordsworth*, 59). Eight days later, "after tea William read Spenser[,] now and then a little aloud to us," his wife and sister (62). And on Thursday, the first of July, 1802, said to be "a very rainy day," we learn that "we had a nice walk, and afterwards sate by a nice snug fire and William read Spenser and I read 'As you like it' " (144). Plainly, Spenser traveled and was seen to belong in some pretty special company. Indeed, the very first poem in *The Complete Poetical Works and Letters of John Keats*, identified therein as "the earliest known composition of Keats," is an "Imitation of Spenser" (1). Spenser's tracks are all over the Keats volume, from a "Spenserian Stanza, written at the close of book v. of THE FAERIE

QUEENE" (8–9), a sonnet "To Spenser" (42), and three more "Spenserian Stanzas" aimed in 1819 at Charles Armitrage Brown, in response (in Keats' own words) to "Brown this morning . . . writing some Spenserian stanzas against Mrs., Miss [Fanny] Brawne and me."

And Spenser's reach extends, as I have indicated, a good century further. In an 1858 letter to his sister, sent from Oxford, John Addington Symonds requests that he be sent his copy of Spenser (the request placed, in sequence, between Chaucer and "the large Milton" (*The Letters of John Addington Symonds*, I, 167). In another letter home the next year, he asks, "Has a small Spenser in 6 diamond volumes, come for me from Jeffries in Redcliffe Street? I ordered it when I was last in Clifton" (I, 200). Nor did Symonds' interest flag in later years. Almost thirty years along, he writes to Edmund Gosse, 16 May 1886, from Germany, expressing genuine concern about the possible misattribution of a sixteenth-century poem the style of which "seems to me suspiciously like that of Spenser" (III, 139). Writing in 1896 from his prison cell in Reading, Oscar Wilde requested "Spenser's Poems," among other books (*The Letters of Oscar Wilde*, 405 n). And, finally, in August 1912 Edward Dowden writes that "most of my reading hours were given to Spenser, and once again I went through the 'Faerie Queene' (though I can't say, as Southey did, that I have read it once a year" (*Letters of Edward Dowden*, 381).

Yet Milton not only participates in a long and strong tradition, connecting to it in more ways than I can here comment upon, but he has always been, and still remains, an immensely significant, powerful contributor to that tradition. He draws upon Shakespeare (he was born eight years before Shakespeare's death), as has everyone else. But he also adds to Shakespeare, as most others neither have done nor could do.

He scarce had ceased when the superior fiend
Was moving toward the shore, his ponderous shield,
Ethereal[1] temper,[2] massy, large, and round,
Behind him cast. The broad circumference
Hung on his shoulders like the moon, whose orb

---

[1] celestial
[2] hardness

Through optic glass the Tuscan[3] artist[4] views
At evening, from the top of Fesolé,
Or in Valdarno, to descry[5] new lands,
Rivers, or mountains in her spotty[6] globe.
His spear—to equal which the tallest pine
Hewn on Norwegian hills to be the mast
Of some great ammiral,[7] were but a wand[8]—
He walked with, to support uneasy[9] steps
Over the burning marl,[10] not like those steps
On Heaven's azure. And the torrid clime
Smote[11] on him sore besides, vaulted[12] with fire.

Paradise Lost, 1:284–98

The sweep and grandeur of this portrait of Satan, struggling to preserve his dignity (not to mention his power) even though newly fallen from the glories of heaven to the sulfurous and smoking fields of hell, is unmatchable in English verse. Virgil and even Homer, had they seen (or heard) Milton's description of the "ponderous shield, / Ethereal temper, massy, large, and round, / Behind him cast," the "broad circumference" of which "Hung on his shoulders like the moon," would have recognized and perhaps envied a colleague in and competitor for poetic glory. Milton's uniquely majestic rhetoric, his commanding poetic "voice," seem almost the effect of some marvelously benign Midas touch, turning even tawdriness into magnificent resonance.

It is not difficult, of course, to find this side of Milton, especially in *Paradise Lost* and *Samson Agonistes* but also, in different and younger ways, in *Lycidas* and, fittingly, in his quite early "On Shakespeare," probably written when he was only twenty-two. This is the Milton of whom Douglas Bush could declare, "Whoever the third of English poets may be [Shakespeare and

---

[3] Italian: Galileo
[4] practical scientist, learned man
[5] discover, make known
[6] spotted, patchy
[7] admiral's ship, flagship
[8] straight slender stick
[9] difficult, troublesome
[10] soil
[11] beat/shone strongly
[12] covered, roofed

Chaucer being overwhelming consensus choices for numbers 1 and 2], Milton's place has been next to the throne" (*English Literature in the Earlier Seventeenth Century*, 359). But whether writing about angels or demons, Milton's touch can also be delicate and lyrically shimmering:

> . . . how he fell
> From Heaven they fabled,[13] thrown by angry Jove
> Sheer[14] o'er the crystal battlements.[15] From morn
> To noon he fell, from noon to dewy eve,
> A summer's day, and with the setting sun
> Dropt from the zenith,[16] like a falling star . . .
>
> *Paradise Lost*, 1:740–45

His psychological insights, as well as his sense of inner drama, exceed those of every English poet or dramatist but Shakespeare. Here is Satan, newly arrived in view of the Garden of Eden:

> . . . Horror and doubt distract
> His troubled thoughts, and from the bottom stir
> The Hell within him, for within him Hell
> He brings, and round about him, nor from Hell
> One step, no more than from himself, can fly
> By change of place.
>
> *Paradise Lost*, 4:18–23

This patient, careful, almost tender delineation of devilish torment is a good deal more impressive even than that offered in Marlowe's fine play *Doctor Faustus*: "How comes it, then," asks Faustus of the devil, "that thou art out of hell?" And the devil replies, "Why, this is hell, nor am I out of it" (*The Works of Christopher Marlowe*, ed. Brooke, 155). Marlowe gives us high drama, as does Milton. But Milton gives us more.

And who can forget, once read, the achingly stupendous close to *Lycidas*, composed when Milton was twenty-nine:

---

[13] talked idly, lied about
[14] steeply, perpendicularly
[15] fortifications placed on top of walls
[16] directly overhead

Thus sang the uncouth[17] swain to th' oaks and rills,[18]
While the still morn went out with sandals gray.
He touched the tender stops of various quills,[19]
With eager thought warbling his Doric[20] lay.
And now the sun had stretched out[21] all the hills,
And now was dropped into the western bay.
At last he rose and twitched[22] his mantle blue:
Tomorrow to fresh woods, and pastures new.

Lycidas, 186–93

The very moment he heard (by e-mail) that this edition was in
preparation, a friend of mine, many years away from any connec-
tion with schools or colleges, promptly wrote out from memory a
remarkably accurate transcript of almost fifty lines of *Lycidas*.
That is exactly the sort of response, and the sort of tribute, that
this edition of Milton's English poems is intended to elicit.

The principal function of the introduction to a book like this is to
inform prospective readers of the editor's goals and intentions
and of the nature of the material offered in support of those goals
and intentions in the pages that follow. Introductions to editions
of Milton customarily explain the editor's view of Milton's theo-
logical concerns, usually discussing the poetry's relationship to
those concerns. Biographical information is often set out as well.
(Biographical material is here offered, in capsule form, in the
Chronology, which immediately follows the Contents listing
above.) In this volume, however, much of the necessary theologi-
cal and other informational material is spread throughout the
book, being contained in the annotations (affixed to the poems
for which such information is necessary), these comprising what-
ever value the book may possess. Those who employ this edition
as a university textbook, which in all likelihood will be its chief
use, will have an informed and communicative instructor to
frame additionally needed contexts. And the brief list of sug-

---

[17] unpolished, rough
[18] streams
[19] reeds, pipes, flutes
[20] pastoral
[21] extended across
[22] pulled around him

gested reading at the end of this volume offers, I trust, whatever further guidance may be required, at least in the initial stages of coming to know John Milton's English poetry. Most of the items there cited, of course, contain references to still further critical and historical materials.

THE ANNOTATED
MILTON

A PARAPHRASE ON PSALM 114
[1624]

When the blest seed of Terah's faithful son[1]
After long toil their liberty had won,
And passed from Pharian[2] fields to Canaan land,
Led by the strength of the Almighty's hand,
Jehovah's wonders were in Israel shown,
His praise and glory was in Israel known.
That saw the troubled sea,[3] and shivering fled,
And sought to hide his froth-becurlèd head
Low in the earth. Jordan's clear streams recoil,
As a faint[4] host[5] that hath received the foil.[6]   10
The high, huge-bellied mountains skip like rams
Amongst their ewes, the little hills like lambs.
Why fled the oceans and why skipped the mountains?
Why turned Jordan toward his crystal fountains?
Shake earth, and at the presence be aghast
Of Him that ever was, and aye[7] shall last,
That[8] glassy floods from ruggèd rocks can crush,
And make soft rills[9] from fiery flint-stones gush.

---

[1] Terah = Abraham's father
[2] Egyptian
[3] i.e., the sea saw the strength of the Almighty's hand
[4] cowardly
[5] army
[6] defeat
[7] always, forever
[8] who
[9] streams, brooks

PSALM 136
[*1624*]

Let us with a gladsome mind
Praise the Lord, for He is kind,
      For His mercies aye endure,
      Ever faithful, ever sure.

Let us blaze[10] His name abroad,[11]
For of gods He is the God,
    . For His, etc.

O let us His praises tell,
Who doth the wrathful tyrants quell,[12]
      For His, etc.   10

That with His miracles doth make
Amazèd Heav'n and earth to shake,
      For His, etc.

Who by His wisdom did create
The painted[13] Heav'ns so full of state,[14]
      For His, etc.

Who did the solid earth ordain
To rise above the wat'ry plain,
      For His, etc.

Who by His all-commanding might   20
Did fill the new-made world with light,
      For His, etc.

---

[10] proclaim
[11] widely, at large
[12] destroy, kill, overcome
[13] brightly colored
[14] greatness, power, dignity

And caused the golden-tressèd sun
All the day long his course to run,
    For His, etc.

The hornèd moon to shine by night,
Amongst her spangled sisters bright,
    For His, etc.

He with His thunder-clasping hand
Smote the first-born of Egypt land,   30
    For His, etc.

And in despite of Pharaoh fell,[15]
He brought from thence His Israel,[16]
    For His, etc.

The ruddy waves He cleft in twain,
Of the Erythraean main,[17]
    For His, etc.

The floods stood still like walls of glass
While the Hebrew bands did pass,
    For His, etc.   40

But full soon they did devour
The tawny[18] king with all his power,
    For His, etc.

His chosen people He did bless
In the wasteful[19] wilderness,
    For His, etc.

In bloody battle He brought down
Kings of prowess and renown,
    For His, etc.

---

[15] cruel, terrible, savage [adjective]
[16] the Hebrew people
[17] the Red Sea
[18] brown-skinned
[19] desolate

He foiled bold Seon and his host,   50
That ruled the Amorrean[20] coast,
      For His, etc.

And large-limbed Og[21] He did subdue,
With all his over-hardy[22] crew,
      For His, etc.

And to His servant Israel[23]
He gave their land, therein to dwell,
      For His, etc.

He hath with a piteous eye
Beheld us in our misery,   60
      For His, etc.

And freed us from the slavery
Of the invading enemy,
      For His, etc.

All living creatures He doth feed,
And with full hand supplies their need,
      For His, etc.

Let us therefore warble[24] forth
His mighty majesty and worth,
      For His, etc.   70

That His mansion hath on high,
Above the reach of mortal eye,
      For His mercies aye endure,
      Ever faithful, ever sure.

---

[20] the Amorites, pre-Israelite dwellers in Canaan
[21] Amorite king, and an exceedingly large man
[22] excessively bold, daring
[23] Jacob
[24] to sing, celebrate in song

ON THE DEATH OF A FAIR INFANT DYING OF A COUGH
[1625–26? 1628?]

I

O fairest flower no sooner blown²⁵ but blasted,²⁶
Soft silken primrose fading timelessly,
Summer's chief honor if thou hadst outlasted
Bleak winter's force, that made thy blossom dry,
For he being amorous on that lovely dye
　　　That did thy cheek envermeil,²⁷ thought to kiss,
But killed, alas, and then bewailed his fatal bliss.

II

For since grim Aquilo,²⁸ his²⁹ charioteer,
By boisterous³⁰ rape th' Athenian damsel³¹ got,
He thought it touched³² his deity full near   10
If likewise he some fair one wedded not,³³
Thereby to wipe away the infamous³⁴ blot
　　　Of long-uncoupled bed and childless eld,³⁵
Which 'mongst the wanton³⁶ gods a foul reproach was held.

III

So mounting up in icy-pearlèd car³⁷
Through middle empire of the freezing air
He wandered long, till thee he spied from far.

---

²⁵ blossomed
²⁶ withered
²⁷ color vermilion
²⁸ the north wind (Aquilo = "eagle")
²⁹ winter's
³⁰ rough, coarse, violent
³¹ Orythia, daughter of the king of Athens
³² affected injuriously
³³ i.e., unless he too wedded some fair one
³⁴ notorious
³⁵ maturity, old age
³⁶ frisky, sportive
³⁷ carriage, chariot

There ended was his quest, there ceased his care:
Down he descended from his snow-soft chair,
      But all unwares with his cold-kind embrace   20
Unhoused thy virgin soul from her fair biding[38] place.

IV

Yet art thou not inglorious[39] in thy fate,
For so Apollo, with unweeting[40] hand,
Whilom[41] did slay his dearly lovèd mate,[42]
Young Hyacinth, born on Eurotas' strand,[43]
Young Hyacinth, the pride of Spartan land,
      But then transformed him to a purple flower:
Alack, that so to change thee winter had no power.

V

Yet can I not persuade me thou art dead
Or that thy corpse corrupts in earth's dark womb,   30
Or that thy beauties lie in wormy bed,
Hid from the world in a low-delvèd[44] tomb.
Could Heav'n, for pity, thee so strictly doom?
      Oh no! for something in thy face did shine
Above mortality that showed thou wast divine.

VI

Resolve[45] me, then, O soul most surely blest
(If so it be that thou these plaints[46] dost hear)!
Tell me, bright spirit, where'er thou hoverest,
Whether above that high, first-moving sphere
Or in the Elysian fields (if such there were),   40

---

[38] dwelling
[39] shamed, disgraced
[40] unknowing, unwitting
[41] once
[42] Zephyr, the west wind, also loved Hyacinth, and in revenge caused a quoit (iron ring thrown at a peg in the ground) thrown by Apollo to swerve, hit, and kill Hyacinth
[43] Eurotas = Laconian river; strand = bank, shore
[44] shallowly dug? or an in-ground grave rather than a properly elevated tomb structure?
[45] explain, clarify
[46] verses, poem

Oh say me true if thou were mortal wight[47]
And why from us so quickly thou didst take thy flight.

VII

Were thou some star which from the ruined roof
Of shaked Olympus by mischance didst fall?
Which careful Jove in Nature's true behoof[48]
Took up, and in fit[49] place did reinstall?
Or did, of late, earth's sons besiege the wall
      Of shiny Heav'n, and thou some goddess fled
Amongst us here below to hide thy nectared head?

VIII

Or were thou that just maid who once before   50
Forsook the hated earth,[50] O tell me sooth,
And cam'st again to visit us once more?
Or wert thou Mercy, that sweet smiling youth?
Or that crowned matron, sage white-robèd Truth?
      Or any other of that heav'nly brood
Let down in cloudy throne to do the world some good?

IX

Or wert thou of the golden-wingèd host,
Who having clad thyself in human weed[51]
To earth from thy prefixèd seat didst post,[52]
And after short abode fly back with speed,   60
As if to show what creatures Heav'n doth breed,
      Thereby to set the hearts of men on fire
To scorn the sordid[53] world, and unto Heav'n aspire?

---

[47] creature, being
[48] benefit, behalf
[49] appropriate, proper
[50] Astraea ("starry maiden"), goddess of justice and the last god to leave the earth
[51] clothing
[52] travel quickly
[53] dirty, repulsive

X

But oh, why didst thou not stay here below
To bless us with thy Heav'n-loved innocence?
To slake his wrath, whom sin hath made our foe?
To turn swift-rushing black perdition hence,
Or drive away the slaughtering pestilence?
  To stand 'twixt us and our deservèd smart?[54]
But thou canst best perform that office where thou art. 70

XI

Then thou, the mother of so sweet a child,
Her false-imagin'd loss cease to lament,
And wisely learn to curb thy sorrows wild.
Think what a present thou to God has sent,
And render Him with patience what he lent.
  This if thou do, He will an offspring give
That till the world's last end shall make thy name to live.

AT A VACATION EXERCISE IN THE COLLEGE, PART LATIN, PART ENGLISH
[1628]

The Latin speeches ended, the English thus began:

Hail, native language, that by sinews weak
Didst move my first endeavoring tongue to speak
And mad'st imperfect words with childish trips,
Half unpronounced, slide through my infant lips,

---

[54] pain, grief

Driving dumb silence from the portal door,
Where he had mutely sat two years before!
Here I salute thee, and thy pardon ask,
That now I use thee in my later task.
Small loss it is that hence can come unto thee:
I know my tongue but little grace can do thee.   10
Thou needst not be ambitious to be first:
Believe me, I have thither[55] packed the worst—
And, if it happen, as I did forecast,
The daintiest dishes shall be served up last.
I pray thee, then, deny me not thy aid
For this same small neglect that I have made,
But haste thee straight to do me once a pleasure,
And from thy wardrobe bring thy chiefest treasure,
Not those new-fangled toys and trimming slight
Which takes our late fantastics with delight,   20
But cull those richest robes and gay'st attire
Which deepest spirits and choicest wits desire.
I have some naked[56] thoughts that rove about
And loudly knock to have their passage out,
And, weary of their place, do only stay
Till thou has decked them in thy best array,
That so they may without suspect[57] or fears
Fly swiftly to this fair assembly's ears.
         Yet I had rather, if I were to choose,
Thy service in some graver subject use,   30
Such as may make thee search thy coffers[58] round[59]
Before thou clothe my fancy in fit sound—
Such where the deep transported mind may soar
Above the wheeling poles, and at Heav'n's door
Look in, and see each blissful deity
How he before the thunderous throne doth lie,
Listening to what unshorn Apollo sings
To the touch of golden wires, while Hebe[60] brings
Immortal nectar to her kingly sire.

---

[55] i.e., in the preceding part, which is a pun-filled "Prolusion"
[56] obvious, bare, plain
[57] suspicion
[58] boxes, chests
[59] thoroughly, all over
[60] Zeus and Hera's daughter; cupbearer to the gods

Then passing through the spheres of watchful fire,   40
And misty regions of wide air next under,
And hills of snow and lofts[61] of pilèd thunder,
May tell at length how green-eyed Neptune raves,
In Heav'n's defiance mustering all his waves.
Then sing of secret things that came to pass
When beldam[62] Nature in her cradle was.
And last, of kings and queens and heroes old,
Such as the wise Demodocus[63] once told,
In solemn songs at king Alcinous' feast,
While sad Ulysses' soul and all the rest   50
Are held with his melodious harmony
In willing chains and sweet captivity.
But fie, my wand'ring muse! How thou dost stray!
Expectance calls thee now another way:
Thou know'st it must be now thy only bent
To keep in compass[64] of thy predicament.[65]
Then quick, about thy purposed business come,
That to the next I may resign my room.[66]

Then Ens is represented as father of the [ten Aristotelian] predica-
ments, his ten sons, whereof the eldest stood for substance, with his
canons, which Ens, thus speaking, explains:

Good luck befriend thee, son, for at thy birth
The fairy ladies danced upon the hearth.   60
Thy drowsy nurse hath sworn she did them spy
Come tripping to the room where thou didst lie,
And sweetly singing round about thy bed
Strew all their blessings on thy sleeping head.
She heard them give thee this: that thou should'st still
From eyes of mortals walk invisible.
Yet there is something that doth force my fear,

---

[61] layers
[62] old woman, grandmother
[63] see Homer's *Odyssey* 8:499ff.
[64] within the boundary
[65] an academic pun: predicament = (1) term used in Aristotelian rhetoric, (2) Milton's difficulty with his "wand'ring muse"
[66] place

For once it was my dismal[67] hap[68] to hear
A sibyl[69] old, bow-bent with crooked age,
That far events full wisely could presage,   70
And in time's long and dark prospective glass
Foresaw what future days should bring to pass:
"Your son," said she, "(nor can you it prevent)
Shall be subject to many an accident.
O'er all his brethren he shall reign as king,
Yet every one shall make him underling,
And those that cannot live from him asunder[70]
Ungratefully shall strive to keep him under.
In worth and excellence he shall out-go[71] them,
Yet being above them, he shall be below them.   80
From others he shall stand in need of nothing,
Yet on his brothers shall depend for clothing.
To find a foe it shall not be his hap,
And peace shall lull him in her flow'ry lap.
Yet shall he live in strife, and at his door
Devouring war shall never cease to roar.
Yea, it shall be his natural property[72]
To harbor those that are at enmity."
What power, what force, what mighty spell, if not
Your learned hands, can loose this Gordian knot?   90

The next, Quantity *and* Quality, *spoke in prose. Then* Relation
was called by his name:

Rivers[73] arise, whether thou be the son
Of utmost[74] Tweed,[75] or Ouse, or gulfy Dun,[76]
Or Trent, who like some earth-born giant spreads
His thirty[77] arms along the indented meads,

---

[67] unlucky, disastrous, dreadful
[68] chance, luck
[69] prophetess, fortune-teller, witch
[70] apart
[71] outdistance, surpass
[72] attribute, quality, nature
[73] one George Rivers (or his brother, Nizell) played the part of Relation
[74] outermost
[75] on the border of England and Scotland
[76] the Don, in Yorkshire
[77] *trente* = "thirty," in French, and the Trent takes its name therefrom

Or sullen Mole, that runneth underneath,
Or Severn swift, guilty of maiden's death,[78]
Or rocky Avon, or of sedgy Lea,
Or coaly Tyne,[79] or ancient hallowed Dee,.
Or Humber loud, that keeps[80] the Scythian's name,
Or Medway smooth, or royal-towered Thame.[81]

ON THE MORNING OF CHRIST'S NATIVITY
[1629]

I

This is the month, and this the happy morn
Wherein the son of Heav'n's eternal king,
Of wedded maid and virgin mother born,
Our great redemption from above did bring.
For so the holy sages once did sing,
   That he our deadly forfeit[82] should release,
And with his Father work us a perpetual peace.

II

That glorious form, that light unsufferable,[83]
And that far-beaming blaze of majesty
Wherewith he wont,[84] at Heav'n's high council-table   10
To sit, the midst of Trinal Unity,
He laid aside, and here with us to be

---

[78] see the story of the river nymph Sabrina in *Comus*, lines 824ff.
[79] the river runs past Newcastle, proverbial for its coal
[80] i.e., is supposedly named for a Scythian chief who drowned in that river
[81] the Thames, which runs past various royal castles
[82] crime, fault, penalty
[83] unbearable, intolerable
[84] was accustomed

Forsook the courts[85] of everlasting day,
And chose with us a darksome house of mortal clay.

III

Say Heavenly Muse, shall not thy sacred vein[86]
Afford[87] a present to the infant God?
Hast thou no verse, no hymn, or solemn strain,[88]
To welcome him to this his new abode,
Now while the Heav'n by the sun's team[89] untrod,
  Hath took no print[90] of the approaching light 20
And all the spangled host keep watch in squadrons bright?

IV

See how, from far, upon the eastern road
The star-led wizards[91] haste, with odors sweet!
O run, prevent[92] them with thy humble ode,
And lay it lowly at his blessèd feet!
Have thou the honor, first thy Lord to greet,
  And join thy voice unto the Angel choir
From out his secret altar, touched with hallowed fire.

THE HYMN

I

It was the winter wild,
While the Heav'n-born child 30
  All meanly[93] wrapped in the rude[94] manger[95] lies.

---

[85] residence/offices of a sovereign
[86] style, talent
[87] effect, accomplish
[88] style, tone
[89] the horses pulling the sun god's chariot
[90] impression, stamp
[91] the three Magi/wise men
[92] come before [*pre* = before, *venir* = come]
[93] poorly, shabbily
[94] rough, coarse, inelegant
[95] feeding trough in stable/barn

Nature in awe[96] to him
Had doffed[97] her gaudy[98] trim,[99]
         With her great master so to sympathize.
It was no season then for her
To wanton with the sun, her lusty[1] paramour.

II

Only with speeches fair
She woos the gentle air
         To hide her guilty front[2] with innocent snow,
And on her naked shame,   40
Pollute[3] with sinful blame,
         The saintly veil of maiden white to throw,
Confounded[4] that her Maker's eyes
Should look so near upon her foul deformities.

III

But he, her fears to cease,
Sent down the meek-eyed Peace.
         She, crowned with olive green, came softly sliding
Down through the turning sphere,
His ready harbinger,[5]
         With turtle wing the amorous clouds dividing,   50
And waving wide her myrtle wand
She strikes a universal peace through sea and land.

IV

No war or battle's sound
Was heard the world around.

---

[96] reverential wonder
[97] laid aside, taken away, taken off
[98] brilliant, fine
[99] adornment
[1] joyful, lively, lustful
[2] forehead, face
[3] corrupted, foul, filthy, stained [adjective]
[4] abashed, ashamed
[5] forerunner (advance person)

The idle spear and shield were high up hung,
The hookèd⁶ chariot stood
Unstained with hostile blood,
     The trumpet spoke not to the armèd throng,
And kings sat still, with awful⁷ eye,
As if they surely knew their sov'reign Lord was by.   60

V

But peaceful was the night
Wherein the Prince of Light
     His reign of peace upon the earth began.
The winds, with wonder whist,⁸
Smoothly the waters kissed,
     Whispering new joys to the mild ocean,
Who now hath quite forgot to rave,⁹
While birds of calm sit brooding on the charmèd wave.

VI

The stars with deep amaze
Stand fixed in steadfast gaze,   70
     Bending one way their precious influence,
And will not take their flight,
For all the morning light,
     Or Lucifer¹⁰ that often warned them thence,
But in their glimmering orbs did glow,
Until their Lord himself bespoke, and bid them go.

VII

And though the shady gloom
Had given day her room,¹¹
     The sun himself withheld his wonted speed,
And hid his head for shame,   80

---

⁶ with hook/scythelike protrusions? a hook-shaped chariot?
⁷ respectful, reverential
⁸ hushed, silent
⁹ rage, roar
¹⁰ the morning star, *not* (in this usage) Satan
¹¹ place

As[12] his inferior flame
    The new-enlightened world no more should need;
He saw a greater sun appear
Than his bright throne or burning axletree could bear.

VIII

The shepherds on the lawn,
Or ere the point[13] of dawn,
    Sat simply chatting in a rustic row.
Full little thought they then
That the mighty Pan
    Was kindly come to live with them below.   90
Perhaps their loves, or else their sheep,
Was all that did their silly[14] thoughts so busy keep.

IX

When such music sweet
Their hearts and ears did greet,
    As never was by mortal finger struck,
Divinely-warbled voice
Answering the stringèd noise
    As all their souls in blissful rapture took.[15]
The air such pleasure loath to lose
With thousand echoes still prolongs each heavenly close.[16]   100

X

Nature that heard such sound
Beneath the hollow round
    Of Cynthia's[17] seat, the airy region thrilling,
Now was almost won
To think her part was done,
    And that her reign had here its last fulfilling.

---

[12] as if
[13] moment, instant
[14] simple, humble
[15] gripped, seized, charmed (the "stringèd noise" took "all their souls in blissful rapture")
[16] cadence
[17] the moon

She knew such harmony alone
Could hold all Heav'n and earth in happier union.

XI

At last surrounds their sight
A globe of circular light,   110
      That with long beams the shame-faced night arrayed.[18]
The helmèd Cherubim
And swordèd Seraphim
      Are seen in glittering ranks, with wings displayed,
Harping in loud and solemn choir,
With unexpressive[19] notes to Heav'n's new-born heir.

XII

Such music (as 'tis said)
Before was never made
      But when of old the sons of morning sung,
While the Creator great   120
His constellations set,
      And the well-balanced world on hinges hung,
And cast the dark foundations deep,
And bid the weltering[20] waves their oozy channel keep.

XIII

Ring out, ye crystal spheres,
Once bless our human ears
      (If ye have power to touch our senses so),
And let your silver chime
Move in melodious time,
      And let the bass of Heav'n's deep organ blow,   130
And with your ninefold harmony
Make up full consort to the angelic symphony.

---

[18] prepared, dressed
[19] inexpressible
[20] rolling, tossing, tumbling

XIV

For if such holy song
Enwrap our fancy long,
      Time will run back and fetch the Age of Gold,
And speckled[21] vanity
Will sicken soon, and die,
      And leprous sin will melt from earthly mould,
And Hell itself will pass away,
And leave her dolorous[22] mansions[23] to the peering day.   140

XV

Yea, Truth and Justice then
Will down return to men,
      Orbed in a rainbow; and like[24] glories wearing
Mercy will sit between,
Throned in celestial sheen,
      With radiant feet the tissued[25] clouds down steering,
And Heav'n, as at some festival,
Will open wide the gates of her high palace hall.

XVI

But wisest Fate says no,
This must not yet be so,   150
      The Babe lies yet in smiling infancy
That on the bitter cross
Must redeem our loss,
      So both himself and us to glorify.
Yet first to those ychained in sleep
The wakeful trump of doom must thunder through the deep

---

[21] full of moral blemishes/defects
[22] suffering, mourning
[23] houses, tents
[24] similar
[25] delicate, gauzy texture

XVII

With such a horrid clang
As on Mount Sinai rang
        While the red fire and smoldering clouds out-break.
The aged earth aghast   160
With terror of that blast
        Shall from the surface to the center shake;
When at the world's last session[26]
The dreadful[27] Judge in middle air shall spread His throne,

XVIII

And then at last our bliss
Full and perfect is—
        But now begins, for from this happy day
Th' old dragon under ground
In straiter[28] limits bound
        Not half so far casts his usurpèd sway,   170
And wroth[29] to see his kingdom fail
Swinges[30] the scaly horror of his folded tail.

XIX

The oracles are dumb;
No voice or hideous hum
        Runs through the archèd roof in words deceiving.
Apollo from his shrine
Can no more divine,[31]
        With hollow shriek the steep[32] of Delphos leaving.
No nightly trance or breathèd spell
Inspires[33] the pale-eyed priest from the prophetic cell.   180

---

[26] meeting of a deliberative council [trisyllabic]
[27] fearful, awe-inspiring
[28] narrower, tighter
[29] wrathful, indignant
[30] lashes, brandishes, whips
[31] prognosticate
[32] slope
[33] prompts, animates

XX

The lonely mountains o'er,
And the resounding shore,
     A voice of weeping heard, and loud lament.
From haunted spring and dale
Edged with poplar pale[34]
     The parting genius[35] is with sighing sent.
With flower-inwoven tresses torn
The Nymphs in twilight shade of tangled thickets mourn.

XXI

In consecrated earth,
And on the holy hearth,
     The lars and lemures[36] moan with midnight plaint.   190
In urns and altars round,
A drear and dying sound
     Affrights the flamens[37] at their service quaint,[38]
And the chill marble seems to sweat,
While each peculiar[39] power[40] forgoes his wonted seat.

XXII

Peor[41] and Baalim[42]
Forsake their temples dim,
     With that twice-battered god of Palestine
And moonèd Ashtaroth,[43]   200
Heav'n's queen and mother both,
     Now sits not girt[44] with tapers' holy shine.

---

[34] silver-leafed?
[35] local spirit (pagan)
[36] Roman household and hearth gods
[37] Roman priests
[38] odd, strange
[39] separate
[40] spiritual/divine being
[41] mountain/Phoenician sun god
[42] followers of Baal
[43] Phoenician moon goddess
[44] encircled

The Libyc Hammon[45] shrinks[46] his horn.
In vain the Tyrian maids their wounded Thammuz[47] mourn,

XXIII

And sullen Moloch,[48] fled,
Hath left in shadows dread
        His burning idol all of blackest hue.
In vain with cymbals' ring
They call the grisly king,
        In dismal dance about the furnace[49] blue.   210
The brutish[50] gods of Nile as fast,
Isis[51] and Orus,[52] and the dog Anubis,[53] haste.

XXIV

Nor is Osiris[54] seen
In Memphian grove or green,
        Trampling th' unshowered grass with lowings loud,
Nor can he be at rest
Within his sacred chest:[55]
        Nought but profoundest Hell can be his shroud.
In vain with timbreled[56] anthems[57] dark
The sable-stolèd[58] sorcerers bear his worshipped ark.   220

XXV

He feels from Judah's land
The dreaded infant's hand,

---

[45] Ammon, Egyptian god with the head of a ram
[46] withers
[47] Phoenician Adonis
[48] deity associated with Baal
[49] into which babies were thrown, as sacrifices to Moloch
[50] animal-like/shaped
[51] Egyptian earth goddess, horned like a cow
[52] Egyptian sun god, Isis' son
[53] son of Orus, dog/jackal-headed
[54] chief of the Egyptian gods, portrayed as a black bull
[55] see line 220, below
[56] percussion instrument, tambourinelike
[57] songs of praise/gladness
[58] robed

The rays of Bethlehem blind his dusky eyn.[59]
Nor all the gods beside
Longer dare abide,
Not Typhon[60] huge, ending in snaky twine.[61]
Our Babe, to show his Godhead true,
Can in his swaddling bands control the damnèd crew.

XXVI

So when the sun in bed,
Curtained with cloudy red,   230
Pillows his chin upon an orient[62] wave,
The flocking shadows pale
Troop to the infernal jail.
Each fettered ghost slips to his several[63] grave
And the yellow-skirted fays[64]
Fly after the night-steeds, leaving their moon-loved maze.[65]

XXVII

But see, the Virgin blest
Hath laid her Babe to rest.
Time is our tedious[66] song should here have ending.
Heav'n's youngest-teemèd[67] star   240
Hath fixed her polished car,
Her sleeping Lord with handmaid lamp attending,
And all about the courtly stable
Bright-harnessed[68] angels sit in order serviceable.[69]

---

[59] eyes
[60] hundred-headed fire-breathing giant, a serpent below the waist
[61] coils
[62] eastern
[63] separate, individual
[64] fairies
[65] labyrinth (as in a fairy ring?)
[66] long and wearisome (used in a jocund rather than literal sense)
[67] youngest-born/produced
[68] i.e., wearing gleaming body armor
[69] ready to be useful [four syllables, first and third accented]

THE PASSION

*[1630: "This subject the author finding to be above the years
he had when he wrote it, and nothing satisfied with what was
begun, left it unfinished."]*

I

Erewhile[70] of music and ethereal mirth,
Wherewith the stage of air and earth did ring,
And joyous news of Heav'nly infant's birth,
My muse with Angels did divide to sing.[71]
But headlong joy is ever on the wing,
　　　In wintry solstice like the shortened light
Soon swallowed up in dark and long outliving night.

II

For now to sorrow must I tune my song,
And set my harp to notes of saddest woe,
Which on our dearest Lord did seize[72] ere long   10
Dangers, and snares, and wrongs, and worse than so,
Which he for us did freely undergo,
　　　Most perfect hero, tried in heaviest[73] plight[74]
Of labors huge and hard, too hard for human wight.[75]

III

He sov'reign priest, stooping his regal head
That dropped with odorous oil down his fair eyes,
Poor fleshly tabernacle[76] entered,
His starry front low-roofed beneath the skies.
Oh what a mask was there, what a disguise!

---

[70] once, formerly, some time ago
[71] to sing in counterpoint
[72] fasten upon, clutch, take hold of
[73] gravest, most severe
[74] peril, danger, risk
[75] creature, being
[76] temporary dwelling, place, abode

Yet more: the stroke of death he must abide,[77]   20
Then lies him meekly down fast by his brethren's side.

IV

These latter scenes confine my roving verse;
To this horizon is my Phoebus[78] bound:
His Godlike acts, and his temptations fierce,
And former sufferings otherwhere are found.
Loud o'er the rest Cremona's trump doth sound.[79]
  Me softer airs befit,[80] and softer strings
Of lute, or viol still,[81] more apt for mournful things.

V

Befriend me, night, best patroness of grief,
Over the pole thy thickest mantle throw,   30
And work my flattered fancy to belief
That Heav'n and earth are colored with my woe,
My sorrows are too dark for day to know.
  The leaves should all be black wheron I write,
And letters, where my tears have washed, a wannish white.

VI

See, see the chariot, and those rushing wheels
That whirled the prophet[82] up, at Chebar flood!
My spirit some transporting Cherub feels,
To bear me where the towers of Salem[83] stood,
Once glorious towers, now sunk in guiltless blood.   40
  There doth my soul in holy vision sit,
In pensive[84] trance,[85] and anguish, and ecstatic fit.[86]

---

[77] put up with, endure
[78] Phoebus Apollo, god of (among other things) poetry
[79] Marco Girolamo Vida's *Christiad*; he was a native of Cremona
[80] proper to
[81] subdued
[82] Ezekiel
[83] Jerusalem (Shalem = ancient Semitic god)
[84] anxiously thoughtful
[85] absorption
[86] mood? seizure?

VII

Mine eye hath found that sad sepulchral rock
That was the casket of Heav'n's richest store,[87]
And here though grief my feeble hands uplock[88]
Yet on the softened quarry[89] would I score[90]
My plaining[91] verse, as lively[92] as before,
     For sure so well instructed are my tears
That they would fitly fall in ordered characters.[93]

VIII

Or should I, thence hurried on viewless wing,   50
Take up a weeping on the mountains wild,
The gentle neighborhood of grove and spring
Would soon unbosom all their echoes mild,
And I (for grief is easily beguiled)
     Might think th' infection[94] of my sorrows loud
Had got a race of mourners on some pregnant cloud.

---

[87] treasures
[88] i.e., as in prayer
[89] mass of stone
[90] mark, engrave
[91] lamenting
[92] vivid, fresh, brightly gay
[93] letters of the alphabet
[94] i.e., infections being carried by some germlike agent, the poet's tears of sorrow, like a sort of sickly semen, spawn "a race of mourners" on that which carries water down on men, namely, a cloud

SONG: ON MAY MORNING
[1630–31]

Now the bright morning star, day's harbinger,[95]
Comes dancing from the east, and leads with her
The flow'ry May, who from her green lap throws
The yellow cowslip, and the pale primrose.
        Hail bounteous May, that dost inspire
        Mirth and youth and warm desire,
        Woods and groves are of thy dressing,[96]
        Hill and dale[97] doth boast thy blessing.
Thus we salute thee with our early song,
And welcome thee, and wish thee long.

---

[95] forerunner (literally)
[96] attiring, arraying
[97] valley, hollow

ENGLISH 98 SONNETS 99

SONNET 1
[1628? 1630?]

O nightingale, that on yon bloomy spray¹
  Warblest at eve, when all the woods are still,
  Thou with fresh hope the lover's heart dost fill,
  While the jolly hours lead on propitious² May.
Thy liquid notes that close the eye of day,
  First heard before the shallow cuckoo's bill,
  Portend success in love. O if Jove's will
  Have linked that amorous power to thy soft lay³
Now timely⁴ sing, ere the rude⁵ bird of hate⁶
  Foretell my hopeless doom, in some grove nigh, 10
  As thou from year to year hast sung too late
For my relief, yet hadst no reason why.
  Whether the muse or love call thee his mate,
  Both them I serve, and of their train⁷ am I.

---

⁹⁸ Sonnets 2–6, written in Italian, are not here included
⁹⁹ arranged by compositional order rather than chronologically; dates of composition are,
as usual, indicated with the title of each poem
¹ twig, shoot
² gracious, favorably inclined
³ song
⁴ soon/soon enough (opportunely)
⁵ barbarous, ignorant
⁶ the cuckoo, linked to sexual jealousy/betrayal
⁷ retinue, attendants

SONNET 7
[*1632*]

How soon hath time, the subtle[8] thief of youth,
  Stol'n on his wing my three and twentieth year!
  My hasting days fly on, with full career,[9]
  But my late spring no bud or blossom show'th.
Perhaps my semblance might deceive the truth
  That I to manhood am arrived so near,
  And inward ripeness doth much less appear,
  That some more timely-happy spirits indu'th.[10]
Yet be it less or more, or soon or slow,
  It shall be still[11] in strictest measure ev'n[12]   10
  To that same lot,[13] however mean[14] or high,
Towards which time leads me, and the will of Heav'n.
  All is, if I have grace to use it so,
  As ever in my great task-master's eye.

---

[8] ingenious, cunning, tricky
[9] speed, impetus
[10] are invested with
[11] yet? always?
[12] equal, proportionate
[13] destiny
[14] low

SONNET 8
[1642]

Captain or colonel,[15] or knight in arms,
  Whose chance[16] on these defenseless doors may seize,[17]
  If ever deed of honor did thee please
  Guard them, and him within[18] protect from harms.
He can requite[19] thee, for he knows the charms
  That call fame on such gentle[20] acts as these,
  And he can spread thy name o'er lands and seas,
  · Whatever clime the sun's bright circle warms.
Lift not thy spear against the muses' bow'r![21]
  The great Emathian conqueror[22] bid spare   10
  The house of Pindarus,[23] when temple and tow'r
Went to the ground, and the repeated air[24]
  Of sad Electra's poet[25] had the power
  To save th' Athenian walls from ruin bare.

---

[15] [trisyllabic]
[16] luck, fortuitous circumstance
[17] In October 1642, during the early days of England's civil war, the royalist army almost reached London; Milton's house lay just outside the city walls
[18] Milton himself
[19] repay
[20] noble, honorable, gentlemanly
[21] dwelling
[22] Alexander the Great: Emathia was a Macedonian province
[23] Pindar, Greek poet
[24] music: in Athenian Greece, the chorus referred to in the next footnote would have been sung
[25] Euripides: a chorus from the play is said to have persuaded the Spartans not to sack Athens, in 404 B.C.

SONNET 9
[1643–45]

Lady,[26] that in the prime of earliest youth
      Wisely hath shunned the broad way,[27] and the green,
      And with those few art eminently[28] seen
      That labor up the hill of Heav'nly truth,
The better part with Mary, and with Ruth,[29]
      Chosen thou hast, and they that overween[30]
      And at thy growing virtues fret[31] their spleen
      No anger find in thee, but pity and ruth.[32]
Thy care[33] is fixed, and zealously attends[34]
      To fill thy odorous lamp with deeds of light,   10
      And hope that reaps not shame. Therefore be sure,
Thou, when the bridegroom with his feastful friends
      Passes to bliss, at the mid hour of night,
      Hast gained thy entrance, virgin wise and pure.

---

[26] the lady is unknown
[27] "I will rise now, and go about the city in the streets, and in the broad ways I will seek him" (Song of Solomon 3:2)
[28] conspicuously
[29] "And Jesus . . . said unto her, Martha, Martha, thou art careful and troubled about many things. But one good thing is needful, and Mary hath chosen that good part, which shall not be taken away from her" (Luke 10:41–42); see also Ruth 1:8–18
[30] are arrogant, presumptious
[31] gnaw, wear away at
[32] compassion, pity
[33] concern
[34] follows, waits upon

SONNET 10
[1643–45]

Daughter to that good earl,[35] once president
    Of England's Council and her Treasury,
    Who lived in both unstained with gold or fee,
    And left them both, more in himself content,
Till the sad breaking of that Parliament
    Broke him,[36] as that dishonest victory
    At Chaeronéa,[37] fatal to liberty
    Killed with report that old man, eloquent.[38]
Though later born than to have known the days
    Wherein your father flourished, yet by you,   10
    Madam, methinks I see him living yet,
So well your words his noble virtues praise
    That all both judge you to relate[39] them true
    And to possess them, honored Margaret.

---

[35] Lady Margaret, daughter of the Earl of Marlborough
[36] Marlborough died four days after King Charles dissolved his third Parliament, in 1629
[37] Philip of Macedon's defeat of Thebes and Athens in 338 B.C.
[38] Chaeronéa marked the end of Greek independence; Isocrates committed suicide four days after hearing the news
[39] recount, tell

SONNET 11
[1645?]

I did but prompt the age to quit their clogs[40]
  By the known rules of ancient liberty[41]
  When straight a barbarous noise environs[42] me
  Of owls and cuckoos, asses, apes, and dogs.
As when those hinds[43] that were transformed to frogs
  Railed at Latona's twin-born progeny,[44]
  Which after held the sun and moon in fee.
But this is got by casting pearl to hogs,
That bawl for freedom, in their senseless mood,
  And still[45] revolt when truth would set them free.   10
  Licence, they mean, when they cry "liberty,"
For who loves that must first be wise and good.
  But from that mark how far they rove we see
  For all this waste of wealth and loss of blood.

---

[40] block of wood attached to the feet of men or horses, to impede movement
[41] by the writing of two tracts on divorce, one of which was entitled *Tetrachordon*: see Sonnet 12, below
[42] surrounds, besieges, besets
[43] rustics, boors
[44] Apollo and Diana, twin children of Latona and Jupiter; peasants who refused water to Latona were turned into frogs by Jupiter
[45] yet

SONNET 12
[*1647?*]

A book was writ, of late, called Tetrachordon,[46]
       And woven close both matter, form, and style.
       The subject new, it walked the town a while,
       Numb'ring good intellects—now seldom pored on.[47]
Cries the stall-reader, "Bless us! What a word on
       A title page is this!" And some in file[48]
       Stand spelling false, while[49] one might walk to Mile-
       End Green. Why is it harder, sirs, than Gordon,[50]
Colkitto,[51] or MacDonnell,[52] or Galasp?[53]
       Those rugged names to our like mouths grow
              sleek,   10
       That would have made Quintilian[54] stare and gasp!
Thy age, like ours—O soul of Sir John Cheek!—[55]
       Hated not learning worse than toad or asp,
       When thou taught'st Cambridge, and King Edward,
              Greek.

---

[46] Milton's 1645 book on divorce was shaped by the "foure chief places in Scripture which treat of Marriage"
[47] read, studied
[48] line
[49] in the time that
[50] James Gordon, Lord Aboyne, Scots royalist
[51] Alexander MacDonnell, known also as MacColkitto and MacGillespie, general in the royalist army of James Graham, Earl Montrose
[52] see footnote 50, above
[53] see footnote 50, above
[54] Roman rhetorician
[55] first professor of Greek at Cambridge, and tutor to Prince (later King) Edward

SONNET 13
[*1646*]

Harry,[56] whose tuneful and well-measured[57] song
    First taught our English music how to span[58]
    Words with just[59] note and accent, not to scan
    With Midas ears,[60] committing[61] short and long.
Thy worth and skill exempts thee from the throng,
    With praise enough for envy to look wan.
    To after age thou shalt be writ the man
    That with smooth air[62] couldst humor best our tongue.
Thou honor'st verse, and verse must lend her wing
    To honor thee, the priest of Phoebus choir,   10
    That tun'st their happiest lines, in hymn or story.
Dante shall give Fame leave to set thee higher
    Than his Casella,[63] whom he wooed to sing,
    Met in the milder shades of Purgatory.

---

[56] Henry Lawes, 1596–1662, master musician, who composed the music for *Comus*
[57] rhythmical
[58] measure out, extend
[59] proper, right, correct
[60] Midas having judged Pan a better flutist than Apollo, Apollo gave him donkey ears
[61] perpetrating
[62] melody, tune
[63] musician of Florence, Dante's friend, who appears, and sings, in *Purgatorio* 2:76ff.

SONNET 14
[1646]

When faith and love, which parted from thee[64] never,
    Had ripened thy just soul to dwell with God,
    Meekly thou didst resign this earthly load
Of death, called life, which us from life doth sever.
Thy works and alms, and all thy good endeavor,
    Stayed not behind nor in the grave were trod,
    But as faith pointed with her golden rod
Followed thee up to joy and bliss forever.
Love led them on, and faith, who knew them best—
    Thy handmaids—clad them o'er with purple
        beams   10
    And azure wings, that up they flew, so dressed,
And spoke the truth of thee in glorious themes[65]
    Before the judge, who thenceforth bid thee rest
    And drink thy fill of pure immortal streams.

SONNET 15
[1648]

Fairfax,[66] whose name in arms through Europe rings,
    Filling each mouth with envy, or with praise,
    And all her jealous monarchs with amaze
    And rumors loud, that daunt remotest kings,
Thy firm unshaken virtue ever brings
    Victory home, though new rebellions raise

---

[64] Catherine, wife of George Thomason, London bookseller and publisher; died in 1646
[65] melodies
[66] Sir Thomas Fairfax, commander in chief of the Parliamentarian army

Their hydra heads, and the false North[67] displays
      Her broken league,[68] to imp[69] her serpent wings:[70]
O yet a nobler task awaits thy hand,
        For what can wars but endless wars still breed,   10
        Till truth and right from violence be freed,
And public faith cleared from the shameful brand
        Of public fraud. In vain doth valor bleed
        While avarice and rapine[71] share the land.

SONNET 16
[*1652*]

Cromwell, our chief of men, who through a cloud
      Not of war only, but detractions[72] rude,[73]
      Guided by faith and matchless fortitude
      To peace and truth thy glorious way hath ploughed,
And on the neck of crownèd Fortune proud
      Hast reared God's trophies, and His work pursued,
      While Darwen[74] stream with blood of Scots embru'd,[75]
      And Dunbar[76] field resounds thy praises loud,
And Worcester's[77] laureat wreath, yet much remains
      To conquer still. Peace hath her victories   10

---

[67] Scotland
[68] a covenant of friendship made in 1643 between Parliament and the Scots was broken a month later by a Scottish invasion
[69] to engraft new feathers onto damaged wings
[70] the covenant with Parliament, being unserpentlike, broke Scotland's "serpent wings," but invading England and breaking that covenant restored her native serpentlike qualities
[71] plunder, pillage, robbery
[72] slander, defamations, calumnies
[73] coarse
[74] battle of 1648
[75] soaked
[76] battle of 1650
[77] battle of 1651 [bisyllabic, as if written "WOOSter"]

No less renowned than war, new foes arise,
Threat'ning to bind our souls with secular chains!
      Help us to save free conscience from the paw
      Of hireling wolves, whose gospel is their maw.[78]

SONNET 17
[1652]

Vane,[79] young in years but in sage counsel old,
      Than whom a better senator ne'er held
      The helm of Rome, when gowns,[80] not arms, repelled
      The fierce Epeirut[81] and th' African[82] bold:
Whether to settle peace, or to unfold
      The drift[83] of hollow[84] states, hard to be spelled;[85]
      Then to advise how war may best upheld,
      Move by her two main nerves, iron and gold,
In all her equipage;[86] besides, to know
      Both spiritual power and civil, what each means,   10
      What severs each—thou hast learned, which few have
          done.
The bounds of either sword to thee we owe.
      Therefore, on thy firm hand religion leans
      In peace, and reckons thee her eldest son.

---

[78] mouth, appetite
[79] Sir Henry Vane (the Younger), statesman and councilor
[80] i.e., the togas worn by the senators of Rome
[81] Pyrrhus, king of Epirus, invaded Rome in the third century B.C.
[82] Hannibal of Carthage, in Africa, also invaded Rome in the third century B.C.
[83] purpose, intent
[84] pun on "Holland"
[85] gibe at the spelling and pronunciation of Dutch
[86] equipment

SONNET 18
[*1655*]

Avenge, O Lord, thy slaughtered Saints,[87] whose bones
　　　Lie scattered on the Alpine mountains cold—
　　　Ev'n them who kept thy truth so pure of old,
　　　When all our fathers worshipped stocks and stones!
Forget not! In Thy book record[88] their groans,
　　　Who were Thy sheep, and in their ancient fold[89]
　　　Slain by the bloody Piemontese, who rolled
　　　Mother with infant down the rocks. Their moans
The vales redoubled to the hills, and they
　　　To Heav'n. Their martyred blood and ashes sow　　10
　　　O'er all th' Italian fields where still doth sway
The triple tyrant,[90] that from these may grow
　　　A hundred-fold, who having learned Thy way
　　　Early, may fly[91] the Babylonian woe.[92]

---

[87] the Vaudois, Swiss Protestants, attacked and killed by Catholic partisans in 1655
[88] [verb]
[89] sheep pen: here, of course, metaphorical
[90] the Pope
[91] flee
[92] the papacy

SONNET 19
[1655]

When I consider how my life is spent,[93]
        Ere[94] half my days in this dark world and wide,
        And that one talent[95] which is death to hide
        Lodged with me, useless, though my soul more bent[96]
To serve therewith my Maker, and present[97]
        My true account, lest He, returning,[98] chide — [99]
        "Doth God exact day labor, light denied?"
        I fondly ask, but patience, to prevent
That murmur, soon replies, "God doth not need
        Either man's work or His own gifts. Who best   10
        Bear His mild yoke, they serve Him best. His state
Is kingly. Thousands at His bidding speed
        And post[1] o'er land and ocean, without rest.
        They also serve who only stand and wait."

---

[93] used up, exhausted
[94] before
[95] in biblical times, "talent" also meant a monetary unit: see Matthew 25:14ff, the parable of the talents
[96] devoted, bound
[97] bring/show to God [verb]
[98] as per the parable of the talents
[99] scold, rebuke
[1] hurry

SONNET 20
[*1655*]

Lawrence,[2] of virtuous father, virtuous son,
        Now that the fields are dank, and ways[3] are mire,[4]
        Where shall we sometimes meet, and by the fire
        Help waste a sullen[5] day, what[6] may be won
From the hard season[7] gaining?[8] Time will run
        On smoother, till Favonius[9] re-inspire
        The frozen earth, and clothe in fresh attire
        The lily and rose, that neither sowed nor spun.[10]
What neat[11] repast shall feast us, light and choice,
        Of Attic taste, with wine, whence we may rise   10
        To hear the lute well touched, or artful voice
Warble immortal notes and Tuscan[12] air?
        He who of those delights can judge, and spare[13]
        To interpose[14] them oft, is not unwise.

---

[2] Edward Lawrence, member of Parliament; his father, Henry Lawrence, was president of Cromwell's Council of State
[3] roads, lanes, paths
[4] boggy, slushy, muddy
[5] gloomy, dark, dismal, dull
[6] a day that
[7] winter, with its ice
[8] which is gaining on us/coming closer and closer
[9] the west wind
[10] "Consider the lilies of the field, how they grow; they toil not, neither do they spin": Matthew 6:28
[11] dainty, elegant
[12] Italian
[13] afford? spare time for? leave off, forbear?
[14] introduce, *or* delay

SONNET 21
[*1655*]

Cyriack![15] Whose grandsire on the Royal Bench[16]
       Of British Themis,[17] with no mean[18] applause
       Pronounced[19] and in his volumes[20] taught our laws,
       Which others at their Bar[21] so often wrench[22]—
Today deep thoughts resolve with me to drench[23]
       In mirth, that after no repenting draws.[24]
       Let Euclid rest, and Archimedes pause,
       And what the Swede[25] intends, and what the French!
To measure life, learn thou betimes[26] and know
       Toward solid[27] good what leads the nearest way.   10
       For other things, mild Heav'n a time ordains,
And disapproves that care, though wise in show,
       That with superfluous burden loads the day
       And, when God sends a cheerful hour, refrains!

---

[15] Cyriack Skinner, 1627–1700, Milton's student, friend, helper, and more than likely his amanuensis
[16] Sir Edward Coke, 1552–1634, chief justice of the King's Bench and a legendary figure in the law to this day
[17] goddess of justice
[18] petty, insignificant
[19] as a judge handing down ("pronouncing") decisions
[20] notably *The Institutes of the Law of England*
[21] i.e., other lawyers, members of the bar
[22] twist, stretch, alter
[23] soak, drown
[24] moves
[25] Sweden
[26] speedily, in good time
[27] sober, sound, practical

SONNET 22
[*1655*]

Cyriack, this three years day these eyes, though clear
      To outward view of blemish or of spot,
      Bereft[28] of light their seeing have forgot,
      Nor to their idle[29] orbs doth sight appear
Of sun, or moon, or star throughout the year,
      Or man, or woman. Yet I argue not
      Against Heav'n's hand or will, nor bate[30] a jot[31]
      Of heart or hope, but still bear up and steer
Right onward. What supports me, dost thou ask?
      The conscience, friend, t' have lost them
             overplied[32]   10
      In liberty's defense, my noble task,
Of which all Europe talks from side to side.
      This thought might lead me through the world's vain
             mask,
      Content, though blind, had I no better guide.

---

[28] deprived
[29] useless, inactive, unemployed
[30] lessen, reduce
[31] the smallest of small amounts
[32] overworked/employed/worked/used

SONNET 23
[1656–58?]

Methought I saw my late espousèd saint[33]
      Brought to me, like Alcestis,[34] from the grave,
      Who Jove's great son to her glad husband gave,
      Rescued from death by force, though pale and faint.
Mine as whom, washed from spot of child-bed taint,[35]
      Purification in th' old law[36] did save,
      And such as yet once more I trust to have
      Full sight of her in Heav'n, without restraint,[37]
Came vested[38] all in white, pure as her mind.
      Her face was veiled, yet to my fancied sight   10
      Love, sweetness, goodness in her person shined
So clear, as in no face with more delight.
      But O, as to embrace me she inclined,[39]
      I waked, she fled, and day brought back my night.

---

[33] probably, but not certainly, Milton's second wife, Katherine Woodcock, to whom he was married in 1656, and who died in 1658, not long after giving birth to a daughter
[34] Admetus, her husband, had his life extended in return for her voluntarily dying in his stead; Hercules, Jove's son, successfully wrestled with Death, and then brought her back to life
[35] stain, blemish
[36] see Leviticus 12:5
[37] limitation, reserve
[38] clothed, dressed
[39] bent, leaned

ON SHAKESPEARE
[*1630*]

What needs my Shakespeare, for his honored bones,
The labor of an age in pilèd stones,
Or that his hallowed relics should be hid
Under a star-ypointing pyramid?
Dear son of memory,[40] great heir of fame,
What need'st thou such weak witness of thy name?
Thou in our wonder and astonishment
Hast built thyself a livelong monument!
For whilst to th' shame of slow-endeavoring[41] art
Thy easy numbers[42] flow, and that each heart   10
Hath from the leaves of thy unvalued[43] book
Those Delphic[44] lines with deep[45] impression[46] took,
Then thou our fancy, of itself bereaving,[47]
Dost make us marble[48] with too much conceiving,[49]
And so sepulchred[50] in such pomp[51] dost lie
That kings for such a tomb would wish to die.

---

[40] the Muses were the daughters of Memory
[41] slow-striving
[42] prosody
[43] invaluable, priceless
[44] inspired by Apollo, god of poetry, who lived in the city of Delphi
[45] (1) heavy, (2) profound: see footnote 46, below
[46] (1) mold, cast, copy (as in printing), (2) effect, influence
[47] depriving, stripping
[48] (1) stone, such as is used in tombs and gravestones, or rigid/cold/white like marble, (2) the marbled pattern or paper used in ornamenting/binding books
[49] imagining
[50] buried (metaphorical: "absorbed")
[51] splendor, magnificence

ON THE UNIVERSITY CARRIER[52]
[1631]

who sickened in the time of his vacancy,[53] being forbid to go to London by reason of the Plague.

Here lies old Hobson.[54] Death has broke his girt[55]
And here, alas, hath laid him in the dirt,
Or else the ways[56] being foul, twenty to one
He's here stuck in a slough,[57] and overthrown.
'Twas such a shifter,[58] that if truth were known,
Death was half glad when he had got him down,
For he had any time this ten years full[59]
Dodged[60] with him, betwixt Cambridge and *The Bull.*[61]
And surely, Death could never have prevailed
Had not his weekly course of carriage[62] failed,   10
But lately finding him so long at home,
And thinking now his journey's end was come,
And that he had ta'en up his latest inn,
In the kind office of a chamberlain[63]
Showed him his room where he must lodge that night,
Pulled off his boots, and took away the light.[64]
If any ask for him, it shall be said,
"Hobson has supped, and's newly gone to bed."

---

[52] deliveryman
[53] temporary idleness
[54] also a renter of horses: the proverbial phrase "Hobson's choice" stems from his insisting that a would-be customer either accepted whatever horse was nearest to the door or else got no horse at all
[55] belt or band (leather or cloth) around a horse's body, securing saddle/pack/etc.; possibly also a pun on Hobson's own girt(h) and Death having broken *him*
[56] roads
[57] muddy ditch
[58] trickster, con man
[59] entire
[60] to dodge = to give (someone) the slip, to avoid, to baffle
[61] inn in London, located on a main thoroughfare
[62] habitual path, route
[63] Death = the "kind . . . chamberlain," or inn servant
[64] a candle—but Death extinguishes a person's "light"

ANOTHER ON THE SAME
[*1631*]

Here lieth one who did most truly prove
That he could never die while he could move,
So hung[65] his destiny never to rot[66]
While he might still jog on and keep his trot,
Made of sphere-metal,[67] never to decay
Until his revolution[68] was at stay.[69]
Time numbers[70] motion, yet (without a crime
'Gainst old truth) motion numbered out his time,
And like an engine[71] moved with wheel and weight,
His principles[72] being ceased, he ended straight.[73]   10
Rest that gives all men life, gave him his death,
And too much breathing[74] put him out of breath.
Nor were it contradiction to affirm
Too long vacation hastened on his term.[75]
Merely to drive[76] the time away he sickened,
Fainted, and died, nor would with ale be quickened.[77]
"Nay," quoth he, on his swooning bed outstretched,
"If I may not carry, sure I'll ne'er be fetched,[78]
But vow, though the cross doctors all stood hearers,
For one carrier put down[79] to make six bearers.[80]   20
Ease was his chief disease, and to judge right

---

[65] remained?
[66] decompose, die
[67] the indestructible stuff of which stars and other heavenly bodies are formed
[68] just as stars revolve, so too did Hobson, back and forth, back and forth, back and forth . . .
[69] stopped
[70] measures, assigns values to
[71] any mechanical contrivance/machine
[72] primary cause, which was movement
[73] at once—but also "straight" in the sense of no longer revolving
[74] one sense of the word "breathe," as in "to take breath," is "to rest"
[75] "term" = when college is in session, "vacation" = when college is not in session
[76] "drive the time away" as in "killing time"—but he was literally a "driver" (coachman)
[77] (1) brought to life, (2) made to go faster
[78] "fetch and carry" = common phraseology
[79] abolished, done away with—but also "put down" in the ground, buried
[80] i.e., six men will be required/used to carry him to his grave

He died for heaviness[81] that his cart went light.
His leisure[82] told him that his time was come,
And lack of load[83] made his life burdensome,
That[84] even to his last breath (there be that say't)
As[85] he were pressed to death,[86] he cried, "More weight!"
But had his doings lasted as they were
He had been an immortal carrier.[87]
Obedient to the moon, he spent his date[88]
In course reciprocal,[89] and had his fate
Linked to the mutual flowing of the seas,
Yet (strange to think) his wain[90] was his increase.
His letters are delivered all and gone,
Only remains this superscription.[91]

[81] boredom, sorrow
[82] involving unconcern with time
[83] load = burden
[84] so that
[85] as if
[86] a form of torture
[87] transformed, like so many classical figures, into a star/constellation?
[88] the "date" of a document is the "time" assigned to it (by the calendar)
[89] i.e., as regular as the moon
[90] "wain" = wagon; "wane" = decrease
[91] written on his tomb, or as his funereal inscription generally, just as letters too have their "superscriptions," or inside addresses

AN EPITAPH ON THE MARCHIONESS OF WINCHESTER
[1631]

This rich marble doth inter[92]
The honored wife of Winchester,[93]
A Viscount's daughter,[94] an Earl's heir,[95]
Besides what her virtues fair
Added to her noble birth,
More than she could own from earth.
Summers three times eight save one
She had told[96]—alas, too soon,
And so short time of breath,
To house[97] with darkness and with death.   10
Yet had the number of her days
Been as complete as was her praise,
Nature and Fate had had no strife
In giving limit to her life.
Her high birth and her graces sweet
Quickly found a lover meet;[98]
The virgin choir for her request
The god that sits at marriage feast.[99]
He at their invoking came
But with a scarce well-lighted flame,[1]   20
And in his garland as he stood
Ye might discern a cypress bud.[2]
Once had the early matrons run
To greet her of a lovely son,[3]
And now with second hope she goes,

---

[92] hold/enclose the corpse of
[93] dead in childbirth, together with her child, in 1631, at age twenty-three
[94] Thomas, Viscount of Rock-Savage
[95] on her mother's side, heir of Lord Darcy, Earl of Rivers
[96] counted, reckoned up
[97] dwell
[98] proper, fit
[99] Hymen
[1] she had been married at sixteen; at twenty-three she died
[2] cypress = a funereal wood, its branches and twigs a symbol of mourning
[3] born in 1629

And calls Lucina[4] to her throes.[5]
But whether by mischance or blame
Atropos[6] for Lucina came,
And with remorseless cruelty
Spoiled at once both fruit and tree: 30
The hapless babe before his birth
Had burial, yet not laid in earth,
And the languished mother's womb
Was not long a living tomb.[7]
So have I seen some tender slip[8]
Saved with care from winter's nip,
The pride of her carnation train,[9]
Plucked up by some unheedy[10] swain[11]
Who only thought to crop[12] the flower
New shot up from vernal[13] shower.   40
But the fair blossom hangs the head
Sideways as on a dying bed,
And those pearls of dew she wears
Prove to be presaging[14] tears
Which the sad morn had let fall
On her hastening funeral.
     Gentle lady, may thy grave
Peace and quiet ever have.
After this, thy travail sore,
Sweet rest seize thee evermore,   50
That to give the world increase
Shortened hast thy own life's lease.
Here besides the sorrowing
That thy noble house doth bring,
Here be tears of perfect moan

---

[4] goddess of childbirth
[5] childbirth labor
[6] one of the three Fates, who cut the thread of life
[7] the child was dead before delivery
[8] a cutting from a plant/flower
[9] retinue?
[10] careless
[11] youth, rustic, lover
[12] pluck, cut
[13] springtime, like springtime
[14] predictive, warning

Wept for thee in Helicon,[15]
And some flowers and some bays[16]
For thy hearse to strew the ways,[17]
Sent thee from the banks of Came,[18]
Devoted to thy virtuous name,   60
Whilst thou, bright Saint, high sitt'st in glory,
Next her much like to thee in story,
That fair Syrian shepherdess[19]
Who after years of barrenness
The highly-favored Joseph bore
To him that served for her before,[20]
And at her next birth, much like thee,
Through pangs fled to felicity,[21]
Far within the bosom bright
Of blazing Majesty and Light.   70
There with thee, new-welcome Saint,
Like fortunes may her soul acquaint,
With thee there clad in radiant sheen,
No Marchioness, but now a Queen.

---

[15] the mountain where the Muses dwelled
[16] twigs/sprays used as wreaths
[17] roads
[18] the River Cam, for which Cambridge is named
[19] Rachel
[20] the child she bore was Benjamin
[21] happiness (in heaven)

L'ALLEGRO [22]
[*1631?*]

Hence, loathèd melancholy,
  Of Cerberus [23] and blackest midnight born,
In Stygian [24] cave forlorn
  'Mongst horrid shapes, and shrieks, and sights unholy!
Find out some uncouth [25] cell [26]
  Where brooding darkness spreads his jealous wings,
And the night-raven sings.
  There under ebon shades and low-browed [27] rocks
As ragged as thy locks,
  In dark Cimmerian [28] desert ever dwell.   10

      But come thou, goddess fair and free,
In Heaven yclept [29] Euphrosyne, [30]
And by men heart-easing mirth,
Whom lovely Venus at a birth
With two sister Graces more
To ivy-crownèd Bacchus bore—
Or whether (as some, sager, sing)
The frolic wind that breathes [31] the spring,
Zephyr with Aurora playing,
As he met her once a-Maying,   20
There on beds of violets blue
And fresh-blown roses washed in dew,
Filled her with thee, a daughter fair,

---

[22] (in Italian) lively, cheerful, gay, merry
[23] monstrous dog, guardian of the entrance to Hades
[24] Styx = underground river across which Charon ferried the souls of the dead into Hades
[25] unknown
[26] small, solitary chamber
[27] projecting cliff edges
[28] according to Homer, a people who live at the outer edge of the world and thus are in perpetual darkness
[29] named, called
[30] the three Graces are Agalia, Thalia, and Euphrosyne [four syllables, the second and fourth accented]
[31] exhales

So buxom,[32] blithe,[33] and debonair.[34]
      Haste thee, nymph, and bring with thee
Jest and youthful jollity,
Quips and cranks,[35] and wanton wiles,[36]
Nods, and becks,[37] and wreathèd smiles
Such as hang on Hebe's[38] cheek
And love to live in dimple sleek,   30
Sport[39] that wrinkled care derides,
And laughter, holding both its sides.
Come, and trip it as ye go
On the light-fantastic toe,
And in thy right hand lead with thee
The mountain nymph, sweet liberty.
And if I give thee honor due,
Mirth, admit me of thy crew
To live with her, and live with thee,
In unreprovèd[40] pleasures free,   40
To hear the lark begin his flight
And, singing, startle the dull[41] night
From his watch-tower in the skies,
Till the dappled[42] dawn doth rise,
Then to come, in spite of sorrow,
And at my window bid good-morrow
Through the sweet-briar, or the vine,
Or the twisted eglantine,
While the cock, with lively din,
Scatters the rear of darkness thin,[43]   50
And to the stack[44] or the barn door
Stoutly[45] fierce struts his dames before.[46]

---

[32] jolly, lively, unresisting
[33] merry, gay
[34] affable, graceful
[35] fanciful turns of speech, conceits
[36] sportive/cunning/amorous tricks
[37] nod of the head, signaling either assent or command
[38] goddess of youth [bisyllabic]
[39] frolic, diversion
[40] uncensured
[41] slow, listless
[42] speckled
[43] "rear" as in "rear guard": the image is military
[44] as in "haystack"
[45] brave, fierce, vigorous
[46] "struts his dames before" = struts in front of his lady folk

Oft listening how the hounds and horn
Cheerly rouse the slumbering morn
From the side of some hoar[47] hill,
Through the high wood echoing shrill.
Sometime walking not unseen[48]
By hedgerow elms, on hillocks green,
Right against the eastern gate
Where the great[49] sun begins his state,[50]   60
Robed in flames and amber light,
The clouds in thousand liveries[51] dight,[52]
While the ploughman, near at hand,
Whistles o'er the furrowed land,
And the milkmaid singeth blithe,
And the mower whets[53] his scythe,
And every shepherd tells his tale
Under the hawthorn in the dale.
            Straight, mine eye hath caught new pleasures
Whilst the landscape round it measures,[54]   70
Russet[55] lawns, and fallows[56] gray,
Where the nibbling flocks do stray,
Mountains on whose barren breast
The laboring clouds do often rest,
Meadows trim with daisies pied,[57]
Shallow brooks and rivers wide.
Towers and battlements[58] it sees,
Bosomed high in tufted trees,
Where perhaps some beauty[59] lies,[60]
The cynosure[61] of neighboring eyes.   80

---

[47] light gray
[48] in plain view, openly
[49] elevated, distinguished, of high rank
[50] display of high dignity/rank/wealth
[51] elaborate costumes/uniforms
[52] equipped, ordered
[53] sharpens
[54] appraises
[55] reddish brown
[56] farmland ploughed and harrowed but left uncultivated for a period (usually a year)
[57] spotted, variegated
[58] indented parapets at the tops of walls
[59] i.e., some beautiful woman
[60] dwells
[61] center of attraction

Hard by, a cottage chimney smokes
From betwixt two agèd oaks,
Where Corydon and Thyrsis,[62] met,
Are at their savory dinner set
Of herbs[63] and other country messes,[64]
Which the neat-handed[65] Phyllis dresses.[66]
And then in haste her bow'r[67] she leaves,
With Thestylis to bind[68] the sheaves,[69]
Or if the earlier season[70] lead[71]
To the tanned[72] haycock[73] in the mead,[74]   90
Sometimes with secure[75] delight
The upland[76] hamlets[77] will invite,
When the merry bells ring round,
And the jocund[78] rebecks[79] sound
To many a youth and many a maid,
Dancing in the checkered shade,
And young and old come forth to play
On a sunshine holiday,
Till the livelong daylight fail.
Then to the spicy nut-brown ale,   100
With stories told of many a feat,
How fairy Mab[80] the junkets[81] eat.
She was pinched and pulled, she said,
And he, by friar's lantern led,

---

[62] Corydon and Thyrsis = protypical names for characters in Greek pastorals
[63] leafy edible plants
[64] food
[65] deft, dexterous
[66] prepares
[67] abode, cottage
[68] tie up
[69] bundles made after reaping (usually of grains)
[70] i.e., before harvest time (autumn)
[71] conduct, guide, show the way
[72] browned by exposure
[73] conical heaps of hay, in the fields/pastures
[74] meadow
[75] free from care/doubt/worry
[76] highland
[77] small villages or groups of houses, having no church
[78] merry, joyful, light-hearted
[79] primitive three-stringed fiddle
[80] a principal fairy
[81] cakes, sweetmeats, dainties

Tells how the drudging goblin sweat
To earn his cream-bowl, duly set,
When in one night, ere glimpse of morn,
His shadowy flail[82] hath threshed the corn[83]
That ten day-laborers could not end,
Then lies him down (the lubber fend!)[84]   110
And, stretched out all the chimney's length,
Basks at the fire his hairy strength,
And, crop-full,[85] out of doors he flings,
Ere the first cock his matin[86] rings.
Thus done the tales, to bed they creep,
By whispering winds soon lulled asleep.
        Tow'red cities please us, then,
And the busy hum of men,
Where throngs of knights and barons bold
In weeds[87] of peace high triumphs[88] hold,   120
With store[89] of ladies, whose bright eyes
Rain influence, and judge the prize
Of wit or arms, while both contend
To win her grace, whom all commend.
There let Hymen[90] oft appear
In saffron[91] robe, with taper[92] clear,
And pomp,[93] and feast, and revelry,
With masque and antique pageantry,
Such sights as youthful poets dream
On summer eves by haunted stream.   130
Then to the well-trod stage anon,
If Jonson's[94] learnèd sock be on,[95]

---

[82] threshing tool: a wooden handle to which is tied a free-swinging clublike swingle (or "swipple")
[83] grain
[84] beneficent goblin
[85] stuffed with food
[86] morning call
[87] garments
[88] public spectacle/festivity
[89] sufficient/abundant supply
[90] god of marriage
[91] orange-red/yellow
[92] wax candle
[93] splendor, magnificence
[94] Ben Jonson, 1572–1637, poet, dramatist, critic; friend/colleague of Shakespeare
[95] comedy (in which the actors wore low-heeled slippers, or "socks")

Or sweetest Shakespeare, Fancy's[96] child,
Warble his native wood-notes wild.
And ever, against eating[97] cares,
Lap me in soft Lydian airs,[98]
Married to immortal verse,
Such as the meeting[99] soul may pierce
In notes, with many a winding bout[1]
Of linkèd sweetness long drawn out,   140
With wanton[2] heed[3] and giddy[4] cunning,[5]
The melting voice through mazes running,
Untwisting all the chains that tie
The hidden soul of harmony,
That Orpheus[6] self may heave[7] his head
From golden slumber on a bed
Of heaped Elysian[8] flowers, and hear
Such strains[9] as would have won the ear
Of Pluto,[10] to have quite set free
His half-regained Eurydice.[11]   150
          These delights if thou canst give,
Mirth, with thee I mean to live.[12]

---

[96] imagination
[97] corrosive
[98] the Lydian (ancient Greek) mode (musical scale) was soft, often melancholy; airs = melodies
[99] gentle
[1] round
[2] see footnote 36 to line 27, above
[3] attention, care
[4] whirling, intoxicated
[5] skill, craft
[6] legendary poet/musician
[7] raise, lift
[8] Elysian Fields/Elysium = legendary island of the blessed
[9] melodies
[10] lord of the underworld
[11] Orpheus had won her right to live again, provided he not look back at her as she followed him up into the world of the living. He finally did look back, at her urgent request, and she disappeared forever [four syllables, second and fourth accented]
[12] The reference is to Marlowe's "Passionate Shepherd"; see also lines 37–40, above

IL PENSEROSO[13]
[1631?]

Hence, vain deluding joys,
  The brood of folly without father bred!
How little you bestead,[14]
  Or fill the fixèd[15] mind with all your toys![16]
Dwell in some idle brain,
  And fancies fond[17] with gaudy[18] shapes possess
As thick and numberless
  As the gay motes[19] that people the sun beams,
Or likest hovering dreams,
  The fickle pensioners[20] of Morpheus[21] train.   10

       But hail thou, goddess, sage and holy,
Hail divinest Melancholy,
Whose saintly visage is too bright
To hit[22] the sense of human sight
And, therefore, to our weaker view
O'er laid with black, staid wisdom's hue—
Black, but such as in esteem
Prince Memnon's[23] sister might beseem,[24]
Or that starr'd Ethiope[25] Queen that strove
To set her beauty's praise above   20
The sea nymphs, and their powers offended.
Yet thou art higher far descended,

---

[13] (in Italian) thoughtful, serious, grave
[14] help, assist
[15] resolved, determined
[16] whims
[17] foolish, credulous, idiotic
[18] showy
[19] minute particle (of dust)
[20] hirelings, mercenaries, tools, creatures
[21] son of Hypnos (Sleep), and god of dreams
[22] reach, light upon
[23] a handsome Ethiopian prince; his sister's name is Himera—but the allusion remains obscure
[24] suit
[25] Cassiopeia, queen of Ethiopia, boasted that Andromeda, her daughter, was more beautiful than the Nereids, who responded by turning Andromeda into a constellation ["Ethiope" = bisyllabic—i.e., first syllable stressed, second syllable elided]

Thee, bright-haired Vesta,[26] long of yore
To solitary Saturn bore:
His daughter she (in Saturn's reign
Such mixture was not held a stain),
Oft in glimmering bow'rs and glades
He met her, and in secret shades
Of woody Ida's[27] inmost grove,
While yet there was no fear of Jove.   30
      Come, pensive nun,[28] devout and pure,
Sober, steadfast, and demure,[29]
All in a robe of darkest grain,[30]
Flowing with majestic train,
And sable[31] stole[32] of cypress lawn[33]
Over thy decent[34] shoulders drawn!
Come, but keep thy wonted[35] state
With even step and musing gait,
And looks commercing[36] with the skies,
Thy rapt[37] soul sitting in thine eyes.   40
There held in holy passion still,
Forget thyself to marble, till
With a sad,[38] leaden[39] downward cast[40]
Thou fix them[41] on the earth as fast.[42]
And join with thee calm peace, and quiet,
Spare[43] fast,[44] that oft with gods doth diet,
And hears the Muses in a ring

---

[26] virgin daughter of Saturn (Chronos) and goddess of the hearth
[27] in Crete? where Jove (Zeus) lived—and plotted against Saturn (Chronos)
[28] priestess of a pagan deity
[29] sober, grave, serious, reserved
[30] color
[31] sable-colored: black
[32] mantlelike vestment, worn over the shoulders
[33] fine linen fabric; unlike most linens, cypress lawn is black
[34] comely
[35] usual, habitual, customary
[36] to communicate/hold intercourse with
[37] transported, carried away, enraptured
[38] steadfast, firm, grave, serious
[39] heavy
[40] glance, look
[41] i.e., her eyes
[42] with equal firmness
[43] lean
[44] fasting (abstinence from food)

Aye[45] round about Jove's altar sing.
And add to these retired[46] leisure,
That in trim[47] gardens takes his pleasure.   50
But first, and chiefest, with thee bring
Him[48] that yon soars on golden wing,
Guiding the fiery-wheelèd throne,[49]
The cherub Contemplation,[50]
And the mute silence hist[51] along,
'Less[52] Philomel[53] will deign a song
In her sweetest, saddest plight,[54]
Smoothing the rugged brow of night,
While Cynthia[55] checks[56] her dragon yoke,[57]
Gently o'er th' accustomed oak—   60
Sweet bird that shunn'st the noise of folly,
Most musical, most melancholy!
Thee, chantress,[58] oft the woods among,
I woo[59] to hear thy even song,
And missing thee, I walk unseen
On the dry, smooth-shaven[60] green,
To behold the wand'ring moon
Riding near her highest noon
Like one that had been led astray
Through the Heav'ns' wide pathless way,   70
And oft, as if her head she bowed,
Stooping through a fleecy cloud.

---

[45] always
[46] withdrawn
[47] well-ordered
[48] "the Cherub Contemplation" (line 54, immediately below)
[49] Ezekiel's vision of a heavenly chariot: see Ezekiel 10:1–2 and 9–22
[50] [five syllables, first, third, and fifth accented]
[51] summon (with a whisper)
[52] unless
[53] the nightingale
[54] mood, manner
[55] moon goddess
[56] curbs, restrains
[57] yoke = wooden device for coupling more than one horse or other dray animal to one vehicle
[58] singer (the nightingale)
[59] solicit, entreat
[60] not by lawn cutting but by sheep nibbling

Oft on a plat[61] of rising ground
I hear the far-off curfew sound
Over some wide-watered shore,
Swinging slow with sullen[62] roar.
Or if the air will not permit,
Some still[63] removèd[64] place will fit,
Where glowing embers through the room
Teach light to counterfeit a gloom,[65]　　　　　　　80
Far from all resort of mirth,
Save the cricket on the hearth,
Or the bellman's[66] drowsy charm[67]
To bless the doors from nightly harm.
Or let my lamp, at midnight hour,
Be seen in some high lonely tow'r
Where I may oft out-watch the Bear,[68]
With thrice great Hermes,[69] or unsphere
The spirit of Plato[70] to unfold[71]
What worlds, or what vast regions, hold　　　　　　90
The immortal mind that hath forsook
Her mansion[72] in this fleshly nook,[73]
And of those daemons[74] that are found
In fire, air, flood, or under ground,
Whose power hath a true consent[75]
With planet, or with element.
Sometime let gorgeous[76] tragedy

---

[61] a piece/patch of ground, usually small
[62] deep mournful tone
[63] quiet
[64] remote, secluded
[65] darkness
[66] the night watchman/town crier
[67] incantation
[68] the constellation Ursa Major ("Great Bear"), which never sets
[69] Hermes Trismegistus ("thrice great Hermes"), third-century Neoplatonist
[70] Plato's spirit is assumed, here, to now reside in a planetary sphere: Plato argued that great men's souls do in fact so ascend after their bodies die
[71] explain
[72] dwelling
[73] corner, outlying/remote region
[74] a being intermediate between god and man: an inferior deity
[75] accord, agreement
[76] brilliant, showy

In sceptered[77]pall[78] come sweeping by,
Presenting Thebes',[79] or Pelops' line,[80]
Or the tale of Troy divine.   100
Or what (though rare) of later age
Ennobled hath the buskined[81] stage.
But, O sad virgin, that thy power
Might raise Musaeus[82] from his bower,
Or bid the soul of Orpheus sing
Such notes as, warbled to the string,
Drew iron tears down Pluto's cheek
And made Hell grant what love did seek.
Or call up him[83] that left half told
The story of Cambuscan bold,   110
Of Camball, and of Algarsife,[84]
And who had Canace to wife,
That owned the virtuous ring and glass,
And of the wondrous horse of brass
On which the Tartar king did ride.
And if ought else, great bards beside
In sage and solemn tunes have sung
Of tourneys,[85] and of trophies hung,
Of forests, and enchantments drear,
Where more is meant than meets the ear.[86]   120
Thus night oft see me in thy pale career,[87]
Till civil-suited[88] morn appear,
Not tricked[89] and frounced,[90] as she was wont

---

[77] scepter = ornamental rod/wand
[78] rich purple cloth
[79] of which Oedipus was king
[80] i.e., Agamemnon, Orestes, Electra, Iphigenia
[81] high thick-soled boots worn in tragedies, as opposed to the "sock" (low slipper) worn in comedies
[82] mythical Greek poet, said to have been taught by Orpheus
[83] Geoffrey Chaucer, "Squire's Tale" (in *Canterbury Tales*): the first two parts were finished, but we have only the first two lines of part three
[84] [three syllables, first and third accented]
[85] tournaments
[86] not ironic, but a reference to Spenser, one of Milton's favorite poets, who (in Book IV, canto 2, of *The Fairy Queen*) added allegory to the tale Chaucer left unfinished
[87] path
[88] sober
[89] decked, adorned
[90] pleated, curled

With the Attic boy[91] to hunt,
But kerchiefed in a comely cloud
While rocking winds are piping loud,
Or ushered with a shower still,
When the gust hath blown his fill,
Ending on the rustling leaves,
With minute drops from off the eaves.   130
      And when the sun begins to fling
His flaring beams, me, goddess, bring
To archèd walks of twilight groves
And shadows brown that Sylvan[92] loves
Of pine, or monumental oak,
Where the rude[93] ax, with heavèd[94] stroke,
Was never heard the nymphs to daunt,
Or fright them from their hallowed haunt.[95]
There in close covert,[96] by some brook,
Where no profaner[97] eye may look,   140
Hide me from day's garish[98] eye,
While the bee, with honeyed thigh,
That at her flow'ry work doth sing,
And the waters murmuring
With such consort[99] as they keep,
Entice the dewy-feathered sleep.
And let some strange mysterious dream
Wave at his wings, in airy stream
Of lively portraiture displayed,
Softly on my eye-lids laid.   150
And as I wake, sweet music breathe
Above, about, or underneath,
Sent by some spirit to mortals good,
Or th' unseen genius[1] of the wood.

---

[91] Cephalus, husband of Procris, trapped in an ultimately fatal human-deity triangle when Eos ("dawn") fell in love with him
[92] god of forests
[93] harsh, violent, rugged
[94] lifted, raised
[95] frequently visited place
[96] shelter, covering
[97] unhallowed, polluted, alien
[98] glaringly bright
[99] company? harmony?
[1] tutelary god/spirit

But let my due[2] feet never fail
To walk the studious cloisters' pale[3]
And love the high embowèd[4] roof,
With antic pillars massy[5]-proof,
And storied[6] windows richly dight,[7]
Casting a dim religious light.   160
There let the pealing[8] organ blow
To the full voiced choir below,
In service high, and anthems clear,
As may with sweetness, through mine ear,
Dissolve me into ecstasies
And bring all Heav'n before mine eyes.
And may at last my weary age
Find out the peaceful hermitage,
The hairy gown and mossy cell
Where I may sit and rightly spell[9]   170
Of every star that Heav'n doth shew,[10]
And every herb that sips the dew,
Till old experience do attain
To something like prophetic strain.

      These pleasures, Melancholy, give,
And I with thee will choose to live.

---

[2] proper
[3] bounds [noun]
[4] arched, vaulted
[5] "massily" [adverb]
[6] ornamented with scenes ("stories") from history, legend, etc.
[7] made, ordered, arrayed
[8] resounding, sounding forth
[9] ponder
[10] show

ARCADES
[1633–34?]

Part of an entertainment presented to the Countess Dowager of Darby, at Harefield, by some noble persons of her family, who appear on the scene in pastoral habit, moving toward the seat of state, with this song:

1. Song

Look, nymphs, and shepherds, look!
What sudden blaze of majesty
Is that which we from hence descry,[11]
Too divine to be mistook.
      This, this is she
To whom our vows and wishes bend:
Here our solemn search hath end.

Fame, that her high worth to raise
Seemed erst so lavish and profuse,
We may justly now accuse   10
Of detraction from her praise.
      Less than half we find expressed:
Envy bid conceal the rest.

Mark what radiant state she spreads
In circle round her shining throne,
Shooting her beams like silver threads!
This, this is she alone,
      Sitting like a goddess bright
In the center of her light.

Might she the wise Latona[12] be,   20
Or the towered Cybele,[13]
Mother of a hundred gods?

---

[11] catch sight of
[12] Leto, a Titan, mother of twins, Apollo and Artemis, whose father is Zeus
[13] the Great Mother [trisyllabic, first and third syllables accented]

Juno dares not give her odds.[14]
      Who had thought this clime had held
      A deity so unparall'ed?

As they come forward, the Genius of the Wood appears and, turning toward them, says:

      Gen. Stay, gentle[15] swains,[16] for though in this disguise
I see bright honor sparkle through your eyes.
Of famous Arcady[17] ye are, and sprung
Of that renownèd flood[18] so often sung,
Divine Alphéus, who by secret sluice   30
Stole under seas, to meet his Arethuse.[19]
And ye the breathing roses of the wood,
Fair silver-buskined[20] nymphs as great and good,
I know this quest of yours, and free[21] intent,
Was all in honor and devotion meant
To the great mistress of yon princely shrine,
Whom with low reverence I adore as mine,
And with all helpful service will comply
To further this night's glad solemnity,
And lead ye where you may more near behold   40
What shallow-searching fame hath left untold,
Which I full oft, amidst these shades alone,
Have sat to wonder at and gaze upon.
      For know, by lot[22] from Jove I am the pow'r
Of this fair wood and live in oaken bow'r
To nurse the saplings tall, and curl the grove
With ringlets quaint,[23] and wanton[24] windings wove.

---

[14] i.e., give her any further competitive advantage
[15] gentlemanly, noble, high-born, aristocratic
[16] shepherds, rustics
[17] Arcadia: region of Greece which Virgil's *Eclogues* made the traditional locale of the pastoral ideal
[18] river, stream
[19] river that fell in love with the nymph Arethusa and, after Diana transformed her into a fountain, flowed under the sea to reach her
[20] buskin halfboot
[21] generous, noble, honorable
[22] choice of
[23] skillful, dainty, pretty, elegant
[24] profuse, extravagant, sportive, fanciful

And all my plants I save from nightly ill
Of noisome[25] winds or blasting[26] vapors chill,
And from the boughs brush off the evil dew   50
And heal the harms, of[27] thwarting[28] thunder blew,
Or what the cross, dire-looking planet[29] smites,
Or hurtful worm with cankered[30] venom bites.
When evening gray doth rise, I fetch[31] my round
Over the mount, and all this hallowed ground,
And early, ere the odorous breath of morn
Awakes the slumb'ring leaves, or tasseled horn[32]
Shakes the high thicket, haste I all about,
Number[33] my ranks,[34] and visit every sprout
With puissant[35] words, and murmurs made to bless.   60
But else, in deep of night, when drowsiness
Hath locked up mortal sense, then listen I
To the celestial sirens' harmony,
That sit upon the nine enfoldèd spheres
And sing to those that hold the vital shears[36]
And turn the adamantine[37] spindle round,[38]
On which the fate of gods and men is wound.
Such sweet compulsion doth in music lie
To lull the daughters of Necessity
And keep unsteady[39] Nature to her law,   70
And the low[40] world in measured[41] motion draw
After the heav'nly tune, which none can hear

---

[25] noxious, harmful
[26] blighting, infectious
[27] from
[28] crossing, traversing (the sky)
[29] Saturn
[30] ulcerative, decaying
[31] go
[32] hunting horn
[33] count
[34] rows
[35] potent, powerful
[36] vital shears = shears of life
[37] unbreakable
[38] the Fates, daughters of Necessity
[39] fickle, changeable
[40] (1) below, (2) of humble rank
[41] rhythmical, regular

Of human mould, with gross[42] unpurgèd[43] ear.
And yet such music worthiest were to blaze
The peerless height of her immortal praise,
Whose luster leads us, and for her most fit,
If my inferior hand or voice could hit
Inimitable sounds. Yet as we go
Whate'er the skill of lesser gods can show
I will assay,[44] her worth to celebrate.   80
And so attend[45] ye toward her glittering state,
Where ye may all (that are of noble stem)[46]
Approach, and kiss her sacred vesture's[47] hem.

2. Song

O'er the smooth enamelled[48] green
Where no print of step hath been,
        Follow me as I sing
        And touch the warbled string.
Under the shady roof
Of branching elm, star-proof,[49]
        Follow me: 90
I will bring you where she sits,
Clad in splendor as befits
        Her deity.
        Such a rural queen
All Arcadia hath not seen.

---

[42] coarse
[43] unpurified
[44] try, attempt
[45] direct one's attention
[46] stock
[47] clothing
[48] glossy, variegated
[49] i.e., providing shelter against the malign influence of evil stars

3. Song

Nymphs and shepherds, dance no more
By sandy Ladon's[50] lillied banks.
On old Lycaeus,[51] or Cyllene[52] hoar,[53]
Trip no more in twilight ranks.
Though Erymanth[54] your loss deplore   100
A better soil shall give you thanks.
From the stony Maenalus[55]
Bring your flocks and live with us.
    Here ye shall have greater grace
    To serve the lady of this place.
    Though Syrinx[56] your Pan's mistress were,
    Yet Syrinx well might wait on her.
        Such a rural queen
    All Arcadia hath not seen.

COMUS: A MASQUE[57]
[*1634; revised 1637*]

The Persons

the attendant spirit, afterwards in the habit of Thyrsis
Comus, with his crew

---

[50] the River Ladon runs through Arcadia and joins the Alpheus
[51] Arcadian mountain, birthplace of Pan, associated with the worship of Zeus
[52] Arcadian mountain
[53] gray/grayish white
[54] Arcadian mountain range, where Hercules hunted and killed a fierce wild boar
[55] Arcadian mountain, associated with Pan
[56] nymph beloved by Pan
[57] written to celebrate the Earl of Bridgewater's election as Lord President of Wales. As performed at Lord Bridgewater's Ludlow castle, 29 September 1634, the lady was played by Bridgewater's daughter and the brothers by her brothers. Thyrsis/attendant spirit was

the lady
brother 1 [older]
brother 2 [younger]
Sabrina, the nymph

*The first scene discovers a wild wood. The attendant spirit descends
(or enters):*

Before the starry threshold of Jove's court
My mansion is, where those immortal shapes
Of bright aerial spirits live ensphered
In regions mild, of calm and serene air,
Above the smoke and stir of this dim spot
Which men call earth and, with low-thoughtèd care,
Confined and pestered in this pinfold[58] here,
Strive to keep up a frail and fev'rish being,
Unmindful of the crown that virtue gives,
After this mortal change, to her true servants,   10
Amongst the enthronèd gods, on sainted seats.
Yet some there be that by due steps aspire
To lay their just hands on that golden key
That opes the palace of eternity:
To such my errand is, and but for such
I would not soil these pure ambrosial weeds
With the rank vapors of this sin-worn mould.
          But to my task. Neptune—besides the sway
Of every salt flood, and each ebbing stream—
Took in, by lot twixt high and nether Jove,[59]   20
Imperial rule of all the sea-girt isles
That, like to rich and various gems, inlay
The unadornèd bosom of the deep,
Which he, to grace his tributary gods,
By course[60] commits to several government
And gives them leave to wear their sapphire crowns
And wield their little tridents. But this isle,
The greatest and the best of all the main,[61]

---

played by the composer of the masque's music (and music tutor to the family), Henry
Lawes.
[58] cattle pen
[59] Pluto, lord of the underworld, as Jove was lord of that above ground
[60] custom, practice
[61] i.e., the main sea, the ocean

He quarters to his blue-haired deities,
And all this tract that fronts the falling sun   30
A noble peer, of mickle[62] trust and power,
Has in his charge, with tempered[63] awe[64] to guide
An old and haughty nation, proud in arms,
Where his fair offspring, nursed in princely lore,
Are coming to attend their father's state
And new-entrusted scepter. But their way
Lies through the perplex'd[65] paths of this drear Wood,
The nodding horror of whose shady brows
Threats the forlorn and wand'ring passenger.
And here their tender age might suffer peril,   40
But that by quick command from sov'reign Jove
I was dispatched for their defence and guard.
And listen why, for I will tell you now
What never yet was heard in tale or song
From old or modern bard, in hall or bow'r.
              Bacchus, that first from out the purple grape
Crushed the sweet poison of mis-used wine,
After the Tuscan mariners transformed,
Coasting the Tyrrhene shore, as the winds listed
On Circe's island fell (who knows not Circe,   50
The daughter of the sun? whose charmèd cup
Whoever tasted lost his upright shape
And downward fell, into a grovelling swine).
This nymph that gazed upon his[66] clust'ring locks
With ivy berries wreathed, and his blithe youth,
Had by him, ere he parted thence, a son
Much like his father, but his mother more,
Whom therefore she brought up and Comus named,
Who ripe and frolic[67] of[68] his full-grown age,
Roving the Celtic and Iberian fields,   60
At last betakes him to this ominous[69] Wood

---

[62] much, great
[63] temperate
[64] power
[65] intricate, entangled
[66] Bacchus
[67] free
[68] with
[69] menacing, inauspicious

And, in thick shelter of black shade embow'red,
Excells his mother at her mighty art,
Off'ring to every weary traveller
His orient[70] liquor, in a crystal glass,
To quench the drought of Phoebus, which as they taste
(For most do taste, through fond,[71] intemperate thirst),
Soon as the potion works, their human count'nance—
Th' express resemblance of the gods—is changed
Into some brutish form of wolf or bear   70
Or ounce,[72] or tiger, hog, or bearded goat,
All other parts remaining as they were.
And they, so perfect is their misery,
Not once perceive their foul disfigurement,
But boast themselves more comely[73] than before
And all their friends and native home forget,
To roll with pleasure in a sensual sty.
Therefore, when any favored of high Jove
Chances to pass through this advent'rous glade,
Swift as the sparkle of a glancing star   80
I shoot from Heav'n, to give him safe convoy—
As now I do. But first I must put off
These my sky robes, spun out of Iris[74] woof,
And take the weeds[75] and likeness of a swain[76]
That to the service of this house belongs,
Who with his soft pipe[77] and smooth-dittied song
Well knows to still the wild winds when they roar,
And hush the waving woods, nor of less faith,
And in this office of his mountain watch
Likeliest and nearest to the present aid   90
Of this occasion.
                         But I hear the tread
Of hateful steps. I must be viewless, now.

---

[70] brilliant, precious
[71] foolish
[72] lynx
[73] fair, pleasing, proper
[74] goddess of the rainbow
[75] garments
[76] male servant, attendant, rustic, shepherd
[77] reed flute

Comus enters, with a charming[78] *rod in one hand, his glass in the other. With him a rout*[79] *of monsters headed*[80] *like sundry sorts of wild beasts, but otherwise like men and women, their apparel glistening. They come in, making a riotous and unruly noise, with torches in their hands.*

Comus. The star that bids[81] the shepherd fold,[82]
Now the top of Heav'n doth hold,
And the gilded car of day
His glowing axle doth allay[83]
In the steep Atlantic stream,
And the slope[84] sun his upward beam
Shoots against the dusky pole,
Pacing toward the other goal   100
Of his chamber in the east.
Meanwhile, welcome joy and feast,
Midnight shout and revelry,
Tipsy dance and jollity!
Braid your locks with rosy twine,[85]
Dropping[86] odors, dropping wine.
Rigor now is gone to bed,
And advice, with scrupulous head.
Strict age, and sour severity
With their grave saws[87] in slumber lie.   110
We that are of purer fire
Imitate the starry choir
Who in their nightly watchful spheres
Lead in swift round the months and years.
The sounds[88] and seas, with all their finny drove,[89]

---

[78] magical, enchanting
[79] band, crowd, herd
[80] having the heads of
[81] commands
[82] to shut up sheep in a fold (pen, enclosure)
[83] (1) temper, abate, mitigate, (2) lay down
[84] sloping, slanting
[85] threads, cords
[86] sprinkling down
[87] proverbs, maxims
[88] channels, inlets
[89] herd, flock, multitude

Now to the moon in wavering morris[90] move,
And on the tawny sands and shelves
Trip the pert[91] fairies and the dapper[92] elves.
By dimpled[93] brook and fountain brim
The wood nymphs, decked with daisies trim,   120
Their merry wakes[94] and pastimes keep.
What has night to do with sleep?
Night has better sweets to prove:
Venus now wakes, and wakens love.
       Come, let us our rites begin!
'Tis only daylight that makes sin—
Which these dun shades will ne'er report.
Hail, goddess of nocturnal sport,
Dark-veil'd Cotytto,[95] t'whom the secret flame
Of midnight torches burns! Mysterious dame   130
That ne'er art called but[96] when the dragon womb
Of Stygian darkness spits her thickest gloom
And makes one blot of all the air!
Stay thy cloudy ebon[97] chair,
Wherein thou rid'st with Hecat,[98] and befriend
Us, thy vowèd priests, till utmost end
Of all thy dues be done, and none left out,
Ere the blabbing[99] eastern scout,[1]
The nice[2] morn on th' Indian steep
From her cabined loop-hole peep,   140
And to the tell-tale sun descry[3]
Our conceal'd solemnity.
Come, knit hands and beat the ground
In a light fantastic round!

---

[90] morris dance: traditional English country dance, especially associated with May Day celebrations
[91] lively, skilled
[92] lively, spruce
[93] rippling
[94] festivals, holidays
[95] Thracian goddess of orgies
[96] except
[97] black
[98] Hecate [trisyllabic], ghost-world goddess
[99] blabbering
[1] spy
[2] fussy, overly refined
[3] announce

The measure.[4]

Break off, break off! I feel the different pace
Of some chaste footing near about this ground.
Run to your shrouds,[5] within these brakes[6] and trees:
Our number may affright. Some virgin, sure
(For so I can distinguish, by mine art),
Benighted[7] in these woods. Now to my charms,   150
And to my wily trains.[8] I shall ere long
Be well-stocked with as fair a herd as grazed
About my mother, Circe. Thus I hurl
My dazzling spells into the spongey[9] air,
Of power to cheat the eye with blear[10] illusion
And give it false presentments,[11] lest the place
And my quaint[12] habits breed astonishment
And put the damsel to suspicious flight,
Which must not be, for that's against my course.
I under fair pretence of friendly ends   160
And well-placed words of glozing[13] courtesy,
Baited with reasons not implausible,
Wind me into the easy-hearted man,
And hug him into snares. When once her eye
Hath met the virtue of this magic dust,
I shall appear some harmless villager
Whom thrift[14] keeps up about[15] his country gear.
But here she comes. I fairly[16] step aside
And hearken, if I may, her business here.

The lady enters.

---

[4] i.e., they dance
[5] shelter, hiding place
[6] thickets
[7] overtaken by darkness
[8] tricks, traps, snares
[9] elastic, impressionable
[10] dim
[11] appearances, form
[12] crafty, clever, skillful
[13] flattering, coaxing, specious
[14] prosperity
[15] maintains in connection with
[16] (1) completely, (2) becomingly

    Lady. This way the noise was, if mine ear be true: 170
My best guide, now. Methought it was the sound
Of riot and ill-managed merriment,
Such as the jocund[17] flute or gamesome[18] pipe
Stirs up amongst the loose, unlettered hinds,[19]
When for their teeming flocks and granges full
In wanton[20] dance they praise the bounteous Pan
And thank the gods amiss.[21] I should be loath
To meet the rudeness[22] and swill'd insolence
Of such late wassailers.[23] Yet where else
Shall I inform my unacquainted feet   180
In the blind maze of this tangled Wood?
My brothers, when they saw me wearied out
With this long way, resolving here to lodge
Under the spreading favor of these pines,
Stepped, as they said, to the next thicket side,
To bring me berries, or such cooling fruit
As the kind, hospitable woods provide.
They left me then, when the gray-hooded ev'n
Like a sad votarist[24] in palmer's[25] weeds[26]
Rose from the hindmost wheels of Phoebus' wain.[27]   190
But where they are, and why they came not back,
Is now the labor of my thoughts. 'Tis likeliest
They had engaged their wand'ring steps too far,
And envious darkness, ere they could return,
Had stol'n them from me—else, O thievish night!
Why shouldst thou, but for some felonious end,
In thy dark lantern thus close up the stars
That Nature hung in Heav'n, and filled their lamps
With everlasting oil, to give due light
To the misled and lonely traveller?   200

---

[17] merry
[18] sportive
[19] rustics, farmhands
[20] frisky, unregulated
[21] in error
[22] uncivilized/coarse behavior
[23] drinkers
[24] devotee
[25] pilgrim
[26] clothing, garments, dress
[27] wagon

This is the place, as well as I may guess,
Whence ev'n now the tumult of loud mirth
Was rife[28] and perfect[29] in my list'ning ear.
Yet nought but single[30] darkness do I find.
What might this be? A thousand fantasies
Begin to throng into my memory,
Of calling shapes and beck'ning shadows dire,
And airy tongues that syllable men's names
On sands and shores, and desert wildernesses.
    These thoughts may startle well, but not astound   210
The virtuous mind, that ever walks attended
By a strong siding[31] champion, conscience—
O welcome, pure-eyed faith, white-handed hope,
Thou flittering Angel girt with golden wings!
And thou, unblemished form of chastity,
I see ye visibly, and now believe
That He, the supreme good, t' whom all things ill
Are but as slavish officers of vengeance,
Would send a glist'ring[32] guardian, if need were,
To keep my life and honor unassailed.   220
    Was I deceived, or did a sable cloud
Turn forth her silver lining on the night?
I did not err: there does a sable cloud
Turn forth her silver lining on the night,
And casts a gleam over this tufted grove.
I cannot halloo to my brothers, but
Such noise as I can make, to be heard farthest,
I'll venture, for my new-enlivened spirits
Prompt me, and they perhaps are not far off.

Song

    Sweet Echo, sweetest nymph that liv'st unseen   230
        Within thy airy cell
      By slow Maeander's[33] margent green,

---

[28] abundant
[29] complete
[30] unbroken, absolute
[31] supporting
[32] glittering, gleaming
[33] river in western Asia Minor, flowing into the Aegean

> And in the violet-embroidered vale
> Where the love-lorn nightingale
> Nightly to thee her sad song mourneth well,
> Canst thou not tell me of a gentle pair
> That likest thy Narcissus[34] are?
> O if thou have
> Hid them in some flow'ry cave,
> Tell me but where,   240
> Sweet queen of parley,[35] daughter of the sphere,
> So may'st thou be translated to the skies,
> And give resounding grace to all Heav'n's harmonies.

Comus. Can any mortal mixture of earth's mould
Breathe such divine, enchanting ravishment?
Sure, something holy lodges in that breast
And with these raptures moves the vocal[36] air
To testify his hidden residence!
How sweetly did they float upon the wings
Of silence, through the empty-vaulted night,   250
At every fall[37] smoothing the raven down[38]
Of darkness, till she smiled. I have oft heard
My mother, Circe, with the Sirens three,
Amidst the flow'ry-kirtled Naiades,[39]
Culling their potent[40] herbs and baleful drugs,
Who as they sung would take the prisoned soul
And lap it in Elysium. Scylla[41] wept
And chid her barking waves into attention,
And fell Charybdis[42] murmured soft applause!
Yet they in pleasing slumber lulled the sense,   260
And in sweet madness robbed it of itself.
But such a sacred and home-felt[43] delight,
Such sober certainty of waking bliss,

---

[34] beloved by Echo, and punished for rejecting her
[35] speech
[36] resounding
[37] drop in pitch
[38] [noun]
[39] water nymphs [trisyllabic, first and third syllables accented]
[40] powerful, mighty
[41] multiheaded, voracious monster
[42] deadly whirlpool, located opposite Scylla
[43] felt intimately/in the heart

I never heard till now. I'll speak to her
And she shall be my queen.
                                    Hail, foreign wonder!
Whom certain these rough shades did never breed—
Unless the goddess that in rural shrine
Dwell'st here with Pan[44] or Silvan,[45] by blest song
Forbidding every bleak unkindly fog
To touch the prosperous growth of this tall Wood!   270
          Lady. Nay, gentle shepherd, ill is lost that praise
That is addressed to unattending ears.
Not any boast of skill, but extreme shift[46]
How to regain my severed company
Compelled me to awake the courteous Echo
To give me answer from her mossy couch.
          Comus. What chance, good lady, hath bereft you thus?
          Lady. Dim darkness, and this leafy labyrinth.
          Comus. Could that divide you from near-ushering[47]
                    guides?
          Lady. They left me, weary, on a grassy turf.   280
          Comus. By falsehood, or discourtesy, or why?
          Lady. To seek i' th' valley some cool friendly spring.
          Comus. And left your fair side all unguarded, lady?
          Lady. They were but twain, and purposed quick return.
          Comus. Perhaps forestalling night prevented them?
          Lady. How easy my misfortune is to hit![48]
          Comus. Imports[49] their loss, beside the present need?
          Lady. No less than if I should my brothers lose.
          Comus. Were they of manly prime, or youthful bloom?
          Lady. As smooth as Hebe's,[50] their unrazored lips.   290
          Comus. Two such I saw, what time the labored ox[51]
In his loose traces[51] from the furrow came,
And the swinked[52] hedger[53] at his supper sat.

---

[44] god of shepherds, flocks, and their fertility; half human, half goat
[45] god of wilderness
[46] expedient, device
[47] ushering = escorting
[48] hit/come upon, guess
[49] to be important, to signify/matter
[50] daughter of Zeus and Hera, cupbearer of the gods [bisyllabic, first accented]
[51] straps, ropes, harness
[52] wearied, overworked
[53] tender/cutter of hedges

I saw 'em under a green mantling[54] vine
That crawls along the side of yon small hill,
Plucking ripe clusters from the tender shoots.
Their port[55] was more than human, as they stood:
I took it for a fairy vision
Of some gay[56] creatures of the element
That in the colors of the rainbow live   300
And play i' th' pleated clouds. I was awe-struck,
And as I passed I worshipped! If those you seek,
It were a journey like the path to Heav'n
To help you find them.
       Lady.   Gentle villager,
What readiest way would bring me to that place?
      Comus. Due west it rises, from this shrubby point.
      Lady. To find out that, good shepherd, I suppose,
In such a scant allowance of star-light,
Would overtask the best land-pilot's art,
Without the sure guess of well-practiced feet.   310
      Comus. I know each lane, and every alley green,
Dingle[57] or bushy dell[58] of this wide wood,
And every bosky[59] bourn,[60] from side to side
My daily walks and ancient neighborhood,
And if your stray attendance[61] be yet lodged[62]
Or shroud[63] within these limits, I shall know
Ere morrow wake or the low-roosted lark
From her thatched pallet[64] rouse. If otherwise,
I can conduct you, lady, to a low[65]
But loyal[66] cottage, where you may be safe   320
Till further quest.

---

[54] covering, as by a mantle/cloak
[55] bearing, carriage
[56] airy, joyful, bright, etc.
[57] dell, hollow, cleft between hills
[58] shallow hollow or pit
[59] bushy
[60] brook
[61] escort
[62] residing
[63] sheltered
[64] straw bed
[65] poor, humble, inferior
[66] dutiful, faithful

  Lady.   Shepherd, I take thy word
And trust thy honest offered courtesy,
Which oft is sooner found in lowly sheds
With smoky rafters than in tap'stry halls
And courts of princes, where it first was named
And yet is most pretended. In a place
Less warranted[67] than this, or less secure,
I cannot be, that I should fear to change it.
Eye me, blest providence, and square[68] my trial
To my proportioned strength!
        Shepherd, lead on.— 330

The two brothers.

  Brother 1. Unmuffle, ye faint stars, and thou fair moon
That wont'st[69] to love the traveller's benison,[70]
Stoop thy pale visage through an amber cloud
And disinherit chaos, that reigns here
In double night of darkness and of shades!
Or if your influence be quite dammed up
With black, usurping mists, some gentle taper[71]
Through a rush[72] candle from the wicker hole[73]
Of some clay habitation visit us
With thy long levelled rule of streaming light, 340
And thou shalt be our star of Arcady[74]
Or Tyrian[75] Cynosure.[76]
  Brother 2. Or if our eyes
Be barred that happiness, might we but hear
The folded[77] flocks penned in their wattled[78] cotes,[79]

---

[67] guaranteed, attested
[68] adapt, regulate
[69] are in the habit/practice of
[70] blessing
[71] (1) wax wick/candle, (2) a light
[72] reed
[73] small door
[74] Arcadia (site of proverbial pastoral simplicity)
[75] Tyre = ancient Phoenician city
[76] Callisto, raped and impregnated by Jupiter, is turned by Juno into Ursa Minor: the Pole Star is in its tail
[77] shut into their folds/enclosures/pens
[78] interlaced twigs, sprigs, and the like
[79] sheds, stalls

Or sound of pastoral reed[80] with oaten[81] stops,[82]
Or whistle from the lodge, or village cock
Count the night watches to his feathery dames,
It would be some solace yet, some little cheering
In this close[83] dungeon of innumerous boughs.
But O, that hapless virgin, our lost sister!   350
Where may she wander now? Whither betake her
From the chill dew, amongst rude burrs and thistles?
Perhaps some cold bank[84] is her bolster,[85] now,
Or 'gainst the rugged bark of some broad elm
Leans her unpillowed head, fraught[86] with sad fears.
What if in wild amazement and affright,
Or while we speak, within the direful grasp
Of savage hunger, or of savage heat?
      Brother 1. Peace, brother: be not over-exquisite[87]
To cast[88] the fashion[89] of uncertain evils,   360
For grant they be so, while they rest unknown
What need a man forestall his date of grief
And run to meet what he would most avoid?
Or if they be but false alarms of fear,
How bitter is such self-delusion?
I do not think my sister so to seek,[90]
Or so unprincipled in virtue's book
And the sweet peace that goodness bosoms[91] ever,
As that the single want of light and noise
(Not being in danger, as I trust she is not)   370
Could stir the constant[92] mood of her calm thoughts
And put them into misbecoming[93] plight.[94]

---

[80] flute
[81] made of oat stems/straw
[82] that which forms/encloses a fingerhole
[83] narrow, enclosed, confined
[84] ridge
[85] large pillow
[86] filled
[87] overexcited/intense
[88] reckon, resolve
[89] form, shape
[90] i.e., I do not plan to look for her in that spirit
[91] embraces, hides
[92] fixed, steadfast
[93] unsuitable
[94] peril, danger, risk

Virtue could see to do what virtue would,
By her own radiant light, though sun and moon
Were in the flat sea sunk. And wisdom's self
Oft seeks to sweet, retired solitude,
Where with her best nurse, contemplation,[95]
She plumes[96] her feathers and lets grow her wings
That in the various bustle of resort[97]
Were all too ruffled,[98] and sometimes impaired.   380
He that has light within his own clear breast
May sit i' th' center[99] and enjoy bright day,
But he that hides a dark soul, and foul thoughts,
Benighted[1] walks under the midday sun—
Himself is his own dungeon.
         Brother 2.   'Tis most true
That musing meditation most affects[2]
The pensive secrecy of desert cell,[3]
Far from the cheerful haunt[4] of men and herds,
And sits as safe as in a Senate house—
For who would rob a hermit of his weeds,[5]   390
His few books, or his beads,[6] or maple dish,
Or do his gray hairs any violence?
But beauty, like the fair Hesperian tree
Laden with blooming gold, had need the guard
Of dragon watch with unenchanted eye,
To save her blossoms and defend her fruit
From the rash hand of bold incontinence.[7]
You may as well spread out the unsunned heaps
Of miser's treasure by an outlaw's den
And tell me it is safe, as bid me hope   400

---

[95] [five syllables, first, third, and fifth accented]
[96] preens
[97] quotidian activities
[98] confused
[99] of the earth
[1] blinded, clouded
[2] likes, seeks
[3] single-person solitary dwelling
[4] place of frequent resort
[5] garments
[6] prayer beads
[7] unchastity

Danger will wink on opportunity
And let a single helpless maiden pass
Uninjured, in this wild surrounding waste.
Of night or loneliness, it recks me not:
I fear the dread events that dog them both,
Lest some ill greeting touch attempt[8] the person[9]
Of our unownèd[10] sister.

    Brother 1. I do not, brother,
Infer,[11] as if I thought my sister's state
Secure without all doubt or controversy.
Yet where an equal poise[12] of hope and fear   410
Does arbitrate[13] th' event, my nature is
That I incline to hope rather than fear
And banish, gladly, squint[14] suspicion.
My sister is not so defenceless left
As you imagine. She has a hidden strength
Which you remember not.

    Brother 2.   What hidden strength,
Unless the strength of Heav'n, if you mean that?

    Brother 1. I mean that too, but yet a hidden strength
Which, if Heav'n gave it, may be termed her own.
'Tis chastity, my brother, chastity.   420
She that has that is clad in complete steel,
And like a quivered nymph with arrows keen
May trace[15] huge forests and unharbored[16] heaths,[17]
Infamous hills and sandy perilous wilds,
Where through the sacred rays of chastity
No savage fierce, bandit or mountaineer,
Will dare to soil her virgin purity.
Yea, there where very desolation dwells,

---

[8] assault
[9] body
[10] unacknowledged? unaccompanied?
[11] conclude
[12] balance
[13] govern
[14] indirect, oblique
[15] travel, tread
[16] having no shelter
[17] open uncultivated ground

By grots[18] and caverns shagged[19] with horrid[20] shades,
She may pass on with unblenched[21] majesty—　　　　　　430
Be it not done in pride or in presumption.
Some say no evil thing that walks by night
In fog, or fire, by lake or moory[22] fen,[23]
Blue meager hag or stubborn unlaid[24] ghost
That breaks his chains at curfew time,
No goblin or swart[25] fairy of the mine,[26]
Has hurtful power o'er true virginity.
　　　　　　Do you believe me yet, or shall I call
Antiquity from the old schools of Greece
To testify the arms[27] of chastity?　　　　　　　　440
Hence had the huntress Dian her dread bow,
Fair silver-shafted queen, forever chaste,
Wherewith she tamed the brinded[28] lioness
And spotted mountain pard,[29] but set at naught
The frivolous bolt[30] of Cupid. Gods and men
Feared her stern frown, and she was queen o' th' woods.
What was that snaky-headed Gorgon shield
That wise Minerva wore, unconquered virgin,
Wherewith she freezed her foes to congealed stone,
But rigid looks of chaste austerity,　　　　　　　　450
And noble grace that dashed[31] brute violence
With sudden adoration and blank[32] awe!
So dear to Heav'n is saintly chastity
That when a soul is found sincerely so

---

[18] grotto = cave, excavation
[19] covered
[20] bristling, frightful
[21] not disconcerted/deceived
[22] marshy, moorlike
[23] swampland, marsh
[24] unexorcised
[25] dark, swarthy
[26] from underground
[27] weapons
[28] tawny-spotted/streaked
[29] leopard, panther
[30] arrow
[31] to frustrate, destroy
[32] absolute, sheer

A thousand liveried[33] Angels lackey[34] her,
Driving far off each thing of sin and guilt,
And in clear dream and solemn vision
Tell her of things that no gross ear can hear,
Till oft converse with Heav'nly habitants
Begin to cast a beam on th' outward shape,   460
The unpolluted temple of the mind,
And turns it by degrees to the soul's essence,
Till all be made immortal. But when lust
By unchaste looks, loose gestures, and foul talk,
But most by lewd and lavish[35] act of sin
Lets in[36] defilement to the inward parts,
The soul grows clotted by contagion,[37]
Embodies[38] and embrutes[39] till she quite lose
The divine property of her first being.
Such are those thick and gloomy shadows damp,   470
Oft seen in charnel[40] vaults and sepulchers
Hovering, and sitting by a new-made grave,
As[41] loath to leave the body that it loved
And linked itself, by carnal sensual'ty,
To a degenerate and degraded state.
          Brother 2. How charming is divine[42] philosophy!
Not harsh and crabbèd, as dull fools suppose,
But musical as is Apollo's lute,
And a perpetual feast of nectared sweets,
Where no crude surfeit reigns.
          Brother 1.   List, list! I hear   480
Some faroff halloo break the silent air.
          Brother 2. Methought so too. What should it be?
          Brother 1.   For certain,
Either someone, like us night-foundered here,
Or else some neighbor woodman—or, at worst,

---

[33] dressed in livery (distinctive uniform of servants)
[34] serve, wait upon
[35] unrestrained, profuse
[36] admits
[37] [four syllables, second and fourth accented]
[38] incorporates
[39] degrade, make bestial
[40] cemetery
[41] as if
[42] sacred, holy, religious

Some roving robber calling to his fellows.
        Brother 2. Heav'n keep my sister! Again: again, and
               near!
Best draw[43] and stand upon our guard.
        Brother 1.   I'll halloo.
If he be friendly, he comes well. If not,
Defence is a good cause, and Heav'n be for us.

The attendant spirit [enters], habited like a shepherd.

That halloo I should know. What are you? Speak!   490
Come not too near: you fall on iron stakes,[44] else!
        Spirit. What voice is that, my young lord? Speak again.
        Brother 2. O brother, 'tis my father's shepherd—sure!
        Brother 1. Thyrsis? Whose artful strains[45] have oft
            delayed
The huddling[46] brook, to hear his madrigal,
And sweetened every muskrose of the dale.
How cam'st thou here, good swain? Hath any ram
Slipped from his fold, or young kid lost his dam,[47]
Or straggling[48] weather the pent flock forsook?[49]
How could'st thou find this dark, sequestered nook?   500
        Spirit. O my loved master's heir, and his next[50] joy,
I came not here on such a trivial toy
As a strayed ewe, or to pursue the stealth
Of pilfering wolf. Not all the fleecy wealth
That doth enrich these downs[51] is worth a thought
To this my errand, and the care[52] it brought!
But O, my virgin lady: where is she?
How chance she is not in your company?
        Brother 1. To tell thee sadly, shepherd, without blame
Or our neglect we lost her as we came.   510

---

[43] unsheathe a sword
[44] i.e., swords
[45] melodies, tunes
[46] pushing, hurrying
[47] mother
[48] irregular
[49] caused to be abandoned
[50] nearest, closest
[51] open expanse of upland
[52] concern, fear

Spirit. Aye me, unhappy! Then my fears are true.
Brother 1. What fears, good Thyrsis? Prithee, briefly
    show.
Spirit. I'll tell you. 'Tis not vain or fabulous[53]
(Though so esteemed by shallow ignorance),
What the sage poets, taught by th' Heav'nly Muse,
Storied[54] of old in high immortal verse
Of dire chimeras[55] and enchanted isles,
And rifted[56] rocks whose entrance leads to Hell,
For such there be. But unbelief is blind.
    Within the navel of this hideous Wood,   520
Immured in cypress shades, a sorcerer dwells,
Of Bacchus and of Circe born, great Comus,
Deep skilled in all his mother's witcheries,
And here to every thirsty wanderer
By sly enticement gives his baneful[57] cup,
With many murmurs[58] mixed, whose pleasing poison
The visage quite transforms of him who drinks,
And the inglorious likeness of a beast
Fixes instead, unmoulding[59] reason's mintage[60]
Charactered[61] in the face. This have I learned,   530
Tending my flocks hard by, i' th' hilly crofts[62]
That brow this bottom glade, whence night by night
He and his monstrous rout[63] are heard to howl
Like stabled[64] wolves or tigers at their prey,
Doing abhorrèd rites to Hecate[65]
In their obscurèd haunts of inmost[66] bow'rs.
Yet have they many baits and guileful spells
T' inveigle and invite th' unwary sense

---

[53] fanciful, incredible
[54] [verb]
[55] monsters with lion heads, goat bodies, and serpent tails
[56] split
[57] poisonous, life-destroying
[58] whispered charms/spells
[59] undoing
[60] coinage, stamp
[61] engraved, written
[62] pastures, fields
[63] crowd
[64] domesticated
[65] [trisyllabic]
[66] most remote (farthest in)

Of them that pass, unweeting,[67] by the way.
This evening, late—by then the chewing flocks   540
Had ta'n their supper on the savory herb—
I sat me down to watch, upon a bank
With ivy canopied and interwove
With flaunting[68] honeysuckle, and began,
Wrapped in a pleasing fit of melancholy,
To meditate my rural minstrelsy
Till Fancy had her fill, but ere a close[69]
The wonted[70] roar was up amidst the woods
And filled the air with barbarous dissonance,   550
At which I ceased and listened them a while,
Till an unusual stop of sudden silence
Gave respite to the drowsy, frightened steeds
That draw the litter of close-curtained sleep.
At last a soft and solemn breathing sound
Rose like a steam of rich distilled perfumes
And stole upon the air, that even silence
Was took, ere she was ware, and wished she might
Deny her nature and be never more
Still to be so displaced. I was all ear,   560
And took in strains that might create a soul
Under the ribs of Death. But O, ere long
Too well I did perceive it was the voice
Of my most honored lady, your dear sister.
Amazed I stood, harrowed with grief and fear,
And O, poor hapless nightingale, thought I,
How sweet thou sing'st, how near the deadly snare!
Then down the lawns I ran, with headlong haste,
Through paths and turnings often trod by day,
Till guided by mine ear I found the place   570
Where that damned wizard, hid in sly disguise
(For so by certain signs I knew), had met
Already, ere my best speed could prevent,[71]
The aidless innocent lady, his wished prey,

---

[67] unwitting
[68] waving
[69] conclusion, end
[70] familiar
[71] forestall

Who gently asked if he had seen such two,
Supposing him some neighbor villager.
Longer I durst not stay, but soon I guessed
Ye were the two she meant. With that I sprung
Into swift flight, till I had found you here.
But further know I not.

      Brother 2.   O night and shades,   580
How are ye joined with Hell in triple knot
Against the unarmed weakness of one virgin,
Alone and helpless! Is this the confidence
You gave me, brother?

      Brother 2. Yes, and keep it still,
Lean on it safely: not a period[72]
Shall be unsaid for me! Against the threats
Of malice or of sorcery, or that power
Which erring men call chance, this I hold firm:
Virtue may be assailed, but never hurt,
Surprised by unjust force—but not enthralled.[73]   590
Yea, even that which mischief[74] meant most harm
Shall in the happy trial prove most glory,
But evil on itself shall back recoil
And mix no more with goodness, when at last
Gathered like scum, and settled to itself,
It shall be in eternal restless change
Self-fed and self-consumed. If this fail,
The pillared firmament is rottenness
And earth's base built on stubble. But come, let's on!
Against th' opposing will and arm of Heav'n   600
May never this just sword be lifted up
But for that damned magician, let him be girt
With all the grisly legions[75] that troop
Under the sooty flag of Acheron,[76]
Harpies[77] and hydras,[78] or all the monstrous bugs[79]

---

[72] a sentence [trisyllabic, first and third accented]
[73] enslaved
[74] evil
[75] [trisyllabic, first and third accented]
[76] the underworld, Hades
[77] monsters, part woman, part bird
[78] many-headed snakes
[79] hobgoblins

'Twixt Africa and Ind! I'll find him out
And force him to restore his purchase[80] back,
Or drag him by the curls and cleave his scalp
Down to the hips!
    Spirit.   Alas, good vent'rous youth,
I love thy courage yet, and bold emprise,[81]   610
But here thy sword can do thee little stead.[82]
Far other arms and other weapons must
Be those that quell the might of hellish charms.
He with his bare wand can unthread thy joints
And crumble all thy sinews!
    Brother 1.   Why prithee, shepherd,
How durst thou then thyself approach so near
As to make this relation?[83]
    Spirit.   Care and utmost shifts![84]
How to secure the lady from surprisal
Brought to my mind a certain shepherd lad
Of small regard[85] to see to, yet well skilled   620
In every virtuous[86] plant and healing herb
That spreads her verdant leaf to th' morning ray.
He loved me well, and oft would beg me sing,
Which when I did, he on the tender grass
Would sit and hearken e'en to ecstasy,
And in requital ope his leathern scrip[87]
And show me simples[88] of a thousand names,
Telling their strange and vigorous faculties.
Amongst the rest a small unsightly root,
But of divine effect, he culled[89] me out.   630
The leaf was darkish and had prickles on it,
But in another country, as he said,
Bore a bright golden flow'r—but not in this soil—
Unknown, and like esteemed—and the dull swain

---

[80] booty
[81] prowess
[82] profit, advantage
[83] "as to tell us this story/narrative"
[84] tricks, stratagems
[85] value, merit
[86] strong, powerful, magically endowed
[87] pouch
[88] herbs, medicinal plants
[89] picked, chose

Treads on it daily with his clouted[90] shoon.
And yet more med'cinal is it than that Moly[91]
Which Hermes[92] once to wise Ulysses gave.
He[93] called it Haemony, and gave it me,
And bade me keep it as of sov'reign[94] use
'Gainst all enchantments, mildew blast,[95] or damp,   640
Or ghastly Furies apparition.[96]
I pursed it up, but little reck'ning made,
Till now that this extremity compelled.
But now I find it true, for by this means
I knew the foul enchanter, though disguised—
Entered the very lime-twigs[97] of his spells
And yet came off.[98] If you have this about you
(As I will give you when we go) you may
Boldly assault the necromancer's hall—
Where if he be, with dauntless hardihood   650
And brandished blade rush on him, break his glass
And shed the luscious[99] liquor on the ground.
But seize his wand. Though he and his cursed crew
Fierce sign of battle make, and menace high,
Or like the sons of Vulcan vomit smoke,
Yet will they soon retire,[1] if he but shrink.[2]

     Brother 1. Thyrsis, lead on apace.[3] I'll follow thee.
And some good Angel bear a shield before us!

The scene changes to a stately palace, set out with all manner of deliciousness: soft music, tables spread with all dainties. Comus appears, with his rabble, and the lady set in an enchanted chair, to whom he offers his glass, which she puts by and goes about to rise.

---

[90] studded
[91] a fabled and fabulous plant
[92] fabulous plant given to Odysseus by the god Hermes [bisyllabic]
[93] the shepherd lad
[94] supreme
[95] blasting influence, curse
[96] [five syllables, first, third, and fifth accented]
[97] entanglements
[98] retired, came away
[99] sweet, pleasing
[1] withdraw, vanish
[2] retreat, recoil, slip away
[3] quickly, at once

    Comus. Nay, lady. Sit. If I but wave this wand
Your nerves are all chained up in alabaster   660
And you a statue—or as Daphne was,
Root-bound, that fled Apollo.
    Lady.   Fool, do not boast.
Thou canst not touch the freedom of my mind
With all thy charms, although this corporal rind
Thou has emmanacled, while Heav'n sees good.
    Comus. Why are you vexed, lady? Why do you frown?
Here dwell no frowns, nor anger. From these gates
Sorrow flies far. See here be all the pleasures
That Fancy can beget on youthful thoughts,
When the fresh blood grows lively and returns   670
Brisk as the April buds in primrose season.
And first behold this cordial[4] julip,[5] here,
That flames and dances in his crystal bounds,[6]
With spirits of balm and fragrant syrups mixed.
Not that nepenthes[7] which the wife of Thon[8]
In Egypt gave to Jove-born Helena
Is of such power to stir up joy as this—
To life so friendly, or so cool to thirst.
Why should you be so cruel to yourself,
And to those dainty limbs which Nature lent   680
For gentle usage and soft delicacy?
But you invert the cov'nants[9] of her trust,
And harshly deal like an ill borrower
With that which you received on other terms,
Scorning the unexempt[10] condition[11]
By which all mortal frailty must subsist,
Refreshment after toil, ease after pain,
That[12] have been tired all day without repast,
And timely rest have wanted. But, fair virgin,

---

[4] stimulating, envigorating
[5] sweet drink
[6] boundaries, limits
[7] grief-banishing drug
[8] wife of Thon = Polydamna
[9] terms, promises
[10] not privileged, not freed from
[11] [four syllables, second and fourth accented]
[12] those who

This will restore all soon.[13]
      Lady.   'Twill not, false traitor!   690
'Twill not restore the truth and honesty
That thou hast banished from thy tongue with lies.
Was this the "cottage," and the "safe abode"
Thou toldst me of? What grim aspects[14] are these,
These ugly-headed monsters? Mercy guard me!
Hence with thy brewed enchantments, foul deceiver!
Hast thou betrayed my credulous innocence
With visored[15] falsehood and base forgeries
And wouldst thou seek again to trap me, here,
With liquorish baits, fit to ensnare a brute?   700
Were it a draught for Juno, when she banquets,
I would not taste thy treasonous offer! None
But such as are good men can give good things,
And that which is not good is not delicious
To a well-governed and wise appetite.
      Comus. O foolishness of men! that lend their ears
To those budge[16] doctors of the stoic fur,
And fetch their precepts from the cynic tub,[17]
Praising the lean and sallow abstinence.
Wherefore did Nature pour her bounties forth   710
With such a full and unwithdrawing hand,
Covering the earth with odors, fruits, and flocks,
Thronging the seas with spawn[18] innumerable,
But all to please and sate the curious taste?
And set to work millions of spinning worms
That in their green shops wave the smooth-haired silk
To deck her sons. And that no corner might
Be vacant of her plenty in her own loins
She hutched[19] th' all-worshipped ore and precious gems
To store[20] her children with. If all the world   720

---

[13] quickly
[14] looks, faces
[15] masked, disguised
[16] pompous, formal, solemn
[17] Diogenes, Cynic philosopher who lived in a tub
[18] offspring
[19] stored
[20] furnish

Should in a pet[21] of temperance feed on pulse,[22]
Drink the clear stream, and nothing wear but frieze,[23]
Th' all-giver would be unthanked, would be unpraised,
Not half His riches known, and yet despised,
And we would serve Him as a grudging master,
As a penurious niggard[24] of His wealth,
And live like Nature's bastards, not her sons,
Who[25] would be quite surcharged[26] with her own weight
And strangled with her waste fertility,
Th' earth cumbered, and the winged air darked with
                    plumes.[27]   730
The herds would over-multitude their lords,
The sea o'er-fraught[28] would swell, and th' unsought diamonds
Would so emblaze the forehead of the deep,
And so be-stud with stars, that they below
Would grow inured to light, and come at last
To gaze upon the sun with shameless brows.
List, lady. Be not coy, and be not cozened[29]
With that same vaunted[30] name, virginity.
Beauty is Nature's coin, must not be hoarded,
But must be current,[31] and the good thereof   740
Consists in mutual and partaken bliss,
Unsavory in th' enjoyment of itself.
If you let slip time, like a neglected rose
It withers on the stalk, with languished head.
Beauty is Nature's brag,[32] and must be shown
In courts, at feasts, on high solemnities
Where most may wonder at the workmanship.
It is for homely[33] features to keep home:

---

[21] sulk
[22] peas, beans, lentils, etc.
[23] coarse wool
[24] miser
[25] Nature
[26] overburdened
[27] feathers [the line, having ten syllables, *can* be scanned as iambic pentameter—but not easily]
[28] overfreighted, overloaded
[29] duped
[30] boasted of, praised
[31] in general use, passing/flowing from hand to hand
[32] show
[33] plain, simple, unpolished

They had their name thence. Coarse complexions[34]
And cheeks of sorry[35] grain[36] will serve to ply[37]   750
The sampler[38] or to tease[39] the housewife's wool.
What need a vermeil-tinctured lip for that?
Love-darting eyes, or tresses like the morn?
There was another meaning in those gifts!
Think what, and be advised.[40] You are but young yet.
     Lady. I had not thought to have unlocked my lips
In this unhallowed air, but[41] that this juggler[42]
Would think to charm my judgment as[43] mine eyes,
Obtruding[44] false rules pranked[45] in reason's garb!
I hate when vice can bolt[46] her arguments   760
And virtue has no tongue to check her[47] pride.
     Impostor! Do not charge[48] most innocent Nature,
As if she would[49] her children should be riotous
With her abundance! She, good cateress,[50]
Means her provision only to the good
That live according to her sober laws
And holy dictate of spare temperance.
If every just man that now pines with want
Had but a moderate and beseeming[51] share
Of that which lewdly-pampered luxury   770
Now heaps upon some few with vast excess,
Nature's full blessings would be well dispensed

---

[34] [four syllables, second and fourth accented]
[35] vile, wretched, worthless
[36] color
[37] work busily at
[38] embroidery
[39] to separate, to card
[40] judicious
[41] except
[42] magician, trickster, buffoon
[43] as he has
[44] thrusting forward, intruding
[45] decked, dressed
[46] sift, examine
[47] vice's
[48] blame, burden
[49] wished
[50] provider
[51] suitable, seemly

In unsuperfluous,[52] ev'n proportion,[53]
And she no whit encumbered with her store.
And then the giver would be better thanked,
His praise due paid—for winish gluttony
N'er looks to Heav'n, amidst his gorgeous[54] feast,
But with besotted base ingratitude
Crams, and blasphemes his feeder.
                                        Shall I go on?
Or have I said enough? To him that dares   780
Arm his profuse tongue with contemptuous words
Against the sun-clad power of chastity
Fain would I something say—yet to what end?
Thou hast nor ear nor soul to apprehend
The sublime notion and high mystery[55]
That must be uttered, to unfold the sage
And serious doctrine of virginity.
And thou art worthy that thou shouldst not know
More happiness than this thy present lot.
Enjoy your dear wit and gay rhetoric   790
That hath so well been taught her dazzling fence![56]
Thou art not fit to hear thyself convinced.
Yet should I try, the uncontrollèd worth
Of this pure cause would kindle my rapt spirits
To such a flame of sacred vehemence
That dumb things would be moved to sympathize,
And the brute earth would lend her nerves,[57] and shake
Till all thy magic structures reared so high
Were shattered into heaps o'er thy false head!
          Comus. She fables not. I feel that I do fear   800
Her words, set off by some superior power.
And, though not mortal, yet a cold shudd'ring dew
Dips me all o'er, as when the wrath of Jove
Speaks thunder and the chains of Erebus[58]
To some of Saturn's crew. I must dissemble

---

[52] [four syllables, first and third accented]
[53] [four syllables, second and fourth accented]
[54] showy, dazzling
[55] holy secret
[56] the practice of swordplay
[57] sinews
[58] i.e., Jove consigns the rebels against him to "the chains" of Hell

And try[59] her yet more strongly.
                              Come, no more.
This is mere moral babble and direct
Against the canon laws of our foundation.[60]
I must not suffer this, yet 'tis but the lees[61]
And settlings of a melancholy blood.   810
But this will cure all straight![62] One sip of this
Will bathe the drooping spirits in delight
Beyond the bliss of dreams. Be wise, and taste.

*The brothers rush in, with swords drawn, wrest his glass out of his
hand, and break it against the ground. His rout makes sign of resis-
tance, but all are driven in. The attendant spirit comes in.*

        Spirit. What? Have you let the false enchanter scape?
O ye mistook, ye should have snatched his wand
And bound him fast. Without his rod reversed,
And backward mutters of dissevering[63] power,
We cannot free the lady that sits here,
In stony fetters fixed and motionless.
Yet stay,[64] be not disturbed. Now I bethink me: 820
Some other means I have which may be used,
Which once of Melibaeus[65] old I learned—
The soothest[66] shepherd that e'er piped[67] on plains.
        There is a gentle nymph, not far from hence,
That with moist curb[68] sways[69] the smooth Severn[70] stream.
Sabrina is her name, a virgin pure.
Whilom[71] she was the daughter of Locrine,[72]

---

[59] test, afflict
[60] i.e., creation
[61] sediments, dregs
[62] at once
[63] disjoining, parting, separating
[64] stop
[65] character in Spenser's *Fairy Queen*
[66] truest, most genuine
[67] played his pipe/flute
[68] check, restraint
[69] governs
[70] river flowing out of Wales, ending in Bristol Channel
[71] once upon a time
[72] son of Brutus, legendary founder of Britain

That had the scepter from his father Brute.[73]
She, guiltless damsel, flying the mad pursuit
Of her enragèd stepdam, Gwendolen,   830
Commended her fair innocence to the flood[74]
That stayed her flight with his cross-flowing course.
The water nymphs that in the bottom[75] played
Held up their pearlèd wrists, and took her in,
Bearing her straight to agèd Nereus[76] hall,
Who, piteous of her woes, reared her lank[77] head
And gave her to his daughters to embathe
In nectared lavers,[78] strewn with asphodil,
And through the porch[79] and inlet of each sense
Dropped in ambrosial oils, till she revived   840
And underwent a quick immortal change,
Made goddess of the river. Still she retains
Her maiden gentleness, and oft at eve
Visits the herds along the twilight meadows,
Helping all urchin[80] blasts[81] and ill luck signs
That the shrewd meddling elf delights to make,
Which she with precious vialed liquors heals.
For which the shepherds at their festivals
Carol[82] her goodness, loud in rustic lays,[83]
And throw sweet garland wreaths into her stream,   850
Of pansies, pinks, and gaudy daffodils.
And, as the old swain said, she can unlock
The clasping[84] charm and thaw the numbing spell,
If she be right invoked in warbled song,
For maidenhood she loves, and will be swift
To aid a virgin such as was herself,

---

[73] Brutus
[74] river
[75] depths
[76] sea god, father of the Nereids
[77] limp, loose
[78] spiritual cleansers
[79] vestibule
[80] elf, goblin
[81] breaths of malignant air, curses, infections
[82] sing joyously
[83] songs
[84] encircling

In hard besetting[85] need. This will I try
And add the power of some adjuring[86] verse.

Song

> *Sabrina, fair,*
>> *Listen where thou are sitting*   860
> *Under the glassy, cool, translucent wave,*
>> *In twisted braids of lillies knitting*
> *The loose train of the amber-dropping hair.*
>> *Listen for dear honor's sake,*
>> *Goddess of the silver lake,*
>>> *Listen and save.*

Listen and appear to us
In name of great Oceanus[87] —
By th' earth-shaking Neptune's mace,
And Tethys' grave, majestic pace —   870
By hoary Nereus' wrinkled look,
And the Carpathian wizard's hook —
By scaly Triton's winding[88] shell,
And old sooth-saying Glaucus' spell —
By Leucothea's[89] lovely hands,
And her son that rules the strands[90] —
By Thetis' tinsel-slippered feet,
And the songs of Sirens' sweet —
By dead Parthenope's[91] dear tomb,
And fair Ligéa's golden comb,   880
Wherewith she sits on diamond rocks,
Sleeking her soft, alluring locks —

---

[85] surrounding, hemming in
[86] exorcising
[87] [four syllables, second and fourth accented] Oceanus' wife, mother of rivers, is Tethys; Neptune = Poseidon, god of the sea and of earthquakes; Nereus is father of the Nereids, one of whom is Thetis; the "Carpathian wizard" is Proteus, a shape-shifter; Triton is son of Poseidon and Amphitrite, human from the waist up, fish below; Glaucus is a fisherman who became immortal and a sea god; Leucothea is a Greek sea goddess; Parthenope is a Siren, as is Ligèa.
[88] blown, sounded
[89] [four syllables, first and third accented]
[90] beaches, shores
[91] [four syllables, second and fourth accented]

By all the nymphs that nightly dance
Upon thy streams, with wily[92] glance!
Rise, rise, and heave[93] thy rosy head
From thy coral-paven bed,
And bridle[94] in thy headlong wave
Till thou our summons answered have.
                              Listen and save.

Sabrina rises, attended by water-nymphs, and sings:

    By the rushy-fringèd bank,   890
        Where grows the willow and the osier dank,
    My sliding chariot stays,
    Thick set with agate and the azure sheen
        Of turquoise blue, and emerald green
          That in the channel strays,
      Whilst from off the waters fleet[95]
      Thus I set my printless feet
        O'er the cowslips' velvet head,
        That bends not as I tread.

Gentle swain, at thy request   900
I am here.
     Spirit. Goddess dear,
We implore thy powerful hand
To undo the charmèd band[96]
Of true virgin, here distressed[97]
Through the force and through the wile
Of unblessed enchanter vile.
     Sabrina. Shepherd, it is my office[98] best
To help ensnarèd chastity.
Brightest lady, look on me!   910
Thus I sprinkle on thy breast

---

[92] sly, artful
[93] raise, lift
[94] toss one's head
[95] [adjective]
[96] shackle, chain, fetter, etc.
[97] constrained, pressed tightly
[98] duty

Drops that from my fountain pure
I have kept, of precious cure.[99]
Thrice upon thy finger's tip,
Thrice upon thy rubied lip!
Next, this marble-venomed seat
Smeared with gums[1] of glutinous[2] heat
I touch with chaste palms, moist and cold.
Now the spell hath lost his hold—
And I must haste, ere morning hour,   920
To wait[3] in Amphritite's[4] bow'r.

Sabrina descends, and the lady rises out of her seat.

  Spirit. Virgin, daughter of Locrine,
Sprung of old Anchises'[5] line,
May thy brimmèd waves, for this,
Their full tribute never miss
From a thousand petty[6] rills[7]
That tumble down the snowy hills.
Summer drought or singèd air
Never scorch thy tresses fair,
Nor wet October's torrent flood   930
Thy molten crystal fill[8] with mud.
May thy billows roll ashore
The beryl[9] and the golden ore.
May thy lofty head be crowned
With many a tow'r and terrace round,
And here and there thy banks upon
With groves of myrrh and cinnamon.

  Come lady, while Heav'n lends us grace
Let us fly this cursèd place,

---

[99] healing effect
[1] viscous resinlike secretions
[2] sticky
[3] serve
[4] Neptune's wife [four syllables, first and third accented]
[5] Trojan prince, father of Aeneas
[6] small, minor
[7] small streams, brooks
[8] headwaters
[9] transparent pale green precious stone

Lest the sorcerer us entice 940
With some other new device.
Not a taste or needless sound
Till we come to holier ground.
I shall be your faithful guide
Through this gloomy covert[10] wide,
And not many furlongs thence
Is your father's residence,
Where this night are met in state
Many a friend to gratulate
His wishèd presence, and beside 950
All the swains that there abide,
With jigs and rural dance resort.[11]
We shall catch them at their sport,
And our sudden coming there
Will double all their mirth and cheer.
Come, let us haste! The stars grow high—
But night sits monarch yet in the mid-sky.

The scene changes, presenting Ludlow Town and the [Lord] Presi-
dent's castle. Then come in country dancers. After them, the atten-
dant spirit, with the two brothers and the lady.

Song

     Spirit. Back, shepherds, back! Enough, your play,
Till next sunshine holiday.
Here be, without duck[12] or nod, 960
Other trippings to be trod
Of lighter toes, and such court guise[13]
As Mercury did first devise[14]
With the mincing[15] Dryades,[16]
On the lawns and on the leas.[17]

---

[10] thicket
[11] come, congregate
[12] quick, abrupt lowering of head or body
[13] customs, behavior
[14] prepare, invent
[15] affectedly elegant or dainty
[16] tree nymphs [trisyllabic, first and third accented]
[17] open ground, grassy pasture

This second song presents them to their father and mother:

[Song 2]

> *Noble lord, and lady bright,*
> *I have brought ye new delight.*
> *Here behold so goodly grown*
> *Three fair branches of your own.*
> *Heav'n hath timely tried their youth,* 970
> *Their faith, their patience, and their truth,*
> *And sent them here, through hard assays,*[18]
> *With a crown of deathless praise,*
> > *To triumph in victorious dance*
> *O'er sensual folly and intemperance.*

The dances ended, the spirit epiloguizes:

> *Spirit.* To the ocean now I fly,
> And those happy climes that lie
> Where day never shuts his eye,
> Up in the broad fields of the sky.
> There I suck the liquid air 980
> All amidst the gardens fair
> Of Hesperus and his daughters three,
> That sing about the golden tree.
> Along the crispèd[19] shades and bow'rs
> Revels the spruce[20] and jocund spring.
> The Graces, and the rosy-bosomed Hours,
> Thither all their bounties bring,
> That[21] there eternal summer dwells,
> And west winds, with musky wing,
> About the cedarn alleys[22] fling 990
> Nard,[23] and cassia's balmy smells.

---

[18] tests, trials
[19] rippling
[20] trim, dapper, neat
[21] so that
[22] walkways, passages
[23] aromatic balsam

Iris[24] there with humid bow
Waters the odorous banks that blow[25]
Flowers of more mingled hue
Than her purflèd[26] scarf can shew,
And drenches with Elysian dew
(List, mortals, if your ears be true)
Beds of hyacinth and roses,
Where young Adonis[27] oft reposes,
Waxing[28] well of his deep wound   1000
In slumber soft, and on the ground
Sadly sits the Assyrian queen.[29]
But far above, in spangled sheen,
Celestial Cupid, her fair son advanced,[30]
Holds his dear Psyche,[31] sweet[32] entranced
After her wand'ring labors long,
Till free consent the gods among
Make her his eternal bride
And from her fair, unspotted side
Two blissful twins are to be born,   1010
Youth and Joy. So Jove hath sworn.
        But now my task is smoothly[33] done.
I can fly or I can run
Quickly to the green earth's end,
Where the bowed welkin[34] slow doth bend,
And from thence can soar as soon
To the corners[35] of the moon.
        Mortals that would follow me,

---

[24] goddess of the rainbow
[25] cause to blossom/bloom
[26] embroidered, trimmed
[27] wonderfully handsome youth: one day while he was hunting, he was seen by
Aphrodite/Venus, who fell in love with him—and when he was killed by a wild boar,
from his blood grew the rose, and from her tears, the anemone
[28] growing
[29] Aphrodite/Venus
[30] raised
[31] Cupid falls in love with Psyche, a mortal; she disobeys him and is deserted by him;
thereafter she goes through trial after trial and, eventually, reclaims and is married to
him [bisyllabic; the first letter is silent]
[32] [adverb]
[33] pleasantly
[34] sky
[35] ends

Love virtue: she alone is free.
She can teach ye how to climb   1020
Higher than the sphery chime—[36]
Or, if virtue feeble[37] were,
Heav'n itself would stoop to her.

ON TIME[38]
[1633–37?]

Fly, envious time, till thou run out thy race!
Call on the lazy leaden-stepping[39] hours,
Whose speed is but the heavy plummet's[40] pace,
And glut thyself with what thy womb[41] devours—
Which is no more than what is false and vain
And merely mortal dross.[42]
So little is our loss,
So little is thy gain.
For when as each thing bad thou hast entombed,
And last of all thy greedy self consumed,   10
Then long eternity shall greet our bliss
With an individual kiss.[43]
And joy shall overtake us as a flood
When everything that is sincerely good
And perfectly divine
With truth, and peace, and love shall ever shine
About the supreme throne
Of Him t' whose happy-making sight alone,

---

[36] the music of the spheres
[37] weak, infirm
[38] the poem was intended to be "set on a clock case"
[39] see footnote 40 immediately below
[40] the leaden weight that animates the clock's works
[41] (1) womb, (2) stomach, belly
[42] scum, rubbish, dregs
[43] indivisible?

When once our Heav'nly-guided soul shall climb,
Then all this earthy grossness quit,[44]   20
Attired with stars we shall forever sit,
      Triumphing over death, and chance, and thee, O
         time!

UPON THE CIRCUMCISION
[1633–37]

      Ye flaming powers[45] and wingèd warriors bright
That erst with music and triumphant song
First heard by happy watchful shepherd's ear,
So sweetly sung your joy the clouds along,
Through the soft silence of the list'ning night,
Now mourn, and if sad share with us to bear
Your fiery essence can distill no tear,
Burn in your sighs and borrow
Seas wept from our deep sorrow.
He who with all Heav'n's heraldry[46] whilere[47]   10
Entered the world, now bleeds to give us ease.
Alas, how soon our sin
      Sore[48] doth begin
His infancy to cease![49]
      O more exceeding love or law more just?
Just law, indeed—but more exceeding love!
For we, by rightful doom[50] remediless,
Were lost in death till He that dwelt above,

---

[44] left behind [adjective]
[45] sixth order in the nine ranks of the celestial hierarchy
[46] heraldic pomp ("herald" = officer who makes state pronouncements and delivers state messages)
[47] erewhile, once
[48] [adjective, modifying "sin"]
[49] spelled in Milton's manuscript "sease," this word could be either "seize" or "cease"
[50] judgment, sentence

High-throned in secret bliss, for us frail dust
Emptied His glory, ev'n to nakedness,   20
And that great cov'nant[51] which we still transgress
Entirely satisfied,
And the full wrath beside
Of vengeful justice bore for our excess,
And seals obedience, first, with wounding smart
This day, but O, ere long
       Huge pangs, and strong,
Will pierce more near His heart.

AT A SOLEMN MUSIC
[*1637*]

Blest pair of Sirens, pledges of Heav'n's joy,
Sphere-born, harmonious sisters, voice and verse,
Wed your divine sounds, and mixed power employ,
Dead things with inbreathed sense able to pierce
And to our high-raised fantasy present
That undisturbèd song of pure content[52]
Aye[53] sung before the sapphire-colored throne
To Him that sits thereon,
With saintly shout and solemn jubilee,
Where the bright Seraphim in burning row   10
Their loud up-lifted Angel trumpets blow
And the Cherubic host, in thousand choirs,
Touch their golden harps of immortal wires,
With those just Spirits that wear victorious palms
Hymns devout and holy psalms
Singing everlastingly,

---

[51] "And I [God] will establish my covenant between me and thee [Abraham] and thy seed after thee in their generations, for an everlasting covenant" (Genesis 17:7)
[52] [adjective]
[53] always

That we on earth with undiscording[54] voice
May rightly answer that melodious noise,
As once we did, till disproportioned sin
Jarred against Nature's chime and with harsh din   20
Broke the fair music that all creatures made
To their great Lord, whose love their motion swayed
In perfect diapason,[55] whilst they stood
In first[56] obedience and their state of good.
O may we soon again renew that song
And keep in tune with Heav'n, till God ere long
To His celestial consort[57] us unite
                    To live with Him, and sing in endless morn of light.

---

[54] not discordant
[55] concord, harmony [four syllables, first and third accented]
[56] primal, original
[57] (1) fellowship, (2) company of musicians

LYCIDAS [58]
[1637]

In this monody[59] the author bewails a learnèd friend,[60] unfortunately drowned in his passage from Chester [in W. England] on the Irish seas, 1637. And by occasion[61] foretells the ruin of our corrupted clergy, then in their height.

Yet once more, O ye laurels,[62] and once more,
Ye myrtles[63] brown, with ivy[64] never sear,[65]
I come to pluck your berries harsh and crude[66]
And with forced[67] fingers rude[68]
Shatter your leaves before the mellowing[69] year.
Bitter constraint,[70] and sad occasion dear,
Compels me to disturb your season due,
For Lycidas is dead, dead ere his prime,
Young Lycidas, and hath not left his peer.
Who would not sing for Lycidas? He well knew   10
Himself to sing, and build the lofty rhyme.
He must not float upon his wat'ry bier
Unwept, and welter[71] to the parching[72] wind,
Without the meed[73] of some melodious tear.

---

[58] a generic shepherd's name—announcing, as it were, that the genre of the poem is the classic pastoral
[59] lyric ode sung by a single voice; in the pastoral tradition, an interior monologue or soliloquy
[60] Edward King, a fellow student at Cambridge
[61] by occasion = the poem, written because of this fatal occasion . . .
[62] (1) symbolic of poetry, (2) symbolic of fame: the laurel, an evergreen, is sacred to Apollo, god of poetry
[63] sacred to Venus
[64] sacred to Bacchus, the god of wine
[65] dry, withered
[66] unripe
[67] constrained
[68] inexperienced, unskilled
[69] ripening
[70] obligation, necessity
[71] roll to and fro
[72] withering, shriveling
[73] recompense, reward, honor

Begin then, sisters of the sacred well,[74]
That from beneath the seat of Jove doth spring,
Begin, and somewhat[75] loudly sweep the string.
Hence with denial vain, and coy[76] excuse!
So may[77] some gentle[78] muse
With lucky[79] words favor[80] my destined[81] urn[82]   20
And, as he passes, turn
And bid fair peace be to my sable shroud.[83]
     For we were nursed upon the self-same hill,
Fed the same flock, by fountain, shade, and rill.[84]
Together both, ere the high lawns[85] appeared
Under the opening eye-lids of the morn,
We drove[86] afield, and both together heard
What time[87] the gray-fly[88] winds[89] her sultry[90] horn,
Batt'ning[91] our flocks with the fresh dews of night,
Oft till the star[92] that rose at ev'ning bright   30
Toward Heav'n's descent had sloped his westering wheel.[93]
Meanwhile, the rural ditties were not mute,
Tempered[94] to th' oaten[95] flute.
Rough satyrs[96] danced, and fauns with clov'n heel
From the glad sound would not be absent long.

---

[74] the Muses
[75] a bit
[76] disdainful
[77] so may = in the future, when Milton dies, he too may be thus mourned by "some gentle muse"
[78] noble, excellent, honorable
[79] fortunate, successful
[80] approve of, regard with kindness
[81] ordained, predetermined, fated
[82] holding funereal ashes
[83] black burial sheet
[84] brook, stream
[85] meadows, glades
[86] their flocks
[87] what time = when, at the time when
[88] a brownish beetle known as a cockchafer or dorfly/dorhawk
[89] blows (strictly, "hums" or "buzzes")
[90] summertime/hot-weather heat
[91] fattening? feeding? watering?
[92] Hesperus (Venus)
[93] "wheel" because heavenly objects were thought to be located in "spheres"
[94] tuned, in harmony with
[95] oat stems/straws
[96] woodland gods/demons, part human, part beast

And old Damoetas[97] loved to hear our song.
        But O the heavy change, now thou art gone,
Now thou art gone and never must return!
Thee, shepherd, thee the woods and desert caves,
With wild thyme and the gadding[98] vine o'er-grown,   40
And all their echoes mourn.
The willows, and the hazel copses green,
Shall now no more be seen
Fanning their joyous leaves to thy soft lays.[99]
As killing as the canker[1] to the rose,
Or taint-worm[2] to the weanling[3] herds that graze,
Or frost to flow'rs, that their gay wardrobe wear,
When first the white thorn blows—[4]
Such, Lycidas, thy loss to shepherd's ear.
        Where were ye, nymphs, when the remorseless
               deep   50
Closed o'er the head of your loved Lycidas?
For neither were ye playing on the steep,[5]
Where your old bards,[6] the famous Druids lie,
Nor on the shaggy top of Mona[7] high,
Nor yet where Deva[8] spreads her wizard[9] stream:
Aye me, I fondly dream!
Had ye been there, for what could that have done?
What could the muse[10] herself, that[11] Orpheus bore,[12]
The muse herself, for her enchanting[13] son
Whom universal[14] nature did lament,   60

---

[97] a tutor at Cambridge?
[98] straggling
[99] poems, songs
[1] plant-disease of an ulcerous sort
[2] worm or crawling larva, an intestinal parasite thought to infect sheep, cattle, etc.
[3] recently weaned
[4] blossoms
[5] slopes, hills, mountains, cliffs, etc.
[6] Celtic minstrel-poets
[7] the island of Anglesey, in the Irish Sea
[8] the River Dee
[9] magic
[10] Calliope [four syllables, second and fourth accented]
[11] i.e., she who bore Orpheus
[12] was mother to
[13] (1) performing magic, (2) entrancing, charming
[14] all of

When by the rout[15] that made the hideous roar
His goary visage[16] down the stream was sent,
Down the swift Hebrus to the Lesbian shore.
                    Alas! What boots[17] it, with incessant care
To tend the homely[18] slighted shepherd's trade,
And strictly meditate the thankless muse?
Were it not better done, as others use,
To sport[19] with Amaryllis[20] in the shade,
Or with the tangles of Neaera's[21] hair?
Fame is the spur that the clear[22] spirit doth raise[23]   70
(That last infirmity of noble mind!)
To scorn delights, and live laborious days.
But the fair guerdon,[24] when we hope to find,[25]
And think to burst out into sudden blaze,
Comes the blind Fury[26] with th' abhorrèd shears
And slits the thin-spun life. But not the praise,
Phoebus[27] replied, and touched my trembling ears.
Fame is no plant that grows on mortal soil,
Nor in the glistering[28] foil[29]
Set off to th' world, nor in broad rumor[30] lies,   80
But lives and spreads aloft by those pure eyes
And perfect witness of all-judging Jove,
As he pronounces lastly[31] on each deed.

---

[15] mob, throng, crowd, rabble, etc., all female, though it is unclear whether they were (1) Thracian women jealous of Eurydice or (2) Maenads angry that Orpheus did not properly honor their god, Dionysus
[16] his head had been cut off; in some versions of the story, the severed head continued to sing
[17] profits, avails
[18] simple, plain
[19] frolic
[20] generic shepherdess name
[21] see footnote 20, immediately above
[22] positive, determined, unobstructed, pure
[23] stimulate, incite
[24] reward
[25] find it
[26] Atropus ("irresistible")
[27] Phoebus Apollo, god of poetry
[28] glittering
[29] metal hammered into very thin sheets and used to set off some gem or glittering stone
[30] talk
[31] ultimately

Of so much fame in Heav'n expect thy meed.[32]
      O fountain Arethuse,[33] and thou honored flood,[34]
Smooth-sliding Mincius,[35] crowned with vocal reeds,
That strain I heard was of a higher mood.
But now my oat[36] proceeds
And listens to the herald of the sea[37]
That came in Neptune's plea.   90
He asked the waves, and asked the felon[38] winds,
What hard mishap hath doomed this gentle swain?
And questioned every gust of rugged[39] wings[40]
That blows from off each beakèd[41] promontory.
They knew not of his story,
And sage Hippotades[42] their answer brings,
That not a blast was from his dungeon strayed,
The air was calm, and on the level brine
Sleek Panope[43] with all her sisters played.
It was that fatal and perfidious bark,   100
Built in[44] th' eclipse[45] and rigged with curses dark,[46]
That sunk so low that sacred head of thine.
      Next Camus,[47] reverend sire, went footing slow,
His mantle hairy, and his bonnet[48] sedge,[49]
Inwrought[50] with figures dim, and on the edge

---

[32] recompense, reward
[33] the nymph Arethusa fled from a sea god, Alpheus; Diana turned her into a fountain, but he—a river—flowed under the sea and was thus united with her
[34] river, stream
[35] river running through Mantua, home of Virgil
[36] pastoral song
[37] Triton, a merman, son of Poseidon and Amphitrite, a Nereid
[38] cruel, terrible, wicked
[39] rough, stormy, strong
[40] winds represented as great birds
[41] pointed, hooked
[42] god of the winds [four syllables, second and fourth accented]
[43] water nymph [trisyllabic, first and third accented]
[44] during, subject to
[45] "Eclipses are misfortunes . . ." *Funk & Wagnalls Standard Dictionary of Folklore, Mythology, and Legend*, ed. Maria Leach (New York: Harper, 1972), p. 337
[46] secret, foul, evil
[47] River Cam, which flows through Cambridge (and from which, of course, the town takes its name)
[48] cap
[49] made of reedlike plants
[50] worked

Like to that sanguine flower[51] inscribed with woe.
"Ah! Who hath reft[52] (quoth he) my dearest pledge?"[53]
Last came, and last did go,
The pilot of the Galilean lake.[54]
Two massy keys he bore, of metals twain,   110
(The golden opes, the iron shuts amain).[55]
He shook his mitered locks, and stern bespake:
"How well could I have spared for thee, young swain,
Anow[56] of such as for their belly's sake
Creep and intrude, and climb into the fold?
Of other care they little reck'ning make
Than how to scramble at the shearers' feast
And shove away the worthy bidden[57] guest.
Blind mouths! that scarce themselves know how to hold
A sheep-hook, or have learned ought else the least   120
That to the faithfull herdsman's art belongs!
What recks it them? What need they? They are[58] sped,[59]
And when they list,[60] their lean and flashy[61] songs
Grate on their scrannel[62] pipes of wretched straw.
The hungry sheep look up, and are not fed,
But swoll'n with wind and the rank[63] mist[64] they draw,[65]
Rot inwardly, and foul contagion[66] spread,
Besides what the grim[67] wolf with privy[68] paw
Daily devours apace,[69] and nothing said!

---

[51] the hyacinth
[52] robbed
[53] child
[54] St. Peter, wearing a bishop's miter (headdress) and carrying the keys to Heaven's gates
[55] violently
[56] enough
[57] invited
[58] the prosody is helped if "they are" is contracted: did Milton perhaps intend it to be sounded as spoken?
[59] successful, prosperous
[60] like
[61] trifling, showy
[62] feeble
[63] corrupt, foul, festering, virulent
[64] vapor
[65] breathe
[66] plague, pestilence, moral corruption
[67] savage, cruel
[68] secret
[69] at a rapid pace, swiftly, right away

But that two-handed engine[70] at the door   130
Stands ready to smite once, and smite no more."
               Return, Alpheus,[71] the dread[72] voice is past
That shrunk thy streams. Return, Sicilian muse,[73]
And call the vales[74] and bid them hither cast
Their bells[75] and flowrets[76] of a thousand hues.
Ye valleys low, where the mild whispers use[77]
Of shades and wanton[78] winds, and gushing brooks,
On whose fresh[79] lap[80] the swart star[81] sparely[82] looks,
Throw hither all your quaint[83] enamelled eyes[84]
That on the green turf suck the honeyed show'rs   140
And purple all the ground with vernal[85] flow'rs.
Bring the rath[86] primrose that forsaken dies,
The tufted crow-toe, and pale gessamine,
The white pink, and the pansy freaked[87] with jet,
The glowing violet,
The muskrose, and the well attired woodbine,
With cowslips wan that hang the pensive head
And every flower that sad[88] embroidery wears:
Bid amaranthus all his beauties shed,
And daffodillies fill their cups with tears,   150
To strew the laureate[89] hearse[90] where Lycid' lies.

---

[70] as Roy Flannagan has said, "perhaps the most famous crux in English literature"
[71] see note 33 to line 85, above
[72] revered, authoritative
[73] uncertain: perhaps Theocritus, pastoral poet, who may have been born in Sicily
[74] valleys
[75] as in "bluebells," "harebells," etc.
[76] small flowers
[77] are customary
[78] playful, sportive
[79] new, green
[80] a hollow among hills
[81] the Dog Star, Sirius
[82] frugally, abstemiously
[83] clever, lovely, dainty
[84] the colored center of flowers
[85] spring, springlike
[86] early
[87] flecked
[88] sober, steadfast, constant, mournful
[89] crowned with laurel
[90] wood frame to hold flowers; funeral carriage

For so to interpose[91] a little ease
Let our frail thoughts dally with false surmise.
Aye me! Whilst thee the shores and sounding seas
Wash far away, where'er thy bones are hurled,
Whether beyond the stormy Hebrides[92]
Where thou perhaps under the whelming[93] tide
Visit'st the bottom of the monstrous[94] world,
Or whether thou to our moist[95] vows denied[96]
Sleep'st, by the fable of Bellerus[97] old,   160
Where the great vision of the guarded mount[98]
Looks toward Namancos[99] and Bayona's[1] hold—
Look homeward, Angel, now, and melt with ruth,[2]
And O, ye dolphins, waft[3] the hapless youth.
            Weep no more, woeful shepherds, weep no more,
For Lycidas your sorrow is not dead,
Sunk though he be beneath the wat'ry floor!
So sinks the day-star[4] in the ocean bed
And yet anon[5] repairs[6] his drooping head
And tricks[7] his beams, and with new spangled ore[8]   170
Flames in the forehead of the morning sky.
So Lycidas sunk low, but mounted high,
Through the dear might of Him that walked the waves!
Where other groves and other streams along

---

[91] introduce, put forward
[92] islands off the Scottish coast
[93] engulfing, submerging
[94] the sea was thought to be full of monsters
[95] tear-strewn
[96] i.e., we pray for you to be returned, but our prayers ("vows") are denied
[97] the Roman name for Land's End, in Cornwall; perhaps a reference to some Cornish giant—or perhaps (since Milton first wrote and then crossed out "Corineus") inserted strictly for prosodic reasons
[98] Mount St. Michael's, near Land's End in Cornwall, and across the English Channel from Mont-St.-Michel, in France
[99] in Spain
[1] a fortress ("hold") near Cape Finisterre, in Spain
[2] pity, compassion
[3] carry, transport
[4] i.e., the sun
[5] soon, in a little while
[6] to restore, renew, mend
[7] dresses
[8] precious metal, here clearly "gold"

With nectar pure his oozy[9] locks he laves[10]
And hears the unexpressive[11] nuptial song
In the blest kingdoms meek, of joy and love.
There entertain him all the saints above,
In solemn[12] troops,[13] and sweet societies[14]
That sing, and singing in their glory move,[15]   180
And wipe the tears forever from his eyes.
Now, Lycidas, the shepherds weep no more!
Henceforth thou art the genius[16] of the shore
In thy large[17] recompense,[18] and shalt be good
To all that wander in that perilous flood.

      Thus sang the uncouth[19] swain to th' oaks and rills,[20]
While the still morn went out with sandals gray.
He touched the tender stops of various quills,[21]
With eager thought warbling his Doric[22] lay.
And now the sun had stretched out[23] all the hills,   190
And now was dropped into the western bay.
At last he rose and twitched[24] his mantle blue:
Tomorrow to fresh woods, and pastures new.

---

[9] muddy, damp
[10] bathes, washes
[11] inexpressible
[12] grand, sacred, formal
[13] companies, groups, bands
[14] fellowships
[15] go
[16] guardian spirit
[17] ample
[18] reparation, compensation
[19] unpolished, rough
[20] streams
[21] reeds, pipes, flutes
[22] pastoral
[23] extended across
[24] pulled around him

THE FIFTH ODE OF HORACE, BOOK ONE
[1646–48?]

Quis multa gracilis te puer in rosa, rendered almost word for word, without rhyme, according to the Latin measure,[25] as near as the [English] language will permit.

What slender youth, bedewed with liquid odors,
Courts[26] thee on roses in some pleasant cave,
    Pyrrha? For whom bind'st thou
    In wreaths thy golden hair,
Plain[27] in thy neatness?[28] O how oft shall he
On faith and changèd gods complain, and seas
    Rough with black winds and storms
    Unwonted[29] shall admire,[30]
Who now enjoys thee credulous[31] all gold?
Who always vacant,[32] always amiable,   10
    Hopes thee, of flattering gales
    Unmindful? Hapless[33] they
To whom thou, untried,[34] seem'st fair. Me in my vowed[35]
Picture[36] the sacred wall declares t' have hung[37]
    My dank and drooping weeds[38]
    To the stern god of sea.

---

[25] prosody
[26] the Latin *urget,* which Horace uses here, means "presses down on"
[27] simple
[28] elegance, style
[29] unaccustomed
[30] to be surprised, astonished, to marvel at
[31] too readily believed
[32] at leisure, unoccupied
[33] luckless
[34] untested
[35] votive offering
[36] [noun: the Latin is *tabula sacer votiva*]: David Ferry's 1997 translation renders these lines "The votive tablet on the temple wall / Is witness that in tribute to the god / I have hung up my sea-soaked garment there."
[37] i.e., dedicated/given them to the god
[38] clothing

ON THE NEW FORCERS OF CONSCIENCE, UNDER THE LONG PARLIAMENT
[1647?]

Because you have thrown off your prelate[39] lord
      And with stiff[40] vows renounced his liturgy,[41]
      To seize the widowed whore, plurality[42]
From them whose sin ye envied, not abhorred,
Dare ye for this adjure[43] the civil sword
      To force our consciences that Christ set free,
      And ride us with a classic[44] hierarchy
Taught ye by mere A.S.[45] and Rutherford?[46]
Men whose life, learning, faith, and pure intent
      Would have been held in high esteem with Paul   10
      Must now be named and printed heretics
By shallow Edwards[47] and Scotch what d'ye call.[48]
      But we do hope to find out all your tricks,
      Your plots and packings, worse than those of Trent,[49]
                  That so the Parliament
May with their wholesome and preventive shears
Clip your phylactries[50] (though bauk[51] your ears),

---

[39] (1) episcopacy had been formally abolished in 1643 (bishops having been members of the House of Lords); (2) in addition, the chief prelate had been the much-hated Archbishop William Laud—whose name, in British English, is virtually a homonym of "lord"

[40] resolute, inflexible

[41] in 1645 the House of Commons banned either public or private use of the *Book of Common Prayer*

[42] i.e., holding more than one clerical post at a time, as Anglicans had, was a practice being indulged in by Presbyterian clergymen as well

[43] swear an oath (to)

[44] presbyterian synod (unit of administration)

[45] Adam Stewart, member of Parliament and propagandist for orthodox Presbyterianism; he affixed only his initials to the pamphlets he published

[46] Samuel Rutherford, a Scot, author of *Plea for Presbytery* (1642)

[47] Thomas Edwards, author of *Gangraena: a catalogue and discovery of many of the errors, heresies, blasphemies, and pernicious practices of the sectaries of this time* (1646)

[48] Robert Baillie, a Scot who attacked the Independents

[49] the Council of Trent, 1545–63, attempted but failed to effect Church reforms

[50] leather accouterments worn, at prayer, by Jews: here, a symbol of open hypocrisy

[51] already cropped: William Prynne (a barrister), the onetime Puritan pamphleteer and then member of the House of Commons, had been thus punished in 1634 (and

                              And succor our just fears
When they shall read this clearly in your charge:
New presbyter is but old priest writ large.   20

PSALMS 1–8[52]
[*August 1653*]

                                  1

Blessèd is the man who hath not walked astray
In counsel of the wicked, and i' th' way
Of sinners hath not stood, and in the seat
Of scorners hath not sat. But in the great
Jehovah's Law is ever his delight,
And in His Law he studies day and night.
He shall be as a tree which, planted, grows
By wat'ry streams, and in his season knows
To yield his fruit, and his leaf shall not fall,
And what he takes in hand shall prosper all.   10
Not so the wicked, but as chaff[53] which fanned[54]
The wind drives, so the wicked shall not stand[55]
In judgment, or abide[56] their trial then,
Nor sinners in the assembly of just men.
For the Lord knows th' upright way of the just,
And the way of bad men to ruin[57] must.

---

punished again, for the same offense, in 1637, at which time his cheeks were branded)
for criticizing the bishops
[52] Psalms 80–88, rather dully translated in 1648—that is, five years earlier than Psalms
1–8—are here omitted; they make no significant contribution either to Milton's English
poetry or to the study thereof
[53] grain husks, separated out by threshing or winnowing
[54] winnowed, threshed
[55] endure, withstand
[56] put up with, endure
[57] [noun]

2

Why do the gentiles[58] tumult,[59] and the nations
      Muse[60] a vain thing? The kings of the earth upstand[61]
      With power, and princes in their congregations[62]
Lay deep their plots together, through each land,
      Against the Lord and His Messiah dear.
      Let us break off, say they, by strength of hand,
Their bonds, and cast from us, no more to wear,
      Their twisted cords. He who in Heav'n doth dwell
      Shall laugh. The Lord shall scoff[63] them, then, severe,[64]
Speak to them in His wrath, and in His fell[65]   10
      And fierce[66] ire[67] trouble[68] them. But I saith He
      Anointed hath my King (though ye rebel)
On Sion, my holy hill. A firm decree
      I will declare. The Lord to me hath said
      Thou art my Son, I have begotten thee
This day. Ask of me, and the grant is made.
      As thy possession I on thee bestow
      Th' heathen, and as thy conquest (to be swayed[69])
Earth's utmost bounds. Them shalt thou bring full low,
      With iron scepters bruised,[70] and them disperse   20
      Like to a potter's vessel, shivered so.
And now be wise at length,[71] ye kings averse,[72]
      Be taught, ye judges of the earth—with fear
      Jehovah serve, and let your joy converse[73]
With trembling. Kiss the Son, lest he appear

---

[58] heathen, pagans
[59] [verb]
[60] ponder
[61] stand erect
[62] meetings, assemblies
[63] deride, mock
[64] rigorous, unsparing
[65] fierce, terrible, dire
[66] merciless
[67] anger, wrath
[68] afflict
[69] ruled, governed
[70] crushed
[71] (1) fully, (2) finally, at last
[72] disinclined
[73] be conversant with

In anger and ye perish in the way,[74]
If once his wrath take fire, like fuel sere.[75]
Happy all those who have him in their stay.[76]

3

When he[77] fled from Absalom.[78]

Lord, how many are my foes,
                    How many those
          That in arms against me rise.
                    Many are they
          That of my life distrustfully thus say:
No help for him in God there lies.
But thou, Lord, art my shield, my glory,
                    Thee through my story[79]
          Th' exalter of my head I count.
                    Aloud I cried   10
          Unto Jehovah. He full soon[80] replied
And heard me from His holy mount.
I lay and slept, I waked again,
                    For my sustain
          Was the Lord. Of many millions
                    The populous rout[81]
          I fear not, though encamping round about
They pitch[82] against me their pavilions.[83]
Rise, Lord. Save me, my God, for Thou
                    Hast smote[84] ere now   20
          On the cheek-bone all my foes,
                    Of men abhorred

---

[74] in the way = thereby
[75] dry
[76] support, reliance
[77] King David
[78] his rebellious son
[79] life
[80] quickly
[81] mob, rabble, herd
[82] set, arrange
[83] tents
[84] struck

Hast broke the teeth. This help was from the Lord,
Thy blessing on Thy people flows.

4

Answer me when I call,
God of my righteousness.[85]
In straits[86] and in distress
Thou didst me disenthrall[87]
And set at large.[88] Now spare,
　　　Now pity me, and hear my earnest prayer.
Great ones, how long will ye
My glory have in scorn?
How long be this forborn[89]
Still to love vanity,　　　　　　　　　　　　　　　　　　10
To love, to seek, to prize
　　　Things false and nothing else but lies?
Yet know the Lord hath chose,
Chose to Himself apart
The good and meek of heart
(For whom to choose He knows).
Jehovah from on high
　　　Will hear my voice, what time[90] to Him I cry.
Be awed,[91] and do not sin.
Speak to your hearts alone,　　　　　　　　　　　　　　　20
Upon your beds, each one,
And be at peace within.
Offer the offerings just[92]
　　　Of righteousness, and in Jehovah trust.
Many there be that say
"Who yet will show us good?"
Talking like this world's brood![93]

---

[85] righteous deeds, conformity to the requirements of divine law
[86] sore need, difficulties
[87] liberate, deliver from bondage
[88] free
[89] tolerated, endured
[90] what time = when
[91] terrified, filled with reverential fear
[92] faithful, rightful, correct, appropriate [adjective]
[93] kind, crowd

But Lord, thus let me pray:
On us lift up the light,
  Lift up the favor of Thy count'nance bright.   30
Into my heart more joy
And gladness Thou has put
Than when a year of glut[94]
Their stores[95] doth over-cloy[96]
And from their plenteous grounds[97]
  With vast increase their corn[98] and wine abounds.
In peace at once will I
Both lay me down and sleep,
For Thou alone dost keep
Me safe, where ere I lie.   40
As in a rocky cell
  Thou, Lord, alone in safety mak'st me dwell.

5

  Jehovah, to my words give ear,
    My meditation[99] weigh,[1]
  The voice of my complaining hear,
My King and God, for unto Thee I pray.
  Jehovah, Thou my early voice
    Shalt in the morning hear.
I' th' morning I to Thee, with choice,[2]
Will rank[3] my prayers and watch till Thou appear.
  For Thou art not a God that takes
    In wickedness delight.   10
  Evil with Thee no biding[4] makes.
Fools or madmen stand[5] not within Thy sight.

---

[94] excessive quantity
[95] supplies, stocks
[96] clog
[97] lands
[98] grains
[99] devotional/contemplative exercise
[1] i.e., "give weight to my meditations"
[2] deliberate judgment
[3] arrange
[4] tarrying, expectation
[5] endure

All workers of iniquity[6]
>>Thou hat'st, and them unblessed
>Thou wilt destroy that speak a lie.
The bloodi' and guileful[7] man God doth detest.
>>But I will in Thy mercies dear,
>>>Thy numerous mercies go
>Into Thy house, I in Thy fear[8]
Will towards Thy holy temple worship low.[9]
>>Lord, lead me in Thy righteousness,
>>>Lead me because of those
>That do observe[10] if I transgress.[11]
Set Thy right ways before[12] where my step goes.
>>For in his[13] falt'ring mouth unstable[14]
>>>No word is firm or sooth:[15]
>Their inside troubles miserable,
An open grave their throat; their tongue they smooth.
>>God, find them guilty, let them fall
>>>By their own counsels quelled,[16]
>Push them in their rebellions all
Still on, for against Thee they have rebelled.
>>Then all who trust in Thee shall bring
>>>Their joy, while Thou from blame
>Defend'st them. They shall ever sing
And shall triumph in Thee, who love Thy name.
>>For Thou, Jehovah, wilt be found
>>>To bless the just man still,[17]
>As with a shield Thou will surround
Him with Thy lasting favor and good will.

20

30

40

---

[6] wickedness
[7] deceitful, treacherous
[8] in Thy fear = in fear of You
[9] humbly
[10] watch, notice, inspect
[11] sin
[12] in front of (the place)
[13] i.e., he who has a . . .
[14] unreliable, vacillating
[15] true
[16] destroyed, crushed
[17] continually, always

6

Lord, in Thine anger do not reprehend[18] me,
     Nor in Thy hot displeasure me correct.
Pity me, Lord, for I am much deject,
     Am very weak and faint. Heal and amend me,
For all my bones that even with anguish ache
     Are troubled, yea, my soul is troubled sore.
And Thou, O Lord, how long? Turn, Lord, restore[19]
     My soul, O save me for Thy goodness sake,
For in death is no remembrance of Thee.
     Who in the grave can celebrate Thy praise?   10
Wearied I am with sighing out my days,
     Nightly my couch[20] I make a kind of sea,
My bed I water with my tears, mine eye
     Through grief consumes,[21] is waxen[22] old and dark
I' th' midst of all mine enemies, that mark.[23]
     Depart all ye that work iniquity![24]
Depart from me, for the voice of my weeping
     The Lord hath heard, the Lord hath heard my prayer,
My supplication[25] with acceptance fair
     The Lord will own,[26] and have me in His keeping.   20
Mine enemies shall be all blank[27] and dashed[28]
     With much confusion, then grown red with shame
They shall return in haste the way they came,
     And in a moment shall be quite abashed.[29]

---

[18] rebuke, find fault with
[19] set right, repair
[20] bed
[21] wastes, burns away
[22] grown
[23] watch, notice
[24] wickedness
[25] petition, entreaty
[26] acknowledge
[27] nonplussed, prostrated
[28] struck, destroyed, confounded, frustrated
[29] disconcerted

7

Upon the words of Chush, the Benjamite,[30] *against him.*[31]

Lord, my God, to Thee I fly,
Save me and secure me under
Thy protection, while I cry,
Lest as a lion (and no wonder)
He haste to tear my soul asunder—
Tearing, and no rescue nigh.

Lord, my God, if I have thought
Or done this, if wickedness
Be in my hands, if I have wrought[32]
Ill to him that meant me peace,   10
Or to him have rendered[33] less
And not freed my foe for naught,[34]

Let th' enemy pursue my soul
And overtake it, let me tread[35]
My life down to the earth and roll
In the dust my glory dead—
In the dust, and there outspread
Lodge[36] it with dishonor foul.

Rise, Jehovah, in Thine ire,[37]
Rouse Thyself amidst the rage   20
Of my foes, that urge[38] like fire,
And wake[39] for me, their furi'[40] assuage.[41]

---

[30] belonging to the tribe of Benjamin, one of the twelve tribes of ancient Israel
[31] King David, the Psalmist
[32] worked, done
[33] given in return
[34] nothing—i.e., without any fee or ransom
[35] crush
[36] deposit, place
[37] anger, wrath
[38] press forward, drive, pursue
[39] keep watch
[40] fury
[41] appease, soften, mitigate

Judgment here[42] thou didst engage[43]
And command, which I desire.

So th' assemblies of each nation
Will surround Thee, seeking right.
Thence to Thy glorious habitation
Return on high, and in their sight.
Jehovah judgeth most upright
All people, from this world's foundation.[44]   30

Judge me, Lord, be judge in this
According to my righteousness
And the innocence which is
Upon me. Cause at length to cease
Of evil men the wickedness,
And their power, that do amiss.[45]

But the just establish[46] fast,[47]
Since Thou art the just God that tries[48]
Hearts and reins.[49] On God is cast
My defence, and in Him lies,   40
In Him who both just and wise
Saves th' upright of heart at last.[50]

God is a just judge, and severe,[51]
And God is every day offended.
If th' unjust will not forbear[52]
His sword He whets,[53] His bow hath bended

---

[42] i.e., on earth
[43] pledge, promise
[44] creation
[45] wrongly ("do" = "act")
[46] set up, place
[47] securely
[48] separates, distinguishes
[49] kidneys
[50] ultimately, in the end
[51] strict, rigorous, unsparing
[52] desist, abstain
[53] sharpens

Already, and for him intended
The tools of death, that waits[54] Him near.

(His arrows purposely made He
For them that persecute.)[55] Behold,   50
He[56] travels big[57] with vanity,
Trouble he hath conceived of old
As in a womb, and from that mould
Hath at length brought forth a lie.

He digged a pit, and delved[58] it deep,
And fell into the pit he made.
His mischief that due[59] course[60] doth keep,
Turns on his head, and his ill trade[61]
Of violence will undelayed
Fall on his crown[62] with ruin steep.[63]   60

Then will I Jehovah's praise
According to His justice raise,[64]
And sing the name and deity
Of Jehovah, the most high.

8

O Jehovah, our Lord, how wondrous great
          And glorious is Thy name through all the earth!
So as above the Heav'ns Thy praise to set
          Out of the tender mouths of latest birth.

---

[54] remains
[55] pursue (maliciously), hunt, harass, oppress
[56] he who (*not* God)
[57] pompous
[58] dug
[59] appropriate, fitting
[60] path
[61] track, way of life
[62] head
[63] precipitous, headlong
[64] stir up, incite, stimulate

Out of the mouths of babes and sucklings Thou
        Hast founded[65] strength, because of all Thy foes,
To stint[66] th' enemy and slack[67] th' avenger's brow
        That bends his rage Thy providence t' oppose.

When I behold Thy Heav'ns, Thy fingers' art,
        The moon and stars which Thou so bright hast set   10
In the pure firmament, then saith my heart:
        O what is man, that Thou remembrest yet

And think'st upon him, or of man begot[68]
        That him Thou visit'st and of[69] him art found.
Scarce to be less than gods Thou mad'st his lot,
        With honor and with state[70] Thou hast him crowned.

O'er the works of Thy hand Thou mad'st him lord.
        Thou hast put all under his lordly feet
All flocks, and herds, by Thy commanding word,
        All beasts that in the field or forest meet,[71]   20

Fowl of the Heav'ns, and fish that through the wet
        Sea-paths in shoals do slide. And know no dearth.[72]
O Jehovah, our Lord, how wondrous great
        And glorious is Thy name through all the earth.

---

[65] molded
[66] cut short, check
[67] weaken
[68] called into being
[69] by
[70] (1) high rank, power, (2) pomp, dignity
[71] i.e., are met
[72] scarcity

PARADISE LOST

[1642?–1665?]

THE VERSE

The measure[1] is English heroic verse[2] without rhyme, as that of Homer in Greek and of Virgil in Latin, rhyme being no necessary adjunct or true ornament of poem or good verse (in longer works especially) but the invention of a barbarous Age, to set off wretched matter[3] and lame meter—graced indeed, since, by the use of some famous modern poets, carried away by custom, but much to their own vexation, hindrance, and constraint to express many things otherwise[4] and for the most part worse than they would have expressed them. Not without cause, therefore, some both Italian and Spanish poets of prime note have rejected rhyme both in longer and shorter works, as have also long since our best English tragedies, as a thing of itself to all judicious ears trivial and of no musical delight, which [delight] consists only in apt numbers,[5] fit[6] quantity of syllables, and the sense variously drawn out from one verse into another, not in the jingling sound of like endings, a fault avoided by the ancients both in poetry and all good oratory. This neglect, then, of rhyme so little is to be taken for a defect—though it may seem so, perhaps, to vulgar[7] readers—that it rather is to be esteemed[8] an example set, the first in English, of ancient liberty recovered to heroic poem from the troublesome and modern bondage of rhyming.

---

[1] metric
[2] iambic pentameter
[3] substance, content
[4] differently
[5] prosody
[6] proper, appropriate
[7] common, ordinary, uneducated
[8] considered

BOOK I

THE ARGUMENT

THIS FIRST BOOK proposes first in brief the whole subject, man's disobedience, and the loss thereupon of Paradise wherein he was placed; then touches the prime cause of his fall, the Serpent, or rather Satan in the Serpent, who, revolting from God, and drawing to his side many legions of Angels, was by the command of God driven out of Heaven with all his crew into the great deep. Which action past over, the poem hastes into the midst of things, presenting Satan with his Angels now fallen into Hell, described here not in the center (for Heaven and Earth may be supposed as yet not made, certainly not yet accursed) but in a place of utter darkness, fitliest[9] called Chaos. Here Satan with his Angels lying on the burning lake, thunder-struck and astonished, after a certain space[10] recovers, as from confusion, calls up him who next in order and dignity lay by him.

They confer of[11] their miserable fall. Satan awakens all his legions, who lay till then in the same manner confounded. They rise, their numbers, array of battle, their chief leaders named, according to the idols known afterwards in Canaan[12] and the countries adjoining. To these Satan directs his speech, comforts them with hope yet of regaining Heaven, but tells them lastly of a new world and new kind of creature to be created, according to an ancient prophecy or report in Heaven—for that Angels *were*, long

---

[9] most appropriately
[10] time
[11] about
[12] ancient Israel

before this visible Creation, was the opinion of many ancient Fathers. To find out the truth of this prophecy, and what to determine thereon, he refers to a full council.

What his associates thence attempt. Pandemonium, the palace of Satan, rises, suddenly built out of the deep. The infernal peers there sit in council.

1　　　　　Of man's first disobedience, and the fruit
2　　Of that forbidden tree whose mortal[13] taste
3　　Brought Death into the world, and all our woe,
4　　With loss of Eden, till one greater Man[14]
5　　Restore us and regain the blissful seat,
6　　Sing, Heavenly Muse, that on the secret top
7　　Of Oreb,[15] or of Sinai, didst inspire
8　　That shepherd[16] who first taught the chosen seed[17]
9　　In the beginning how the heavens and earth
10　　Rose out of Chaos. Or if Sion hill[18]
11　　Delight thee more, and Siloa's[19] brook that flowed
12　　Fast by[20] the oracle of God,[21] I thence
13　　Invoke thy aid to my adventurous[22] song
14　　That with no middle flight intends to soar
15　　Above th' Aonian mount,[23] while it pursues
16　　Things unattempted yet in prose or rhyme.
17　　　　　And chiefly thou, O Spirit,[24] that dost prefer
18　　Before[25] all temples th' upright heart and pure,
19　　Instruct me, for Thou know'st, Thou from the first
20　　Wast present and, with mighty wings outspread,
21　　Dove-like sat'st brooding[26] on the vast abyss,
22　　And mad'st it pregnant. What in me is dark[27]
23　　Illumine, what is low raise and support,
24　　That, to the height of this great argument,
25　　I may assert Eternal Providence
26　　And justify the ways of God to men.
27　　　　　Say first—for Heav'n hides nothing from thy
　　　　　　　　view,

---

[13] deadly, fatal
[14] Christ
[15] Horeb = Sinai, in Exodus and Deuteronomy
[16] Moses, who was thought to have been the author of Genesis
[17] the Jews
[18] site of the Temple, in Jerusalem
[19] Siolam, near Jerusalem
[20] fast by = close, very near
[21] the temple
[22] (1) perilous, rash, risky, (2) enterprising
[23] Mount Parnassus, sacred to Apollo and to the Muses
[24] not specified: the basic nature of the Godhead?
[25] in preference to, rather than
[26] (1) hatching eggs by sitting on them, (2) meditating
[27] ignorant, obscure, blind

28 Nor the deep tract of Hell—say first what cause
29 Moved our grand[28] parents, in that happy state
30 Favored of Heav'n so highly, to fall off[29]
31 From their Creator and transgress His will
32 For[30] one restraint, lords of the world besides.
33 Who first seduced them to that foul revolt?
34 Th' infernal Serpent, he it was whose guile,
35 Stirred up with envy and revenge, deceived
36 The mother of mankind, what time his pride
37 Had cast him out from Heav'n, with all his host
38 Of rebel Angels, by whose aid, aspiring
39 To set himself in glory above his peers,
40 He trusted to have equalled the Most High,
41 If he opposed and with ambitious aim
42 Against the throne and monarchy of God
43 Raised impious war in Heav'n and battle proud,
44 With vain attempt. Him the Almighty Power
45 Hurled headlong flaming from th' ethereal[31] sky,
46 With hideous[32] ruin and combustion,[33] down
47 To bottomless perdition,[34] there to dwell
48 In adamantine[35] chains and penal[36] fire,
49 Who durst defy th' Omnipotent to arms.
50   Nine times the space that measures day and
night
51 To mortal men, he, with his horrid[37] crew,[38]
52 Lay vanquished, rolling in the fiery gulf,[39]
53 Confounded,[40] though immortal. But his doom[41]
54 Reserved[42] him to more wrath, for now the thought

---

[28] great, original
[29] move away
[30] on account of
[31] celestial
[32] horrible, frightful, terrific
[33] conflagration, burning
[34] final damnation
[35] unbreakable
[36] (1) punishing, (2) severe
[37] detestable, abominable
[38] army, band, gang, mob
[39] abyss
[40] brought to nought, shamed
[41] sentence, judgment (punishment)
[42] kept, retained, preserved

55   Both of lost happiness and lasting pain
56   Torments him. Round he throws his baleful[43] eyes,
57   That witnessed[44] huge affliction and dismay,
58   Mixed with obdurate[45] pride and steadfast hate.
59   At once, as far as Angels ken,[46] he views
60   The dismal[47] situation waste[48] and wild.[49]
61   A dungeon horrible, on all sides round
62   As one great furnace flamed, yet from those flames
63   No light but rather darkness visible
64   Served only to discover[50] sights of woe,
65   Regions of sorrow, doleful shades, where peace
66   And rest can never dwell, hope never comes
67   That comes to all, but torture without end
68   Still urges,[51] and a fiery deluge, fed
69   With ever-burning sulphur unconsumed.[52]
70   Such place Eternal Justice had prepared
71   For those rebellious, here their prison ordained
72   In utter darkness, and their portion[53] set,
73   As far removed from God and light of Heav'n
74   As from the center thrice to th' utmost pole.
75   Oh how unlike the place from whence they fell!
76   There the companions of his fall, o'erwhelmed
77   With floods and whirlwinds of tempestuous fire,
78   He soon discerns and, weltering[54] by his side,
79   One next himself in power, and next in crime,
80   Long after known in Palestine, and named
81   Beelzebub.[55] To whom th' arch-enemy,
82   And thence in Heav'n called Satan, with bold words
83   Breaking the horrid silence, thus began:

---

[43] (1) full of active evil, (2) full of pain and suffering
[44] attested to, were evidence of
[45] hardened to evil, unyielding
[46] power of vision
[47] disastrous, dreadful, calamitous
[48] barren
[49] (1) desolate, (2) fantastic
[50] reveal, show
[51] presses forward
[52] never used up
[53] lot, destiny, fate
[54] rolling, tumbling
[55] Beëlzebub

84   "If thou beest he—but O how fallen! how
                   changed
85   From him who, in the happy[56] realms of light
86   Clothed with transcendent brightness, didst outshine
87   Myriads,[57] though bright!—if he whom mutual league,[58]
88   United thoughts and counsels, equal hope
89   And hazard in the glorious enterprise
90   Joined with me once, now misery hath joined
91   In equal ruin—into what pit thou seest
92   From what height fall'n, so much the stronger proved
93   He with His thunder. And till then who knew
94   The force of those dire arms? Yet not for those,
95   Nor what the potent victor in His rage
96   Can else inflict, do I repent, or change
97   (Though changed in outward luster) that fixed mind
98   And high disdain from sense of injured merit
99   That with the Mightiest raised me to contend,
100   And to the fierce contentions[59] brought along
101   Innumerable[60] force of Spirits armed,
102   That durst dislike His reign and, me preferring,
103   His utmost power with adverse[61] power opposed
104   In dubious[62] battle on the plains of Heav'n,
105   And shook His throne. What though the field be lost?
106   All is not lost—the unconquerable will,
107   And study[63] of revenge, immortal hate,
108   And courage never to submit or yield:
109   And what is else not to be overcome?
110   That glory never shall His wrath or might
111   Extort from me. To bow and sue[64] for grace[65]
112   With suppliant[66] knee, and deify His power

---

[56] blessèd, fortunate
[57] countless numbers
[58] covenant
[59] strife
[60] [five syllables, second and fourth accented]
[61] hostile
[62] uncertain, undetermined
[63] cultivation
[64] to petition, beg
[65] favor, pardon, mercy
[66] humbly petitioning, bent

113   Who, from[67] the terror[68] of this arm, so late[69]
114   Doubted[70] His empire: that were low indeed,
115   That were an ignominy and shame beneath
116   This downfall, since, by fate, the strength of gods,
117   And this empyreal[71] substance, cannot fail;
118   Since, through experience of this great event,
119   In arms not worse, in foresight[72] much advanced,[73]
120   We may with more successful hope resolve
121   To wage by force or guile eternal war,
122   Irreconcilable to our grand foe,
123   Who now triumphs, and in th' excess of joy
124   Sole reigning holds the tyranny of Heav'n."
125   So spoke th' apostate Angel, though in pain,
126   Vaunting[74] aloud, but racked with deep despair.
127   And him thus answered, soon, his bold compeer:[75]
128   "O Prince, O chief of many thronèd Powers[76]
129   That led th' embattled Seraphim[77] to war
130   Under thy conduct[78] and, in dreadful deeds
131   Fearless, endangered Heav'n's perpetual[79] King,
132   And put to proof[80] His high supremacy,
133   Whether upheld by strength, or chance, or fate:
134   Too well I see and rue[81] the dire event
135   That, with sad overthrow and foul defeat,
136   Hath lost us Heav'n, and all this mighty host
137   In horrible destruction laid thus low,
138   As far as gods and Heav'nly Essences[82]
139   Can perish—for the mind and spirit remains

---

[67] because of
[68] fear
[69] recently
[70] feared for
[71] heavenly, pure fire
[72] care for/prediction of the future
[73] raised, moved forward
[74] boasting, bragging
[75] comrade, of equal rank
[76] sixth of the nine angelic orders
[77] first of the nine angelic orders
[78] guidance, leadership
[79] eternal, everlasting
[80] test, trial
[81] regret
[82] entities, beings

140 Invincible,[83] and vigor soon returns,
141 Though all our glory extinct, and happy state
142 Here swallowed up in endless misery.
143 But what if He our conqueror (whom I now
144 Of force[84] believe almighty, since no less
145 Than such could have o'erpowered such force as ours)
146 Have left us this our spirit and strength entire,[85]
147 Strongly to suffer[86] and support[87] our pains,
148 That we may so suffice[88] His vengeful ire,
149 Or do Him mightier service as His thralls[89]
150 By right of war, whate'er His business be,
151 Here in the heart of Hell to work in fire,
152 Or do His errands in the gloomy deep?
153 What can it then avail, though yet we feel
154 Strength undiminshed, or eternal being,
155 To undergo eternal punishment?"
156 Whereto with speedy words th' arch-fiend replied:
157   "Fall'n Cherub, to be weak is miserable,
158 Doing or suffering. But of this be sure—
159 To do aught[90] good never will be our task,
160 But ever to do ill our sole delight,
161 As being the contrary to His high will
162 Whom we resist. If then His providence
163 Out of our evil seek to bring forth good,
164 Our labor must be to pervert that end
165 And out of good still[91] to find means of evil,
166 Which oft-times may succeed so as, perhaps,
167 Shall grieve Him, if I fail not, and disturb[92]
168 His inmost counsels[93] from their destined[94] aim.
169   "But see! the angry victor hath recalled

---

[83] unconquerable
[84] perforce, of necessity
[85] whole
[86] permit, allow
[87] strengthen
[88] satisfy
[89] slaves, bondsmen
[90] anything
[91] always
[92] interfere with, interrupt
[93] purposes, directions
[94] intended, designed

170 His ministers of vengeance and pursuit
171 Back to the gates of Heav'n. The sulphurous hail,
172 Shot after us in storm[95] o'erblown, hath laid[96]
173 The fiery surge[97] that from the precipice
174 Of Heav'n received us falling, and the thunder,
175 Winged with red lightning and impetuous rage,
176 Perhaps hath spent his shafts, and ceases now
177 To bellow through the vast and boundless deep.
178 Let us not slip[98] th' occasion, whether scorn
179 Or satiate[99] fury yield it from our foe.
180   "Seest thou yon dreary plain, forlorn and wild,
181 The seat of desolation, void of light,
182 Save what the glimmering of these livid[100] flames
183 Casts pale and dreadful? Thither let us tend[101]
184 From off the tossing of these fiery waves,
185 There rest, if any rest can harbor[102] there,
186 And, re-assembling our afflicted[103] Powers,
187 Consult how we may henceforth most offend[104]
188 Our enemy, our own loss how repair,
189 How overcome this dire calamity,
190 What reinforcement we may gain from hope,
191 If not, what resolution from despair."
192   Thus Satan, talking to his nearest mate,[105]
193 With head uplift above the wave, and eyes
194 That sparkling blazed, his other parts besides
195 Prone on the flood,[106] extended long and large,
196 Lay floating many a rood,[107] in bulk as huge
197 As whom the fables name of monstrous size,

---

[95] discharge
[96] caused to subside, laid to rest
[97] billows, waves
[98] waste
[99] satiated, glutted
[100] bluish leaden-colored
[101] direct our course, move toward
[102] lodge, take shelter, be contained
[103] mortified, troubled
[104] attack, hurt, damage
[105] companion, associate
[106] water
[107] rod = 5½ yards

198 Titanian[108] or earth-born,[109] that warred on Jove,
199 Briareos or Typhon, whom the den
200 By ancient Tarsus[110] held,[111] or that sea-beast
201 Leviathan,[112] which God of all His works
202 Created hugest that swim th' ocean-stream.
203 Him, haply[113] slumbering on the Norway foam,[114]
204 The pilot of some small night-foundered[115] skiff,
205 Deeming[116] some island, oft, as seamen tell,
206 With fixed anchor in his scaly rind,[117]
207 Moors by his side under the lee,[118] while night
208 Invests[119] the sea, and wishèd morn delays.
209 So stretched out huge in length the arch-fiend lay,
210 Chained on the burning lake, nor ever thence
211 Had risen or heaved[120] his head, but that the will
212 And high permission of all-ruling Heav'n
213 Left him at large to his own dark designs,
214 That with reiterated crimes he might
215 Heap on himself damnation, while he sought
216 Evil to others, and enraged might see
217 How all his malice served but to bring forth
218 Infinite goodness, grace, and mercy, shown
219 On man by him seduced, but on himself
220 Treble confusion,[121] wrath, and vengeance poured.
221   Forthwith[122] upright he rears from off the pool
222 His mighty stature. On each hand the flames
223 Driv'n backward slope their pointing spires and, rolled
224 In billows, leave in th' midst a horrid vale.

---

[108] Titans: Briareos, in the next line, is one
[109] giants: Typhon, in the next line, is one
[110] biblical city in Cilicia (Asia Minor), north of Cyprus
[111] had
[112] (1) sea monster often analogized and linked to Satan, (2) whale
[113] perhaps, by chance
[114] foaming water, the sea
[115] "foundered" can mean "sunk"; here, it may mean "stuck, mired"
[116] concluding, considering, thinking that it (i.e., Leviathan)
[117] skin, outer surface
[118] on the sheltered side, the side away from the wind
[119] covers, clothes
[120] lifted, raised
[121] discomfiture, ruin, perplexity
[122] immediately, at once

225 Then with expanded[123] wings he steers his flight
226 Aloft, incumbent[124] on the dusky air,
227 That felt unusual weight, till on dry land
228 He lights[125] —if it were land that ever burned
229 With solid, as the lake with liquid fire,
230 And such[126] appeared in hue[127] as when the force
231 Of subterranean wind transports a hill
232 Torn from Pelorus,[128] or the shattered side
233 Of thundering Etna, whose combustible
234 And fuellèd entrails thence conceiving fire
235 Sublimed[129] with mineral fury, aid the winds
236 And leave a singèd bottom[130] all involved[131]
237 With stench and smoke. Such resting found the sole
238 Of unblest feet. Him followed his next mate,
239 Both glorying to have scaped the Stygian[132] flood[133]
240 As[134] gods, and by their own recovered strength,
241 Not by the sufferance[135] of supernal[136] power.
242   "Is this the region, this the soil, the clime,"
243 Said then the lost Archangel, "this the seat[137]
244 That we must change for Heav'n?—this mournful gloom
245 For that celestial light? Be it so, since He
246 Who now is sov'reign can dispose[138] and bid[139]
247 What shall be right. Farthest from Him is best
248 Whom reason hath equalled, force hath made supreme
249 Above His equals. Farewell, happy fields,

---

[123] spread out
[124] lying his weight upon
[125] descends, settles
[126] so, the like
[127] form, appearance
[128] Sicilian promontory, near Mount Etna (an active volcano, then and now)
[129] (1) vaporized, (2) transmuted
[130] lowland
[131] wrapped, enfolded
[132] infernal, hellish
[133] (1) literally, the River Styx, but metaphorically death, (2) by analogy, this particular burning lake
[134] still being
[135] consent, toleration
[136] heavenly
[137] residence
[138] regulate, control
[139] command

250 Where joy forever dwells! Hail, horrors! hail,
251 Infernal world! and thou, profoundest[140] Hell,
252 Receive thy new possessor—one who brings
253 A mind not to be changed by place or time.
254 The mind is its own place, and in itself
255 Can make a Heav'n of Hell, a Hell of Heav'n.
256 What matter where, if I be still the same,
257 And what I should be, all but[141] less than He
258 Whom thunder hath made greater? Here at least
259 We shall be free. Th' Almighty hath not built
260 Here for His envy, will not drive us hence.
261 Here we may reign secure and, in my choice,
262 To reign is worth ambition, though in Hell:
263 Better to reign in Hell than serve in Heav'n!
264   "But wherefore let we then our faithful friends,
265 Th' associates and co-partners of our loss,
266 Lie thus astonished[142] on th' oblivious[143] pool,
267 And call them not to share with us their part
268 In this unhappy mansion,[144] or once more
269 With rallied arms to try what may be yet
270 Regained in Heav'n, or what more lost in Hell?"
271   So Satan spoke; and him Beelzebub
272 Thus answered: "Leader of those armies bright
273 Which, but th' Omnipotent, none could have foiled![145]
274 If once they hear that voice, their liveliest pledge[146]
275 Of hope in fears and dangers—heard so oft
276 In worst extremes, and on the perilous edge
277 Of battle, when it raged, in all assaults
278 Their surest signal—they will soon resume
279 New courage and revive, though now they lie
280 Grovelling and prostrate on yon lake of fire,
281 As we erewhile, astounded[147] and amazed.[148]

---

[140] deepest
[141] just barely
[142] stunned, bewildered
[143] unmindful: this is not Lethe, which induces forgetting (oblivion), as Milton makes clear, later, in Book 2, lines 606–10
[144] abode
[145] defeated, overthrown, balked, frustrated
[146] a guarantee, security
[147] stunned
[148] overwhelmed

282   No wonder, fall'n such a pernicious[149] height!"
283   He scarce had ceased when the superior fiend
284   Was moving toward the shore, his ponderous shield,
285   Ethereal[150] temper,[151] massy, large, and round,
286   Behind him cast. The broad circumference
287   Hung on his shoulders like the moon, whose orb
288   Through optic glass the Tuscan[152] artist[153] views
289   At evening, from the top of Fesolé,
290   Or in Valdarno, to descry[154] new lands,
291   Rivers, or mountains in her spotty[155] globe.
292   His spear—to equal which the tallest pine
293   Hewn on Norwegian hills to be the mast
294   Of some great ammiral,[156] were but a wand—[157]
295   He walked with, to support uneasy[158] steps
296   Over the burning marl,[159] not like those steps
297   On Heaven's azure. And the torrid clime
298   Smote[160] on him sore besides, vaulted[161] with fire.
299   Nathless[162] he so endured, till on the beach
300   Of that inflamèd[163] sea he stood, and called
301   His legions, Angel forms, who lay entranced[164]
302   Thick as autumnal leaves that strew the brooks
303   In Vallombrosa,[165] where th' Etrurian[166] shades,
304   High over-arched, embow'r[167]—or scattered sedge[168]

---

[149] wicked, fatal
[150] celestial
[151] hardness
[152] Italian: Galileo
[153] practical scientist, learned man
[154] discover, make known
[155] spotted, patchy
[156] admiral's ship, flagship
[157] straight slender stick
[158] difficult, troublesome
[159] soil
[160] beat/shone strongly
[161] covered, roofed
[162] nevertheless
[163] burning, glowing
[164] in a trance, overpowered
[165] monastery south of Florence
[166] Etruscan
[167] give shelter
[168] rushlike/reedlike plants

305 Afloat, when with fierce winds Orion armed[169]
306 Hath vexed[170] the Red-Sea coast, whose waves o'erthrew
307 Busiris[171] and his Memphian[172] chivalry,[173]
308 While with perfidious[174] hatred they pursued
309 The sojourners[175] of Goshen,[176] who beheld
310 From the safe shore their floating carcases
311 And broken chariot-wheels. So thick bestrewn,
312 Abject[177] and lost, lay these, covering the flood,
313 Under amazement[178] of their hideous[179] change.
314   He called so loud that all the hollow deep
315 Of Hell resounded: "Princes, Potentates,[180]
316 Warriors, the Flow'r of Heav'n—once yours, now lost,
317 If such astonishment[181] as this can seize
318 Eternal Spirits! Or have ye chosen this place
319 After the toil of battle to repose
320 Your wearied virtue,[182] for the ease you find
321 To slumber here, as in the vales of Heav'n?
322 Or in this abject posture have ye sworn
323 To adore the conqueror, who now beholds
324 Cherub and Seraph rolling in the flood
325 With scattered arms and ensigns,[183] till anon[184]
326 His swift pursuers from Heav'n-gates discern
327 Th' advantage, and descending, tread us down
328 Thus drooping, or with linkèd thunderbolts
329 Transfix[185] us to the bottom of this gulf?[186]

---

[169] the constellation of Orion is associated with winter storms
[170] troubled, agitated
[171] Egyptian pharaoh who oppressed the captive Israelites
[172] Egyptian (Memphis = city in ancient Egypt)
[173] knights, horsemen
[174] treacherous
[175] temporary residents
[176] where the captive Israelites lived, in Egypt
[177] brought low, cast down
[178] stupefaction
[179] revolting, immense
[180] rulers
[181] insensibility, mental prostration
[182] power, force, strength
[183] banners, flags
[184] soon
[185] impale, pierce through
[186] abyss

330   Awake, arise, or be for ever fall'n!"
331   They heard, and were abashed, and up they
                        sprung
332   Upon the wing,[187] as when men wont[188] to watch
333   On duty, sleeping found by whom they dread,
334   Rouse and bestir themselves ere well awake.
335   Nor did they not perceive the evil plight
336   In which they were, or the fierce pains not feel,
337   Yet to their general's voice they soon obeyed
338   Innumerable. As when the potent rod
339   Of Amram's son,[189] in Egypt's evil day,
340   Waved round the coast, up-called a pitchy[190] cloud
341   Of locusts, warping[191] on the eastern wind,
342   That o'er the realm of impious Pharaoh hung
343   Like night, and darkened all the land of Nile—
344   So numberless were those bad Angels seen
345   Hovering on wing under the cope[192] of Hell
346   'Twixt upper, nether, and surrounding fires,
347   Till, as a signal giv'n, th' uplifted spear
348   Of their great sultan waving to direct
349   Their course, in even balance down they light[193]
350   On the firm[194] brimstone,[195] and fill all the plain:
351   A multitude like which the populous North[196]
352   Poured never from her frozen loins to pass
353   Rhine or the Danau,[197] when her barbarous sons
354   Came like a deluge on the South and spread
355   Beneath[198] Gibraltar to the Libyan sands.
356   Forthwith,[199] from every squadron and each band
357   The heads and leaders thither haste, where stood

---

[187] briskly, quickly
[188] accustomed
[189] Moses
[190] black
[191] floating/whirling through the air
[192] vault
[193] descend, settle
[194] solid
[195] burning stone, sulfur
[196] Goths and Vikings
[197] Danube
[198] down from
[199] at once

358   Their great commander—godlike shapes, and forms

359   Excelling[200] human; princely Dignities

360   And Powers that erst[201] in Heav'n sat on thrones,

361   Though of their names in Heav'nly records now

362   Be no memorial, blotted out and razed,

363   By their rebellion, from the Books of Life.[202]

364   Nor had they yet among the sons of Eve

365   Got them new names, till wand'ring o'er the earth

366   (Through God's high sufferance)[203] for the trial[204] of man,

367   By falsities and lies the greatest part

368   Of mankind they corrupted to forsake

369   God their Creator, and th' invisible

370   Glory of Him that made them to transform

371   Oft to the image of a brute, adorned

372   With gay[205] religions full of pomp and gold,

373   And devils to adore for deities.

374   Then were they known to men by various names,

375   And various idols through the heathen world.

376   Say, Muse, their names then known, who first, who last,

377   Roused from their slumber on that fiery couch,[206]

378   At their great emperor's call, as next in worth

379   Came singly where he stood on the bare strand,[207]

380   While the promiscuous[208] crowd stood yet aloof[209]

381   The chief[210] were those who, from the pit of Hell

382   Roaming to seek their prey on Earth, durst fix[211]

383   Their seats, long after, next the seat of God,

384   Their altars by His altar, gods adored

385   Among the nations round, and durst abide[212]

---

[200] surpassing

[201] at first, originally

[202] God's record of the righteous

[203] toleration, consent

[204] testing

[205] showy

[206] bed

[207] shore

[208] of mixed and disorderly composition

[209] at a distance

[210] most, the bulk

[211] place

[212] to face (defiantly)? await?

386 Jehovah thundering out of Sion, throned
387 Between the Cherubim, yea, often placed
388 Within His sanctuary itself their shrines—
389 Abominations!—and with cursèd things
390 His holy rites and solemn feasts profaned,[213]
391 And with their darkness durst affront[214] His light.
392   First, Moloch, horrid king, besmeared with blood
393 Of human sacrifice, and parents' tears,
394 Though, for the noise of drums and timbrels[215] loud,
395 Their children's cries unheard that passed through fire
396 To his grim[216] idol. Him the Ammonite[217]
397 Worshipped in Rabba[218] and her wat'ry plain,
398 In Argob[219] and in Basan,[220] to the stream
399 Of utmost Arnon.[221] Nor content with such
400 Audacious[222] neighbourhood, the wisest heart
401 Of Solomon he led by fraud to build
402 His[223] temple right against the temple of God
403 On that opprobrious[224] hill, and made his grove
404 The pleasant valley of Hinnom,[225] Tophet[226] thence
405 And black Gehenna[227] called, the type[228] of Hell.
406   Next Chemos,[229] th' obscene[230] dread[231] of
                    Moab's[232] sons,

---

[213] desecrated, violated
[214] to insult, defy
[215] percussion instrument, tambourinelike
[216] savage, cruel, fierce, harsh
[217] a Semitic people who lived in Jordan; they were related to the Israelites but often at war with them
[218] now Amman
[219] in Bashan region; included in the sixth province of Solomon's kingdom
[220] modern Bashan
[221] river flowing into the Dead Sea
[222] shameless, daring
[223] Moloch's
[224] scandalous, disgraceful
[225] Gehinnom, valley SW of Jerusalem
[226] high place in the valley of Hinnom, where children were sacrificed to Moloch
[227] place of future torment, hell
[228] symbol, model
[229] the Moabites' god
[230] filthy
[231] object of fear/reverence
[232] like the Ammonites, the Moabites were located in Jordan and related to the Israelites, with whom they often warred

407   From Aroar[233] to Nebo[234] and the wild
408   Of southmost Abarim,[235] in Hesebon[236]
409   And Horonaim,[237] Seon's[238] realm, beyond
410   The flow'ry dale of Sibma[239] clad with vines,
411   And Eléalé[240] to th' asphaltic pool.[241]
412   Peor[242] his other name, when he enticed
413   Israel in Sittim,[243] on their march from Nile,[244]
414   To do him wanton[245] rites, which cost them woe.
415   Yet thence his lustful orgies he enlarged
416   Ev'n to that hill of scandal,[246] by the grove
417   Of Moloch homicide, lust hard by[247] hate,
418   Till good Josiah[248] drove them thence to Hell.
419   With these came they who, from the bord'ring flood
420   Of old Euphrates[249] to the brook[250] that parts
421   Egypt from Syrian ground, had general names
422   Of Baalim[251] and Ashtaroth[252] — those male,
423   These feminine. For Spirits, when they please,
424   Can either sex assume, or both, so soft
425   And uncompounded[253] is their essence pure,
426   Not tied or manacled with joint or limb,
427   Nor founded[254] on the brittle strength of bones,

---

[233] see Deuteronomy 3:12
[234] a mountain in the Moabite region: see Isaiah 15:2
[235] linked to Nebo (see footnote 219, above)
[236] Hesebon = Moabite city
[237] see Isaiah 15:5
[238] Sehon = king of the Amorites, the pre-Israelite people of Canaan
[239] Moabite town
[240] Moabite city
[241] the Dead Sea
[242] Peor = Baal-Peor, Canaanite god associated with sexual orgies on Mt. Peor, in the Moabite region
[243] Israelite campsite near Jericho
[244] i.e., Egypt
[245] lewd, lascivious
[246] the Mount of Olives: see also line 403, above, and the footnote thereto
[247] hard by = close to
[248] king of Judea, 637–608 B.C., a religious reformer
[249] a major Mesopotamian river
[250] the River Esor
[251] plural of "Baal," in Hebrew
[252] plural of "Ashtoreth," in Hebrew
[253] uncombined, unmixed
[254] based

428 Like cumbrous[255] flesh, but in what shape they choose,
429 Dilated[256] or condensed, bright or obscure,
430 Can execute their airy purposes
431 And works of love or enmity[257] fulfil.
432 For those the race of Israel oft forsook
433 Their Living Strength, and unfrequented[258] left
434 His righteous altar, bowing lowly down
435 To bestial gods, for which their heads as low
436 Bowed down in battle, sunk before the spear
437 Of despicable[259] foes.
                                  With these in troop
438 Came Astoreth,[260] whom the Phoenicians called
439 Astarté, queen of heaven, with crescent horns,
440 To whose bright image nightly by the moon
441 Sidonian[261] virgins paid their vows and songs;
442 In Sion[262] also not unsung, where stood
443 Her temple on th' offensive[263] mountain, built
444 By that uxorious[264] king[265] whose heart, though large,
445 Beguiled by fair idolatresses, fell
446 To idols foul.
                                  Thammuz[266] came next behind,
447 Whose annual wound in Lebanon allured
448 The Syrian damsels to lament his fate
449 In amorous ditties all a summer's day,
450 While smooth Adonis[267] from his native rock
451 Ran purple to the sea, supposed with blood
452 Of Thammuz yearly wounded. The love-tale
453 Infected Sion's daughters with like heat,

---

[255] cumbersome: clumsy, unwieldy
[256] expanded
[257] ill will, hatred
[258] unfilled, uncrowded
[259] vile, wretched [four syllables, first and third accented]
[260] see line 422, above
[261] Sidon, Syrian city of the Phoenicians; now in Lebanon
[262] hill in Jerusalem, site of the Temple
[263] displeasing
[264] excessively fond of one's wife
[265] Solomon
[266] or Tammuz, Babylonian-Sumerian god (known elsewhere as Adonis, Osiris, etc.), carried off to the underworld but redeemed by Ishtar, chief Babylonian-Sumerian goddess, because life on earth had withered in his absence
[267] the river, which originates in Lebanon

454   Whose wanton passions in the sacred porch[268]
455   Ezekiel[269] saw, when by the vision led
456   His eye surveyed the dark idolatries
457   Of alienated Judah.[270]

                                   Next came one
458   Who mourned in earnest, when the captive ark[271]
459   Maimed his brute image, head and hands lopped off
460   In his own temple,[272] on the grunsel-edge,[273]
461   Where he fell flat and shamed his worshippers:
462   Dagon his name, sea-monster, upward man
463   And downward fish, yet[274] had his temple high
464   Reared in Azotus,[275] dreaded through the coast
465   Of Palestine, in Gath[276] and Ascalon,[277]
466   And Accaron[278] and Gaza's[279] frontier bounds.
467   Him followed Rimmon,[280] whose delightful seat
468   Was fair Damascus, on the fertile banks
469   Of Abbana[281] and Pharphar,[282] lucid[283] streams.[284]
470   He also against the house of God was bold.
471   A leper[285] once he lost, and gained a king—
472   Ahaz,[286] his[287] sottish[288] conqueror, whom he drew[289]

---

[268] antechamber/entranceway to the temple
[269] prophet of the Babylonian exile of the Israelites, sixth century B.C.
[270] the southern of the two kingdoms into which Israel was divided, after Solomon's death; the northern kingdom retained the name Israel
[271] captured by the Philistines
[272] placed in Dagon's temple, overnight the ark toppled Dagon's statue, knocking off the head and both hands
[273] threshold-edge
[274] (1) still, at that time, (2) nevertheless
[275] Ashdod, major Philistine city
[276] a major Philistine city
[277] a major Philistine city
[278] Ekron: a major Philistine city
[279] a major Philistine city
[280] Syrian god
[281] river in Damascus [trisyllabic, first and third accented]
[282] river near Damascus
[283] clear, pellucid, translucent, shining
[284] rivers
[285] Naaman, cured by Elisha, ninth century B.C. prophet of Israel, disciple of and successor to Elijah
[286] Ahaz, king of Judah, eighth century B.C.
[287] i.e., Rimmon's
[288] stupid, foolish
[289] induced

473 God's altar to disparage and displace
474 For one of Syrian mode, whereon to burn
475 His odious offerings, and adore the gods
476 Whom he[290] had vanquished.

                              After these appeared
477 A crew who, under names of old renown—
478 Osiris, Isis, Orus, and their train—[291]
479 With monstrous shapes and sorceries abused[292]
480 Fanatic Egypt and her priests to seek
481 Their wand'ring gods disguised in brutish forms
482 Rather than human. Nor did Israel scape
483 Th' infection, when their borrowed gold composed[293]
484 The calf[294] in Oreb,[295] and the rebel king[296]
485 Doubled that sin in Bethel[297] and in Dan,[298]
486 Lik'ning his Maker to the grazèd ox—[299]
487 Jehovah, who in one night, when he[300] passed
488 From Egypt marching, equalled[301] with one stroke[302]
489 Both her first-born and all her bleating gods.
490   Belial[303] came last, than whom a Spirit more lewd
491 Fell not from Heaven, or more gross[304] to love
492 Vice for itself. To him no temple stood

---

[290] i.e., Ahaz

[291] Osiris was husband to Isis; Horus (Orus) was their son

[292] tricked, deceived, imposed upon

[293] produced, made up

[294] linked to Apis, the sacred bull of Egypt

[295] Horeb: the mountain where God gave Moses the Ten Commandments; the Israelites waiting below demanded an idol to worship and Aaron, taking their gold jewelry, melted it and made them a golden calf

[296] Jeroboam, king of Judah, 930–910 B.C., made not one but two golden calves for his people to worship

[297] holy site, north of Jerusalem

[298] holy site in far northern Palestine

[299] "They made a calf in Horeb, and worshiped the molten [golden] image,/ Thus they changed their glory [i.e., God] into the similitude of an ox that eateth grass." Psalm 106:19–20

[300] by extension, the Israelites

[301] made equal

[302] "For I [the Lord] will pass through the land of Egypt this night, and will smite all the firstborn in the land of Egypt, both man and beast, and against all the gods of Egypt I will execute judgment." Exodus 12:12

[303] "wickedness"

[304] monstrous, flagrant

493 Or altar smoked, yet who more oft than he
494 In temples and at altars, when the priest
495 Turns atheist, as did Eli's sons, who filled
496 With lust and violence the house of God?[305]
497 In courts and palaces he also reigns,
498 And in luxurious[306] cities, where the noise
499 Of riot[307] ascends above their loftiest tow'rs,
500 And injury[308] and outrage.[309] And when night
501 Darkens the streets, then wander forth the sons
502 Of Belial,[310] flown[311] with insolence and wine.
503 Witness the streets of Sodom,[312] and that night
504 In Gibeah,[313] when the hospitable door
505 Exposed[314] a matron,[315] to avoid worse rape.[316]
506   These were the prime[317] in order and in might.
507 The rest were long to tell, though far[318] renowned,[319]
508 Th' Ionian gods—of Javan's issue[320] held
509 Gods, yet confessed[321] later than Heav'n and Earth,
510 Their boasted parents; Titan,[322] Heav'n's first-born,
511 With his enormous brood, and birthright seized
512 By younger Saturn. He[323] from mightier Jove,
513 His own and Rhea's[324] son, like measure[325] found:
514 So Jove usurping reigned. These first in Crete

[305] see 1 Samuel 2:12–17
[306] (1) lecherous, unchaste, outrageous, (2) given to luxury
[307] debauchery, dissipation, extravagance, loose living, etc.
[308] wrongful treatment, violation of another's rights
[309] intemperance, excess, violent/disorderly behavior
[310] a common Puritan insult, borrowed from the Hebrew *bene Belial*, "sons of Belial"
[311] inflated
[312] a city in the Jordan plain, destroyed by God because of its wickedness
[313] see Judges 19:22–30
[314] cast out
[315] married woman (though in fact the woman was a concubine)
[316] i.e., homosexual rape of a man
[317] primary
[318] widely
[319] celebrated, famous
[320] Javan = Ion: his issue were the Ionian (western Asia Minor) Greeks
[321] admitted, acknowledged
[322] Uranus' oldest son, Saturn's older brother
[323] Saturn, overthrown by Jove
[324] Uranus' daughter, Cronus' wife
[325] like measure = equal treatment

515   And Ida[326] known, thence on the snowy top
516   Of cold Olympus[327] ruled the middle air,[328]
517   Their highest heav'n, or[329] on the Delphian cliff,[330]
518   Or in Dodona,[331] and through all the bounds[332]
519   Of Doric land,[333] or who with Saturn old
520   Fled over Adria[334] to th' Hesperian[335] fields,
521   And o'er the Celtic roamed the utmost isles.[336]
522   All these and more came flocking, but with looks
523   Downcast and damp,[337] yet such wherein appeared
524   Obscure[338] some glimpse of joy to have found their
                chief[339]
525   Not in despair, to have found themselves not lost
526   In loss itself, which on his countenance cast
527   Like[340] doubtful[341] hue.[342] But he, his wonted[343] pride
528   Soon recollecting, with high words that bore
529   Semblance[344] of worth, not substance, gently raised
530   Their fainting courage and dispelled their fears,
531   Then straight[345] commands that, at the warlike sound
532   Of trumpets loud, and clarions,[346] be upreared[347]
533   His mighty standard.[348] That proud honor claimed

---

[326] Mount Ida (in Crete)
[327] mountain in Thessaly: the gods' home
[328] true heaven is the highest; the middle air is for demons—and for the Greek gods, according to Milton; in the lower air is the earth (and Hades underneath it)
[329] or = whether
[330] the oracle of Apollo at Delphi
[331] the oracle of Zeus at Dodona
[332] boundaries, limits
[333] Doric land = southern Greece
[334] the Adriatic Sea
[335] western, Italian
[336] i.e., Britain and Ireland
[337] dejected
[338] hidden
[339] Satan
[340] a similar
[341] uncertain, unsettled
[342] appearance
[343] accustomed
[344] appearance
[345] immediately
[346] a form of trumpet, shrill-sounding
[347] raised
[348] banner, flag

534   Azazel[349] as his right, a Cherub tall,
535   Who forthwith from the glittering staff[350] unfurled
536   Th' imperial ensign, which, full high advanced,[351]
537   Shone like a meteor streaming to the wind,
538   With gems and golden luster rich emblazed,
539   Seraphic arms and trophies, all the while
540   Sonorous metal blowing martial sounds.
541   At which the universal host up-sent
542   A shout that tore Hell's concave,[352] and beyond
543   Frighted the reign[353] of Chaos and old Night.
544   All in a moment through the gloom were seen
545   Ten thousand banners rise into the air,
546   With orient[354] colors waving. With them rose
547   A forest huge of spears, and thronging helms[355]
548   Appeared, and serried[356] shields in thick array
549   Of depth immeasurable. Anon[357] they move
550   In perfect phalanx[358] to the Dorian mood[359]
551   Of flutes and soft recorders[360] — such as raised
552   To height of noblest temper[361] heroes old
553   Arming to battle, and instead of rage
554   Deliberate valour breathed, firm, and unmoved
555   With dread of death to flight or foul retreat,
556   Nor wanting[362] power to mitigate[363] and suage[364]
557   With solemn touches troubled thoughts, and chase
558   Anguish and doubt and fear and sorrow and pain
559   From mortal or immortal minds. Thus they,
560   Breathing united force with fixèd thought,

---

[349] in Judaism, the very personification of impurity, an archdemon
[350] flagpole
[351] presented, put forward
[352] vault, hollow
[353] realm
[354] brilliant, sparkling, radiant, lustrous
[355] helmets
[356] pressed close together
[357] quickly
[358] close-packed battle array, sixteen-man-deep square, perfected by the Romans
[359] mode, scale
[360] wooden flutes, not held transversely, as is the flute properly so called
[361] composure, state of mind
[362] lacking
[363] mollify, appease
[364] assuage: soften, pacify

561   Moved on in silence to soft pipes that charmed
562   Their painful steps o'er the burnt soil.

And now
563   Advanced in view they stand—a horrid[365] front[366]
564   Of dreadful length[367] and dazzling arms,[368] in guise[369]
565   Of warriors old, with ordered[370] spear and shield,
566   Awaiting what command their mighty chief
567   Had to impose.[371] He through the armèd files[372]
568   Darts his experienced eye, and soon traverse[373]
569   The whole battalion views—their order due,[374]
570   Their visages and stature as of gods.
571   Their number last he sums.[375] And now his heart
572   Distends[376] with pride and hard'ning in his strength
573   Glories, for never since created man
574   Met such embodied[377] force as, named[378] with these,
575   Could merit[379] more than[380] that small infantry
576   Warred on by cranes[381]—though all the giant brood
577   Of Phlegra[382] with th' heroic race were joined
578   That fought at Thebes[383] and Ilium,[384] on each side
579   Mixed with auxiliar[385] gods, and what resounds[386]
580   In fable or romance of Uther's son,[387]

---

[365] bristling, frightful
[366] battle line
[367] fearfully/exceedingly long
[368] weapons
[369] semblance, external appearance
[370] arranged
[371] lay on, give
[372] rows
[373] passing across, side to side (in ranks) rather than front to back (in files)
[374] proper
[375] counts up
[376] swells, expands
[377] (1) actual, concrete, (2) joined in one group/body
[378] mentioned (for purposes of comparison)
[379] be entitled to, be deserving of
[380] i.e., any more than
[381] pygmies: the battle is in Homer's *Iliad*, III:1–5; Milton returns to it in lines 780–81, below
[382] in Chalcidice, where the giants warred with the gods
[383] part of the Oedipus story: see Aeschylus, *The Seven Against Thebes*
[384] Troy
[385] auxiliary
[386] echoes, rings
[387] King Arthur

581	Begirt with[388] British and Armoric[389] knights,
582	And all who since, baptized or infidel,
583	Jousted[390] in Aspramont,[391] or Montalban,[392]
584	Damasco,[393] or Marocco,[394] or Trebisond,[395]
585	Or whom Biserta[396] sent from Afric shore
586	When Charlemain with all his peerage fell
587	By Fontarabbia.[397] Thus far these, beyond
588	Compare of[398] mortal prowess, yet observed
589	Their dread[399] commander. He, above the rest
590	In shape and gesture proudly eminent,
591	Stood like a tow'r. His form had yet not lost
592	All her original brightness, nor appeared
593	Less than Archangel ruined, and th' excess
594	Of glory obscured, as when the sun new-ris'n
595	Looks through the horizontal misty air
596	Shorn of his beams, or from behind the moon,
597	In dim eclipse, disastrous[400] twilight sheds[401]
598	On half the nations, and with fear of change
599	Perplexes[402] monarchs. Darkened so, yet shone
600	Above them all th' Archangel, but his face
601	Deep scars of thunder had intrenched,[403] and care
602	Sat on his faded cheek, but under brows
603	Of dauntless courage, and considerate[404] pride
604	Waiting revenge. Cruel his eye, but cast[405]
605	Signs of remorse and passion, to behold

---

[388] surrounded by

[389] of Brittany

[390] knightly combat (pronounced "justed")

[391] castle near Nice, where Charlemagne fought

[392] Rinaldo's castle: see Ariosto, *Orlando Furioso*

[393] Damascus, where Moslem and Christian knights jousted, in *Orlando Furioso*

[394] Morocco (city): see footnote 396, below

[395] on the southern coast of the Black Sea

[396] Bizerta, in Tunisia, like Morocco a famous site of knightly tournaments

[397] in *La Chanson de Roland*, it is Roland rather than Charlemagne who dies at Roncevaux, not far from Fontarabbia

[398] with (merely)

[399] revered, feared

[400] ominous, ill-boding

[401] sprinkles, lets fall on, pours out, drops

[402] confuses, makes uncertain

[403] furrowed

[404] deliberate, prudent

[405] dropped

606 The fellows[406] of his crime, the followers rather
607 (Far other once beheld in bliss), condemned
608 For ever now to have their lot[407] in pain.
609 Millions of Spirits for his fault amerced[408]
610 Of Heav'n, and from eternal splendors flung
611 For his revolt, yet faithful how they stood,
612 Their glory withered—as when Heaven's fire
613 Hath scathed[409] the forest oaks or mountain pines,
614 With singèd top their stately[410] growth, though bare,
615 Stands on the blasted[411] heath. He now prepared
616 To speak, whereat their doubled ranks they bend
617 From wing to wing, and half enclose him round
618 With all his peers. Attention held them mute.
619 Thrice he assayed,[412] and thrice, in spite of[413] scorn,
620 Tears, such as Angels weep, burst forth. At last
621 Words interwove with sighs found out their way:
622   "O myriads of immortal Spirits! O Powers
623 Matchless, but[414] with th' Almighty! And that strife
624 Was not inglorious, though th' event[415] was dire,[416]
625 As this place testifies, and this dire change,
626 Hateful to utter. But what power of mind,
627 Foreseeing or presaging,[417] from the depth
628 Of knowledge past or present, could have feared
629 How such united force of gods, how such
630 As stood like these, could ever know repulse?[418]
631 For who can yet believe, though after loss,
632 That all these puissant[419] legions,[420] whose exile
633 Hath emptied Heav'n, shall fail to re-ascend,

---

[406] partners, colleagues
[407] fate, destiny
[408] punished
[409] blast/scorch/sear with fire/heat
[410] noble, majestic, imposing
[411] blighted, withered
[412] tried, attempted
[413] in spite of = with contempt for
[414] except
[415] outcome
[416] dreadful, terrible
[417] predicting
[418] rebuff, being forced/driven back
[419] powerful
[420] armies

634   Self-raised, and repossess their native seat?
635   For me, be witness all the host of Heav'n,
636   If counsels[421] different, or danger shunned
637   By me, have lost our hopes. But He who reigns
638   Monarch in Heav'n till then as one secure
639   Sat on His throne, upheld by old repute,
640   Consent or custom, and His regal state
641   Put forth at full,[422] but still His strength concealed—
642   Which tempted our attempt, and wrought[423] our fall.
643   Henceforth His[424] might we know, and know our own,
644   So as not either to provoke, or dread
645   New war provoked. Our better part[425] remains
646   To work in close[426] design,[427] by fraud or guile,
647   What force effected[428] not, that He no less
648   At length from us may find:[429] who overcomes
649   By force hath overcome but half his foe.
650   Space may produce new worlds—whereof so rife[430]
651   There went a fame[431] in Heav'n that He ere long
652   Intended to create, and therein plant
653   A generation whom His choice[432] regard[433]
654   Should favor equal to the sons of Heav'n.
655   Thither, if but to pry, shall be perhaps
656   Our first eruption[434]—thither, or elsewhere,
657   For this infernal pit shall never hold
658   Celestial Spirits in bondage, nor th' abyss
659   Long under darkness cover.[435]

                              "But these thoughts
660   Full counsel must mature. Peace is despaired,

---

[421] judgment, opinion, direction
[422] at full = completely
[423] worked
[424] "His strength"
[425] act, business
[426] secret, confidential
[427] plan, scheme
[428] brought about, accomplished
[429] discover
[430] common, prevalent
[431] rumor
[432] special, select [adjective]
[433] attention, consideration
[434] breaking/bursting forth
[435] hide, wrap

661   For who can think submission? War, then, war
662   Open or understood, must be resolved."
663   He spoke and, to confirm his words, outflew
664   Millions of flaming swords, drawn from the thighs[436]
665   Of mighty Cherubim: the sudden blaze
666   Far round illumined Hell. Highly[437] they raged
667   Against the Highest, and fierce with graspèd[438] arms
668   Clashed on their sounding[439] shields the din of war,
669   Hurling defiance toward the vault of Heav'n.
670   There stood a hill not far, whose grisly[440] top
671   Belched fire and rolling smoke; the rest entire[441]
672   Shone with a glossy scurf[442]—undoubted sign
673   That in his womb was hid metallic ore,
674   The work of sulphur.[443] Thither, winged with speed,
675   A numerous brigade hastened: as when bands
676   Of pioneers,[444] with spade and pickaxe armed,
677   Forerun[445] the royal camp, to trench[446] a field
678   Or cast[447] a rampart.[448] Mammon led them on—
679   Mammon, the least erected[449] Spirit that fell
680   From Heav'n, for even in Heav'n his looks and thoughts
681   Were always downward bent, admiring more
682   The riches of Heav'n's pavement, trodden gold,
683   Than aught divine or holy else[450] enjoyed
684   In vision beatific.[451] By him first
685   Men also, and by his suggestion taught,
686   Ransacked the center,[452] and with impious hands

---

[436] i.e., from scabbards strapped to their thighs
[437] (1) very much, (2) proudly, arrogantly
[438] clutched and held firmly
[439] reverberating, sonorous
[440] ugly, horrible
[441] "the whole rest"
[442] a scale/crust (of hardened sulfur, combined with volcanic flow)
[443] current science taught that metals formed by mercury combining with sulfur
[444] soldiers with shovels and axes
[445] run in front of, precede
[446] dig trenches in
[447] to throw up, with shovels or spades
[448] defensive mound, usually of earth
[449] upright, elevated
[450] aught . . . else = anyone else
[451] blessed
[452] (of the earth)

687	Rifled[453] the bowels of their mother earth
688	For treasures better hid. Soon had his crew
689	Opened into the hill a spacious wound,
690	And digged out ribs[454] of gold. Let none admire[455]
691	That riches grow in Hell: that soil may best
692	Deserve the precious bane.[456] And here let those
693	Who boast in[457] mortal things, and wond'ring tell
694	Of Babel, and the works of Memphian[458] kings,
695	Learn how their greatest monuments of fame
696	And strength, and art, are easily outdone
697	By Spirits reprobate,[459] and in an hour
698	What in an age they,[460] with incessant toil
699	And hands innumerable, scarce perform.
700	Nigh[461] on the plain, in many cells[462] prepared,
701	That underneath had veins of liquid fire
702	Sluiced[463] from the lake, a second multitude
703	With wondrous art[464] founded[465] the massy[466] ore,
704	Severing[467] each kind, and scummed[468] the bullion-dross.[469]
705	A third as soon[470] had formed within the ground
706	A various[471] mould, and from the boiling cells
707	By strange[472] conveyance filled each hollow nook,
708	As in an organ, from one blast of wind,
709	To many a row of pipes the sound-board breathes.

---

[453] plundered, robbed
[454] veins (of ore)
[455] be surprised/amazed/astonished
[456] curse
[457] (1) brag of, (2) glory in
[458] Egyptian
[459] condemned, depraved, rejected by God
[460] i.e., Memphian kings et al.
[461] near
[462] pits
[463] drawn
[464] skill
[465] melted
[466] dense
[467] separating
[468] skimmed
[469] golden dregs
[470] as soon = quickly
[471] versatile
[472] unknown

710   Anon[473] out of the earth a fabric[474] huge
711   Rose like an exhalation with the sound
712   Of dulcet[475] symphonies[476] and voices sweet—
713   Built like a temple, where pilasters[477] round
714   Were set, and Doric[478] pillars overlaid
715   With golden architrave,[479] nor did there want[480]
716   Cornice[481] or frieze,[482] with bossy sculptures[483] grav'n.
717   The roof was fretted[484] gold. Not Babylon
718   Nor great Alcairo[485] such magnificence
719   Equaled in all their glories, to enshrine
720   Belus or Serapis[486] their gods, or seat[487]
721   Their kings, when Egypt with Assyria strove
722   In wealth and luxury. Th' ascending pile[488]
723   Stood fixed[489] her stately height, and straight the doors,
724   Opening their brazen[490] folds, discover,[491] wide
725   Within, her ample spaces o'er the smooth
726   And level pavement. From the archèd roof,
727   Pendant[492] by subtle[493] magic, many a row
728   Of starry lamps and blazing cressets,[494] fed
729   With naphtha and asphaltus, yielded light
730   As from a sky. The hasty[495] multitude
731   Admiring entered, and the work some praise,

---

[473] soon
[474] structure, building
[475] sweet, pleasing
[476] harmonious music
[477] pillars, columns
[478] a form of Greek architecture
[479] support beams of various types
[480] lack
[481] ornamental molding
[482] decoration applied between the architrave and the cornice
[483] bossy scultures = bas-relief sculptures
[484] adorned, carved
[485] ancient Memphis, near modern Cairo
[486] Belus or Serapis = Baal or Osiris
[487] enthrone, establish
[488] lofty/large building/structure
[489] (1) located, established, (2) firm, stable
[490] (1) brass, (2) hardened in their effrontery
[491] reveal
[492] suspended, hung
[493] intricate, delicate, skillful, expert, ingenious
[494] firepots
[495] swift, hurrying

732 And some the architect. His hand was known
733 In Heav'n by many a tow'red structure high,
734 Where sceptered Angels held their residence
735 And sat as Princes, whom the supreme King
736 Exalted to such power, and gave to rule,
737 Each in his hierarchy, the Orders bright.
738 Nor was his name unheard or unadored
739 In ancient Greece. And in Ausonian[496] land
740 Men called him Mulciber,[497] and how he fell
741 From Heav'n they fabled,[498] thrown by angry Jove
742 Sheer[499] o'er the crystal battlements.[500] From morn
743 To noon he fell, from noon to dewy eve,
744 A summer's day, and with the setting sun
745 Dropt from the zenith[501] like a falling star,
746 On Lemnos, th' Aegean isle. Thus they relate,[502]
747 Erring, for he with this rebellious rout[503]
748 Fell long before, nor aught availed him now
749 To have built in Heav'n high tow'rs, nor did he scape
750 By all his engines,[504] but was headlong sent,
751 With his industrious[505] crew, to build in Hell.
752 Meanwhile the wingèd heralds, by command
753 Of sov'reign power, with awful[506] ceremony
754 And trumpet's sound throughout the host[507] proclaim
755 A solemn council forthwith to be held
756 At Pandemonium, the high capital
757 Of Satan and his peers.[508] Their summons called
758 From every band and squarèd[509] regiment

---

[496] Italian
[497] Mulciber = Hephaestus/Vulcan
[498] talked idly, lied about
[499] steeply, perpendicularly
[500] fortifications placed on top of walls
[501] directly overhead
[502] tell, recount
[503] mob, rabble
[504] machines, devices
[505] hardworking, skillful, ingenious
[506] solemnly impressive/majestic
[507] multitude
[508] i.e., all the spirits/demons
[509] precisely formed

759   By place[510] or choice the worthiest. They anon[511]
760   With hundreds and with thousands trooping came
761   Attended.[512] All access[513] was thronged, the gates
762   And porches wide, but chief the spacious hall
763   (Though like a covered field, where champions bold
764   Wont[514] ride in armed, and at the Soldan's[515] chair
765   Defied the best of Paynim[516] chivalry
766   To mortal combat, or career[517] with lance),
767   Thick swarmed, both on the ground and in the air,
768   Brushed with the hiss of rustling wings. As bees
769   In spring-time, when the sun with Taurus rides,
770   Pour forth their populous youth about the hive
771   In clusters, they among fresh dews and flowers
772   Fly to and fro, or on the smoothèd plank,
773   The suburb[518] of their straw-built citadel,
774   New rubbed with balm, expatiate[519] and confer
775   Their state-affairs. So thick the airy crowd
776   Swarmed and were straitened,[520] till, the signal given,
777   Behold a wonder! They but now who seemed
778   In bigness to surpass earth's giant sons,
779   Now less than smallest dwarfs in narrow room
780   Throng numberless—like that pygmean race
781   Beyond the Indian mount,[521] or faery elves,
782   Whose midnight revels[522] by a forest-side
783   Or fountain some belated[523] peasant sees,
784   Or dreams he sees, while overhead the moon
785   Sits arbitress,[524] and nearer to the earth

---

[510] position, post, rank
[511] soon, quickly
[512] escorted
[513] approaches
[514] were in the habit, accustomed to
[515] Sultan's
[516] pagan
[517] encounter, charge
[518] outskirts
[519] walk and speak
[520] closed in, compacted
[521] the Himalayas
[522] merrymaking
[523] tardy, late-coming
[524] person in charge

786   Wheels[525] her pale course.[526] They, on their mirth and
                          dance
787   Intent, with jocund[527] music charm his[528] ear;
788   At once with joy and fear his heart rebounds.
789   Thus incorporeal Spirits to smallest forms
790   Reduced their shapes immense, and were at large,[529]
791   Though without number still, amidst the hall
792   Of that infernal court.[530] But far within,
793   And in their own dimensions like themselves,
794   The great Seraphic Lords and Cherubim
795   In close recess and secret conclave[531] sat,
796   A thousand demi-gods on golden seats,
797   Frequent[532] and full. After short silence, then,
798   And summons read, the great consult began.

The End of the First Book

---

[525] revolves, turns, rolls, moves
[526] way, onward movement
[527] joyful
[528] i.e., the watching peasant
[529] at large = at liberty, free
[530] sovereign establishment
[531] assembly
[532] crowded

·BOOK II·

THE ARGUMENT

THE CONSULTATION BEGUN, Satan debates whether another battle be[1] to be hazarded for the recovery of Heaven. Some advise it, others dissuade. A third proposal is preferred,[2] mentioned before by Satan, to search the truth of that prophesy or tradition in Heaven concerning another world, and another kind of creature equal or not much inferior to themselves, about this time to be created.

Their doubt who shall be sent on this difficult search.

Satan, their chief, undertakes alone the voyage, is honored and applauded. The council thus ended, the rest betake them several ways and to several employments, as their inclinations lead them, to entertain[3] the time till Satan return. He passes on his journey to Hell Gates, finds them shut, and who sat there to guard them, by whom at length they are opened, and discover to him the great gulf[4] between Hell and Heaven.

With what difficulty he passes through, directed by Chaos, the Power of that place, to the sight of this new world which he sought.

---

[1] is
[2] put forward
[3] occupy
[4] abyss

1	High on a throne of royal state, which far
2	Outshone the wealth of Ormus[5] and of Ind,[6]
3	Or where the gorgeous[7] East with richest hand
4	Show'rs on her kings barbaric pearl and gold,
5	Satan exalted sat, by merit raised
6	To that bad eminence and, from despair
7	Thus high uplifted beyond hope, aspires
8	Beyond thus high, insatiate[8] to pursue
9	Vain war with Heav'n and, by success[9] untaught,
10	His proud imaginations thus displayed:
11	"Powers and Dominions, Deities of Heav'n!—
12	For since no deep within her gulf[10] can hold
13	Immortal vigor,[11] though oppressed and fall'n,
14	I give not Heav'n for lost. From this descent
15	Celestial Virtues[12] rising will appear
16	More glorious and more dread than from no fall,
17	And trust themselves to fear no second fate!—
18	Me, though, just right[13] and the fixed laws of Heav'n
19	Did first create your leader, next free choice,
20	With what besides in council or in fight
21	Hath been achieved of merit, yet this loss,
22	Thus far at least recovered,[14] hath much more
23	Established in a safe, unenvied throne,
24	Yielded with full consent. The happier[15] state
25	In Heav'n, which follows[16] dignity,[17] might draw
26	Envy from each inferior. But who here
27	Will envy whom the highest place exposes
28	Foremost to stand against the Thunderer's aim
29	Your bulwark,[18] and condemns to greatest share

---

[5] Persian Gulf city of great wealth
[6] India
[7] showy, magnificent
[8] unsatisfiable
[9] (1) failure, misfortune, (2) result, sequel (to the first attempt)
[10] abyss
[11] (1) strength, energy, (2) mental acuity
[12] the seventh of the nine angelic orders
[13] "Although just right [fair law] at first created me . . ."
[14] regained
[15] luckier, more fortunate
[16] goes along with, depends on
[17] rank, worth, honor, excellence
[18] defensive structure, rampart

30 Of endless pain? Where there is then no good
31 For which to strive, no strife can grow up there
32 From faction,[19] for none sure will claim in Hell
33 Precedence, none whose portion is so small
34 Of present pain that with ambitious mind
35 Will covet more! With this advantage, then,
36 To union, and firm faith, and firm accord,
37 More than can be in Heav'n, we now return
38 To claim our just inheritance of old,
39 Surer to prosper than prosperity
40 Could have assured us. And by what best way,
41 Whether of open war or covert guile,
42 We now debate. Who can advise may speak."
43   He ceased. And next[20] him Moloch, sceptered
            king,
44 Stood up—the strongest and the fiercest Spirit
45 That fought in Heav'n, now fiercer by despair.
46 His trust[21] was with th' Eternal to be deemed
47 Equal in strength, and rather than be less
48 Cared not to be at all. With that care lost
49 Went all his fear—of God, or Hell, or worse,
50 He recked[22] not—and these words thereafter spoke:
51   "My sentence[23] is for open war. Of wiles
52 More unexpert, I boast not. Them let those
53 Contrive who need, or when they need; not now.
54 For while they sit contriving, shall the rest—
55 Millions that stand in arms, and longing wait
56 The signal to ascend—sit ling'ring here,
57 Heav'n's fugitives? and for their dwelling-place
58 Accept this dark opprobrious[24] den of shame,
59 The prison of His tyranny who reigns
60 By our delay? No! Let us rather choose,
61 Armed with Hell-flames and fury, all at once
62 O'er Heav'n's high tow'rs to force resistless way,
63 Turning our tortures into horrid arms

---

[19] political parties, intrigue, strife
[20] after
[21] (1) hope, (2) confidence, confident expectation
[22] cared
[23] opinion, judgment
[24] injurious, abusive, disgraceful

64   Against the Torturer! When to meet the noise
65   Of His almighty engine,[25] He shall hear
66   Infernal thunder and, for lightning, see
67   Black fire and horror shot with equal rage
68   Among His Angels, and His throne itself
69   Mixed with Tartarean[26] sulphur and strange[27] fire,
70   His own invented torments. But perhaps
71   The way seems difficult, and steep to scale
72   With upright wing against a higher foe?
73   Let such bethink them, if the sleepy drench[28]
74   Of that forgetful[29] lake benumb not still,
75   That in our proper[30] motion we ascend
76   Up to our native seat; descent and fall
77   To us is adverse.[31] Who but felt of late,
78   When the fierce foe hung on our broken rear[32]
79   Insulting,[33] and pursued us through the deep,
80   With what compulsion and laborious flight
81   We sunk thus low? Th' ascent is easy, then;
82   Th' event[34] is feared! Should we again provoke
83   Our stronger, some worse way His wrath may find
84   To our destruction, if there be in Hell
85   Fear to be worse destroyed! What can be worse
86   Than to dwell here, driv'n out from bliss, condemned
87   In this abhorrèd[35] deep to utter[36] woe!
88   Where pain of unextinguishable fire
89   Must exercise[37] us without hope of end,
90   The vassals[38] of His anger, when the scourge
91   Inexorably, and the torturing hour,
92   Calls us to penance? More destroyed than thus

---

[25] engine = mechanical device: God's chariot?
[26] the deepest region of Hades
[27] unknown, unfamiliar
[28] drug, potion
[29] in book 1, line 266, an "oblivious pool"
[30] intrinsic—i.e., that which inheres in Spirits/Angels, etc.
[31] actively opposed (i.e., unnatural)
[32] the hindmost portion of their army
[33] attacking, assaulting
[34] result, outcome
[35] horrible, disgusting
[36] [adjective]
[37] harass, oppress
[38] slaves, serfs

93   We should be quite abolished, and expire.
94   What fear we then? What doubt we to incense[39]
95   His utmost ire? which, to the height enraged,
96   Will either quite consume us, and reduce
97   To nothing this essential[40]—happier far
98   Than miserable to have eternal being!—
99   Or if our substance be indeed divine,
100   And cannot cease to be, we are at worst
101   On this side nothing. And by proof we feel
102   Our power sufficient to disturb His Heav'n,
103   And with perpetual inroads to alarm,
104   Though inaccessible, His fatal throne—
105   Which if not victory, is yet revenge."
106   He ended frowning, and his look denounced[41]
107   Desperate revenge, and battle dangerous
108   To less than gods. On th' other side up rose
109   Belial, in act more graceful and humane.
110   A fairer person lost not Heav'n. He seemed
111   For dignity composed, and high exploit.
112   But all was false and hollow, though his tongue
113   Dropped manna[42] and could make the worse appear
114   The better reason, to perplex[43] and dash[44]
115   Maturest counsels, for his thoughts were low—
116   To vice industrious, but to nobler deeds
117   Timorous and slothful. Yet he pleased the ear,
118   And with persuasive accent thus began:
119   "I should be much for open war, O peers,[45]
120   As not behind in hate, if what was urged,
121   Main reason to persuade immediate war,
122   Did not dissuade me most, and seem to cast
123   Ominous conjecture[46] on the whole success,[47]
124   When he who most excels in fact[48] of arms,

---

[39] kindle, inflame
[40] essence, being
[41] proclaimed, threatened
[42] as God had dropped manna to the Israelites, in the desert, when they fled from Egypt
[43] complicate, confuse
[44] frustrate, destroy
[45] (1) companions, (2) high lords
[46] prognostication
[47] result
[48] feats, deeds, actions

125   In what he counsels and in what excels
126   Mistrustful, grounds his courage on despair
127   And utter dissolution[49] as the scope[50]
128   Of all his aim,[51] after some dire revenge.
129   First, what revenge? The tow'rs of Heav'n are filled
130   With armèd watch that render all access
131   Impregnable. Oft on the bordering deep
132   Encamp their legions, or with obscure[52] wing
133   Scout far and wide into the realm of Night,
134   Scorning surprise. Or could[53] we break our way
135   By force, and at our heels all Hell should rise
136   With blackest insurrection to confound[54]
137   Heav'n's purest light, yet our great enemy,
138   All incorruptible, would on His throne
139   Sit unpolluted, and th' ethereal[55] mould,[56]
140   Incapable of stain, would soon expel
141   Her mischief,[57] and purge off the baser[58] fire,
142   Victorious. Thus repulsed, our final hope
143   Is flat[59] despair: we must exasperate
144   Th' Almighty victor to spend[60] all His rage;
145   And that must end us, that must be our cure—
146   To be no more. Sad cure! for who would lose,[61]
147   Though full of pain, this intellectual being,[62]
148   Those thoughts that wander through eternity,
149   To perish rather, swallowed up and lost
150   In the wide womb of uncreated Night,
151   Devoid of sense and motion? And who knows,
152   Let this be good, whether our angry foe
153   Can give it, or will ever? How He can

---

[49] being brought to an end, death
[50] goal, purpose
[51] object
[52] dark, secret
[53] "if we could"
[54] overthrow, defeat
[55] celestial
[56] distinctive nature/shape
[57] evil, harm
[58] low, inferior, degraded
[59] absolute, lifeless, spiritless
[60] employ, exercise
[61] undo, release
[62] (1) intelligent existence, (2) superior intelligent existence

154 Is doubtful; that He never will is sure.
155 Will He, so wise, let loose at once His ire,
156 Belike[63] through impotence or unaware,
157 To give His enemies their wish, and end
158 Them in His anger, whom His anger saves
159 To punish endless? 'Wherefore cease we, then?'
160 Say they who counsel war: 'we are decreed,[64]
161 Reserved,[65] and destined to eternal woe.
162 Whatever doing, what can we suffer more,
163 What can we suffer worse?' Is this, then, worst—
164 Thus sitting, thus consulting, thus in arms?
165 What when we fled amain,[66] pursued and struck
166 With Heav'n's afflicting thunder, and besought
167 The deep to shelter us? This Hell then seemed
168 A refuge from those wounds. Or when we lay
169 Chained on the burning lake? That sure was worse.
170 What if the breath that kindled those grim fires,
171 Awaked, should blow them into sevenfold rage,
172 And plunge us in the flames? Or from above
173 Should intermitted[67] vengeance arm again
174 His red right hand to plague us? What if all
175 Her stores were opened, and this firmament
176 Of Hell should spout her cataracts of fire,
177 Impendent[68] horrors, threat'ning hideous fall
178 One day upon our heads, while we, perhaps
179 Designing or exhorting glorious war,
180 Caught in a fiery tempest, shall be hurled,
181 Each on his rock transfixed, the sport and prey
182 Of racking[69] whirlwinds, or for ever sunk
183 Under yon boiling ocean, wrapped in chains,
184 There to converse with everlasting groans,
185 Unrespited,[70] unpitied, unreprieved,
186 Ages of hopeless end? This would be worse.

---

[63] possibly, probably
[64] ordained
[65] set apart
[66] in full force of numbers
[67] interrupted
[68] overhanging, near
[69] afflicting, shaking
[70] without reprieve/delay

187 War, therefore, open or concealed, alike
188 My voice dissuades. For what can force or guile
189 With Him, or who deceive His mind, whose eye
190 Views all things at one view? He from Heav'n's height
191 All these our motions vain sees and derides,
192 Not more Almighty to resist our might
193 Than wise to frustrate all our plots and wiles.
194 Shall we, then, live thus vile—the race of Heav'n
195 Thus trampled, thus expelled, to suffer here
196 Chains and these torments? Better these than worse,
197 By my advice, since fate inevitable
198 Subdues us, and omnipotent decree,
199 The victor's will. To suffer, as to do,
200 Our strength is equal, nor the law unjust
201 That so ordains. This was at first resolved,
202 If we were wise, against so great a foe
203 Contending,[71] and so[72] doubtful what might fall.[73]
204 I laugh when those who at the spear are bold
205 And vent'rous, if that fail them, shrink, and fear
206 What yet they know must follow—to endure
207 Exile, or ignominy,[74] or bonds, or pain,
208 The sentence of their conqueror. This is now
209 Our doom,[75] which if we can sustain and bear,
210 Our Supreme foe in time may much remit[76]
211 His anger, and perhaps, thus far removed,[77]
212 Not mind[78] us, not offending, satisfied
213 With what is punished, whence these raging fires
214 Will slacken, if His breath stir not their flames.
215 Our purer essence then will overcome
216 Their noxious[79] vapor or, inured,[80] not feel.
217 Or, changed at length, and to the place conformed[81]

---

[71] struggling, fighting
[72] therefore
[73] occur, come to pass, result
[74] dishonor, disgrace
[75] sentence, judgment, destiny
[76] discharge, withdraw, cancel
[77] distant
[78] remember, notice
[79] unwholesome
[80] habituated, accustomed
[81] adapted

218   In temper and in nature, will receive
219   Familiar the fierce heat, and void of pain.
220   This horror will grow mild, this darkness light,
221   Besides what hope the never-ending flight
222   Of future days may bring, what chance, what change
223   Worth waiting—since our present lot appears
224   For happy though but ill, for ill not worst,
225   If we procure not to ourselves more woe."
226   Thus Belial, with words clothed in reason's garb,
227   Counselled ignoble ease and peaceful sloth,
228   Not peace. And after him thus Mammon spoke:
229   "Either to disenthrone the King of Heav'n
230   We war, if war be best, or to regain
231   Our own right lost. Him to unthrone we then
232   May hope, when everlasting Fate shall yield
233   To fickle Chance, and Chaos judge the strife.
234   The former, vain to hope, argues as vain
235   The latter—for what place can be for us
236   Within Heav'n's bound, unless Heav'n's Lord supreme
237   We overpower? Suppose He should relent
238   And publish[82] grace to all, on promise made
239   Of new subjection?[83] With what eyes could we
240   Stand in His presence humble, and receive
241   Strict laws imposed, to celebrate His throne
242   With warbled hymns, and to His Godhead sing
243   Forced hallelujahs, while He lordly sits,
244   Our envied sov'reign, and His altar breathes
245   Ambrosial odors and ambrosial flowers,
246   Our servile offerings? This must be our task
247   In Heav'n, this our delight. How wearisome
248   Eternity so spent in worship paid
249   To whom we hate! Let us not then pursue,
250   By force impossible, by leave obtained
251   Unacceptable, though in Heav'n, our state
252   Of splendid vassalage, but rather seek
253   Our own good from ourselves, and from our own
254   Live to[84] ourselves, though in this vast recess,

---

[82] announce, proclaim
[83] submission, obedience, homage
[84] for/by

255 Free and to none accountable, preferring
256 Hard liberty before the easy yoke
257 Of servile pomp. Our greatness will appear
258 Then most conspicuous when great things of[85] small,
259 Useful of hurtful, prosperous of adverse,[86]
260 We can create, and in what place soe'er
261 Thrive under evil, and work ease out of pain
262 Through labor and endurance. This deep world
263 Of darkness do we dread? How oft amidst
264 Thick clouds and dark doth Heav'n's all-ruling Sire
265 Choose to reside, His glory unobscured,
266 And with the majesty of darkness round
267 Covers His throne, from whence deep thunders roar,
268 Must'ring[87] their rage, and Heav'n resembles Hell!
269 As He our darkness, cannot we His light
270 Imitate when we please? This desert soil
271 Wants[88] not her hidden luster, gems and gold,
272 Nor want[89] we skill or art from whence to raise
273 Magnificence. And what can Heav'n show more?
274 Our torments also may, in length of time,
275 Become our elements,[90] these piercing fires
276 As soft as now severe, our temper changed
277 Into their temper, which must needs remove
278 The sensible[91] of pain. All things invite
279 To peaceful counsels, and the settled state
280 Of order, how in safety best we may
281 Compose[92] our present evils, with regard
282 Of what we are and where, dismissing quite
283 All thoughts of war. Ye have what I advise."
284   He scarce had finished, when such murmur filled
285 Th' assembly as when hollow rocks retain
286 The sound of blust'ring winds, which all night long

---

[85] from
[86] unfavorable
[87] showing, displaying, exhibiting
[88] lacks
[89] lack
[90] component parts
[91] perception, awareness, feeling [noun]
[92] arrange, adjust

287 Had roused the sea, now with hoarse cadence lull
288 Seafaring men o'erwatched,[93] whose barque[94] by chance,
289 Or pinnace,[95] anchors in a craggy bay
290 After the tempest. Such applause was heard
291 As Mammon ended, and his sentence[96] pleased,
292 Advising peace, for such another field[97]
293 They dreaded worse than Hell, so much the fear
294 Of thunder and the sword of Michael
295 Wrought[98] still within them, and no less desire
296 To found[99] this nether[100] empire, which might rise,
297 By policy[101] and long process[102] of time,
298 In emulation[103] opposite[104] to Heav'n.
299 Which when Beelzebub perceived—than whom,
300 Satan except, none higher sat—with grave
301 Aspect he rose, and in his rising seemed
302 A pillar of state. Deep on his front[105] engrav'n
303 Deliberation sat, and public care,
304 And princely counsel in his face yet shone,
305 Majestic, though in ruin. Sage he stood
306 With Atlantean[106] shoulders, fit to bear
307 The weight of mightiest monarchies. His look
308 Drew audience[107] and attention still as night
309 Or summer's noontide air, while thus he spoke:
310   "Thrones and Imperial Powers, offspring of
              Heav'n,
311 Ethereal Virtues! Or these titles now
312 Must we renounce and, changing style, be called
313 Princes of Hell? For so the popular vote

---

[93] exhausted after watching all night
[94] sailing vessel (usually small)
[95] small boat, schooner-rigged, often with two masts
[96] opinion, judgment
[97] battlefield
[98] worked
[99] create, begin the building of
[100] lower
[101] statecraft, stratagem
[102] course, lapse
[103] ambitious rivalry
[104] opposed, hostile
[105] face
[106] the Titan Atlas, on whose shoulders the entire world rested
[107] (1) the state of hearing, (2) reception

314   Inclines—here to continue, and build up here
315   A growing empire. Doubtless! While we dream,
316   And know not that the King of Heav'n hath doomed[108]
317   This place our dungeon, not our safe retreat
318   Beyond His potent arm, to live exempt
319   From Heav'n's high jurisdiction, in new league
320   Banded against His throne, but to remain
321   In strictest bondage, though thus far removed,
322   Under th' inevitable[109] curb,[110] reserved[111]
323   His captive multitude. For He, to be sure,
324   In height or depth, still first and last will reign
325   Sole king, and of His Kingdom lose no part
326   By our revolt, but over Hell extend
327   His empire, and with iron scepter rule
328   Us here, as with His golden[112] those in Heav'n.
329   What sit we then projecting peace and war?
330   War hath determined[113] us and foiled[114] with loss
331   Irreparable; terms of peace yet none
332   Vouchsafed[115] or sought. For what peace will be giv'n
333   To us enslaved, but custody severe,
334   And stripes[116] and arbitrary punishment
335   Inflicted? And what peace can we return,[117]
336   But, to our power, hostility and hate,
337   Untamed reluctance,[118] and revenge, though slow,
338   Yet ever plotting how the conqueror least
339   May reap[119] His conquest, and may least rejoice
340   In doing what we most in suffering feel?
341   Nor will occasion[120] want,[121] nor shall we need

---

[108] pronounced, judged
[109] [five syllables, second and fourth accented]
[110] chain or strap fastened to the bit of a horse, in order to restrain it
[111] kept, stored
[112] golden scepter
[113] settled, fixed, resolved
[114] overthrown, defeated, repulsed
[115] conferred, granted, allowed, permitted
[116] whip-strokes/lashes
[117] exchange, give back
[118] resistance, opposition
[119] harvest, gain from
[120] opportunity
[121] be lacking

342   With dangerous expedition[122] to invade
343   Heav'n, whose high walls fear no assault or siege,
344   Or ambush from the deep. What if we find
345   Some easier enterprise?[123] There is a place
346   (If ancient and prophetic fame[124] in Heav'n
347   Err not)—another world, the happy seat
348   Of some new race, called man, about this time
349   To be created like to us, though less
350   In power and excellence, but favored more
351   Of Him who rules above. So was His will
352   Pronounced among the gods, and by an oath
353   That shook Heav'n's whole circumference[125] confirmed.
354   Thither let us bend all our thoughts, to learn
355   What creatures there inhabit, of what mould[126]
356   Or substance, how endued,[127] and what their power
357   And where their weakness: how attempted best,
358   By force or subtlety. Though Heav'n be shut,
359   And Heav'n's high arbitrator[128] sit secure
360   In His own strength, this place[129] may lie exposed,
361   The utmost border of His Kingdom, left
362   To their defence who hold it. Here, perhaps,
363   Some advantageous act may be achieved
364   By sudden onset[130]—either with Hell-fire
365   To waste[131] His whole creation, or possess
366   All as our own, and drive,[132] as we were driven,
367   The puny[133] habitants, or if not drive,
368   Seduce them to our party, that their God
369   May prove their foe, and with repenting hand
370   Abolish His own works. This would surpass
371   Common revenge, and interrupt His joy

---

[122] speed, promptness
[123] bold/daring task
[124] report, talk
[125] [four syllables, second and fourth accented]
[126] form
[127] endowed
[128] (1) judge, (2) sole and absolute ruler
[129] the world of man
[130] attack, assault
[131] ruin, destroy
[132] direct (like cattle)
[133] (1) inexperienced, (2) undersized

372 In our confusion, and our joy upraise
373 In His disturbance, when His darling sons,
374 Hurled headlong to partake with us, shall curse
375 Their frail original,[134] and faded bliss—
376 Faded so soon! Advise if this be worth
377 Attempting, or to sit in darkness here
378 Hatching vain empires." Thus Beelzebub
379 Pleaded his devilish counsel—first devised
380 By Satan, and in part proposed, for whence
381 But from the author of all ill could spring
382 So deep a malice, to confound[135] the race
383 Of mankind in one root,[136] and earth with Hell
384 To mingle and involve, done all to spite
385 The great Creator? But their spite still serves
386 His glory to augment. The bold design
387 Pleased highly those infernal States,[137] and joy
388 Sparkled in all their eyes. With full assent
389 They vote, whereat his speech he thus renews:
390   "Well have ye judged, well ended long debate,
391 Synod[138] of gods, and, like to what ye are,
392 Great things resolved, which from the lowest deep
393 Will once more lift us up, in spite of fate,
394 Nearer our ancient seat—perhaps in view
395 Of those bright confines, whence, with neighboring arms,
396 And opportune[139] excursion, we may chance
397 Re-enter Heav'n, or else in some mild zone
398 Dwell not unvisited of Heav'n's fair light
399 Secure,[140] and at the bright'ning orient[141] beam
400 Purge off this gloom. The soft delicious air,
401 To heal the scar of these corrosive fires,
402 Shall breathe her balm. But first, whom shall we send
403 In search of this new world? whom shall we find

---

[134] i.e., the first man, Adam
[135] overthrow, defeat
[136] Adam and Eve combined, metaphorically the root of all mankind
[137] high-ranking powers, beings of rank/status/importance
[138] assembly
[139] suitable, timely
[140] safe
[141] precious, lustrous

404   Sufficient? who shall tempt[142] with wand'ring feet
405   The dark, unbottomed, infinite abyss,
406   And through the palpable[143] obscure[144] find out
407   His uncouth[145] way, or spread his airy flight,
408   Upborne with indefatigable wings
409   Over the vast abrupt,[146] ere he arrive
410   The happy isle?[147] What strength, what art, can then
411   Suffice, or what evasion bear him safe,
412   Through the strict senteries[148] and stations thick
413   Of Angels watching round? Here he had need
414   All circumspection, and we now no less
415   Choice in our suffrage,[149] for on whom we send
416   The weight of all, and our last hope, relies."
417   This said, he sat, and expectation held
418   His look suspense,[150] awaiting who appeared
419   To second, or oppose, or undertake
420   The perilous attempt. But all sat mute,
421   Pondering the danger with deep thoughts, and each
422   In other's count'nance read his own dismay,
423   Astonished.[151] None among the choice[152] and prime[153]
424   Of those Heav'n-warring champions could be found
425   So hardy[154] as to proffer or accept,
426   Alone, the dreadful voyage, till at last
427   Satan, whom now transcendent glory raised
428   Above his fellows, with monarchal pride
429   Conscious of highest worth, unmoved[155] thus spoke:
430   "O progeny[156] of Heaven! Empyreal[157] Thrones!

---

[142] test
[143] touchable, tangible, perceptible
[144] darkness
[145] unknown
[146] abyss
[147] (metaphorical)
[148] sentries [Milton's spelling = prosodically necessary]
[149] vote, collective decision
[150] cautious, doubtful, uncertain
[151] stunned, paralyzed
[152] worthy, select
[153] first in rank/degree
[154] bold
[155] calm, collected
[156] descendants
[157] celestial

431 With reason hath deep silence and demur[158]
432 Seized us, though undismayed. Long is the way
433 And hard, that out of Hell leads up to light.
434 Our prison strong, this huge convex[159] of fire,
435 Outrageous[160] to devour, immures[161] us round
436 Ninefold, and gates of burning adamant,[162]
437 Barred[163] over us, prohibit all egress.[164]
438 These passed, if any pass, the void[165] profound[166]
439 Of unessential[167] Night receives him next,
440 Wide-gaping, and with utter loss of being
441 Threatens him, plunged in that abortive[168] gulf.[169]
442 If thence he scape, into whatever world
443 Or unknown region, what remains him less
444 Than unknown dangers, and as hard escape?
445 But I should ill become this throne, O peers,
446 And this imperial sov'reignty, adorned
447 With splendor, armed with power, if aught proposed
448 And judged of public moment[170] in the shape
449 Of difficulty or danger, could deter
450 Me from attempting. Wherefore do I assume
451 These royalties,[171] and not refuse to reign,
452 Refusing to accept as great a share
453 Of hazard as of honor, due alike
454 To him who reigns, and so much to him due
455 Of hazard more as he above the rest
456 High honored sits? Go therefore, mighty Powers,
457 Terror of Heav'n, though fall'n. Intend[172] at home,
458 While here shall be our home, what best may ease

---

[158] hesitancy
[159] the high vault of hell
[160] excessive, cruel
[161] walls in, surrounds, imprisons
[162] material of impregnable hardness
[163] shut
[164] exit
[165] emptiness, vacuum
[166] vast, deep
[167] immaterial
[168] miscarrying, bringing to nothing
[169] great depth, abyss
[170] weight, importance
[171] sovereignty, pomp
[172] consider assiduously, apply oneself to thinking about

459   The present misery, and render Hell
460   More tolerable,[173] if there be cure[174] or charm[175]
461   To respite,[176] or deceive, or slack[177] the pain
462   Of this ill[178] mansion.[179] Intermit[180] no watch
463   Against a wakeful foe, while I abroad
464   Through all the coasts[181] of dark destruction seek
465   Deliverance for us all. This enterprise
466   None shall partake[182] with me." Thus saying, rose
467   The monarch, and prevented all reply,
468   Prudent, lest from[183] his resolution raised,[184]
469   Others among the chief might offer now,
470   Certain to be refused, what erst they feared,
471   And so refused, might in opinion[185] stand
472   His rivals, winning cheap the high repute
473   Which he through hazard huge must earn. But they
474   Dreaded not more th' adventure than his voice
475   Forbidding, and at once with him they rose.
476   Their rising all at once was as the sound
477   Of thunder heard remote. Towards him they bend
478   With awful[186] reverence prone, and as a god
479   Extol him equal to the Highest in Heav'n.
480   Nor failed they to express how much they praised
481   That for the general safety he despised
482   His own, for neither do the Spirits damned
483   Lose all their virtue, lest bad men should boast
484   Their specious[187] deeds on earth, which glory excites,[188]

---

[173] [four syllables, first and third accented]
[174] remedy
[175] incantation, spell
[176] relieve, delay, suspend
[177] reduce/diminish
[178] wretched, difficult, troublesome
[179] abode
[180] omit
[181] border (-lands)
[182] participate in, share
[183] by
[184] restored, roused, stirred up, animated, stimulated
[185] esteem, reputation
[186] profoundly respectful
[187] plausible but false [by A.D. 1651 the modern meaning]
[188] incites, sets in motion

485   Or close[189] ambition varnished o'er with zeal.
486   Thus they their doubtful consultations dark[190]
487   Ended, rejoicing in their matchless chief—
488   As when from mountain-tops the dusky clouds
489   Ascending, while the north wind sleeps, o'erspread
490   Heav'n's cheerful face, the louring[191] element[192]
491   Scowls o'er the darkened landscape, snow or shower.
492   If chance the radiant sun, with farewell sweet,
493   Extend[193] his evening beam, the fields revive,
494   The birds their notes renew, and bleating herds
495   Attest[194] their joy, that hill and valley rings.
496   O shame to men! Devil with devil damned
497   Firm[195] concord[196] holds. Men only[197] disagree
498   Of creatures rational, though under[198] hope
499   Of Heav'nly grace. And God proclaiming peace,
500   Yet live in hatred, enmity, and strife
501   Among themselves, and levy[199] cruel wars,
502   Wasting the earth, each other to destroy,
503   As if (which might induce us to accord[200])
504   Man had not hellish foes enow[201] besides,
505   That day and night for his destruction wait!
506   The Stygian[202] council thus dissolved, and forth
507   In order came the grand infernal peers.
508   Midst came their mighty Paramount,[203] and seemed
509   Alone th' antagonist of Heav'n, nor less
510   Than Hell's dread emperor, with pomp supreme,
511   And god-like imitated state. Him round

---

[189] secret, hidden
[190] somber, wicked
[191] frowning, sullen
[192] atmospheric agency (the weather)
[193] spreads out, stretches forth
[194] bear witness to
[195] settled, secure, steadfast, unwavering
[196] harmony, agreement, peace
[197] alone
[198] possessed of, protected by
[199] undertake, impose
[200] reconciliation, agreement
[201] enough
[202] infernal, hellish
[203] overlord

512 A globe[204] of fiery Seraphim enclosed
513 With bright emblazonry,[205] and horrent[206] arms.
514 Then of their session ended they bid cry,[207]
515 With trumpet's regal[208] sound, the great result.
516 Toward the four winds four speedy Cherubim
517 Put to their mouths the sounding[209] alchemy,[210]
518 By herald's voice explained. The hollow abyss
519 Heard far and wide, and all the host of Hell
520 With deaf'ning shout returned[211] them loud acclaim.
521 Thence more at ease their minds, and somewhat raised
522 By false presumptuous hope, the rangèd[212] Powers
523 Disband and, wand'ring, each his several way
524 Pursues, as inclination or sad choice
525 Leads him, perplexed,[213] where he may likeliest find
526 Truce to his restless thoughts, and entertain
527 The irksome hours till his great chief return.
528 Part on the plain, or in the air sublime,[214]
529 Upon the wing or in swift race contend,[215]
530 As at th' Olympian[216] games or Pythian[217] fields.
531 Part curb[218] their fiery steeds, or shun[219] the goal[220]
532 With rapid wheels, or fronted[221] brigades form—
533 As when, to warn proud cities, war appears,
534 Waged in the troubled sky, and armies rush

---

[204] having a spherical form (or, in this case, a spherical arrangement/order)
[205] heraldic devices
[206] bristling
[207] pronounce, announce
[208] kingly, magnificent
[209] resonant, sonorous
[210] trumpet made of a composite brass-based metal, shining like gold
[211] sent back, reflected
[212] drawn up in ranks
[213] anxious, in doubt, troubled
[214] high up
[215] compete, strive earnestly
[216] i.e., the games held at Olympia, in Elis
[217] second most important site of Greek games, held at Pythia, in Delphi, and in honor of Apollo
[218] practice checking/managing/controlling
[219] avoid
[220] column making a turn, in a chariot race
[221] facing

535 To battle in the clouds. Before each van[222]
536 Prick[223] forth the airy knights, and couch[224] their spears,
537 Till thickest[225] legions close.[226] With feats of arms
538 From either end of Heav'n the welkin[227] burns.
539 Others, with vast Typhoean[228] rage, more fell,[229]
540 Rend[230] up both rocks and hills, and ride the air
541 In whirlwind. Hell scarce holds the wild uproar,
542 As when Alcides,[231] from Oechalia[232] crowned
543 With conquest, felt th' envenomed robe,[233] and tore
544 Through pain up by the roots Thessalian[234] pines,
545 And Lichas[235] from the top of Oeta[236] threw
546 Into th' Euboic sea.[237] Others, more mild,
547 Retreated[238] in a silent valley, sing
548 With notes angelical to many a harp
549 Their own heroic deeds and hapless[239] fall
550 By doom[240] of battle, and complain that Fate
551 Free virtue should enthrall[241] to force or chance.[242]
552 Their song was partial,[243] but the harmony
553 (What could it less when Spirits immortal sing?)

---

[222] vanguard
[223] spur/urge forward their horses
[224] lower (into fighting position)
[225] densest
[226] come together, grapple
[227] sky
[228] Typhon/Typhoeus, a hundred-serpent-headed giant with a great voice, who fought against and was killed by Jove as soon as he was born
[229] fierce, savage, cruel, terrible
[230] tear
[231] Hercules
[232] a kingdom on the large Greek island of Euboea, ruled by Eurytus, whose daughter, Iolé, was beloved by Hercules; Hercules was married and neither the girl's father nor Hercules' wife was pleased
[233] sent to him by his wife, Deianeira, who believed (erroneously) it would win her back his love
[234] Thessaly, in NE Greece
[235] the innocent messenger who had brought him the poisoned robe
[236] mountain in south Thessaly
[237] the southern Aegean
[238] withdrawn, retired [adjective]
[239] unlucky
[240] judgment
[241] enslave
[242] they complained that, at Fate's hands, free virtue was put in bondage to force or chance
[243] prejudiced, biased

554   Suspended[244] Hell, and took[245] with ravishment
555   The thronging audience. In discourse[246] more sweet
556   (For eloquence the soul,[247] song charms the sense)
557   Others apart sat on a hill retired,[248]
558   In thoughts more elevate, and reasoned high
559   Of providence, foreknowledge, will, and fate—
560   Fixed fate, free will, foreknowledge absolute,
561   And found no end, in wand'ring mazes lost.
562   Of good and evil much they argued then,
563   Of happiness and final misery,
564   Passion and apathy, and glory and shame:
565   Vain wisdom all, and false philosophy
566   Yet with a pleasing sorcery could charm
567   Pain for a while, or anguish, and excite
568   Fallacious hope, or arm th' obdurèd[249] breast
569   With stubborn patience, as with triple steel.
570   Another part, in squadrons and gross[250] bands,
571   On bold[251] adventure to discover[252] wide[253]
572   That dismal world, if any clime perhaps
573   Might yield them easier habitation, bend
574   Four ways their flying[254] march, along the banks
575   Of four infernal rivers, that disgorge
576   Into the burning lake their baleful[255] streams—
577   Abhorrèd Styx, the flood[256] of deadly hate;
578   Sad Acheron of sorrow, black and deep;
579   Cocytus,[257] named of[258] lamentation loud

---

[244] riveted the attention of
[245] seized
[246] communication of thought by speech
[247] "eloquence charms the soul, but . . ."
[248] secluded
[249] unyielding, hardened in evil, insensible to moral influence
[250] dense, compact
[251] confident, daring
[252] reconnoiter
[253] extensively [adverb]
[254] swift, rapid
[255] full of active evil
[256] river
[257] [trisyllabic, second accented]
[258] for

580   Heard on the rueful[259] stream; fierce Phlegeton,[260]
581   Whose waves of torrent[261] fire inflame[262] with rage.[263]
582   Far off from these, a slow and silent stream,
583   Lethe,[264] the river of oblivion, rolls
584   Her wat'ry labyrinth,[265] whereof who drinks
585   Forthwith[266] his former state and being forgets—
586   Forgets both joy and grief, pleasure and pain.
587   Beyond this flood[267] a frozen continent
588   Lies dark and wild, beat with perpetual storms
589   Of whirlwind and dire hail, which on firm land
590   Thaws not, but gathers heap,[268] and ruin seems
591   Of ancient pile,[269] all else deep snow and ice,
592   A gulf[270] profound[271] as that Serbonian bog[272]
593   Betwixt Damiata[273] and Mount Casius[274] old,
594   Where armies whole have sunk. The parching[275] air
595   Burns frore,[276] and cold performs[277] th' effect of fire.
596   Thither, by harpy-footed Furies haled,[278]
597   At certain revolutions[279] all the damned
598   Are brought and feel by turns the bitter change
599   Of fierce extremes, extremes by change more fierce,
600   From[280] beds of raging fire to starve[281] in ice

---

[259] sorrowful
[260] [trisyllabic, first—with "ph" pronounced as "f"—and third accented]
[261] swift-flowing [adjective]
[262] blaze up
[263] with rage = violently
[264] [bisyllabic, first accented]
[265] like error, the river follows "a devious or wandering course"; labyrinth = a maze
[266] at once
[267] river
[268] mass, form
[269] large structure, building
[270] abyss
[271] deep
[272] Egyptian lake, bordered by quicksand
[273] Damietta/ Tamiathis: city at the mouth of the Nile
[274] mountain range bordering on Egypt
[275] to dry/shrivel/wither with cold
[276] intensely cold, frostlike
[277] brings about, works, achieves
[278] dragged
[279] turnings of celestial bodies, times
[280] i.e., going from
[281] wither, perish

601 Their soft ethereal warmth, and there to pine[282]
602 Immovable, infixed, and frozen round,
603 Periods[283] of time, thence hurried back to fire.
604 They ferry over this Lethean sound
605 Both to and fro, their sorrow to augment,
606 And wish and struggle, as they pass, to reach
607 The tempting stream, with one small drop to lose
608 In sweet forgetfulness all pain and woe,
609 All in one moment, and so near the brink.
610 But Fate withstands[284] and, to oppose th' attempt,
611 Medusa,[285] with Gorgonian terror, guards
612 The ford, and of itself the water flies[286]
613 All taste of living wight,[287] as once it fled
614 The lip of Tantalus.[288] Thus roving on
615 In confused[289] march forlorn, th' adventurous bands,
616 With shuddering horror pale and eyes aghast,
617 Viewed first their lamentable[290] lot, and found
618 No rest. Through many a dark and dreary vale
619 They passed, and many a region dolorous,
620 O'er many a frozen, many a fiery alp,
621 Rocks, caves, lakes, fens, bogs, dens, and shades of
                  death—
622 A universe of death, which God by curse
623 Created evil, for evil only good,[291]
624 Where all life dies, death lives, and Nature breeds,
625 Perverse, all monstrous, all prodigious[292] things,
626 Abominable, inutterable, and worse
627 Than fables yet have feigned[293] or fear conceived,

---

[282] suffer, languish
[283] for periods
[284] resists, stands in the way, opposes
[285] one of three Gorgons; there are writhing serpents all over her head; those who look at her are turned to stone
[286] flees
[287] creature, living being
[288] condemned to remain in a pool filled with water that moves away whenever he attempts to drink
[289] [first syllable accented]
[290] [four syllables, first and third accented]
[291] for evil only good = good only for evil
[292] abnormal, unnatural
[293] pretended, invented

628	Gorgons,[294] and Hydras,[295] and Chimeras[296] dire.
629	Meanwhile the adversary of God and man,
630	Satan, with thoughts inflamed of highest design,[297]
631	Puts on[298] swift wings, and toward the gates of Hell
632	Explores[299] his solitary flight. Sometimes
633	He scours[300] the right-hand coast, sometimes the left,
634	Now shaves[301] with level wing the deep, then soars
635	Up to the fiery concave[302] towering high.
636	As when far off at sea a fleet descried[303]
637	Hangs in the clouds, by[304] equinoctial[305] winds
638	Close sailing[306] from Bengala,[307] or the isles
639	Of Ternate and Tidore,[308] whence merchants bring
640	Their spicy drugs—they on the trading[309] flood,[310]
641	Through the wide Ethiopian[311] to the Cape[312]
642	Ply[313] stemming[314] nightly toward the pole:[315] so seemed
643	Far off the flying fiend. At last appear
644	Hell-bounds,[316] high reaching to the horrid roof,
645	And thrice threefold the gates. Three folds[317] were brass,
646	Three iron, three of adamantine rock,

---

[294] see line 611, above

[295] many-headed serpent; the heads immediately grow back if cut off

[296] fire-breathing monster with a lion's head, a goat's body, and a serpent's tail

[297] purpose, intention

[298] brings to bear (as one "puts on" speed)

[299] conducts

[300] moves rapidly along

[301] comes exceedingly close

[302] vault of hell

[303] caught sight of

[304] by means of

[305] equatorial

[306] i.e., close to the wind, with sail tacks hauled close

[307] Bengal

[308] Ternate and Tidore = Moluccan (spice) islands

[309] winds that blow steadily in one direction are "trade winds"—i.e., useful for trading vessels

[310] moving water, "tide" (metaphorical)

[311] Indian Ocean, near northeastern Africa

[312] Cape of Good Hope, at the southern tip of Africa

[313] steer, direct their course

[314] making headway

[315] the South Pole

[316] hell's boundaries

[317] leaves of a folding door, gates

647   Impenetrable, impaled[318] with circling fire,
648   Yet unconsumed. Before the gates there sat
649   On either side a formidable[319] shape.
650   The one seemed woman to the waist, and fair,
651   But ended foul in many a scaly fold,
652   Voluminous and vast—a serpent armed
653   With mortal sting. About her middle round
654   A cry[320] of Hell-hounds never-ceasing barked
655   With wide Cerberean mouths full loud, and rung
656   A hideous peal,[321] yet when they list,[322] would creep,
657   If aught disturbed their noise, into her womb,
658   And kennel[323] there, yet there still barked and howled
659   Within unseen. Far less abhorred than these
660   Vexed[324] Scylla,[325] bathing in the sea that parts
661   Calabria[326] from the hoarse[327] Trinacrian[328] shore.
662   Nor uglier follow[329] the night-hag,[330] when called
663   In secret, riding through the air she comes,
664   Lured with the smell of infant blood, to dance
665   With Lapland[331] witches, while the laboring moon[332]
666   Eclipses at[333] their charms. The other shape—
667   If shape it might be called, that shape had none
668   Distinguishable in member,[334] joint, or limb,
669   Or substance might be called that shadow seemed,[335]
670   For each seemed either—black it stood as Night,
671   Fierce as ten Furies, terrible as Hell,

---

[318] enclosed
[319] alarming
[320] pack
[321] outburst of sound
[322] wanted to
[323] [verb]
[324] grieved, distressed, agitated
[325] six-headed monster, each head having triple rows of teeth
[326] the extreme south of Italy
[327] rough
[328] Sicilian
[329] is ("comes after")
[330] Hecate [trisyllabic, first and third accented]
[331] extreme north of Scandinavia, associated with storm-causing witches and wizards
[332] *labores lunæ* (Latin) = the moon in eclipse
[333] because of
[334] part (of the body)
[335] "or might be called a substance: it seemed a shadow"

672   And shook a dreadful dart.[336] What seemed his head
673   The likeness of a kingly crown had on.
674   Satan was now at hand, and from his seat
675   The monster moving onward came as fast[337]
676   With horrid strides. Hell trembled as he strode.
677   Th' undaunted fiend what this might be admired—[338]
678   Admired, not feared (God and His Son except,
679   Created thing naught valued[339] he nor shunned),[340]
680   And with disdainful look thus first began:
681   "Whence and what art thou, execrable[341] shape,
682   That dar'st, though grim[342] and terrible, advance
683   Thy miscreated[343] front[344] athwart[345] my way
684   To yonder gates? Through them I mean to pass,
685   That be assured, without leave asked of thee.
686   Retire, or taste thy folly, and learn by proof,
687   Hell-born, not to contend with Spirits of Heav'n."
688   To whom the goblin,[346] full of wrath, replied:
689   "Art thou that traitor Angel? Art thou he
690   Who first broke peace in Heav'n, and faith, till then
691   Unbroken, and in proud rebellious arms
692   Drew after him the third part of Heav'n's sons,
693   Conjured[347] against the Highest—for which both thou
694   And they, outcast from God, are here condemned
695   To waste[348] eternal days in woe and pain?
696   And reckon'st[349] thou thyself with Spirits of Heav'n,
697   Hell-doomed, and breath'st defiance here and scorn,
698   Where I reign king and, to enrage thee more,
699   Thy king and lord? Back to thy punishment,
700   False fugitive, and to thy speed add wings,

---

[336] spear
[337] i.e., as fast as Satan
[338] wondered
[339] took account of, heeded, was worried about
[340] fled from, avoided
[341] detestable
[342] fierce, cruel, savage
[343] misshapen
[344] (1) impudence, effrontery, (2) face
[345] across
[346] ugly demon
[347] sworn, conspiring
[348] spend, use up, consume
[349] count, consider

701 Lest with a whip of scorpions I pursue
702 Thy ling'ring, or with one stroke of this dart
703 Strange[350] horror seize thee, and pangs unfelt before."
704   So spoke the grisly terror, and in shape,
705 So speaking and so threat'ning, grew tenfold
706 More dreadful and deform. On th' other side,
707 Incensed with indignation, Satan stood
708 Unterrified, and like a comet burned,
709 That fires the length of Ophiuchus[351] huge
710 In th' arctic sky, and from his horrid hair
711 Shakes pestilence and war. Each at the head
712 Levelled his deadly aim. Their fatal[352] hands
713 No second stroke intend. And such a frown
714 Each cast at th' other as when two black clouds,
715 With Heav'n's artillery fraught,[353] come rattling on
716 Over the Caspian,[354] then stand front to front,
717 Hov'ring a space,[355] till winds the signal blow
718 To join[356] their dark encounter in mid-air.
719 So frowned the mighty combatants, that Hell
720 Grew darker at their frown. So matched they stood,
721 For never but once more was either like
722 To meet so great a foe.[357] And now great deeds
723 Had been achieved, whereof all Hell had rung,
724 Had not the snaky sorceress, that sat
725 Fast by[358] Hell-gate and kept the fatal key,
726 Ris'n, and with hideous outcry rushed between.
727   "O father, what intends thy hand," she cried,
728 "Against thy only son? What fury, O son,
729 Possesses thee to bend[359] that mortal[360] dart
730 Against thy father's head? And know'st for whom?
731 For Him who sits above, and laughs the while

---

[350] unknown, unfamiliar, never experienced
[351] Ophiuchus = "serpent-bearer," a vast northern constellation
[352] deadly
[353] filled
[354] the Caspian Sea, between Iran and Turkestan
[355] a space = a time, a while
[356] engage in
[357] i.e., Christ
[358] fast by = close, very near
[359] aim, direct
[360] fatal

732 At thee, ordained His drudge to execute
733 Whate'er His wrath, which He calls justice, bids—
734 His wrath, which one day will destroy ye both!"
735   She spoke, and at her words the hellish pest[361]
736 Forbore.[362] Then these[363] to her Satan returned:
737   "So strange thy outcry, and thy words so strange
738 Thou interposest,[364] that my sudden[365] hand,
739 Prevented, spares[366] to tell thee yet by deeds
740 What it intends, till first I know of thee
741 What thing thou art, thus double-formed, and why,
742 In this infernal vale first met, thou call'st
743 Me father, and that phantasm call'st my son?
744 I know thee not, nor ever saw till now
745 Sight more detestable than him and thee."
746 T' whom thus the portress[367] of Hell-gate replied:—
747   "Hast thou forgot me, then? and do I seem
748 Now in thine eye so foul?—once deemed so fair
749 In Heav'n when at th' assembly, and in sight
750 Of all the Seraphim with thee combined
751 In bold conspiracy against Heav'n's King,
752 All on a sudden miserable pain
753 Surprised thee, dim thine eyes, and dizzy swum
754 In darkness, while thy head flames[368] thick and fast
755 Threw forth, till on the left side op'ning wide,
756 Likest to thee in shape and count'nance bright,
757 Then shining heavenly fair, a goddess armed,
758 Out of thy head I sprung. Amazement seized
759 All th' host of Heav'n. Back they recoiled, afraid
760 At first, and called me Sin, and for a sign
761 Portentous[369] held me. But, familiar grown,
762 I pleased, and with attractive graces won
763 The most averse—thee chiefly, who full oft

---

[361] scourge, plague ("pestilence")
[362] desisted
[363] these = these words
[364] puts forth, interrupts with
[365] quick, speedy
[366] refrains, abstains
[367] female porter, gatekeeper
[368] [noun]
[369] ominous, warning

764 Thyself in me thy perfect image viewing,
765 Becam'st enamored, and such joy thou took'st
766 With me in secret that my womb conceived
767 A growing burden. Meanwhile war arose,
768 And fields were fought in Heav'n, wherein remained
769 (For what could else?) to our Almighty foe
770 Clear victory, to our part loss and rout[370]
771 Through all the Empyrean.[371] Down they fell,
772 Driv'n headlong from the pitch[372] of Heaven, down
773 Into this deep, and in the general fall
774 I also, at which time this powerful key
775 Into my hands was giv'n, with charge to keep
776 These gates forever shut, which none can pass
777 Without my op'ning. Pensive[373] here I sat
778 Alone, but long I sat not, till my womb,
779 Pregnant by thee, and now excessive grown,
780 Prodigious[374] motion felt and rueful[375] throes.[376]
781 At last this odious[377] offspring whom thou seest,
782 Thine own begotten, breaking violent way,[378]
783 Tore through my entrails that,[379] with fear and pain
784 Distorted, all my nether shape thus grew
785 Transformed. But he my inbred enemy
786 Forth issued, brandishing[380] his fatal dart,
787 Made to destroy. I fled, and cried out 'Death!'
788 Hell trembled at the hideous name, and sighed
789 From all her caves, and back resounded 'Death!'
790 I fled, but he pursued (though more, it seems,
791 Inflamed with lust than rage), and swifter far,
792 Me overtook, his mother, all dismayed,[381]
793 And in embraces forcible and foul

---

[370] complete overthrow, disorderly retreat
[371] heaven
[372] highest point
[373] (1) melancholy, sorrowful, (2) reflective
[374] vast, enormous, powerful
[375] dismal, pitiable
[376] labor pangs
[377] repulsive, hateful
[378] path
[379] so that
[380] waving, flourishing
[381] paralyzed with fear

794   Engend'ring[382] with me, of that rape begot
795   These yelling monsters, that with ceaseless cry
796   Surround me, as thou saw'st—hourly conceived
797   And hourly born, with sorrow infinite
798   To me, for when they list[383] into the womb
799   That bred them they return, and howl, and gnaw
800   My bowels, their repast.[384] Then bursting forth
801   Afresh, with conscious terrors vex me round,
802   That rest or intermission none I find.
803   Before mine eyes in opposition[385] sits
804   Grim Death, my son and foe, who set them on,
805   And me, his parent, would full soon devour
806   For want of other prey, but that he knows
807   His end with mine involved, and knows that I
808   Should prove a bitter morsel, and his bane,[386]
809   Whenever that shall be. So Fate pronounced.
810   But thou, O father, I forewarn thee, shun
811   His deadly arrow. Neither[387] vainly hope
812   To be invulnerable in those bright arms,[388]
813   Though tempered[389] Heav'nly, for that mortal dint,[390]
814   Save He who reigns above, none can resist."
815   She finished, and the subtle fiend, his lore[391]
816   Soon learned, now milder, and thus answered smooth:
817   "Dear daughter—since thou claim'st me for thy
                          sire,
818   And my fair son here show'st me, the dear pledge[392]
819   Of dalliance[393] had with thee in Heav'n, and joys
820   Then sweet, now sad to mention, through dire change
821   Befall'n us unforeseen, unthought-of—know
822   I come no enemy, but to set free

---

[382] copulating
[383] wish
[384] food, meal
[385] in opposition = placed opposite
[386] destruction, ruin, death
[387] nor
[388] those bright arms = that bright armor
[389] constituted, endowed
[390] violence, force
[391] lesson
[392] (1) love token, (2) hostage given to fortune
[393] amorous play

823   From out this dark and dismal house of pain
824   Both him and thee, and all the Heav'nly host
825   Of Spirits that, in our just pretences[394] armed,
826   Fell with us from on high. From them I go
827   This uncouth[395] errand sole,[396] and one for all
828   Myself expose, with lonely steps to tread
829   Th' unfounded[397] deep, and through the void immense
830   To search, with wand'ring quest, a place foretold
831   Should be—and by concurring signs, ere now
832   Created vast and round—a place of bliss
833   In the purlieus[398] of Heav'n, and therein placed
834   A race of upstart creatures, to supply
835   Perhaps our vacant room,[399] though more removed,[400]
836   Lest Heav'n, surcharged[401] with potent[402] multitude,
837   Might hap to move[403] new broils.[404] Be this, or aught
838   Than this more secret, now designed,[405] I haste
839   To know, and this once known shall soon return
840   And bring ye to the place where thou and Death
841   Shall dwell at ease, and up and down unseen
842   Wing silently the buxom[406] air, embalmed
843   With odors. There ye shall be fed and filled
844   Immeasurably; all things shall be your prey."
845   He ceased, for both seemed highly pleased, and Death
846   Grinned horrible a ghastly smile, to hear
847   His famine[407] should be filled, and blessed his maw[408]
848   Destined to that good hour. No less rejoiced

---

[394] claims
[395] unknown, strange
[396] alone
[397] bottomless
[398] outskirts
[399] place
[400] distant
[401] overstocked, overpopulated
[402] mighty, powerful
[403] actuate
[404] quarrels, tumults
[405] intended
[406] unresisting
[407] extreme scarcity of food, hunger
[408] throat, stomach

849   His mother bad, and thus bespoke[409] her sire:
850   "The key of this infernal pit, by due[410]
851   And by command of Heav'n's all-powerful King,
852   I keep, by Him forbidden to unlock
853   These adamantine gates. Against all force
854   Death ready stands to interpose[411] his dart,[412]
855   Fearless to be o'ermatched by living might.
856   But what owe I to His commands above,
857   Who hates me, and hath hither thrust me down
858   Into this gloom of Tartarus[413] profound,[414]
859   To sit in hateful office here confined,
860   Inhabitant of Heav'n and Heav'nly born—
861   Here in perpetual agony and pain,
862   With terrors and with clamors compassed round[415]
863   Of mine own brood, that on my bowels feed?
864   Thou art my father, thou my author, thou
865   My being gav'st me. Whom should I obey
866   But thee? whom follow? Thou wilt bring me soon
867   To that new world of light and bliss, among
868   The gods who live at ease, where I shall reign
869   At thy right hand voluptuous,[416] as beseems[417]
870   Thy daughter and thy darling, without end."
871   Thus saying, from her side the fatal key,
872   Sad instrument of all our woe, she took,
873   And towards the gate rolling her bestial train,[418]
874   Forthwith the huge portcullis[419] high up-drew,
875   Which, but herself, not all the Stygian[420] Powers
876   Could once have moved, then in the key-hole turns
877   Th' intricate wards,[421] and every bolt and bar

---

[409] said to
[410] right
[411] put forward
[412] spear
[413] underworld place of punishment for the sinful
[414] deep
[415] compassed round = surrounded
[416] luxuriously sensuous
[417] suits, becomes, fits
[418] as per lines 651–53, above, she has a serpentine tail
[419] lattice gate
[420] infernal, hellish
[421] notches cut in the key

878 Of massy iron or solid rock with ease
879 Unfastens. On a sudden, open fly
880 (With impetuous[422] recoil and jarring sound)
881 Th' infernal doors, and on their hinges grate
882 Harsh thunder, that the lowest bottom shook
883 Of Erebus.[423] She opened—but to shut
884 Excelled[424] her power. The gates wide open stood,
885 That with extended wings a bannered host,
886 Under spread ensigns marching, might pass through
887 With horse and chariots ranked in loose array.
888 So wide they stood, and like a furnace-mouth
889 Cast forth redounding[425] smoke and ruddy flame.
890 Before their eyes in sudden view appear
891 The secrets of the hoary deep—a dark
892 Illimitable ocean, without bound,
893 Without dimension, where length, breadth, and height,
894 And time, and place, are lost, where eldest Night
895 And Chaos, ancestors of Nature, hold
896 Eternal anarchy, amidst the noise
897 Of endless wars, and by confusion[426] stand.
898 For hot, cold, moist, and dry, four champions fierce,
899 Strive here for mast'ry, and to battle bring
900 Their embryon[427] atoms. They around the flag
901 Of each his faction, in their several clans,
902 Light-armed or heavy, sharp, smooth, swift, or slow,
903 Swarm populous, unnumbered as the sands
904 Of Barca[428] or Cyrene's[429] torrid soil,
905 Levied[430] to side with warring winds, and poise[431]
906 Their lighter wings. To whom these most adhere,[432]
907 He rules a moment. Chaos umpire sits,

---

[422] rapid, violent
[423] Hell
[424] surpassed
[425] surging, overflowing
[426] tumult, civil commotion
[427] embryonic, not yet created
[428] Egyptian/Tunisian desert
[429] city located near modern Tripoli [trisyllabic, second accented]
[430] enlisted, enrolled
[431] to add weight to (*"avoir du pois"* = to have weight)
[432] follow, side with, cleave/cling to

908 And by decision more embroils⁴³³ the fray
909 By which he reigns. Next him, high arbiter,
910 Chance governs all. Into this wild abyss,
911 The womb of Nature, and perhaps her grave,
912 Of neither sea, nor shore, nor air, nor fire,
913 But all these in their pregnant causes mixed
914 Confus'dly, and which thus must ever fight,
915 Unless th' Almighty Maker them ordain⁴³⁴
916 His dark materials to create more worlds—
917 Into this wild abyss the wary⁴³⁵ fiend
918 Stood on the brink of Hell and looked a while,
919 Pondering his voyage, for no narrow frith⁴³⁶
920 He had to cross. Nor was his ear less pealed⁴³⁷
921 With noises loud and ruinous⁴³⁸ (to compare
922 Great things with small) than when Bellona⁴³⁹ storms
923 With all her battering engines,⁴⁴⁰ bent⁴⁴¹ to raze⁴⁴²
924 Some capital city; or less than if this frame
925 Of Heav'n were falling, and these elements
926 In mutiny had from her axle torn
927 The steadfast earth. At last his sail-broad vans⁴⁴³
928 He spread for flight and, in the surging smoke
929 Uplifted, spurns⁴⁴⁴ the ground, thence many a league,
930 As in a cloudy chair, ascending rides
931 Audacious,⁴⁴⁵ but that seat soon failing, meets
932 A vast vacuity. All unawares,
933 Flutt'ring his pennons⁴⁴⁶ vain,⁴⁴⁷ plumb-down he drops
934 Ten thousand fathom deep, and to this hour
935 Down had been falling, had not, by ill chance,

---

⁴³³ heats up, adds discord/hostility/dissension to
⁴³⁴ decree, order [verb]
⁴³⁵ cautious
⁴³⁶ estuary, arm of the sea
⁴³⁷ assailed
⁴³⁸ crashing
⁴³⁹ Roman goddess of war
⁴⁴⁰ contrivances, machines
⁴⁴¹ leveled, wound up
⁴⁴² destroy
⁴⁴³ wings
⁴⁴⁴ kicks off from
⁴⁴⁵ daring, confident
⁴⁴⁶ wings
⁴⁴⁷ [adjective]

936 The strong rebuff[448] of some tumultuous cloud,
937 Instinct[449] with fire and niter,[450] hurried him
938 As many miles aloft. That fury[451] stayed—[452]
939 Quenched in a boggy Syrtis,[453] neither sea,
940 Nor good dry land—nigh[454] foundered,[455] on he fares,
941 Treading the crude[456] consistence,[457] half on foot,
942 Half flying. Behoves him now[458] both oar and sail.
943 As when a gryphon[459] through the wilderness
944 With wingèd course, o'er hill or moory dale,
945 Pursues the Arimaspian,[460] who by stealth
946 Had from his[461] wakeful[462] custody purloined[463]
947 The guarded gold, so eagerly the fiend
948 O'er bog or steep, through strait, rough, dense, or rare,
949 With head, hands, wings, or feet, pursues his way,
950 And swims, or sinks, or wades, or creeps, or flies.
951   At length a universal hubbub wild
952 Of stunning sounds, and voices all confused,
953 Borne through the hollow dark, assaults his ear
954 With loudest vehemence.[464] Thither he plies[465]
955 Undaunted, to meet there whatever Power
956 Or Spirit of the nethermost abyss
957 Might in that noise reside, of whom to ask
958 Which way the nearest coast of darkness lies,
959 Bord'ring on light: When straight behold the throne
960 Of Chaos, and his dark pavilion spread

---

[448] blow
[449] imbued, charged
[450] saltpeter, potassium nitrate
[451] infernal spirit (Satan)
[452] checked
[453] stretch of sandbanks off North Africa
[454] almost
[455] sent to the bottom, sunk
[456] not fully developed
[457] material coherence
[458] behoves him now = now he needed
[459] half lion, half eagle
[460] Scythian
[461] the gryphon's
[462] vigilant
[463] stolen
[464] intensity, strength
[465] steers

961 Wide on the wasteful deep! With him enthroned
962 Sat sable-vested Night, eldest of things,
963 The consort[466] of his reign; and by them stood
964 Orcus and Adès,[467] and the dreaded name
965 Of Demogorgon,[468] Rumor next, and Chance,
966 And Tumult, and Confusion, all embroiled,[469]
967 And Discord with a thousand various[470] mouths.
968   T' whom Satan, turning boldly, thus: "Ye Powers
969 And Spirits of this nethermost abyss,
970 Chaos and ancient Night, I come no spy
971 With purpose to explore or to disturb
972 The secrets of your realm, but by constraint
973 Wand'ring this darksome desert, as my way
974 Lies through your spacious empire up to light,
975 Alone and without guide, half lost, I seek
976 What readiest path leads where your gloomy bounds
977 Confine[471] with Heav'n, or if some other place
978 From your dominion won,[472] th' Ethereal King
979 Possesses lately, thither to arrive
980 I travel this profound,[473] direct[474] my course:
981 Directed, no mean[475] recompense it brings
982 To your behoof,[476] if I that region lost,[477]
983 All usurpation[478] thence expelled, reduce
984 To her original darkness, and your sway
985 (Which is my present journey), and once more
986 Erect the standard[479] there of ancient Night.
987 Yours be th' advantage all, mine the revenge!"
988   Thus Satan; and him thus the Anarch[480] old,

---

[466] partner
[467] Orcus = Pluto/Hades, Adès = Pluto/Hades
[468] ancestor of all the gods
[469] entangled in disorder
[470] changing, unstable
[471] have a border with
[472] reached
[473] depth [noun]
[474] "guide (if you would/please)"
[475] small, petty
[476] benefit
[477] loosed, freed [adjective]
[478] unlawful seizure
[479] flag
[480] author of anarchy

989   With falt'ring speech and visage incomposed,[481]
990   Answered: "I know thee, stranger, who thou art—
991   That mighty leading Angel, who of late
992   Made head[482] against Heav'n's King, though overthrown.
993   I saw and heard, for such a numerous host
994   Fled not in silence through the frighted deep,
995   With ruin upon ruin, rout on rout,[483]
996   Confusion worse confounded.[484] And Heav'n-gates
997   Poured out by millions her victorious bands,
998   Pursuing. I upon my frontiers here
999   Keep residence; if all I can[485] will serve
1000 That little which is left so[486] to defend,
1001 Encroached on still through our intestine[487] broils,[488]
1002 Weakening the scepter of old Night. First Hell,
1003 Your dungeon, stretching far and wide beneath;
1004 Now lately Heav'n and earth, another world
1005 Hung o'er my realm, linked in a golden chain
1006 To that side Heav'n from whence your legions fell!
1007 If that way be your walk, you have not far;
1008 So much the nearer danger. Go, and speed;[489]
1009 Havoc, and spoil, and ruin, are my gain."
1010   He ceased, and Satan stayed not to reply,
1011 But glad that now his sea should find a shore,
1012 With fresh alacrity and force renewed
1013 Springs upward like a pyramid of fire,
1014 Into the wild expanse, and through the shock[490]
1015 Of fighting elements, on all sides round
1016 Environed,[491] wins his way, harder beset[492]
1017 And more endangered than when Argo[493] passed

---

[481] agitated
[482] insurrection
[483] fleeing bands
[484] mixed up
[485] can do
[486] thus
[487] internal, inner
[488] quarrels
[489] be successful
[490] clashing
[491] surrounded
[492] closed round, hemmed in
[493] ship of Jason and the Argonauts

1018 Through Bosphorus betwixt the jostling rocks,
1019 Or when Ulysses on the larboard[494] shunned
1020 Charybdis, and by th' other whirlpool steered.
1021 So he[495] with difficulty and labor hard
1022 Moved on, with difficulty and labor he.[496]
1023 But he once passed,[497] soon after, when man fell,
1024 Strange alteration! Sin and Death amain[498]
1025 Following his track (such was the will of Heav'n)
1026 Paved after him a broad and beaten way
1027 Over the dark abyss, whose boiling gulf
1028 Tamely endured a bridge of wondrous length,
1029 From Hell continued, reaching th' utmost orb[499]
1030 Of this frail world, by which the Spirits perverse[500]
1031 With easy intercourse pass to and fro
1032 To tempt or punish mortals, except whom
1033 God and good Angels guard by special grace.
1034   But now at last the sacred influence[501]
1035 Of light appears, and from the walls of Heav'n
1036 Shoots far into the bosom of dim Night
1037 A glimmering dawn. Here Nature first begins
1038 Her farthest verge,[502] and Chaos to retire[503]
1039 As from her outmost works, a broken foe,
1040 With tumult less and with less hostile din,
1041 That Satan with less toil, and now with ease,
1042 Wafts[504] on the calmer wave by dubious[505] light,
1043 And like a weather-beaten vessel holds
1044 Gladly the port, though shrouds[506] and tackle[507] torn,
1045 Or in the emptier waste, resembling air,

---

[494] the left side of a ship, when looking forward
[495] Ulysses
[496] Satan
[497] having passed
[498] rapidly
[499] sphere, circle
[500] wicked
[501] emanation
[502] rim, edge, border
[503] to retire = begins to retire
[504] sails, floats
[505] vague, uncertain
[506] mainmast ropes
[507] rigging

1046 Weighs[508] his spread wings, at leisure to behold
1047 Far off th' empyreal Heav'n, extended wide
1048 In circuit, undetermined[509] square or round,
1049 With opal towers and battlements adorned
1050 Of living sapphire, once his native seat,
1051 And fast by,[510] hanging in a golden chain,
1052 This pendant world, in bigness as a star
1053 Of smallest magnitude close by the moon.
1054 Thither, full fraught[511] with mischievous revenge,
1055 Accursed, and in a cursèd hour, he hies.[512]

The End of the Second Book

---

[508] balances
[509] not fixed, not settled
[510] fast by = close by
[511] filled
[512] hastens

BOOK III

THE ARGUMENT

GOD SITTING ON His throne sees Satan flying towards this world, then newly created; shews him to the Son who sat at His right hand; foretells the success of Satan in perverting mankind; clears His own justice and wisdom from all imputation, having created man free and able enough to have withstood his tempter; yet declares His purpose of grace towards him, in regard he fell not of his own malice, as did Satan, but by him seduced.

The Son of God renders praises to His Father for the manifestation of His gracious purpose towards man, but God again declares that grace cannot be extended towards man without the satisfaction of divine justice. Man hath offended the majesty of God by aspiring to Godhead, and therefore with all his progeny devoted to Death must die, unless some one can be found sufficient to answer for his offence, and undergo his punishment.

The Son of God freely offers himself a ransom for man. The Father accepts him, ordains his incarnation, pronounces his exaltation above all names in Heaven and earth; commands all the Angels to adore him. They obey, and hymning to their harps in full choir, celebrate the Father and the Son.

Meanwhile Satan alights upon the bare convex of this world's outermost orb, where wandring he first finds a place since called the Limbo of Vanity; what persons and things fly up thither. Thence [Satan] comes to the Gate of Heaven, described ascending by stairs, and the waters above the firmament that flow about it. His passage thence to the orb of the sun; he finds there Uriel the Regent of that orb, but first changes himself into the shape of

a meaner Angel and, pretending a zealous desire to behold the
new creation, and man whom God had placed here, inquires of
him the place of his habitation, and is directed; alights first on
Mount Niphates.

1   Hail holy light, offspring of Heav'n first-born,
2   Or of the Eternal Coeternal beam
3   May I express thee unblamed? since God is light,
4   And never but in unapproachèd light
5   Dwelt from eternity, dwelt then in thee
6   Bright effluence[1] of bright essence increate.[2]
7   Or hear'st[3] thou rather pure ethereal stream,
8   Whose fountain who shall tell? Before the sun,
9   Before the Heav'ns thou wert, and at the voice
10   Of God, as with a mantle, didst invest[4]
11   The rising world of waters dark and deep,
12   Won from the void and formless infinite.
13   Thee I re-visit now with bolder wing,
14   Escaped the Stygian[5] pool, though long detained
15   In that obscure sojourn,[6] while in my flight
16   Through utter and through middle darkness borne,
17   With other notes than to the Orphean[7] lyre[8]
18   I sung of Chaos and eternal Night,
19   Taught by the Heav'nly Muse to venture down
20   The dark descent, and up to re-ascend,
21   Though hard and rare.[9] Thee I re-visit safe,
22   And feel thy sov'reign vital lamp,[10] but thou
23   Re-visit'st not these eyes, that roll in vain
24   To find thy piercing ray, and find no dawn,
25   So thick a drop serene[11] hath quenched[12] their orbs,
26   Or dim suffusion[13] veiled.[14] Yet not the more
27   Cease I to wander where the Muses haunt,
28   Clear spring, or shady grove, or sunny hill,

---

[1] a flowing out, emanation
[2] uncreated
[3] "would you rather hear"
[4] cover
[5] infernal, hellish
[6] visit
[7] Orphean = belonging to Orpheus
[8] harplike musical instrument used to accompany poetry
[9] unusual, uncommon
[10] the sun
[11] pure, clear
[12] extinguished, killed
[13] a fluid that spreads over some part of the body
[14] i.e., veiled them (his eyes)

29   Smit[15] with the love of sacred song. But chief
30   Thee, Sion,[16] and the flow'ry brooks beneath
31   That wash thy hallowed feet, and warbling flow,
32   Nightly I visit, nor sometimes forget
33   Those other two, equaled with[17] me in fate
34   (So were I equaled with them in renown),
35   Blind Thamyris,[18] and blind Maeonides,[19]
36   And Tiresias,[20] and Phineus,[21] prophets old.
37   Then feed[22] on thoughts, that voluntary move
38   Harmonious numbers,[23] as the wakeful bird[24]
39   Sings darkling,[25] and in shadiest covert[26] hid
40   Tunes her nocturnal note. Thus with the year
41   Seasons return, but not to me returns
42   Day, or the sweet approach of ev'n or morn,
43   Or sight of vernal bloom, or summer's rose,
44   Or flocks, or herds, or human face divine,
45   But cloud instead, and ever-during[27] dark
46   Surrounds me, from the cheerful ways of men
47   Cut off, and for the book of knowledge fair
48   Presented with a universal blank
49   Of Nature's works to me expunged[28] and razed,[29]
50   And wisdom at one entrance quite shut out.
51   So much the rather thou, celestial light,
52   Shine inward, and the mind through all her powers
53   Irradiate.[30] There plant[31] eyes, all mist from thence
54   Purge and disperse, that I may see and tell

---

[15] struck, impressed, inspired
[16] site of the Temple, in Jerusalem
[17] equaled with = the same as
[18] legendary Thracian poet
[19] Homer
[20] blind seer of Thebes
[21] Thracian king and prophet
[22] "I feed"
[23] poetry
[24] the nightingale, which does not sleep at night
[25] in the dark [adverb]
[26] cover
[27] during = lasting, continuing
[28] blotted out, erased
[29] destroyed
[30] illuminate, shine light upon [three syllables, second accented]
[31] [verb]

55 Of things invisible to mortal sight.
56   Now had the Almighty Father from above,
57 From the pure empyrean where He sits
58 High throned above all height, bent down His eye,
59 His own works and their works at once to view.
60 About Him all the Sanctities of Heav'n
61 Stood thick as stars, and from His sight received
62 Beatitude[32] past utterance.[33] On His right
63 The radiant image of His glory sat,
64 His only Son. On earth He first beheld
65 Our two first parents, yet[34] the only two
66 Of mankind in the happy garden placed,
67 Reaping immortal fruits of joy and love,
68 Uninterrupted joy, unrivaled love,
69 In blissful solitude. He then surveyed
70 Hell and the gulf between, and Satan there
71 Coasting the wall of Heav'n on this side Night
72 In the dun[35] air sublime,[36] and ready now
73 To stoop with wearied wings and willing feet
74 On the bare outside of this world, that seemed
75 Firm land embosomed,[37] without firmament,[38]
76 Uncertain which, in ocean or in air.
77 Him God beholding, from His prospect[39] high,
78 Wherein past, present, future, He beholds,
79 Thus to His only Son foreseeing spoke:
80   "Only-begotten Son, seest thou what rage
81 Transports[40] our adversary? whom no bounds
82 Prescribed, no bars of Hell, nor all the chains
83 Heaped on him there, nor yet the main abyss
84 Wide interrupt,[41] can hold, so bent he seems
85 On desperate revenge, that shall redound
86 Upon his own rebellious head. And now,

---

[32] supreme blessing/happiness
[33] [bisyllabic, first accented]
[34] as yet, still
[35] dark, dusky, murky
[36] high up
[37] enclosed
[38] substratum, support
[39] a place affording an open view
[40] carries away
[41] broken open

87	Through all restraint broke[42] loose, he wings his way
88	Not far off Heav'n, in the precincts[43] of light,
89	Directly towards the new created world,
90	And man there placed, with purpose to assay[44]
91	If him by force he can destroy or, worse,
92	By some false guile pervert. And shall pervert,
93	For man will hearken to his glozing[45] lies,
94	And easily transgress[46] the sole command,
95	Sole pledge[47] of his obedience: So will fall
96	He and his faithless progeny. Whose fault?
97	Whose but his own? Ingrate, he had of me
98	All he could have. I made him just and right,
99	Sufficient to have stood,[48] though free to fall.
100	Such I created all the ethereal Powers
101	And Spirits, both them who stood and them who failed.
102	Freely they stood who stood, and fell who fell.
103	Not free, what proof could they have given sincere
104	Of true allegiance, constant faith, or love,
105	Where only what they needs must do appeared,
106	Not what they would? What praise could they receive?
107	What pleasure I, from such obedience paid,
108	When will and reason (reason also is choice)
109	Useless and vain, of freedom both despoiled,[49]
110	Made passive both, had served necessity,
111	Not me? They therefore, as to right belonged,
112	So were created, nor can justly accuse
113	Their Maker, or their making, or their fate,
114	As if predestination over-ruled
115	Their will, disposed[50] by absolute decree
116	Or high foreknowledge. They themselves decreed
117	Their own revolt, not I: if I foreknew,
118	Foreknowledge had no influence on their fault,

---

[42] having broken
[43] environs, neighborhoods, districts
[44] try, attempt
[45] specious, flattering
[46] violate, break
[47] (1) vow, promise, (2) surety
[48] stayed erect, endured
[49] plundered, robbed
[50] controlled

119   Which had no less proved certain unforeknown.
120   So without least impulse or shadow of Fate,
121   Or aught by me immutably[51] foreseen,
122   They trespass, authors[52] to themselves in all
123   Both what they judge and what they choose. For so
124   I formed them free, and free they must remain,
125   Till they enthrall[53] themselves. I else must change
126   Their nature, and revoke the high decree
127   Unchangeable, eternal, which ordained
128   Their freedom. They themselves ordained their fall.
129   The first sort[54] by their own suggestion fell,
130   Self-tempted, self-depraved. Man falls deceived
131   By the other first. Man therefore shall find grace,
132   The other none. In mercy and justice both,
133   Through Heav'n and earth, so shall my glory excel,
134   But mercy, first and last, shall brightest shine."
135   Thus while God spoke,[55] ambrosial fragrance filled
136   All Heav'n, and in the blessèd Spirits elect
137   Sense of new joy ineffable diffused.
138   Beyond compare, the Son of God was seen
139   Most glorious. In him all His Father shone,
140   Substantially[56] expressed, and in his face
141   Divine compassion visibly appeared,
142   Love without end, and without measure grace,
143   Which uttering thus he to his Father spoke:
144   "O Father, gracious was that word which closed
145   Thy sov'reign[57] sentence,[58] that man should find grace.
146   For which both Heav'n and earth shall high extol
147   Thy praises, with th' innumerable sound
148   Of hymns and sacred songs, wherewith Thy throne
149   Encompassed[59] shall resound[60] Thee ever blessed.

---

[51] unalterably
[52] founder, instigator, father, ancestor
[53] enslave
[54] Satan and his followers
[55] "while God spoke thus"
[56] (1) not imaginary, (2) real, (3) amply
[57] paramount, supreme
[58] authoritative decision
[59] encircled
[60] proclaim, celebrate

150 For should man finally be lost? Should man,
151 Thy creature late so loved, Thy youngest son,
152 Fall circumvented⁶¹ thus by fraud, though joined
153 With his own folly? That be from Thee far,
154 That far be from Thee, Father, who art judge
155 Of all things made, and judgest only right.
156 Or shall the adversary⁶² thus obtain
157 His end, and frustrate Thine? Shall he fulfill
158 His malice, and Thy goodness bring to nought?
159 Or proud return, though to his heavier doom,⁶³
160 Yet with revenge accomplished, and to Hell
161 Draw after him the whole race of mankind,
162 By him corrupted? Or wilt Thou Thyself
163 Abolish Thy creation, and unmake
164 For him, what for Thy glory Thou hast made?
165 So should Thy goodness and Thy greatness both
166 Be questioned and blasphemed without defence."
167 To whom the great Creator thus replied:
168   "O Son, in whom my soul hath chief delight,
169 Son of my bosom, Son who art alone.
170 My word, my wisdom, and effectual⁶⁴ might,
171 All hast thou spoken as my thoughts are, all
172 As my eternal purpose hath decreed.
173 Man shall not quite be lost, but saved who will,
174 Yet not of will in him, but grace in me
175 Freely vouchsafed.⁶⁵ Once more I will renew
176 His lapsèd⁶⁶ powers, though forfeit⁶⁷ and enthralled
177 By Sin to foul exorbitant desires.
178 Upheld by me, yet once more he shall stand
179 On even ground against his mortal foe,
180 By me upheld, that he may know how frail
181 His fall'n condition is, and to me owe
182 All his deliverance, and to none but me.

---

⁶¹ surrounded
⁶² Satan
⁶³ sentence, final fate
⁶⁴ conclusive
⁶⁵ conferred, bestowed
⁶⁶ fallen
⁶⁷ lost by misconduct

183   Some I have chosen of peculiar[68] grace,
184   Elect[69] above the rest; so is my will.
185   The rest shall hear me call, and oft be warned
186   Their sinful state, and to appease betimes[70]
187   The incensed[71] Deity, while offered[72] grace
188   Invites, for I will clear their senses dark,
189   What may suffice, and soften stony hearts
190   To pray, repent, and bring obedience due.[73]
191   To prayer, repentance, and obedience due,
192   Though but endeavored with sincere intent,
193   Mine ear shall not be slow, mine eye not shut.
194   And I will place within them as a guide
195   My umpire[74] Conscience, whom if they will hear,
196   Light[75] after light, well used, they shall attain,
197   And to the end, persisting, safe arrive.
198   This my long sufferance,[76] and my day of grace,
199   They who neglect and scorn shall never taste,
200   But hard be hardened, blind be blinded more,
201   That they may stumble on, and deeper fall.
202   And none but such from mercy I exclude.
203   "But yet all is not done. Man disobeying,
204   Disloyal, breaks his fealty[77] and sins
205   Against the high supremacy of Heav'n,
206   Affecting[78] God-head and, so losing all,
207   To expiate his treason hath nought left,
208   But to destruction sacred[79] and devote,
209   He, with his whole posterity, must die.
210   Die he or justice must; unless for him
211   Some other able, and as willing, pay

---

[68] particular, special
[69] chosen
[70] (1) in good time, (2) at an early time, speedily
[71] inflamed, angered
[72] [adjective]
[73] proper, fitting, right
[74] arbitrator
[75] enlightenment, the brightness of Heaven
[76] patient endurance/toleration
[77] sworn fidelity
[78] loving
[79] consecrated

212 The rigid[80] satisfaction,[81] death for death.
213 Say, Heav'nly Powers, where shall we find such love?
214 Which of you will be mortal, to redeem
215 Man's mortal crime and, just, the unjust to save?
216 Dwells in all Heav'n charity[82] so dear?"
217   He asked, but all the Heav'nly choir[83] stood mute,
218 And silence was in Heav'n: on man's behalf
219 Patron[84] or intercessor[85] none appeared,
220 Much less that durst upon his own head draw
221 The deadly forfeiture and ransom set.
222 And now without redemption all mankind
223 Must have been lost, adjudged to Death and Hell
224 By doom[86] severe, had not the Son of God,
225 In whom the fullness dwells of love divine,
226 His dearest mediation thus renewed:
227   "Father, Thy word is past, man shall find grace;
228 And shall grace not find means? that finds her way,
229 The speediest of Thy wingèd messengers,
230 To visit all Thy creatures, and to all
231 Comes unprevented,[87] unimplored, unsought?
232 Happy for man, so coming. He her aid
233 Can never seek, once dead in sins, and lost:
234 Atonement for himself, or offering meet,[88]
235 Indebted and undone, hath none to bring.
236 Behold me, then: me for him, life for life
237 I offer. On me let Thine anger fall;
238 Account[89] me man. I for his sake will leave
239 Thy bosom, and this glory next to Thee
240 Freely put off, and for him lastly[90] die

---

[80] unyielding, strict, firm
[81] payment of a debt [legal/theological]
[82] love, spontaneous goodness, benevolence
[83] company
[84] protector, advocate
[85] mediator
[86] sentence, judgment
[87] not anticipated, not won by prayer
[88] fit, suitable, appropriate [adjective]
[89] hold, reckon
[90] ultimately

241 Well pleased. On me let Death wreak[91] all his rage.
242 Under his gloomy power I shall not long
243 Lie vanquished. Thou hast giv'n me to possess
244 Life in myself forever. By Thee I live,
245 Though now to Death I yield, and am his due[92]
246 (All that of me can die), yet that debt paid,
247 Thou wilt not leave me in the loathsome grave
248 His prey, nor suffer my unspotted soul
249 Forever with corruption there to dwell,
250 But I shall rise victorious, and subdue
251 My vanquisher, spoiled of his vaunted[93] spoil.
252 Death his Death's wound shall then receive, and stoop[94]
253 Inglorious, of his mortal sting disarmed.
254 I through the ample[95] air in triumph high
255 Shall lead Hell captive maugre[96] Hell, and show[97]
256 The powers of darkness bound. Thou, at the sight
257 Pleased, out of Heaven shalt look down and smile,
258 While, by Thee raised, I ruin[98] all my foes,
259 Death last, and with his carcass glut[99] the grave.
260 Then with the multitude of my redeemed
261 Shall enter Heav'n, long absent, and return,
262 Father, to see Thy face, wherein no cloud
263 Of anger shall remain, but peace assured
264 And reconcilement. Wrath shall be no more,
265 Thenceforth, but in Thy presence joy entire."[100]
266   His words here ended, but his meek aspect,
267 Silent, yet spoke, and breathed immortal love
268 To mortal men, above which only shone
269 Filial obedience. As a sacrifice
270 Glad to be offered, he attends the will
271 Of his great Father. Admiration[101] seized

---

[91] give vent to
[92] tribute, right
[93] boasted of
[94] bow, submit
[95] broad, spacious
[96] in spite of
[97] exhibit, display
[98] destroy
[99] overfill, surfeit
[100] complete
[101] wonder mixed with reverence

272 All Heav'n, what this might mean, and whither tend,[102]
273 Wond'ring. But soon[103] th' Almighty thus replied:
274   "O thou, in Heav'n and earth the only peace
275 Found out for mankind under wrath, O thou
276 My sole complacence![104] Well thou know'st how dear
277 To me are all my works, nor man the least;
278 Though last created, that for him I spare
279 Thee from my bosom and right hand, to save,
280 By losing thee a while, the whole race lost.
281 Thou, therefore, whom thou only canst redeem,[105]
282 Their nature also to thy nature join,
283 And be thyself man among men on earth,
284 Made flesh, when time shall be, of virgin seed,
285 By wondrous birth. Be thou in Adam's room[106]
286 The head of all mankind, though Adam's son.
287 As in him perish all men, so in thee,
288 As from a second root, shall be restored
289 As many as are restored, without thee none.
290 His crime makes guilty all his sons: thy merit,
291 Imputed,[107] shall absolve them[108] who renounce
292 Their own both righteous and unrighteous deeds,
293 And live in thee transplanted, and from thee
294 Receive new life. So man, as is most just,
295 Shall satisfy for man, be judged and die,
296 And dying rise, and rising with him raise
297 His brethren, ransomed with his own dear life.
298 So Heav'nly love shall outdo hellish hate,
299 Giving to death, and dying to redeem,
300 So dearly[109] to redeem what hellish hate
301 So easily destroyed, and still destroys
302 In those who, when they may, accept not grace.
303 Nor shalt thou, by descending to assume
304 Man's nature, lessen or degrade thine own.

---

[102] to lead, result
[103] quickly, at once
[104] pleasure, delight
[105] ransom
[106] place
[107] transferred
[108] those among them
[109] expensively, at such a high price

305 Because thou hast, though throned in highest bliss
306 Equal to God, and equally enjoying
307 God-like fruition,[110] quitted[111] all, to save
308 A world from utter loss, and hast been found
309 By merit more than birthright Son of God,
310 Found worthiest to be so by being good,
311 Far more than great or high—because in thee
312 Love hath abounded more than glory abounds.
313 Therefore thy humiliation shall exalt
314 With thee thy manhood also to this throne.
315 Here shalt thou sit incarnate,[112] here shalt reign
316 Both God and man, Son both of God and man,
317 Anointed universal King. All power
318 I give thee: reign forever, and assume
319 Thy merits.[113] Under thee, as head supreme,
320 Thrones, Princedoms, Powers, Dominions, I reduce.[114]
321 All knees to thee shall bow, of them that bide[115]
322 In Heav'n, or earth, or under earth in Hell.
323 When thou, attended gloriously from Heav'n
324 Shalt in the sky appear, and from thee send
325 The summoning Arch-Angels to proclaim
326 Thy dread tribunal, forthwith from all winds
327 The living, and forthwith the cited[116] dead
328 Of all past ages, to the general doom[117]
329 Shall hasten. Such a peal[118] shall rouse their sleep.
330 Then all thy Saints assembled, thou shalt judge
331 Bad men and Angels. They, arraigned,[119] shall sink
332 Beneath thy sentence. Hell, her numbers full,
333 Thenceforth shall be forever shut. Meanwhile
334 The world shall burn, and from her ashes spring
335 New Heav'n and earth, wherein the just shall dwell
336 And after all their tribulations long

---

[110] pleasurable possession
[111] renounced, given up
[112] embodied
[113] reward
[114] make subject, subdue, constrain, lower
[115] dwell
[116] summoned
[117] judgment
[118] outburst/volley of sound
[119] called to account

337 See golden days, fruitful of golden deeds,
338 With joy and peace triumphing, and fair truth.
339 Then thou thy regal scepter shalt lay by,
340 For regal scepter then no more shall need:
341 God shall be all in all. But all ye gods,
342 Adore him, who to compass[120] all this dies,
343 Adore the Son, and honor him as me."
344   No sooner had the Almighty ceased, but all
345 The multitude of Angels, with a shout
346 Loud as from numbers without number, sweet
347 As from blest voices, uttering joy, Heav'n rung
348 With jubilee,[121] and loud hosannas[122] filled
349 The eternal regions. Lowly reverent
350 Towards either throne they bow, and to the ground
351 With solemn adoration down they cast
352 Their crowns inwove with amarant[123] and gold,
353 Immortal amarant, a flower which once
354 In Paradise, fast by the Tree of Life,
355 Began to bloom, but soon for man's offence
356 To Heav'n removed, where first it grew, there grows,
357 And flow'rs aloft, shading the Fount of Life,
358 And where the river of bliss through midst of Heav'n
359 Rolls o'er Elysian flow'rs her amber stream.
360 With these that never fade the Spirits elect[124]
361 Bind their resplendent locks inwreathed with beams,
362 Now in loose garlands thick thrown off, the bright
363 Pavement,[125] that like a sea of jasper shone,
364 Impurpled with celestial roses smiled.
365 Then, crowned again, their golden harps they took,
366 Harps ever tuned, that glittering by their side
367 Like quivers hung, and with preamble sweet
368 Of charming symphony[126] they introduce
369 Their sacred song, and waken raptures high.

---

[120] accomplish
[121] wild cries, shouts
[122] cries of praise to God
[123] mythical flower that never fades
[124] [adjective]
[125] floor [noun, and grammatical subject; the verb is "smiled," at the end of the next line]
[126] harmony, music in parts

370	No voice exempt, no voice but well could join
371	Melodious part, such concord[127] is in Heav'n.
372	Thee, Father, first they sung Omnipotent,
373	Immutable, Immortal, Infinite,
374	Eternal King, Thee Author of all being,
375	Fountain of light, Thyself invisible
376	Amidst the glorious brightness where Thou sit'st
377	Throned inaccessible, but[128] when Thou shad'st
378	The full blaze of thy beams and, through a cloud
379	Drawn round about Thee like a radiant shrine,
380	Dark with excessive bright Thy skirts[129] appear,
381	Yet[130] dazzle Heav'n, that brightest Seraphim
382	Approach not, but with both wings veil their eyes.
383	Thee[131] next they sang of all creation first,
384	Begotten Son, Divine Similitude,
385	In whose conspicuous[132] count'nance, without cloud
386	Made visible, the Almighty Father shines,
387	Whom else no creature can behold. On thee
388	Impressed[133] the effulgence[134] of His glory abides,
389	Transfused on thee His ample[135] Spirit rests.
390	He Heav'n of Heav'ns and all the Powers therein
391	By thee created; and by thee threw down
392	Th' aspiring Dominations.[136] Thou that day
393	Thy Father's dreadful thunder didst not spare,
394	Nor stop thy flaming chariot-wheels, that shook
395	Heav'n's everlasting frame, while o'er the necks
396	Thou drov'st of warring Angels disarrayed.
397	Back from pursuit, thy Powers[137] with loud acclaim
398	Thee only extolled, Son of thy Father's might,
399	To execute fierce vengeance on His foes,

---

[127] harmoniousness
[128] except
[129] lower part of a robe
[130] still
[131] Christ
[132] eminent
[133] stamped
[134] splendid radiance
[135] full whole
[136] fourth of the nine orders of angels
[137] sixth of the nine orders of angels

400   Not so on man. Him through their[138] malice fallen,
401   Father of mercy and grace, Thou didst not doom[139]
402   So strictly, but much more to pity inclined.
403   No sooner did Thy dear and only Son
404   Perceive Thee purposed not to doom frail man
405   So strictly, but much more to pity inclined,
406   He to appease Thy wrath, and end the strife
407   Of mercy and justice in Thy face discerned,
408   Regardless of the bliss wherein he sat
409   Second to Thee, offered himself to die
410   For man's offence. O unexampled love,
411   Love nowhere to be found less than Divine!
412   Hail, Son of God, Savior of men! Thy name
413   Shall be the copious matter of my song
414   Henceforth, and never shall my heart thy praise
415   Forget, nor from thy Father's praise disjoin.[140]
416   Thus they in Heav'n, above the starry sphere,
417   Their happy hours in joy and hymning spent.
418   Meanwhile, upon the firm opacious[141] globe
419   Of this round world, whose first convex[142] divides
420   The luminous inferior orbs, enclosed[143]
421   From Chaos and th' inroad[144] of Darkness old,
422   Satan alighted walks. A globe far off
423   It seemed, now seems a boundless continent
424   Dark, waste, and wild, under the frown of Night
425   Starless exposed, and ever-threat'ning storms
426   Of Chaos blust'ring round, inclement[145] sky,
427   Save on that side which from the wall of Heav'n,
428   Though distant far, some small reflection gains
429   Of glimmering air less vexed with tempest loud.
430   Here walked the fiend at large[146] in spacious field.
431   As when a vulture on Imaus[147] bred,

---

[138] the fallen angels
[139] sentence, judge
[140] separate
[141] opaque
[142] curved surface
[143] fenced in
[144] (1) sudden incursion, raid, (2) a road in, entranceway
[145] harsh, severe, pitiless
[146] at large = unconfined, at liberty
[147] Himalayan mountain

432 Whose snowy ridge the roving Tartar bounds,[148]
433 Dislodging[149] from a region scarce of prey
434 To gorge the flesh of lambs or yeanling[150] kids,
435 On hills where flocks are fed, flies toward the springs[151]
436 Of Ganges or Hydaspes, Indian streams,
437 But in[152] his way lights[153] on the barren plains
438 Of Sericana,[154] where Chineses drive
439 With sails and wind their cany[155] waggons light.[156]
440 So on this windy sea of land, the fiend
441 Walked up and down alone, bent on his prey—
442 Alone, for other creature in this place,
443 Living or lifeless, to be found was none,
444 None yet, but store[157] hereafter from the earth
445 Up hither like aereal vapors flew
446 Of all things transitory and vain, when Sin
447 With vanity had filled the works of men:
448 Both all things vain, and all who in vain things
449 Built their fond hopes of glory or lasting fame,
450 Or[158] happiness in this or th' other life,
451 All who have their reward on earth, the fruits
452 Of painful superstition and blind zeal,
453 Nought seeking but the praise of men, here find
454 Fit retribution, empty as their deeds.
455 All th' unaccomplished[159] works of Nature's hand,
456 Abortive, monstrous, or unkindly[160] mixed,
457 Dissolved on earth, fleet[161] hither, and in vain,
458 Till final dissolution, wander here,
459 Not in the neighboring moon, as some have dreamed.

---

[148] leaps, often on horseback [verb]
[149] leaving his usual surroundings, shifting
[150] springtime
[151] origins, sources
[152] on, along
[153] descends
[154] partly in China, partly in Tibet
[155] cane, bamboo
[156] [adjective]
[157] plenty, abundance
[158] whether
[159] incomplete
[160] unnaturally
[161] hurry [verb]

460   Those argent[162] fields' more likely habitants,
461   Translated[163] Saints,[164] or middle Spirits hold
462   Betwixt th' angelical and human kind.
463   Hither of ill-joined sons and daughters born
464   First from the ancient world those giants came,
465   With many a vain exploit, though then renowned.
466   The builders next of Babel on the plain
467   Of Sennaär,[165] and still with vain design,
468   New Babels, had[166] they wherewithal,[167] would build.
469   Others came single:[168] he,[169] who to be deemed[170]
470   A god, leaped fondly[171] into Aetna's flames,
471   Empedocles; and he,[172] who to enjoy
472   Plato's Elysium,[173] leaped into the sea,
473   Cleombrotus; and many more too long,[174]
474   Embryos and idiots, eremites,[175] and friars
475   White,[176] black,[177] and gray,[178] with all their trumpery.[179]
476   Here pilgrims roam, that strayed so far to seek
477   In Golgotha[180] him dead who lives in Heav'n,
478   And they who to be sure of Paradise,
479   Dying, put on the weeds[181] of Dominick,[182]
480   Or in Franciscan[183] think to pass disguised.
481   They pass the planets seven, and pass the fixed,

---

[162] silvery
[163] transported
[164] Enoch and Elijah: see Genesis 5:24 and 2 Kings 2:11
[165] Shinar, in Babylonia
[166] if they had
[167] means, resources
[168] singly, one by one
[169] he = as per line 471, below: Empedocles
[170] considered, judged, thought
[171] foolishly credulous/sanguine
[172] he = as per line 473, below: Cleombrotus
[173] as described in Plato's *Phaedo*, which he had just read
[174] too long to tell of
[175] hermits
[176] Carmelite
[177] Dominican
[178] Franciscan
[179] frauds, trash
[180] where Christ was crucified
[181] clothes, habits
[182] Dominicans
[183] i.e., in Franciscan garments

482   And that crystalline sphere whose balance weighs
483   The trepidation talked,[184] and that first moved.[185]
484   And now Saint Peter at Heav'n's wicket[186] seems
485   To wait[187] them with his keys, and now at foot
486   Of Heav'n's ascent they lift their feet, when lo!
487   A violent[188] cross wind from either coast
488   Blows them transverse,[189] ten thousand leagues[190] awry[191]
489   Into the devious[192] air. Then might ye see
490   Cowls, hoods, and habits, with their wearers, tossed
491   And fluttered into rags, then relics, beads,
492   Indulgences, dispenses,[193] pardons, bulls,
493   The sport of winds. All these, upwhirled aloft,
494   Fly o'er the backside[194] of the world far off
495   Into a limbo large and broad, since called
496   The Paradise of Fools, to few unknown
497   Long after, now unpeopled, and untrod.
498   All this dark globe the fiend found as he passed,
499   And long he wandered, till at last a gleam
500   Of dawning light[195] turned thitherward in haste
501   His travelled steps. Far distant he descries,[196]
502   Ascending by degrees[197] magnificent
503   Up to the wall of Heav'n, a structure high
504   At top whereof, but far more rich, appeared
505   The work as of a kingly palace-gate,
506   With frontispiece[198] of diamond and gold
507   Embellished. Thick with sparkling orient[199] gems

---

[184] i.e., "or so they said," proposed, prated
[185] all as in Ptolemaic astronomy: the "trepidation" was the shaking of the spheres
[186] small door/gate
[187] await
[188] [trisyllabic, first and third accented]
[189] sideways, across
[190] one league = ca. three miles
[191] askew, out of the right course
[192] remote
[193] dispensations
[194] [the pun is surely deliberate]
[195] [noun, and subject of the verb "turned," immediately following]
[196] sees
[197] steps
[198] the decorated entrance of a building
[199] lustrous

508   The portal[200] shone, inimitable on earth
509   By model or by shading[201] pencil drawn.
510   These stairs were such as whereon Jacob saw
511   Angels ascending and descending, bands
512   Of guardians bright, when he from Esau fled
513   To Padan-Aram,[202] in the field of Luz,[203]
514   Dreaming by night under the open sky
515   And waking cried, "This is the gate of Heav'n!"
516   Each stair mysteriously[204] was meant, nor stood
517   There always, but drawn up[205] to Heav'n sometimes,
518   Viewless.[206] And underneath a bright sea flowed
519   Of jasper, or of liquid pearl, whereon
520   Who after came from earth, sailing arrived,
521   Wafted by Angels, or flew o'er the lake
522   Rapt[207] in a chariot drawn by fiery steeds.
523   The stairs were then let down, whether to dare
524   The fiend by easy ascent, or aggravate[208]
525   His sad exclusion from the doors of bliss,
526   Direct against which opened from beneath,
527   Just o'er the blissful seat of Paradise,
528   A passage down to th' earth, a passage wide,
529   Wider by far than that of after-times
530   Over Mount Sion and, though that were large,
531   Over the Promised Land, to God so dear,
532   By which, to visit oft those happy tribes,
533   On high behests[209] His Angels to and fro
534   Passed frequent, and His eye with choice regard[210]
535   From Paneas,[211] the fount[212] of Jordan's flood,[213]

---

[200] gateway
[201] i.e., making the distinctions of dark and light that indicate depth, color, etc.
[202] [both bisyllabic, first accented]
[203] see Genesis 28
[204] mystically, allegorically
[205] i.e., this is Jacob's "ladder"
[206] invisible
[207] carried
[208] worsen
[209] commands, injunctions
[210] (1) choice regard = well-chosen/careful attention *or* (less likely) (2) choice regard = deliberately observed
[211] Paneas = "spring of Dan"; a city near Mt. Hermon, in northern Palestine, at a spring of the River Jordan; now Banias
[212] source
[213] river

536   To Beersaba,[214] where the Holy Land
537   Borders on Egypt and th' Arabian shore.
538   So wide the op'ning seemed, where bounds were set
539   To darkness, such as bound the ocean wave.
540   Satan from hence, now on the lower stair
541   That scaled by steps of gold to Heav'n-gate,
542   Looks down with wonder at the sudden view
543   Of all this world at once. As when a scout,[215]
544   Through dark and desert ways with peril gone
545   All night, at last by break of cheerful dawn
546   Obtains the brow of some high-climbing hill,
547   Which to his eye discovers[216] unaware
548   The goodly[217] prospect[218] of some foreign land
549   First seen, or some renowned metropolis
550   With glistering spires and pinnacles adorned,
551   Which now the rising sun gilds with his beams,
552   Such wonder seized, though after Heaven seen,
553   The Spirit malign, but much more envy seized,
554   At sight of all this world beheld so fair.
555   Round he surveys (and well might, where he stood
556   So high above the circling canopy
557   Of Night's extended shade), from eastern point
558   Of Libra[219] to the fleecy star[220] that bears
559   Andromeda[221] far off Atlantic seas
560   Beyond th' horizon. Then from pole to pole
561   He views in breadth, and without longer pause
562   Down right into the world's first region throws
563   His flight precipitant,[222] and winds[223] with ease
564   Through the pure marble[224] air his oblique way
565   Amongst innumerable stars, that shone
566   Stars distant, but nigh hand seemed other worlds—

---

[214] Beersheba, in southern Palestine
[215] spy
[216] reveals
[217] (1) of good appearance, (2) large
[218] view
[219] constellation, the Scales
[220] Aries, the Ram
[221] nebula
[222] headlong
[223] [verb; rhymes with "finds, minds, binds," etc.]
[224] smooth as marble

567   Or[225] other worlds they seemed, or happy isles,
568   Like those Hesperian gardens[226] famed of old,
569   Fortunate fields, and groves, and flowery vales,
570   Thrice happy isles. But who dwelt happy there
571   He stayed[227] not to inquire. Above them all
572   The golden sun, in splendor likest Heav'n,
573   Allured his eye. Thither his course he bends
574   Through the calm firmament, but up or down,
575   By center, or eccentric,[228] hard to tell,[229]
576   Or longitude, where the great luminary[230]
577   Aloof[231] the vulgar[232] constellations thick,[233]
578   That from his[234] lordly eye keep distance due,[235]
579   Dispenses light from far. They as they move
580   Their starry dance in numbers that compute
581   Days, months, and years, towards his all-cheering lamp
582   Turn swift their various[236] motions, or are turned
583   By his magnetic beam, that gently warms
584   The universe, and to each inward part
585   With gentle penetration, though unseen,
586   Shoots invisible virtue[237] ev'n to the deep,
587   So wondrously was set his station bright.
588   There lands the fiend, a spot like which perhaps
589   Astronomer in the sun's lucent[238] orb
590   Through his glazed[239] optic tube[240] yet never saw.
591   The place he found beyond expression[241] bright,
592   Compared with aught on earth, metal or stone,

---

[225] either
[226] in which the Hesperides, daughters of Night and Darkness, guarded a tree that bore golden apples
[227] stopped
[228] "away from the center," which in this astronomy = the earth
[229] i.e., whether Ptolemaic or Copernican
[230] the sun
[231] at a distance from
[232] common
[233] dense
[234] the sun's
[235] proper, fitting
[236] changing
[237] powers, qualities
[238] luminous
[239] made of glass
[240] telescope: Milton had visited Galileo and looked through his telescope
[241] utterance

593 Not all parts like, but all alike informed[242]
594 With radiant light, as glowing iron with fire.
595 If metal, part seemed gold, part silver clear;
596 If stone, carbuncle most or chrysolite,
597 Ruby or topaz, to the twelve that shone
598 In Aaron's breast-plate,[243] and a stone besides
599 Imagined rather oft than elsewhere seen,[244]
600 That stone, or like to that which here below
601 Philosophers in vain so long have sought—
602 In vain, though by their powerful art they bind
603 Volatile Hermes,[245] and call up unbound
604 In various shapes old Proteus[246] from the sea,
605 Drained through a limbic[247] to his native form.
606 What wonder then if fields and regions here
607 Breathe forth elixir[248] pure, and rivers run
608 Potable[249] gold? when with one virtuous[250] touch
609 The arch-chemic[251] sun, so far from us remote,[252]
610 Produces, with terrestrial humor[253] mixed,
611 Here in the dark so many precious things
612 Of color glorious, and effect so rare?
613 Here matter new to gaze the Devil met,
614 Undazzled. Far and wide his eye commands,
615 For sight no obstacle found here, nor shade,
616 But all sun-shine, as when his beams at noon
617 Culminate[254] from th'equator, as they now
618 Shot upward still direct, whence no way round
619 Shadow from body opaque can fall, and the air,
620 Nowhere so clear, sharpened his[255] visual ray[256]
621 To objects distant far, whereby he soon

---

[242] stamped, impressed
[243] see Exodus 28:17–20
[244] i.e., the so-called philosopher's stone
[245] the god also known as Mercury, "volatile" because fond of trickery and furtiveness
[246] sea god, a shape-shifter
[247] glass vessel with a beak, used by alchemists for distilling operations
[248] mythical essence
[249] liquid, drinkable
[250] powerful
[251] master chemist (or alchemist)
[252] distant
[253] fluid
[254] reach
[255] Satan's
[256] line (of sight)

622   Saw within ken[257] a glorious Angel stand,
623   The same whom John saw also in the sun.[258]
624   His back was turned, but not his brightness hid.
625   Of beaming sunny rays a golden tiar[259]
626   Circled his head, nor less his locks behind
627   Illustrious[260] on his shoulders fledge[261] with wings
628   Lay waving round. On some great charge[262] employed
629   He seemed, or fixed in cogitation[263] deep.
630   Glad was the Spirit impure, as now in hope
631   To find who might direct his wandering flight
632   To Paradise, the happy seat of man,
633   His journey's end and our beginning woe.
634   But first he casts[264] to change his proper shape,
635   Which else might work him danger or delay.
636   And now a stripling[265] Cherub he appears,
637   Not of the prime,[266] yet such as in his face
638   Youth smiled celestial, and to every limb
639   Suitable grace diffused,[267] so well he feigned.
640   Under a coronet[268] his flowing hair
641   In curls on either cheek played; wings he wore
642   Of many a colored plume,[269] sprinkled with gold;
643   His habit fit for speed succinct,[270] and held
644   Before his decent[271] steps a silver wand.
645   He drew not nigh unheard. The Angel bright,
646   Ere he[272] drew nigh, his radiant visage turned,
647   Admonished by his ear, and straight was known
648   The Arch-Angel Uriel, one of the seven

---

[257] identifiable distance
[258] see Revelation 19:17
[259] tiara, headdress
[260] luminous, shining brightly
[261] furnished
[262] commission, mandate, responsibility
[263] thought, reflection
[264] contrives
[265] youthful
[266] fully grown, mature
[267] spread, shed [verb]
[268] a small, inferior crown
[269] feather
[270] not cut full, close-fitting
[271] respectable
[272] Satan

649 Who in God's presence, nearest to His throne,
650 Stand ready at command, and are His eyes
651 That run through all the Heav'ns, or down to th' earth
652 Bear His swift errands over moist and dry,
653 O'er sea and land. Him Satan thus accosts:[273]
654   "Uriel, for thou of those sev'n Spirits that stand
655 In sight of God's high throne, gloriously bright,
656 The first art wont[274] His great authentic[275] will
657 Interpreter[276] through highest Heav'n to bring,
658 Where all His sons thy embassy[277] attend,
659 And here art likeliest by supreme decree
660 Like honor to obtain, and as His eye
661 To visit oft this new creation round.
662 Unspeakable desire to see,[278] and know
663 All these His wondrous works, but chiefly man,
664 His chief delight and favor, him for whom
665 All these His works so wondrous He ordained,
666 Hath brought me from the choirs[279] of Cherubim
667 Alone thus wand'ring. Brightest Seraph, tell
668 In which of all these shining orbs hath man
669 His fixèd seat, or fixèd seat hath none,
670 But all these shining orbs his choice to dwell,
671 That I may find him, and with secret gaze
672 Or open admiration[280] him behold,
673 On whom the great Creator hath bestowed
674 Worlds, and on whom hath all these graces poured,
675 That both in him and all things, as is meet,[281]
676 The universal Maker we may praise,
677 Who justly hath driven out His rebel foes
678 To deepest Hell and, to repair that loss,
679 Created this new happy race of men
680 To serve Him better. Wise are all His ways."

---

[273] addresses
[274] usually
[275] authoritative
[276] one who makes another's will known, a messenger
[277] message, business
[278] "unspeakable desire to see" = subject; the verb is "hath brought me," in line 666, below
[279] companies
[280] wonder, marveling
[281] proper

681   So spoke the false dissembler unperceived,
682   For neither man nor Angel can discern
683   Hypocrisy, the only evil that walks
684   Invisible, except to God alone,
685   By His permissive will, through Heav'n and earth,
686   And oft, though wisdom wake, suspicion sleeps
687   At wisdom's gate, and to simplicity[282]
688   Resigns her charge, while goodness thinks no ill
689   Where no ill seems. Which now for once beguiled
690   Uriel, though regent[283] of the sun, and held[284]
691   The sharpest-sighted Spirit of all in Heav'n,
692   Who to the fraudulent impostor foul,
693   In his[285] uprightness,[286] answer thus returned:
694   "Fair Angel, thy desire, which tends to know
695   The works of God, thereby to glorify
696   The great work-master, leads to no excess
697   That reaches[287] blame, but rather merits praise
698   The more it seems excess, that led thee hither
699   From thy empyreal[288] mansion[289] thus alone,
700   To witness with thine eyes what some perhaps,
701   Contented with report, hear only in Heav'n.
702   For wonderful indeed are all His works,
703   Pleasant[290] to know, and worthiest to be all
704   Had in remembrance always with delight.
705   But what created mind can comprehend
706   Their number, or the wisdom infinite
707   That brought them forth, but hid their causes deep?
708   I saw when at His word the formless mass,
709   This world's material mould, came to a heap.[291]
710   Confusion heard His voice, and wild uproar

---

[282] sincerity, innocence, ignorance
[283] controller
[284] considered
[285] Uriel's
[286] integrity
[287] attains to, brings
[288] celestial
[289] home, residence
[290] pleasing
[291] collected into a form

711   Stood[292] ruled,[293] stood vast infinitude confined,
712   Till at His second bidding darkness fled,
713   Light shone, and order from disorder sprung.
714   Swift to their several quarters hasted then
715   The cumbrous[294] elements, earth, flood, air, fire,
716   And this ethereal[295] quintessence[296] of Heav'n
717   Flew upward, spirited[297] with various forms,
718   That rolled orbicular,[298] and turned to stars
719   Numberless, as thou seest, and how they move.
720   Each had his place appointed, each his course.
721   The rest, in circuit, walls[299] this universe.
722   Look downward on that globe, whose hither side
723   With light from hence, though but reflected, shines.
724   That place is earth, the seat of man, that light
725   His day, which else, as th' other hemisphere,
726   Night would invade, but there the neighboring moon
727   (So call that opposite fair star) her aid
728   Timely interposes,[300] and her monthly round
729   Still ending, still renewing, through mid Heav'n,
730   With borrowed light her countenance triform[301]
731   Hence fills and empties to enlighten[302] th' earth,
732   And in her pale dominion[303] checks[304] the night.
733   That spot, to which I point, is Paradise,
734   Adam's abode; those lofty shades, his bow'r.
735   Thy way thou canst not miss, me mine requires."
736   Thus said, he turned, and Satan, bowing low,
737   As to superior Spirits is wont[305] in Heav'n,

---

[292] stopped in its tracks
[293] controlled
[294] cumbersome
[295] airy, impalpable
[296] the fifth essence, of which substance the heavenly bodies were thought to be composed
[297] infused, animated
[298] in a circle
[299] furnishes walls for [verb]
[300] puts forth, introduces
[301] the goddess of the moon, Diana, had three distinct shapes ("triform"), representing the moon's three phases: Luna, Diana, and Hecate/Proserpine
[302] to give light to
[303] control, rule
[304] holds back, retards
[305] customary

738   Where honor due[306] and reverence none neglects,
739   Took leave, and toward the coast of earth beneath,
740   Down from th' ecliptic,[307] sped with hoped success,
741   Throws[308] his steep flight in many an airy wheel,[309]
742   Nor stayed,[310] till on Niphates'[311] top he lights.

The End of the Third Book

---

[306] (1) appropriate, (2) owed
[307] the orbit of the sun around the earth; earth's great circle
[308] twists
[309] circular movement
[310] stopped
[311] Armenian mountain, near the Assyrian/Mesopotamian border; it is the source of the River Tigris

BOOK IV

THE ARGUMENT

SATAN NOW IN prospect[1] of Eden, and nigh the place where he must now attempt the bold enterprize which he undertook alone against God and man, falls into many doubts with himself, and many passions, fear, envy, and despair, but at length confirms himself in evil. Journey[ing] on to Paradise, whose outward prospect and situation is described, [he] overleaps the bounds[2] [and] sits in the shape of a cormorant on the Tree of Life, as highest in the Garden, [in order] to look about him. The Garden described; Satan's first sight of Adam and Eve; his wonder at their excellent form and happy state, but with resolution to work their fall; [he] overhears their discourse, thence gathers that the Tree of Knowledge was forbidden them to eat of, under penalty of death; and thereon intends to found his temptation, by seducing them to transgress. Then [he] leaves them a while, to know further of their state by some other means.

Meanwhile Uriel descending on a Sun-beam warns Gabriel, who had in charge the Gate of Paradise, that some evil spirit had escaped the deep, and passed at Noon, by his sphere, in the shape of a good Angel, down to Paradise, [as] discovered[3] after[wards] by his[4] furious gestures in the Mount. Gabriel promises to find him out ere morning.

Night coming on, Adam and Eve discourse of going to their

---

[1] expectation, looking forward to
[2] boundary markers
[3] shown, disclosed
[4] i.e., Satan's

rest; their bower describ'd; their evening worship. Gabriel draw-
ing forth his bands of night-watch to walk the round of Paradise,
appoints[5] two strong Angels to Adam's bower, lest the evil spirit
should be there doing some harm to Adam or Eve sleeping.
There they find him at the ear of Eve, tempting her in a dream,
and bring him, though unwilling, to Gabriel, by whom ques-
tioned, he scornfully answers, prepares resistance, but hindered
by a sign from Heaven, flies out of Paradise.

---

[5] orders

1   O, for that warning voice, which he, who saw
2   The Apocalypse, heard cry in Heaven aloud,
3   Then when the dragon, put to second rout,
4   Came furious down to be revenged on men,
5   "Woe to the inhabitants on earth!"[6] that[7] now,
6   While time was,[8] our first parents had been warned
7   The coming of their secret foe, and 'scaped,
8   Haply[9] so 'scaped, his mortal snare. For now
9   Satan, now first inflamed with rage, came down,
10   The tempter ere[10] the accuser of mankind,
11   To wreak[11] on innocent frail man his[12] loss
12   Of that first battle, and his flight to Hell.
13   Yet, not rejoicing in his speed, though bold,
14   Far off and fearless, nor with cause to boast,
15   Begins his dire attempt, which nigh the birth
16   Now rolling,[13] boils in his tumultuous breast,
17   And like a devilish engine[14] back recoils
18   Upon himself. Horror and doubt distract
19   His troubled thoughts, and from the bottom stir
20   The Hell within him, for within him Hell
21   He brings, and round about him, nor from Hell
22   One step, no more than from himself, can fly
23   By change of place. Now conscience wakes despair
24   That slumbered, wakes the bitter memory
25   Of what he was, what is, and what must be
26   Worse: of[15] worse deeds, worse sufferings must ensue.[16]
27   Sometimes towards Eden, which now in his view
28   Lay pleasant, his grieved look he fixes sad,
29   Sometimes towards Heav'n and the full-blazing sun,
30   Which now sat high in his[17] meridian[18] tower.

---

[6] see Revelation 12:10–12
[7] so that
[8] while there was still time
[9] perhaps
[10] before he became
[11] (1) give vent to, (2) take revenge on
[12] Satan's
[13] moving, forming, advancing, sweeping upward
[14] a cannon
[15] from
[16] result, follow
[17] the sun's
[18] noontime

31   Then much[19] revolving,[20] thus in sighs began:
32   "O thou,[21] that with surpassing glory crowned,
33   Look'st from thy sole dominion like the god
34   Of this new world, at whose sight all the stars
35   Hide their diminished heads, to thee I call,
36   But with no friendly voice, and add thy name,
37   O Sun! to tell thee how I hate thy beams,
38   That bring to my remembrance from what state
39   I fell, how glorious once above thy sphere,[22]
40   Till pride and worse ambition threw me down,
41   Warring in Heav'n against Heav'n's matchless King.
42   Ah, wherefore! He deserved no such return
43   From me, whom He created what I was
44   In that bright eminence,[23] and with His good
45   Upbraided[24] none. Nor was His service hard.
46   What could be less than to afford[25] Him praise,
47   The easiest recompense,[26] and pay Him thanks—
48   How due![27] Yet all His good proved ill in me,
49   And wrought[28] but malice. Lifted up so high
50   I 'sdained[29] subjection,[30] and thought one step higher
51   Would set me highest, and in a moment quit[31]
52   The debt immense of endless gratitude,
53   So burdensome still[32] paying, still to owe,
54   Forgetful what from Him I still received,
55   And understood not that a grateful mind
56   By owing owes not, but still pays, at once
57   Indebted and discharged. What burden then?
58   O, had His powerful destiny ordained

---

[19] many things/thoughts
[20] turning over in his mind
[21] the sun
[22] above thy sphere = (1) above your position/status, (2) literally, in Heaven above the sphere which you are in
[23] (1) height, (2) distinction
[24] He (God) reproached/scolded/censured
[25] to give/yield
[26] repayment
[27] (1) owed, (2) right, proper
[28] worked
[29] disdained [probably from the Italian *sdegnare*, "to disdain/despise/scorn"]
[30] submission, obedience
[31] get rid of, release
[32] (1) yet, (2) always

59   Me some inferior Angel, I had stood[33]
60   Then happy: no unbounded[34] hope had raised
61   Ambition! Yet why not? Some other Power[35]
62   As great might have aspired, and me, though mean,[36]
63   Drawn[37] to his part.[38] But other Powers as great
64   Fell not, but stand unshaken from within
65   Or from without, to all temptations armed.[39]
66   Hadst thou the same free will and power to stand?[40]
67   Thou hadst: whom hast thou then or what t' accuse,
68   But Heav'n's free[41] love dealt equally to all?
69   Be then His love accursed, since love or hate,
70   To me alike, it deals[42] eternal woe.
71   Nay, cursed be thou,[43] since against His thy will
72   Chose freely what it now so justly[44] rues![45]
73   "Me miserable![46] Which way shall I fly[47]
74   Infinite wrath, and infinite despair?
75   Which[48] way I fly is Hell. Myself am Hell,
76   And in the lowest deep a lower deep
77   Still threat'ning to devour me opens wide,
78   To which the Hell I suffer seems a Heav'n.
79   O then, at last relent![49] Is there no place
80   Left for repentance, none for pardon left?
81   None left but by submission, and that word
82   Disdain forbids me, and my dread of shame
83   Among the Spirits beneath, whom I seduced

---

[33] remained
[34] unlimited, uncontrolled
[35] sixth of the nine angelic orders
[36] lowly
[37] might have been drawn
[38] side, cause
[39] (1) having weapons, (2) having protective qualities/characteristics
[40] to remain steadfast/firm
[41] honorable, generous
[42] gives, brings
[43] himself
[44] rightfully, properly
[45] regrets
[46] i.e., "O how miserable I am!" [four syllables, first and third accented]
[47] flee
[48] whichever
[49] yield

84   With other promises and other vaunts[50]
85   Than to submit, boasting I could subdue
86   The Omnipotent. Ay me! they little know
87   How dearly[51] I abide[52] that boast so vain,
88   Under what torments inwardly I groan,
89   While they adore me on the throne of Hell!
90   With diadem and scepter high advanced[53]
91   The lower still I fall, only supreme
92   In misery. Such joy ambition finds![54]
93   But say I could repent, and could obtain,
94   By act of grace, my former state, how soon
95   Would height recall high thoughts, how soon unsay
96   What feigned[55] submission swore? Ease would recant[56]
97   Vows made in pain, as violent[57] and void.
98   For never can true reconcilement grow
99   Where wounds of deadly hate have pierced so deep,
100   Which would but lead me to a worse relapse
101   And heavier fall. So should I purchase dear[58]
102   Short intermission, bought with double smart.[59]
103   This knows my punisher, therefore as far
104   From granting He, as I from begging, peace.
105   All hope excluded thus, behold, instead
106   Of us[60] out-cast, exiled, his new delight,
107   Mankind created, and for him[61] this world.
108   So farewell hope and, with hope, farewell fear,
109   Farewell remorse! All good to me is lost.
110   Evil, be thou my good: by thee at least
111   Divided empire with Heav'n's King I hold—
112   By thee, and more than half[62] perhaps will reign,
113   As man ere long, and this new world, shall know."

---

[50] boasts
[51] at a high price
[52] face, put up with
[53] raised
[54] obtains, gains
[55] pretended
[56] withdraw, disavow, retract
[57] forced
[58] at high cost, great expense
[59] pain, suffering
[60] instead of us = replacing us
[61] man
[62] more than half of the empire

114   Thus while he spoke, each passion dimmed his
             face
115 Thrice changed with pale,[63] ire,[64] envy, and despair,
116 Which marred[65] his borrowed visage, and betrayed
117 Him counterfeit, if any eye beheld.
118 For Heav'nly minds from such distempers[66] foul
119 Are ever clear.[67] Whereof he soon aware,
120 Each perturbation[68] smoothed with outward calm,
121 Artificer[69] of fraud, and[70] was the first
122 That practised falsehood under saintly show,
123 Deep malice to conceal, couched[71] with revenge.
124 Yet not enough had practised[72] to deceive
125 Uriel, once warned, whose eye pursued him down
126 The way he went, and on the Assyrian mount
127 Saw him disfigured, more than could befall[73]
128 Spirit of happy sort. His gestures fierce
129 He marked, and mad demeanour,[74] then alone,
130 As he supposed, all unobserved, unseen.
131   So on he fares,[75] and to the border comes
132 Of Eden, where delicious Paradise,
133 Now nearer, crowns with her enclosure green,
134 As with a rural mound, the champaign[76] head[77]
135 Of a steep wilderness, whose hairy sides
136 With thicket overgrown, grotesque and wild,
137 Access denied.[78] And overhead up grew
138 Insuperable[79] height of loftiest shade,

---

[63] pallor
[64] anger
[65] spoiled, disfigured
[66] ill tempers, ill humors, disorders, derangements
[67] innocent
[68] agitation
[69] mechanic-inventor
[70] i.e., "who"
[71] hidden, joined in concealment
[72] put into practice
[73] happen to
[74] conduct, behavior
[75] travels
[76] expanse of open land
[77] top
[78] access denied to him (Satan)
[79] impossible to overcome/surmount

139   Cedar, and pine, and fir, and branching palm,
140   A sylvan[80] scene, and as the ranks[81] ascend,
141   Shade above shade, a woody theater[82]
142   Of stateliest[83] view. Yet higher than their tops
143   The verdurous wall of Paradise upsprung,
144   Which to our general[84] sire gave prospect large[85]
145   Into his[86] nether[87] empire neighboring round.
146   And higher than that wall a circling row
147   Of goodliest[88] trees, loaden with fairest fruit,
148   Blossoms and fruits at once[89] of golden hue
149   Appeared, with gay enamelled[90] colours mixed,
150   On which the sun more glad impressed[91] his beams
151   Than in fair evening cloud, or humid bow,[92]
152   When God hath show'red the earth. So lovely seemed
153   That landscape. And of pure now purer[93] air
154   Meets his approach, and to the heart inspires
155   Vernal[94] delight and joy, able to drive[95]
156   All sadness but despair. Now gentle gales,[96]
157   Fanning their odoriferous[97] wings, dispense[98]
158   Native[99] perfumes, and whisper whence they stole
159   Those balmy spoils.[100] As when to them who sail
160   Beyond the Cape of Hope,[101] and now are past

---

[80] rustic
[81] rows
[82] place where action occurs
[83] noble, majestic
[84] common
[85] prospect large = extensive view
[86] Adam's
[87] lower
[88] handsome, large
[89] at the same time, simultaneously
[90] any smooth, lustrous surface
[91] imprinted, stamped
[92] rainbow
[93] of pure now purer = purer still
[94] springlike
[95] chase, expel
[96] a wind not much stronger than a breeze
[97] fragrant
[98] bestow, distribute
[99] natural
[100] loot, plunder, booty
[101] Cape of Good Hope, at the southern tip of Africa

161	Mozambique,[102] off at sea north-east winds blow
162	Sabean[103] odors from the spicy shore
163	Of Araby the blest,[104] with such delay
164	Well pleased they slack[105] their course,[106] and many a league[107]
165	Cheered with the grateful[108] smell old ocean smiles.
166	So entertained[109] those odorous sweets the fiend,
167	Who came their bane,[110] though with them better pleased
168	Than Asmodeus[111] with the fishy fume[112]
169	That drove him, though enamored, from the spouse
170	Of Tobit's son, and with a vengeance sent[113]
171	From Media post[114] to Egypt, there fast bound.[115]
172	Now to the ascent of that steep savage[116] hill
173	Satan had journeyed on, pensive and slow,
174	But further way found none, so thick entwined,
175	As one continued brake,[117] the undergrowth
176	Of shrubs and tangling bushes had perplexed[118]
177	All path of man or beast that passed that way.
178	One gate there only was, and that looked east
179	On th' other side. Which when the arch-felon saw,
180	Due entrance he disdained and, in contempt,
181	At one slight[119] bound high over-leaped all bound
182	Of hill or highest wall, and sheer[120] within

---

[102] [trisyllabic, second accented]
[103] Saba, in modern Yemen
[104] Arabia, called at the time, in Latin, *Arabia felix*, "happy/blessed Arabia"
[105] abate, let slacken
[106] onward movement
[107] one league = ca. three miles
[108] pleasing, agreeable
[109] experienced with pleasure
[110] slayer
[111] evil demon in Apocryphal book of the Bible, Tobit, who has seven times killed the husbands of Sarah, daughter of Tobit's relative, with whom the demon is in love; he is finally driven off by fish smells
[112] vapor
[113] sent him, the demon, away from Media, where Tobit, his son, and his wife lived
[114] hurriedly
[115] by the Angel Raphael, sent by God
[116] wild, uncultivated
[117] thicket
[118] troubled, entangled
[119] easy
[120] completely

183 Lights on his feet. As when a prowling wolf,
184 Whom hunger drives to seek new haunt for prey,
185 Watching where shepherds pen their flocks at eve
186 In hurdled[121] cotes[122] amid the field secure,
187 Leaps o'er the fence with ease into the fold—
188 Or as a thief, bent to unhoard[123] the cash
189 Of some rich burgher, whose substantial doors,
190 Cross-barred and bolted fast, fear no assault,
191 In at the window climbs, or o'er the tiles,[124]
192 So clomb[125] this first grand thief into God's fold.
193 So since into His church lewd hirelings climb.
194 Thence up he flew, and on the Tree of Life,
195 The middle tree and highest there that grew,
196 Sat like a cormorant, yet not true life
197 Thereby regained, but sat devising death
198 To them who lived, nor on the virtue thought
199 Of that life-giving plant, but only used
200 For prospect,[126] what well-used had been[127] the pledge[128]
201 Of immortality. So little knows
202 Any, but God alone, to value right
203 The good before him, but perverts best things
204 To worst abuse, or to their meanest[129] use.
205   Beneath him with new wonder now he views,
206 To all delight of human sense exposed
207 In narrow room,[130] Nature's whole wealth, yea more,
208 A Heav'n on earth. For blissful Paradise
209 Of God the garden was, by Him in th' east
210 Of Eden planted. Eden stretched her line[131]
211 From Auran[132] eastward to the royal tow'rs

---

[121] made of interwoven branches
[122] stalls, pens
[123] reduce the store of money
[124] of the roof
[125] climbed
[126] the view it afforded him
[127] had been = would have been
[128] guarantee, promise
[129] lowest
[130] space
[131] contours
[132] Haran, city on the River Euphrates, in Mesopotamia

212   Of great Seleucia,[133] built by Grecian kings,
213   Or where the sons of Eden long before
214   Dwelt in Telassar.[134] In this pleasant soil
215   His far more pleasant garden God ordained.
216   Out of the fertile ground He caused to grow
217   All trees of noblest kind for sight, smell, taste,
218   And all amid them stood the Tree of Life,
219   High eminent, blooming ambrosial fruit
220   Of vegetable[135] gold. And next to life
221   Our death, the Tree of Knowledge, grew fast by,
222   Knowledge of good bought dear by knowing ill.
223   Southward through Eden went a river large,
224   Nor changed his course, but through the shaggy[136] hill
225   Passed underneath engulfed,[137] for God had thrown[138]
226   That mountain as His garden-mold[139] high raised
227   Upon the rapid current, which through veins
228   Of porous earth with kindly[140] thirst up-drawn,
229   Rose a fresh fountain, and with many a rill[141]
230   Watered the garden, thence united fell
231   Down the steep glade, and met the nether[142] flood,[143]
232   Which from his darksome passage now appears,
233   And now, divided into four main streams,
234   Runs diverse,[144] wand'ring many a famous realm
235   And country, whereof here needs no account,
236   But rather to tell how, if art[145] could tell,
237   How from that sapphire fount the crispèd[146] brooks,
238   Rolling on orient[147] pearl and sands of gold,

---

[133] city near Babylon, on the River Tigris
[134] city in Eden
[135] [four syllables, first and third accented]
[136] tangled, heavily wooded
[137] swallowed up
[138] formed, fashioned (as a potter "throws" a pot)
[139] garden topsoil
[140] natural
[141] brook
[142] underground
[143] river
[144] in different directions [bisyllabic, first accented]
[145] skill
[146] rippling
[147] gleaming

239 With mazy[148] error[149] under pendant shades
240 Ran nectar, visiting each plant, and fed
241 Flow'rs worthy of Paradise, which not nice[150] art
242 In beds and curious[151] knots, but Nature boon[152]
243 Poured forth profuse on hill and dale and plain,
244 Both where the morning sun first warmly smote
245 The open field, and where the unpierced shade
246 Imbrowned[153] the noontide bow'rs. Thus was this place
247 A happy rural seat of various view,
248 Groves whose rich trees wept odorous gums and balm,
249 Others whose fruit, burnished with golden rind,
250 Hung amiable,[154] Hesperian[155] fables true,
251 If true, here only, and of delicious taste.
252 Betwixt them lawns, or level downs,[156] and flocks
253 Grazing the tender herb,[157] were interposed,
254 Or palmy[158] hillock, or the flowery lap[159]
255 Of some irriguous[160] valley spread her store,
256 Flow'rs of all hue, and without thorn the rose.
257 Another side, umbrageous[161] grots and caves
258 Of cool recess, o'er which the mantling[162] vine
259 Lays forth her purple grape, and gently creeps
260 Luxuriant. Meanwhile murmuring waters fall
261 Down the slope hills, dispersed, or in a lake,
262 That to the fringèd bank with myrtle crowned
263 Her crystal mirror holds, unite their streams.
264 The birds their choir[163] apply,[164] airs, vernal airs,

---

[148] winding, labyrinthine
[149] wandering
[150] fussy, fastidious
[151] skillful, choice, exquisite
[152] gracious, bountiful, jolly
[153] i.e., darkened
[154] [four syllables, first and third accented]
[155] legendary garden in which the Hesperides, daughters of Night and Darkness, guarded a tree that bore golden apples
[156] open expanse of treeless pastureland
[157] grass
[158] bearing palm trees
[159] a hollow among hills
[160] irrigated [probably trisyllabic, second accented]
[161] shady
[162] covering
[163] chorus
[164] bring into operation

265   Breathing the smell of field and grove, attune[165]
266   The trembling leaves, while universal Pan,
267   Knit[166] with the Graces[167] and the Hours[168] in dance,
268   Led on th' eternal Spring. Not that fair field
269   Of Enna,[169] where Proserpine, gath'ring flow'rs,
270   Herself a fairer flow'r by gloomy Dis[170]
271   Was gathered, which cost Ceres[171] all that pain
272   To seek her through the world. Nor that sweet grove
273   Of Daphne[172] by Orontes,[173] and the inspired[174]
274   Castalian spring,[175] might with this Paradise
275   Of Eden strive,[176] nor that Nyseian[177] isle
276   Girt[178] with the river Triton, where old Cham,[179]
277   Whom gentiles Ammon call, and Libyan Jove,
278   Hid Amalthea[180] and her florid[181] son
279   Young Bacchus from his stepdame Rhea's eye,
280   Nor where Abassin[182] kings their issue[183] guard,
281   Mount Amara,[184] though this by some supposed
282   True Paradise under the Ethiop line[185]
283   By Nilus[186] head,[187] enclosed with shining rock,
284   A whole day's journey high, but wide remote
285   From this Assyrian garden, where the fiend
286   Saw, undelighted, all delight, all kind

---

[165] make tuneful/harmonious
[166] joined
[167] Aglaia (brilliance), Euphrosyne (joy), Thalia (blossoming)
[168] female divinities presiding over seasonal changes
[169] in Sicily
[170] Dis = Pluto = Hades
[171] Nature/earth goddess, later Demeter; mother of Proserpine/Persephone
[172] like Proserpine, pursued by lustful gods
[173] river in Syria
[174] the grove of Daphne contained an oracle dedicated to Apollo
[175] named after the spring at the oracle in Delphi, also dedicated to Apollo
[176] compete
[177] the island of Nysa, in the River Triton in Tunisia
[178] encircled, surrounded
[179] Ammon
[180] Zeus' nurse, mother of Bacchus by Ammon
[181] red-faced (from wine)
[182] Abyssinian/Ethiopian
[183] offspring, children
[184] in Abyssinia
[185] contours
[186] River Nile
[187] source

287 Of living creatures, new to sight, and strange.
288   Two of far nobler shape, erect and tall,
289 Godlike erect, with native honor clad
290 In naked majesty, seemed lords of all.
291 And worthy seemed, for in their looks divine
292 The image of their glorious Maker shone,
293 Truth, wisdom, sanctitude severe and pure
294 (Severe, but in true filial freedom placed),
295 Whence true authority in men. Though both
296 Not equal, as their sex not equal seemed:
297 For contemplation he, and valor, formed;
298 For softness she and sweet attractive grace;
299 He for God only, she for God in him.
300 His fair large front[188] and eye sublime[189] declared[190]
301 Absolute rule, and hyacinthine[191] locks
302 Round from his parted forelock[192] manly hung
303 Clust'ring, but not beneath his shoulders broad.
304 She as a veil down to the slender waist
305 Her unadornèd golden tresses wore
306 Dishevelled,[193] but in wanton[194] ringlets waved
307 As the vine curls her tendrils, which implied
308 Subjection, but required[195] with gentle sway,[196]
309 And by her yielded, by him best received,
310 Yielded with coy[197] submission, modest pride,
311 And sweet, reluctant, amorous delay.
312 Nor those mysterious parts[198] were then concealed.
313 Then was not guilty shame, dishonest[199] shame
314 Of Nature's works. Honor dishonorable,
315 Sin-bred, how have ye troubled all mankind

---

[188] forehead
[189] exalted, lofty
[190] manifested, made plain/clear
[191] (1) curled, *or* (2) scented, *or* (3) dark-colored
[192] lock of hair in front
[193] loosened
[194] frisky, sportive
[195] requested, demanded
[196] authority, rule
[197] shy, modest
[198] mysterious parts = genitalia
[199] i.e., unchaste

316   With shows[200] instead, mere shows of seeming pure,
317   And banished from man's life his happiest life,
318   Simplicity and spotless innocence!
319   So passed they naked on, nor shunned the sight
320   Of God or Angel, for they thought no ill:
321   So hand in hand they passed, the loveliest pair
322   That ever since in love's embraces met,
323   Adam the goodliest man of men, since born
324   His sons, the fairest of her daughters Eve.
325   Under a tuft[201] of shade that on a green[202]
326   Stood whispering soft, by a fresh fountain side
327   They sat them down and, after no more toil
328   Of their sweet gardening labor than sufficed
329   To recommend[203] cool Zephyr,[204] and made ease
330   More easy, wholesome thirst and appetite
331   More grateful, to their supper-fruits they fell,
332   Nectarine[205] fruits which the compliant[206] boughs
333   Yielded them, side-long as they sat recline
334   On the soft downy bank, damasked[207] with flow'rs.
335   The savory pulp they chew, and in the rind,
336   Still as they thirsted, scoop the brimming stream,
337   Nor gentle purpose,[208] nor endearing smiles
338   Wanted,[209] nor youthful dalliance, as beseems
339   Fair couple, linked in happy nuptial league,
340   Alone as they. About them frisking played
341   All beasts of the earth, since wild, and of all chase[210]
342   In wood or wilderness, forest or den.
343   Sporting,[211] the lion ramped,[212] and in his paw

---

[200] externals, displays
[201] patch
[202] grassy spot
[203] commend
[204] the west wind
[205] sweet as nectar [adjective]
[206] obliging, yielding
[207] variegated
[208] discourse, speech
[209] lacked
[210] animals that are hunted [noun]
[211] playing
[212] bounded

344   Dandled[213] the kid; bears, tigers, ounces,[214] pards,[215]
345   Gambolled[216] before them; the unwieldy elephant,
346   To make them mirth, used all his might, and wreathed[217]
347   His lithe[218] proboscis;[219] close,[220] the serpent sly
348   Insinuating[221] wove with Gordian[222] twine[223]
349   His braided[224] train,[225] and of his fatal[226] guile
350   Gave proof unheeded; others on the grass
351   Couched,[227] and now filled with pasture[228] gazing sat,
352   Or bedward ruminating,[229] for the sun,
353   Declined,[230] was hasting now with prone[231] career[232]
354   To th' ocean isles,[233] and in the ascending scale[234]
355   Of Heav'n the stars that usher evening rose.
356   When Satan still in gaze, as first he stood,
357   Scarce thus at length failed speech recovered, sad:
358   "O Hell! What do mine eyes with grief behold!
359   Into our room[235] of bliss thus high advanced
360   Creatures of other mould, earth-born perhaps,
361   Not Spirits, yet to Heav'nly Spirits bright
362   Little inferior, whom my thoughts pursue
363   With wonder, and could love, so lively shines
364   In them divine resemblance, and such grace

---

[213] moving lightly up and down
[214] (1) lynx, (2) panther
[215] leopards
[216] capered, danced
[217] coiled, twisted
[218] flexible, pliant, supple
[219] trunk, nose
[220] close by
[221] sinuously
[222] intricate
[223] rope, twine, knots
[224] intertwined, braided
[225] tail, long dragging body
[226] destined, fated
[227] lay
[228] i.e., with eating the grass that grows on pastureland
[229] (1) digesting, as ruminants do, (2) reflecting
[230] slanting down
[231] steeply downward
[232] racelike, galloping speed
[233] the Azores, to the west
[234] with a scale having two weighing pans, when one (lighter) goes up the other (heavier) necessarily goes down
[235] place, position

365   The hand that formed them on their shape hath
                    poured.[236]
366   Ah! gentle[237] pair, ye little think how nigh[238]
367   Your change approaches, when all these delights
368   Will vanish, and deliver ye to woe,
369   More woe, the more your taste is now of joy,
370   Happy, but for so happy ill secured[239]
371   Long to continue, and this high seat your Heav'n
372   Ill fenced for Heav'n to keep out such a foe
373   As now is entered. Yet no purposed[240] foe
374   To you, whom I could pity thus forlorn,[241]
375   Though I[242] unpitied. League[243] with you I seek,
376   And mutual amity, so straight,[244] so close,
377   That I with you must dwell, or you with me
378   Henceforth. My dwelling haply[245] may not please
379   (Like this fair Paradise) your sense, yet such
380   Accept your Maker's work. He gave it me,
381   Which I as freely give: Hell shall unfold,
382   To entertain[246] you two, her widest gates,
383   And send forth all her kings. There will be room,
384   Not like these narrow limits, to receive
385   Your numerous offspring. If no better place,
386   Thank Him who puts me, loath, to this revenge
387   On you (who wrong me not), for Him who wronged.[247]
388   And should I at your harmless innocence
389   Melt,[248] as I do, yet public[249] reason just,
390   Honor and empire with revenge enlarged,
391   By conquering this new world, compels me now
392   To do what else, though damned, I should abhor."

---

[236] "hath poured on their shape"
[237] noble, excellent
[238] close
[239] firmly fixed, safe
[240] deliberate
[241] abandoned, lost, doomed
[242] I am myself
[243] alliance
[244] direct, honest
[245] perhaps
[246] hold, keep
[247] did wrong me
[248] soften
[249] common, community, patriotic

393   So spoke the fiend, and with necessity
394 (The tyrant's plea) excused his devilish deeds.
395 Then from his lofty stand on that high tree
396 Down he alights among the sportful[250] herd
397 Of those four-footed kinds, himself now one,
398 Now other, as their shape served best his end
399 Nearer to view his prey, and unespied
400 To mark what of their state[251] he more might learn,
401 By word or action marked.[252] About them round
402 A lion[253] now he stalks with fiery glare,
403 Then as a tiger, who by chance hath spied
404 In some purlieu[254] two gentle fawns at play,
405 Straight couches[255] close, then rising, changes oft
406 His couchant watch, as one who chose his ground,
407 Whence rushing, he might surest seize them both,
408 Gripped in each paw: When Adam, first of men,
409 To first of women Eve, thus moving[256] speech,
410 Turned him[257] all ear[258] to hear new utterance flow:
411   "Sole partner, and sole part,[259] of all these joys,
412 Dearer thyself than all! Needs must the Power
413 That made us, and for us this ample world,
414 Be infinitely good, and of His good
415 As liberal and free as infinite,
416 That raised us from the dust, and placed us here
417 In all this happiness, who at His hand
418 Have nothing merited,[260] nor can perform
419 Aught whereof He hath need, He who requires
420 From us no other service than to keep
421 This one, this easy charge:[261] of all the trees
422 In Paradise that bear delicious fruit

---

[250] frolicking
[251] condition, circumstances
[252] noted, observed
[253] as a lion
[254] rangeland
[255] lies
[256] uttering
[257] Satan
[258] all ear = eagerly attentive
[259] participant
[260] deserved
[261] mandate, order, instruction, admonition

423   So various, not to taste that only Tree
424   Of Knowledge, planted by[262] the Tree of Life.
425   So near grows death to life, whate'er death is,
426   Some dreadful thing no doubt, for well thou know'st
427   God hath pronounced it death to taste that tree,
428   The only sign of our obedience left
429   Among so many signs of power and rule
430   Conferred upon us, and dominion[263] giv'n
431   Over all other creatures that possess
432   Earth, air, and sea. Then let us not think hard
433   One easy prohibition, who enjoy
434   Free leave so large to all things else, and choice
435   Unlimited of manifold delights,
436   But let us ever praise Him, and extol
437   His bounty, following our delightful task,
438   To prune these growing plants, and tend these flow'rs,
439   Which were it toilsome, yet with thee were sweet."
440   To whom thus Eve replied: "O thou for whom
441   And from whom I was formed, flesh of thy flesh,
442   And without whom am to no end,[264] my guide
443   And head! What thou hast said is just and right.
444   For we to Him indeed all praises owe,
445   And daily thanks—I chiefly, who enjoy
446   So far the happier lot, enjoying thee
447   Pre-eminent by so much odds,[265] while thou
448   Like[266] consort[267] to thyself canst nowhere find.
449   That day I oft remember, when from sleep
450   I first awaked, and found myself reposed
451   Under a shade[268] on flow'rs, much wond'ring where
452   And what I was, whence thither brought, and how.
453   Not distant far from thence a murmuring sound
454   Of waters issued from a cave, and spread
455   Into a liquid plain, then stood unmoved,[269]

---

[262] near, alongside
[263] rule, control, government
[264] purpose
[265] preeminent by so much odds = superior by such a high percentage/amount
[266] similar
[267] companion
[268] shady cover (from the sun)
[269] unmoving, fixed

456 Pure as th' expanse of Heav'n. I thither[270] went
457 With unexperienced[271] thought, and laid me down
458 On the green bank, to look into the clear
459 Smooth lake, that to me seemed another sky.
460 As I bent down to look, just opposite
461 A shape within the wat'ry gleam appeared,
462 Bending to look on me. I started back—
463 It started back—but pleased I soon returned,
464 Pleased it returned as soon, with answering looks
465 Of sympathy and love. There I had fixed
466 Mine eyes till now, and pined[272] with vain desire,
467 Had not a voice thus warned me: 'What thou see'st,
468 What there thou see'st, fair creature, is thyself.
469 With thee it came and goes. But follow me
470 And I will bring thee where no shadow stays[273]
471 Thy coming, and thy soft embraces, he
472 Whose image thou art, him thou shalt enjoy
473 Inseparably thine, to him shalt bear
474 Multitudes like thyself, and thence be called
475 Mother of human race.' What could I do,
476 But follow straight,[274] invisibly thus led?
477 Till I espied thee, fair indeed and tall,
478 Under a platane,[275] yet methought less fair,
479 Less winning soft, less amiably mild,
480 Than that smooth wat'ry image. Back I turned.
481 Thou following cried'st aloud, 'Return, fair Eve.
482 Whom fly'st[276] thou? Whom thou fly'st, of him thou art,
483 His flesh, his bone. To give thee being I lent
484 Out of my side to thee, nearest my heart,
485 Substantial[277] life, to[278] have thee by my side
486 Henceforth an individual[279] solace[280] dear.

---

[270] i.e., to the pool
[271] inexperienced
[272] languished
[273] awaits
[274] at once
[275] plane tree (e.g., the sycamore)
[276] flee
[277] solid, true, real
[278] in order to
[279] inseparable, indivisible, special
[280] (1) comfort, pleasure, delight, (2) entertainment, recreation, amusement

487 Part of my soul, I seek thee! and thee claim[281]
488 My other half.' With that thy gentle hand
489 Seized mine, I yielded, and from that time see
490 How beauty is excelled by manly grace,
491 And wisdom, which alone is truly fair."
492   So spoke our general[282] mother, and with eyes
493 Of conjugal attraction unreproved,
494 And meek surrender, half-embracing leaned
495 On our first father. Half her swelling breast
496 Naked met his, under the flowing gold
497 Of her loose tresses hid. He in delight
498 Both of her beauty and submissive charms,
499 Smiled with superior love, as Jupiter
500 On Juno smiles, when he impregns[283] the clouds
501 That shed May flowers, and pressed her matron lip
502 With kisses pure. Aside the Devil turned
503 For envy, yet with jealous leer malign
504 Eyed them askance, and to himself thus plained:[284]
505 "Sight hateful, sight tormenting! Thus these two,
506 Imparadised in one another's arms,
507 The happier Eden, shall enjoy their fill
508 Of bliss on bliss, while I to Hell am thrust,
509 Where neither joy nor love, but fierce desire,
510 Among our other torments not the least,
511 Still unfulfilled with pain of longing pines.[285]
512 Yet let me not forget what I have gained
513 From their own mouths. All is not theirs, it seems.
514 One fatal tree there stands, of knowledge called,
515 Forbidden them to taste. Knowledge forbidden?
516 Suspicious, reasonless. Why should their Lord
517 Envy them that? Can it be sin to know?
518 Can it be death? And do they only stand[286]
519 By ignorance? Is that their happy state,
520 The proof of their obedience and their faith?
521 O fair foundation laid whereon to build

---

[281] claim as
[282] universal, common
[283] impregnates
[284] complained
[285] wastes away
[286] endure

522   Their ruin! Hence I will excite[287] their minds
523   With more desire to know, and to reject
524   Envious commands, invented with design
525   To keep them low, whom knowledge might exalt
526   Equal with gods. Aspiring to be such,
527   They taste and die. What likelier can ensue?
528   But first with narrow[288] search I must walk round
529   This garden, and no corner leave unspied.
530   A chance (but chance)[289] may lead where I may meet
531   Some wand'ring Spirit of Heav'n by fountain side,
532   Or in thick shade retired, from him to draw
533   What further would be learned. Live while ye may,
534   Yet happy pair—enjoy, till I return,
535   Short pleasures, for long woes are to succeed!"[290]
536   So saying, his proud step he scornful turned,
537   But with sly circumspection,[291] and began
538   Through wood, through waste,[292] o'er hill, o'er dale, his
        roam.[293]
539   Meanwhile in utmost longitude,[294] where Heav'n
540   With earth and ocean meets, the setting sun
541   Slowly descended, and with right aspect[295]
542   Against the eastern gate of Paradise
543   Leveled his evening rays. It was a rock
544   Of alabaster, piled up to the clouds,
545   Conspicuous[296] far, winding with one ascent
546   Accessible from earth, one entrance high.
547   The rest was craggy cliff, that overhung
548   Still as it rose, impossible to climb.
549   Betwixt these rocky pillars, Gabriel sat,
550   Chief of the Angelic guards, awaiting night.
551   About him exercised[297] heroic games

---

[287] rouse/stir up
[288] close, careful
[289] but only a chance
[290] follow
[291] vigilant/cautious observation
[292] wild, uncultivated land
[293] [noun]
[294] extreme/outermost west
[295] astronomical orientation: directly opposite
[296] visible
[297] practiced

552 Th' unarmed youth of Heav'n, but nigh[298] at hand
553 Celestial armory—shields, helms, and spears,
554 Hung high with diamond flaming, and with gold.
555 Thither came Uriel, gliding through the ev'n[299]
556 On a sun-beam, swift as a shooting star
557 In autumn thwarts[300] the night (when vapors fired[301]
558 Impress[302] the air) and shows the mariner
559 From what point of his compass to beware
560 Impetuous[303] winds. He thus began in haste:
561   "Gabriel, to thee thy course by lot[304] hath given
562 Charge[305] and strict watch, that to this happy place
563 No evil thing approach or enter in.
564 This day at height of noon came to my sphere
565 A Spirit, zealous, as he seemed, to know
566 More of the Almighty's works, and chiefly man,
567 God's latest image. I described[306] his way
568 Bent all on speed, and marked[307] his airy gait,[308]
569 But in the mount that lies from Eden north,
570 Where he first lighted, soon discerned his looks
571 Alien[309] from Heav'n, with passions foul obscured.[310]
572 Mine eye pursued him still, but under shade
573 Lost sight of him. One of the banished crew,
574 I fear, hath ventured from the deep, to raise[311]
575 New troubles. Him thy care must be to find."
576 To whom the wingèd warrior thus returned:
577   "Uriel, no wonder if thy perfect sight,
578 Amid the sun's bright circle where thou sit'st,
579 See far and wide. In at this gate none pass

---

[298] close
[299] evening, twilight
[300] crosses, traverses
[301] burning
[302] stamp, imprint on
[303] violently forceful
[304] destiny
[305] responsibility
[306] traced
[307] noted
[308] (1) course, (2) carriage: i.e., through the air, as spirits move
[309] foreign, inconsistent, repugnant
[310] darkened
[311] stir up, cause

580   The vigilance[312] here placed, but such as come
581   Well known from Heav'n. And since meridian hour[313]
582   No creature thence. If Spirit of other sort,
583   So minded,[314] have o'er-leaped these earthly bounds
584   On purpose, hard thou know'st it to exclude
585   Spiritual substance with corporeal bar.
586   But if within the circuit of these walks,
587   In whatsoever shape he lurk, of whom
588   Thou tell'st, by morrow dawning I shall know."
589   So promised he, and Uriel to his charge[315]
590   Returned on that bright beam, whose point now raised
591   Bore him slope downward to the sun now fall'n
592   Beneath the Azores, whither the prime orb,
593   Incredible how swift, had thither rolled
594   Diurnal,[316] or[317] this less voluble[318] earth,
595   By shorter flight to the east, had left him there,
596   Arraying with reflected purple and gold
597   The clouds that on his western throne attend.
598   Now came still[319] ev'ning on, and twilight gray
599   Had in her sober livery[320] all things clad.[321]
600   Silence accompanied, for beast and bird,
601   They to their grassy couch, these to their nests
602   Were slunk, all but the wakeful nightingale:
603   She all night long her amorous descant[322] sung.
604   Silence was pleased. Now glowed the firmament
605   With living sapphires. Hesperus,[323] that led
606   The starry host, rode brightest, till the moon,
607   Rising in clouded majesty, at length
608   (Apparent[324] queen) unveiled her peerless light,

---

[312] watch, guard
[313] meridian hour = noon
[314] disposed, thinking, intending
[315] responsibility: i.e., to his post
[316] daily: i.e., as it does every day
[317] or else
[318] rolling, revolving
[319] silent, quiet [adjective]
[320] sober livery = grave/solemn/sedate uniform/style of dress
[321] "had clad all things in her sober livery"
[322] melodious song
[323] brightest of the early evening stars
[324] manifest, obvious

609	And o'er the dark her silver mantle threw.
610	When Adam thus to Eve: "Fair consort, th' hour
611	Of night, and all things now retired to rest,
612	Mind[325] us of like[326] repose, since God hath set
613	Labor and rest, as day and night, to men
614	Successive,[327] and the timely dew of sleep,
615	Now falling with soft slumbrous weight, inclines[328]
616	Our eye-lids. Other creatures all day long
617	Rove idle, unemployed, and less need rest;
618	Man hath his daily work of body or mind
619	Appointed, which declares[329] his dignity,
620	And the regard[330] of Heav'n on all his ways,
621	While other animals unactive range,[331]
622	And of their doings God takes no account.
623	To-morrow, ere fresh morning streak the east
624	With first approach of light, we must be ris'n,
625	And at our pleasant labor, to reform[332]
626	Yon flow'ry arbors, yonder alleys[333] green,
627	Our walk at noon, with branches overgrown,
628	That mock our scant manuring,[334] and require
629	More hands than ours to lop their wanton[335] growth.
630	Those blossoms also, and those dropping gums,
631	That lie bestrewn, unsightly and unsmooth,
632	Ask riddance, if we mean to tread with ease.
633	Meanwhile, as Nature wills, night bids us rest."
634	To whom thus Eve, with perfect beauty adorned:
635	"My author and disposer, what thou bid'st
636	Unargued I obey. So God ordains:
637	God is thy law, thou mine. To know no more
638	Is woman's happiest knowledge, and her praise.
639	With thee conversing I forget all time;

---

[325] think, remind
[326] similar
[327] one after another
[328] bends downward
[329] makes known
[330] observant attention
[331] move hither and thither
[332] prune
[333] passages, walks
[334] tilling, cultivating
[335] luxuriant

640   All seasons, and their change, all please alike.
641   Sweet is the breath of morn, her rising sweet,
642   With charm[336] of earliest birds. Pleasant the sun,
643   When first on this delightful land he spreads
644   His orient[337] beams, on herb, tree, fruit, and flow'r,
645   Glistering with dew. Fragrant the fertile earth
646   After soft showers, and sweet the coming on
647   Of grateful[338] evening mild, then silent night,
648   With this her solemn bird, and this fair moon,
649   And these the gems of Heav'n, her starry train.
650   But neither breath of morn, when she ascends
651   With charm[339] of earliest birds, nor rising sun
652   On this delightful land, nor herb, fruit, flow'r,
653   Glistering with dew, nor fragrance after showers,
654   Nor grateful ev'ning mild, nor silent night,
655   With this her solemn bird, nor walk by moon,
656   Or glittering star-light, without thee is sweet.
657   "But wherefore all night long shine these? For whom
658   This glorious sight, when sleep hath shut all eyes?"
659   To whom our general[340] ancestor replied:
660   "Daughter of God and man, accomplished[341] Eve,
661   These have their course to finish round the earth,
662   By morrow ev'ning, and from land to land
663   In order, though to nations yet unborn.
664   Minist'ring[342] light prepared,[343] they set and rise,
665   Lest total darkness should by night regain
666   Her old possession, and extinguish life
667   In Nature and all things, which these soft fires
668   Not only enlighten,[344] but with kindly[345] heat

---

[336] blended song, of multiple origin
[337] bright
[338] pleasing
[339] see footnote 336, above
[340] universal, common
[341] perfect, fulfilled
[342] furnishing, supplying
[343] ready [adjective]
[344] illuminate
[345] (1) natural, (2) benevolent

669 Of various[346] influence[347] foment[348] and warm,
670 Temper or nourish, or in part shed down
671 Their stellar virtue[349] on all kinds[350] that grow
672 On earth, made hereby apter[351] to receive
673 Perfection from the sun's more potent[352] ray.
674 These then, though unbeheld in deep of night,
675 Shine not in vain, nor think,[353] though men were none,
676 That Heav'n would want[354] spectators, God want praise.
677 Millions of spiritual creatures walk the earth
678 Unseen, both when we wake, and when we sleep:
679 All these with ceaseless praise His works behold
680 Both day and night. How often from the steep[355]
681 Of echoing hill or thicket have we heard
682 Celestial voices to the midnight air,
683 Sole, or responsive each to others' note,
684 Singing their great Creator? Oft in bands
685 While they keep watch, or nightly rounding walk,[356]
686 With Heav'nly touch of instrumental sounds
687 In full harmonic number[357] joined, their songs
688 Divide[358] the night, and lift our thoughts to Heav'n."
689   Thus talking, hand in hand alone they passed
690 On to their blissful bower. It was a place
691 Chosen by the sov'reign Planter,[359] when He framed
692 All things to man's delightful use. The roof
693 Of thickest covert[360] was inwoven shade,
694 Laurel and myrtle, and what higher grew
695 Of firm and fragrant leaf, on either side
696 Acanthus, and each odorous bushy shrub,

---

[346] variable, varying
[347] disposition, temperament (i.e., astrologically)
[348] rouse/stir up with heat
[349] qualities, powers
[350] the species
[351] better fit/suited
[352] powerful, mighty
[353] should you think
[354] lack
[355] height, slope
[356] rounding walk = walking round
[357] musical periods/groups of notes
[358] into watches
[359] proprietor
[360] covering

697	Fenced up the verdant wall. Each beauteous flow'r,
698	Iris all hues, roses, and jessamin,
699	Reared high their flourished[361] heads between, and wrought[362]
700	Mosaic. Underfoot the violet,
701	Crocus, and hyacinth, with rich inlay
702	Broidered[363] the ground, more colored than with stone
703	Of costliest emblem.[364] Other creature here,
704	Bird, beast, insect, or worm, durst enter none,
705	Such was their awe of man. In shadier bower
706	More sacred and sequestered, though but feigned,[365]
707	Pan or Sylvanus never slept, nor nymph
708	Nor Faunus[366] haunted. Here, in close[367] recess,[368]
709	With flowers, garlands, and sweet-smelling herbs,
710	Espousèd[369] Eve decked first her nuptial bed,
711	And Heav'nly choirs the hymenaean[370] sung,
712	What day[371] the genial[372] Angel to our sire
713	Brought her in naked beauty more adorned,
714	More lovely, than Pandora,[373] whom the gods
715	Endowed with all their gifts, and O! too like
716	In sad event, when to the unwiser son[374]
717	Of Japhet[375] brought by Hermes,[376] she ensnared
718	Mankind with her fair looks, to be[377] avenged

---

[361] adorned
[362] made, shaped
[363] embroidered
[364] i.e., inlaid with precious gems
[365] though but feigned = even if only in fables
[366] pastoral god of vegetation and agriculture, who had goat horns and legs
[367] intimate
[368] seclusion, withdrawal, retirement
[369] married
[370] wedding hymn
[371] what day = on the day
[372] (1) festive, kindly, (2) nuptial
[373] Pandora ("all gifts"), whose box of gifts, when opened, let loose all ills upon the world
[374] she was brought to Epimetheus ("afterthought"), brother of Prometheus ("forethought")
[375] Iapetus, a Titan
[376] Jove's messenger
[377] to be = in order to be

719   On him[378] who had stole Jove's authentic[379] fire.
720   Thus at their shady lodge[380] arrived, both stood,
721   Both turned, and under open sky adored[381]
722   The God that made both sky, air, earth, and Heav'n,
723   Which they beheld, the moon's resplendent globe
724   And starry pole: "Thou also mad'st the night,
725   Maker Omnipotent, and Thou the day,
726   Which we, in our appointed work employed,
727   Have finished, happy in our mutual help
728   And mutual love, the crown of all our bliss
729   Ordained by Thee. And this delicious[382] place
730   For us too large, where thy abundance wants[383]
731   Partakers, and uncropped[384] falls to the ground.
732   But thou hast promised from us two a race
733   To fill the earth, who shall with us extol
734   Thy goodness infinite, both when we wake,
735   And when we seek, as now, Thy gift of sleep."
736   This said unanimous, and other rites
737   Observing none, but adoration pure
738   (Which God likes best), into their inmost bow'r
739   Handed[385] they went and, eased[386] the putting off
740   These troublesome disguises which we wear,
741   Straight side by side were laid, nor turned, I ween,[387]
742   Adam from his fair spouse, nor Eve the rites
743   Mysterious of connubial love refused,
744   Whatever hypocrites austerely talk
745   Of purity, and place, and innocence,
746   Defaming as impure what God declares
747   Pure, and commands to some, leaves free to all.
748   Our Maker bids increase: who bids abstain
749   But our destroyer, foe to God and man?
750   Hail, wedded love, mysterious law, true source

---

[378] Prometheus
[379] truly created by Jove
[380] hut, cottage, house
[381] venerated
[382] wonderfully pleasant
[383] lacks
[384] unreaped
[385] joined hand in hand
[386] relieved/set free of
[387] believe, suppose

751 Of human offspring, sole propriety[388]
752 In Paradise of all things common[389] else!
753 By thee adulterous lust was driv'n from men
754 Among the bestial herds to range.[390] By thee
755 Founded in reason, loyal, just, and pure,
756 Relations[391] dear, and all the charities[392]
757 Of father, son, and brother, first were known.
758 Far be it, that I should write[393] thee sin or blame,
759 Or think thee unbefitting holiest place,
760 Perpetual fountain of domestic sweets,
761 Whose bed is undefiled and chaste pronounced,
762 Present, or past, as saints and patriarchs used.
763 Here love his golden shafts[394] employs, here lights
764 His constant[395] lamp, and waves his purple wings,
765 Reigns here and revels, not in the bought smile
766 Of harlots, loveless, joyless, unendeared,
767 Casual fruition,[396] nor in court-amours,
768 Mixed dance, or wanton[397] masque, or midnight ball,
769 Or serenade, which the starved lover sings
770 To his proud fair, best quitted with disdain.
771 These, lulled by nightingales, embracing slept,
772 And on their naked limbs the flow'ry roof
773 Show'red roses, which the morn repaired.[398] Sleep on,
774 Blest pair! and O! yet happiest, if ye seek
775 No happier state, and know to know no more!
776 Now had night measured with her shadowy cone[399]
777 Halfway up hill this vast sublunar vault,[400]
778 And from their ivory port[401] the Cherubim,

---

[388] property
[389] held in common
[390] wander
[391] kinship
[392] natural affections
[393] describe, call
[394] arrows
[395] steadfast, faithful, true
[396] enjoyment
[397] unchaste, lascivious
[398] renewed, replaced
[399] the earth's shadow
[400] arch (the sky)
[401] Paradise's eastern gate

779 Forth issuing at the accustomed hour, stood armed
780 To their night watches in warlike parade,
781 When Gabriel to his next in power thus spoke:
782   "Uzziel,[402] half these draw off, and coast the
                south
783 With strictest watch. These other wheel[403] the north;
784 Our circuit meets full west." As[404] flame they part,
785 Half wheeling to the shield, half to the spear.[405]
786 From these, two strong and subtle Spirits he called
787 That near him stood, and gave them thus in charge:
788   "Ithuriel[406] and Zephon,[407] with wingèd speed
789 Search through this garden, leave unsearched no nook,
790 But chiefly where those two fair creatures lodge,
791 Now laid perhaps asleep, secure of[408] harm.
792 This ev'ning from[409] the sun's decline arrived
793 Who tells[410] of some infernal Spirit seen
794 Hitherward bent[411] (who could have thought?), escaped
795 The bars of Hell, on errand bad no doubt.
796 Such, where ye find, seize fast, and hither bring."
797   So saying, on he led his radiant files,[412]
798 Dazzling the moon. These to the bower direct
799 In search of whom they sought, him[413] there they found
800 Squat[414] like a toad, close at[415] the ear of Eve,
801 Assaying[416] by his devilish art to reach
802 The organs of her fancy, and with them forge
803 Illusions, as he list,[417] phantasms and dreams,

---

[402] "Strength of God"
[403] move, turn to
[404] like
[405] the shield was worn on the left arm; the spear was held in the right
[406] "Discovery of God"
[407] "Searcher of Secrets"
[408] secure of = protected/safe from
[409] from the time of
[410] who tells = one (Uriel) who tells
[411] headed, bound
[412] ranks/rows of armed angels
[413] Satan
[414] crouching
[415] close at = near
[416] trying
[417] desired, wished

804 Or if,[418] inspiring[419] venom, he might taint[420]
805 The animal spirits that from pure blood arise
806 Like gentle breaths from rivers pure, thence raise
807 At least distempered,[421] discontented thoughts,
808 Vain hopes, vain aims, inordinate desires,
809 Blown up with high conceits engend'ring pride.
810 Him thus intent, Ithuriel with his spear
811 Touched lightly, for no falsehood can endure
812 Touch of celestial temper,[422] but returns
813 Of force[423] to its own likeness. Up he starts,[424]
814 Discovered and surprised.[425] As when a spark
815 Lights on a heap of nitrous powder,[426] laid[427]
816 Fit for the tun[428] some magazine[429] to store
817 Against a rumored war, the smutty[430] grain,[431]
818 With sudden blaze diffused,[432] inflames the air,
819 So started up in his own shape the fiend.
820 Back stepped those two fair Angels, half amazed[433]
821 So sudden to behold the grisly[434] king,
822 Yet thus, unmoved with fear, accost[435] him soon:[436]
823   "Which of those rebel Spirits adjudged[437] to Hell
824 Com'st thou, escaped thy prison? And, transformed,
825 Why sat'st thou like an enemy in wait,
826 Here watching at the head of these that sleep?"
827   "Know ye not then," said Satan, filled with scorn,

---

[418] whether
[419] blowing, breathing
[420] infect, corrupt
[421] disordered, ill-humored, deranged
[422] hardening
[423] necessity
[424] leaps, bounds, jumps
[425] caught unawares
[426] nitrous powder = gunpowder
[427] piled up, heaped
[428] barrel, cask
[429] military warehouse
[430] blackened
[431] powder of a granular texture: i.e., gunpowder
[432] sent forth
[433] overwhelmed
[434] horrible, ghastly
[435] address
[436] quickly, without delay
[437] sentenced, condemned

828   "Know ye not me? Ye knew me once no mate[438]
829   For you, there[439] sitting where ye durst not soar.
830   Not to know me argues[440] yourselves unknown,
831   The lowest of your throng. Or if ye know,
832   Why ask ye, and superfluous begin
833   Your message, like to end as much in vain?"
834   To whom thus Zephon, answering scorn with scorn:
835   "Think not, revolted[441] Spirit, thy shape the
                     same,
836   Or undiminished brightness, to be known
837   As when thou stood'st in Heav'n upright and pure.
838   That glory then, when thou no more wast good,
839   Departed from thee, and thou resembl'st now
840   Thy sin and place of doom,[442] obscure and foul.
841   But come, for thou, be sure, shalt give account
842   To him who sent us, whose charge is to keep
843   This place inviolable, and these from harm."
844   So spoke the Cherub, and his grave rebuke,
845   Severe in youthful beauty, added grace
846   Invincible. Abashed the Devil stood,
847   And felt how awful[443] goodness is, and saw
848   Virtue in her shape how lovely, saw and pined[444]
849   His loss, but chiefly to find here observed
850   His luster visibly impaired, yet seemed
851   Undaunted. "If I must contend,"[445] said he,
852   "Best with the best, the sender, not the sent,
853   Or all at once. More glory will be won,
854   Or less be lost." "Thy fear," said Zephon bold,
855   "Will save us trial what the least can do
856   Single against thee wicked, and thence weak."
857   The fiend replied not, overcome with rage,
858   But like a proud steed reined, went haughty on,

---

[438] suitable companion
[439] i.e., in Heaven
[440] indicates
[441] rebel
[442] judgment
[443] sublime, majestic, impressive
[444] mourned
[445] fight

859   Champing[446] his iron curb.[447] To strive or fly[448]
860   He held it vain; awe[449] from above had quelled[450]
861   His heart, not else dismayed. Now drew they nigh
862   The western point, where those half-rounding guards
863   Just met, and closing stood in squadron joined,
864   Awaiting next command. To whom their chief,
865   Gabriel, from the front[451] thus called aloud:
866   "O friends! I hear the tread of nimble[452] feet
867   Hasting this way, and now by glimpse discern
868   Ithuriel and Zephon through the shade,
869   And with them comes a third of regal[453] port,[454]
870   But faded splendor wan,[455] who by his gait
871   And fierce demeanor seems the Prince of Hell,
872   Not likely to part[456] hence without contest.
873   Stand firm, for in his look defiance lours."[457]
874   He scarce had ended, when those two
                approached
875   And brief related whom they brought, where found,
876   How busied, in what form and posture couched.[458]
877   To whom with stern regard[459] thus Gabriel spoke:
878   "Why hast thou, Satan, broke the bounds prescribed
879   To thy transgressions, and disturbed the charge[460]
880   Of others, who approve[461] not to transgress
881   By thy example, but have power and right
882   To question thy bold entrance on this place,
883   Employed, it seems, to violate sleep, and those
884   Whose dwelling God hath planted here in bliss!"

---

446 gnashing, rattling
447 the strap/chain of a horse's bit
448 strive or fly = fight or flee
449 dread combined with wonder
450 overcome
451 front line
452 quick
453 royal, stately
454 carriage, bearing
455 pallid, gloomy
456 depart
457 scowls
458 crouching, lurking
459 look
460 responsibility
461 commend

885   To whom thus Satan, with contemptuous brow:

886   "Gabriel, thou had'st in Heav'n th' esteem[462] of wise,

887   And such I held thee. But this question asked

888   Puts me in doubt. Lives there who loves his pain?

889   Who would not, finding way, break loose from Hell,

890   Though thither doomed?[463] Thou would'st thyself, no doubt,

891   And boldly venture to whatever place

892   Farthest from pain, where thou might'st hope to change[464]

893   Torment with ease, and soonest recompense[465]

894   Dole[466] with delight, which in this place I sought.

895   To thee no reason, who know'st only good,

896   But evil hast not tried. And wilt object

897   His will who bound us? Let him surer[467] bar

898   His iron gates, if he intends our stay

899   In that dark durance.[468] Thus much what was asked.

900   The rest is true, they found me where they say,

901   But that implies not violence or harm."

902   Thus he in scorn. The warlike Angel, moved,[469]

903   Disdainfully half smiling, thus replied:

904   "O loss of one in Heav'n to judge of wise,[470]

905   Since Satan fell, whom folly overthrew,

906   And now returns him from his prison 'scaped,

907   Gravely in doubt whether to hold them wise

908   Or not, who ask what boldness brought him hither

909   Unlicensed[471] from his bounds[472] in Hell prescribed.

910   So wise he judges it to fly[473] from pain,

911   However,[474] and to 'scape his punishment!

912   So judge thou still, presumptuous! till the wrath,

---

[462] reputation
[463] sentenced
[464] exchange
[465] compensate, repay
[466] grief, sorrow
[467] more firmly/securely
[468] forced confinement, imprisonment
[469] provoked
[470] "What a loss in Heaven is one who can judge what wisdom is!"
[471] unauthorized, without permission
[472] boundaries, limits
[473] flee
[474] however he can

913   Which thou incurr'st by flying, meet[475] thy flight
914   Sevenfold, and scourge[476] that wisdom back to Hell,
915   Which taught thee yet no better, than no pain
916   Can equal anger infinite provoked.
917   But wherefore thou alone? Wherefore with thee
918   Came not all Hell broke loose? Is pain to them
919   Less pain, less to be fled, or thou than they
920   Less hardy[477] to endure? Courageous chief,
921   The first in flight from pain! Had'st thou alleged[478]
922   To thy deserted host this cause of flight,
923   Thou surely hadst not come sole fugitive."
924   To which the fiend thus answered, frowning
                stern:
925   "Not that I less endure, or shrink from pain,
926   Insulting Angel! Well thou know'st I stood
927   Thy fiercest, when in battle to thy aid
928   The blasting vollied thunder made all speed[479]
929   And seconded[480] thy else[481] not dreaded spear.
930   But still thy words at random,[482] as before,
931   Argue thy inexperience what[483] behooves[484]
932   From hard assays[485] and ill successes[486] past
933   A faithful leader, not to hazard all
934   Through ways[487] of danger by himself untried.
935   I, therefore, I alone first undertook
936   To wing[488] the desolate abyss, and spy
937   This new created world, whereof in Hell
938   Fame[489] is not silent, here in hope to find
939   Better abode, and my afflicted Powers

---

[475] oppose
[476] whip, lash
[477] courageous
[478] declared
[479] hurry
[480] reinforced
[481] otherwise
[482] thy words at random = thy careless/heedless words
[483] as to what
[484] is needful/required of . . . a faithful leader
[485] attempts, experiments
[486] results
[487] courses, directions, roads, paths
[488] fly
[489] rumor, report

940   To settle here on earth, or in mid air,
941   Though[490] for possession put[491] to try once more
942   What thou and thy gay legions dare against,
943   Whose easier business were to serve their Lord
944   High up in Heav'n, with songs to hymn His throne,
945   And practised distances to cringe, not fight."
946   To whom the warrior Angel soon[492] replied:
947   "To say and straight unsay, pretending first
948   Wise to fly[493] pain, professing[494] next the spy,
949   Argues[495] no leader but a liar traced,[496]
950   Satan—and couldst thou faithful add? O name,
951   O sacred name of faithfulness profaned!
952   Faithful to whom? To thy rebellious crew?
953   Army of fiends, fit body to fit head!
954   Was this your discipline and faith engaged,
955   Your military obedience, to dissolve
956   Allegiance to th' acknowledged Power supreme?
957   And thou, sly hypocrite, who now would'st seem
958   Patron of liberty, who more than thou
959   Once fawned, and cringed, and servilely[497] adored
960   Heav'n's awful[498] Monarch? Wherefore,[499] but in hope
961   To dispossess Him, and thyself to reign?
962   But mark what I agreed[500] thee now. Avaunt![501]
963   Fly thither whence thou fled'st! If from this hour
964   Within these hallowed limits[502] thou appear,
965   Back to the infernal pit I drag thee chained,
966   And seal[503] thee so as henceforth not to scorn
967   The facile[504] gates of Hell too slightly barred."

---

[490] even if
[491] forced, pushed
[492] quickly
[493] flee
[494] declare oneself
[495] indicates
[496] found, searched out
[497] slavelike, meanly
[498] dread
[499] why
[500] counsel
[501] leave!
[502] boundaries
[503] fasten
[504] (1) easy, (2) courteous

968   So threatened he, but Satan to no threats
969   Gave heed, but waxing[505] more in rage[506] replied:
970   "Then when I am thy captive, talk of chains,
971   Proud limitary[507] Cherub! But ere then
972   Far heavier load[508] thyself expect to feel
973   From my prevailing[509] arm, though Heaven's King
974   Ride on thy wings, and thou with thy compeers,[510]
975   Used to the yoke, draw'st His triumphant wheels
976   In progress through the road of Heav'n star-paved."
977   While thus he spoke, the angelic squadron bright
978   Turned fiery red, sharp'ning in moonèd horns[511]
979   Their phalanx,[512] and began to hem him round
980   With ported[513] spears, as thick as when a field
981   Of Ceres,[514] ripe for harvest, waving[515] bends
982   Her bearded grove of ears which way the wind
983   Sways[516] them. The careful ploughman doubting stands,
984   Lest on the threshing floor his hopeful sheaves[517]
985   Prove chaff. On th' other side, Satan, alarmed,[518]
986   Collecting all his might, dilated[519] stood,
987   Like Teneriffe[520] or Atlas,[521] unremoved.[522]
988   His stature reached the sky, and on his crest
989   Sat horror plumed,[523] nor wanted[524] in his grasp
990   What seemed both spear and shield. Now dreadful deeds
991   Might have ensued, nor only Paradise

---

[505] growing
[506] in rage = enraged
[507] guardian of boundaries
[508] material force
[509] superior, stronger
[510] comrades
[511] moonèd horns = crescent formation
[512] close-packed battle array, sixteen-man-deep square, perfected by the Romans
[513] raised/lifted and at the ready
[514] grain (metaphorical use of the goddess' name)
[515] [adverb]
[516] swings
[517] bundles
[518] alert
[519] (1) wings extended, (2) expanded in size
[520] high peak in the Canary Islands
[521] Mt. Atlas in Mauritania, Africa
[522] (1) holding his ground, (2) unremovable
[523] helmeted
[524] was lacking

992 In[525] this commotion, but the starry cope[526]
993 Of Heav'n, perhaps, or all the elements
994 At least had gone to wrack,[527] disturbed and torn
995 With violence of this conflict, had not soon[528]
996 Th' Eternal, to prevent such horrid fray,
997 Hung forth in Heav'n His golden scales,[529] yet[530] seen
998 Betwixt Astrea[531] and the Scorpion sign,
999 Wherein all things created first He weighed,
1000 The pendulous round earth with balanced air
1001 In counterpoise, now ponders[532] all events,
1002 Battles and realms. In these[533] he put two weights,
1003 The sequel[534] each of parting[535] and of fight.
1004 The latter quick up flew, and kicked the beam,[536]
1005 Which Gabriel spying, thus bespoke[537] the fiend:
1006   "Satan, I know thy strength, and thou know'st
                   mine—
1007 Neither our own, but giv'n. What folly then
1008 To boast what arms can do? since thine no more
1009 Than Heav'n permits, nor mine, though doubled now
1010 To trample thee as mire.[538] For proof look up,
1011 And read thy lot[539] in yon celestial sign,
1012 Where thou art weighed, and shown how light, how weak,
1013 If thou resist." The fiend looked up, and knew[540]
1014 His mounted scale aloft: nor more, but fled
1015 Murmuring,[541] and with him fled the shades of night.

The End of the Fourth Book

---

[525] involved in
[526] vault
[527] crash, collision, destruction
[528] quickly
[529] the constellation Libra ("the Scales") is between Scorpio and Virgo/Astrea
[530] still
[531] Virgo
[532] reflects upon, weighs
[533] i.e., the two pans of the scale
[534] result
[535] separating, breaking off
[536] the balance beam
[537] addressed
[538] mud
[539] destiny
[540] recognized
[541] grumbling, complaining, muttering

BOOK V

THE ARGUMENT

MORNING APPROACHED, EVE relates to Adam her troublesome dream; he likes it not, yet comforts her. They come forth to their day labors; their morning hymn at the door of their bower.

God to render man inexcusable[1] sends Raphael to admonish him of his obedience, of his free estate, of his enemy near at hand; who he is, and why his enemy, and whatever else may avail Adam to know. Raphael comes down to Paradise, his appearance described, his coming discerned by Adam afar off, sitting at the door of his bower; he goes out to meet him, brings him to his lodge, entertains him with the choicest fruits of Paradise got together by Eve; their discourse at table.

Raphael performs his message, minds Adam of his state and of his enemy; relates at Adam's request who that enemy is, and how he came to be so, beginning from his first revolt in Heaven, and the occasion thereof; how he drew his legions after him to the parts of the North, and there incited them to rebel with him, persuading all but only Abdiel, a Seraph, who in argument dissuades and opposes him, then forsakes him.

---

[1] i.e., responsible, without any excuse

1   Now morn, her rosy steps in the eastern clime[2]
2   Advancing, sowed the earth with orient[3] pearl,
3   When Adam waked, so customed,[4] for his sleep
4   Was airy-light, from pure digestion bred,[5]
5   And temperate[6] vapors[7] bland,[8] which th' only sound
6   Of leaves and fuming[9] rills, Aurora's[10] fan,
7   Lightly dispersed,[11] and the shrill matin[12] song
8   Of birds on every bough, so much the more
9   His wonder was to find unwakened Eve
10   With tresses discomposed, and glowing cheek,
11   As through unquiet rest. He, on his side
12   Leaning half raised, with looks of cordial[13] love
13   Hung over her enamored, and beheld
14   Beauty which, whether waking or asleep,
15   Shot forth peculiar[14] graces. Then with voice
16   Mild, as when Zephyrus[15] on Flora[16] breathes,
17   Her hand soft touching, whispered thus:
                      "Awake,
18   My fairest, my espoused, my latest found,
19   Heav'n's last best gift, my ever new delight!
20   Awake. The morning shines, and the fresh field
21   Calls us. We lose the prime,[17] to mark[18] how spring[19]
22   Our tender plants, how blows the citron grove,
23   What drops the myrrh,[20] and what the balmy reed,[21]

---

[2] region, realm
[3] bright, gleaming
[4] accustomed, in the habit
[5] produced, developed
[6] moderate
[7] exhalations of a digestive kind
[8] soft, mild
[9] giving off vapors—mist and evaporation
[10] goddess of morning
[11] Adam's exhalations were easily "dispersed" (dissipated, scattered) by the "fanning" motion of leaves and the "fuming" of running water
[12] morning
[13] heartfelt
[14] singular, special
[15] west wind/spring breeze
[16] goddess of flowers
[17] early morning (either dawn or about 6 A.M.)
[18] note, observe
[19] [verb]
[20] "what the myrrh tree (a gum resin) drops"
[21] here, a balsam (pine) tree

24 How Nature paints her colors, how the bee
25 Sits on the bloom extracting liquid sweet."
26   Such whispering waked her, but with startled eye
27 On Adam, whom embracing, thus she spoke:
28   "O sole in whom my thoughts find all repose,
29 My glory, my perfection! Glad I see
30 Thy face, and morn returned, for I this night
31 (Such night till this I never passed) have dreamed
32 (If dreamed) not, as I oft am wont,[22] of thee,
33 Works of day past, or morrow's next design,[23]
34 But of offence and trouble, which my mind
35 Knew never till this irksome[24] night. Methought
36 Close at mine ear one called me forth to walk,
37 With gentle voice; I thought it thine. It said,
38 'Why sleep'st thou, Eve? Now is the pleasant time,
39 The cool, the silent, save[25] where silence yields
40 To the night-warbling bird, that now awake
41 Tunes sweetest his love-labored song. Now reigns
42 Full-orbed the moon, and with more pleasing light
43 Shadowy sets off the face of things. In vain,
44 If none regard.[26] Heav'n wakes with all his eyes,
45 Whom to behold but thee, Nature's desire?
46 In whose sight all things joy,[27] with ravishment[28]
47 Attracted by thy beauty still to gaze.'
48 I rose as at thy call, but found thee not;
49 To find thee I directed then my walk,
50 And on, methought, alone I passed through ways
51 That brought me on a sudden to the tree
52 Of interdicted[29] knowledge. Fair it seemed,
53 Much fairer to my fancy than by day,
54 And as I wond'ring looked, beside it stood
55 One shaped and winged like one of those from Heav'n

---

[22] accustomed
[23] plan, aim
[24] wearisome, irritating, tiring, annoying
[25] except
[26] look
[27] [verb]
[28] ecstasy
[29] forbidden

56   By us oft seen. His dewy locks distilled[30]
57   Ambrosia. On that tree he also gazed,
58   And 'O fair plant,' said he, 'with fruit surcharged,[31]
59   Deigns none to ease thy load, and taste thy sweet,
60   Nor god, nor man? Is knowledge so despised?
61   Or envy, or what reserve[32] forbids to taste?
62   Forbid who will, none shall from me withhold
63   Longer thy offered good: why else set[33] here?'
64   This said, he paused not, but with venturous[34] arm
65   He plucked, he tasted; me damp[35] horror chilled
66   At such bold words vouched[36] with a deed so bold,
67   But he thus, overjoyed: 'O fruit divine,
68   Sweet of thyself, but much more sweet thus cropped,[37]
69   Forbidden here, it seems, as only fit
70   For gods, yet able to make gods of men.
71   And why not gods of men? Since good, the more
72   Communicated, more abundant grows,
73   The author[38] not impaired, but honored more?
74   Here, happy creature, fair angelic Eve!
75   Partake thou also. Happy though thou art,
76   Happier thou may'st be, worthier canst not be.
77   Taste this, and be henceforth among the gods
78   Thyself a goddess, not to earth confined,
79   But sometimes in the air, as we, sometimes
80   Ascend to Heav'n, by merit thine, and see
81   What life the gods live there, and such live thou!'
82   "So saying, he drew nigh, and to me held,
83   Ev'n to my mouth of that same fruit held part[39]
84   Which he had plucked. The pleasant savory smell
85   So quickened appetite that I, methought,
86   Could not but taste. Forthwith up to the clouds
87   With him I flew, and underneath beheld

---

[30] exuded, let fall
[31] overloaded
[32] imposition of a limitation
[33] is it set
[34] venturesome
[35] dazed, depressing
[36] declared
[37] plucked
[38] instigator, the Creator
[39] a portion of

88   The earth outstretched immense, a prospect wide
89   And various, wond'ring at my flight and change
90   To this high exaltation. Suddenly
91   My guide was gone, and I, methought, sunk down,
92   And fell asleep. But O, how glad I waked
93   To find this but a dream!" Thus Eve her night
94   Related, and thus Adam answered, sad:[40]
95   "Best image of myself, and dearer half,
96   The trouble of thy thoughts this night in sleep
97   Affects me equally, nor can I like
98   This uncouth[41] dream, of evil sprung, I fear.
99   Yet evil whence? In thee can harbor none,
100 Created pure. But know that in the soul
101 Are many lesser faculties, that serve
102 Reason as chief; among these Fancy[42] next[43]
103 Her office[44] holds. Of all external things
104 Which the five watchful[45] senses represent,[46]
105 She forms imaginations, airy shapes,
106 Which reason, joining or disjoining, frames
107 All what we affirm or what deny, and call[47]
108 Our knowledge or opinion, then retires
109 Into her private cell, when Nature rests.
110 Oft, in her absence, mimic Fancy wakes
111 To imitate her but, misjoining shapes,
112 Wild work produces oft, and most in dreams,
113 Ill matching words and deeds long past or late.[48]
114 Some such resemblances, methinks, I find
115 Of our last evening's talk, in this thy dream,
116 But with addition strange. Yet be not sad.[49]
117 Evil into the mind of god or man
118 May come and go, so unapproved, and leave
119 No spot or blame behind. Which gives me hope

---

[40] firmly, soberly
[41] unusual, unfamiliar, strange
[42] imagination
[43] closest, nearest
[44] function
[45] vigilant
[46] bring before the mind
[47] what we call
[48] recent
[49] dismal

120   That what in sleep thou didst abhor to dream,
121   Waking thou never will consent to do.
122   Be not disheartened, then, nor cloud those looks
123   That wont to be more cheerful and serene
124   Than when fair morning first smiles on the world.
125   And let us to our fresh employments rise
126   Among the groves, the fountains, and the flowers
127   That open now their choicest bosomed[50] smells,
128   Reserved from night, and kept for thee in store."
129   So cheered he his fair spouse, and she was
                                cheered.
130   But silently a gentle tear let fall
131   From either eye, and wiped them with her hair.
132   Two other precious drops that ready stood,
133   Each in their crystal sluice,[51] he ere they fell
134   Kissed, as the gracious signs of sweet remorse
135   And pious awe, that feared to have offended.
136   So all was cleared, and to the field they haste.
137   But first, from under shady arborous roof
138   Soon as they forth were come to open sight
139   Of day-spring, and the sun, who scarce up-risen,
140   With wheels yet hov'ring o'er the ocean-brim,
141   Shot parallel to the earth his dewy ray,
142   Discovering[52] in wide landscape all the east
143   Of Paradise and Eden's happy plains,
144   Lowly they bowed adoring, and began
145   Their orisons,[53] each morning duly paid
146   In various[54] style, for neither various style
147   Nor holy rapture wanted[55] they to praise
148   Their Maker, in fit[56] strains[57] pronounced, or sung
149   Unmeditated, such prompt[58] eloquence
150   Flowed from their lips, in prose or numerous[59] verse,

---

[50] hidden, confined
[51] a dam or any device holding back water
[52] disclosing (i.e., making visible, after the darkness of night)
[53] prayers
[54] different, variable, changing
[55] lacked
[56] suitable, appropriate
[57] (1) flow of impassioned language, (2) style
[58] ready and willing
[59] metrical

151 More tuneable[60] than needed lute or harp
152 To add more sweetness. And they thus began:
153   "These are Thy glorious works, Parent of good,
154 Almighty! Thine this universal frame,[61]
155 Thus wondrous fair. Thyself how wondrous then!
156 Unspeakable, who sit'st above these Heav'ns
157 To us invisible, or dimly seen
158 In these Thy lowest works. Yet these declare
159 Thy goodness beyond thought, and power divine.
160 Speak ye who best can tell, ye sons of light,
161 Angels, for ye behold Him, and with songs
162 And choral symphonies,[62] day without night,
163 Circle His throne rejoicing, ye in Heav'n!
164 On earth join all ye creatures to extol
165 Him first, Him last, Him midst, and without end!
166 Fairest of stars,[63] last in the train of night
167 (If better thou belong not to the dawn),
168 Sure pledge[64] of day that crown'st the smiling morn
169 With thy bright circlet,[65] praise Him in thy sphere,
170 While day arises, that sweet hour of prime.[66]
171 Thou sun, of this great world both eye and soul,
172 Acknowledge Him thy greater, sound His praise
173 In thy eternal course, both when thou climb'st
174 And when high noon hast gained,[67] and when thou fall'st.
175 Moon, that now meet'st the orient[68] sun, now fly'st[69]
176 With the fixed stars, fixed in their orb that flies,[70]
177 And ye five other wand'ring[71] fires[72] that move
178 In mystic dance not without song, resound

---

[60] tuneful, musical
[61] structure, fabric
[62] harmonious music
[63] Venus (as morning star, called Lucifer; as evening star, called Hesperus)
[64] promise
[65] gemlike headband
[66] early morning (either dawn or about 6 A.M.)
[67] attained, achieved, reached
[68] gleaming, bright
[69] flees (it)
[70] moves quickly (rotating once every twenty-four hours)
[71] i.e., not having fixed orbits
[72] the known planets: Mercury, Venus, Mars, Saturn, Jupiter

179   His praise, who out of darkness called up light.
180   Air, and ye Elements, the eldest birth
181   Of Nature's womb, that in quaternion[73] run
182   Perpetual circle, multiform, and mix
183   And nourish all things: let your ceaseless change
184   Vary,[74] to our great Maker still new praise.
185   Ye mists and exhalations that now rise
186   From hill or steaming lake, dusky or gray,
187   Till the sun paint your fleecy skirts with gold,
188   In honor to the world's great Author rise,
189   Whether to deck with clouds the uncolored[75] sky,
190   Or wet the thirsty earth with falling showers,
191   Rising or falling still advance His praise.
192   His praise, ye winds, that from four quarters blow,
193   Breathe soft or loud. And wave your tops, ye pines,
194   With every plant, in sign of worship wave!
195   Fountains,[76] and ye that warble as ye flow,
196   Melodious murmurs, warbling tune[77] His praise.
197   Join voices, all ye living souls! Ye birds,
198   That singing up to Heaven-gate ascend,
199   Bear on your wings, and in your notes, His praise.
200   Ye that in waters glide, and ye that walk
201   The earth, and stately tread, or lowly creep,
202   Witness[78] if I be silent, morn or ev'n,
203   To hill, or valley, fountain, or fresh shade,
204   Made vocal[79] by my song, and taught His praise.
205   Hail, universal Lord, be bounteous still[80]
206   To give us only good. And if the night
207   Have gathered aught of evil, or concealed,
208   Disperse it, as now light dispels the dark!"
209   So prayed they innocent, and to their thoughts

---

[73] in fourfold combination
[74] exhibit divergence
[75] not of different colors, but only of one
[76] more usually used for "streams, brooks," than in the modern meaning of a man-made device
[77] sing
[78] testify, give evidence
[79] made vocal = sounded, turned into/endowed with music
[80] always

210   Firm peace recovered soon, and wonted[81] calm.
211   On to their morning's rural[82] work they haste,
212   Among sweet dews and flow'rs, where any row
213   Of fruit-trees over-woody reached too far
214   Their pampered boughs,[83] and needed hands to check
215   Fruitless[84] embraces.[85] Or they led the vine
216   To wed her elm; she, spoused, about him twines
217   Her marriageable arms, and with him brings
218   Her dow'r, th' adopted[86] clusters,[87] to adorn
219   His barren[88] leaves. Them thus employed beheld
220   With pity Heav'n's high King,[89] and to him called
221   Raphael, the sociable Spirit that deigned
222   To travel with Tobias, and secured
223   His marriage with the seven-times-wedded maid.[90]
224   "Raphael," said He, "thou hear'st what stir on
              earth
225   Satan, from Hell 'scaped through the darksome gulf,
226   Hath raised in Paradise, and how disturbed
227   This night the human pair, how he designs[91]
228   In them at once to ruin all mankind.
229   Go, therefore: half this day as friend with friend
230   Converse with Adam, in what bow'r or shade
231   Thou find'st him from the heat of noon retired,
232   To respite[92] his day-labor with repast[93]
233   Or with repose, and such discourse bring on
234   As may advise him of his happy state,
235   Happiness in his power left free to will,
236   Left to his own free will, his will though free,
237   Yet mutable.[94] Whence warn him to beware

---

[81] accustomed, usual, habitual
[82] agricultural, pastoral
[83] pampered boughs = crammed with boughs
[84] without offspring
[85] entangled branches?
[86] the elm becomes the stepparent of the vine's "children," her bunches of grapes
[87] bunches (of grapes)
[88] unproductive
[89] "With pity, Heaven's High King (God) beheld Adam and Eve thus employed"
[90] see Book IV, above, at lines 168–71
[91] plans, schemes
[92] relieve
[93] food, a meal
[94] unsettled, fickle, variable, subject to change or alteration

238 He swerve not, too secure.[95] Tell him withal[96]
239 His danger, and from whom—what enemy,
240 Late fall'n himself from Heav'n, is plotting now
241 The fall of others from like state of bliss.
242 By violence? No, for that shall be withstood,[97]
243 But by deceit and lies. This let him know
244 Lest, wilfully transgressing, he pretend[98]
245 Surprisal, unadmonished,[99] unforewarned."
246   So spoke the Eternal Father, and fulfilled[100]
247 All justice. Nor delayed the wingèd Saint
248 After his charge[101] received, but from among
249 Thousand celestial Ardors,[102] where he stood
250 Veiled[103] with his gorgeous[104] wings, up springing light,
251 Flew through the midst of Heav'n. Th' angelic choirs,
252 On each hand parting, to his speed gave way
253 Through all th' empyreal road, till at the gate
254 Of Heav'n arrived, the gate self-opened wide
255 On golden hinges turning, as by work
256 Divine the sov'reign Architect had framed.[105]
257 From hence no cloud, or to obstruct his sight,
258 Star interposed,[106] however small, he sees,
259 Not unconform[107] to other shining globes,
260 Earth, and the garden of God, with cedars crowned
261 Above all hills. As when by night the glass
262 Of Galileo, less assured,[108] observes
263 Imagined lands and regions in the moon,
264 Or pilot from amidst the Cyclades[109]

---

[95] confident
[96] moreover, in addition
[97] resisted
[98] claim, put forward as an excuse
[99] unexhorted, uninformed
[100] satisfied, did, performed
[101] order, responsibility
[102] radiant spirits
[103] shrouded, covered
[104] brilliant, magnificent
[105] contrived, built, intended
[106] placed between
[107] corresponding
[108] competent
[109] islands in the south Aegean Sea

265   Delos[110] or Samos[111] first appearing, kens[112]
266   A cloudy spot. Down thither prone[113] in flight
267   He speeds, and through the vast ethereal sky
268   Sails between worlds and worlds, with steady wing
269   Now on the polar winds, then with quick fan[114]
270   Winnows[115] the buxom[116] air, till within soar[117]
271   Of tow'ring eagles, to all the fowls he seems
272   A phoenix,[118] gazed[119] by all as that sole[120] bird,
273   When, to enshrine his[121] relics in the sun's
274   Bright temple, to Egyptian Thebes he flies.
275   At once on th' eastern cliff of Paradise
276   He[122] lights, and to his proper shape returns,
277   A Seraph winged. Six wings he wore, to shade
278   His lineaments[123] divine. The pair that clad
279   Each shoulder broad, came mantling[124] o'er his breast
280   With regal ornament; the middle pair
281   Girt like a starry zone[125] his waist, and round
282   Skirted[126] his loins and thighs with downy[127] gold
283   And colors dipped[128] in Heav'n; the third his feet
284   Shadowed from either heel with feathered mail,
285   Sky-tinctured[129] grain.[130] Like Maia's son[131] he stood

---

[110] Greek island
[111] island off the coast of Asia Minor
[112] sees, identifies
[113] headlong
[114] wing
[115] beats
[116] flexible, unresisting
[117] the altitude attained in soaring
[118] mythical bird that perpetually renews its life, first burning its old body, then being reborn from the ashes
[119] stared at
[120] solitary
[121] the phoenix's
[122] Raphael
[123] features
[124] draped
[125] belt
[126] covered, bordered, edged
[127] soft
[128] dyed (by immersion)
[129] colored
[130] dye
[131] Hermes

286   And shook his plumes,[132] that[133] Heav'nly fragrance filled
287   The circuit wide.[134] Straight knew him all the bands
288   Of Angels under[135] watch, and to his state,
289   And to his message high, in honor rise,
290   For on some message high they guessed him bound.
291   Their glittering tents he passed, and now is come
292   Into the blissful[136] field, through groves of myrrh,
293   And flowering odors, cassia, nard,[137] and balm—
294   A wilderness of sweets. For Nature here
295   Wantoned[138] as in her prime, and played at will
296   Her virgin fancies, pouring forth more sweet,
297   Wild above[139] rule or art, enormous bliss.
298   Him through the spicy[140] forest onward come
299   Adam discerned, as in the door he sat
300   Of his cool bow'r, while now the mounted sun
301   Shot down direct his fervid[141] rays to warm
302   Earth's inmost womb, more warmth than Adam needs.
303   And Eve within, due[142] at her hour prepared
304   For dinner savory fruits, of taste to please
305   True appetite, and not disrelish[143] thirst
306   Of nectarous draughts between, from milky stream,
307   Berry or grape. To whom thus Adam called:
308   "Haste hither, Eve, and worth thy sight behold
309   Eastward among those trees, what glorious shape
310   Comes this way moving, seems another morn
311   Ris'n on mid-noon! Some great behest[144] from Heav'n
312   To us perhaps he brings, and will vouchsafe[145]
313   This day to be our guest. But go with speed,
314   And what thy stores contain bring forth, and pour

---

[132] plumage, feathers
[133] so that
[134] circuit wide = wide surrounding space
[135] participating in, performing
[136] blessed, beatified
[137] an aromatic balsam
[138] sported, played
[139] beyond
[140] aromatic
[141] burning, glowing
[142] properly
[143] render distasteful
[144] command
[145] condescend

315 Abundance, fit to honor and receive
316 Our Heav'nly stranger. Well we may afford
317 Our givers their own gifts, and large bestow[146]
318 From large[147] bestowed, where Nature multiplies
319 Her fertile growth, and by disburthening[148] grows
320 More fruitful, which instructs us not to spare."[149]
321 To whom thus Eve:
           "Adam, earth's hallowed[150] mold,[151]
322 Of God inspired, small store[152] will serve,[153] where store,
323 All seasons, ripe for use hangs on the stalk,
324 Save what by frugal[154] storing[155] firmness gains
325 To nourish, and superfluous[156] moist[157] consumes.
326 But I will haste, and from each bough and brake,[158]
327 Each plant and juiciest gourd, will pluck such choice
328 To entertain our Angel-guest, as he
329 Beholding shall confess, that here on earth
330 God hath dispensed His bounties as in Heav'n."'
331   So saying, with dispatchful[159] looks in haste
332 She turns, on hospitable[160] thoughts intent
333 What choice to choose for delicacy best,
334 What order, so contrived as not to mix
335 Tastes not well joined, inelegant, but bring
336 Taste after taste upheld[161] with kindliest[162] change.
337 Bestirs[163] her then, and from each tender stalk

---

[146] confer as a gift
[147] liberality, bounty
[148] discharging its load
[149] hoard
[150] holy, sanctified
[151] soil
[152] supply
[153] suffice
[154] careful
[155] laying by
[156] (1) unneeded, (2) excessive
[157] moisture
[158] thicket
[159] hurried, quick
[160] [four syllables, first and third accented]
[161] sustained, supported, confirmed
[162] most natural
[163] busies

338   Whatever earth, all-bearing mother, yields

339   In India east or west, or middle shore[164]

340   In Pontus[165] or the Punic[166] coast, or where

341   Alcinous[167] reigned, fruit of all kinds, in coat

342   Rough, or smooth rind, or bearded husk, or shell,

343   She gathers tribute[168] large, and on the board[169]

344   Heaps with unsparing hand. For drink the grape

345   She crushes, inoffensive must,[170] and mead

346   From many a berry, and from sweet kernels pressed

347   She tempers[171] dulcet[172] creams.[173] Nor these to hold

348   Wants[174] her fit[175] vessels pure. Then strews the ground

349   With rose and odors from the shrub unfumed.[176]

350   Meanwhile our primitive[177] great sire, to meet

351   His god-like guest, walks forth, without more train

352   Accompanied than with his own complete

353   Perfections. In himself was all his state,

354   More solemn[178] than the tedious pomp that waits

355   On princes, when their rich retinue long

356   Of horses led, and grooms besmeared with gold,

357   Dazzles the crowd, and sets them all agape.

358   Nearer his presence Adam, though not awed,

359   Yet with submiss[179] approach and reverence meek,

360   As to a superior nature bowing low,

361   Thus said:

                "Native of Heav'n, for other place

362   None can than Heav'n such glorious shape contain,

363   Since by descending from the thrones above

---

[164] Mediterranean

[165] the Black Sea

[166] Carthaginian/Phoenician (North African)

[167] king of the Phaeacian island, now Corfu

[168] homage, tax

[169] table

[170] unfermented juice

[171] mixes

[172] sweet

[173] smooth (creamy) and frothing liquids

[174] lacks

[175] suitable, appropriate

[176] not burned, as incense would be, since there was as yet no fire available to burn them

[177] original

[178] grand, imposing

[179] submissive, subdued

364 Those happy places thou hast deigned a while
365 To want,[180] and honor these, vouchsafe[181] with us
366 Two only, who yet by sov'reign gift possess
367 This spacious ground, in yonder shady bow'r
368 To rest, and what the garden choicest bears
369 To sit and taste, till this meridian[182] heat
370 Be over, and the sun more cool decline."[183]
371 Whom thus the angelic Virtue[184] answered mild:
372   "Adam, I therefore came, nor art thou such
373 Created, or such place hast here to dwell,
374 As may not oft invite, though Spirits of Heav'n,
375 To visit thee. Lead on, then, where thy bow'r
376 O'ershades, for these mid-hours, till evening rise,
377 I have at will."[185] So to the sylvan[186] lodge
378 They came, that like Pomona's[187] arbor[188] smiled,
379 With flow'rets decked, and fragrant smells. But Eve,
380 Undecked save with herself, more lovely fair
381 Than wood-nymph, or the fairest goddess feigned[189]
382 Of three that in mount Ida naked strove,[190]
383 Stood to entertain her guest from Heav'n. No veil[191]
384 She needed, virtue-proof: no thought infirm[192]
385 Altered her cheek. On whom the Angel "Hail"
386 Bestowed, the holy salutation used
387 Long after to blest Mary, second Eve:
388   "Hail, mother of mankind, whose fruitful womb
389 Shall fill the world more numerous with thy sons,
390 Than with these various fruits the trees of God
391 Have heaped this table!"
                    —Raised of grassy turf

---

[180] lack
[181] condescend
[182] noontime, midday
[183] sink down
[184] seventh of the nine angelic orders
[185] at will = as I please
[186] pastoral
[187] Roman goddess of fruits
[188] orchard, bower
[189] (1) from fables rather than real, (2) sham, because pagan
[190] a beauty competition among Hera, Athena, and Aphrodite; Paris, son of King Priam of Troy, gave the prize to Aphrodite
[191] "veil" could then mean "cloak" or "mantle"
[192] weak, shaky

392 Their table was, and mossy seats had round,
393 And on her ample square[193] from side to side
394 All autumn piled, though spring and autumn here
395 Danced hand in hand. A while discourse they hold—
396 No fear lest dinner cool—when thus began
397 Our author:[194]

                 "Heav'nly stranger, please to taste
398 These bounties,[195] which our Nourisher, from whom
399 All perfect good, unmeasured out, descends,
400 To us for food and for delight hath caused
401 The earth to yield—unsavory food perhaps
402 To spiritual natures. Only this I know,
403 That one celestial Father gives to all."
404 To whom the Angel:

               "Therefore what He gives
405 (Whose praise be ever sung) to man in part[196]
406 Spiritual, may of purest Spirits be found
407 No ungrateful[197] food. And food alike those pure
408 Intelligential substances require,
409 As doth your rational,[198] and both[199] contain
410 Within them every lower faculty
411 Of sense, whereby they hear, see, smell, touch, taste,
412 Tasting concoct,[200] digest, assimilate,
413 And corporeal to incorporeal turn.
414 For know, whatever was created, needs
415 To be sustained and fed. Of elements
416 The grosser feeds the purer, earth the sea,
417 Earth and the sea feed air, the air those fires
418 Ethereal, and as lowest first the moon,
419 Whence in her visage round[201] those spots, unpurged[202]

---

[193] table
[194] Adam
[195] generous gifts
[196] in part = who is in part
[197] distasteful, unwelcome
[198] as "rational" creatures, human beings are required to (and can) think in order to know; their knowledge is therefore of necessity partial. "Intelligential" creatures, however, are endowed with complete knowledge that is of their very essence
[199] both angels and men
[200] heat for digestive purposes
[201] [adjective]
[202] unpurified

420   Vapors not yet into her substance turned.
421   Nor doth the moon no nourishment exhale
422   From her moist continent[203] to higher orbs.
423   The sun, that light imparts to all, receives
424   From all[204] his alimental[205] recompence
425   In humid exhalations, and at ev'n[206]
426   Sups[207] with the ocean. Though in Heav'n the trees
427   Of life ambrosial fruitage bear, and vines
428   Yield nectar; though from off the boughs each morn
429   We brush mellifluous[208] dews, and find the ground
430   Covered with pearly grain; yet God hath here[209]
431   Varied His bounty so with new delights
432   As may compare with Heaven, and to taste
433   Think not I shall be nice."[210] So down they sat,
434   And to their viands[211] fell, nor seemingly[212]
435   The Angel, nor in mist,[213] the common gloss[214]
436   Of theologians, but with keen dispatch
437   Of real[215] hunger, and concoctive[216] heat
438   To transubstantiate.[217] What redounds,[218] transpires[219]
439   Through Spirits with ease—nor wonder, if by fire
440   Of sooty coal the empiric[220] alchemist
441   Can turn, or holds it possible to turn,
442   Metals of drossiest ore to perfect gold,
443   As from[221] the mine. Meanwhile at table Eve

---

[203] land
[204] everything else
[205] nutritional
[206] evening
[207] dines
[208] flowing as sweet as honey
[209] on earth, in the Garden of Eden
[210] fussy
[211] food
[212] so far as one can judge
[213] in mist = blurred (as an immaterial object)
[214] interpretation, explanation
[215] [bisyllabic]
[216] see footnote 200, above
[217] to turn corporeal to incorporeal, i.e., to make spiritual that which was material
[218] is excessive, superfluous
[219] is emitted/breathed/vaporized (i.e., passes through their "bodies," is excreted)
[220] lower-ranking, merely experimentally oriented (rather than the higher, theoretically oriented)
[221] as from = just as if it had come from

444   Ministered²²² naked, and their flowing cups
445   With pleasant liquors crowned.²²³ O innocence
446   Deserving Paradise! If ever, then,
447   Then had the sons of God excuse to have been
448   Enamored at that sight. But in those hearts
449   Love unlibidinous²²⁴ reigned, nor jealousy
450   Was understood, the injured lover's hell.
451   Thus when with meats²²⁵ and drinks they had
           sufficed,
452   Not burdened Nature,²²⁶ sudden mind arose
453   In Adam, not to let th' occasion pass
454   Giv'n him by this great conference²²⁷ to know
455   Of things above his world, and of their being
456   Who dwell in Heav'n, whose excellence he saw
457   Transcend his own so far, whose radiant forms,
458   Divine effulgence,²²⁸ whose high power, so far
459   Exceeded human. And his wary²²⁹ speech
460   Thus to the empyreal minister he framed:²³⁰
461   "Inhabitant with God, now know I well
462   Thy favor, in this honor done to man,
463   Under whose lowly roof thou hast vouchsafed²³¹
464   To enter, and these earthly fruits to taste,
465   Food not of Angels, yet accepted so
466   As that more willingly thou could'st not seem
467   At Heav'n's high feasts t' have fed. Yet what compare?"
468   To whom the wingèd Hierarch²³² replied:
469   "O Adam, one Almighty is, from whom
470   All things proceed, and up to Him return,
471   If not depraved²³³ from good, created all

---

²²² served
²²³ filled to overflowing
²²⁴ unlustful, unlecherous
²²⁵ food
²²⁶ i.e., their natures
²²⁷ conversation, meeting [trisyllabic, second accented]
²²⁸ splendid radiance
²²⁹ careful
²³⁰ shaped, articulated
²³¹ condescended
²³² member of the hierarch (order) of angels [trisyllabic, first and third accented]
²³³ perverted, corrupted

472   Such to perfection, one first[234] matter all,
473   Endued[235] with various forms, various degrees
474   Of substance and, in things that live, of life,
475   But more refined, more spiritous, and pure,
476   As nearer to Him placed, or nearer tending
477   Each in their several active spheres assigned,
478   Till body up to spirit work, in bounds[236]
479   Proportioned to each kind. So from the root
480   Springs lighter the green stalk, from thence the leaves
481   More airy, last the bright consummate[237] flower
482   Spirits odorous breathes. Flow'rs and their fruit,
483   Man's nourishment, by gradual scale sublimed,[238]
484   To vital spirits aspire, to animal,
485   To intellectual, give both life and sense,
486   Fancy and understanding, whence the soul
487   Reason receives, and reason is her being,
488   Discursive, or intuitive.[239] Discourse
489   Is oftest yours, the latter most is ours,
490   Differing but in degree, of kind the same.
491   Wonder not then, what God for you saw good
492   If I refuse not, but convert, as you,
493   To proper substance. Time may come when men
494   With Angels may participate, and find
495   No inconvenient[240] diet, nor too light fare.
496   And from these corporal nutriments perhaps
497   Your bodies may at last turn all to spirit,
498   Improved by tract[241] of time and, winged, ascend
499   Ethereal, as we. Or may, at choice,
500   Here or in Heav'nly Paradises dwell,
501   If ye be found obedient, and retain
502   Unalterably firm His love entire,
503   Whose[242] progeny[243] you are. Meanwhile enjoy

---

[234] earliest (primeval)
[235] invested, supplied
[236] upward jumps
[237] completed, perfected, supreme
[238] elevated, refined, purified
[239] complete instantaneous knowledge requiring no prior thought
[240] unsuitable, inappropriate
[241] duration
[242] He whose
[243] offspring

504   Your fill what[244] happiness this happy state
505   Can comprehend, incapable of more."
506   To whom the patriarch of mankind replied:
507   "O favorable Spirit, propitious[245] guest,
508   Well hast thou taught the way that might direct
509   Our knowledge, and the scale of Nature set
510   From center to circumference, whereon,
511   In contemplation of created things,
512   By steps we may ascend to God. But say,
513   What meant that caution joined,[246] 'If ye be found
514   Obedient?' Can we want[247] obedience then
515   To Him, or possibly His love desert,
516   Who formed us from the dust and placed us here
517   Full to the utmost measure of what bliss
518   Human desires can seek or apprehend?"
519   To whom the Angel:
                    "Son of Heav'n and earth,
520   Attend:[248] that thou art happy, owe to God;
521   That thou continuest such, owe to thyself—
522   That is, to thy obedience: therein stand.[249]
523   This was that caution given thee: be advised.[250]
524   God made thee perfect,[251] not immutable,[252]
525   And good He made thee, but to persevere
526   He left it in thy power, ordained thy will
527   By nature free, not overruled by fate
528   Inextricable,[253] or strict necessity.
529   Our voluntary service He requires,
530   Not our necessitated. Such with Him
531   Finds no acceptance, nor can find, for how
532   Can hearts, not free, be tried[254] whether they serve

---

[244] of what
[245] gracious, helpful
[246] added, annexed
[247] lack
[248] listen, follow me closely/carefully
[249] remain firm/steady
[250] hereby notified, warned
[251] complete
[252] unalterable
[253] from which one cannot extricate oneself
[254] tested

533 Willing or no, who will but what they must[255]
534 By destiny, and can no other choose?
535 Myself, and all th' Angelic host that stand
536 In sight of God enthroned, our happy state
537 Hold, as you yours, while our obedience holds,
538 On other surety[256] none. Freely we serve,
539 Because we freely love, as in our will
540 To love or not. In this we stand or fall,
541 And some are fall'n, to disobedience fall'n,
542 And so from Heav'n to deepest Hell. O fall[257]
543 From what high state of bliss, into what woe!"
544 To whom our great progenitor:[258]

                          "Thy words
545 Attentive, and with more delighted ear,
546 Divine instructor, I have heard, than when
547 Cherubic songs by night from neighboring hills
548 Aerial music send. Nor knew I not
549 To be both will and deed created free.
550 Yet that we never shall forget to love
551 Our Maker, and obey Him whose command,
552 Single,[259] is yet so just, my constant thoughts
553 Assured me, and still assure. Though what thou tellest
554 Hath passed in Heav'n, some doubt within me move,[260]
555 But more desire to hear, if thou consent,
556 The full relation,[261] which must needs be strange,
557 Worthy of sacred[262] silence to be heard.
558 And we have yet large[263] day,[264] for scarce the sun
559 Hath finished half his journey, and scarce begins
560 His other half in the great zone[265] of Heav'n."
561   Thus Adam made request, and Raphael,

---

[255] must will
[256] guarantee
[257] [noun]
[258] ancestor, forefather
[259] command, single = single command
[260] raise, stir up
[261] narrative
[262] dedicated
[263] ample, abundant
[264] daylight hours (since the angel has said, in line 376, that he will stay on earth "till evening rise")
[265] region, encircling band

562   After short pause assenting, thus began:
563   "High matter thou enjoin'st[266] me, O prime[267] of
                        men,
564   Sad[268] task and hard. For how shall I relate
565   To human sense the invisible exploits
566   Of warring Spirits? How, without remorse,[269]
567   The ruin of so many, glorious once,
568   And perfect while they stood? How last[270] unfold
569   The secrets of another world, perhaps
570   Not lawful to reveal? Yet for thy good
571   This is dispensed,[271] and what surmounts the reach
572   Of human sense I shall delineate[272] so,
573   By lik'ning spiritual to corporal forms,
574   As may express them best. Though what if earth
575   Be but a shadow[273] of Heav'n, and things therein
576   Each t' other like, more than on earth is thought?
577   "As yet this world was not, and Chaos wild
578   Reigned where these Heav'ns now roll, where earth now
                        rests
579   Upon her center poised, when on a day
580   (For time, though in eternity, applied
581   To motion, measures all things durable
582   By present, past, and future), on such day
583   As Heav'n's great year[274] brings forth, the empyreal[275] host
584   Of Angels by imperial summons called,
585   Innumerable before the Almighty's throne
586   Forthwith, from all the ends of Heav'n, appeared
587   Under their Hierarchs[276] in orders bright.
588   Ten thousand thousand ensigns[277] high advanced,

---

[266] impose on
[267] first, original
[268] sober, serious
[269] regretful remembrance
[270] finally, last of all
[271] permitted
[272] sketch, draw, portray
[273] for men, a foreshadowing
[274] calculated by Plato, in his *Republic*, as approximately thirty-six thousand years (i.e., when all the heavenly bodies have returned to their created starting points)
[275] celestial
[276] archangels
[277] banners, flags

589   Standards[278] and gonfalons[279] 'twixt van[280] and rear
590   Stream in the air, and for distinction serve[281]
591   Of hierarchies, of orders, and degrees,
592   Or in their glittering tissues[282] bear emblazed[283]
593   Holy memorials,[284] acts of zeal and love
594   Recorded eminent.[285] Thus when in orbs
595   Of circuit inexpressible they stood,
596   Orb within orb, the Father Infinite,
597   By whom in bliss embosomed[286] sat the Son,
598   Amidst as[287] from a flaming mount whose top
599   Brightness had made invisible, thus spoke:
600   " 'Hear, all ye Angels, progeny[288] of light,
601   Thrones, Dominations, Princedoms, Virtues, Powers!
602   Hear my decree, which unrevoked shall stand.[289]
603   This day I have begot[290] whom[291] I declare
604   My only Son, and on this holy hill
605   Him have anointed, whom ye now behold
606   At my right hand. Your head I him appoint,
607   And by myself have sworn, to him shall bow
608   All knees in Heav'n, and shall confess[292] him Lord.
609   Under his great vice-gerent[293] reign abide
610   United, as one individual soul,
611   Forever happy. Him who disobeys,
612   Me disobeys, breaks union, and that day,
613   Cast out from God and blessèd vision, falls

---

[278] military banner or flag
[279] banners with tails/streamers, suspended from a crossbar rather than a pole
[280] front, foremost
[281] for distinction serve = used in order to distinguish
[282] fabric, cloth
[283] inscribed
[284] [trisyllabic, second accented]
[285] prominently
[286] enclosed
[287] as if
[288] offspring
[289] unrevoked shall stand = shall stand unrevoked (not rescinded/annulled/withdrawn, etc.)
[290] called into being
[291] he whom
[292] acknowledge, avow
[293] gerent = ruler, manager

614   Into utter darkness, deep engulfed,[294] his place
615   Ordained without redemption, without end.'
616   "So spoke the Omnipotent, and with His words
617   All seemed well pleased—all seemed, but were not all.
618   That day, as other solemn days, they spent
619   In song and dance about the sacred hill,
620   Mystical dance, which yonder starry sphere
621   Of planets, and of fixed,[295] in all her wheels
622   Resembles nearest, mazes intricate,
623   Eccentric,[296] intervolved,[297] yet regular
624   Then most when most irregular they seem.
625   And in their motions harmony divine
626   So smooths[298] her[299] charming tones,[300] that God's own ear
627   Listens delighted. Ev'ning now approached
628   (For we have also our ev'ning and our morn,
629   We ours for change delectable,[301] not need).
630   Forthwith from dance to sweet repast they turn
631   Desirous, all in circles as they stood.
632   Tables are set, and on a sudden piled
633   With Angels' food, and rubied nectar flows
634   In pearl, in diamond,[302] and massy gold,
635   Fruit of delicious vines, the growth[303] of Heav'n.
636   On flow'rs reposed,[304] and with fresh flow'rets crowned,
637   They eat, they drink, and in communion[305] sweet
638   Quaff[306] immortality and joy, secure
639   Of[307] surfeit where full measure only bounds[308]
640   Excess, before the all-bounteous King, who show'red

---

[294] swallowed, buried
[295] fixed stars
[296] elliptical, irregular
[297] interwound
[298] frees from difficulties, invests with calm/placidity
[299] harmony divine's
[300] musical intervals
[301] delightful
[302] [trisyllabic, first and third accented]
[303] produce, product
[304] inclining, resting
[305] fellowship, sharing
[306] drink deeply of
[307] secure of = safe from
[308] limits

641   With copious[309] hand, rejoicing in their joy.
642   Now when ambrosial[310] night with clouds
                    exhaled
643   From that high mount of God, whence light and shade
644   Spring both, the face of brightest Heav'n had changed
645   To grateful[311] twilight (for night comes not there
646   In darker veil), and roseate[312] dews disposed[313]
647   All but the unsleeping eyes of God to rest.
648   Wide over all the plain, and wider far
649   Than all this globous[314] earth in plain outspread
650   (Such are the courts of God), th' Angelic throng,
651   Dispersed in bands and files, their camp extend
652   By living[315] streams among the trees of life,
653   Pavilions[316] numberless, and sudden reared,
654   Celestial tabernacles[317] where they slept,
655   Fanned with cool winds, save those who, in their
                    course,[318]
656   Melodious hymns about the sov'reign throne
657   Alternate all night long. But not so waked
658   Satan—so call him now, his former name
659   Is heard no more in Heav'n. He of[319] the first,
660   If not the first Arch-Angel, great in power,
661   In favor and pre-eminence, yet fraught[320]
662   With envy against the Son of God, that day
663   Honored by his great Father, and proclaimed
664   Messiah, King anointed, could not bear
665   Through pride that sight, and thought himself
                    impaired.[321]
666   Deep malice thence conceiving, and disdain,

---

[309] abundant
[310] (1) celestial, (2) divinely fragrant
[311] pleasing, agreeable
[312] (1) rose-colored, (2) rose-scented
[313] inclined, prepared
[314] spherical, globular
[315] (1) constantly flowing, (2) refreshing
[316] a kind of large tent
[317] tents
[318] turn, customary practice
[319] among
[320] filled
[321] lessened

667 Soon as midnight brought on the dusky hour
668 Friendliest to sleep and silence, he resolved
669 With all his legions to dislodge,[322] and leave
670 Unworshipped, unobeyed, the throne supreme,
671 Contemptuous. And his next subordinate[323]
672 Awak'ning, thus to him in secret spoke:
673   " 'Sleep'st thou, companion dear? What sleep
                  can close
674 Thy eye-lids, and[324] rememb'rest what decree
675 Of yesterday, so late hath passed the lips
676 Of Heav'n's Almighty? Thou to me thy thoughts
677 Wast wont,[325] I mine to thee was wont t' impart.[326]
678 Both waking,[327] we were one. How then can now
679 Thy sleep dissent?[328] New laws thou see'st imposed:
680 New laws from Him who reigns, new minds may raise
681 In us who serve, new counsels to debate
682 What doubtful may ensue. More in this place
683 To utter is not safe. Assemble thou
684 Of all those myriads[329] which we lead the chief.[330]
685 Tell them that by command, ere yet dim night
686 Her shadowy cloud withdraws, I am to haste,[331]
687 And all who under me their banners wave,
688 Homeward, with flying[332] march, where we possess[333]
689 The quarters[334] of the North, there to prepare
690 Fit entertainment to receive our King,
691 The great Messiah, and his new commands,
692 Who speedily through all the hierarchies[335]
693 Intends to pass triumphant, and give laws.'

---

[322] leave one's place of lodging (break camp)
[323] Beelzebub
[324] if you
[325] in the habit of
[326] make known, communicate
[327] both waking = both of us awake
[328] disagree, be at variance
[329] countless numbers
[330] the chief = the best part
[331] I am to haste . . . homeward = I will hurry . . . home
[332] (1) swift, (2) literally flying (through the air)
[333] hold, occupy
[334] (1) headquarters, (2) regions
[335] angelic orders

694   "So spoke the false Arch-Angel, and infused[336]
695   Bad influence[337] into th' unwary breast
696   Of his associate. He[338] together calls,
697   Or several[339] one by one,[340] the regent[341] Powers
698   Under him Regent;[342] tells, as he was taught,
699   That the Most High commanding, now ere night,
700   Now ere dim night had disincumbered[343] Heav'n,
701   The great hierarchal standard[344] was to move;
702   Tells the suggested cause, and casts between
703   Ambiguous words and jealousies, to sound[345]
704   Or taint[346] integrity. But all obeyed
705   The wonted[347] signal and superior voice[348]
706   Of their great Potentate,[349] for great indeed
707   His name, and high was his degree[350] in Heav'n.
708   His count'nance, as the morning-star that guides
709   The starry flock, allured[351] them, and with lies
710   Drew after him the third part of Heav'n's host.
711   Meanwhile th' Eternal eye, whose sight discerns
712   Abstrusest[352] thoughts, from forth His holy mount
713   And from within the golden lamps that burn
714   Nightly before Him, saw without their light
715   Rebellion rising, saw in whom, how spread
716   Among the sons of morn, what multitudes
717   Were banded to oppose His high decree
718   And, smiling, to His only Son thus said:
719   "'Son, thou in whom my glory I behold

---

[336] insinuated
[337] [trisyllabic, second accented]
[338] Beelzebub
[339] separately
[340] "He calls together, or else speaks to them separately, or one by one"
[341] controlling, governing
[342] under him Regent = which were Regents under him
[343] freed
[344] ensign of the hierarchy
[345] test
[346] corrupt
[347] familiar
[348] command, will, right
[349] person with great and independent power, a ruler
[350] rank
[351] charmed, tempted
[352] the most hidden

720　In full resplendence, heir of all my might,
721　Nearly[353] it now concerns us to be sure
722　Of our omnipotence, and with what arms
723　We mean to hold what anciently[354] we claim
724　Of deity or empire. Such a foe
725　Is rising who intends t' erect his throne
726　Equal to ours, throughout the spacious North,
727　Nor so content, hath in his thought to try
728　In battle what our power is, or our right.
729　Let us advise,[355] and to this hazard[356] draw
730　With speed what force is left, and all employ
731　In our defence, lest unawares we lose
732　This our high place, our sanctuary, our hill.'
733　To whom the Son with calm aspect and clear,
734　Ligh'tning divine, ineffable,[357] serene,
735　Made answer:

　　　　　　　'Mighty Father, Thou Thy foes
736　Justly hast in derision and, secure,[358]
737　Laugh'st at their vain designs and tumults[359] vain,
738　Matter to me of glory, whom their hate
739　Illustrates,[360] when they see all regal power
740　Giv'n me, to quell[361] their pride,[362] and in event[363]
741　Know whether I be dextrous[364] to subdue
742　Thy rebels, or be found the worst in Heav'n.'
743　　　　　"So spoke the Son. But Satan, with his Powers,
744　Far was advanced on[365] wingèd speed, an host
745　Innumerable[366] as the stars of night,
746　Or stars of morning, dew-drops, which the sun
747　Impearls on every leaf and every flower.

---

[353] particularly
[354] of long standing
[355] consider, reflect
[356] peril
[357] inexpressible
[358] safe
[359] commotions, agitations
[360] makes illustrious
[361] put an end to, suppress, destroy
[362] matter to me of glory . . . to quell their pride
[363] in event = in the occurrence
[364] adroit, skillful
[365] with
[366] [five syllables, second and fourth accented]

748   Regions they passed, the mighty regencies
749   Of Seraphim, and Potentates, and Thrones
750   In their triple degrees[367]—regions to which
751   All thy dominion, Adam, is no more
752   Than what this garden is to all the earth
753   And all the sea, from one entire globose[368]
754   Stretched into longitude[369]—which, having passed,
755   At length into the limits[370] of the North
756   They came. And Satan to his royal seat
757   High on a hill, far blazing, as a mount
758   Raised on a mount, with pyramids and tow'rs
759   From diamond quarries hewn, and rocks of gold,
760   The palace of great Lucifer (so call
761   That structure, in the dialect of men
762   Interpreted)[371] which, not long after, he
763   (Affecting all equality with God)
764   In imitation of that mount whereon
765   Messiah was declared, in sight of Heav'n,
766   The Mountain of the Congregation called,
767   For thither he assembled all his train,
768   Pretending[372] so commanded to consult
769   About the great reception of their King,
770   Thither to come, and with calumnious[373] art
771   Of counterfeited truth thus held their ears:
772   " "Thrones, Dominations, Princedoms, Virtues,
                      Powers—
773   If these magnific titles yet remain
774   Not merely titular,[374] since by decree
775   Another now hath to himself engrossed[375]
776   All power, and us eclipsed under the name
777   Of King anointed, for whom all this haste
778   Of midnight-march and hurried meeting here,

---

[367] the nine angelic orders were at one time said to be divided into three subgroupings
[368] having the form of a globe
[369] stretched into longitude = stretched lengthwise
[370] territories, bounds
[371] explained, translated
[372] claiming, feigning
[373] false, slanderous
[374] having the name, but not the reality
[375] collected

779   This only to consult how we may best,
780   With what may be devised of honors new,
781   Receive him coming to receive from us
782   Knee-tribute yet unpaid, prostration vile!
783   Too much to one! But double how endured,
784   To one and to His image[376] now proclaimed?
785   But what if better counsels might erect[377]
786   Our minds, and teach us to cast off this yoke?
787   Will ye submit your necks, and choose to bend
788   The supple knee? Ye will not, if I trust
789   To know ye right, or if ye know yourselves
790   Natives and sons of Heav'n, possessed before
791   By none, and if not equal all, yet free,
792   Equally free, for orders and degrees
793   Jar not with liberty, but well consist.[378]
794   Who can in reason, then, or right, assume
795   Monarchy over such as live by right
796   His equals, if in power and splendor less,
797   In freedom equal? Or can introduce
798   Law and edict on us, who without law
799   Err not? Much less for this to be our Lord
800   And look for adoration, to th' abuse[379]
801   Of those imperial titles which assert
802   Our being ordained to govern, not to serve.'
803   "Thus far his bold discourse without control[380]
804   Had audience, when among the Seraphim
805   Abdiel,[381] than whom none with more zeal adored
806   The Deity, and divine commands obeyed,
807   Stood up, and in a flame of zeal severe[382]
808   The current[383] of his fury thus opposed:
809   " 'O argument blasphemous, false, and proud!
810   Words which no ear ever to hear in Heav'n
811   Expected, least of all from thee, ingrate,

---

[376] artificial representation, copy, counterpart, portrait
[377] raise
[378] well consist = are consistent
[379] perversion, corruption, misuse
[380] check
[381] "to boil"
[382] stringent, rigorous
[383] flowing

812   In place thyself so high above thy peers.
813   Canst thou with impious obloquy[384] condemn
814   The just decree of God, pronounced and sworn,
815   That to His only Son, by right endued[385]
816   With regal scepter, every soul in Heav'n
817   Shall bend the knee, and in that honor due[386]
818   Confess[387] him rightful King? Unjust, thou say'st,
819   Flatly unjust, to bind with laws the free,
820   And equal over equals to let reign,
821   One over all with unsucceeded[388] power.
822   Shalt thou give law to God? Shalt thou dispute
823   With Him the points of liberty, who made
824   Thee what thou art, and formed the Powers of Heav'n
825   Such as He pleased, and circumscribed[389] their being?
826   Yet, by experience taught, we know how good,
827   And of our good and of our dignity
828   How provident[390] He is, how far from thought
829   To make us less, bent[391] rather to exalt
830   Our happy state, under one head more near[392]
831   United. But to grant it thee unjust[393]
832   That equal over equals monarch reign:
833   Thyself, though great and glorious, dost thou count—
834   Or all Angelic nature joined in one—
835   Equal to him, begotten Son? By whom,
836   As by His Word, the Mighty Father made
837   All things, ev'n thee, and all the Spirits of Heav'n
838   By Him created in their bright degrees,
839   Crowned them with glory, and to their glory named
840   Thrones, Dominations, Princedoms, Virtues, Powers,
841   Essential Powers, nor by His reign obscured[394]

---

[384] speaking evil
[385] invested
[386] fit, proper, owed
[387] acknowledge, avow
[388] uninherited
[389] marked out the limits of
[390] careful
[391] inclined
[392] nearly
[393] to be unjust
[394] dimmed, darkened

842   But more illustrious made, since He the head
843   One of our number thus reduced becomes,
844   His laws our laws, all honor to Him done
845   Returns our own. Cease then this impious rage,
846   And tempt not these,[395] but hasten to appease[396]
847   Th' incensèd Father and th' incensèd Son,
848   While pardon may be found, in time[397] besought.'
849   "So spoke the fervent[398] Angel, but his zeal
850   None seconded, as out of season[399] judged,
851   Or singular[400] and rash.[401] Whereat rejoiced
852   Th' apostate and, more haughty, thus replied:
853   " 'That we were formed then, say'st thou? And
              the work
854   Of secondary[402] hands, by task transferred
855   From Father to His Son? Strange[403] point and new!
856   Doctrine which we would know whence learned. Who
              saw
857   When this creation was? Remember'st thou
858   Thy making, while the Maker gave thee being?
859   We know no time when we were not as now,
860   Know none before us, self-begot, self-raised
861   By our own quick'ning[404] power, when fatal[405] course
862   Had circled his full orb, the birth mature[406]
863   Of this our native Heav'n, ethereal[407] sons.
864   Our puissance[408] is our own: our own right hand
865   Shall teach us highest deeds, by proof to try
866   Who is our equal. Then thou shalt behold
867   Whether by supplication we intend

---

[395] these others
[396] pacify, mollify
[397] in time = if in time
[398] ardent, intensely earnest
[399] out of season = inopportune, unseasonable, not at the right time
[400] just him
[401] hasty, impetuous
[402] second-best, second-class, subsidiary, auxiliary
[403] unfamiliar
[404] life-giving, animating
[405] destined, fated
[406] complete
[407] celestial
[408] power

868   Address,[409] and to begirt[410] th' Almighty throne
869   Beseeching or besieging. This report,
870   These tidings carry to th' anointed King,
871   And fly,[411] ere evil intercept thy flight.'
872   "He said, and as the sound of waters deep
873   Hoarse murmur echoed to his words applause,[412]
874   Through the infinite host. Nor less for that
875   The flaming Seraph fearless, though alone,
876   Encompassed round with foes, thus answered bold:
877   "'O alienate[413] from God, O Spirit accursed,
878   Forsaken of all good! I see thy fall
879   Determined,[414] and thy hapless[415] crew involved
880   In this perfidious fraud, contagion spread
881   Both of thy crime and punishment. Henceforth
882   No more be troubled how to quit the yoke
883   Of God's Messiah. Those indulgent[416] laws
884   Will not be now vouchsafed;[417] other decrees
885   Against thee are gone forth without recall.
886   That golden scepter, which thou did'st reject,
887   Is now an iron rod to bruise[418] and break
888   Thy disobedience. Well thou didst advise.[419]
889   Yet not for thy advice or threats I fly
890   These wicked tents devoted,[420] lest the wrath
891   Impendent,[421] raging into sudden flame,
892   Distinguish not.[422] For soon expect to feel
893   His thunder on thy head, devouring fire.
894   Then who created thee lamenting learn,
895   When who can uncreate thee thou shalt know.'
896   "So spoke the Seraph Abdiel, faithful found

---

[409] the act of addressing someone
[410] surround
[411] (1) flee, (2) fly on wings
[412] "hoarse murmur echoed applause to his words"
[413] estranged
[414] settled, decided
[415] luckless
[416] lenient
[417] bestowed, conferred
[418] crush, smash
[419] advise me (to leave)
[420] (1) dedicated (to evil), (2) doomed
[421] overhanging, imminent
[422] distinguish not = not distinguish between you and me

897 Among the faithless, faithful only he,
898 Among innumerable false. Unmoved,
899 Unshaken, unseduced, unterrified,
900 His loyalty he kept, his love, his zeal,
901 Nor number, nor example, with him wrought[423]
902 To swerve from truth, or change his constant mind,
903 Though single.[424] From amidst them forth he passed,
904 Long way through hostile scorn, which he sustained
905 Superior, nor of violence[425] feared aught,
906 And with retorted[426] scorn, his back he turned
907 On those proud tow'rs to swift destruction doomed."

The End of the Fifth Book

---

[423] worked
[424] alone
[425] [trisyllabic, first and third accented]
[426] returned, cast back

BOOK VI

THE ARGUMENT

RAPHAEL CONTINUES TO relate how Michael and Gabriel were sent forth to battle against Satan and his Angels. The first fight described: Satan and his Powers retire under night; he calls a council, invents devilish engines,[1] which in the second day's fight put Michael and his Angels to some disorder, but they at length, pulling up mountains, overwhelmed both the force and machines of Satan.

Yet the tumult not so ending, God on the third day sends Messiah his Son, for whom he had reserved the glory of that victory. He in the power of his Father coming to the place, and causing all his legions to stand still on either side, with his chariot and thunder driving into the midst of his enemies, pursues them unable to resist towards the wall of Heaven; which opening, they leap down with horror and confusion into the place of punishment prepared for them in the deep. Messiah returns with triumph to his Father.

---

[1] machines, mechanical devices

1   "All night the dreadless[2] Angel,[3] unpursued,
2   Through Heav'n's wide champaign[4] held his way, till
              morn,
3   Waked by the circling hours, with rosy hand
4   Unbarred the gates of light. There is a cave
5   Within the mount of God, fast by[5] His throne,
6   Where light and darkness in perpetual round
7   Lodge[6] and dislodge[7] by turns, which makes through
              Heav'n
8   Grateful[8] vicissitude,[9] like day and night.
9   Light issues forth, and at the other door
10   Obsequious[10] darkness enters, till her hour
11   To veil the Heav'n, though darkness there might well
12   Seem twilight here. And now went forth the morn
13   Such as[11] in highest Heav'n, arrayed in gold
14   Empyreal.[12] From before her vanished night,
15   Shot through with orient[13] beams. When all the plain[14]
16   Covered with thick embattled squadrons bright,
17   Chariots, and flaming arms, and fiery steeds,
18   Reflecting blaze on blaze, first met his[15] view,
19   War he perceived, war in procinct,[16] and found
20   Already known what he for news had thought
21   To have reported. Gladly then he mixed
22   Among those friendly Powers, who him received
23   With joy and acclamations loud—that one
24   That of so many myriads[17] fall'n—yet one
25   Returned not lost. On to the sacred hill

---

[2] fearless
[3] Abdiel
[4] open country
[5] fast by = very near
[6] reside
[7] go away
[8] pleasing
[9] mutation
[10] obedient, dutiful
[11] as it is
[12] celestial
[13] brightly shining
[14] [when all the plain (lines 15 ff.) = subject; met his view (line 18) = verb]
[15] Abdiel's
[16] readiness, preparation
[17] countless numbers

26　They led him, high applauded, and present[18]
27　Before the seat supreme, from whence a voice,
28　From midst a golden cloud, thus mild was heard:
29　　　　" 'Servant of God, well done, well hast thou
　　　　　　fought
30　The better fight, who single hast maintained
31　Against revolted multitudes the cause
32　Of truth, in word mightier than they in arms,
33　And for the testimony of truth hast borne
34　Universal reproach, far worse to bear
35　Than violence. For this was all thy care,
36　To stand approved[19] in sight of God, though worlds
37　Judged thee perverse.[20] The easier conquest now
38　Remains[21] thee, aided by this host of friends,
39　Back on thy foes more glorious to return
40　Than, scorned, thou didst depart, and to subdue
41　By force, who reason for their law refuse,
42　Right reason for their law, and for their King
43　Messiah, who by right of merit reigns.
44　　　　" 'Go, Michael, of celestial armies prince,
45　And thou, in military prowess next,
46　Gabriel, lead forth to battle these my sons
47　Invincible, lead forth my armèd Saints,
48　By thousands and by millions, ranged for fight,
49　Equal in number to that Godless crew
50　Rebellious. Them with fire and hostile arms
51　Fearless assault,[22] and to the brow[23] of Heav'n
52　Pursuing, drive them out from God and bliss,
53　Into their place of punishment, the gulf
54　Of Tartarus,[24] which ready opens wide
55　His fiery chaos to receive their fall.'
56　　　　"So spoke the Sov'reign Voice, and clouds began
57　To darken all the hill, and smoke to roll

---

[18] present him [verb, in the present tense]
[19] valued, good
[20] incorrect, wicked
[21] remains to
[22] [verb]
[23] cliff edge
[24] lowest region of Hades/Hell

58   In dusky wreaths, reluctant[25] flames, the sign
59   Of wrath awaked, nor with less dread[26] the loud
60   Ethereal trumpet from on high 'gan blow.
61   At which command the Powers militant
62   That stood[27] for Heav'n, in mighty quadrate[28] joined
63   Of union irresistible, moved on
64   In silence their bright legions, to the sound
65   Of instrumental harmony that breathed
66   Heroic ardor to advent'rous deeds
67   Under their god-like leaders, in the cause
68   Of God and His Messiah. On they move
69   Indissolubly firm, nor[29] obvious[30] hill,
70   Nor straitening[31] vale, nor wood, nor stream, divides
71   Their perfect ranks, for high above the ground
72   Their march was, and the passive[32] air upbore
73   Their nimble[33] tread. As when the total kind[34]
74   Of birds, in orderly array on wing,
75   Came summoned over Eden to receive
76   Their names of thee,[35] so over many a tract[36]
77   Of Heav'n they marched, and many a province wide,
78   Tenfold the length of this terrene.[37] At last,
79   Far in the horizon to the north appeared
80   From skirt[38] to skirt a fiery region, stretched
81   In battailous[39] aspect, and nearer view[40]
82   Bristled with upright beams[41] innumerable

---

[25] writhing
[26] fear, awe, reverence
[27] were drawn up for battle
[28] square formation
[29] and neither
[30] obstructing
[31] constricting
[32] quiescent, unresisting
[33] quick
[34] race, species
[35] Adam
[36] stretch/extent of land, region
[37] earth
[38] border
[39] ready/eager for battle [trisyllabic, first and third accented]
[40] on nearer view
[41] upright beams = the upright poles

83   Of rigid spears, and helmets thronged,[42] and shields
84   Various, with boastful argument[43] portrayed,[44]
85   The banded Powers of Satan hasting on
86   With furious[45] expedition,[46] for they weened[47]
87   That self-same day, by fight or by surprise,
88   To win the mount of God, and on His throne
89   To set the envier of His state, the proud
90   Aspirer. But their thoughts proved fond[48] and vain
91   In the mid way,[49] though strange to us it seemed
92   At first, that Angel should with Angel war,
93   And in fierce hosting[50] meet, who wont to[51] meet
94   So oft in festivals of joy and love
95   Unanimous,[52] as sons of one great Sire,
96   Hymning th' Eternal Father. But the shout
97   Of battle now began, and rushing sound
98   Of onset ended soon each milder thought.
99   High in the midst, exalted as a god,
100   Th' apostate in his sun-bright chariot sat,
101   Idol of majesty divine, enclosed
102   With flaming Cherubim, and golden shields.
103   Then lighted[53] from his gorgeous throne, for now
104   'Twixt host and host but narrow space was left,
105   A dreadful[54] interval,[55] and front to front
106   Presented stood in terrible array
107   Of hideous length. Before the cloudy[56] van,[57]
108   On the rough[58] edge of battle ere it joined,

---

[42] crowded
[43] statements, slogans, arguments
[44] painted, adorned
[45] wild, mad
[46] speed
[47] thought, expected
[48] foolish
[49] "when they were halfway there"
[50] hostile encounter
[51] wont to = usually
[52] like-minded
[53] descended
[54] fearful, terrible
[55] open space
[56] darkened by ignorance, anger, etc.
[57] foremost part
[58] bristling

109   Satan, with vast and haughty strides advanced,
110   Came tow'ring, armed in adamant and gold.
111   Abdiel that sight endured not, where he stood
112   Among the mightiest, bent on highest deeds,
113   And thus his own undaunted heart explores:
114   " 'O Heav'n! that such resemblance of the
                  Highest
115   Should yet remain, where faith and realty[59]
116   Remain not. Wherefore should not strength and might
117   There fail where virtue fails, or weakest prove
118   Where boldest, though to fight unconquerable?
119   His puissance, trusting[60] in th' Almighty's aid,
120   I mean to try,[61] whose reason I have tried
121   Unsound and false, nor is it aught but just
122   That he, who in debate of truth hath won,
123   Should win in arms, in both disputes alike
124   Victor, though brutish[62] that contest[63] and foul,[64]
125   When reason hath to deal with force, yet so
126   Most reason is that reason overcome.'
127   So pondering, and from his armèd peers
128   Forth stepping opposite, half-way he met
129   His daring foe, at this prevention[65] more
130   Incensed,[66] and thus securely him[67] defied:
131   " 'Proud, art thou met? Thy hope was to have
                  reached
132   The height of thy aspiring unopposed,
133   The throne of God unguarded, and His side
134   Abandoned, at the terror of thy power
135   Or potent tongue. Fool! Not to think how vain
136   Against the Omnipotent to rise in arms,
137   Who out of smallest things could, without end,
138   Have raised incessant armies to defeat

---

[59] loyalty, devotion, honesty [trisyllabic, first and third accented]
[60] (Abdiel, not Satan, is trusting in God)
[61] test, probe
[62] savage
[63] [second syllable accented]
[64] wicked, dirty, offensive
[65] (1) obstruction, obstacle, (2) confrontation
[66] is Abdiel incensed at Satan? or Satan at Abdiel?
[67] Satan

139   Thy folly, or with solitary hand,
140   Reaching beyond all limit, at one blow
141   Unaided could have finished thee, and whelmed[68]
142   Thy legions under darkness. But thou see'st
143   All are not of thy train.[69] There be who[70] faith
144   Prefer, and piety to God, though then
145   To thee not visible when I alone
146   Seemed in thy world erroneous[71] to dissent
147   From all. My sect[72] thou see'st. Now learn too late
148   How few[73] sometimes may know, when thousands err.'
149   Whom the grand[74] foe, with scornful eye askance,[75]
150   Thus answered:
                " 'Ill for thee, but in wished hour
151   Of my revenge, first sought for. Thou return'st
152   From flight, seditious[76] Angel! to receive
153   Thy merited reward, the first assay[77]
154   Of this right hand provoked, since first that tongue,
155   Inspired with contradiction, durst oppose
156   A third part of the gods, in synod met
157   Their deities to assert,[78] who while they feel
158   Vigor divine within them, can allow
159   Omnipotence to none. But well thou com'st
160   Before thy fellows, ambitious to win
161   From me some plume,[79] that thy success[80] may show
162   Destruction[81] to the rest. This pause between
163   (Unanswered lest thou boast) to let thee know:
164   At first I thought that liberty and Heav'n
165   To Heav'nly souls had been all one, but now
166   I see that most through sloth had rather serve,

---

[68] submerged, buried, completely covered
[69] (1) course, (2) following
[70] those who
[71] misguided, mistaken
[72] party
[73] a few
[74] principal, great
[75] (1) sideways, (2) askew, asquint
[76] rebelling
[77] (1) assault, (2) test
[78] (1) free, (2) claim
[79] reward
[80] result, outcome
[81] slaughter

167 Minist'ring Spirits, trained up in feast and song!
168 Such hast thou armed, the minstrelsy of Heav'n,
169 Servility with freedom to contend,
170 As both their deeds compared this day shall prove.'
171 To whom in brief thus Abdiel stern replied:
172   " 'Apostate! Still thou err'st, nor end wilt find
173 Of erring, from the path of truth remote.
174 Unjustly thou deprav'st[82] it with the name
175 Of servitude, to serve whom God ordains,
176 Or Nature: God and Nature bid[83] the same,
177 When he who rules is worthiest, and excels
178 Them whom he governs. This is servitude,
179 To serve the unwise, or him who hath rebelled
180 Against his worthier, as thine now serve thee,
181 Thyself not free, but to thyself enthralled.[84]
182 Yet lewdly[85] dar'st our minist'ring[86] upbraid.[87]
183 Reign thou in Hell, thy kingdom! Let me serve
184 In Heav'n God ever blest, and His divine
185 Behests[88] obey, worthiest to be obeyed.
186 Yet chains in Hell, not realms, expect. Meanwhile,
187 From me returned, as erst thou saidst, from flight,
188 This greeting on thy impious crest[89] receive.'
189   "So saying, a noble stroke he lifted high,
190 Which hung not, but so swift with tempest[90] fell
191 On the proud crest of Satan, that no sight
192 Nor motion of swift thought, less could his shield,
193 Such ruin[91] intercept. Ten paces huge[92]
194 He back recoiled; the tenth on bended knee,
195 His massy spear upstaid,[93] as if on earth
196 Winds under ground, or waters forcing way,

---

[82] corrupt
[83] command
[84] enslaved
[85] wickedly, basely
[86] serving
[87] censure, reproach
[88] commands
[89] heraldic device on the top of his helmet
[90] violent speed
[91] injury, damage
[92] "ten large paces"
[93] held up

197   Sidelong had pushed a mountain from his seat,
198   Half sunk with all his pines. Amazement seized
199   The rebel Thrones, but greater rage, to see
200   Thus foiled[94] their mightiest; ours joy filled, and shout,
201   Presage of victory,[95] and fierce desire
202   Of battle. Whereat Michael[96] bid sound
203   The Arch-Angel trumpet. Through the vast[97] of Heav'n
204   It sounded, and the faithful armies rung
205   Hosanna to the Highest.
                     "Nor stood at gaze[98]
206   The adverse legions, nor less hideous, joined,[99]
207   The horrid shock. Now storming fury rose,
208   And clamor such as heard in Heav'n till now
209   Was never. Arms on armor clashing brayed[100]
210   Horrible discord, and the madding[101] wheels
211   Of brazen[102] chariots raged. Dire[103] was the noise
212   Of conflict. Overhead the dismal hiss
213   Of fiery darts[104] in flaming vollies flew,
214   And flying vaulted[105] either host with fire.
215   So under fiery cope[106] together rushed
216   Both battles[107] main,[108] with ruinous assault
217   And inextinguishable rage. All Heav'n
218   Resounded, and had earth been then, all earth
219   Had to her center shook.
                     "What wonder, when
220   Millions of fierce encount'ring Angels fought
221   On either side, the least of whom could wield
222   These elements, and arm him with the force

---

[94] discomfited, overthrown
[95] [trisyllabic]
[96] [trisyllabic?]
[97] vastness
[98] in wonder/amazement
[99] met, now engaged in combat
[100] made a harsh, clashing sound
[101] frenzied, turning furiously
[102] brasslike, brass-hard
[103] horrible, dreadful
[104] spears, javelins, arrows
[105] covered
[106] canopy
[107] armies
[108] mighty

223   Of all their regions? How much more of power
224   Army against army numberless to raise
225   Dreadful combustion[109] warring, and disturb,
226   Though not destroy, their happy native seat,
227   Had not the Eternal King Omnipotent,
228   From His stronghold of Heav'n high, over-ruled[110]
229   And limited their might, though numbered[111] such
230   As each divided[112] legion might have seemed
231   A numerous host, in strength each armèd band
232   A legion. Led in fight, yet leader seemed
233   Each warrior single as in chief, expert
234   When to advance, or stand, or turn the sway
235   Of battle, open when, and when to close
236   The ridges[113] of grim[114] war. No thought of flight,
237   None of retreat, no unbecoming deed
238   That argued fear. Each on himself relied,
239   As[115] only in his arm the moment[116] lay
240   Of victory. Deeds of eternal fame
241   Were done, but infinite, for wide was spread
242   That war and various. Sometimes on firm ground
243   A standing fight; then soaring on main[117] wing
244   Tormented[118] all the air. All air seemed then
245   Conflicting[119] fire.
                      "Long time in even scale
246   The battle hung, till Satan, who that day
247   Prodigious[120] power had shown, and met in arms
248   No equal, ranging through the dire attack
249   Of fighting Seraphim confused,[121] at length
250   Saw where the sword of Michael smote, and felled

---

[109] tumultuous conflagration
[110] controlled, ruled against
[111] of such numbers
[112] split into factions, discordant
[113] battle lines
[114] fierce, cruel
[115] as if
[116] cause, influence, turning point
[117] mighty, vigorous
[118] shaking, stirring
[119] battling
[120] marvelous, amazing
[121] disorderly

251 Squadrons at once: with huge two-handed sway[122]
252 Brandished aloft, the horrid[123] edge came down
253 Wide-wasting. Such destruction to withstand
254 He hasted, and opposed[124] the rocky orb
255 Of tenfold adamant, his ample shield,
256 A vast circumference. At his approach
257 The great Arch-Angel from his warlike toil
258 Surceased,[125] and glad, as hoping here to end
259 Intestine[126] war in Heav'n, th' arch-foe subdued
260 Or captive dragged in chains, with hostile frown
261 And visage all inflamed first thus began:
262   " 'Author of evil, unknown till thy revolt,
263 Unnamed in Heav'n, now plenteous, as thou see'st—
264 These acts of hateful strife, hateful to all,
265 Though heaviest by just measure[127] on thyself
266 And thy adherents! How hast thou disturbed
267 Heav'n's blessèd peace, and into Nature brought
268 Misery, uncreated till the crime
269 Of thy rebellion! How hast thou instilled
270 Thy malice into thousands, once upright
271 And faithful, now proved false! But think not here
272 To trouble holy rest.[128] Heav'n casts thee out
273 From all her confines.[129] Heav'n, the seat of bliss,
274 Brooks[130] not the works of violence and war.
275 Hence then, and evil go with thee along,
276 Thy offspring, to the place of evil, Hell,
277 Thou and thy wicked crew! There mingle[131] broils,[132]
278 Ere this avenging sword begin thy doom,
279 Or some more sudden vengeance, winged from God,
280 Precipitate thee with augmented pain.'
281   "So spoke the Prince of Angels, to whom thus

---

[122] motion, force
[123] frightful
[124] set in opposition, put in the way
[125] left off
[126] internal
[127] quantity, degree, proportion
[128] spiritual/mental peace
[129] borders
[130] puts up with
[131] join together
[132] quarrels

282 The adversary:

> " 'Nor think thou with wind

283 Of airy threats to awe whom yet with deeds

284 Thou canst not. Hast thou turned the least of these

285 To flight, or if to fall, but that they rise

286 Unvanquished? Easier to transact[133] with me

287 That thou shouldst hope, imperious, and with threats

288 To chase me hence? Err not, that so shall end

289 The strife which thou call'st evil, but we style

290 The strife of glory, which we mean to win,

291 Or turn this Heav'n itself into the Hell

292 Thou fablest, here however to dwell free,

293 If not to reign. Meanwhile, thy utmost force

294 (And join Him named Almighty to thy aid)

295 I fly not, but have sought thee far and nigh.'

296 > "They ended parle,[134] and both addressed[135] for fight

297 Unspeakable, for who, though with the tongue

298 Of Angels, can relate, or to what things

299 Liken on earth conspicuous,[136] that may lift

300 Human imagination to such height

301 Of godlike power? For likest gods they seemed,

302 Stood they or moved, in stature, motion, arms,

303 Fit to decide the empire of great Heav'n.

304 Now waved their fiery swords, and in the air

305 Made horrid circles: two broad suns their shields

306 Blazed opposite, while expectation stood

307 In horror. From each hand[137] with speed retired,

308 Where erst was thickest[138] fight, th' Angelic throng,

309 And left large field,[139] unsafe within the wind[140]

310 Of such commotion—such as, to set forth

311 Great things by small, if Nature's concord broke,

312 Among the constellations war were sprung,

---

[133] negotiate
[134] parley
[135] readied
[136] visible
[137] side, direction
[138] most dense
[139] space, room
[140] (1) wind, (2) violence

313 Two planets, rushing from aspect[141] malign
314 Of fiercest opposition, in mid sky
315 Should combat, and their jarring spheres confound.[142]
316 Together both with next to almighty arm
317 Up-lifted imminent, one stroke they aimed
318 That might determine,[143] and not need repeat,
319 As not of power at once, nor odds[144] appeared
320 In might or swift prevention.[145] But the sword
321 Of Michael from the armory of God
322 Was giv'n him tempered so that neither keen
323 Nor solid might resist that edge. It met
324 The sword of Satan, with steep force to smite
325 Descending, and in half cut sheer,[146] nor stayed,
326 But with swift wheel reverse, deep ent'ring, shared[147]
327 All his right side. Then Satan first knew pain,
328 And writhed him to and fro convolved,[148] so sore
329 The griding[149] sword with discontinuous[150] wound
330 Passed through him. But the ethereal substance closed,
331 Not long divisible, and from the gash
332 A stream of nectarous humor[151] issuing flowed
333 Sanguine,[152] such as celestial Spirits may bleed,
334 And all his armor stained, erewhile so bright.
335 Forthwith on all sides to his aid was run
336 By Angels many and strong, who interposed
337 Defence, while others bore him on their shields
338 Back to his chariot, where it stood retired[153]
339 From off the files of war.[154] There they him laid
340 Gnashing for anguish and despite[155] and shame

---

[141] bearing, relative position
[142] destroy one another?
[143] settle/put an end to/decide/resolve
[144] advantage
[145] blocking, parrying
[146] completely
[147] divided
[148] coiling, twisting
[149] piercing
[150] breaking the organic continuity of Satan's bodily substance
[151] fluid, essence
[152] bloody
[153] withdrawn
[154] files of war = rows/ranks of fighters
[155] outrage, anger

341   To find himself not matchless, and his pride
342   Humbled by such rebuke,[156] so far beneath
343   His confidence to equal God in power.
344   Yet soon he healed, for Spirits that live throughout
345   Vital in every part, not as frail man
346   In entrails, heart or head, liver or reins,[157]
347   Cannot but[158] by annihilating die,
348   Nor in their liquid texture mortal wound
349   Receive, no more than can the fluid air.
350   All heart they live, all head, all eye, all ear,
351   All intellect, all sense, and as they please
352   They limb themselves, and color, shape, or size
353   Assume, as likes them best, condense or rare.
354   "Meanwhile in other parts like[159] deeds deserved
355   Memorial, where the might of Gabriel fought,
356   And with fierce ensigns[160] pierced the deep array[161]
357   Of Moloch, furious king, who him defied,
358   And at his chariot-wheels to drag him bound
359   Threat'ned, nor from the Holy One of Heav'n
360   Refrained his tongue blasphemous. But anon[162]
361   Down cloven to the waist, with shattered arms
362   And uncouth[163] pain, fled bellowing. On each wing[164]
363   Uriel and Raphael his[165] vaunting[166] foe,
364   Though huge and in a rock of diamond armed,
365   Vanquished Adramelech[167] and Asmadai,[168]
366   Two potent Thrones,[169] that to be less than gods
367   Disdained, but meaner[170] thoughts learned in their flight,

---

[156] disgrace
[157] kidneys
[158] except
[159] similar [adjective]
[160] troops serving under a single ensign/banner/flag
[161] ranks
[162] soon, at once
[163] unfamiliar, never experienced
[164] of the army: military formation
[165] their: i.e., each of them vanquished "his" boasting opponent
[166] boasting
[167] Assyrian sun god
[168] Asmodeus, the demon in the Apocryphal Book of Tobit: see Book 4, line 168, above
[169] third of the nine angelic orders
[170] inferior, lower

368   Mangled[171] with ghastly wounds through plate and mail.
369   Nor stood unmindful Abdiel to annoy
370   The atheist crew, but with redoubled blow
371   Ariel,[172] and Arioch,[173] and the violence
372   Of Ramiel[174] scorched and blasted, overthrew.
373   "I might relate of thousands, and their names
374   Eternize here on earth, but those elect
375   Angels, contented with their fame in Heav'n,
376   Seek not the praise of men. The other sort,
377   In might though wondrous and in acts of war,
378   Nor of renown less eager, yet by doom[175]
379   Cancelled from Heav'n and sacred memory,
380   Nameless in dark oblivion let them dwell.
381   For strength from truth divided, and from just,[176]
382   Illaudable,[177] nought merits but dispraise
383   And ignominy,[178] yet to glory aspires,
384   Vain-glorious, and through infamy seeks fame.
385   Therefore eternal silence be their doom.[179]
386   "And now, their mightiest quelled,[180] the battle
               swerved,[181]
387   With many an inroad[182] gored.[183] Deformèd[184] rout
388   Entered, and foul disorder, all the ground
389   With shivered armor strewn, and on a heap
390   Chariot and charioteer lay overturned,
391   And fiery-foaming steeds. What stood, recoiled
392   O'er-wearied, through the faint[185] Satanic host

---

[171] cut, hacked
[172] "lion of God"
[173] a Spirit of revenge; Arioch is mentioned in Genesis 14:1 as a "king of Ellasar"
[174] "exaltation of God"—although in the Apocryphal Book of Enoch, Ramiel's lustfulness with mortal women causes him to fall from Heaven
[175] judgment, sentence
[176] that which is just
[177] unworthy
[178] dishonor, disgrace
[179] fate, destiny
[180] crushed
[181] changed
[182] raid
[183] stuck, stabbed, pierced: i.e., into the rebel ranks
[184] hideous
[185] spiritless, feeble

393　　Defensive scarce, or with pale[186] fear surprised[187]
394　　(Then first with fear surprised, and sense of pain)
395　　Fled ignominious, to such evil brought
396　　By sin of disobedience, till that hour
397　　Not liable to fear, or flight, or pain.
398　　Far otherwise th' inviolable[188] Saints,
399　　In cubic phalanx[189] firm, advanced entire,[190]
400　　Invulnerable, impenetrably armed,
401　　Such high advantages their innocence
402　　Gave them above their foes, not to have sinned,
403　　Not to have disobeyed. In fight they stood
404　　Unwearied, unobnoxious[191] to be pained
405　　By wound, though from their place by violence moved.
406　　　　　　"Now Night her course began and, over Heav'n
407　　Inducing darkness, grateful truce imposed,
408　　And silence on the odious[192] din of war.
409　　Under her cloudy covert both retired,
410　　Victor and vanquished. On the foughten field
411　　Michael and his Angels prevalent[193]
412　　Encamping, placed in guard their watches round,[194]
413　　Cherubic[195] waving fires. On th' other part,[196]
414　　Satan with his rebellious disappeared,
415　　Far in the dark dislodged[197] and, void[198] of rest,
416　　His potentates to council called by night,
417　　And in the midst thus, undismayed, began:
418　　　　　　" 'O now in danger tried, now known in arms
419　　Not to be overpowered, companions dear,
420　　Found worthy not of liberty alone,

---

[186] ashen
[187] attacked, captured
[188] unable to be violated/broken/injured [five syllables, second and fourth accented]
[189] close-packed battle array, sixteen-man-deep square, perfected by the Romans
[190] as a whole
[191] not exposed/liable
[192] hateful
[193] victorious, dominant
[194] around
[195] red
[196] side
[197] gone away
[198] devoid

421 Too mean pretence![199] but what we more affect,[200]
422 Honor, dominion, glory, and renown,
423 Who have sustained one day in doubtful[201] fight
424 (And if one day, why not eternal days?)
425 What Heaven's Lord had powerfullest to send
426 Against us from about His throne, and judged
427 Sufficient to subdue us to His will,
428 But proves not so. Then fallible, it seems,
429 Of future we may deem Him, though till now
430 Omniscient thought. True is, less firmly armed,
431 Some disadvantage we endured and pain,
432 Till now not known, but known, as soon contemned,[202]
433 Since now we find this our empyreal[203] form
434 Incapable of mortal injury,
435 Imperishable, and though pierced with wound,
436 Soon closing, and by native vigor healed.
437 Of evil then so small, as easy think[204]
438 The remedy. Perhaps more valid[205] arms,
439 Weapons more violent, when next we meet,
440 May serve to better us, and worse our foes,
441 Or equal what between us made the odds,
442 In Nature none. If other hidden cause
443 Left them superior, while we can preserve
444 Unhurt our minds, and understanding sound,
445 Due search and consultation will disclose.'
446   "He sat; and in the assembly next upstood
447 Nisroch,[206] of Principalities[207] the prime.[208]
448 As one he stood escaped from cruel fight,
449 Sore toiled,[209] his riven[210] arms[211] to havoc[212] hewn,

---

[199] claim
[200] seek, aim at
[201] uncertain
[202] disdained
[203] celestial
[204] ponder
[205] effective, technically perfect
[206] an Assyrian deity
[207] fifth of the nine angelic orders
[208] principal, first
[209] fatigued
[210] split, cracked open
[211] weapons, armor
[212] destruction

450　　And cloudy[213] in aspect[214] thus answering spoke:
451　　　　　　" 'Deliverer from new Lords, leader to free
452　　Enjoyment of our right as gods! Yet hard
453　　For gods, and too unequal work we find,
454　　Against unequal arms to fight in pain,
455　　Against unpained, impassive,[215] from which evil
456　　Ruin must needs ensue. For what avails
457　　Valor or strength, though matchless, quelled[216] with pain
458　　Which all subdues, and makes remiss[217] the hands
459　　Of mightiest? Sense of pleasure we may well
460　　Spare[218] out of life, perhaps, and not repine,[219]
461　　But live content, which is the calmest life.
462　　But pain is perfect misery, the worst
463　　Of evils and, excessive, overturns
464　　All patience. He who therefore can invent[220]
465　　With what more forcible we may offend[221]
466　　Our yet unwounded enemies, or arm
467　　Ourselves with like defence, to me deserves
468　　No less than for deliverance what we owe.'
469　　Whereto with look composed Satan replied:
470　　　　　　" 'Not uninvented that, which thou aright[222]
471　　Believ'st so main[223] to our success, I bring.
472　　Which of us who beholds the bright surface
473　　Of this ethereous[224] mould[225] whereon we stand,
474　　This continent of spacious Heav'n, adorned
475　　With plant, fruit, flow'r ambrosial, gems, and gold—
476　　Whose eye so superficially[226] surveys

---

[213] darkened
[214] countenance, face
[215] invulnerable
[216] vanquished, crushed
[217] weak
[218] dispense with
[219] complain
[220] find, discover, produce
[221] attack
[222] correctly
[223] important
[224] composed of ether or similar celestial material [trisyllabic, second accented, "-eous" elided]
[225] ground
[226] only seeing the surface (an erudite pun)

477   These things, as not to mind[227] from whence they grow
478   Deep under ground, materials dark and crude,
479   Of spiritous and fiery spume,[228] till touched
480   With Heav'n's ray, and tempered,[229] they shoot forth
481   So beauteous, opening to the ambient[230] light?
482   These in their dark nativity[231] the deep
483   Shall yield us, pregnant with infernal flame,
484   Which into hollow engines, long and round,
485   Thick rammed,[232] at th' other bore[233] with touch of fire
486   Dilated[234] and infuriate, shall send forth
487   From far, with thund'ring noise, among our foes
488   Such implements of mischief as shall dash
489   To pieces and o'erwhelm whatever stands
490   Adverse,[235] that they shall fear we have disarmed
491   The Thunderer of His only dreaded bolt.
492   Nor long shall be our labor: yet ere dawn,
493   Effect[236] shall end our wish. Meanwhile revive,
494   Abandon fear, to strength and counsel joined
495   Think nothing hard, much less to be despaired.'
496   "He ended, and his words their drooping cheer[237]
497   Enlightened,[238] and their languished[239] hope revived.
498   Th' invention all admired, and each, how he
499   To be the inventer missed, so easy it seemed
500   Once found, which yet unfound most would have
                         thought
501   Impossible. Yet, haply,[240] of thy race
502   In future days, if malice should abound,
503   Someone intent on mischief, or inspired

---

[227] think
[228] foam
[229] modified, worked
[230] surrounding
[231] birthplace
[232] stuffed
[233] aperture, hole
[234] (1) distended, amplified, enlarged, (2) spread abroad
[235] (1) opposite, (2) hostile
[236] accomplishment
[237] countenances
[238] lit up, illuminated
[239] drooping
[240] perhaps

504   With devilish machination,[241] might devise
505   Like[242] instrument to plague the sons of men
506   For sin, on war and mutual slaughter bent.
507   Forthwith from council to the work they flew.
508   None arguing stood; innumerable hands
509   Were ready. In a moment up they turned
510   Wide the celestial soil, and saw beneath
511   The originals[243] of Nature in their crude
512   Conception. Sulphurous and nitrous foam
513   They found, they mingled and, with subtle art,
514   Concocted[244] and adjusted,[245] they reduced
515   To blackest grain,[246] and into store conveyed.
516   Part[247] hidden veins digged up (nor hath this earth
517   Entrails unlike) of mineral and stone,
518   Whereof to found[248] their engines and their balls
519   Of missive ruin;[249] part incentive[250] reed
520   Provide, pernicious[251] with one touch to fire.
521   So all ere day-spring, under conscious Night,[252]
522   Secret they finished, and in order set,
523   With silent circumspection,[253] unespied.
524   "Now when fair morn orient[254] in Heav'n
                        appeared,
525   Up rose the victor-Angels, and to arms
526   The matin trumpet sung. In arms they stood
527   Of golden panoply,[255] refulgent[256] host,[257]

---

[241] contrivance
[242] similar
[243] original elements
[244] mixed
[245] arranged, systematized
[246] granules
[247] some of them
[248] melt and mold, build
[249] missive ruin = missilelike destruction
[250] kindling
[251] swift
[252] conscious Night = Night, aware of what they were doing
[253] caution
[254] bright
[255] armor
[256] gleaming, radiant, resplendent
[257] army

528   Soon banded.[258] Others from the dawning hills
529   Look round, and scouts each coast light-armèd scour,
530   Each quarter to descry[259] the distant foe,
531   Where lodged, or whither fled, or if for fight,
532   In motion or in halt. Him soon they met
533   Under spread ensigns moving nigh, in slow
534   But firm battalion. Back with speediest sail
535   Zophiel,[260] of Cherubim the swiftest wing,
536   Came flying, and in mid air aloud thus cried:
537   " 'Arm, warriors, arm for fight! The foe at hand,
538   Whom fled we thought, will save us long pursuit
539   This day. Fear not his flight: so thick a cloud
540   He comes, and settled in his face I see
541   Sad[261] resolution, and secure.[262] Let each
542   His adamantine coat gird[263] well, and each
543   Fit well his helm, grip fast his orbèd shield,
544   Borne ev'n[264] or high, for this day will pour down,
545   If I conjecture[265] aught, no drizzling shower,
546   But rattling storm of arrows barbed with fire.'
547   "So warned he them, aware themselves, and soon
548   In order, quit of all impediment,
549   Instant without disturb they took alarm,[266]
550   And onward moved embattled.[267] When behold!
551   Not distant far with heavy[268] pace the foe
552   Approaching, gross[269] and huge,[270] in hollow cube
553   Training[271] his devilish enginery, impaled[272]
554   On every side with shadowing squadrons deep,

---

[258] joined/formed into a company
[259] discover
[260] "spy of God"
[261] sober, serious, firm
[262] confident [adjective, modifying "resolution"]
[263] buckle
[264] level, horizontal
[265] can predict
[266] the call to arms
[267] in battle order
[268] slow
[269] massive
[270] of great size
[271] pulling
[272] surrounded, enclosed

555   To hide the fraud. At interview[273] both stood
556   A while, but suddenly at head appeared
557   Satan, and thus was heard commanding loud:
558   " 'Vanguard, to right and left the front unfold,[274]
559   That all may see, who hate us, how we seek
560   Peace and composure,[275] and with open breast
561   Stand ready to receive them, if they like
562   Our overture,[276] and turn not back perverse.[277]
563   But that I doubt. However, witness, Heav'n!
564   Heav'n, witness thou anon![278] while we discharge
565   Freely our part. Ye who appointed stand
566   Do as you have in charge, and briefly touch
567   What we propound,[279] and loud that all may hear!'
568   "So scoffing in ambiguous words, he scarce
569   Had ended, when to right and left the front
570   Divided, and to either flank retired,
571   Which to our eyes discovered, new and strange,
572   A triple mounted row of pillars laid
573   On wheels (for like to pillars most they seemed,
574   Or hollowed bodies made of oak or fir,
575   With branches lopped, in wood or mountain felled),
576   Brass, iron, stony mould,[280] had not their mouths
577   With hideous orifice[281] gaped on us wide,
578   Portending hollow truce. At each, behind,
579   A Seraph stood, and in his hand a reed
580   Stood waving, tipped with fire, while we, suspense,[282]
581   Collected stood, within our thoughts amused.[283]
582   Not long, for sudden all at once their reeds
583   Put forth, and to a narrow vent[284] applied

---

[273] their face-to-face meeting
[274] open
[275] agreement, settlement
[276] opening, revelation
[277] obstinate
[278] at once
[279] bring forward
[280] forms
[281] opening, aperture
[282] uncertain, doubtful
[283] staring, puzzled
[284] vent = hole, here the "touch-hole"

584   With nicest[285] touch. Immediate in a flame,
585   But soon obscured with smoke all Heav'n appeared,
586   From those deep-throated engines belched,[286] whose roar
587   Emboweled[287] with outrageous[288] noise the air
588   And all her entrails tore, disgorging foul
589   Their devilish glut,[289] chained thunderbolts and hail
590   Of iron globes which, on the victor host
591   Levelled, with such impetuous[290] fury smote
592   That, whom they hit, none on their feet might stand,
593   Though standing else as rocks, but down they fell
594   By thousands, Angel on Arch-Angel rolled,
595   The sooner for[291] their arms.[292] Unarmed, they might
596   Have easily, as Spirits, evaded swift
597   By quick contraction or remove, but now
598   Foul dissipation[293] followed, and forced rout,
599   Nor served it to relax[294] their serried[295] files.[296]
600   What should they do? If on they rushed, repulse
601   Repeated, and indecent[297] overthrow
602   Doubled, would render them yet more despised,
603   And to their foes a laughter, for in view
604   Stood ranked of Seraphim another row,
605   In posture to displode[298] their second tire[299]
606   Of thunder. Back defeated to return
607   They worse abhorred. Satan beheld their plight,
608   And to his mates thus in derision called:
609   " 'O friends! Why come not on, these victors
                            proud?
610   Erewhile they fierce were coming, and when we,

---

[285] most precise, delicate
[286] vomited
[287] filled
[288] enormous
[289] overflowing amount
[290] violent, forceful, rapid
[291] because of
[292] armor
[293] scattering
[294] loosen, open
[295] pressed close together
[296] ranks
[297] unseemly
[298] discharge, explode
[299] volley

611   To entertain them fair, with open front
612   And breast (what could we more?), propounded terms
613   Of composition, straight they changed their minds,
614   Flew off, and into strange vagaries[300] fell,
615   As they would dance. Yet for a dance they seemed
616   Somewhat extravagant and wild—perhaps
617   For joy of offered peace. But I suppose,
618   If our proposals once again were heard,
619   We should compel them to a quick result.'
620   To whom thus Belial, in like gamesome mood:
621   " 'Leader! the terms we sent were terms of
                 weight,
622   Of hard contents, and full of force urged home,
623   Such as we might perceive amused[301] them all,
624   And stumbled[302] many. Who receives them right
625   Had need from head to foot well understand.[303]
626   Not understood, this gift they have besides,
627   They show us when our foes walk not upright.'
628   "So they among themselves in pleasant vein
629   Stood scoffing, heightened[304] in their thoughts beyond
630   All doubt of victory. Eternal Might
631   To match with their inventions they presumed
632   So easy, and of His thunder made a scorn,
633   And all His host derided, while they stood
634   A while in trouble. But they[305] stood not long.
635   Rage prompted them at length, and found them arms
636   Against such hellish mischief fit t' oppose.
637   Forthwith (behold the excellence, the power,
638   Which God hath in His mighty Angels placed!)
639   Their arms away they threw, and to the hills
640   (For earth hath this variety from Heav'n,
641   Of pleasure situate[306] in hill and dale)
642   Light[307] as the lightning glimpse they ran, they flew.

---

[300] frolicking
[301] amazed
[302] overthrew
[303] (1) comprehend, (2) be supported ("stand under")
[304] excited
[305] the angels
[306] located
[307] swiftly/easily

643   From their foundations loos'ning to and fro,
644   They plucked the seated hills, with all their load,
645   Rocks, waters, woods, and by the shaggy tops
646   Up-lifting bore them in their hands. Amaze,
647   Be sure, and terror, seized the rebel host,
648   When coming towards them so dread they saw[308]
649   The bottom of the mountains upward turned,
650   Till on those cursed engines' triple-row
651   They saw them whelmed,[309] and all their confidence
652   Under the weight of mountains buried deep,
653   Themselves invaded[310] next, and on their heads
654   Main[311] promontories[312] flung, which in the air
655   Came shadowing, and oppressed[313] whole legions armed.
656   Their armor helped their harm, crushed in and bruised
657   Into their substance pent,[314] which wrought them pain
658   Implacable,[315] and many a dolorous groan,
659   Long struggling underneath, ere they could wind
660   Out of such prison, though Spirits of purest light,
661   Purest at first, now gross by sinning grown.
662   The rest, in imitation, to like arms
663   Betook them, and the neighboring hills uptore.
664   So hills amid the air encountered hills,
665   Hurled to and fro with jaculation[316] dire,[317]
666   That under ground they fought in dismal shade.
667   Infernal noise! War seemed a civil game
668   To this uproar. Horrid confusion heaped
669   Upon confusion rose.
                              "And now all Heav'n
670   Had gone to wrack,[318] with ruin overspread,
671   Had not th' Almighty Father, where He sits
672   Shrined in His sanctuary of Heav'n secure,

---

[308] [prosodically, "When *coming towards* them so *dread* they *saw*"]
[309] thrown, so as to cover
[310] attacked, intruded upon
[311] great, solid
[312] headlands
[313] weighed down, crushed
[314] distended
[315] inexorable
[316] hurling, throwing
[317] horrible
[318] disaster, wreck, ruin

673   Consulting on the sum of things, foreseen
674   This tumult, and permitted all, advised,[319]
675   That His great purpose He might so fulfil,
676   To honor His anointed Son avenged
677   Upon his enemies, and to declare
678   All power on him transferred. Whence to His Son,
679   The assessor[320] of His throne, He thus began:
680   " 'Effulgence[321] of my glory, Son belov'd,
681   Son, in whose face invisible is beheld
682   Visibly, what by Deity I am,
683   And in whose hand what by decree I do,
684   Second Omnipotence! Two days are past,
685   Two days, as we compute the days of Heav'n,
686   Since Michael and his Powers went forth to tame
687   These disobedient. Sore hath been their fight,
688   As likeliest was, when two such foes met armed,
689   For to themselves I left them, and thou know'st
690   Equal in their creation they were formed,
691   Save what sin hath impaired, which yet hath wrought
692   Insensibly, for I suspend their doom.[322]
693   Whence in perpetual fight they needs must last[323]
694   Endless, and no solution will be found.
695   War wearied hath performed what war can do,
696   And to disordered rage let loose the reins
697   With mountains, as with weapons, armed, which makes
698   Wild work in Heav'n, and dangerous to the main.[324]
699   Two days are therefore past, the third is thine,
700   For thee I have ordained it, and thus far
701   Have suffered[325] that the glory may be thine
702   Of ending this great war, since none but thou
703   Can end it. Into thee such virtue and grace
704   Immense I have transfused,[326] that all may know
705   In Heav'n and Hell thy power above compare

---

[319] judicious, deliberate
[320] associate, sharer
[321] radiance
[322] sentence, judgment
[323] hold out
[324] the whole, the rest of Heaven
[325] tolerated, allowed
[326] poured, instilled

706 And, this perverse[327] commotion[328] governed[329] thus,
707 To manifest thee worthiest to be heir
708 Of all things, to be heir, and to be King
709 By sacred unction,[330] thy deservèd right.
710 Go then, thou mightiest, in thy Father's might.
711 Ascend my chariot, guide the rapid wheels
712 That shake Heav'n's basis, bring forth all my war,
713 My bow and thunder. My almighty arms
714 Gird on, and sword upon thy puissant thigh.
715 Pursue these sons of darkness, drive them out
716 From all Heav'n's bounds into the utter deep.
717 There let them learn, as likes them,[331] to despise
718 God, and Messiah his anointed King.'
719   "He said, and on His Son with rays direct
720 Shone full. He all his Father full expressed
721 Ineffably[332] into his face received,
722 And thus the Filial Godhead, answering, spoke:
723   " 'O Father, O Supreme of Heav'nly Thrones,
724 First, Highest, Holiest, Best! Thou always seek'st
725 To glorify Thy Son, I always Thee,
726 As is most just. This I my glory account,[333]
727 My exaltation, and my whole delight,
728 That Thou, in me well pleased, declar'st Thy will
729 Fulfilled, which to fulfil is all my bliss.
730 Scepter and power, Thy giving, I assume,
731 And gladlier shall resign, when in the end
732 Thou shalt be all in all, and I in Thee
733 Forever, and in me all whom Thou lov'st.
734 But whom Thou hat'st, I hate, and can put on
735 Thy terrors, as I put Thy mildness on,
736 Image of Thee in all things, and shall soon,
737 Armed with Thy might, rid Heav'n of these rebelled,
738 To their prepared ill mansion driven down,

---

[327] wicked, stubborn
[328] disturbance, sedition
[329] curbed, checked
[330] anointing
[331] as likes them = as they please
[332] beyond the power of words
[333] consider, value

739 To chains of darkness, and th' undying worm,[334]
740 That from Thy just obedience could revolt,
741 Whom to obey is happiness entire,
742 Then shall Thy Saints unmixed,[335] and from th' impure
743 Far separate, circling Thy holy mount,
744 Unfeignèd Halleluiahs to Thee sing,
745 Hymns of high praise, and I among them chief.'
746   "So said, he o'er his scepter bowing, rose
747 From the right hand of Glory where he sat.
748 And the third sacred morn began to shine,
749 Dawning through Heav'n. Forth rushed with whirlwind sound
750 The chariot of paternal Deity,
751 Flashing thick flames, wheel within wheel undrawn,[336]
752 Itself instinct[337] with Spirit, but convoyed[338]
753 By four Cherubic shapes. Four faces each
754 Had wondrous. As with stars, their bodies all
755 And wings were set with eyes, with eyes the wheels
756 Of beryl, and careering[339] fires between.
757 Over their heads a crystal firmament,
758 Whereon a sapphire throne, inlaid with pure
759 Amber, and colors of the showery[340] arch.[341]
760 He in celestial panoply all armed
761 Of radiant Urim,[342] work divinely wrought,
762 Ascended. At his right hand victory
763 Sat eagle-winged; beside him hung his bow
764 And quiver with three-bolted thunder stored,
765 And from about him fierce effusion[343] rolled
766 Of smoke, and bickering[344] flame, and sparkles dire.
767 Attended with ten thousand thousand Saints,
768 He onward came. Far off his coming shone,

---

[334] serpent, snake
[335] purified
[336] undreamed
[337] innate
[338] carried, conveyed
[339] racing
[340] i.e., resembling a shower
[341] the heavens
[342] the jewels on the high priest Aaron's breastplate: see Exodus 28:30
[343] pouring-out
[344] flashing, glistening, quivering

769   And twenty thousand (I their number heard)
770   Chariots of God, half on each hand, were seen.
771   He on the wings of Cherub rode sublime[345]
772   On the crystalline sky, in sapphire throned,
773   Illustrious[346] far and wide, but by his own
774   First seen. Them unexpected joy surprised,
775   When the great ensign of Messiah blazed
776   Aloft, by Angels borne, his sign in Heav'n,
777   Under whose conduct Michael soon reduced[347]
778   His army, circumfused[348] on either wing,
779   Under their head[349] embodied[350] all in one.
780   Before him Power Divine his way prepared;
781   At his command the uprooted hills retired[351]
782   Each to his place. They heard his voice, and went
783   Obsequious.[352] Heav'n his wonted[353] face renewed,
784   And with fresh flow'rets hill and valley smiled.
785   This saw his hapless[354] foes, but stood obdured,[355]
786   And to rebellious fight rallied their Powers,
787   Insensate,[356] hope conceiving[357] from despair.
788   "In Heav'nly Spirits could such perverseness dwell?
789   But to convince the proud what signs avail,
790   Or wonders move th' obdurate to relent?
791   They, hardened more by what might most reclaim,[358]
792   Grieving to see his glory, at the sight
793   Took envy and, aspiring to his height,
794   Stood re-embattled fierce, by force or fraud
795   Weening[359] to prosper, and at length prevail

---

[345] exalted
[346] luminous, gleaming
[347] drew/led back
[348] diffused around
[349] leader
[350] united
[351] withdrew
[352] dutiful, obedient
[353] usual, habitual, familiar
[354] unlucky
[355] unyielding
[356] foolish
[357] forming, taking
[358] reform, win back
[359] thinking

796 Against God and Messiah, or to fall
797 In universal ruin last.[360] And now
798 To final battle drew, disdaining flight,
799 Or faint retreat. When the great Son of God
800 To all his host on either hand thus spoke:
801   " 'Stand still in bright array, ye Saints; here stand,
802 Ye Angels armed; this day from battle rest.
803 Faithful hath been your warfare, and of God
804 Accepted, fearless in His righteous cause,
805 And as ye have received, so have ye done,
806 Invincibly. But of this cursèd crew
807 The punishment to other hand belongs.
808 Vengeance is His, or whose He sole appoints.
809 Number to this day's work is not ordained,
810 Nor multitude. Stand only, and behold
811 God's indignation on these godless poured
812 By me. Not you, but me, they have despised,
813 Yet envied. Against me is all their rage,
814 Because the Father, to whom in Heav'n supreme
815 Kingdom, and power, and glory appertains,
816 Hath honored me, according to His will.
817 Therefore to me their doom[361] He hath assigned,
818 That they may have their wish, to try[362] with me
819 In battle which the stronger proves, they all,
820 Or I alone against them, since by strength
821 They measure all, of other excellence
822 Not emulous,[363] nor care who them excels.
823 Nor other strife with them do I vouchsafe.' "[364]
824   "So spoke the Son, and into terror changed
825 His count'nance, too severe to be beheld,
826 And full of wrath bent on his enemies.
827 At once the Four spread out their starry wings
828 With dreadful shade contiguous, and the orbs
829 Of his fierce chariot rolled, as with the sound
830 Of torrent floods, or of a numerous host.[365]

---

[360] finally, in the end
[361] fate
[362] test
[363] desirous
[364] grant
[365] army

831   He on his impious foes right onward drove,
832   Gloomy[366] as night. Under his burning wheels
833   The steadfast empyrean[367] shook throughout,
834   All but the throne itself of God. Full soon
835   Among them he arrived, in his right hand
836   Grasping ten thousand thunders, which he sent
837   Before him, such as in their souls infixed
838   Plagues.[368] They astonished[369] all resistance lost,
839   All courage. Down their idle[370] weapons dropped.
840   O'er shields, and helms, and helmèd heads he rode
841   Of Thrones and mighty Seraphim prostrate,
842   That wished the mountains now might be again
843   Thrown on them, as a shelter from his ire.[371]
844   Nor less on either side tempestuous fell
845   His arrows, from the fourfold-visaged Four
846   Distinct[372] with eyes, and from the living wheels
847   Distinct alike with multitude of eyes.
848   One Spirit in them ruled; and every eye
849   Glared lightning, and shot forth pernicious[373] fire
850   Among the accursed, that withered all their strength,
851   And of their wonted[374] vigor left them drained,
852   Exhausted, spiritless, afflicted, fall'n.
853   Yet half his strength he put not forth, but checked
854   His thunder in mid volley, for he meant
855   Not to destroy, but root them out of Heav'n.
856   The overthrown he raised, and as a herd
857   Of goats or timorous flock together thronged
858   Drove them before him thunder-struck, pursued
859   With terrors, and with furies, to the bounds
860   And crystal wall of Heav'n, which op'ning wide,
861   Rolled inward, and a spacious gap disclosed
862   Into the wasteful[375] deep. The monstrous sight

---

[366] dark, dismal
[367] [four syllables, first and third accented]
[368] scourges, wounds, afflictions
[369] stunned
[370] useless
[371] wrath
[372] adorned
[373] rapid
[374] customary
[375] empty

863   Struck them with horror backward, but far worse
864   Urged them behind. Headlong themselves they threw
865   Down from the verge[376] of Heav'n. Eternal wrath
866   Burnt after them to the bottomless pit.
867   "Hell heard th' unsufferable[377] noise, Hell saw
868   Heav'n ruining[378] from Heav'n, and would have fled
869   Affrighted, but strict[379] Fate had cast too deep
870   Her dark foundations, and too fast had bound.
871   Nine days they fell. Confounded[380] Chaos roared,
872   And felt tenfold confusion in their fall
873   Through his wild anarchy, so huge a rout[381]
874   Encumbered him with ruin. Hell at last
875   Yawning[382] received them whole, and on them closed,
876   Hell their fit habitation, fraught[383] with fire
877   Unquenchable, the house of woe and pain.
878   Disburdened Heav'n rejoiced, and soon repaired
879   Her mural[384] breach, returning whence it rolled.
880   "Sole victor, from th' expulsion of his foes,
881   Messiah his triumphal chariot turned.
882   To meet him all his Saints, who silent stood
883   Eye-witnesses of his almighty acts,
884   With jubilee[385] advanced and, as they went,
885   Shaded with branching palm, each Order bright
886   Sung triumph, and him sung victorious King,
887   Son, heir, and Lord, to him dominion giv'n,
888   Worthiest to reign. He celebrated rode
889   Triumphant through mid Heav'n, into the courts
890   And temple of his Mighty Father throned
891   On high, who into glory him received,
892   Where now he sits at the right hand of bliss.
893   "Thus, measuring things in Heav'n by things on earth,

---

[376] edge
[377] unbearable, intolerable
[378] falling headlong, falling into ruins [trisyllabic, first and third accented]
[379] rigorous
[380] disordered, confused
[381] defeated army
[382] opening wide
[383] filled
[384] walled
[385] joyful shouts

894   At thy[386] request, and that thou may'st beware[387]
895   By what is past, to thee I have revealed
896   What might have else to human race been hid,
897   The discord which befell,[388] and war in Heav'n
898   Among th' angelic Powers, and the deep fall
899   Of those too high aspiring, who rebelled
900   With Satan—he who envies now thy state,
901   Who now is plotting how he may seduce
902   Thee also from obedience, that[389] with[390] him
903   Bereaved[391] of happiness, thou may'st partake
904   His punishment, eternal misery,
905   Which would be all his solace and revenge,
906   As a despite[392] done against the Most High,
907   Thee once[393] to gain companion[394] of his woe.
908   But listen not to his temptations, warn
909   Thy weaker.[395] Let it profit thee t' have heard,
910   By terrible example, the reward
911   Of disobedience. Firm they might have stood,
912   Yet fell. Remember, and fear to transgress."

The End of the Sixth Book

---

[386] Adam's
[387] be cautious, take warning
[388] occurred
[389] so that
[390] like him, together with him
[391] deprived
[392] spiteful injury
[393] once and for all, forever
[394] as companion
[395] weaker partner, Eve

BOOK VII

THE ARGUMENT

RAPHAEL AT THE request of Adam relates how and wherefore this world was first created; that God, after the expelling of Satan and his Angels out of Heaven, declared His pleasure to create another world and other creatures to dwell therein; sends His Son with glory and attendance of Angels to perform the work of Creation in six days.

The Angels celebrate with hymns the performance thereof, and his[1] re-ascension into Heaven.

---

[1] i.e., Christ

1   Descend from Heav'n, Urania,[2] by that name
2   If rightly thou art called, whose voice divine
3   Following, above the Olympian hill I soar,
4   Above the flight of Pegasean[3] wing![4]
5   The meaning, not the name, I call, for thou
6   Nor of the Muses nine, nor on the top
7   Of old Olympus, dwell'st, but Heav'nly-born,
8   Before the hills appeared, or fountain flowed,
9   Thou with eternal wisdom didst converse,[5]
10   Wisdom thy sister, and with her did'st play
11   In presence of th' Almighty Father, pleased
12   With thy celestial song. Up led by thee
13   Into the Heav'n of Heav'ns I have presumed,
14   An earthly guest, and drawn[6] empyreal air,
15   Thy temp'ring.[7] With like safety guided down,
16   Return me to my native element,[8]
17   Lest from this flying steed unreined (as once
18   Bellerophon, though from a lower clime)
19   Dismounted,[9] on the Aleian field[10] I fall,
20   Erroneous[11] there to wander, and forlorn.[12]
21   Half yet remains unsung, but narrower bound[13]
22   Within the visible diurnal sphere:[14]
23   Standing on earth, not rapt[15] above the pole,[16]
24   More safe I sing with mortal voice, unchanged
25   To hoarse or mute, though fall'n on evil days,
26   On evil days though fall'n, and evil tongues,
27   In darkness, and with dangers compassed round,[17]

---

[2] "heavenly": muse of astronomy
[3] Bellerophon's flying horse
[4] i.e., "above" (beyond) pagan inspiration
[5] live, keep company
[6] breathed in
[7] of thy blending/alloying/preparation
[8] surroundings
[9] Bellerophon was unhorsed by Zeus, when attempting to fly up to the gods' home
[10] to which Bellerophon fell when unhorsed
[11] wandering aimless, straying (as Bellerophon had done)
[12] lost, abandoned
[13] enclosed, contained, confined
[14] diurnal sphere: the sphere that revolves daily around the earth
[15] swept away, carried
[16] above the pole = into Heaven
[17] compassed round = surrounded

28 And solitude. Yet not alone while thou
29 Visit'st my slumbers nightly, or when morn
30 Purples the east. Still govern thou my song,
31 Urania, and fit audience find, though few.
32 But drive far off the barbarous dissonance
33 Of Bacchus and his revellers, the race[18]
34 Of that wild rout that tore the Thracian bard[19]
35 In Rhodopé,[20] where woods and rocks had ears
36 To rapture,[21] till the savage clamor drowned
37 Both harp and voice. Nor could the Muse defend
38 Her son.[22] So fail not thou, who thee implores,
39 For thou art Heav'nly, she an empty dream.
40   Say, goddess, what ensued when Raphael,
41 The affable Arch-Angel, had forewarned
42 Adam, by dire example, to beware
43 Apostasy, by what befell[23] in Heav'n
44 To those apostates, lest the like befall
45 In Paradise to Adam or his race,
46 Charged not to touch the interdicted tree,
47 If they transgress, and slight[24] that sole command,
48 So easily obeyed amid the choice
49 Of all tastes else to please their appetite,
50 Though wand'ring.[25] He with his consorted[26] Eve
51 The story heard, attentive, and was filled
52 With admiration[27] and deep muse[28] to hear
53 Of things so high[29] and strange[30] — things to their thought
54 So unimaginable, as hate in Heav'n,
55 And war so near the peace of God in bliss,
56 With such confusion,[31] but the evil, soon

---

[18] group or class of persons, here Bacchantes or worshipers of Bacchus
[19] Orpheus
[20] mountain range in Thrace, sacred to Bacchus
[21] ecstasy
[22] Calliope, muse of epic poetry
[23] happened
[24] ignore, disdain
[25] unsteady, not fixed
[26] partner in marriage
[27] wonder
[28] pensiveness
[29] exalted
[30] astonishing, unknown
[31] disorder, commotion

57 Driv'n back, redounded[32] as a flood on those
58 From whom it sprung, impossible to mix
59 With blessedness. Whence Adam soon repealed[33]
60 The doubts that in his heart arose, and now
61 Led on, yet sinless, with desire to know
62 What nearer might concern him, how this world
63 Of Heav'n and earth conspicuous[34] first began,
64 When, and whereof created, for what cause,
65 What within Eden, or without, was done
66 Before his memory—as one whose drought
67 Yet scarce allayed, still eyes the current[35] stream,
68 Whose liquid murmur heard, new thirst excites,
69 Proceeded thus to ask his Heav'nly guest:
70   "Great things, and full of wonder in our ears,
71 Far differing from this world, thou hast revealed,
72 Divine interpreter![36] by favor sent
73 Down from the empyrean, to forewarn
74 Us timely of what might else have been our loss,
75 Unknown, which human knowledge could not reach.
76 For which to the infinitely Good we owe
77 Immortal thanks, and His admonishment
78 Receive, with solemn purpose to observe
79 Immutably His sov'reign will, the end[37]
80 Of what we are. But since thou hast vouchsafed[38]
81 Gently,[39] for our instruction, to impart
82 Things above earthly thought, which yet concerned
83 Our knowing, as to highest wisdom seemed,
84 Deign to descend now lower, and relate
85 What may no less perhaps avail us, known,
86 How first began this Heav'n which we behold
87 Distant so high, with moving fires adorned
88 Innumerable, and this which yields or fills

---

[32] turned back
[33] dismissed, abandoned
[34] visible
[35] flowing
[36] messenger
[37] purpose
[38] deigned, condescended
[39] courteously, generously

89 All space, the ambient[40] air wide interfused[41]
90 Embracing round this florid[42] earth. What cause
91 Moved the Creator, in His holy rest[43]
92 Through all eternity, so late[44] to build
93 In Chaos, and the work begun, how soon
94 Absolved.[45] If unforbid thou may'st unfold
95 What we, not to explore the secrets, ask
96 Of His eternal empire, but the more
97 To magnify His works, the more we know.
98 And the great light of day yet wants[46] to run
99 Much of his race, though steep. Suspense in Heav'n,
100 Held by thy voice, thy potent voice he hears,
101 And longer will delay to hear thee tell
102 His generation,[47] and the rising birth
103 Of Nature from the unapparent[48] deep.[49]
104 Or if the star of ev'ning and the moon
105 Haste to thy audience, night with her will bring
106 Silence—and sleep, list'ning to thee, will watch,[50]
107 Or we can bid[51] his absence till thy song
108 End, and dismiss[52] thee ere the morning shine."
109 Thus Adam his illustrious guest besought,[53]
110 And thus the godlike Angel answered mild:
111   "This also thy request, with caution asked,
112 Obtain, though to recount Almighty works
113 What words or tongue of Seraph can suffice,
114 Or heart of man suffice to comprehend?
115 Yet what thou canst attain,[54] which best may serve

---

[40] encompassing
[41] interspersed, poured in
[42] flowering, blooming, bright
[43] repose
[44] recently
[45] completed
[46] lacks
[47] creating, begetting
[48] invisible
[49] Chaos
[50] stay awake
[51] ask
[52] send away, allow to depart
[53] supplicated
[54] gain, reach

116　To glorify the Maker, and infer[55]
117　Thee also happier, shall not be withheld
118　Thy hearing. Such commission from above
119　I have received, to answer thy desire
120　Of knowledge within bounds. Beyond,[56] abstain
121　To ask, nor let thine own inventions[57] hope
122　Things not revealed, which the invisible King,
123　Only[58] Omniscient, hath suppressed[59] in night,
124　To none communicable in earth or Heaven:
125　Enough is left besides to search and know.
126　But knowledge is as food, and needs no less
127　Her temp'rance over appetite, to know
128　In measure what the mind may well contain,
129　Oppresses else with surfeit, and soon turns
130　Wisdom to folly, as nourishment to wind.
131　　　　　"Know then, that after Lucifer from Heav'n
132　(So call him, brighter once amidst the host
133　Of Angels than that star[60] the stars among)
134　Fell with his flaming legions through the deep
135　Into his place, and the great Son returned
136　Victorious with his Saints, the Omnipotent
137　Eternal Father from His throne beheld
138　Their multitude, and to His Son thus spoke:
139　　　　　" 'At last our envious foe hath failed, who
　　　　　　　　　thought
140　All[61] like himself rebellious, by whose aid
141　This inaccessible high strength, the seat
142　Of Deity supreme, us dispossessed,
143　He trusted to have seized, and into fraud
144　Drew many, whom their place knows here no more.
145　Yet far the greater part have kept, I see,
146　Their station.[62] Heaven, yet populous, retains

---

[55] make, show, prove
[56] further
[57] imagining
[58] the only
[59] hidden, kept secret
[60] Lucifer, the morning star
[61] all were
[62] position, place

147	Number sufficient to possess[63] her realms
148	Though wide, and this high temple to frequent[64]
149	With ministeries[65] due, and solemn rites.
150	But lest his heart exalt him in the harm
151	Already done, to have dispeopled Heav'n,
152	My damage fondly[66] deemed,[67] I can repair
153	That detriment,[68] if such it be to lose
154	Self-lost, and in a moment will create
155	Another world, out of one man a race
156	Of men innumerable, there to dwell,
157	Not here, till by degrees of merit raised
158	They open to themselves at length the way
159	Up hither, under long obedience tried,[69]
160	And earth be changed to Heav'n, and Heav'n to earth,
161	One kingdom, joy and union without end.
162	Meanwhile inhabit lax,[70] ye Powers of Heav'n,
163	And thou my Word, begotten Son, by thee
164	This I perform. Speak thou, and be it done!
165	My overshadowing[71] Spirit and Might with thee
166	I send along. Ride forth, and bid the deep
167	Within appointed bounds be Heav'n and earth—
168	Boundless the deep, because I Am who fill
169	Infinitude, nor vacuous the space.
170	Though I, uncircumscribed myself, retire,
171	And put not forth my goodness, which is free
172	To act or not, necessity and chance
173	Approach not me, and what I will is fate.'
174	"So spoke th' Almighty and, to what He spoke,
175	His Word, the Filial Godhead gave effect.
176	Immediate are the acts of God, more swift
177	Than time or motion, but to human ears
178	Cannot without process of speech be told,

---

[63] occupy, hold
[64] [frequent]
[65] services (in the religious sense)
[66] foolishly
[67] surmised
[68] loss
[69] tested
[70] loosely, at ease
[71] protecting

179   So told as earthly notion can receive.
180   Great triumph and rejoicing was in Heav'n,
181   When such was heard declared th' Almighty's will.
182   Glory they sung to the Most High, good will
183   To future men, and in their dwellings peace—
184   Glory to Him, whose just avenging ire
185   Had driven out the ungodly from His sight
186   And th' habitations of the just; to Him
187 · Glory and praise, whose wisdom had ordained
188   Good out of evil to create, instead
189   Of Spirits malign a better race to bring
190   Into their vacant room,[72] and thence diffuse
191   His good to worlds and ages infinite.
192   So sang the Hierarchies.[73]
                              "Meanwhile the Son
193   On his great expedition now appeared,
194   Girt with Omnipotence, with radiance crowned
195   Of Majesty Divine. Sapience[74] and love
196   Immense, and all his Father in him shone.
197   About his chariot numberless were poured
198   Cherub, and Seraph, Potentates, and Thrones,
199   And Virtues, wingèd Spirits, and chariots winged
200   From th' armory[75] of God, where stand of old
201   Myriads, between two brazen[76] mountains lodged[77]
202   Against a solemn day, harnessed at hand,
203   Celestial equipage,[78] and now came forth
204   Spontaneous,[79] for within them Spirit lived,
205   Attendant on their Lord. Heav'n op'ned wide
206   Her ever-during[80] gates, harmonious sound
207   On golden hinges moving, to let forth
208   The King of Glory, in his powerful Word
209   And Spirit, coming to create new worlds.

---

[72] place
[73] of angels
[74] wisdom
[75] arsenal
[76] like brass
[77] deposited
[78] apparatus
[79] naturally [trisyllabic, second accented, "-eous" elided]
[80] enduring

210   On Heav'nly ground they stood, and from the shore
211   They viewed the vast immeasurable abyss
212   Outrageous[81] as a sea, dark, wasteful,[82] wild,
213   Up from the bottom turned by furious winds
214   And surging waves, as mountains, to assault
215   Heav'n's height, and with the center mix the pole.
216   " 'Silence, ye troubled waves, and thou, deep:
                                         peace!'
217   Said then the Omnific[83] Word. 'Your discord end!'
218   Nor stayed but on the wings of Cherubim
219   Uplifted, in paternal glory rode
220   Far into Chaos and the world unborn,
221   For Chaos heard His voice. Him all his train
222   Followed in bright procession, to behold
223   Creation, and the wonders of His might.
224   Then stayed the fervid[84] wheels, and in His hand
225   He took the golden compasses, prepared
226   In God's eternal store, to circumscribe[85]
227   This universe, and all created things.
228   One foot He centered, and the other turned
229   Round through the vast profundity[86] obscure.
230   And said: 'Thus far extend, thus far thy bounds,
231   This be thy just circumference, O world!'
232   Thus God the Heav'n created, thus the earth,
233   Matter unformed and void. Darkness profound[87]
234   Covered the abyss, but on the wat'ry calm
235   His brooding wings the Spirit of God outspread,
236   And vital virtue infused, and vital warmth
237   Throughout the fluid mass, but downward purged[88]
238   The black tartareous[89] cold infernal dregs,
239   Adverse to life. Then founded,[90] then conglobed[91]

---

[81] enormous
[82] desolate
[83] all-creating
[84] glowing
[85] inscribe/draw a circular line/boundary
[86] depth
[87] deep
[88] removed
[89] (1) earthy, gritty, sedimentary, (2) hellish
[90] created
[91] collected and compacted

240   Like things to like; the rest to several place
241   Disparted,[92] and between[93] spun out the air,
242   And earth self-balanced on her center hung.
243   'Let there be light,' said God, and forthwith light
244   Ethereal,[94] first of things, quintessence[95] pure,
245   Sprung from the deep, and from her native east
246   To journey through the airy gloom began,
247   Sphered in a radiant cloud, for yet the sun
248   Was not; she[96] in a cloudy tabernacle[97]
249   Sojourned[98] the while. God saw the light was good,
250   And light from darkness by the hemisphere
251   Divided: light the Day, and darkness Night
252   He named. Thus was the first day, ev'n and morn,
253   Nor passed uncelebrated, nor unsung
254   By the celestial choirs, when orient[99] light
255   Exhaling[100] first from darkness they beheld,
256   Birth-day of Heav'n and earth. With joy and shout
257   The hollow universal orb they filled,
258   And touched their golden harps, and hymning praised
259   God and His works. Creator Him they sung,
260   Both when first ev'ning was, and when first morn.
261   Again, God said: 'Let there be firmament[101]
262   Amid the waters, and let it divide
263   The waters from the waters.' And God made
264   The firmament, expanse of liquid, pure,
265   Transparent, elemental air, diffused
266   In circuit to the uttermost convex
267   Of this great round, partition[102] firm and sure,
268   The waters underneath from those above
269   Dividing, for as earth, so He the world

---

[92] separated
[93] in between
[94] spiritlike
[95] the fifth essence, of which substance the heavenly bodies were thought to be composed
[96] the sun
[97] tent
[98] stayed for a while, tarried
[99] gleaming
[100] blowing, sent out
[101] firm or solid structure
[102] division, distribution

270 Built on circumfluous[103] waters calm, in wide
271 Crystalline ocean, and the loud[104] misrule[105]
272 Of Chaos far removed,[106] lest fierce extremes
273 Contiguous[107] might distemper[108] the whole frame.
274 And Heav'n He named the firmament. So ev'n
275 And morning chorus sung the second day.
276   "The earth was formed, but in the womb as yet
277 Of waters, embryon[109] immature involved,[110]
278 Appeared not. Over all the face of earth
279 Main ocean flowed, not idle[111] but with warm
280 Prolific[112] humor[113] soft'ning all her globe,
281 Fermented[114] the great mother to conceive,
282 Satiate with genial[115] moisture, when God said:
283 'Be gathered now ye waters under Heav'n
284 Into one place, and let dry land appear.'
285 Immediately the mountains huge appear
286 Emergent, and their broad bare backs upheave
287 Into the clouds, their tops ascend the sky,
288 So high as heaved the tumid[116] hills, so low
289 Down sunk a hollow bottom broad and deep,
290 Capacious bed of waters. Thither they[117]
291 Hasted with glad precipitance,[118] uprolled[119]
292 As drops on dust conglobing[120] from the dry.
293 Part rise in crystal wall, or ridge[121] direct,

---

[103] ambient, flowing around
[104] offensive
[105] disorder
[106] took away
[107] [trisyllabic, second accented, "-uous" elided]
[108] disturb, disorder, derange
[109] embryo [trisyllabic, second accented]
[110] reserved
[111] uselessly, pointless
[112] fertilizing
[113] fluids, essences
[114] stirred
[115] generative
[116] swelling, bulging
[117] the waters
[118] great speed
[119] rolled up
[120] collecting
[121] beds, lines

294 For haste: such flight the great command impressed
295 On the swift floods. As armies at the call
296 Of trumpet (for of armies thou hast heard)
297 Troop[122] to their standard, so the wat'ry throng,
298 Wave rolling after wave, where way they found,
299 If steep, with torrent[123] rapture,[124] if through plain,
300 Soft-ebbing,[125] nor withstood them rock or hill,
301 But they, or[126] under ground, or circuit wide
302 With serpent error[127] wand'ring, found their way,
303 And on the washy[128] ooze deep channels wore—
304 Easy,[129] ere God had bid the ground be dry,
305 All but within those banks, where rivers now
306 Stream and perpetual draw their humid train.[130]
307 The dry land, earth,[131] and the great receptacle
308 Of congregated waters, He called seas,
309 And saw that it was good. And said: 'Let th' earth
310 Put forth the verdant[132] grass, herb yielding seed,
311 And fruit-tree yielding fruit after her kind,
312 Whose seed is in herself upon the earth.'
313 He scarce had said, when the bare earth, till then
314 Desert and bare, unsightly, unadorned,
315 Brought forth the tender grass, whose verdure clad
316 Her universal face with pleasant green.
317 Then herbs of every leaf, that sudden flowered
318 Op'ning their various colours, and made gay
319 Her bosom, smelling sweet, and these scarce blown,[133]
320 Forth flourished thick the clust'ring vine, forth crept
321 The swelling gourd, up stood the corny[134] reed

---

[122] [verb]
[123] rushing [adjective]
[124] force of movement
[125] flowing back
[126] whether, either
[127] winding
[128] waterlogged
[129] comfortable
[130] current
[131] "He called the dry land 'earth'"
[132] green
[133] formed
[134] grainlike

322   Embattled[135] in her field, and the humble shrub,
323   And bush with frizzled hair implicit.[136] Last
324   Rose, as in dance, the stately trees, and spread
325   Their branches hung with copious fruit, or gemmed[137]
326   Their blossoms. With high woods the hills were crowned,
327   With tufts[138] the valleys, and each fountain-side,
328   With borders long[139] the rivers, that earth now
329   Seemed like to Heav'n, a seat where gods might dwell,
330   Or wander with delight, and love to haunt[140]
331   Her sacred shades, though God had yet not rained
332   Upon the earth, and man to till the ground
333   None was. But from the earth a dewy mist
334   Went up, and watered all the ground, and each
335   Plant of the field, which ere it was in th' earth
336   God made, and every herb, before it grew
337   On the green stem. God saw that it was good.
338   So ev'n and morn recorded the third day.
339   "Again th' Almighty spoke: 'Let there be lights
340   High in th' expanse of Heaven, to divide
341   The day from night, and let them be for signs,
342   For seasons, and for days, and circling years,
343   And let them be for lights, as I ordain
344   Their office in the firmament of Heav'n,
345   To give light on the earth.' And it was so.
346   And God made two great lights, great for their use
347   To man, the greater to have rule by day,
348   The less by night, altern.[141] And made the stars,
349   And set them in the firmament of Heav'n
350   T' illuminate the earth, and rule the day
351   In their vicissitude,[142] and rule the night,
352   And light from darkness to divide. God saw,
353   Surveying His great work, that it was good,
354   For of celestial bodies first the sun

---

[35] crenellated, having battlements
[36] entangled, entwined
[37] budded
[38] groups of trees/shrubs
[39] along
[40] visit, habituate
[41] alternately
[42] mutation, sequence

355   A mighty sphere He framed, unlightsome[143] first,[144]
356   Though of ethereal mould, then formed the moon
357   Globose,[145] and every magnitude of stars,
358   And sowed with stars the Heav'n, thick as a field.
359   Of light by far the greater part He took,
360   Transplanted from her cloudy shrine, and placed
361   In the sun's orb, made porous to receive
362   And drink the liquid light, firm to retain
363   Her gathered beams, great palace[146] now of light.
364   Hither, as to their fountain, other stars
365   Repairing,[147] in their golden urns draw light,
366   And hence the morning-planet[148] gilds her horns.[149]
367   By tincture[150] or reflection they augment
368   Their small peculiar,[151] though from human sight
369   So far remote, with diminution seen.[152]
370   First in his east the glorious lamp was seen,
371   Regent[153] of day, and all th' horizon round
372   Invested[154] with bright rays, jocund[155] to run
373   His longitude[156] through Heav'n's high road. The gray
374   Dawn and the Pleiades before him danced,
375   Shedding sweet influence.[157] Less bright the moon,
376   But opposite in levelled[158] west was set,
377   His[159] mirror, with full face borrowing her light
378   From him, for other light she needed none
379   In that aspect,[160] and still that distance keeps

---

[143] not luminous
[144] at first
[145] of globular shape
[146] residence
[147] going, resorting
[148] Venus
[149] Galileo discovered that Venus, like the moon, had phases (then commonly spoken of as "horns")
[150] extraction, infusion, absorption
[151] private property
[152] with diminution seen = seen with lessened light
[153] ruler, governor, controller
[154] clothed, vested
[155] glad
[156] east-west course
[157] flowing forces
[158] horizontal
[159] the sun's
[160] position

380 Till night, then in the east her turn she shines,
381 Revolved on Heav'n's great axle, and her reign
382 With thousand lesser lights dividual[161] holds,
383 With thousand thousand stars, that then appeared
384 Spangling[162] the hemisphere. Then first adorned
385 With their bright luminaries that set and rose,
386 Glad ev'ning and glad morn crowned the fourth day.
387   "And God said: 'Let the waters generate
388 Reptile with spawn abundant, living soul,
389 And let fowl fly above the earth, with wings
390 Displayed on the open firmament of Heav'n.'
391 And God created the great whales, and each
392 Soul living, each that crept, which plenteously
393 The waters generated by their kinds,
394 And every bird of wing after his kind,
395 And saw that it was good, and blessed them, saying:
396 'Be fruitful, multiply, and in the seas,
397 And lakes, and running streams, the waters fill,
398 And let the fowl be multiplied on th' earth.'
399 Forthwith the sounds[163] and seas, each creek and bay,
400 With fry[164] innumerable swarm, and shoals
401 Of fish that with their fins, and shining scales,
402 Glide under the green wave, in sculls[165] that oft
403 Bank[166] the mid sea, part single, or with mate,
404 Graze the sea-weed their pasture, and through groves
405 Of coral stray, or sporting[167] with quick glance,
406 Show to the sun their waved coats dropped[168] with gold,
407 Or in their pearly shells at ease, attend[169]
408 Moist nutriment, or under rocks their food
409 In jointed armour watch.[170] On smooth[171] the seal

---

[161] divided, separate
[162] decorating
[163] channels, inlets
[164] smaller fish
[165] schools
[166] form a mass/mound in
[167] frolicking
[168] sprinkled, flecked
[169] look for
[170] watch for
[171] smooth water

410   And bended[172] dolphins play, part huge of bulk,
411   Wallowing[173] unwieldy,[174] enormous in their gait
412   Tempest[175] the ocean. There Leviathan,
413   Hugest of living creatures, on the deep
414   Stretched like a promontory sleeps or swims,
415   And seems a moving land, and at his gills
416   Draws in, and at his trunk spouts out, a sea.
417   Meanwhile the tepid[176] caves, and fens,[177] and shores
418   Their brood as numerous hatch, from th' egg that soon
419   Bursting with kindly[178] rupture forth disclosed
420   Their callow[179] young, but feathered soon and fledge[180]
421   They summed[181] their pens[182] and, soaring the air sublime,[183]
422   With clang[184] despised[185] the ground, under a cloud
423   In prospect.[186] There the eagle and the stork
424   On cliffs and cedar tops their eyries build.
425   Part loosely wing the region,[187] part more wise
426   In common, ranged[188] in figure,[189] wedge[190] their way,
427   Intelligent[191] of seasons, and set forth
428   Their airy caravan, high over seas
429   Flying, and over lands, with mutual[192] wing
430   Easing their flight. So steers the prudent crane
431   Her annual voyage, borne on winds. The air

---

[172] striped
[173] rolling, surging
[174] ungraceful
[175] disturb violently [verb]
[176] lukewarm
[177] marshes
[178] natural
[179] downy, unfledged
[180] maturely feathered
[181] collect
[182] full-grown feathers
[183] high
[184] harsh birdcalls
[185] looked down on
[186] in visual survey from the ground, the mass of birds resembles a cloud
[187] i.e., of the sky
[188] arranged
[189] a pattern
[190] cleave, drive (as per their wedgelike, triangular formation)
[191] understanding
[192] reciprocal: those behind, it was said, rested their heads on those in front

432 Floats[193] as they pass, fanned with unnumbered plumes.
433 From branch to branch the smaller birds with song
434 Solaced[194] the woods, and spread their painted wings
435 Till ev'n,[195] nor then the solemn[196] nightingale
436 Ceased warbling, but all night tuned her soft lays.[197]
437 Others, on silver lakes and rivers, bathed
438 Their downy breast; the swan with archèd neck,
439 Between her white wings mantling[198] proudly, rows
440 Her state with oary feet; yet oft they quit
441 The dank[199] and, rising on stiff pennons, tow'r[200]
442 The mid aereal sky. Others on ground
443 Walked firm, the crested cock whose clarion[201] sounds
444 The silent hours, and th' other[202] whose gay train
445 Adorns him, colored with the florid hue
446 Of rainbows and starry eyes. The waters thus
447 With fish replenished,[203] and the air with fowl,
448 Ev'ning and morn solemnized[204] the fifth day.
449   "The sixth, and of Creation last, arose
450 With ev'ning harps, and matin,[205] when God said:
451 'Let th' earth bring forth soul living, in her kind,[206]
452 Cattle, and creeping things, and beast of th' earth,
453 Each in their kind.' The earth obeyed, and straight
454 Op'ning her fertile womb teemed[207] at a birth
455 Innumerous living creatures, perfect forms,
456 Limbed and full grown. Out of the ground up rose,
457 As from his lair, the wild beast where he wons[208]

---

[193] moves gently, undulates
[194] made a cheerful place of
[195] evening
[196] grave, impressive
[197] songs
[198] spread out, one after the other
[199] wet spot, wetness
[200] [verb]
[201] trumpetlike call [noun]
[202] the peacock
[203] filled
[204] proclaimed, honored
[205] (1) birdsong [if a noun], or (2) morning [if an adjective modifying "harps"]
[206] of her sort/kind/species
[207] brought forth
[208] dwells

458   In forest wild, in thicket, brake,[209] or den.
459   Among the trees in pairs they rose, they walked,
460   The cattle in the fields and meadows green,
461   Those[210] rare and solitary, these[211] in flocks
462   Pasturing at once, and in broad herds upsprung.[212]
463   The grassy clods[213] now calved: now half appeared
464   The tawny lion, pawing to get free
465   His hinder parts, then springs as broke from bonds,
466   And rampant[214] shakes his brinded[215] mane. The ounce,[216]
467   The libbard,[217] and the tiger, as the mole
468   Rising, the crumbled earth above them threw
469   In hillocks. The swift stag from under ground
470   Bore up his branching head. Scarce from his mould
471   Behemoth,[218] biggest born of earth, upheaved
472   His vastness. Fleeced the flocks, and bleating rose
473   As[219] plants. Ambiguous[220] between[221] sea and land
474   The river-horse,[222] and scaly crocodile.
475   At once came forth whatever creeps the ground,
476   Insect or worm. Those waved their limber[223] fans[224]
477   For wings, and smallest lineaments[225] exact[226]
478   In all the liveries decked of summer's pride
479   With spots of gold and purple, azure and green.
480   These as a line their long dimension drew,
481   Streaking[227] the ground with sinuous trace.[228] Not all

---

[209] brushwood
[210] the wild beasts of the wood
[211] cattle
[212] come into being
[213] earth
[214] rearing
[215] brindled, streaked
[216] lynx
[217] leopard
[218] see Job 40:15–24
[219] like
[220] hesitating
[221] [*between*]
[222] hippo = horse, potamus = of the river: Milton here translates the Greek
[223] flexible
[224] tails
[225] parts of the body
[226] finishèd, perfect
[227] marking with stripes
[228] tracks

482   Minims[229] of Nature: some of serpent-kind,
483   Wondrous in length and corpulence,[230] involved[231]
484   Their snaky folds, and added[232] wings. First crept
485   The parsimonious emmet,[233] provident
486   Of future, in small room large heart enclosed,
487   Pattern of just equality perhaps
488   Hereafter, joined in her popular[234] tribes
489   Of commonalty. Swarming, next appeared
490   The female bee, that feeds her husband drone
491   Deliciously, and builds her waxen cells
492   With honey stored. The rest are numberless,
493   And thou their natures know'st, and gav'st them names,
494   Needless to thee repeated. Nor unknown
495   The serpent, subtlest[235] beast of all the field,
496   Of huge extent sometimes, with brazen eyes
497   And hairy mane terrific,[236] though to thee
498   Not noxious,[237] but obedient at thy call.
499   "Now Heav'n in all her glory shone, and rolled
500   Her motions, as the great first Mover's hand
501   First wheeled their course. Earth in her rich attire
502   Consummate[238] lovely smiled. Air, water, earth,
503   By fowl, fish, beast, was flown, was swum, was walked,
504   Frequent, and of the sixth day yet remained.
505   There wanted yet the master-work, the end[239]
506   Of all yet done, a creature who not prone[240]
507   And brute[241] as other creatures, but endued
508   With sanctity[242] of reason, might erect
509   His stature, and upright with front[243] serene

---

[229] very small creatures
[230] size
[231] enwrapped
[232] [adjective]
[233] ant
[234] crowded [popular?]
[235] most artful, trickiest
[236] frightful, terrorizing
[237] hurtful
[238] supremely, perfected
[239] goal, purpose
[240] face down
[241] savage
[242] holy feelings
[243] face

510   Govern the rest, self-knowing, and from thence
511   Magnanimous[244] to correspond[245] with Heav'n,
512   But grateful to acknowledge whence his good
513   Descends, thither with heart, and voice, and eyes
514   Directed in devotion, to adore
515   And worship God Supreme, who made him chief
516   Of all His works. Therefore th' Omnipotent
517   Eternal Father (for where is not He
518   Present?) thus to His Son audibly spoke:
519   " 'Let us make now man in our image, man
520   In our similitude,[246] and let them[247] rule
521   Over the fish and fowl of sea and air,
522   Beast of the field, and over all the earth,
523   And every creeping thing that creeps the ground.'
524   This said, He formed thee, Adam, thee, O man,
525   Dust of the ground, and in thy nostrils breathed
526   The breath of life. In His own image He
527   Created thee, in the image of God
528   Express,[248] and thou becam'st a living soul.
529   Male He created thee, but thy consort
530   Female, for race,[249] then blessed mankind, and said:
531   'Be fruitful, multiply, and fill the earth;
532   Subdue[250] it, and throughout dominion hold
533   Over fish of the sea, and fowl of the air,
534   And every living thing that moves on th' earth.'
535   Wherever thus created, for no place
536   Is yet distinct[251] by name, thence, as thou know'st,
537   He brought thee into this delicious grove,
538   This garden, planted with the trees of God,
539   Delectable both to behold and taste,
540   And freely all their pleasant fruit for food
541   Gave thee. All sorts are here that all th' earth yields,
542   Variety without end. But of the tree

---

[244] noble
[245] be harmonious with, answer to
[246] likeness
[247] men
[248] exact [adjective]
[249] breeding, generation
[250] control, cultivate
[251] differentiated, distinguishable

543 Which tasted, works knowledge of good and evil,
544 Thou may'st not. In the day thou eat'st, thou di'st.[252]
545 Death is the penalty imposed. Beware,
546 And govern well thy appetite, lest Sin
547 Surprise thee, and her black attendant, Death.
548　　　　"Here finished He, and all that He had made
549 Viewed, and behold all was entirely good.
550 So ev'n and morn accomplished the sixth day.
551　　　　"Yet not till the Creator from His work
552 Desisting, though unwearied, up returned,
553 Up to the Heav'n of Heav'ns, His high abode,
554 Thence to behold this new created world,
555 Th' addition of His empire, how it showed
556 In prospect from His throne, how good, how fair,
557 Answering[253] His great idea.[254] Up He rode
558 Followed with acclamation, and the sound
559 Symphonious of ten thousand harps, that tuned
560 Angelic harmonies. The earth, the air
561 Resounded (thou rememb'rest, for thou heard'st),
562 The Heav'ns and all the constellations rung,
563 The planets in their station listening stood,
564 While the bright pomp[255] ascended jubilant.
565 'Open, ye everlasting gates!' they sung,
566 'Open, ye Heav'ns! your living doors! Let in
567 The great Creator from His work returned
568 Magnificent, His six days work, a world!
569 Open, and henceforth oft, for God will deign
570 To visit oft the dwellings of just men,
571 Delighted, and with frequent intercourse
572 Thither will send His wingèd messengers
573 On errands of supernal[256] grace.' So sung
574 The glorious train[257] ascending. He through Heav'n,
575 That opened wide her blazing portals, led
576 To God's eternal house direct the way,
577 A broad and ample road, whose dust is gold

---

[252] die-est
[253] fulfilling
[254] [the syntax here is uncertain, though the intended meaning is not]
[255] procession
[256] heavenly, exalted
[257] procession

578   And pavement stars, as stars to thee appear,
579   Seen in the galaxy, that milky way
580   Which nightly, as a circling zone,[258] thou see'st
581   Powdered with stars. And now on earth the seventh
582   Ev'ning arose in Eden, for the sun
583   Was set, and twilight from the east came on,
584   Forerunning night, when at the holy mount
585   Of Heav'n's high-seated top, the imperial throne
586   Of Godhead, fixed for ever firm and sure,
587   The Filial Power arrived, and sat him down
588   With his great Father, for he also went
589   Invisible, yet stayed[259] (such privilege
590   Hath Omnipresence), and the work ordained,
591   Author and End of all things, and from work
592   Now resting, blessed and hallowed the sev'nth day,
593   As resting on that day from all His work,
594   But not in silence holy kept. The harp
595   Had work and rested not, the solemn pipe,
596   And dulcimer, all organs of sweet stop,
597   All sounds on fret[260] by string or golden wire,
598   Tempered[261] soft tunings, intermixed with voice
599   Choral or unison. Of incense clouds,
600   Fuming from golden censers, hid the mount.
601   Creation and the six days acts they sung:
602   " 'Great are thy works, Jehovah! Infinite
603   Thy power! What thought can measure Thee, or tongue
604   Relate thee? Greater now in Thy return
605   Than from the giant Angels. Thee that day
606   Thy thunders magnified, but to create
607   Is greater than created[262] to destroy.
608   Who can impair[263] Thee, Mighty King, or bound[264]
609   Thy empire? Easily the proud attempt
610   Of Spirits apostate, and their counsels vain,
611   Thou hast repelled, while impiously they thought

---

[258] belt, girdle
[259] abided
[260] the stop on a stringed instrument
[261] produced
[262] that which is created
[263] injure
[264] limit

612 Thee to diminish, and from Thee withdraw
613 The number of Thy worshippers. Who seeks
614 To lessen Thee, against his purpose serves
615 To manifest the more Thy might. His evil
616 Thou usest, and from thence creat'st more good.
617 Witness this new-made world, another Heav'n
618 From Heaven-gate not far, founded in view
619 On the clear hyaline,[265] the glassy sea,
620 Of amplitude almost immense,[266] with stars
621 Numerous, and every star perhaps a world
622 Of destined habitation. But thou know'st
623 Their seasons. Among[267] these the seat of men,
624 Earth, with her nether[268] ocean circumfused,[269]
625 Their pleasant dwelling-place. Thrice happy men,
626 And sons of men, whom God hath thus advanced![270]
627 Created in His image, there to dwell
628 And worship Him, and in reward to rule
629 Over His works, on earth, in sea, or air,
630 And multiply a race of worshippers
631 Holy and just. Thrice happy, if they know
632 Their happiness, and persevere upright!'
633   "So sung they, and the empyrean rung
634 With hallelujahs. Thus was sabbath kept.
635 And thy request think now fulfilled, that asked
636 How first this world and face[271] of things began,
637 And what before thy memory was done
638 From the beginning, that[272] posterity,
639 Informed by thee, might know. If else thou seek'st
640 Aught, not surpassing human measure,[273] say."

The End of the Seventh Book

---

[265] the waters above the firmament
[266] boundless, immeasurable: the reference is to the new world, not to the hyaline
[267] [first syllable accented]
[268] lower
[269] surrounded
[270] raised
[271] visible state, external appearance
[272] so that
[273] need

BOOK VIII

THE ARGUMENT

ADAM INQUIRES CONCERNING celestial motions, is doubtfully answered, and exhorted to search rather things more worthy of knowledge. Adam assents, and still desirous to detain Raphael, relates to him what he remembered since his own creation, his placing in Paradise, his talk with God concerning solitude and fit society, his first meeting and nuptials with Eve, his discourse with the Angel thereupon, who after admonitions repeated departs.

1   The Angel ended, and in Adam's ear
2 So charming[1] left his voice, that he a while
3 Thought him still speaking, still stood fixed[2] to hear,
4 Then, as new waked, thus gratefully replied:
5   "What thanks sufficient, or what recompence
6 Equal, have I to render thee, divine
7 Historian,[3] who thus largely[4] hast allayed
8 The thirst I had of knowledge, and vouchsafed
9 This friendly condescension to relate
10 Things else by me unsearchable?[5] now heard
11 With wonder, but delight, and as is due
12 With glory attributed to the high
13 Creator! Something yet of doubt remains,
14 Which only thy solution[6] can resolve.
15 When I behold this goodly frame,[7] this world,
16 Of Heav'n and earth consisting, and compute
17 Their magnitudes, this earth, a spot, a grain,
18 An atom, with the firmament compared
19 And all her numbered stars, that seem to roll
20 Spaces incomprehensible (for such
21 Their distance argues,[8] and their swift return
22 Diurnal)[9] merely to officiate[10] light
23 Round this opaceous[11] earth, this punctual[12] spot,
24 One day and night, in all her vast survey[13]
25 Useless besides, reasoning I oft admire[14]
26 How Nature wise and frugal could commit
27 Such disproportions, with superfluous hand
28 So many nobler bodies to create,
29 Greater so manifold, to this one use

---

[1] under a spell: i.e., "charm," as in magic spells
[2] immobile
[3] (1) teller of history, (2) teller of stories
[4] amply, fully
[5] inscrutable
[6] solving
[7] structure, fabric
[8] indicates
[9] daily
[10] provide, supply
[11] dark ("opaque")
[12] like a point, a dot
[13] viewing
[14] wonder

30 (For aught appears), and on their orbs impose
31 Such restless[15] revolution[16] day by day
32 Repeated, while the sedentary[17] earth,
33 That better might with far less compass[18] move,
34 Served by more[19] noble than herself, attains
35 Her end without least motion, and receives,
36 As tribute, such a sumless[20] journey brought[21]
37 Of incorporeal speed, her warmth and light—
38 Speed, to describe whose swiftness number fails."
39   So spoke our sire, and by his count'nance
              seemed
40 Entering on studious thoughts abstruse,[22] which Eve
41 Perceiving, where she sat retired in[23] sight,
42 With lowliness[24] majestic from her seat,
43 And grace that won[25] who[26] saw to wish her stay,
44 Rose and went forth among her fruits and flow'rs,
45 To visit[27] how they prospered, bud and bloom,
46 Her nursery. They at her coming sprung
47 And, touched by her fair tendance,[28] gladlier grew.
48 Yet went she not, as not with such discourse
49 Delighted, or not capable her ear
50 Of what was high: such pleasure she reserved,[29]
51 Adam relating,[30] she sole auditress.[31]
52 Her husband the relater she preferred
53 Before the Angel, and of him to ask

---

[15] constant, unceasing
[16] revolving, turning
[17] inactive
[18] ingenuity, craft, artifice
[19] those more
[20] immeasurable
[21] caused
[22] remote from understanding, recondite
[23] from ("out of")
[24] humility
[25] won over
[26] whoever
[27] examine, inspect
[28] care
[29] held back, kept apart
[30] telling
[31] hearer, listener

54   Chose[32] rather. He, she knew, would intermix
55   Grateful[33] digressions, and solve high dispute
56   With conjugal caresses: from his lip
57   Not words alone pleased her. (O! when meet[34] now
58   Such pairs, in love and mutual honor joined?)
59   With goddess-like demeanor forth she went,
60   Not unattended, for on her, as queen,
61   A pomp[35] of winning graces waited still,
62   And from about her shot darts of desire
63   Into all eyes, to wish her still in sight.
64   And Raphael now, to Adam's doubt proposed,
65   Benevolent and facile,[36] thus replied:
66   "To ask or search, I blame thee not, for Heav'n
67   Is as the book of God before thee set,
68   Wherein to read His wondrous works, and learn
69   His seasons, hours, or days, or months, or years.
70   This to attain,[37] whether Heav'n move or earth,
71   Imports[38] not if[39] thou reckon[40] right. The rest
72   From man or Angel the great Architect
73   Did wisely to conceal, and not divulge
74   His secrets to be scanned[41] by them who ought
75   Rather admire,[42] or if they list[43] to try
76   Conjecture, He His fabric of the Heav'ns
77   Hath left to their disputes, perhaps to move
78   His laughter at their quaint[44] opinions wide[45]
79   Hereafter. When they come to model[46] Heav'n
80   And calculate the stars, how they will wield[47]

---

[32] [verb]
[33] pleasing
[34] [verb]
[35] procession
[36] mild of manner
[37] find out
[38] matters, signifies
[39] whether or not
[40] calculate, estimate
[41] analyze, scrutinize, examine carefully
[42] wonder, marvel at
[43] desire, wish
[44] clever, ingenious
[45] mistaken
[46] portray
[47] express

81   The mighty frame, how build, unbuild, contrive
82   To save[48] appearances,[49] how gird[50] the sphere
83   With centric[51] and eccentric[52] scribbled o'er,
84   Cycle[53] and epicycle,[54] orb[55] in orb.
85   Already by thy reasoning this I guess,
86   Who[56] art to lead thy offspring, and supposest
87   That bodies bright and greater should not serve
88   The less not bright, nor Heav'n such journeys run,
89   Earth sitting still, when she alone receives
90   The benefit.
                              "Consider, first, that great
91   Or bright infers[57] not excellence. The earth,
92   Though in comparison of Heav'n so small,
93   Nor glistering,[58] may of solid good contain
94   More plenty than the sun that barren shines,
95   Whose virtue[59] on itself works no effect,
96   But in the fruitful earth, there first received,
97   His beams, unactive[60] else,[61] their vigor[62] find.
98   Yet not to earth are those bright luminaries
99   Officious,[63] but to thee, earth's habitant.
100 And for the Heav'n's wide circuit, let it speak
101 The Maker's high magnificence, who built
102 So spacious, and His line stretched out so far
103 That man may know he dwells not in his own,
104 An edifice too large for him to fill,
105 Lodged in a small partition,[64] and the rest

---

[48] preserve, keep
[49] likelihood
[50] encircle
[51] at the center
[52] not centrally placed
[53] recurrent sequence
[54] small circle, with its center on the circumference of another circle
[55] circle
[56] you who
[57] implies
[58] gleaming, bright
[59] power
[60] ineffective
[61] otherwise
[62] active force
[63] in service/office
[64] part

106	Ordained for uses to his Lord best known.
107	The swiftness of those circles attribute,[65]
108	Though numberless, to His Omnipotence,
109	That to corporeal substances could add
110	Speed almost spiritual. Me thou think'st not slow,
111	Who since the morning-hour set out from Heav'n
112	Where God resides, and ere mid-day arrived
113	In Eden—distance inexpressible
114	By numbers that have name. But this I urge,[66]
115	Admitting[67] motion in the Heav'ns, to show
116	Invalid that which thee to doubt it moved.[68]
117	Not that I so affirm,[69] though so it seem
118	To thee who hast thy dwelling here on earth.
119	God, to remove His ways from human sense,
120	Placed Heav'n from earth so far, that earthly sight,
121	If it presume, might err in things too high,
122	And no advantage gain. What if the sun
123	Be center to the world? and other stars,
124	By his[70] attractive[71] virtue[72] and their own
125	Incited, dance about him various rounds?
126	Their wand'ring course now high, now low, then hid,
127	Progressive,[73] retrograde,[74] or standing still,
128	In six[75] thou see'st? And what if sev'nth to these
129	The planet earth, so steadfast though she seem,
130	Insensibly three different motions move,
131	Which else to several spheres thou must ascribe,
132	Moved contrary with thwart[76] obliquities,[77]
133	Or save the sun his labor, and that swift

---

[65] [trisyllabic, first and third accented]
[66] allege, say
[67] conceding (arguendo: for the purposes of argument)
[68] said
[69] confirm, ratify
[70] the sun's
[71] magnetic
[72] power
[73] continually moving forward/larger
[74] continually moving backward/smaller
[75] six planets
[76] transverse, crossways
[77] angles

134   Nocturnal and diurnal rhomb[78] supposed,
135   Invisible[79] else above all stars, the wheel
136   Of day and night, which needs not thy belief
137   If earth, industrious[80] of herself, fetch[81] day
138   Travelling east, and with her part averse
139   From the sun's beam meet night, her other part
140   Still luminous by his[82] ray? What if that light,
141 · Sent from her[83] through the wide transpicuous[84] air,
142   To the terrestrial moon be as a star,
143   Enlight'ning her[85] by day, as she[86] by night
144   This earth, reciprocal, if land be there,
145   Fields and inhabitants? Her spots thou see'st
146   As clouds, and clouds may rain, and rain produce
147   Fruits in her softened soil for some to eat
148   Allotted[87] there. And other suns perhaps,
149   With their attendant moons, thou wilt descry,
150   Communicating male and female light,[88]
151   Which two great sexes animate the world,
152   Stored in each orb perhaps with some that live.
153   For such vast room[89] in Nature unpossessed
154   By living soul, desert[90] and desolate,
155   Only to shine, yet scarce to contribute[91]
156   Each orb a glimpse of light, conveyed so far
157   Down to this habitable,[92] which returns
158   Light back to them, is obvious to dispute.[93]
159   But whether thus these things, or whether not—

---

[78] the tenth and outermost sphere, the primum mobile, which kept the other spheres in motion
[79] [trisyllabic, second accented, "-ible" elided]
[80] zealous
[81] reaches, meets
[82] the sun's
[83] the earth
[84] clear, transparent
[85] the moon
[86] the moon
[87] assigned, destined
[88] male light = original, female light = reflected
[89] space
[90] deserted [*desert*]
[91] [trisyllabic, first and third accented]
[92] habitable earth [four syllables, first and third accented]
[93] obvious to dispute = obviously disputable

160   But whether the sun, predominant in Heav'n,
161   Rise on the earth, or earth rise on the sun—
162   He from the east his flaming road begin,
163   Or she from west her silent course advance,
164   With inoffensive[94] pace that spinning sleeps
165   On her soft axle, while she paces ev'n,[95]
166   And bears thee soft with the smooth air along—
167   Solicit[96] not thy thoughts with matters hid.
168   Leave them to God above. Him serve, and fear!
169   Of other creatures, as Him pleases best,
170   Wherever placed, let Him dispose. Joy thou
171   In what He gives to thee, this Paradise
172   And thy fair Eve. Heav'n is for thee too high
173   To know what passes there. Be lowly[97] wise,
174   Think only what concerns thee, and thy being.
175   Dream not of other worlds, what creatures there
176   Live, in what state,[98] condition,[99] or degree,[100]
177   Contented that thus far hath been revealed
178   Not of earth only, but of highest Heav'n."
179   To whom thus Adam, cleared of doubt, replied:
180   "How fully hast thou satisfied me, pure
181   Intelligence of Heav'n, Angel serene!
182   And, freed from intricacies,[101] taught to live
183   The easiest way, nor with perplexing thoughts
184   To interrupt the sweet of life, from which
185   God hath bid dwell far off all anxious cares,
186   And not molest[102] us, unless we ourselves
187   Seek them with wand'ring thoughts, and notions vain.
188   But apt the mind or fancy is to rove
189   Unchecked, and of her roving is no end,
190   Till warned, or by experience taught, she learn
191   That not to know at large[103]of things remote

---

[94] harmless
[95] evenly
[96] disturb, make anxious
[97] humbly
[98] manner
[99] circumstances (i.e., rich or poor)
[100] a point on some scale of measurement
[101] complications
[102] afflict, trouble
[103] at large = fully, amply

192   From use, obscure and subtle,[104] but to know
193   That which before us lies in daily life,
194   Is the prime wisdom. What is more, is fume[105]
195   Or emptiness, or fond[106] impertinence,[107]
196   And renders us, in things that most concern
197   Unpractised, unprepared, and still to seek.
198   Therefore from this high pitch[108] let us descend[109]
199   A lower flight, and speak of things at hand
200   Useful, whence haply,[110] mention may arise
201   Of something not unseasonable to ask,
202   By sufferance,[111] and thy wonted[112] favor, deigned.
203   "Thee I have heard relating what was done
204   Ere my remembrance. Now, hear me relate
205   My story, which perhaps thou hast not heard.
206   And day is not yet spent—till then thou see'st
207   How subtly to detain thee I devise,
208   Inviting thee to hear while I relate.
209   Fond![113] were it not in hope of thy reply,
210   For while I sit with thee, I seem in Heav'n,
211   And sweeter thy discourse is to my ear
212   Than fruits of palm-tree pleasantest to thirst
213   And hunger both, from[114] labor, at the hour
214   Of sweet repast.[115] They satiate,[116] and soon fill,
215   Though pleasant, but thy words, with grace divine
216   Imbued,[117] bring to their sweetness no satiety."[118]
217   To whom thus Raphael answered, Heav'nly meek:[119]
218   "Nor are thy lips ungraceful, sire of men,

---

[104] abstruse
[105] smoke, vapor
[106] foolish
[107] irrelevance, presumption
[108] point, elevation
[109] descend to
[110] perhaps
[111] permission [bisyllabic: *suff*rance]
[112] usual, customary, habitual
[113] foolish
[114] after
[115] meal, food
[116] [bisyllabic: *satiate*]
[117] permeated, inspired
[118] [trisyllabic: second accented: *satiety*]
[119] courteous, indulgent

219   Nor tongue ineloquent. For God on thee
220   Abundantly His gifts hath also poured
221   Inward and outward both, His image fair.
222   Speaking or mute,[120] all comeliness and grace
223   Attends thee, and each word, each motion[121] forms.[122]
224   Nor less think we in Heav'n of thee on earth
225   Than of our fellow-servant, and inquire
226   Gladly into the ways of God with man,
227   For God, we see, hath honored thee, and set
228   On man His equal love. Say therefore on,
229   For I that day was absent, as befell,[123]
230   Bound on a voyage uncouth[124] and obscure,[125]
231   Far on excursion[126] toward the gates of Hell,
232   Squared[127] in full legion[128] (such command we had)
233   To see that none thence issued forth a spy
234   Or enemy, while God was in His work,
235   Lest He, incensed at such eruption[129] bold,
236   Destruction with creation might have mixed.
237   Not that they durst without His leave attempt—
238   But us He sends upon His high behests
239   For state, as Sov'reign King, and to inure[130]
240   Our prompt obedience.[131] Fast we found, fast shut,
241   The dismal gates, and barricado'd[132] strong,
242   But long ere our approaching heard within
243   Noise, other than the sound of dance or song,
244   Torment, and loud lament, and furious rage.
245   Glad we returned up to the coasts of light
246   Ere sabbath-ev'ning: so we had in charge.[133]

---

[120] silent
[121] proposition
[122] is in order/form/a structure
[123] it happened
[124] unfamiliar, strange [*uncouth*]
[125] dark, hidden
[126] a journey
[127] arranged, formed
[128] military formation
[129] breaking out
[130] accustom
[131] [trisyllabic, second accented, "-ience" elided]
[132] barricaded
[133] ordered, commanded

247 But thy relation[134] now, for I attend,[135]
248 Pleased with thy words no less than thou with mine."
249 So spoke the godlike Power, and thus our sire:
250   "For man to tell how human life began
251 Is hard, for who himself beginning knew?
252 Desire with thee still longer to converse
253 Induced[136] me. As new waked from soundest sleep,
254 Soft on the flow'ry herb[137] I found me laid,
255 In balmy[138] sweat, which with his beams the sun
256 Soon dried, and on the reeking[139] moisture fed.
257 Straight toward Heav'n my wond'ring eyes I turned,
258 And gazed a while the ample sky, till raised
259 By quick instinctive motion, up I sprung,
260 As thitherward endeavoring, and upright
261 Stood on my feet. About me round I saw
262 Hill, dale, and shady woods, and sunny plains,
263 And liquid lapse[140] of murmuring streams. By[141] these,
264 Creatures that lived and moved, and walked, or flew,
265 Birds on the branches warbling—all things smiled.
266 With fragrance and with joy my heart o'erflowed.
267 Myself I then perused, and limb by limb
268 Surveyed, and sometimes went,[142] and sometimes ran
269 With supple joints, as lively vigor led.
270 But who I was, or where, or from what cause,
271 Knew not. To speak I tried, and forthwith spoke.
272 My tongue obeyed, and readily could name
273 Whate'er I saw. 'Thou Sun,' said I, 'fair light,
274 And thou enlight'ned[143] earth, so fresh and gay,
275 Ye hills and dales, ye rivers, woods, and plains,
276 And ye that live and move, fair creatures, tell,
277 Tell, if ye saw, how I came thus, how here?—
278 Not of myself—by some great Maker, then,

---

[134] narration
[135] listen
[136] led, prevailed upon
[137] herbage, grass
[138] mild, soft
[139] steaming
[140] gliding flow
[141] near, alongside
[142] moved, walked
[143] illuminated (literally: by sunlight)

279   In goodness and in power preëminent.
280   Tell me, how may I know Him, how adore,
281   From whom I have that thus I move and live,
282   And feel that I am happier than I know.'
283   While thus I called, and strayed I knew not whither
284   From where I first drew air, and first beheld
285   This happy light—when, answer none returned,
286   On a green shady bank, profuse of flowers,
287   Pensive I sat me down. There gentle sleep
288   First found me, and with soft oppression[144] seized
289   My drowsèd[145] sense, untroubled, though I thought
290   I then was passing to my former state
291   Insensible, and forthwith to dissolve.
292   When suddenly stood at my head a dream,
293   Whose inward apparition[146] gently moved
294   My fancy to believe I yet had being,
295   And lived. One came, methought, of shape divine,
296   And said, 'Thy mansion[147] wants[148] thee, Adam. Rise,
297   First man, of men innumerable ordained
298   First father! Called by thee, I come thy guide
299   To the garden of bliss, thy seat prepared.'
300   So saying, by the hand He took me raised,
301   And over fields and waters, as in air
302   Smooth-sliding without step, last led me up
303   A woody mountain, whose high top was plain,
304   A circuit wide, enclosed with goodliest trees
305   Planted, with walks, and bowers, that what I saw
306   Of earth before scarce pleasant seemed. Each tree,
307   Loaden with fairest fruit that hung to the eye
308   Tempting, stirred in me sudden appetite
309   To pluck and eat, whereat I waked, and found
310   Before mine eyes all real,[149] as the dream
311   Had lively[150] shadowed.[151] Here had new begun

---

[144] weight
[145] soporific, sleepy
[146] manifestation
[147] dwelling, habitation
[148] needs, requires
[149] [bisyllabic, first accented]
[150] vividly, lifelike
[151] depicted

312 My wand'ring, had not He, who was my guide
313 Up hither, from among the trees appeared,
314 Presence Divine. Rejoicing, but with awe,
315 In adoration at His feet I fell
316 Submiss. He reared me, and 'Whom thou sought'st I am,'
317 Said mildly, 'Author of all this thou see'st
318 Above, or round about thee, or beneath.
319 This Paradise I give thee, count it thine
320 To till[152] and keep, and of the fruit to eat.
321 Of every tree that in the garden grows
322 Eat freely with glad heart, fear here no dearth.[153]
323 But of the tree whose operation[154] brings
324 Knowledge of good and ill, which I have set
325 The pledge[155] of thy obedience and thy faith,
326 Amid the garden by[156] the Tree of Life,
327 Remember what I warn thee: shun to taste,
328 And shun the bitter consequence. For know,
329 The day thou eat'st thereof, my sole command
330 Transgressed, inevitably[157] thou shalt die,
331 From that day mortal, and this happy state
332 Shalt lose, expelled from hence into a world
333 Of woe and sorrow.' Sternly He pronounced
334 The rigid interdiction, which resounds
335 Yet dreadful in mine ear, though in my choice
336 Not to incur. But soon His clear aspect[158]
337 Returned, and gracious purpose[159] thus renewed:
338 'Not only these fair bounds,[160] but all the earth
339 To thee and to thy race I give. As lords
340 Possess it, and all things that therein live,
341 Or live in sea, or air, beast, fish, and fowl.
342 In sign whereof each bird and beast behold

---

[152] cultivate
[153] famine, shortage
[154] effect, power
[155] guarantee
[156] close by, near
[157] [five syllables, second and fourth accented]
[158] look, countenance
[159] discourse
[160] lands, territory

343   After their kinds; I bring them to receive
344   From thee their names, and pay thee fealty[161]
345   With low subjection. Understand the same
346   Of fish within their wat'ry residence,
347   Not hither summoned, since they cannot change
348   Their element, to draw[162] the thinner air.'
349   As thus he spoke, each bird and beast behold
350   Approaching two and two, these[163] cowering low
351   With blandishment,[164] each bird stooped on his wing.
352   I named them, as they passed, and understood
353   Their nature, with such knowledge God endued[165]
354   My sudden apprehension.[166] But in these
355   I found not what methought I wanted still,
356   And to the Heav'nly vision thus presumed:[167]
357   " 'O by what name, for Thou above all these,
358   Above mankind, or aught than mankind higher,
359   Surpassest far my naming? How may I
360   Adore Thee, Author of this universe,
361   And all this good to man? for whose well being
362   So amply, and with hands so liberal,
363   Thou hast provided all things. But with me
364   I see not who partakes. In solitude
365   What happiness? Who can enjoy alone,
366   Or all enjoying, what contentment find?'
367   Thus I presumptuous, and the Vision bright,
368   As with a smile more bright'ned, thus replied:
369   " 'What call'st thou solitude? Is not the earth
370   With various living creatures, and the air
371   Replenished,[168] and all these at thy command
372   To come and play[169] before thee? Know'st thou not
373   Their language and their ways? They also know,
374   And reason not contemptibly. With these

---

[161] oath/acknowledgment of loyalty
[162] breathe
[163] some (the land-bound animals)
[164] whatever please
[165] invested, endowed
[166] understanding
[167] pressed forward, presumptuously
[168] filled, fully stocked
[169] exercise, frolic

375 Find pastime,[170] and bear[171] rule. Thy realm is large.'
376 So spoke the Universal Lord, and seemed
377 So ordering. I, with leave of speech implored,
378 And humble deprecation,[172] thus replied:
379   " 'Let not my words offend Thee, Heav'nly
                         Power.
380 My Maker, be propitious[173] while I speak.
381 Hast Thou not made me here Thy substitute,
382 And these inferior far beneath me set?
383 Among unequals what society
384 Can sort,[174] what harmony or true delight?
385 Which must be mutual, in proportion due
386 Giv'n and received. But in disparity
387 The one intense,[175] the other still remiss,[176]
388 Cannot well suit with either, but soon prove
389 Tedious[177] alike.[178] Of fellowship I speak
390 Such as I seek, fit to participate[179]
391 All rational delight, wherein the brute
392 Cannot be human consort.[180] They rejoice
393 Each with their kind, lion with lioness,
394 So fitly[181] them in pairs Thou hast combined.
395 Much less can bird with beast, or fish with fowl
396 So well converse,[182] nor with the ox the ape.
397 Worse then can man with beast, and least of all.'
398 Whereto the Almighty answered, not displeased:
399   " 'A nice[183] and subtle happiness, I see,
400 Thou to thyself proposest, in the choice
401 Of thy associates, Adam! And wilt taste
402 No pleasure, though in pleasure, solitary.

---

[170] diversion, entertainment
[171] wield, sustain
[172] intercessory prayer
[173] favorably inclined
[174] be suitable
[175] eager, ardent
[176] lacking force/energy
[177] wearisome, annoying, disagreeable
[178] mutually, to each
[179] share
[180] companion, partner
[181] suitably
[182] live
[183] closely reasoned, discriminating

403 What think'st thou then of me, and this my state?
404 Seem I to thee sufficiently possessed
405 Of happiness, or not? who am alone
406 From all eternity? For none I know
407 Second to me or like, equal much less.
408 How have I then with whom to hold converse,[184]
409 Save with the creatures which I made, and those
410 To me inferior, infinite descents
411 Beneath what other creatures are to thee?'
412 He ceased; I lowly answered:
                                              " 'To attain
413 The height and depth of Thy eternal ways
414 All human thoughts come short, Supreme of things!
415 Thou in Thyself art perfect, and in Thee
416 Is no deficience found. Not so is man,
417 But in degree, the cause of his desire
418 By conversation[185] with his like to help
419 Or solace[186] his defects. No need that Thou
420 Should'st propagate, already Infinite,
421 And through all numbers Absolute,[187] though One.
422 But man by number is to manifest[188]
423 His single imperfection,[189] and beget
424 Like of his like, his image multiplied,
425 In unity defective, which requires
426 Collateral[190] love, and dearest amity.[191]
427 Thou in Thy secrecy[192] although alone,
428 Best with Thyself accompanied, seek'st not
429 Social communication, yet, so pleased,
430 Canst raise Thy creature to what height Thou wilt
431 Of union or communion, deified.
432 I by conversing cannot these[193] erect

---

[184] communion
[185] discourse, interchange of thoughts and words
[186] comfort, alleviate, soothe
[187] complete, perfect
[188] display, prove
[189] imperfection in being single/solitary
[190] parallel
[191] friendship
[192] seclusion, mysteriousness
[193] birds, beasts, fish, etc.

433　From prone, nor in their ways complacence[194] find.'
434　Thus I embold'ned spoke, and freedom used
435　Permissive, and acceptance found, which gained
436　This answer from the gracious voice Divine:
437　　　" 'Thus far to try[195] thee, Adam, I was pleased,
438　And find thee knowing, not of beasts alone,
439　Which thou hast rightly named, but of thyself,
440　Expressing well the spirit within thee free,
441　My image, not imparted to the brute,
442　Whose fellowship therefore unmeet[196] for thee
443　Good reason was thou freely should'st dislike,
444　And be so minded still.[197] I ere thou spok'st
445　Knew it not good for man to be alone,
446　And no such company as then thou saw'st
447　Intended thee—for trial only brought,[198]
448　To see how thou could'st judge of fit and meet.
449　What next I bring shall please thee, be assured,
550　Thy likeness, thy fit help, thy other self,
451　Thy wish exactly to thy heart's desire.'
452　He ended, or I heard no more, for now
453　My earthly by His Heav'nly overpowered,
454　Which it had long stood[199] under, strained to the height
455　In that celestial colloquy[200] sublime,[201]
456　As with an object that excels[202] the sense,
457　Dazzled and spent, sunk down, and sought repair[203]
458　Of sleep, which instantly fell on me, called
459　By Nature as in aid, and closed mine eyes.
460　　　"Mine eyes He closed, but open left the cell
461　Of fancy, my internal sight, by which,
462　Abstract[204] as in a trance, methought I saw,[205]

---

[194] pleasure
[195] test
[196] unsuitable
[197] always
[198] adduced, proposed
[199] remained, endured
[200] dialogue
[201] lofty
[202] surpasses, is superior to
[203] restoration
[204] held apart, separated
[205] was able to see

463   Though sleeping where I lay, and saw the shape
464   Still glorious before whom awake I stood,
465   Who stooping op'ned my left side, and took
466   From thence a rib, with cordial[206] spirits warm,
467   And life-blood streaming fresh. Wide was the wound,
468   But suddenly with flesh filled up and healed.
469   The rib He formed and fashioned with His hands.
470   Under His forming hands a creature grew,
471   Man-like, but different sex, so lovely fair
472   That what seemed fair in all the world seemed now
473   Mean[207] or in her summed up, in her contained
474   And in her looks, which from that time infused[208]
475   Sweetness into my heart, unfelt before,
476   And into all things from her air[209] inspired
477   The spirit of love and amorous delight.
478   She disappeared, and left me dark; I waked
479   To[210] find her, or for ever to deplore
480   Her loss, and other pleasures all abjure—[211]
481   When, out of hope, behold her, not far off,
482   Such as I saw her in my dream, adorned
483   With what all earth or Heav'n could bestow
484   To make her amiable.[212] On she came,
485   Led by her Heav'nly Maker, though unseen,
486   And guided by His voice, nor uninformed
487   Of nuptial sanctity and marriage rites.
488   Grace was in all her steps, Heav'n in her eye,
489   In every gesture dignity and love.
490   I overjoyed could not forbear[213] aloud:
491   " "This turn[214] hath made amends! Thou hast
                      fulfilled
492   Thy words, Creator bounteous and benign,
493   Giver of all things fair! But fairest this

---

[206] restorative
[207] inferior, poor
[208] instilled, insinuated
[209] manner, appearance
[210] in order to
[211] renounce
[212] lovable
[213] desist
[214] change

494   Of all Thy gifts, nor enviest.[215] I now see
495   Bone of my bone, flesh of my flesh, myself
496   Before me. Woman is her name, of man
497   Extracted.[216] For this cause he shall forego
498   Father and mother, and to his wife adhere,
499   And they shall be one flesh, one heart, one soul.'
500   "She heard me thus, and though divinely brought[217]
501   Yet innocence, and virgin modesty,
502   Her virtue, and the conscience[218] of her worth,
503   That would be wooed, and not unsought be won,
504   Not obvious,[219] not obtrusive,[220] but retired,[221]
505   The more desirable—or, to say all,
506   Nature herself, though pure of sinful thought,
507   Wrought[222] in her so that, seeing me, she turned.
508   I followed her. She what was honor knew,
509   And with obsequious[223] majesty approved[224]
510   My pleaded[225] reason.[226] To the nuptial bow'r
511   I led her blushing like the morn. All Heav'n,
512   And happy constellations, on that hour
513   Shed their selectest[227] influence, the earth
514   Gave sign of gratulation,[228] and each hill;
515   Joyous the birds; fresh gales and gentle airs
516   Whispered it to the woods, and from their wings
517   Flung rose, flung odors from the spicy[229] shrub,
518   Disporting,[230] till the amorous bird of night[231]

---

[215] "given (by You) grudgingly/with reluctance"
[216] drawn forth, obtained
[217] brought forth, produced, created
[218] knowledge
[219] open, bold
[220] forward
[221] reserved
[222] worked
[223] dutiful, compliant
[224] confirmed
[225] urged
[226] statement/speech/discourse
[227] most choice
[228] joyous feeling
[229] aromatic
[230] frolicking, gamboling
[231] nightingale

519   Sung spousal,[232] and bid haste the ev'ning-star[233]
520   On his hill top, to light the bridal lamp.
521   "Thus have I told thee all my state, and brought
522   My story to the sum of earthly bliss
523   Which I enjoy, and must confess to find
524   In all things else delight indeed, but such
525   As, used or not, works in the mind no change,
526   Nor vehement[234] desire—these delicacies
527   I mean of taste, sight, smell, herbs, fruits, and flow'rs,
528   Walks, and the melody of birds. But here
529   Far otherwise, transported[235] I behold,
530   Transported touch;[236] here passion first I felt,
531   Commotion[237] strange! in all enjoyments else
532   Superior and unmoved, here only weak
533   Against the charm of beauty's powerful glance.
534   Or[238] Nature failed in me, and left some part
535   Not proof enough such object to sustain,[239]
536   Or, from my side subducting,[240] took perhaps
537   More than enough, at least on her bestowed
538   Too much of ornament, in outward show
539   Elaborate,[241] of inward less exact.
540   For well I understand in the prime end[242]
541   Of Nature her th' inferior, in the mind
542   And inward faculties, which most excel.[243]
543   In outward also her resembling less
544   His image who made both, and less expressing
545   The character of that dominion giv'n
546   O'er other creatures. Yet when I approach
547   Her loveliness, so absolute[244] she seems

---

[232] a marriage poem
[233] Venus
[234] strong, passionate
[235] enraptured
[236] I touch
[237] agitation
[238] either
[239] support
[240] removing
[241] highly finished
[242] principal goal
[243] which most excel = which are by and large those that are superior
[244] perfect

548 And in herself complete, so well to know
549 Her own, that what she wills to do or say
550 Seems wisest, virtuousest, discreetest, best.
551 All higher knowledge in her presence falls
552 Degraded,[245] wisdom in discourse with her
553 Looses[246] discount'nanced,[247] and like folly shows.[248]
554 Authority and reason on her wait,
555 As[249] one intended first, not after made[250]
556 Occasionally.[251] And, to consummate[252] all,
557 Greatness of mind and nobleness their seat
558 Build in her loveliest, and create an awe
559 About her, as[253] a guard Angelic placed."
560 To whom the Angel with contracted brow:
561   "Accuse not Nature. She hath done her part;
562 Do thou but thine, and be not diffident[254]
563 Of wisdom. She deserts thee not, if thou
564 Dismiss[255] not her, when most thou need'st her nigh,
565 By attributing[256] overmuch to things
566 Less excellent, as thou thyself perceiv'st.
567 For what admir'st thou, what transports thee so?
568 An outside? Fair, no doubt, and worthy well
569 Thy cherishing, thy honoring, and thy love.
570 Not thy subjection. Weigh with her thyself,
571 Then value. Oft-times nothing profits more
572 Than self-esteem, grounded on just and right
573 Well managed. Of that skill[257] the more thou know'st
574 The more she will acknowledge thee her head,[258]
575 And to realities yield all her shows.[259]

---

[245] reduced, lowered
[246] loosens, goes slack
[247] shamed
[248] appears
[249] as if she were
[250] created
[251] incidentally
[252] finish, complete
[253] like
[254] distrusting, lacking confidence in
[255] discard, reject, send away
[256] ascribing, assigning
[257] i.e., self-esteem
[258] master
[259] appearances

576   Made so adorn for thy delight the more,

577   So awful[260] that with honor thou may'st love

578   Thy mate, who sees when thou art seen least wise.

579   But if the sense of touch, whereby mankind

580   Is propagated, seem such dear delight

581   Beyond all other, think the same vouchsafed

582   To cattle and each beast, which would not be

583   To them made common and divulged, if aught

584   Therein enjoyed were worthy to subdue

585   The soul of man, or passion in him move.

586   What higher in her society thou find'st

587   Attractive, human, rational, love still.[261]

588   In loving thou dost well, in passion not,

589   Wherein true love consists not. Love refines

590   The thoughts, and heart enlarges, hath his seat

591   In reason, and is judicious, is the scale

592   By which to Heav'nly love thou may'st ascend,

593   Not sunk in carnal pleasure. For which cause

594   Among the beasts no mate for thee was found."

595   To whom thus, half abashed, Adam replied:

596   "Neither her outside formed so fair, nor aught

597   In procreation common to all kinds

598   (Though higher of the genial[262] bed by far,

599   And with mysterious reverence, I deem)[263]

600   So much delights me as those graceful[264] acts,

601   Those thousand decencies,[265] that daily flow

602   From all her words and actions, mixed with love

603   And sweet compliance, which declare unfeigned

604   Union of mind, or in us both one soul.

605   Harmony to behold in wedded pair

606   More grateful[266] than harmonious sound to th' ear.

607   Yet these subject[267] not. I to thee disclose

---

[260] worthy of/commanding profound respect
[261] always
[262] procreative
[263] judge, consider
[264] full of divine grace
[265] acts of decorum, proprieties
[266] pleasing
[267] [verb, second syllable accented]

608 What inward thence I feel, not therefore foiled,[268]
609 Who meet with various objects[269] from the sense
610 Variously representing,[270] yet still free
611 Approve the best, and follow what I approve.
612 To love, thou blam'st me not, for love, thou say'st,
613 Leads up to Heav'n, is both the way and guide.
614 Bear with me, then, if lawful what I ask:
615 Love not the Heav'nly Spirits, and how their love
616 Express they? by looks only? or do they mix
617 Irradiance,[271] virtual[272] or immediate touch?"
618 To whom the Angel, with a smile that glowed
619 Celestial rosy red, love's proper hue,
620 Answered:
                  "Let it suffice thee that thou know'st
621 Us happy, and without love no happiness.
622 Whatever pure thou in the body enjoy'st
623 (And pure thou wert created), we enjoy
624 In eminence,[273] and obstacle find none
625 Of membrane, joint, or limb, exclusive[274] bars.
626 Easier than air with air, if Spirits embrace:
627 Total they mix, union of pure with pure
628 Desiring, nor restrained[275] conveyance[276] need,
629 As flesh to mix with flesh, or soul with soul.
630 But I can now no more. The parting sun
631 Beyond the earth's green cape and verdant isles[277]
632 Hesperian[278] sets: my signal to depart.
633 Be strong, live happy, and love! But first of all[279]
634 Him whom to love is to obey, and keep
635 His great command. Take heed lest passion sway

---

[268] frustrated, defeated
[269] statements, arguments
[270] lines 609–10: "I who deal with all sorts of arguments, presented to me (my mind) by my bodily senses . . ."
[271] emitted radiance
[272] having virtues/powers
[273] in eminence = in eminent measure (i.e., even more)
[274] exclusionary, excluding
[275] restricting, limited
[276] (1) conducting way, passage, (2) management, skill, artifice
[277] Cape Verde Islands, in the Atlantic off northwestern Africa
[278] in the west
[279] first of all = primarily

636   Thy judgment to do aught which else free will
637   Would not admit.[280] Thine, and of all thy sons,
638   The weal[281] or woe in thee is placed. Beware!
639   I in thy persevering shall rejoice,
640   And all the Blest. Stand fast! To stand or fall
641   Free in thine own arbitrement[282] it lies.
642   Perfect[283] within, no outward aid require,
643   And all temptation to transgress repel."
644   So saying, he arose, whom Adam thus
645   Followed with benediction. "Since to part,
646   Go, Heav'nly guest, ethereal messenger,
647   Sent from whose sov'reign goodness I adore!
648   Gentle[284] to me and affable hath been
649   Thy condescension, and shall be honored ever
650   With grateful memory. Thou to mankind
651   Be good and friendly still,[285] and oft return!"
652   So parted they, the Angel up to Heav'n
653   From the thick shade, and Adam to his bow'r.

The End of the Eighth Book

---

[280] allow, permit, consent to
[281] happiness, welfare
[282] free choice
[283] [verb]
[284] courteous, noble
[285] always

BOOK IX

THE ARGUMENT

SATAN HAVING COMPASSED[1] the earth, with meditated guile returns as a mist by night into Paradise, enters into the serpent sleeping.[2] Adam and Eve in the morning go forth to their labors, which Eve proposes to divide in[3] several places, each laboring apart. Adam consents not, alleging the danger, lest that enemy, of whom they were forewarned, should attempt[4] her, found alone. Eve, loath to be thought not circumspect or firm enough, urges her going apart, the rather desirous to make trial of her strength. Adam at last yields.

The serpent finds her alone; his subtle approach, first gazing, then speaking, with much flattery extolling Eve above all other creatures. Eve wondering to hear the serpent speak, asks how he attained to human speech and such understanding not till now. The serpent answers that by tasting of a certain tree in the garden he attained both to speech and reason, till then void of both. Eve requires him to bring her to that tree, and finds it to be the Tree of Knowledge, forbidden.

The serpent, now grown bolder, with many wiles and arguments induces her at length[5] to eat. She, pleased with the taste, deliberates awhile whether to impart thereof to Adam or not, at last brings him of the fruit, relates what persuaded her to eat

---

[1] circled around
[2] i.e., while the serpent is sleeping
[3] among
[4] attack, assault, try to seduce
[5] finally

thereof. Adam at first amaz'd, but perceiving her lost, resolves through vehemence[6] of love to perish with her and, extenuating the trespass, eats also of the fruit.

The effects thereof in them both; they seek to cover their nakedness, then fall to variance[7] and accusation of one another.

---

[6] intensity, strength, ardor

[7] i.e., quarrel, disagree

1   No more of talk where God or Angel guest
2   With man, as with his[8] friend, familiar used,[9]
3   To sit indulgent,[10] and with him[11] partake
4   Rural[12] repast, permitting him[13] the while
5   Venial[14] discourse unblamed.[15] I now must change
6   Those notes[16] to tragic, foul distrust, and breach[17]
7   Disloyal on the part of man, revolt,
8   And disobedience; on the part of Heav'n,
9   Now alienated,[18] distance and distaste,
10   Anger and just rebuke, and judgment giv'n,
11   That brought into this world a world of woe,
12   Sin and her shadow Death, and misery,
13   Death's harbinger[19]—sad task, yet argument[20]
14   Not less but more heroic than the wrath
15   Of stern[21] Achilles on his foe[22] pursued
16   Thrice fugitive[23] about Troy wall, or rage
17   Of Turnus[24] for Lavinia[25] disespoused,[26]
18   Or Neptune's ire,[27] or Juno's,[28] that so long
19   Perplexed[29] the Greek,[30] and Cytherea's son.[31]

---

[8] i.e., God or an Angel guest "sitting indulgent" with Adam, as with a friend
[9] familiar used = treated affably, intimately, courteously
[10] good-humored
[11] Adam
[12] country-style
[13] Adam
[14] pardonable
[15] unreproved
[16] (of poetry/music)
[17] breaking of relations
[18] estranged
[19] forerunner
[20] theme, subject
[21] fierce, hard, merciless
[22] Hector, prince of Troy
[23] Hector, in great fear, tried to escape Achilles by running away, and was caught after a chase that went three times around Troy's walls
[24] Italian king
[25] Turnus' promised bride, given to Aeneas instead
[26] betrothal (engagement) broken off
[27] Neptune's ire = Neptune's anger at Odysseus for killing Neptune's son, Polyphemus
[28] Juno's anger stems from (1) the beauty contest, which she did not win, and which Venus did, the judge being Aeneas' brother, Paris, and (2) the peril Aeneas poses to Carthage, a city sacred to Juno
[29] puzzled, entangled
[30] Odysseus
[31] Cytherea = Venus; Aeneas was her son

20   If answerable[32] style I can obtain
21   Of[33] my celestial patroness,[34] who deigns[35]
22   Her nightly visitation unimplored,
23   And dictates to me slumb'ring, or inspires
24   Easy[36] my unpremeditated[37] verse,
25   Since first this subject for heroic song
26   Pleased me, long choosing, and beginning late,[38]
27   Not sedulous[39] by nature to indite[40]
28   Wars, hitherto the only argument[41]
29   Heroic deemed,[42] chief mastery[43] to dissect[44]
30   With long and tedious havoc[45] fabled knights
31   In battles feigned[46]—the better fortitude
32   Of patience and heroic martyrdom
33   Unsung—or to describe races and games,
34   Or tilting[47] furniture,[48] emblazoned[49] shields,
35   Impresses[50] quaint,[51] caparisons[52] and steeds,
36   Bases[53] and tinsel[54] trappings, gorgeous[55] knights
37   At joust and tournament, then marshalled[56] feast
38   Served up in hall with sewers[57] and senechals,[58]

---

[32] appropriate [four syllables, first and third accented]
[33] from
[34] Urania, muse of epic poetry
[35] condescends, vouchsafes
[36] quietly, comfortably
[37] not planned out in advance
[38] i.e., taking a long time to choose his course, his subject matter, and starting late in life
[39] diligent, assiduous
[40] write about, in a literary composition
[41] theme, subject
[42] judged, considered
[43] skill, knowledge
[44] analyze, anatomize
[45] destruction
[46] imaginary, not real
[47] knightly combat, jousting
[48] equipment, furnishings
[49] adorned (painted)
[50] devices/insignia painted on shields
[51] ingenious, skillful
[52] harnesses
[53] the lower part of a shield
[54] showy, glittering
[55] magnificent, rich
[56] properly ordered
[57] attendants
[58] stewards

39   The skill of artifice[59] or office[60] mean,[61]
40   Not that which justly gives heroic name
41   To person or to poem. Me, of these
42   Nor skilled nor studious, higher argument
43   Remains, sufficient of itself to raise[62]
44   That name,[63] unless an age too late, or cold
45   Climate, or years, damp my intended wing[64]
46   Depressed.[65] And much they may, if all be mine,
47   Not hers, who brings it nightly to my ear.
48   The sun was sunk, and after him the star
49   Of Hesperus,[66] whose office[67] is to bring
50   Twilight upon the earth, short arbiter[68]
51   'Twixt day and night. And now from end to end
52   Night's hemisphere had veiled th' horizon round,
53   When Satan, who late[69] fled before the threats
54   Of Gabriel out of Eden, now improved[70]
55   In meditated fraud and malice, bent
56   On man's destruction, maugre[71] what might hap[72]
57   Of heavier on himself, fearless returned.
58   By night he fled, and at midnight returned
59   From compassing[73] the earth, cautious of day,
60   Since Uriel, regent of the sun, descried[74]
61   His entrance, and forewarned the Cherubim
62   That kept their watch. Thence full of anguish driv'n,
63   The space of seven continued nights he rode[75]

---

[59] clever trickery/devices
[60] duty, service
[61] low
[62] inspire
[63] i.e., "heroic poem"
[64] flight
[65] held/forced down
[66] evening star
[67] duty, function
[68] mediator
[69] not long before
[70] enhanced, advanced, made better
[71] despite
[72] come about, happen
[73] circling
[74] had observed
[75] traveled

64   With darkness. Thrice the equinoctial[76] line
65   He circled, four times crossed the car[77] of night
66   From pole to pole, traversing each colure.[78]
67   On the eighth returned and, on the coast averse[79]
68   From entrance or Cherubic watch, by stealth
69   Found unsuspected[80] way.[81]
                                 There was a place,
70   Now not, though Sin, not time, first wrought the change,
71   Where Tigris,[82] at the foot of Paradise,
72   Into a gulf[83] shot[84] under ground, till part
73   Rose up a fountain by the Tree of Life.
74   In with the river sunk, and with it rose
75   Satan, involved[85] in rising mist, then sought
76   Where to lie hid. Sea he had searched, and land,
77   From Eden over Pontus[86] and the pool
78   Maeotis,[87] up beyond the river Ob,[88]
79   Downward as far Antarctic, and in length
80   West from Orontes[89] to the ocean barred
81   At Darien,[90] thence to the land where flows
82   Ganges and Indus. Thus the orb[91] he roamed
83   With narrow[92] search, and with inspection deep
84   Considered every creature, which of all
85   Most opportune might serve his wiles, and found
86   The serpent, subtlest beast of all the field.
87   Him after long debate, irresolute

---

[76] equatorial
[77] chariot
[78] great circle
[79] coast averse = side opposite
[80] that which does not arouse suspicion
[81] path
[82] Mesopotamian river, which watered Eden
[83] profound depth in a body of water
[84] passing swiftly/suddenly
[85] enwrapped
[86] the Black Sea
[87] the Sea of Azov (a lake, in fact)
[88] flowing into the Arctic Sea
[89] Syrian river
[90] Isthmus of Panama, northeastern (Atlantic) side
[91] sphere, globe
[92] close, careful

88 Of thoughts revolved, his final sentence[93] chose
89 Fit vessel, fittest imp[94] of fraud, in whom
90 To enter, and his dark suggestions hide
91 From sharpest sight, for in the wily snake,
92 Whatever sleights,[95] none would suspicious mark,[96]
93 As from his wit and native subtlety
94 Proceeding, which in other beasts observed
95 Doubt might beget[97] of diabolic power
96 Active within, beyond the sense[98] of brute.
97 Thus he resolved, but first from inward grief
98 His bursting passion into plaints[99] thus poured:
99   "O earth, how like to Heav'n, if not preferred
100 More justly, seat worthier of gods, as built
101 With second thoughts, reforming[100] what was old!
102 For what god, after better, worse would build?
103 Terrestrial Heav'n, danced round by other Heav'ns
104 That shine, yet bear their bright officious[101] lamps,
105 Light above light, for thee[102] alone, as seems,
106 In thee concent'ring all their precious beams
107 Of sacred influence! As God in Heav'n
108 Is center, yet extends to all, so thou,
109 Cent'ring, receiv'st from all those orbs. In thee,
110 Not in themselves, all their known virtue[103] appears
111 Productive in herb, plant, and nobler birth
112 Of creatures animate with gradual[104] life
113 Of growth, sense, reason, all summed up in man.
114 With what delight could I have walked thee round
115 (If I could joy in aught), sweet interchange[105]

---

[93] judgment, opinion
[94] urchin, little devil/demon
[95] tricks
[96] note, notice
[97] create
[98] mental capacity
[99] complaints
[100] correcting
[101] dutiful
[102] earth
[103] power
[104] graded, degrees of
[105] succession

116   Of hill, and valley, rivers, woods, and plains,
117   Now land, now sea and shores with forest crowned,
118   Rocks, dens, and caves! But I in none of these
119   Find place or refuge, and the more I see
120   Pleasures about me, so much more I feel
121   Torment within me, as from the hateful siege
122   Of contraries.[106] All good to me becomes
123   Bane[107]—and in Heav'n much worse would be my state.
124   "But neither here seek I, no, nor in Heav'n
125   To dwell, unless by mast'ring Heav'n's Supreme,[108]
126   Nor hope to be myself less miserable
127   By what I seek, but others to make such
128   As I, though thereby worse to me redound.[109]
129   For only in destroying I find ease
130   To my relentless thoughts and, him[110] destroyed,
131   Or won to what may work his utter loss,
132   For whom all this was made, all this will soon
133   Follow, as to him linked in weal[111] or woe.
134   In woe then. That destruction wide may range:[112]
135   To me shall be the glory sole among
136   Th' infernal Powers, in one day to have marred[113]
137   What He, Almighty styled, six nights and days
138   Continued making—and who knows how long
139   Before had been contriving? Though perhaps
140   Not longer than since I, in one night, freed
141   From servitude inglorious well nigh half
142   Th' Angelic name, and thinner left the throng
143   Of His adorers. He, to be avenged,
144   And to repair His numbers thus impaired,
145   Whether such virtue spent of old now failed
146   More Angels to create (if they at least
147   Are His created) or, to spite us more,

---

[106] enemies
[107] destruction, ruin, woe
[108] God
[109] come back
[110] i.e., man
[111] happiness, welfare
[112] extend
[113] harmed, spoiled

148 Determined to advance into our room[114]
149 A creature formed of earth, and him endow,
150 Exalted from so base original,[115]
151 With Heav'nly spoils—our spoils. What He decreed,
152 He effected. Man He made, and for him built
153 Magnificent this world, and earth his seat,
154 Him lord pronounced and, O indignity!
155 Subjected to his service angel-wings,
156 And flaming ministers[116] to watch and tend
157 Their earthly charge. Of these the vigilance
158 I dread and, to elude, thus wrapped in mist
159 Of midnight vapor glide obscure,[117] and pry[118]
160 In every bush and brake,[119] where hap[120] may find
161 The serpent sleeping, in whose mazy folds[121]
162 To hide me, and the dark intent I bring.

163   "O foul descent! that I, who erst contended
164 With gods to sit the highest, am now constrained[122]
165 Into a beast and, mixed with bestial slime,
166 This essence to incarnate[123] and imbrute[124]
167 That[125] to the height of Deity aspired!
168 But what will not ambition and revenge
169 Descend to? Who[126] aspires, must down[127] as low
170 As high he soared, obnoxious,[128] first or last,
171 To basest things. Revenge, at first though sweet,
172 Bitter ere long, back on itself recoils.
173 Let it. I reck[129] not, so it light[130] well aimed,

---

[114] place
[115] an origin
[116] attendants
[117] hidden, secret
[118] peer
[119] thicket
[120] chance, fortune
[121] mazy folds = mazelike object, bent/folded
[122] forcibly compressed
[123] convert into flesh
[124] degrade to the level of an animal
[125] he whom
[126] whoever
[127] go down
[128] liable, subject
[129] care
[130] descend, fall

174 Since higher I fall short, on him who next
175 Provokes my envy, this new favorite
176 Of Heav'n, this man of clay, son of despite[131]
177 Whom us the more to spite his Maker raised
178 From dust. Spite then with spite is best repaid."
179   So saying, through each thicket dank or dry,
180 Like a black mist low-creeping, he held[132] on
181 His midnight-search, where soonest he might find
182 The serpent. Him fast-sleeping soon he found
183 In labyrinth of many a round[133] self-rolled,
184 His head the midst, well stored with subtle wiles,
185 Not yet in horrid[134] shade or dismal den,[135]
186 Nor nocent[136] yet, but on the grassy herb,
187 Fearless unfeared he slept. In at his mouth
188 The Devil entered and his[137] brutal sense,
189 In heart or head, possessing, soon inspired
190 With act intelligential, but his sleep
191 Disturbed not, waiting close[138] the approach of morn.
192   Now when as sacred light began to dawn
193 In Eden on the humid flow'rs, that breathed
194 Their morning incense,[139] when all things that breathe
195 From th' earth's great altar send up silent praise
196 To the Creator, and His nostrils fill
197 With grateful[140] smell, forth came the human pair
198 And joined their vocal worship to the choir
199 Of creatures wanting[141] voice. That done, partake[142]
200 The season prime for sweetest scents and airs,
201 Then commune[143] how that day they best may ply[144]
202 Their growing work, for much their work out-grew

---

[131] insult, contempt
[132] continued
[133] circle
[134] frightful, detestable
[135] wild beast's lair
[136] harmful
[137] the serpent's
[138] secretly
[139] perfume
[140] (1) pleasing, (2) thankful
[141] lacking
[142] they partake, share in
[143] discuss
[144] work at, continue

203   The hands' dispatch[145] of two gard'ning so wide.[146]
204   And Eve first to her husband thus began:
205   "Adam, well may we labor still[147] to dress[148]
206   This garden, still to tend plant, herb, and flow'r,
207   Our pleasant task enjoined,[149] but till more hands
208   Aid us the work under our labor grows
209   Luxurious[150] by restraint. What we by day
210   Lop overgrown, or prune, or prop, or bind,
211   One night or two with wanton[151] growth derides,[152]
212   Tending[153] to wild. Thou therefore now advise,[154]
213   Or hear what to my mind first thoughts present.
214   Let us divide our labors—thou where choice
215   Leads thee, or where most needs, whether to wind
216   The woodbine round this arbor, or direct
217   The clasping ivy where to climb, while I,
218   In yonder spring[155] of roses intermixed
219   With myrtle, find what to redress[156] till noon.
220   For while so near each other thus all day
221   Our task we choose, what wonder if so near
222   Looks intervene and smiles, or object new
223   Casual discourse draw on, which intermits[157]
224   Our day's work, brought to little, though begun
225   Early, and th' hour of supper comes unearned?"
226   To whom mild answer Adam thus returned:
227   "Sole Eve, associate sole, to me beyond
228   Compare above all living creatures dear!
229   Well hast thou motioned,[158] well thy thoughts employed,
230   How we might best fulfil the work which here
231   God hath assigned us, nor of me shalt pass

---

[145] getting, doing
[146] widely, extensively
[147] continually
[148] make straight/right
[149] prescribed authoritatively
[150] luxuriant
[151] rebellious, unmanageable
[152] mocks us
[153] inclining
[154] consider
[155] bursting forth
[156] set right
[157] interrupts, stops
[158] proposed

232   Unpraised, for nothing lovelier can be found
233   In woman, than to study houshold good,
234   And good works in her husband to promote.
235   Yet not so strictly hath our Lord imposed
236   Labor, as to debar us when we need
237   Refreshment, whether food, or talk between,
238   Food of the mind, or this sweet intercourse
239   Of looks and smiles, for smiles from reason flow,
240   To brute denied, and are of love the food—
241   Love, not the lowest end[159] of human life.
242   For not to irksome[160] toil, but to delight
243   He made us, and delight to reason joined.
244   These paths and bowers[161] doubt not but our joint hands
245   Will keep from wilderness with ease, as wide
246   As we need walk, till younger hands ere long
247   Assist us. But if much converse perhaps
248   Thee satiate, to short absence I could yield,[162]
249   For solitude sometimes is best society,
250   And short retirement[163] urges sweet return.
251   "But other doubt possesses me, lest harm
252   Befall thee, severed from me, for thou know'st
253   What hath been warned us, what malicious foe
254   Envying our happiness, and of his own
255   Despairing, seeks to work us woe and shame
256   By sly assault. And somewhere nigh at hand
257   Watches, no doubt, with greedy hope to find
258   His wish and best advantage, us asunder.
259   Hopeless to circumvent us joined, where each
260   To other speedy aid might lend at need,
261   Whether his first design be to withdraw
262   Our fealty from God, or to disturb
263   Conjugal love, than which perhaps no bliss
264   Enjoyed by us excites his envy more.
265   Or[164] this, or worse, leave not the faithful side
266   That gave thee being, still shades thee, and protects.

---

[159] purpose
[160] tedious
[161] shady paths
[162] assent
[163] withdrawal
[164] whether

267   The wife, where danger or dishonor lurks,
268   Safest and seemliest[165] by her husband stays,
269   Who guards her, or with her the worst endures."
270   To whom the virgin[166] majesty of Eve,
271   As one who loves, and some unkindness meets,
272   With sweet austere[167] composure thus replied:
273   "Offspring of Heav'n and earth, and all earth's
                            lord!
274   That such an enemy we have, who seeks
275   Our ruin, both by thee informed I learn,
276   And from the parting Angel over-heard,
277   As in a shady nook I stood behind,
278   Just then returned at shut of evening flow'rs.
279   But that thou should'st my firmness[168] therefore doubt
280   To God or thee, because we have a foe
281   May tempt it, I expected not to hear.
282   His violence thou fear'st not, being such
283   As we, not capable of death or pain,
284   Can either not receive, or can repel.
285   His fraud is then thy fear, which plain infers
286   Thy equal fear that my firm faith and love
287   Can by his fraud be shaken or seduced,
288   Thoughts which how found they harbor in thy breast,
289   Adam, mis-thought of her to thee so dear?"
290   To whom with healing words Adam replied:
291   "Daughter of God and man, immortal Eve!
292   For such thou art, from sin and blame entire.[169]
293   Not diffident[170] of thee do I dissuade
294   Thy absence from my sight, but to avoid
295   Th' attempt itself, intended by our foe.
296   For he who tempts, though in vain, at least asperses[171]
297   The tempted with dishonor foul, supposed
298   Not incorruptible of faith, not proof
299   Against temptation. Thou thyself with scorn

---

[165] most appropriately
[166] pure, innocent, unstained
[167] grave, sober
[168] steadiness, constancy
[169] intact, free, untouched
[170] wanting confidence
[171] bespatters

300 And anger would'st resent the offered wrong,
301 Though ineffectual found. Misdeem not, then,
302 If such affront I labor to avert
303 From thee alone, which on us both at once
304 The enemy, though bold, will hardly dare,
305 Or daring, first on me th' assault shall light.
306 Nor thou his malice and false guile contemn.[172]
307 Subtle he needs must be, who could seduce
308 Angels, nor think superfluous others' aid.
309 I, from the influence of thy looks, receive
310 Access[173] in every virtue, in thy sight
311 More wise, more watchful, stronger, if need were
312 Of outward strength, while shame, thou looking on,
313 Shame to be overcome or over-reached,[174]
314 Would utmost vigor raise, and raised unite.[175]
315 Why should'st not thou like[176] sense within thee feel
316 When I am present, and thy trial[177] choose
317 With me, best witness of thy virtue tried?"
318   So spoke domestic[178] Adam in his care
319 And matrimonial love. But Eve, who thought
320 Less attributed[179] to her faith sincere,
321 Thus her reply with accent sweet renewed:
322   "If this be our condition, thus to dwell
323 In narrow circuit, straitened[180] by a foe,
324 Subtle or violent, we not endued
325 Single[181] with like[182] defence, wherever met,
326 How are we happy, still in fear of harm?
327 But harm precedes not sin. Only our foe
328 Tempting affronts[183] us with his foul esteem[184]

---

[172] despise
[173] increase
[174] overpowered
[175] bring to bear
[176] similar, equivalent
[177] test, endeavor, effort
[178] attached to his home
[179] [four syllables, first and third accented]
[180] made narrower
[181] alone
[182] equivalent, equal
[183] insults, confronts
[184] judgment, estimate

329   Of our integrity. His foul esteem
330   Sticks no dishonor on our front,[185] but turns
331   Foul on himself. Then wherefore shunned or feared
332   By us? who rather double honor gain
333   From his surmise[186] proved false, find peace within,
334   Favor from Heav'n, our witness, from th' event.
335   And what is faith, love, virtue, unassayed
336   Alone, without exterior help sustained?
337   Let us not then suspect[187] our happy state
338   Left so imperfect by the Maker wise
339   As not secure[188] to[189] single or combined.
340   Frail is our happiness, if this be so,
341   And Eden were no Eden, thus exposed."
342   To whom thus Adam fervently[190] replied:
343   "O woman, best are all things as the will
344   Of God ordained them! His creating hand
345   Nothing imperfect or deficient left
346   Of all that He created, much less man,
347   Or aught that might his[191] happy state secure,
348   Secure from outward force. Within himself
349   The danger lies, yet lies within his power.
350   Against his will he can receive no harm.
351   But God left free the will, for what obeys
352   Reason, is free; and reason He made right,
353   But bid her well beware, and still erect,[192]
354   Lest, by some fair-appearing good surprised,
355   She dictate[193] false, and mis-inform the will
356   To do what God expressly hath forbid.
357   Not then mistrust, but tender love, enjoins[194]
358   That I should mind[195] thee oft, and mind thou me.

---

[185] forehead, face
[186] allegation, suspicion
[187] imagine, fancy
[188] certain, safe
[189] to either
[190] intensely earnest
[191] man's
[192] alert
[193] prescribe, direct
[194] prescribes
[195] (1) attend to, take care of, (2) remind

359	Firm we subsist,[196] yet possible to swerve,
360	Since reason not impossibly may meet
361	Some specious[197] object by the foe suborned,[198]
362	And fall into deception unaware,
363	Not keeping strictest watch, as she[199] was warned.
364	Seek not temptation, then, which to avoid
365	Were better, and most likely if from me
366	Thou sever not. Trial will come unsought.
367	Would'st[200] thou approve[201] thy constancy, approve
368	First thy obedience. Th' other who can know,
369	Not seeing thee attempted, who attest?
370	But if thou think trial unsought may find
371	Us both securer[202] than thus warned thou seem'st,
372	Go, for thy stay not free absents thee more.
373	Go in thy native innocence, rely
374	On what thou hast of virtue, summon all!
375	For God towards thee hath done His part. Do thine."
376	So spoke the patriarch of mankind. But Eve
377	Persisted, yet[203] submiss, though last[204] replied:
378	"With thy permission, then, and thus forewarned
379	Chiefly by what thy own last reasoning words
380	Touched[205] only, that our trial, when least sought,
381	May find us both perhaps far less prepared,
382	The willinger I go, nor much expect
383	A foe so proud will first the weaker seek.
384	So bent,[206] the more shall shame him his repulse."
385	Thus saying, from her husband's hand her hand
386	Soft she withdrew and, like a wood-nymph light,
387	Oread[207] or dryad,[208] or of Delia's[209] train,

---

[196] remain, exist
[197] outwardly respectable but in fact not
[198] bribed
[199] reason
[200] if you would
[201] attest, demonstrate
[202] more certain/confident
[203] though still
[204] i.e., Eve has the last word
[205] mentioned, noticed in passing
[206] inclined, determined
[207] a mountain nymph
[208] a tree nymph
[209] Diana's

388 Betook her to the groves, but Delia's self
389 In gait surpassed, and goddess-like deport,[210]
390 Though not as she with bow and quiver armed,
391 But with such gard'ning tools as art[211] yet rude,[212]
392 Guiltless[213] of fire, had formed, or Angels brought.
393 To Pales,[214] or Pomona,[215] thus adorned,
394 Likest she seemed, Pomona when she fled
395 Vertumnus,[216] or to Ceres[217] in her prime,
396 Yet virgin[218] of Proserpina from Jove,
397 Her long with ardent look his eye pursued,
398 Delighted, but desiring more her stay.
399 Oft he to her his charge[219] of quick return
400 Repeated; she to him as oft engaged[220]
401 To be returned by noon amid the bow'r,
402 And all things in best order to invite[221]
403 Noontide repast, or afternoon's repose.
404   O much deceived, much failing, hapless[222] Eve,
405 Of thy presumed[223] return! Event perverse![224]
406 Thou never from that hour in Paradise
407 Found'st either sweet repast, or sound repose.
408 Such ambush, hid among sweet flow'rs and shades,
409 Waited with hellish rancor[225] imminent
410 To intercept thy way, or send thee back
411 Despoiled of innocence, of faith, of bliss!
412   For now, and since first break of dawn the fiend,
413 Mere serpent in appearance, forth was come,
414 And on his quest, where likeliest he might find

---

[210] deportment, manner
[211] skill [noun]
[212] coarse, inelegant
[213] innocent
[214] goddess of flocks and herds
[215] goddess of fruit
[216] god of the orchards and fruit, husband of Pomona
[217] Ceres/Demeter, goddess of Nature's generative power
[218] not maternal/the mother of
[219] injunction
[220] promised, pledged
[221] ask him to come to
[222] luckless, unfortunate
[223] anticipated
[224] wicked, wrong, stubborn
[225] bitter grudge

415   The only two of mankind, but in them
416   The whole included race, his purposed prey.
417   In bow'r and field he sought, where any tuft
418   Of grove or garden-plot more pleasant lay,
419   Their tendance or plantation[226] for delight.
420   By fountain or by shady rivulet
421   He sought them both, but wished his hap[227] might find
422   Eve separate. He wished, but not with hope
423   Of what so seldom chanced, when to his wish,
424   Beyond his hope, Eve separate he spies,
425   Veiled in a cloud of fragrance, where she stood,
426   Half spied, so thick the roses bushing round
427   About her glowed, oft stooping to support
428   Each flower of slender stalk, whose head, though gay
429   Carnation, purple, azure, or specked with gold,
430   Hung drooping unsustained. Them she upstays
431   Gently with myrtle band, mindless the while
432   Herself, though fairest unsupported flower,
433   From her best prop so far, and storm so nigh.
434   Nearer he drew, and many a walk traversed
435   Of stateliest covert,[228] cedar, pine, or palm,
436   Then voluble[229] and bold, now hid, now seen
437   Among thick-woven arborets,[230] and flow'rs
438   Imbordered on each bank, the hand[231] of Eve—
439   Spot more delicious than those gardens feigned[232]
440   Or[233] of revived Adonis,[234] or renowned
441   Alcinous,[235] host of old Laertes' son,[236]
442   Or that, not mystic,[237] where the sapient[238] king[239]

---

[226] planting
[227] chance, luck, fortune
[228] cover, overhang, shelter
[229] gliding
[230] shrubbery
[231] work
[232] imaginary, fabled
[233] whether
[234] for whom, and in whose honor, "gardens of Adonis" were planted
[235] king of the Phaeacians, in Scheria
[236] Odysseus
[237] mythical, fabled
[238] wise
[239] Solomon

443 Held dalliance[240] with his fair Egyptian spouse.[241]
444 Much he the place admired,[242] the person more.
445 As one who long in populous city pent,[243]
446 Where houses thick and sewers annoy[244] the air,
447 Forth issuing on a summer's morn to breathe
448 Among the pleasant villages and farms
449 Adjoined, from each thing met conceives delight,
450 The smell of grain, or tedded grass,[245] or kine,[246]
451 Or dairy,[247] each rural sight, each rural sound.
452 If chance, with nymph-like step, fair virgin pass,
453 What pleasing seemed, for her[248] now pleases more,
454 She most, and in her look sums all delight.
455 Such pleasure took the serpent to behold
456 This flowery plat,[249] the sweet recess[250] of Eve
457 Thus early, thus alone. Her Heav'nly form
458 Angelic, but more soft, and feminine,
459 Her graceful innocence, her every air
460 Of gesture, or least action, overawed[251]
461 His malice, and with rapine[252] sweet bereaved[253]
462 His fierceness of the fierce intent it brought.
463 That space[254] the Evil One abstracted[255] stood
464 From his own evil, and for the time remained
465 Stupidly[256] good, of enmity disarmed,
466 Of guile, of hate, of envy, of revenge.
467 But the hot Hell that always in him burns,
468 Though in mid Heav'n, soon ended his delight,

---

[240] amorous play
[241] see 1 Kings 3:1; Solomon's wife is not named
[242] marveled at
[243] confined, shut up
[244] injure, trouble
[245] tedded grass = grass spread out for drying
[246] cattle
[247] place where milk and cream are stored, butter and cheese are made
[248] for her = on her account
[249] plot
[250] hidden place
[251] restrained/suppressed/controlled by awe
[252] pillage, robbery [noun]
[253] deprived, robbed
[254] interval
[255] withdrawn, absent in mind
[256] dully, stupefiedly

469 And tortures him now more, the more he sees
470 Of pleasure, not for him ordained. Then soon
471 Fierce hate he recollects, and all his thoughts
472 Of mischief, gratulating,[257] thus excites:[258]
473   "Thoughts, whither have ye led me! with what sweet
474 Compulsion thus transported, to forget
475 What hither brought us! Hate, not love, nor hope
476 Of Paradise for Hell, hope here to taste
477 Of pleasure, but all pleasure to destroy,
478 Save what is in destroying. Other joy
479 To me is lost. Then let me not let pass[259]
480 Occasion[260] which now smiles. Behold alone
481 The woman, opportune[261] to all attempts,
482 Her husband, for I view far round, not nigh,
483 Whose higher intellectual[262] more I shun,
484 And strength, of courage haughty,[263] and of limb
485 Heroic built, though of terrestrial mould,
486 Foe not informidable![264] exempt from wound,
487 I not, so much hath Hell debased, and pain
488 Enfeebled me, to what I was in Heav'n.
489 She fair, divinely fair, fit love for Gods!
490 Not terrible, though terror be in love
491 And beauty, not[265] approached[266] by stronger hate,
492 Hate stronger, under show of love well feigned,
493 The way which to her ruin now I tend."[267]
494   So spoke the enemy of mankind, enclosed
495 In serpent, inmate[268] bad! and toward Eve
496 Addressed[269] his way, not with indented[270] wave,

---

[257] (1) in compensation, (2) joyously, welcoming
[258] stirs, rouses
[259] diverge/depart from
[260] opportunity
[261] convenient
[262] mind
[263] exalted, eminent
[264] unformidable, to be dreaded
[265] if not
[266] equaled
[267] turn
[268] lodger
[269] directed
[270] zigzag, wavy

497 Prone on the ground, as since, but on his rear,
498 Circular base of rising folds, that tow'red
499 Fold above fold, a surging maze! His head
500 Crested aloft, and carbuncle[271] his eyes,
501 With burnished neck of verdant gold, erect
502 Amidst his circling spires,[272] that on the grass
503 Floated[273] redundant.[274] Pleasing was his shape
504 And lovely, never since of serpent-kind
505 Lovelier, not those that in Illyria changed[275]
506 Hermione[276] and Cadmus,[277] or the god
507 In Epidaurus,[278] nor to which transformed
508 Ammonian Jove,[279] or Capitoline,[280] was seen,
509 He with Olympias, this with her who bore
510 Scipio, the height[281] of Rome. With tract[282] oblique[283]
511 At first, as one who sought access[284] but feared
512 To interrupt, sidelong he works his way.
513 As when a ship, by skilful steersman wrought
514 Nigh river's mouth or foreland,[285] where the wind
515 Veers oft, as oft so steers, and shifts her sail,
516 So varied he, and of his tortuous[286] train
517 Curled many a wanton[287] wreath[288] in sight of Eve,
518 To lure her eye. She, busied, heard the sound

---

[271] fiery red
[272] spirals? (spires = stems, stalks)
[273] moved gently
[274] copious
[275] transformed into serpents
[276] Hermione/Harmonia = daughter of Ares/Mars and Aphrodite/Venus; Cadmus' wife [four syllables, second and forth accented]
[277] founder and king of Thebes; he and his wife were both turned into snakes by Zeus
[278] Aesculapius, god of healing, portrayed as a serpent at his temple in Epidaurus, in Argos, Greece
[279] Ammonian Jove = Egyptian/African Jove, supposed to be the biological father of Alexander the Great, having slept with Olympias, wife of Philip of Macedonia, in the form of a serpent
[280] Capitoline (Jove) = Roman Jove, supposed to have fathered Scipio Africanus
[281] eminence
[282] track
[283] at an angle, indirect
[284] a way to approach [second syllable accented]
[285] cape, promontory
[286] crooked, twisting
[287] extravagant
[288] ring, band, circle

519   Of rustling leaves, but minded not, as used
520   To such disport before[289] her through the field,
521   From every beast, more duteous[290] at her call
522   Than at Circean call the herd disguised.[291]
523   He, bolder now, uncalled before her stood,
524   But as in gaze admiring. Oft he bowed
525   His turret crest, and sleek enamelled neck,
526   Fawning, and licked the ground whereon she trod.
527   His gentle dumb expression turned at length
528   The eye of Eve to mark his play. He, glad
529   Of her attention gained, with serpent-tongue
530   Organic,[292] or impulse[293] of vocal air,
531   His fraudulent temptation thus began:
532   "Wonder not, sov'reign mistress, if perhaps
533   Thou canst, who art sole[294] wonder! Much less arm
534   Thy looks, the Heav'n of mildness, with disdain,
535   Displeased that I approach thee thus, and gaze
536   Insatiate,[295] I thus single, nor have feared
537   Thy awful[296] brow, more awful thus retired.[297]
538   Fairest resemblance of thy Maker fair,
539   Thee all things living gaze on, all things thine
540   By gift, and thy celestial beauty adore
541   With ravishment[298] beheld! There best beheld,
542   Where universally admired, but here
543   In this enclosure wild, these beasts among,
544   Beholders rude, and shallow[299] to discern
545   Half what in thee is fair, one man except,
546   Who sees thee? And what is one? Who should be seen
547   A goddess among gods, adored and served
548   By Angels numberless, thy daily train."

---

[289] around
[290] obedient [bisyllabic, first accented, "-eous" elided]
[291] herd disguised = Odysseus/Ulysses' men, turned by Circe into swine
[292] like an organ or other similar instrument
[293] thrust, force
[294] unrivaled
[295] insatiable
[296] majestic, commanding
[297] secluded
[298] ecstasy
[299] deficient

549   So glozed[300] the Tempter, and his proem[301]
                    tuned.[302]
550 Into the heart of Eve his words made way,
551 Though at the voice much marvelling. At length,
552 Not unamazed, she thus in answer spoke:
553   "What may this mean? Language of man
                    pronounced
554 By tongue of brute, and human sense expressed?
555 The first, at least, of these I thought denied
556 To beasts, whom God, on their creation-day,
557 Created mute to all articulate sound.
558 The latter I demur,[303] for in their looks
559 Much reason, and in their actions, oft appears.
560 Thee, serpent, subtlest beast of all the field
561 I knew, but not with human voice endued.
562 Redouble then this miracle, and say
563 How cam'st thou speakable[304] of[305] mute, and how
564 To me so friendly grown above the rest
565 Of brutal kind, that daily are in sight?
566 Say, for such wonder[306] claims attention due."
567 To whom the guileful Tempter thus replied:
568   "Empress of this fair world, resplendent Eve!
569 Easy to me it is to tell thee all
570 What thou command'st, and right thou should'st be
                    obeyed.
571 I was at first as other beasts that graze
572 The trodden herb, of abject[307] thoughts and low,
573 As was my food, nor aught but food discerned,
574 Or sex, and apprehended nothing high.
575 Till on a day, roving the field, I chanced
576 A goodly tree far distant to behold,
577 Loaden with fruit of fairest colors mixed,
578 Ruddy and gold. I nearer drew to gaze,

---

[300] veiled with specious comments
[301] prelude, preface, introduction
[302] uttered, gave forth
[303] (1) hesitate, (2) disagree about
[304] capable of speech
[305] from being
[306] a marvel, extraordinary event
[307] despicable

579 When from the boughs a savory odor blown,
580 Grateful[308] to appetite, more pleased my sense
581 Than smell of sweetest fennel,[309] or the teats
582 Of ewe or goat dropping with milk at ev'n,[310]
583 Unsucked of lamb or kid, that tend[311] their play.
584 To satisfy the sharp desire I had
585 Of tasting those fair apples, I resolved
586 Not to defer. Hunger and thirst at once,
587 Powerful persuaders, quick'ned at the scent
588 Of that alluring[312] fruit, urged me so keen.
589 About the mossy trunk I wound me soon,[313]
590 For high from ground the branches would require
591 Thy utmost reach, or Adam's. Round the tree
592 All other beasts that saw, with like desire
593 Longing and envying stood, but could not reach.
594 Amid the tree now got, where plenty hung
595 Tempting so nigh, to pluck and eat my fill
596 I spared not, for such pleasure till that hour,
597 At feed[314] or fountain never had I found.
598 Sated at length, ere long I might[315] perceive
599 Strange alteration in me, to degree
600 Of reason in my inward powers, and speech
601 Wanted[316] not long, though to this shape retained.[317]
602 Thenceforth to speculations high or deep
603 I turned my thoughts, and with capacious mind
604 Considered all things visible in Heav'n,
605 Or earth, or middle,[318] all things fair and good.
606 But all that fair and good in thy divine
607 Semblance, and in thy beauty's Heav'nly ray,
608 United I beheld: no fair to thine
609 Equivalent or second! Which compelled

---

[308] pleasing
[309] snakes were thought to improve their eyesight by rubbing their eyes on fennel
[310] snakes were reputed to suck milk from sheep and goats
[311] are engaged in
[312] tempting, charming
[313] quickly
[314] feeding ground
[315] was able to
[316] lacked
[317] kept, confined
[318] in between

610   Me thus, though importune[319] perhaps, to come
611   And gaze, and worship thee of right declared
612   Sov'reign of creatures, universal Dame!"[320]
613   So talked the spirited[321] sly snake, and Eve,
614   Yet more amazed, unwary thus replied:
615   "Serpent, thy overpraising leaves in doubt
616   The virtue[322] of that fruit, in thee first proved.[323]
617   But say, where grows the tree? from hence how far?
618   For many are the trees of God that grow
619   In Paradise, and various, yet unknown
620   To us. In such abundance lies our choice,
621   As leaves a greater store of fruit untouched,
622   Still hanging incorruptible, till men
623   Grow up to their provision,[324] and more hands
624   Help to disburden Nature of her birth."[325]
625   To whom the wily adder, blithe and glad:
626   "Empress, the way is ready, and not long.
627   Beyond a row of myrtles, on a flat,[326]
628   Fast[327] by a fountain, one small thicket past
629   Of blowing myrrh and balm. If thou accept
630   My conduct,[328] I can bring thee thither soon."
631   "Lead then," said Eve. He, leading, swiftly rolled
632   In tangles, and made intricate seem straight,
633   To mischief swift. Hope elevates, and joy
634   Bright'ns his crest, as when a wand'ring fire,
635   Compact[329] of unctuous[330] vapor, which the night
636   Condenses, and the cold environs[331] round,
637   Kindled through agitation[332] to a flame,

---

[319] vexatious
[320] mistress, woman of rank and power
[321] having a Spirit in his body
[322] power, quality
[323] demonstrated, tested, learned about
[324] due number
[325] that which is born of Nature, Nature's offspring
[326] a flat = level ground
[327] close, near
[328] guidance [second syllable accented]
[329] composed, made [second syllable accented]
[330] oily
[331] envelops
[332] a shaking movement

638   Which oft, they say, some evil Spirit attends,[333]
639   Hovering and blazing with delusive light,
640   Misleads th' amazed night-wanderer from his way
641   To bogs and mires, and oft through pond or pool,
642   There swallowed up and lost, from succor far.
643   So glistered the dire snake, and into fraud
644   Led Eve, our credulous mother, to the tree
645   Of prohibition,[334] root of all our woe,
646   Which when she saw, thus to her guide she spoke:
647   "Serpent, we might have spared our coming hither,
648   Fruitless[335] to me, though fruit be here to excess,
649   The credit[336] of whose virtue rest with thee,
650   Wondrous indeed, if cause of such effects.
651   But of this tree we may not taste nor touch.
652   God so commanded, and left that command
653   Sole daughter[337] of His voice. The rest, we live
654   Law to ourselves. Our reason is our law."
655   To whom the Tempter guilefully replied:
656   "Indeed! Hath God then said that of the fruit
657   Of all these garden-trees ye shall not eat,
658   Yet lords declared of all in earth or air?"
659   To whom thus Eve, yet sinless:
                                 "Of the fruit
660   Of each tree in the garden we may eat,
661   But of the fruit of this fair tree amidst
662   The garden, God hath said, 'Ye shall not eat
663   Thereof, nor shall ye touch it, lest ye die.' "
664   She scarce had said, though brief, when now more bold
665   The Tempter, but with show of zeal and love
666   To man, and indignation at his wrong,
667   New part[338] puts on and, as[339] to passion moved,

---

[333] accompanies
[334] i.e., the order forbidding that its fruit be eaten
[335] useless, wasted
[336] credibility
[337] offspring
[338] role
[339] as if

668 Fluctuates[340] disturbed, yet comely[341] and in act[342]
669 Raised as of some great matter to begin.[343]
670 As when of old some orator renowned,
671 In Athens or free Rome, where eloquence
672 Flourished, since mute! to some great cause addressed,[344]
673 Stood in himself collected, while each part,
674 Motion, each act, won audience ere the tongue,
675 Sometimes in height began, as no delay
676 Of preface brooking, through his zeal of right.[345]
677 So standing, moving, or to height up grown,
678 The Tempter, all impassioned, thus began:
679   "O sacred, wise, and wisdom-giving plant,
680 Mother of science![346] Now I feel thy power
681 Within me clear, not only to discern
682 Things in their causes, but to trace the ways
683 Of highest agents,[347] deemed however[348] wise.
684 Queen of this universe! Do not believe
685 Those rigid threats of death. Ye shall not die.
686 How should you? By the fruit? It gives you life
687 To knowledge. By the threat'ner?[349] Look on me,
688 Me, who have touched and tasted, yet both live,
689 And life more perfect have attained than Fate
690 Meant me, by vent'ring[350] higher than my lot.
691 Shall that be shut to man, which to the beast
692 Is open? Or will God incense[351] His ire
693 For such a petty trespass? and not praise
694 Rather your dauntless virtue, whom the pain
695 Of death denounced,[352] whatever thing death be,
696 Deterred not from achieving what might lead

---

[340] rises and falls [bisyllabic?]
[341] proper, decorous
[342] actions
[343] [raised *as of some matter to begin*]
[344] standing up, rising (to speak)
[345] of right = rightful
[346] knowledge
[347] natural forces/substances that are productive of active phenomena
[348] no matter how
[349] God
[350] venturing
[351] kindle
[352] uttered denunciations against

697   To happier life, knowledge of good and evil?
698   Of good, how just? Of evil, if what is evil
699   Be real, why not known, since easier shunned?
700   God therefore cannot hurt ye, and be just—
701   Not just, not God. Not feared then, nor obeyed:
702   Your fear itself of death removes the fear.
703   Why then was this forbid? Why but to awe?
704   Why but to keep ye low and ignorant,
705   His worshippers? He knows that in the day
706   Ye eat thereof, your eyes that seem so clear,
707   Yet are but dim, shall perfectly be then
708   Op'ned and cleared, and ye shall be as gods,
709   Knowing both good and evil, as they know.
710   That ye should be as gods, since I as man,
711   Internal man, is but proportion meet— [353]
712   I of brute, human; ye of human, gods.
713   So ye shall die, perhaps, by putting off
714   Human, to put on gods—death to be wished,
715   Though threat'ned, which no worse than this can bring.
716   And what are gods, that man may not become
717   As they, participating [354] god-like food?
718   The gods are first, and that advantage use [355]
719   On our belief that all from them proceeds.
720   I question it, for this fair earth I see,
721   Warmed by the sun, producing every kind,
722   Them [356] nothing. If they all things, who enclosed
723   Knowledge of good and evil in this tree,
724   That whoso eats thereof, forthwith attains
725   Wisdom without their leave? And wherein lies
726   Th' offence, that man should thus attain to know?
727   What can your knowledge hurt Him, or this tree
728   Impart against His will, if all be His?
729   Or is it envy? and can envy dwell
730   In Heav'nly breasts? These, these, and many more
731   Causes [357] import [358] your need of this fair fruit.

---

[353] fitting, suitable, proper
[354] sharing
[355] they employ/make use of
[356] the gods
[357] reasons [noun]
[358] signify

732   Goddess humane, reach then, and freely taste!"
733   He ended, and his words replete[359] with guile
734   Into her heart too easy entrance won.
735   Fixed on the fruit she gazed, which to behold
736   Might tempt alone,[360] and in her ears the sound
737   Yet rung of his persuasive words, impregned[361]
738   With reason (to her seeming) and with truth.
739   Meanwhile the hour of noon drew on, and waked
740   An eager appetite, raised by the smell
741   So savory of that fruit, which with desire,
742   Inclinable[362] now grown to touch or taste,
743   Solicited[363] her longing eye. Yet first
744   Pausing a while, thus to herself she mused:
745   "Great are thy virtues, doubtless, best of fruits,
746   Though kept from man, and worthy to be admired,
747   Whose taste, too long forborn, at first assay[364]
748   Gave elocution[365] to the mute, and taught
749   The tongue not made for speech to speak thy praise.
750   Thy praise He also, who forbids thy use,
751   Conceals not from us, naming thee the Tree
752   Of Knowledge, knowledge both of good and evil,
753   Forbids us then to taste! But His forbidding
754   Commends thee more, while it infers the good
755   By thee communicated, and our want.[366]
756   For good unknown sure is not had or, had
757   And yet unknown, is as not had at all.
758   In plain[367] then, what forbids He but to know,
759   Forbids us good, forbids us to be wise?
760   Such prohibitions bind not. But if death
761   Bind us with after-bands, what profits then
762   Our inward freedom? In the day we eat
763   Of this fair fruit, our doom is, we shall die!

---

[359] filled
[360] all by itself
[361] impregnated
[362] favorably disposed, inclining
[363] incited
[364] test, taste
[365] oral utterance
[366] lack, need
[367] plain language/terms

764 How dies the serpent? He hath eaten and lives,
765 And knows, and speaks, and reasons, and discerns,
766 Irrational[368] till then. For us alone
767 Was death invented? Or to us denied
768 This intellectual food, for beasts reserved?
769 For beasts it seems. Yet that one beast which first
770 Hath tasted envies not, but brings with joy
771 The good befall'n him, author unsuspect,[369]
772 Friendly to man, far from deceit or guile.
773 What fear I then? Rather, what know to fear
774 Under this ignorance of good and evil,
775 Of God or death, of law or penalty?
776 Here grows the cure of all, this fruit divine,
777 Fair to the eye, inviting to the taste,
778 Of virtue to make wise. What hinders then
779 To reach, and feed at once both body and mind?"
780   So saying, her rash hand in evil hour
781 Forth reaching to the fruit, she plucked, she ate![370]
782 Earth felt the wound, and Nature from her seat,
783 Sighing through all her works, gave signs of woe,
784 That all was lost. Back to the thicket slunk
785 The guilty[371] serpent, and well might, for Eve,
786 Intent now wholly on her taste, nought else
787 Regarded.[372] Such delight till then, as seemed,
788 In fruit she never tasted, whether true
789 Or fancied so, through expectation high
790 Of knowledge, nor was godhead from her thought.
791 Greedily she ingorged without restraint,
792 And knew not eating death. Satiate at length,
793 And heightened as with wine, jocund and boon,[373]
794 Thus to herself she pleasingly began:
795   "O sov'reign, virtuous, precious of all trees
796 In Paradise! Of operation[374] blest

---

[368] not rational
[369] not to be suspected
[370] [pronounced, in British English both then and now, /et/]
[371] criminal
[372] noticed, paid attention to
[373] convivial
[374] influence, power, effect

797 To sapience,[375] hitherto obscured,[376] infamed,[377]
798 And thy fair fruit let[378] hang, as to no end[379]
799 Created. But henceforth my early care,
800 Not without song, each morning, and due praise,
801 Shall tend thee, and the fertile burden ease
802 Of thy full branches offered free to all,
803 Till dieted[380] by thee I grow mature
804 In knowledge, as the gods, who all things know,
805 Though others envy what they cannot give—
806 For had the gift been theirs, it had not here
807 Thus grown. Experience, next, to thee I owe,
808 Best guide. Not following thee, I had remained
809 In ignorance. Thou op'nest wisdom's way,
810 And giv'st access, though secret she retire.
811 And I perhaps am secret.[381] Heav'n is high,
812 High and remote to see from thence distinct
813 Each thing on earth. And other care perhaps
814 May have diverted from continual watch
815 Our great Forbidder, safe with all His spies
816 About him. But to Adam in what sort[382]
817 Shall I appear? Shall I to him make known
818 As yet my change, and give him to partake[383]
819 Full happiness with me, or rather not,
820 But keep the odds of knowledge in my power
821 Without co-partner? So to add what wants[384]
822 In female sex, the more to draw his love,
823 And render me more equal, and perhaps,
824 A thing not undesirable, sometime
825 Superior—for inferior, who is free?
826 This may be well. But what if God have seen,
827 And death ensue?[385] Then I shall be no more!

---

[375] wisdom, understanding
[376] hidden
[377] defamed
[378] left, allowed to
[379] purpose
[380] fed
[381] concealed
[382] way
[383] share
[384] is lacking
[385] follow

828   And Adam, wedded to another Eve,
829   Shall live with her enjoying, I extinct:
830   A death to think![386] Confirmed then I resolve,
831   Adam shall share with me in bliss or woe!
832   So dear I love him, that with him all deaths
833   I could endure, without him live no life."
834   So saying, from the tree her step she turned,
835   But first low reverence done, as to the power
836   That dwelt within, whose presence had infused
837   Into the plant sciential[387] sap, derived
838   From nectar, drink of gods. Adam the while,
839   Waiting desirous her return, had wove
840   Of choicest flow'rs a garland, to adorn
841   Her tresses, and her rural labors crown,
842   As reapers oft are wont their harvest-queen.
843   Great joy he promised to his thoughts, and new
844   Solace in her return, so long delayed,
845   Yet oft his heart, divine[388] of something ill,
846   Misgave him. He the fault'ring[389] measure[390] felt,[391]
847   And forth to meet her went, the way she took
848   That morn when first they parted. By the Tree
849   Of Knowledge he must pass. There he her met,
850   Scarce from the tree returning, in her hand
851   A bough of fairest fruit, that downy smiled,
852   New gathered, and ambrosial smell diffused.
853   To him she hasted. In her face excuse
854   Came prologue,[392] and apology too prompt,
855   Which, with bland[393] words at will,[394] she thus addressed:
856   "Hast thou not wondered, Adam, at my stay?
857   Thee I have missed, and thought it long, deprived[395]
858   Thy presence. Agony of love till now

---

[386] consider
[387] knowledge-containing
[388] divining, prefiguring
[389] wrongdoing
[390] action
[391] perceived, was conscious of
[392] preface
[393] soft, coaxing
[394] at will = ready
[395] deprived of

859   Not felt, nor shall be twice, for never more
860   Mean I to try, what rash untried I sought,
861   The pain of absence from thy sight. But strange
862   Hath been the cause, and wonderful to hear.
863   This tree is not, as we are told, a tree
864   Of danger tasted, nor to evil unknown
865   Op'ning the way, but of divine effect
866   To open eyes, and make them gods who taste,
867   And hath been tasted such. The serpent wise,
868   Or not restrained as we, or not obeying,
869   Hath eaten of the fruit, and is become—
870   Not dead, as we are threat'ned, but thenceforth
871   Endued[396] with human voice and human sense,
872   Reasoning to admiration,[397] and with me
873   Persuasively hath so prevailed, that I
874   Have also tasted, and have also found
875   Th' effects to correspond.[398] Opener mine eyes,
876   Dim erst, dilated[399] spirits, ampler heart,
877   And growing up to godhead—which for thee
878   Chiefly I sought—without thee can despise.
879   For bliss, as[400] thou hast part,[401] to me is bliss.
880   Tedious, unshared with thee, and odious soon.
881   Thou therefore also taste, that equal lot[402]
882   May join us, equal joy, as equal love,
883   Lest thou not tasting, different degree
884   Disjoin us, and I then too late renounce
885   Deity for thee, when Fate will not permit."
886   Thus Eve with count'nance blithe[403] her story
                 told,
887   But in her cheek distemper[404] flushing glowed.
888   On th' other side Adam, soon as he heard
889   The fatal trespass done by Eve, amazed,

---

[396] endowed, supplied, invested
[397] to admiration = marvelously
[398] to be as he has said they would be
[399] amplified, expanded
[400] to the extent that, if
[401] a share
[402] fortune, destiny
[403] cheerful, gay
[404] intoxication, derangement

890	Astonied[405] stood and blank,[406] while horror chill
891	Ran through his veins, and all his joints relaxed.[407]
892	From his slack hand the garland wreathed for Eve
893	Down dropped, and all the faded roses shed.[408]
894	Speechless he stood and pale, till thus at length
895	First to himself he inward silence broke:
896	"O fairest of Creation, last and best
897	Of all God's works, creature in whom excelled
898	Whatever can to sight or thought be formed,
899	Holy, divine, good, amiable, or sweet!
900	How art thou lost! How on a sudden lost,
901	Defaced, deflow'red, and now to death devote![409]
902	Rather, how hast thou yielded to transgress
903	The strict forbiddance, how to violate
904	The sacred fruit forbidden! Some cursèd fraud
905	Of enemy hath beguiled thee, yet unknown,
906	And me with thee hath ruined, for with thee
907	Certain my resolution is to die!
908	How can I live without thee? How forego
909	Thy sweet converse,[410] and love so dearly joined,
910	To live again in these wild woods forlorn?[411]
911	Should God create another Eve, and I
912	Another rib afford, yet loss of thee
913	Would never[412] from my heart. No, no, I feel
914	The link of Nature draw me. Flesh of flesh,
915	Bone of my bone thou art, and from thy state[413]
916	Mine never shall be parted, bliss or woe."
917	So having said, as one from sad dismay
918	Recomforted,[414] and after thoughts disturbed
919	Submitting to what seemed remediless,
920	Thus in calm mood his words to Eve he turned:
921	"Bold deed thou hast presumed, advent'rous Eve,

---

[405] stunned, astonished
[406] prostrate
[407] went slack
[408] fell off, scattered
[409] doomed
[410] company
[411] abandoned, forsaken, desolate, lost
[412] never be
[413] condition, manner of existing
[414] strengthened, soothed

922   And peril great provoked, who thus hast dared,
923   Had it been only coveting to eye
924   That sacred fruit, sacred to abstinence,
925   Much more to taste it under ban to touch.
926   But past who can recall, or done undo?
927   Not God Omnipotent, nor Fate. Yet so
928   Perhaps thou shalt not die, perhaps the fact
929   Is not so heinous,[415] now, foretasted[416] fruit,
930   Profaned[417] first by the serpent, by him first
931   Made common[418] and unhallowed,[419] ere our taste,
932   Nor yet on him found deadly. Yet he lives,
933   Lives, as thou said'st, and gains to live, as man,
934   Higher degree of life—inducement strong
935   To us, as likely tasting to attain
936   Proportional ascent, which cannot be
937   But to be gods, or Angels, demi-gods.
938   Nor can I think that God, Creator wise,
939   Though threat'ning, will in earnest so destroy
940   Us His prime creatures, dignified so high,
941   Set over all His works, which in our fall,
942   For us created, needs with us must fail,
943   Dependent made. So God shall uncreate,
944   Be frustrate, do, undo, and labor lose—
945   Not well conceived of God, who though His power
946   Creation could repeat, yet would be loath
947   Us to abolish, lest the adversary
948   Triumph, and say: 'Fickle their state whom God
949   Most favors. Who can please Him long? Me first
950   He ruined, now mankind. Whom will He next?'
951   Matter of scorn, not to be giv'n the foe.
952   However, I with thee have fixed my lot,
953   Certain[420] to undergo like[421] doom. If death
954   Consort[422] with thee, death is to me as life,

---

[415] criminal, infamous
[416] already tasted
[417] polluted
[418] accessible, general, free
[419] unsanctified
[420] resolved, determined
[421] equivalent, equal
[422] accompany, attend

955 So forcible[423] within my heart I feel
956 The bond of Nature draw me to my own,
957 My own in thee, for what thou art is mine,
958 Our state cannot be severed. We are one,
959 One flesh. To lose thee were to lose myself."
960 So Adam, and thus Eve to him replied:
961   "O glorious trial of exceeding[424] love,
962 Illustrious evidence,[425] example high!
963 Engaging me to emulate. But short[426]
964 Of thy perfection, how shall I attain,[427]
965 Adam, from whose dear side I boast me sprung,
966 And gladly of our union hear thee speak,
967 One heart, one soul in both—whereof good proof
968 This day affords, declaring thee resolved,
969 Rather than death, or aught than death more dread,
970 Shall separate us, linked in love so dear,
971 To undergo with me one guilt, one crime,
972 If any be, of tasting this fair fruit,
973 Whose virtue, for of good still good proceeds,
974 Direct, or by occasion,[428] hath presented
975 This happy trial of thy love, which else
976 So eminently[429] never had been known?
977 Were it[430] I thought death menaced[431] would ensue[432]
978 This my attempt, I would sustain[433] alone
979 The worst, and not persuade thee, rather die
980 Deserted, than oblige thee with a fact[434]
981 Pernicious[435] to thy peace, chiefly assured
982 Remarkably so late[436] of thy so true,
983 So faithful, love unequalled. But I feel

---

[423] powerful, convincing, unavoidable
[424] extremely great, surpassing excellence
[425] manifestation
[426] but short = but since I am short (have less of)
[427] achieve (such emulation)
[428] circumstance
[429] conspicuously [four syllables, first and third accented]
[430] were it = were it that
[431] as threatened
[432] follow
[433] undergo, endure, bear, experience
[434] deed, action
[435] destructive, fatal
[436] recently

984   Far otherwise th' event. Not death, but life
985   Augmented, opened eyes, new hopes, new joys,
986   Taste so divine, that what of sweet before
987   Hath touched my sense, flat seems to this, and harsh.
988   On my experience, Adam, freely taste,
989   And fear of death deliver to the winds."
990   So saying, she embraced him, and for joy
991   Tenderly wept, much won[437] that he his love
992   Had so ennobled, as of choice to incur
993   Divine displeasure for her sake, or death.
994   In recompense (for such compliance bad,
995   Such recompense best merits) from the bough
996   She gave him of that fair enticing fruit
997   With liberal hand. He scrupled not to eat,
998   Against his better knowledge, not deceived,
999   But fondly[438] overcome with female charm.
1000   Earth trembled from her entrails, as again
1001   In pangs, and Nature gave a second groan,
1002   Sky loured[439] and, muttering thunder, some sad drops
1003   Wept at completing[440] of the mortal sin
1004   Original[441]—while Adam took no thought,
1005   Eating his fill, nor Eve to iterate[442]
1006   Her former trespass feared, the more to soothe
1007   Him with her loved society, that now,
1008   As with new wine intoxicated both,
1009   They swim in mirth, and fancy that they feel
1010   Divinity within them breeding wings
1011   Wherewith to scorn the earth. But that false fruit
1012   Far other operation[443] first displayed,
1013   Carnal desire inflaming. He on Eve
1014   Began to cast lascivious eyes, she him
1015   As wantonly repaid. In lust they burn,
1016   Till Adam thus 'gan Eve to dalliance[444] move:

---

[437] influenced, won over
[438] foolishly
[439] darkened, threatened
[440] finishing
[441] primary, first
[442] repeat
[443] effect
[444] amorous play

1017	"Eve, now I see thou art exact[445] of taste,
1018	And elegant,[446] of[447] sapience[448] no small part.
1019	Since to each meaning savor[449] we apply,
1020	And palate[450] call judicious,[451] I the praise
1021	Yield thee, so well this day thou hast purveyed.[452]
1022	Much pleasure we have lost, while we abstained
1023	From this delightful fruit, nor known till now
1024	True relish,[453] tasting. If such pleasure be
1025	In things to us forbidden, it might be wished
1026	For this one tree had been forbidden ten.
1027	But come, so well refreshed, now let us play,
1028	As meet is, after such delicious fare,
1029	For never did thy beauty, since the day
1030	I saw thee first and wedded thee, adorned
1031	With all perfections, so inflame my sense
1032	With ardor to enjoy thee, fairer now
1033	Than ever—bounty[454] of this virtuous[455] tree!"
1034	So said he, and forbore not glance or toy[456]
1035	Of amorous intent, well understood
1036	Of Eve, whose eye darted contagious fire.
1037	Her hand he seized, and to a shady bank,
1038	Thick overhead with verdant roof embow'red,
1039	He led her, nothing loath. Flow'rs were the couch,
1040	Pansies, and violets, and asphodel,
1041	And hyacinth, earth's freshest softest lap.[457]
1042	There they their fill of love and love's disport[458]
1043	Took largely,[459] of their mutual guilt the seal,

---

[445] strict
[446] correct, delicate, graceful, polite
[447] which is of
[448] wisdom
[449] quality, character
[450] sense of taste
[451] sensible, wise, having sound judgment
[452] furnished, provided
[453] enjoyment of taste
[454] gift, kindness
[455] potent, powerful
[456] caress
[457] a hollow among hills
[458] diversion, sport, games
[459] amply, at length

1044 The solace of their sin, till dewy[460] sleep
1045 Oppressed[461] them, wearied with their amorous play.
1046 Soon as the force of that fallacious[462] fruit,
1047 That with exhilarating vapor bland[463]
1048 About their spirits had played, and inmost powers
1049 Made err, was now exhaled, and grosser sleep,
1050 Bred of unkindly[464] fumes, with conscious dreams
1051 Encumbered,[465] now had left them, up they rose
1052 As from unrest[466] and, each the other viewing,
1053 Soon found their eyes how opened, and their minds
1054 How darkened. Innocence, that as a veil
1055 Had shadowed them from knowing ill, was gone,
1056 Just[467] confidence, and native righteousness,[468]
1057 And honor, from[469] about them, naked left
1058 To guilty shame. He covered,[470] but his robe
1059 Uncovered more. So rose the Danite[471] strong,
1060 Herculean Samson, from the harlot-lap
1061 Of Philistean[472] Dalilah,[473] and waked
1062 Shorn of his strength. They destitute and bare
1063 Of all their virtue, silent, and in face
1064 Confounded,[474] long they sat, as stricken mute,
1065 Till Adam, though not less than Eve abashed,
1066 At length gave utterance to these words constrained:[475]
1067   "O Eve, in evil hour thou did'st give ear
1068 To that false worm, of whomsoever taught
1069 To counterfeit man's voice, true in our fall,
1070 False in our promised rising, since our eyes

---

[460] moist
[461] pressed down on
[462] deceitful
[463] genial
[464] unnatural
[465] burdened, hampered, embarrassed, clogged
[466] turmoil, disturbance
[467] rightful, proper
[468] quality of conforming to moral or divine law
[469] had gone from
[470] covered himself
[471] of the tribe of Dan
[472] Philistine [four syllables, first and third accented]
[473] Samson's traitorous wife [trisyllabic, first and third accented]
[474] defeated, overthrown, brought to nought
[475] afflicted

1071 Op'ned we find, indeed, and find we know
1072 Both good and evil—good lost, and evil got!
1073 Bad fruit of knowledge, if this be to know,
1074 Which leaves us naked thus, of honor void,
1075 Of innocence, of faith, of purity,
1076 Our wonted[476] ornaments now soiled and stained,
1077 And in our faces evident the signs
1078 Of foul concupiscence,[477] whence evil store,[478]
1079 Ev'n shame, the last[479] of evils. Of the first
1080 Be sure then. How shall I behold the face
1081 Henceforth of God or Angel, erst with joy
1082 And rapture so oft beheld? Those Heav'nly shapes
1083 Will dazzle now this earthly with their blaze
1084 Insufferably bright. O! might I here
1085 In solitude live savage, in some glade
1086 Obscured,[480] where highest woods, impenetrable
1087 To star or sun-light, spread their umbrage[481] broad
1088 And brown as evening. Cover me, ye pines!
1089 Ye cedars, with innumerable boughs
1090 Hide me, where I may never see them[482] more!
1091   "But let us now, as in bad plight,[483] devise
1092 What best may for the present serve to hide
1093 The parts of each from other, that seem most
1094 To shame obnoxious,[484] and unseemliest[485] seen.
1095 Some tree, whose broad smooth leaves together sewed,
1096 And girded on our loins, may cover round
1097 Those middle parts, that this newcomer, shame,
1098 There sit not, and reproach us as unclean."
1099   So counselled he, and both together went
1100 Into the thickest wood. There soon they chose
1101 The fig-tree—not that kind for fruit renowned,

---

[476] customary
[477] lust
[478] evil store = an abundance of evil
[479] worst, final
[480] hidden
[481] (1) shade, (2) the foliage that produces shade
[482] God or Angels
[483] peril, danger
[484] offensive
[485] most improperly

1102 But such[486] as at this day, to Indians known,
1103 In Malabar[487] or Deccan[488] spreads her arms
1104 Branching so broad and long, that in the ground
1105 The bended twigs take root, and daughters grow
1106 About the mother tree, a pillared shade
1107 High over-arched, and echoing walks between.
1108 There oft the Indian herdsman, shunning heat,
1109 Shelters in cool, and tends his pasturing herds
1110 At loop-holes cut through thickest shade. Those leaves
1111 They gathered, broad as Amazonian targe[489]
1112 And, with what skill they had, together sewed,
1113 To gird their waist—vain covering, if to hide
1114 Their guilt and dreaded shame! O how unlike
1115 To that first naked glory! Such of late
1116 Columbus found th' American, so girt[490]
1117 With feathered cincture,[491] naked else, and wild
1118 Among the trees on isles and woody shores.
1119 Thus fenced[492] and, as they thought, their shame in part
1120 Covered, but not at rest or ease of mind,
1121 They sat them down to weep, nor only tears
1122 Rained at their eyes, but high winds worse within
1123 Began to rise, high passions, anger, hate,
1124 Mistrust, suspicion, discord, and shook sore
1125 Their inward state of mind, calm region once
1126 And full of peace, now tossed and turbulent,
1127 For understanding ruled not, and the will
1128 Heard not her[493] lore,[494] both[495] in subjection now
1129 To sensual appetite, who from beneath
1130 Usurping over sov'reign reason claimed
1131 Superior sway.[496] From thus distempered[497] breast,

---

[486] the banyan
[487] western India
[488] southern India
[489] shield
[490] belted
[491] belt
[492] screened, shielded, protected
[493] understanding's
[494] counsel, advice
[495] both of them (Adam and Eve)
[496] power, authority, rule
[497] disordered

1132   Adam, estranged[498] in look and altered style,[499]
1133   Speech intermitted[500] thus to Eve renewed:
1134   "Would thou had'st hearkened to my words, and
                       stayed
1135   With me, as I besought[501] thee, when that strange
1136   Desire of wand'ring, this unhappy morn,
1137   I know not whence possessed thee. We had then
1138   Remained still happy—not, as now, despoiled[502]
1139   Of all our good, shamed, naked, miserable!
1140   Let none henceforth seek needless cause t' approve
1141   The faith they owe![503] When earnestly they seek
1142   Such proof, conclude they then begin to fail."
1143   To whom, soon[504] moved with touch of blame, thus Eve:
1144   "What words have passed thy lips, Adam severe!
1145   Imput'st thou that to my default, or will
1146   Of wand'ring, as thou call'st it, which who knows
1147   But might as ill have happened thou being by—
1148   Or to thyself perhaps? Had'st thou been there,
1149   Or here th' attempt, thou could'st not have discerned
1150   Fraud in the serpent, speaking as he spoke.
1151   No ground of enmity between us known,
1152   Why he should mean me ill, or seek to harm?
1153   Was I t' have never parted from thy side?
1154   As good have grown there still, a lifeless rib.
1155   Being as I am, why did'st not thou, the head,
1156   Command me absolutely not to go,
1157   Going into such danger as thou said'st?
1158   Too facile[505] then, thou did'st not much gainsay—[506]
1159   Nay, did'st permit, approve, and fair[507] dismiss.[508]
1160   Had'st thou been firm and fixed in thy dissent,
1161   Neither had I transgressed, nor thou with me."

---

[498] alienated
[499] tone
[500] interrupted
[501] begged earnestly, supplicated
[502] robbed, stripped
[503] own
[504] quickly
[505] easily persuaded
[506] oppose, contradict
[507] clearly, distinctly, openly
[508] send away

1162   To whom, then first incensed, Adam replied:
1163   "Is this the love, is this the recompence
1164 Of mine to thee, ungrateful Eve! expressed
1165 Immutable,[509] when thou wert lost, not I,
1166 Who might have lived, and joyed[510] immortal bliss,
1167 Yet willingly chose rather death with thee?
1168 And am I now upbraided as the cause
1169 Of thy transgressing? Not enough severe,
1170 It seems, in thy restraint. What could I more?
1171 I warned thee, I admonished thee, foretold
1172 The danger, and the lurking enemy
1173 That lay in wait. Beyond this had been force,
1174 And force upon free will hath here no place.
1175 But confidence then bore thee on, secure[511]
1176 Either to meet no danger, or to find
1177 Matter[512] of glorious trial.[513] And perhaps
1178 I also erred, in overmuch admiring
1179 What seemed in thee so perfect that I thought
1180 No evil durst attempt thee. But I rue[514]
1181 The error now, which is become my crime,
1182 And thou th' accuser. Thus it shall befall[515]
1183 Him who, to worth in women overtrusting,
1184 Lets her will[516] rule. Restraint she will not brook
1185 And left t' herself, if evil thence ensue,[517]
1186 She first his weak indulgence will accuse."
1187   Thus they in mutual accusation spent
1188 The fruitless hours, but neither self-condemning,
1189 And of their vain contest[518] appeared no end.

The End of the Ninth Book

---

[509] as unchangeable
[510] enjoyed
[511] confident
[512] thing, affair, events, circumstances
[513] test, endeavor, experiment
[514] regret, repent
[515] happen, occur
[516] [noun]
[517] follow
[518] [*contest*]

BOOK X

THE ARGUMENT

MAN'S TRANSGRESSION KNOWN, the Guardian Angels forsake Paradise, and return up to Heaven to approve[1] their vigilance, and are approved, God declaring that the entrance of Satan could not be by them prevented. He sends his Son to judge the transgressors, who descends and gives sentence accordingly, then in pity clothes them both, and reascends.

Sin and Death sitting till then at the gates of Hell, by wondrous sympathy feeling the success of Satan in this new world, and the sin by man there committed, resolve to sit no longer confined in Hell, but to follow Satan their sire up to the place of man. To make the way easier from Hell to this world, to and fro, they pave a broad highway or bridge over Chaos, according to the track that Satan first made. Then preparing for earth, they meet him, proud of his success, returning to Hell; their mutual gratulation.

Satan arrives at Pandemonium, in full assembly relates with boasting his success against man. Instead of applause is entertained with a general hiss by all his audience, transformed—with himself also—suddenly into serpents, according to his doom, given in Paradise. Then deluded with show of the forbidden tree springing up before them, they greedily reaching to take of the fruit, chew dust and bitter ashes.

The proceedings of Sin and Death; God foretells the final victory of his Son over them, and the renewing of all things, but for

---

[1] confirm, pronounce

the present commands his Angels to make several alterations in the heavens and elements. Adam more and more perceiving his fallen condition heavily bewails, rejects the condolement of Eve. She persists and at length appeases him, then to evade the curse likely to fall on their offspring, proposes to Adam violent ways, which he approves not, but conceiving better hope, puts her in mind of the late promise made them, that her seed should be revenged on the serpent, and exhorts her with him to seek peace of the offended Deity, by repentance and supplication.

1   Meanwhile the heinous[2] and despiteful[3] act
2 Of Satan, done in Paradise, and how
3 He, in the serpent, had perverted[4] Eve,
4 Her husband she, to taste the fatal fruit,
5 Was known in Heav'n, for what can 'scape the eye
6 Of God all-seeing, or deceive His heart
7 Omniscient? Who, in all things wise and just,
8 Hindered not Satan to attempt the mind
9 Of man, with strength entire[5] and free will armed,
10 Complete to have discovered and repulsed
11 Whatever wiles of foe or seeming friend.
12 For still they[6] knew and ought t' have still[7] remembered
13 The high injunction not to taste that fruit,
14 Whoever tempted, which they not obeying,
15 Incurred (what could they less?) the penalty
16 And, manifold[8] in sin, deserved to fall.
17   Up into Heav'n from Paradise in haste
18 The Angelic guards ascended, mute, and sad
19 For man, for of his state by this they knew,
20 Much wond'ring how the subtle fiend had stol'n
21 Entrance unseen. Soon as th' unwelcome news
22 From earth arrived at Heaven-gate, displeased
23 All were who heard. Dim sadness did not spare,
24 That time, celestial visages, yet mixed
25 With pity violated[9] not their bliss.
26 About the new-arrived in multitudes
27 The ethereal people ran, to hear and know
28 How all befell.[10] They towards the Throne Supreme
29 Accountable,[11] made haste to make appear[12]
30 With righteous[13] plea their utmost vigilance,

---

[2] infamous
[3] spiteful
[4] corrupted
[5] complete
[6] Adam and Eve
[7] always
[8] complexly, in multiple fashion
[9] corrupted, injured, broke, destroyed
[10] had happened/occurred
[11] responsible
[12] clear
[13] guiltless

31 And easily approved,[14] when the Most High
32 Eternal Father, from His secret cloud,
33 Amidst in thunder, uttered thus His voice:
34   "Assembled Angels, and ye Powers returned
35 From unsuccessful charge,[15] be not dismayed,
36 Nor troubled at these tidings from the earth,
37 Which your sincerest[16] care could not prevent,
38 Foretold[17] so lately[18] what would come to pass,
39 When first this Tempter crossed the gulf from Hell.
40 I told ye then he should prevail, and speed[19]
41 On his bad errand. Man should[20] be seduced
42 And flattered out of all, believing lies
43 Against his Maker, no decree of mine
44 Concurring to necessitate his fall
45 Or touch with lightest moment[21] of impulse[22]
46 His free will, to her[23] own inclining left
47 In ev'n scale. But fall'n he is. And now
48 What rests[24] but[25] that the mortal[26] sentence pass[27]
49 On his transgression, death denounced[28] that day,
50 Which he presumes already vain and void
51 Because not yet inflicted, as he feared,
52 By some immediate stroke, but soon shall find
53 Forbearance[29] no acquittance,[30] ere day end.
54 Justice shall not return as bounty scorned.[31]
55 But whom send I to judge them? Whom but thee,

---

[14] demonstrated
[15] responsibility, trust
[16] truest, purest
[17] predicted
[18] recently
[19] succeed
[20] had to be
[21] weight
[22] force
[23] his will's
[24] remains
[25] except
[26] deadly
[27] be passed
[28] proclaimed
[29] lenity, mercy, indulgence
[30] release (from a debt)
[31] "Justice must not be scorned (treated with contempt) as the free gift of kindness (bounty) has been"

56   Vice-gerent[32] Son? To thee I have transferred

57   All judgment, whether in Heav'n, or earth, or Hell.

58   Easy it may be seen that I intend

59   Mercy colleague[33] with justice, sending thee

60   Man's friend, his mediator, his designed[34]

61   Both ransom and redeemer voluntary,

62   And destined, man himself, to judge man fallen."

63   So spoke the Father and, unfolding bright

64   Toward the right hand His glory, on the Son

65   Blazed forth unclouded Deity. He full

66   Resplendent all his Father manifest

67   Expressed, and thus divinely answered mild:

68   "Father Eternal, Thine is to decree,

69   Mine, both in Heav'n and earth, to do Thy will

70   Supreme, that Thou in me, Thy Son beloved,

71   May'st ever rest well pleased. I go to judge

72   On earth these Thy transgressors, but Thou know'st,

73   Whoever judged, the worst on me must light,[35]

74   When time shall be, for so I undertook

75   Before Thee, and not repenting, this obtain[36]

76   Of right, that I may mitigate[37] their doom[38]

77   On me derived.[39] Yet I shall temper so

78   Justice with mercy, as may illustrate[40] most

79   Them fully satisfied,[41] and Thee appease.[42]

80   Attendance[43] none shall need,[44] nor train, where none

81   Are to behold the judgment but the judged,

82   Those two. The third,[45] best absent,[46] is condemned,

---

[32] one who rules by deputed power, appointed by a ruler to exercise certain powers

[33] joined

[34] planned, intended

[35] descend, fall

[36] I possess/hold

[37] alleviate, abate

[38] judgment, sentence

[39] conveyed, transferred

[40] explain, make clear, elucidate

[41] set free from doubt, convinced

[42] pacify

[43] escort, attending company

[44] be needed

[45] Satan

[46] i.e., from the process of judgment, as applied to Adam and Eve

83   Convict[47] by flight, and rebel to all law.
84   Conviction[48] to the serpent[49] none belongs."
85   Thus saying, from his radiant seat he rose
86   Of high collateral[50] glory. Him Thrones, and Powers,
87   Princedoms, and Dominations ministrant[51]
88   Accompanied to Heaven-gate, from whence
89   Eden, and all the coast, in prospect lay.
90   Down he descended straight: the speed of gods
91   Time counts not, though with swiftest minutes winged.
92   Now was the sun in western cadence[52] low
93   From noon, and gentle airs, due at their hour,
94   To fan the earth now waked, and usher in
95   The ev'ning cool, when He, from wrath more cool,
96   Came the mild Judge and Intercessor[53] both,
97   To sentence man. The voice of God they heard
98   Now walking in the garden, by soft winds
99   Brought to their ears, while day decline. They heard,
100 And from His presence hid themselves among
101 The thickest trees, both man and wife, till God,
102 Approaching, thus to Adam called aloud:
103   "Where art thou, Adam, wont with joy to meet
104 My coming seen far off? I miss thee here,
105 Not pleased, thus entertained[54] with solitude,
106 Where obvious duty erewhile appeared unsought.
107 Or[55] come I less conspicuous,[56] or what change
108 Absents thee, or what chance detains? Come forth."
109   He came, and with him Eve, more loath, though
                      first
110 T' offend. Discount'nanced[57] both, and discomposed.[58]
111 Love was not in their looks, either to God

---

[47] proved guilty
[48] proof, demonstration
[49] i.e., the animal whose body was appropriated, wrongly and without consent, by Satan
[50] parallel, side by side
[51] attendant
[52] descent
[53] mediator
[54] received
[55] either
[56] visible
[57] disconcerted, abashed
[58] disturbed, unsettled, agitated

112   Or to each other, but apparent[59] guilt,
113   And shame, and perturbation, and despair,
114   Anger, and obstinacy, and hate, and guile.
115   Whence Adam, falt'ring long, thus answered brief:
116   "I heard Thee in the garden, and of Thy voice
117   Afraid, being naked hid myself." To whom
118   The gracious Judge, without revile,[60] replied:
119   "My voice thou oft hast heard, and hast not feared,
120   But still rejoiced, How is it now become
121   So dreadful to thee? That thou art naked, who
122   Hath told thee? Hast thou eaten of the tree
123   Whereof I gave thee charge[61] thou should'st not eat?"
124   To whom thus Adam sore beset[62] replied:
125   "O Heav'n! In evil strait[63] this day I stand
126   Before my Judge, either to undergo[64]
127   Myself the total crime, or to accuse
128   My other self, the partner of my life,
129   Whose failing, while her faith to me remains,
130   I should conceal, and not expose to blame
131   By my complaint. But strict necessity
132   Subdues me, and calamitous[65] constraint,
133   Lest on my head both sin and punishment,
134   However insupportable,[66] be all
135   Devolved.[67] Though should I hold my peace, yet Thou
136   Would'st easily detect what I conceal.
137   "This woman, whom Thou mad'st to be my help,
138   And gav'st me as Thy perfect gift, so good,
139   So fit, so acceptable,[68] so divine,
140   That from her hand I could suspect no ill,
141   And what she did, whatever in itself,

---

[59] visible
[60] abusive language
[61] instruction, order, mandate
[62] assailed
[63] narrow pathway
[64] suffer, bear
[65] miserable
[66] (1) unbearable, unendurable, (2) unjustifiable
[67] come upon
[68] [four syllables, first and third accented]

142   Her doing seemed to justify the deed.
143   She gave me of the tree, and I did eat."
144   To whom the sov'reign Presence thus replied:
145   "Was she thy God, that her thou did'st obey
146   Before His voice? Or was she made thy guide,
147   Superior,[69] or but[70] equal, that to her
148   Thou did'st resign thy manhood, and the place
149   Wherein God set thee above her, made of thee
150   And for thee, whose perfection far excelled
151   Hers in all real[71] dignity?[72] Adorned
152   She was indeed, and lovely, to attract
153   Thy love, not thy subjection, and her gifts
154   Were such, as under government[73] well seemed,
155   Unseemly[74] to bear rule, which was thy part
156   And person,[75] had'st thou known thyself aright."
157   So having said, He thus to Eve in few:
158   "Say, woman, what is this which thou hast
                      done?"
159   To whom sad Eve, with shame nigh
                      overwhelmed,
160   Confessing soon,[76] yet not before her Judge
161   Bold or loquacious,[77] thus abashed replied:
162   "The serpent me beguiled, and I did eat."
163 · Which when the Lord God heard, without delay
164   To judgment He proceeded on th' accused
165   Serpent (though brute, unable to transfer
166   The guilt on him who made him instrument
167   Of mischief, and polluted from the end[78]
168   Of his creation), justly then accursed,
169   As vitiated[79] in Nature. More to know
170   Concerned not man (since he no further knew)

---

[69] [trisyllabic, second accented]
[70] merely, simply
[71] true
[72] worth, excellence, honor
[73] rule, direction
[74] unfit, improper
[75] office, role
[76] quickly
[77] babbling, talkative
[78] polluted from the end = corrupted away from the purpose
[79] faulty, corrupt

171 Nor altered his offense. Yet God at last[80]
172 To Satan (first in sin) his doom[81] applied,
173 Though in mysterious[82] terms, judged as then best,
174 And on the serpent thus His curse let fall:
175   "Because thou hast done this, thou art accursed
176 Above all cattle,[83] each beast of the field.
177 Upon thy belly groveling thou shalt go,
178 And dust shalt eat all the days of thy life.
179 Between thee and the woman I will put
180 Enmity, and between thine and her seed.
181 Her seed shall bruise[84] thy head, thou bruise his heel."
182   So spoke this oracle, then verified
183 When Jesus, Son of Mary, second Eve,
184 Saw Satan fall, like lightning, down from Heav'n,
185 Prince of the air. Then rising from his[85] grave
186 Spoiled[86] Principalities and Powers, triumphed
187 In open show[87] and, with ascension bright,
188 Captivity led captive through the air,
189 The realm itself of Satan, long usurped,[88]
190 Whom he[89] shall tread at last under our feet,
191 Ev'n he,[90] who now foretold his[91] fatal bruise,[92]
192 And to the woman thus His sentence turned:
193   "Thy sorrow I will greatly multiply
194 By thy conception.[93] Children thou shalt bring
195 In sorrow forth, and to thy husband's will
196 Thine shall submit. He over thee shall rule."
197 On Adam last thus judgment He pronounced:
198   "Because thou hast heark'ned to the voice of thy
                    wife,

---

[80] finally
[81] judgment, sentence
[82] occult, obscure
[83] creatures
[84] crush, smash, break
[85] Christ's
[86] captured
[87] display (of force)
[88] wrongfully appropriated
[89] Christ
[90] Christ
[91] the serpent's
[92] his fatal bruise = the Crucifixion
[93] action of conceiving (becoming pregnant)

199   And eaten of the tree, concerning which
200   I charged thee, saying, 'Thou shalt not eat thereof,'
201   Cursed is the ground for thy sake. Thou in sorrow
202   Shalt eat thereof all the days of thy life.
203   Thorns also and thistles it shall bring thee forth
204   Unbid,[94] and thou shalt eat th' herb of the field.
205   In the sweat of thy face shalt thou eat bread,
206   Till thou return unto the ground, for thou
207   Out of the ground wast taken: know thy birth,
208   For dust thou art, and shalt to dust return."
209   So judged He man, both Judge and Savior sent,
210   And th' instant stroke of death denounced[95] that day,
211   Removed far off. Then pitying how they stood
212   Before Him, naked to the air, that now
213   Must suffer change, disdained not to begin
214   Thenceforth the form of servant to assume,
215   As when He washed His servant's feet. So now,
216   As Father of His family, He clad
217   Their nakedness with skins of beasts, or slain,
218   Or as the snake with youthful coat[96] repaid,[97]
219   And thought not much[98] to clothe His enemies.
220   Nor He their outward only with the skins
221   Of beasts, but inward nakedness, much more
222   Opprobrious,[99] with His robe of righteousness
223   Arraying, covered from His Father's sight.
224   To Him with swift ascent he up returned,
225   Into His blissful bosom reassumed
226   In glory, as of old. To Him appeased,[100]
227   All (though all-knowing) what had passed with man
228   Recounted, mixing intercession sweet.
229   Meanwhile, ere thus was sinned and judged on
               earth,
230   Within the gates of Hell sat Sin and Death,

---

[94] unasked, uninvited, uncommanded
[95] proclaimed
[96] youthful coat = sloughed-off skin
[97] exchanged
[98] not much = not at all
[99] shameful, injurious
[100] satisfied [adjective]

231 In counterview[101] within the gates, that now
232 Stood open wide, belching outrageous[102] flame
233 Far into Chaos, since the fiend passed through,
234 Sin opening,[103] who thus now to Death began:
235   "O son, why sit we here, each other viewing
236 Idly, while Satan, our great author, thrives
237 In other worlds, and happier seat[104] provides
238 For us, his offspring dear? It cannot be
239 But that success attends him. If mishap,
240 Ere this he had returned, with fury driv'n
241 By his avengers, since no place like this
242 Can fit his punishment, or their revenge.
243 Methinks I feel new strength within me rise,
244 Wings growing, and dominion[105] giv'n me large[106]
245 Beyond this deep. Whatever draws me on,[107]
246 Or[108] sympathy,[109] or some connatural[110] force,
247 Powerful[111] at greatest distance to unite,
248 With secret amity, things of like kind,
249 By secretest conveyance. Thou, my shade
250 Inseparable, must with me along,
251 For Death from Sin no power can separate.
252 But lest the difficulty of passing back
253 Stay his return, perhaps, over this gulf[112]
254 Impassable, impervious,[113] let us try
255 Advent'rous[114] work, yet to thy power and mine
256 Not unagreeable, to found[115] a path
257 Over this main[116] from Hell to that new world

---

[101] view from opposite sides
[102] extraordinary, enormous, excessive, hyperviolent/gross/wrong
[103] i.e., opening the way (and the gates) for Satan
[104] place, abode
[105] rule, control
[106] [adjective, modifying "dominion"]
[107] draws me on = leads me on
[108] whether, either
[109] affinity, harmony
[110] congenial
[111] is powerful
[112] profound depth
[113] not affording passage
[114] enterprising
[115] create
[116] mainland

258 Where Satan now prevails, a monument
259 Of merit high to all th' infernal host,
260 Easing their passage hence, for intercourse[117]
261 Or transmigration, as their lot shall lead.
262 Nor can I miss[118] the way, so strongly drawn
263 By this new-felt attraction and instinct."
264 Whom thus the meager shadow answered soon:
265   "Go whither Fate and inclination strong
266 Leads thee. I shall not lag behind, nor err[119]
267 The way, thou leading—such a scent I draw[120]
268 Of carnage, prey innumerable, and taste[121]
269 The savor of death from all things there that live.
270 Nor shall I to the work thou enterprisest[122]
271 Be wanting,[123] but afford thee equal aid."
272   So saying, with delight he snuffed the smell
273 Of mortal[124] change on earth. As when a flock
274 Of ravenous fowl, though many a league remote,
275 Against the day of battle, to a field
276 Where armies lie encamped, come flying, lured
277 With scent of living carcasses designed
278 For death the following day, in bloody fight,
279 So scented the grim feature,[125] and upturned
280 His nostril wide into the murky air,
281 Sagacious[126] of his quarry from so far.
282 Then both from out Hell-gates, into the waste,
283 Wide anarchy of Chaos, damp and dark,
284 Flew diverse,[127] and with power (their power was great)
285 Hovering[128] upon the waters, what[129] they met
286 Solid or slimy, as in raging sea

---

[117] communication, passage
[118] mistake
[119] miss, mistake
[120] breathe
[121] I taste
[122] take in hand, attempt
[123] absent
[124] fatal
[125] shape
[126] perceiving by smell
[127] separately
[128] fluttering, flapping
[129] whatever

287 Tossed up and down, together crowded drove,
288 From each side shoaling[130] towards the mouth of Hell,
289 As when two polar winds, blowing adverse
290 Upon the Cronian[131] sea, together drive
291 Mountains of ice, that stop[132] th' imagined[133] way
292 Beyond Petsora[134] eastward, to the rich
293 Cathaian[135] coast. The aggregated soil[136]
294 Death with his mace petrific,[137] cold and dry,
295 As with a trident,[138] smote, and fixed as firm
296 As Delos,[139] floating once. The rest his look
297 Bound with Gorgonian[140] rigor[141] not to move,
298 And with asphaltic[142] slime, broad as the gate,
299 Deep to the roots of Hell the gathered beach[143]
300 They fastened, and the mole[144] immense wrought[145] on
301 Over the foaming deep high-arched, a bridge
302 Of length prodigious, joining to the wall
303 Immoveable[146] of this now fenceless[147] world,
304 Forfeit[148] to Death. From hence a passage broad,
305 Smooth, easy, inoffensive,[149] down to Hell.
306 So (if great things to small may be compared)
307 Xerxes,[150] the liberty of Greece to yoke,

---

[130] swimming together
[131] Arctic, Satanian: frozen, northern
[132] block, close up
[133] fancied
[134] the River Pechora, in Siberia, flowing down from the Urals into the Arctic Ocean
[135] Cathay = China
[136] muddy/wet places
[137] causing things to be petrified/turned to stone
[138] three-pronged fish spear or scepter: wielded by Neptune in creating the Cyclades (islands in the Aegean)
[139] one of the Cyclades: it floated until Zeus fixed it in place, for the birth of Apollo and Diana/Artemis
[140] the most famous (and the only mortal) Gorgon, Medusa, turned to stone anyone who looked at her
[141] harshness, strictness
[142] blackish mineral, containing among other things pitch
[143] seashore
[144] mass, massive structure
[145] worked
[146] the primum mobile or other shell of the universe
[147] (1) without a safeguarding fence, (2) defenseless
[148] given up
[149] easy
[150] Persian king who invaded Greece in 480 B.C.

308	From Susa,[151] his Memnonian palace high,
309	Came to the sea, and over Hellespont[152]
310	Bridging his way, Europe with Asia joined,
311	And scourged[153] with many a stroke th' indignant waves.
312	Now had they brought the work by wondrous art
313	Pontifical,[154] a ridge of pendant[155] rock
314	Over the vexed[156] abyss, following the track
315	Of Satan to the self-same place where he
316	First lighted[157] from his wing,[158] and landed safe
317	From out of Chaos, to the outside bare
318	Of this round world. With pins of adamant
319	And chains they made all fast—too fast they made
320	And durable! And now in little space
321	The confines[159] met of empyrean Heav'n
322	And of this world, and on the left hand Hell
323	With long reach interposed.[160] Three sev'ral[161] ways[162]
324	In sight, to each of these three places led.
325	And now their way to earth they had descried,[163]
326	To Paradise first tending[164]—when, behold!
327	Satan, in likeness of an Angel bright,
328	Betwixt the Centaur and the Scorpion steering
329	His zenith,[165] while the sun in Aries rose.[166]
330	Disguised he came, but those his children dear
331	Their parent soon discerned,[167] though in disguise.
332	He, after Eve seduced, unminded[168] slunk

---

[151] biblical Shushan, founded by Tithonus, Memnon's father
[152] the Dardenelles, the strait between Turkey and southeastern Europe
[153] beat, whip
[154] bridge-making
[155] suspended, hanging
[156] disturbed
[157] descended
[158] flying, flight
[159] regions, borders
[160] pushed itself in
[161] different
[162] roads, paths
[163] discovered
[164] turning, moving
[165] i.e., steering a central course, through the high point of the sky
[166] the sun (Uriel) rises under the sign of Aries; it is opposite to Scorpion, which is near Centaurus
[167] recognized
[168] unnoticed

333 Into the wood fast by and, changing shape
334 T' observe the sequel, saw his guileful act
335 By Eve, though all unweeting,[169] seconded
336 Upon her husband, saw their shame that sought
337 Vain covertures,[170] but when he saw descend
338 The Son of God to judge them, terrified
339 He fled, not hoping to escape, but shun
340 The present, fearing, guilty, what His[171] wrath
341 Might suddenly inflict. That past, returned[172]
342 By night, and list'ning where the hapless[173] pair
343 Sat in their sad discourse and various plaint,
344 Thence gathered his own doom, which understood
345 Not instant, but of future time. With joy
346 And tidings fraught,[174] to Hell he now returned,
347 And at the brink of Chaos, near the foot
348 Of this new wondrous pontifice, unhoped
349 Met who to meet him came, his offspring dear.
350 Great joy was at their meeting, and at sight
351 Of that stupendious bridge his joy increased.
352 Long he admiring stood, till Sin, his fair
353 Enchanting daughter, thus the silence broke:
354   "O parent, these are thy magnific deeds,
355 Thy trophies! which thou view'st as not thine own.
356 Thou art their author and prime architect,
357 For I no sooner in my heart divined
358 (My heart, which by a secret harmony
359 Still moves with thine, joined in connection sweet)
360 That thou on earth had'st prospered, which thy looks
361 Now also evidence, but straight I felt
362 (Though distant from thee worlds between), yet felt
363 That I must after[175] thee, with this thy son,
364 Such fatal[176] consequence[177] unites us three!

---

[169] unknowing
[170] covering
[171] Christ's/God's
[172] he (Satan) returned
[173] luckless
[174] filled
[175] follow after
[176] inevitable, deadly
[177] relationship, connection

365 Hell could no longer hold us in our bounds,
366 Nor this unvoyageable gulf obscure
367 Detain from following thy illustrious track.
368 Thou hast achieved our liberty, confined
369 Within Hell-gates till now. Thou us empowered
370 To fortify[178] thus far, and overlay,
371 With this portentous[179] bridge, the dark abyss.
372 Thine now is all this world. Thy virtue hath won
373 What thy hands builded not, thy wisdom gained
374 With odds[180] what war hath lost, and fully avenged
375 Our foil[181] in Heav'n. Here thou shalt monarch reign,
376 There did'st not. There let Him still victor sway,[182]
377 As battle hath adjudged, from this new world
378 Retiring, by His own doom[183] alienated,[184]
379 And henceforth monarchy with thee divide
380 Of all things, parted by the empyreal bounds,
381 His quadrature,[185] from thy orbicular[186] world—
382 Or try[187] thee, now more dang'rous to His throne."
383 Whom thus the Prince of darkness answered glad:
384   "Fair daughter, and thou son and grandchild
       both:
385 High proof ye now have giv'n to be the race
386 Of Satan (for I glory in the name,
387 Antagonist of Heaven's Almighty King).
388 Amply have merited of me, of all
389 Th' infernal empire, that so near Heav'n's door
390 Triumphal with triumphal act have met,
391 Mine[188] with this glorious work, and made one realm,
392 Hell and this world, one realm, one continent
393 Of easy thoroughfare. Therefore, while I
394 Descend through darkness, on your road with ease,

---

[178] (1) to build/establish a position/structure of defense, (2) to become powerful
[179] (1) marvelous, prodigious, (2) bearing portents, omens, signs
[180] with odds = and more ("and then some!")
[181] defeat, repulse
[182] rule
[183] decision, judgment
[184] turned away
[185] Heaven is square
[186] the earth and all our world/universe is round/globular
[187] test
[188] i.e., on earth

395 To my associate Powers, them to acquaint
396 With these successes, and with them rejoice,
397 You two this way, among these numerous orbs,
398 All yours, right down to Paradise descend.
399 There dwell, and reign in bliss, thence on the earth
400 Dominion exercise and in the air,
401 Chiefly on man, sole lord of all declared.
402 Him first make sure your thrall,[189] and lastly kill.
403 My substitutes I send ye, and create
404 Plenipotent[190] on earth, of matchless might
405 Issuing from me. On your joint vigor now
406 My hold of this new kingdom all depends,
407 Through Sin to Death exposed[191] by my exploit.[192]
408 If your joint power prevail, th' affairs of Hell
409 No detriment[193] need fear. Go, and be strong!"
410   So saying he dismissed them. They with speed
411 Their course through thickest constellations held,
412 Spreading their bane.[194] The blasted[195] stars looked wan,
413 And planets, planet-struck,[196] real[197] eclipse[198]
414 Then suffered. Th' other way Satan went down
415 The causey[199] to Hell-gate. On either side
416 Disparted[200] Chaos overbuilt exclaimed[201]
417 And with rebounding surge the bars[202] assailed,
418 That scorned his indignation. Through the gate,
419 Wide open and unguarded, Satan passed,
420 And all about found desolate, for those
421 Appointed to sit there had left their charge,
422 Flown to the upper world. The rest were all

---

[189] slave
[190] invested with full power/authority
[191] i.e., the "new kingdom" has, by his action, been exposed to sin and death
[192] action
[193] loss, damage
[194] poison, destruction
[195] suddenly infected
[196] (though planets usually influence the earth, they are now struck, in their turn, by the activities of Sin and Death)
[197] [bisyllabic, second accented]
[198] darkening, loss of splendor
[199] causeway
[200] divided-into-parts
[201] cried out
[202] walls, gates

423   Far to the inland retired,[203] about the walls
424   Of Pandemonium, city and proud seat
425   Of Lucifer, so by allusion called
426   Of that bright star to Satan paragoned.[204]
427   There kept their watch the legions, while the grand
428   In council sat, solicitous[205] what chance
429   Might intercept[206] their emperor sent.[207] So he
430   Departing gave[208] command, and they observed.
431   As when the Tartar from his Russian foe
432   By Astrakhan[209] over the snowy plains
433   Retires, or Bactrin Sophi,[210] from the horns
434   Of Turkish crescent, leaves all waste beyond
435   The realm of Aladule,[211] in his retreat
436   To Tauris[212] or Casbeen,[213] so these, the late[214]
437   Heav'n-banished host left desert[215] utmost[216] Hell
438   Many a dark league, reduced[217] in careful watch
439   Round their metropolis, and now expecting
440   Each hour their great adventurer, from the search
441   Of foreign worlds. He through the midst unmarked,[218]
442   In show[219] plebeian[220] Angel militant[221]
443   Of lowest order, passed, and from the door
444   Of that Plutonian hall, invisible
445   Ascended his high throne, which under state[222]
446   Of richest texture spread, at th' upper end

---

[203] withdrawn
[204] compared
[205] anxious, apprehensive
[206] cut off, stop, hinder
[207] [adjective, modifying "emperor"]
[208] i.e., had earlier commanded
[209] near the mouth of the Volga
[210] Persian ruler
[211] greater Armenia
[212] Tabriz, in northwestern Persia
[213] Kazvin, in northern Persia
[214] recently
[215] deserted
[216] outermost
[217] drawing together
[218] unnoticed
[219] appearance
[220] of low rank
[221] soldier
[222] canopy

447 Was placed in regal luster. Down a while
448 He sat, and round about him saw unseen.
449 At last, as from a cloud, his fulgent[223] head
450 And shape star-bright appeared, or brighter, clad
451 With what permissive glory since his fall
452 Was left him, or false glitter. All amazed
453 At that so sudden blaze, the Stygian[224] throng
454 Bent[225] their aspect,[226] and whom they wished beheld,
455 Their mighty chief returned. Loud was th' acclaim!
456 Forth rushed in haste the great consulting peers,
457 Raised from their dark divan,[227] and with like joy
458 Congratulant approached him, who with hand
459 Silence, and with these words attention won:
460   "Thrones, Dominations, Princedoms, Virtues, Powers!
461 For in possession such, not only of right,
462 I call ye and declare ye now, returned
463 Successful beyond hope, to lead ye forth
464 Triumphant out of this infernal pit
465 Abominable, accursed, the house of woe
466 And dungeon of our tyrant. Now possess,
467 As lords, a spacious world, t' our native Heav'n
468 Little inferior, by my adventure hard
469 With peril great achieved. Long were to tell
470 What I have done, what suffered, with what pain
471 Voyaged th' unreal,[228] vast, unbounded deep
472 Of horrible confusion, over which
473 By Sin and Death a broad way now is paved,
474 To expedite your glorious march. But I
475 Toiled out my uncouth[229] passage, forced to ride[230]
476 The untractable[231] abyss, plunged in the womb
477 Of unoriginal[232] Night and Chaos wild

---

[223] gleaming
[224] hellish
[225] directed, turned
[226] gaze
[227] (1) hall of state, (2) raised floor area, used (with pillows) as a kind of couch or sofa
[228] unformed
[229] unknown
[230] travel
[231] stubborn, difficult, unmanageable
[232] possessing no creator, since existing from the very beginning

478 That, jealous of their secrets, fiercely opposed
479 My journey strange,[233] with clamorous uproar
480 Protesting Fate supreme. Thence how I found
481 The new created world, which fame[234] in Heav'n
482 Long had foretold, a fabric[235] wonderful
483 Of absolute[236] perfection, therein man
484 Placed in a Paradise, by our exile
485 Made happy. Him by fraud I have seduced[237]
486 From his Creator and, the more to increase
487 Your wonder, with an apple.[238] He,[239] thereat
488 Offended (worth your laughter!) hath given up
489 Both His belovèd man and all his world
490 To Sin and Death a prey, and so to us,
491 Without our hazard, labor, or alarm,[240]
492 To range[241] in, and to dwell, and over man
493 To rule, as over all He should have ruled.
494   "True is, me also He hath judged, or rather
495 Me not, but the brute serpent in whose shape
496 Man I deceived. That which to me belongs
497 Is enmity, which He will put between
498 Me and mankind. I am to bruise[242] his heel.
499 His seed (when is not set[243]) shall bruise my head.
500 A world who would not purchase with a bruise,
501 Or much more grievous pain?
               "Ye have th' account
502 Of my performance. What remains, ye Gods,
503 But up, and enter now into full bliss?"
504   So having said, a while he stood, expecting
505 Their universal shout and high applause
506 To fill his ear—when, contrary, he hears

---

[233] unfamiliar
[234] rumor, report
[235] product
[236] complete
[237] beguiled, led astray
[238] (although there are no stage directions, this being an epic poem and not a drama, Milton clearly intends at this point a burst of laughter from Satan's devilish audience)
[239] God
[240] sudden attack
[241] move hither and thither
[242] break, smash, crush
[243] ordained, established, fixed

507   On all sides, from innumerable tongues,
508   A dismal universal hiss, the sound
509   Of public scorn. He wondered, but not long
510   Had leisure, wond'ring at himself now more.
511   His visage drawn he felt to sharp and spare;
512   His arms clung to his ribs, his legs entwining
513   Each other, till supplanted[244] down he fell,
514   A monstrous serpent on his belly prone,
515   Reluctant,[245] but in vain. A greater power
516   Now ruled him, punished in the shape he sinned,
517   According to his doom.[246] He would have spoke,
518   But hiss for hiss returned with forkèd tongue
519   To forkèd tongue, for now were all transformed
520   Alike, to serpents all, as accessories
521   To his bold[247] riot.[248] Dreadful was the din
522   Of hissing through the hall, thick swarming now
523   With complicated[249] monsters head and tail,
524   Scorpion, and asp, and amphisbaena[250] dire,
525   Cerastes hornèd, hydrus,[251] and elops[252] drear,[253]
526   And dipsas[254] (not so thick swarmed once the soil
527   Bedropped with blood of Gorgon,[255] or the isle
528   Ophiusa),[256] but still greatest he the midst,
529   Now dragon grown, larger than whom[257] the sun
530   Engendered in the Pythian[258] vale on slime,[259]
531   Huge python, and his[260] power no less he seemed
532   Above the rest still to retain. They all

---

[244] brought low, stumbling
[245] struggling
[246] sentence
[247] presumptuous, audacious
[248] tumult, disorder, violence
[249] twisted/twined together
[250] mythical serpent with a head at each end
[251] mythical water snake
[252] swordfish?
[253] dismal, melancholy
[254] the bite of which caused intense thirst
[255] serpents grew from Gorgon blood
[256] "full of snakes": one of the Balearic Islands
[257] the dragon whom
[258] the Pythia = the prophetess of Apollo
[259] i.e., the sun's heat engenders the monster in the mud ("slime") of the Nile River
[260] Satan

533   Him followed, issuing forth to th' open field,
534   Where all yet left of that revolted rout,[261]
535   Heav'n-fall'n, in station[262] stood or just[263] array,
536   Sublime[264] with expectation when to see
537   In triumph issuing forth their glorious chief.
538   They saw, but other sight instead! a crowd
539   Of ugly serpents. Horror on them fell,
540   And horrid sympathy, for what they saw
541   They felt themselves now changing. Down their arms,
542   Down fell both spear and shield, down they as fast,
543   And the dire hiss renewed, and the dire form
544   Catched by contagion,[265] like[266] in punishment
545   As in their crime. Thus was th' applause they meant
546   Turned to exploding hiss, triumph to shame
547   Cast on themselves from their own mouths.

                                There stood

548   A grove hard by, sprung up with[267] this their change
549   (His will who reigns above, to aggravate[268]
550   Their penance), laden with fair fruit, like that
551   Which grew in Paradise, the bait of Eve
552   Used by the Tempter. On that prospect[269] strange[270]
553   Their earnest eyes they fixed, imagining
554   For one forbidden tree a multitude
555   Now ris'n, to work them further woe or shame.
556   Yet parched with scalding thirst and hunger fierce,
557   Though to delude them sent, could not abstain,
558   But on they rolled in heaps, and up the trees
559   Climbing, sat thicker than the snaky locks
560   That curled Megaera.[271] Greedily they plucked
561   The fruitage fair to sight, like that which grew

---

[261] mob, crowd
[262] in station = at their proper post
[263] proper
[264] proud, erect
[265] corruption
[266] alike
[267] along with
[268] make worse, weigh down, exasperate
[269] view
[270] unfamiliar
[271] a Fury, all three of whom had snakes in their hair

562 Near that bituminous[272] lake[273] where Sodom flamed—
563 This more delusive, not the touch, but taste
564 Deceived. They fondly[274] thinking to allay
565 Their appetite with gust,[275] instead of fruit
566 Chewed bitter ashes, which th' offended taste
567 With spattering noise rejected. Oft they assayed,
568 Hunger and thirst constraining, drugged[276] as oft,
569 With hatefullest disrelish[277] writhed their jaws,
570 With soot and cinders filled. So oft they fell
571 Into the same illusion, not as man
572 Whom they triumphed[278] once[279] lapsed. Thus were they
          plagued
573 And worn with famine,[280] long and ceaseless hiss,
574 Till their lost shape, permitted, they resumed,
575 Yearly enjoined, some say, to undergo
576 This annual humbling certain[281] numbered days,
577 To dash[282] their pride and joy for man seduced.
578 However, some tradition[283] they dispersed[284]
579 Among the heathen, of their purchase[285] got,
580 And fabled how the serpent, whom they called
581 Ophion,[286] with Eurynome[287] (the wide-
582 Encroaching Eve,[288] perhaps), had first the rule
583 Of high Olympus, thence by Saturn driv'n
584 And Ops,[289] ere yet Dictaean Jove[290] was born.
585   Meanwhile in Paradise the hellish pair

---

[272] pitchy
[273] the Dead Sea
[274] foolishly
[275] gusto
[276] nauseated
[277] aversion, disgust
[278] triumphed over
[279] i.e., only once
[280] extreme hunger
[281] on certain
[282] depress, frustrate
[283] relate/transmit as a tradition [verb]
[284] spread about
[285] booty
[286] "snake": a Titan, first ruler of Olympus
[287] "wide-ruling": Ophion's wife
[288] i.e., more or less the pagan equivalent of Eve?
[289] Ops/Rhea/Cybele: wife of Cronos
[290] Dictaean Jove = Dicte, mountain in Crete, where Jove/Jupiter/Zeus grew up

586 Too soon arrived, Sin there in power before,
587 Once[291] actual,[292] now in body, and to dwell
588 Habitual habitant; behind her Death,
589 Close following pace for pace, not mounted yet
590 On his pale horse.[293] To whom Sin thus began:
591   "Second of Satan sprung, all-conquering Death!
592 What think'st thou of our empire now, though earned
593 With travel difficult, not better far
594 Than still at Hell's dark threshold to have sat watch,
595 Unnamed, undreaded, and thyself half starved?"
596 Whom thus the Sin-born monster answered soon:[294]
597   "To me, who with eternal famine pine,[295]
598 Alike is Hell, or Paradise, or Heaven—
599 There best, where most with ravine[296] I may meet,
600 Which here, though plenteous, all too little seems
601 To stuff this maw, this vast unhide-bound[297] corpse."[298]
602 To whom th' incestuous mother thus replied:
603   "Thou therefore on these herbs, and fruits, and
              flow'rs
604 Feed first. On each beast next, and fish, and fowl—
605 No homely[299] morsels! And whatever thing
606 The scythe of Time mows down, devour unspared,[300]
607 Till I, in man residing through the race,
608 His thoughts, his looks, words, actions, all infect,
609 And season him thy last and sweetest prey."
610   This said, they both betook them several[301] ways,
611 Both to destroy, or unimmortal make
612 All kinds, and for destruction to mature[302]
613 Sooner or later.
              Which th' Almighty seeing,

---

[291] at one time
[292] actuated/made actual by Adam and Eve
[293] see Revelation 6:8
[294] quickly
[295] suffer, am tormented/troubled
[296] prey
[297] not limited/bound by his body
[298] a body, living or dead
[299] plain, rude
[300] mercilessly
[301] in different
[302] ripen

614　From His transcendent seat the Saints among,
615　To those bright orders uttered thus His voice:
616　　　　　"See with what heat these dogs of Hell advance
617　To waste[303] and havoc[304] yonder world, which I
618　So fair and good created, and had still
619　Kept in that state, had not the folly of man
620　Let in these wasteful Furies, who impute[305]
621　Folly to me! So doth the Prince of Hell
622　And his adherents, that with so much ease
623　I suffer[306] them to enter and possess
624　A place so Heav'nly, and conniving[307] seem
625　To gratify[308] my scornful enemies,
626　That laugh, as if transported[309] with some fit
627　Of passion, I to them had quitted[310] all,
628　At random[311] yielded up to their misrule,
629　And know not that I called, and drew them thither,
630　My Hell-hounds, to lick up the draff[312] and filth
631　Which man's polluting sin with taint hath shed
632　On what was pure, till[313] crammed[314] and gorged,[315] nigh[316] burst
633　With sucked[317] and glutted[318] offal,[319] at one sling[320]
634　Of thy victorious arm, well-pleasing Son,
635　Both Sin and Death, and yawning[321] grave at last
636　Through Chaos hurled, obstruct[322] the mouth of Hell

---

[303] consume, diminish, destroy
[304] devastate, destroy
[305] attribute, ascribe
[306] permit, allow
[307] winking, tacitly permitting
[308] reward, oblige
[309] carried away
[310] renounced, abandoned
[311] at random = without consideration/care/control, purposelessly, heedlessly
[312] dregs, refuse
[313] till the time when
[314] filled/stuffed to excess
[315] glutted, satiated
[316] almost
[317] sucked-dry?
[318] chokingly/sickeningly overfilled
[319] garbage, rubbish, putrid flesh
[320] throw, fling
[321] gaping
[322] will obstruct

637   Forever, and seal up his ravenous jaws.
638   Then Heav'n and earth renewed shall be made pure
639   To sanctity[323] that shall receive no stain:
640   Till then, the curse pronounced on both precedes."[324]
641   He ended, and the Heav'nly audience loud
642   Sung Hallelujah, as[325] the sound of seas,
643   Through multitude that sung:
                                 "Just are Thy ways,
644   Righteous are Thy decrees on all Thy works.
645   Who can extenuate[326] Thee?" Next,[327] to the Son,
646   Destined Restorer of mankind, by whom
647   New Heav'n and earth shall to the ages rise,
648   Or down from Heav'n descend.
                                 Such was their song,
649   While the Creator, calling forth by name
650   His mighty Angels, gave them several charge,[328]
651   As sorted[329] best with present things. The sun
652   Had first his precept[330] so to move, so shine,
653   As might affect the earth with cold and heat
654   Scarce tolerable, and from the north to call
655   Decrepit[331] winter, from the south to bring
656   Solstitial[332] summer's heat. To the blanc[333] moon
657   Her office they prescribed; to th' other five[334]
658   Their planetary motions, and aspects,[335]
659   In sextile,[336] square,[337] and trine,[338] and opposite,[339]

---

[323] saintliness, holiness
[324] takes precedence
[325] like
[326] weaken, lessen
[327] i.e., next they sang
[328] different tasks/responsibilities/mandates
[329] fitted
[330] order, authoritative command
[331] feeble, worn out
[332] connected with the solstice, i.e., when the sun is halfway between the two equinoxes and, in the summer, at its farthest point from the equator
[333] pale, white
[334] planets
[335] relative positions of the planets, as seen from the earth
[336] two heavenly bodies at 60-degree angles from one another (60 degrees = one-sixth of the whole zodiac)
[337] two heavenly bodies at 90-degree angles from one another
[338] two heavenly bodies at 120-degree angles from one another
[339] two heavenly bodies at 180-degree angles from one another

660   Of noxious[340] efficacy, and when to join
661   In synod[341] unbenign, and taught the fixed[342]
662   Their influence malignant when to shower,
663   Which of them rising with the sun, or falling,
664   Should prove tempestuous.[343] To the winds they set
665   Their corners,[344] when with bluster[345] to confound[346]
666   Sea, air, and shore; the thunder when to roll
667   With terror through the dark aereal hall.
668   Some say He bid his Angels turn askance[347]
669   The poles of earth, twice ten degrees and more
670   From the sun's axle. They with labor pushed
671   Oblique[348] the centric globe.[349] Some say the sun[350]
672   Was bid turn reins from th' equinoctial[351] road
673   Like[352] distant breadth to Taurus[353] with the Sev'n
674   Atlantic Sisters,[354] and the Spartan Twins,[355]
675   Up to the Tropic Crab,[356] thence down amain[357]
676   By Leo,[358] and the Virgin,[359] and the Scales,[360]
677   As deep as Capricorn, to bring in change
678   Of seasons to each clime. Else[361] had the Spring
679   Perpetual smiled on earth with vernant[362] flowers,
680   Equal in days and nights, except to those
681   Beyond the polar circles: to them day

---

[340] harmful, unwholesome
[341] conjunction
[342] the fixed = the fixed stars, in the eighth of the heavenly spheres
[343] stormy, passionate [trisyllabic, second accented, "-uous" elided]
[344] north, east, south, west
[345] storming, raging
[346] throw into confusion/disorder
[347] sideways
[348] at a slanting angle
[349] centric globe = the earth, which was at the center
[350] Apollo's chariot
[351] celestial equator
[352] equally
[353] the Bull
[354] the Pleiades
[355] Gemini
[356] Cancer
[357] (1) without delay, rapidly, (2) exceedingly
[358] the Lion
[359] Virgo
[360] Libra
[361] otherwise
[362] blossoming

682   Had unbenighted[363] shone, while the low sun,
683   To recompense[364] his distance, in their sight
684   Had rounded still the horizon, and not known
685   Or east or west, which had forbid the snow
686   From cold Estotiland,[365] and south as far
687   Beneath Magellan.[366] At that tasted fruit[367]
688   The sun, as from Thyestean banquet,[368] turned
689   His course intended: else how had the world
690   Inhabited,[369] though sinless more than now,
691   Avoided pinching[370] cold and scorching heat?
692   These changes in the heav'ns, though slow, produced
693   Like[371] change on sea and land, sideral[372] blast,
694   Vapor, and mist, and exhalation hot,
695   Corrupt and pestilent. Now from the north
696   Of Norumbega,[373] and the Samoed shore,[374]
697   Bursting their brazen dungeon,[375] armed with ice,
698   And snow, and hail, and stormy gust and flaw,[376]
699   Boreas,[377] and Caecias,[378] and Argestes[379] loud,
700   And Thrascias,[380] rend the woods, and seas upturn.
701   With adverse[381] blast upturns them from the south
702   Notus,[382] and Afer,[383] black with thund'rous clouds

---

[363] undarkened
[364] make up for
[365] Labrador
[366] strait at the extreme southern tip of South America
[367] i.e., when Adam and Eve ate the forbidden fruit
[368] Atreus, Thyestes' brother, killed Thyestes' sons and served them to their father at a banquet
[369] world inhabited = inhabited world
[370] nipping, painful
[371] equivalent
[372] from the malign stars
[373] New England
[374] Samoed shore = Siberia
[375] i.e., the cave of the winds, in which Aeolus, god of the winds, kept the winds in confinement, when they were not blowing
[376] burst of wind
[377] a north wind
[378] a north wind
[379] a north wind
[380] a north wind
[381] the opposite
[382] a south wind
[383] a south wind

703   From Serraliona.[384] Thwart of [385] these, as[386] fierce,
704   Forth rush the Levant[387] and the Ponent[388] winds,
705   Eurus and Zephyr, with their lateral[389] noise,[390]
706   Sirocco[391] and Libecchio.[392]

                          Thus began
707   Outrage[393] from lifeless things, but Discord first,
708   Daughter of Sin, among th' irrational[394]
709   Death introduced, through fierce antipathy.[395]
710   Beast now with beast 'gan war, and fowl with fowl,
711   And fish with fish. To graze the herb all leaving,[396]
712   Devoured each other, nor stood much in awe
713   Of man, but fled him or, with count'nance grim,[397]
714   Glared on him passing.

                          These were from without[398]
715   The growing miseries, which Adam saw
716   Already in part, though hid in gloomiest shade,
717   To sorrow abandoned, but worse felt within,
718   And in a troubled sea of passion tossed,
719   Thus to disburden sought[399] with sad complaint:
720   "O miserable of[400] happy! Is this the end
721   Of this new glorious world, and me so late[401]
722   The glory of that glory, who now become
723   Accursed, of[402] blessèd? Hide me from the face
724   Of God, whom to behold was then my height

---

[384] Sierra Leone, in Africa
[385] thwart of = across
[386] equally
[387] Euras/Levant is an east wind
[388] Ponent/Zephyr is a west wind
[389] coming from the horizon: east/west rather than north/south
[390] clamor, loud/harsh sound
[391] a southeast wind
[392] a southwest wind
[393] riot, violence
[394] irrational creatures [probably, from Latin influence, four syllables, first and third accented]
[395] settled aversion, contrariety of feeling/disposition
[396] leaving off
[397] fierce, savage
[398] from without = in addition to
[399] "he, Adam, sought"
[400] from, instead of
[401] recently
[402] from, instead of

725   Of happiness! Yet well,[403] if here would end
726   The misery. I deserved it, and would[404] bear
727   My own deservings. But this will not serve:[405]
728   All that I eat or drink, or shall beget,
729   Is propagated[406] curse. O voice, once heard
730   Delightfully, 'Increase and multiply,'
731   Now death to hear! For what can I increase
732   Or multiply, but curses on my head?
733   Who of all ages to succeed,[407] but feeling
734   The evil on him brought by me, will curse
735   My head? 'Ill fare our ancestor impure,
736   For this we may thank Adam!' But his thanks
737   Shall be the execration.[408] So, besides
738   Mine own[409] that bide[410] upon me, all from me
739   Shall with a fierce reflux[411] on me redound — [412]
740   On me, as on their natural center, light[413]
741   Heavy, though in their place.[414] O fleeting joys
742   Of Paradise, dear bought with lasting woes!
743   Did I request thee, Maker, from my clay
744   To mould me man? Did I solicit Thee
745   From darkness to promote[415] me, or here place
746   In this delicious[416] garden? As my will
747   Concurred[417] not to my being, it were but right
748   And equal to reduce me to my dust,
749   Desirous to resign[418] and render back
750   All I received, unable to perform
751   Thy terms too hard, by which I was to hold

---

[403] it would be well/all right
[404] want to
[405] satisfy, be useful, answer the requirements, meet the needs of the case, suit, fit
[406] multiplied, spread
[407] follow
[408] curse
[409] mine own = mine own curses
[410] remain, continue
[411] flowing back
[412] surge, turn back
[413] fall, descend
[414] proper order
[415] advance
[416] luxurious, highly pleasing
[417] agreed
[418] surrender

752   The good I sought not. To the loss of that,
753   Sufficient penalty: why hast Thou added
754   The sense of endless woes? Inexplicable
755   Thy Justice seems. Yet to say truth, too late
756   I thus contest. Then should have been refused
757   Those terms whatever, when they were proposed.
758   Thou[419] didst accept them. Wilt thou[420] enjoy the good,
759   Then cavil[421] the conditions? And though God
760   Made thee without thy leave,[422] what if thy[423] son
761   Prove disobedient, and reproved, retort,
762   'Wherefore did'st thou beget me? I sought it not.'
763   Would'st thou admit[424] for his contempt of thee
764   That proud excuse? Yet him not thy election[425]
765   But natural necessity begot.[426]
766   God made thee of choice His own, and of His own
767   To serve Him: thy reward was of His grace,
768   Thy punishment then justly is at His will.
769   "Be it so, for I submit: His doom[427] is fair,
770   That dust I am, and shall to dust return.
771   O welcome hour whenever! Why delays
772   His hand to execute what His decree
773   Fixed[428] on this day?[429] Why do I overlive,[430]
774   Why am I mocked with death, and lengthened out
775   To deathless pain? How gladly would I meet
776   Mortality, my sentence, and be earth
777   Insensible![431] How glad would lay me down
778   As in my mother's lap! There I should rest,
779   And sleep secure.[432] His dreadful voice no more
780   Would thunder in my ears. No fear of worse

---

[419] himself, Adam
[420] himself, Adam
[421] captiously object to/find fault with
[422] permission
[423] himself, Adam
[424] receive, permit
[425] choice
[426] procreated, generated
[427] judgment
[428] settled, determined
[429] this day = today
[430] live too long
[431] deprived of sensation, unconscious
[432] confident, safe, free from fear/anxiety

781 To me, and to my offspring, would torment me
782 With cruel expectation.

                              "Yet one doubt
783 Pursues me still, lest all[433] I cannot die,
784 Lest that pure breath of life, the spirit of man
785 Which God inspired, cannot together perish
786 With this corporeal clod.[434] Then in the grave,
787 Or in some other dismal place, who knows
788 But I shall die a living death? O thought
789 Horrid, if true! Yet why? It was but breath
790 Of life that sinned. What dies but what had life
791 And sin? The body properly had neither.
792 All of me then shall die: let this appease[435]
793 The doubt, since human reach no further knows.
794 For though the Lord of all be infinite,
795 Is His wrath also? Be it, man is not so,
796 But mortal doomed.[436] How can He exercise
797 Wrath without end on man, whom death must end?
798 Can He make deathless death? That were to make
799 Strange contradiction, which to God Himself
800 Impossible is held,[437] as argument[438]
801 Of weakness, not of power. Will He draw out,
802 For anger's sake, finite to infinite,
803 In punished man, to satisfy His rigor,[439]
804 Satisfied never? That were to extend
805 His sentence beyond dust and Nature's law,
806 By which all causes else,[440] according still
807 To the reception[441] of their matter, act,[442]
808 Not to th' extent of their own sphere.

                                           "But say
809 That death be not one stroke, as I supposed,

---

[433] completely, entirely
[434] corporeal clod = earthen body
[435] relieve, calm
[436] fated, destined
[437] considered, thought
[438] fact, proof
[439] severity
[440] all causes else = all other causes
[441] absorption, taking in
[442] i.e., causes act according to the capacity of what they *work upon;* what the *cause* of something may be capable of is, in this sense, irrelevant

810 Bereaving[443] sense, but endless misery
811 From this day onward, which I feel begun
812 From in[444] me, and without[445] me—and so last
813 To perpetuity. Aye me, that fear
814 Comes thundering back with dreadful revolution[446]
815 On my defenceless head. Both Death and I
816 Am found eternal, and incorporate[447] both,
817 Nor I on my part single.[448] In me all
818 Posterity stands cursed: fair patrimony
819 That I must leave ye, sons. O were I able
820 To waste[449] it all myself, and leave ye none!
821 So disinherited, how would you bless
822 Me, now your curse! Ah, why should all mankind,
823 For one man's fault, thus guiltless be condemned—
824 If guiltless? But from me what can proceed,
825 But all corrupt, both mind and will depraved[450]
826 Not to do only, but to will the same
827 With[451] me? How can they then acquitted stand
828 In sight of God? Him after all disputes,
829 Forced[452] I absolve. All my evasions vain,
830 And reasonings, though through mazes, lead me still
831 But to my own conviction: first and last
832 On me, me only, as the source and spring
833 Of all corruption, all the blame lights[453] due.
834 So might the wrath. Fond[454] wish! Could'st thou[455]
                                                         support
835 That burden, heavier than the earth to bear,
836 Than all the world much heavier, though divided[456]

---

[443] depriving, taking away
[444] inside
[445] outside
[446] turning/spinning motion
[447] immaterial (spiritual) rather than material (bodily)
[448] alone
[449] use up, consume
[450] corrupted
[451] along with me, just as I do/have
[452] of necessity
[453] falls
[454] foolish
[455] himself, Adam
[456] shared

837   With that bad woman?[457] Thus what thou desir'st,
838   And what thou fear'st, alike destroys all hope
839   Of refuge, and concludes thee miserable
840   Beyond all past example and future.
841   To Satan only like[458] both crime and doom.[459]
842   O Conscience! Into what abyss of fears
843   And horrors hast thou[460] driv'n me, out of which
844   I find no way, from deep to deeper plunged!"
845   Thus Adam to himself lamented loud
846   Through the still night—not now, as ere[461] man fell,
847   Wholesome, and cool, and mild, but with black air
848   Accompanied, with damps,[462] and dreadful gloom,
849   Which to his[463] evil conscience represented[464]
850   All things with double terror. On the ground
851   Outstretched he lay, on the cold ground, and oft
852   Cursed his creation, Death as oft accused
853   Of tardy execution, since denounced[465]
854   The day of his offence. "Why comes not Death,"
855   Said he, "with one thrice-acceptable[466] stroke
856   To end me? Shall truth fail to keep her word,
857   Justice Divine not hasten to be just?
858   But Death comes not at call, Justice Divine
859   Mends[467] not her slowest pace for prayers or cries.
860   O woods, O fountains, hillocks, dales, and bow'rs!
861   With other echo late[468] I taught your shades
862   To answer, and resound[469] far other song!"
863   Whom thus afflicted when sad Eve beheld,
864   Desolate where she sat, approaching nigh
865   Soft words to his fierce passion she assayed,[470]

---

[457] Eve
[458] similar
[459] sentence, judgment
[460] conscience
[461] before
[462] noxious exhalations/vapors
[463] Adam's
[464] exhibited, showed
[465] already announced/proclaimed
[466] [four syllables, first and third accented: ACCepTABle]
[467] sets right
[468] not long ago
[469] ring out, reëcho
[470] attempted

866　　But her with stern regard he thus repelled:
867　　　　　"Out of my sight, thou serpent! That name best
868　　Befits[471] thee, with him leagued,[472] thyself as false
869　　And hateful.[473] Nothing wants,[474] but that thy shape,
870　　Like his, and color serpentine, may show
871　　Thy inward fraud, to warn all creatures from thee
872　　Henceforth, lest that too Heav'nly form, pretended[475]
873　　To hellish falsehood, snare them! But[476] for thee
874　　I had[477] persisted[478] happy, had not thy pride
875　　And wand'ring[479] vanity, when least was safe,
876　　Rejected my forewarning and disdained
877　　Not to be trusted—longing to be seen,
878　　Though by the Devil himself, him overweening[480]
879　　To over-reach,[481] but with the serpent meeting
880　　Fooled and beguiled. By him, thou, I by thee.
881　　To trust thee from my side, imagined[482] wise,
882　　Constant, mature, proof against all assaults,
883　　And understood not[483] all was but a show
884　　Rather than solid virtue, all but a rib
885　　Crookèd by nature, bent, as now appears,
886　　More to the part sinister,[484] from me drawn,[485]
887　　Well if thrown out, as supernumerary[486]
888　　To my just number found.[487] O why did God,
889　　Creator wise, that peopled highest Heav'n
890　　With Spirits masculine, create at last

---

[471] suits
[472] allied
[473] as Satan is
[474] is missing
[475] held, as if a mask or screen, in front of her, to conceal the "hellish falsehood" behind it
[476] except
[477] would have
[478] remained
[479] vagrant, wanton, uncertain
[480] thinking arrogantly/presumptuously
[481] overpower, outdo, get the better of
[482] imagined by me
[483] not understood by me
[484] (1) the left side, (2) darkly suspicious/dishonest/corrupt
[485] withdrawn, taken
[486] unnecessary, superfluous [five syllables, first, third, and fifth accented]
[487] i.e., his correct/right/true number is one (only himself), not two (with her—superfluously—added)

891   This novelty on earth, this fair defect
892   Of Nature, and not fill the world at once
893   With men, as[488] Angels without feminine,
894   Or find some other way to generate[489]
895   Mankind? This mischief had not been befallen,[490]
896   And more that shall befall, innumerable
897   Disturbances on earth through female snares,
898   And strait conjunction[491] with this sex. For either
899   He never shall find out fit[492] mate, but such
900   As some misfortune brings him, or mistake,
901   Or whom[493] he wishes most shall seldom gain,
902   Through her perverseness,[494] but shall see her gained
903   By a far worse,[495] or if she love,[496] withheld
904   By parents, or his happiest choice too late
905   Shall meet, already linked and wedlock-bound
906   To a fell[497] adversary,[498] his hate or shame.
907   Which infinite calamity shall cause
908   To human life, and household peace confound."[499]
909   He added not, and from her turned, but Eve,
910   Not so[500] repulsed, with tears that ceased not flowing
911   And tresses all disordered, at his feet
912   Fell humble and, embracing them, besought[501]
913   His peace,[502] and thus proceeded in her plaint:
914   "Forsake[503] me not thus, Adam! Witness Heav'n
915   What love sincere, and reverence in my heart

---

[488] like
[489] procreate
[490] been befallen = happened, occurred
[491] strait conjunction = narrow connection ("conjunction" carrying heavy sexual overtones)
[492] proper, suitable
[493] the woman
[494] obstinacy, contrariness, wickedness
[495] a far worse = a far worse man than himself
[496] him
[497] (1) fierce, cruel, (2) clever
[498] antagonist, enemy
[499] destroy
[500] thus, thereby
[501] begged earnestly for
[502] amity, end of hostilities
[503] renounce, abandon

916   I bear thee, and unweeting⁵⁰⁴ have offended,
917   Unhappily deceived! Thy suppliant
918   I beg, and clasp thy knees. Bereave⁵⁰⁵ me not
919   Whereon I live,⁵⁰⁶ thy gentle⁵⁰⁷ looks, thy aid,
920   Thy counsel, in this uttermost⁵⁰⁸ distress,
921   My only strength and stay.⁵⁰⁹ Forlorn⁵¹⁰ of thee,
922   Whither shall I betake⁵¹¹ me, where subsist?⁵¹²
923   While yet we live, scarce one short hour perhaps,
924   Between us two let there be peace, both joining,
925   As joined in injuries, one enmity
926   Against a foe by doom express⁵¹³ assigned us,
927   That cruel serpent. On me exercise not
928   Thy hatred for this misery befall'n,
929   On me already lost, me than thyself
930   More miserable! Both have sinned, but thou
931   Against God only, I against God and thee,
932   And to the place of judgement will return,
933   There with my cries importune Heav'n that all
934   The sentence, from thy head removed, may light⁵¹⁴
935   On me, sole cause to thee of all this woe—
936   Me, me only, just object of His ire!"
937   She ended weeping, and her lowly⁵¹⁵ plight,⁵¹⁶
938   Immoveable,⁵¹⁷ till peace obtained from fault
939   Acknowledged and deplored,⁵¹⁸ in Adam wrought⁵¹⁹
940   Commiseration.⁵²⁰ Soon his heart relented

---

⁵⁰⁴ unknowingly
⁵⁰⁵ deprive
⁵⁰⁶ whereon I live = of that upon which I live
⁵⁰⁷ mild, generous, courteous
⁵⁰⁸ extreme, greatest
⁵⁰⁹ support
⁵¹⁰ forsaken, abandoned
⁵¹¹ go, turn
⁵¹² exist, live
⁵¹³ definite, fixed, exact
⁵¹⁴ fall, descend
⁵¹⁵ abject, humble
⁵¹⁶ (1) condition, state, (2) pledge, undertaking
⁵¹⁷ (1) stationary, fixed, (2) unalterable, not subject to change
⁵¹⁸ lamented, deeply regretted
⁵¹⁹ worked
⁵²⁰ compassion, pity, sorrow

941   Towards her, his life so late,[521] and sole delight,
942   Now at his feet submissive in distress,
943   Creature so fair his reconcilement seeking,
944   His counsel, whom she had displeased, his aid.
945   As one disarmed, his anger all he lost,
946   And thus with peaceful words upraised her soon:[522]
947   "Unwary, and too desirous, as before,
948   So now of what thou know'st not, who desir'st
949   The punishment all on thyself! Alas!
950   Bear thine own first, ill able to sustain
951   His full wrath, whose thou feel'st as yet least part,
952   And my displeasure bear'st so ill. If prayers
953   Could alter high decrees, I to that place
954   Would speed before thee, and be louder heard,
955   That on my head all might be visited,
956   Thy frailty[523] and infirmer[524] sex forgiv'n,
957   To me committed[525] and by me exposed.[526]
958   But rise, let us no more contend,[527] nor blame
959   Each other, blamed enough elsewhere, but strive
960   In offices[528] of love, how we may lighten
961   Each other's burden in our share of woe,
962   Since this day's death denounced,[529] if aught I see,[530]
963   Will prove no sudden but a slow-paced evil,
964   A long day's dying, to augment our pain,
965   And to our seed (O hapless Seed!) derived."[531]
966   To whom thus Eve, recovering heart, replied:
967   "Adam, by sad experiment I know
968   How little weight my words with thee can find,
969   Found so erroneous, thence by just event[532]

---

[521] recently
[522] quickly
[523] moral weakness, instability of mind
[524] weaker
[525] entrusted
[526] imperiled, made subject/open to danger (since he allowed her to go to her labor alone that day)
[527] fight
[528] services, duties, attentions
[529] proclaimed
[530] apprehend, understand
[531] transmitted
[532] just event = equitable/impartial/rightful result/outcome

970 Found so unfortunate. Nevertheless,
971 Restored by thee, vile as I am, to place
972 Of new acceptance, hopeful to regain
973 Thy love, the sole contentment of my heart
974 Living or dying, from thee I will not hide
975 What thoughts in my unquiet breast are ris'n,
976 Tending to some relief of our extremes,
977 Or end, though sharp and sad, yet tolerable,
978 As in our evils, and of easier choice.
979 If care of our descent perplex us most,
980 Which must be born to certain woe, devoured
981 By Death at last (and miserable it is
982 To be to others cause of misery,
983 Our own begotten, and of our loins to bring
984 Into this cursèd world a woeful race,
985 That after wretched life must be at last
986 Food for so foul a monster), in thy power
987 It lies, yet ere conception, to prevent
988 The race unblest, to being yet unbegot.
989 Childless thou art: childless remain. So Death
990 Shall be deceived[533] his glut, and with us two
991 Be forced to satisfy his ravenous maw.
992 But if thou judge it hard and difficult,
993 Conversing, looking, loving, to abstain
994 From love's due[534] rites, nuptial embraces sweet,
995 And with desire to languish[535] without hope,
996 Before the present object[536] languishing
997 With like desire, which would be misery
998 And torment less than none of what we dread,
999 Then both ourselves and seed at once to free
1000 From what we fear for both, let us make short[537] —
1001 Let us seek Death, or he not found, supply
1002 With our own hands his office[538] on ourselves.
1003 Why stand we longer shivering under fears
1004 That show no end but death, and have the power

---

[533] defrauded, beguiled of
[534] (1) proper, (2) necessary, (3) owed
[535] to be depressed/sick/weak
[536] person, body: Eve herself
[537] short work (of it)
[538] function, service

1005 Of many ways to die the shortest choosing,
1006 Destruction with destruction to destroy?"
1007   She ended here, or vehement[539] despair
1008 Broke off the rest: so much of death her thoughts
1009 Had entertained[540] as dyed her cheeks with pale.
1010 But Adam, with such counsel nothing swayed,[541]
1011 To better hopes his more attentive[542] mind
1012 Laboring had raised, and thus to Eve replied:
1013   "Eve, thy contempt of life and pleasure seems
1014 To argue in thee something more sublime
1015 And excellent than what thy mind contemns.[543]
1016 But self-destruction therefore sought refutes
1017 That excellence thought in thee, and implies,
1018 Not thy contempt, but anguish and regret
1019 For loss of life and pleasure overloved.
1020 Or if thou covet death, as utmost end
1021 Of misery, so thinking to evade
1022 The penalty pronounced, doubt not but God
1023 Hath wiselier armed His vengeful ire, than so
1024 To be forestalled. Much more I fear lest death,
1025 So snatched, will not exempt us from the pain
1026 We are by doom[544] to pay. Rather, such acts
1027 Of contumacy[545] will provoke the Highest
1028 To make death in us live. Then let us seek
1029 Some safer resolution, which methinks
1030 I have in view, calling to mind with heed
1031 Part of our sentence, that thy seed shall bruise[546]
1032 The serpent's head. Piteous amends! unless
1033 Be meant, whom I conjecture, our grand foe,
1034 Satan, who in the serpent hath contrived
1035 Against us this deceit. To crush his head
1036 Would be revenge indeed! Which will be lost
1037 By death brought on ourselves, or childless days

---

[539] intense, passionate, excited
[540] maintained, experienced
[541] moved, ruled, diverted (turned)
[542] more attentive = steadier
[543] despises
[544] sentence, judgment
[545] willful disobedience, perversity
[546] smash, destroy, break

1038 Resolved,[547] as thou proposest. So[548] our foe
1039 Shall 'scape his punishment ordained, and we
1040 Instead shall double ours upon our heads.
1041 No more be mentioned then of violence
1042 Against ourselves, and wilful barrenness,
1043 That cuts us off from hope, and savors[549] only
1044 Rancor[550] and pride, impatience and despite,[551]
1045 Reluctance[552] against God and His just yoke
1046 Laid on our necks. Remember with what mild
1047 And gracious temper He both heard and judged,
1048 Without wrath or reviling. We expected
1049 Immediate dissolution,[553] which we thought
1050 Was meant by death that day, when lo, to thee
1051 Pains only in child-bearing were foretold,
1052 And bringing forth, soon recompensed with joy,
1053 Fruit of thy womb. On me the curse aslope[554]
1054 Glanced[555] on the ground: with labor I must earn
1055 My bread. What harm? Idleness had been worse.
1056 My labor will sustain me and, lest cold
1057 Or heat should injure us, His timely[556] care
1058 Hath, unbesought, provided, and His hands
1059 Clothed us unworthy, pitying while He judged.
1060 How much more, if we pray Him, will His ear
1061 Be open, and His heart to pity incline,
1062 And teach us further by what means to shun
1063 Th' inclement[557] seasons, rain, ice, hail, and snow,
1064 Which now the sky, with various[558] face, begins
1065 To show us in this mountain, while the winds
1066 Blow moist and keen, shattering the graceful locks
1067 Of these fair spreading trees—which bids us seek

---

[547] resolved/decided on
[548] thus
[549] (1) concerns [verb], (2) pleases [verb]
[550] bitterness, spitefulness
[551] spite
[552] resistance
[553] disintegration, decomposition
[554] slantwise
[555] struck and glided, passed quickly
[556] (1) well-timed, (2) early
[557] harsh, pitiless
[558] unstable, changeable

1068	Some better shroud,[559] some better warmth to cherish
1069	Our limbs benumbed, ere this diurnal[560] star[561]
1070	Leave cold the night, how we his gathered beams
1071	Reflected may with matter sere[562] foment[563]
1072	Or, by collision of two bodies, grind[564]
1073	The air attrite[565] to fire; as late[566] the clouds
1074	Jostling,[567] or pushed with winds, rude[568] in their shock,
1075	Tine[569] the slant lightning, whose thwart[570] flame, driv'n down,
1076	Kindles the gummy bark of fir or pine
1077	And sends a comfortable heat from far,
1078	Which might supply the sun. Such fire to use,
1079	And what may else be remedy or cure
1080	To evils which our own misdeeds have wrought,
1081	He will instruct us, praying,[571] and of grace
1082	Beseeching Him, so as we need not fear
1083	To pass commodiously[572] this life, sustained
1084	By Him with many comforts, till we end
1085	In dust, our final rest and native home.
1086	What better can we do than, to the place
1087	Repairing[573] where He judged us, prostrate fall
1088	Before Him reverent, and there confess
1089	Humbly our faults, and pardon beg, with tears
1090	Watering the ground, and with our sighs the air
1091	Frequenting,[574] sent from hearts contrite, in sign
1092	Of sorrow unfeigned and humiliation[575] meek?

---

[559] dwelling, cover
[560] of/belonging to the day
[561] the sun
[562] dry
[563] rouse, excite
[564] rub, harass
[565] by friction
[566] recently
[567] pushing, shoving, knocking against
[568] violent, harsh
[569] kindle
[570] transverse
[571] if we pray to Him
[572] conveniently
[573] going
[574] often, habitually
[575] [four syllables, first and third accented]

1093 Undoubtedly He will relent and turn
1094 From His displeasure, in whose look serene,
1095 When angry most He seemed, and most severe,
1096 What else but favor, grace, and mercy shone?"
1097   So spoke our father penitent, nor Eve
1098 Felt less remorse. They forthwith to the place
1099 Repairing where He judged them, prostrate fell
1100 Before Him reverent, and both confessed
1101 Humbly their faults, and pardon begged, with tears
1102 Watering the ground, and with their sighs the air
1103 Frequenting, sent from hearts contrite, in sign
1104 Of sorrow unfeigned, and humiliation meek.

The End of the Tenth Book

BOOK XI

THE ARGUMENT

THE SON OF GOD presents to his Father the prayers of our first parents, now repenting, and intercedes for them. God accepts them,[1] but declares they[2] must no longer abide in Paradise; sends Michael with a band of Cherubim to dispossess them, but first to reveal to Adam future things.

Michael's coming down.

Adam shews to Eve certain ominous signs; he discerns Michael's approach, goes out to meet him. The Angel denounces their departure.

Eve's lamentation. Adam pleads, but submits. The Angel leads him up to a high Hill, sets before him in vision what shall happen till the Flood.

---

[1] i.e., the prayers
[2] i.e., Adam and Eve

1   Thus they, in lowliest plight, repentant stood
2   Praying, for from the mercy-seat[3] above
3   Prevenient[4] grace descending had removed
4   The stony from their hearts, and made new flesh
5   Regenerate[5] grow instead, that sighs now breathed
6   Unutterable,[6] which the spirit of prayer
7   Inspired, and winged for Heav'n with speedier flight
8   Than loudest oratory. Yet their port[7]
9   Not of mean[8] suitors, nor important less
10   Seemed their petition than when the ancient pair
11   In fables old, less ancient yet than these,
12   Deucalion[9] and chaste Pyrrha,[10] to restore
13   The race of mankind drowned,[11] before the shrine
14   Of Themis[12] stood devout. To Heav'n their prayers
15   Flew up, nor missed the way, by envious winds
16   Blown vagabond[13] or frustrate. In they[14] passed
17   Dimensionless[15] through Heav'nly doors, then clad
18   With incense, where the golden altar fumed[16]
19   By[17] their great Intercessor,[18] came in sight
20   Before the Father's throne. Them the glad Son
21   Presenting, thus to intercede began:
22   "See, Father, what first-fruits on earth are sprung
23   From Thy implanted grace in man! These sighs
24   And prayers, which in this golden censer[19] mixed
25   With incense, I Thy priest, before Thee bring,

---

[3] golden covering placed over the Ark of the Covenant; regarded as God's resting place and thus the seat of mercy
[4] anticipatory
[5] reborn, reformed, restored
[6] [five syllables, second and fourth accented]
[7] demeanor
[8] inferior, poor
[9] Prometheus' son, and the "Noah" of classical myth
[10] Deucalion's wife
[11] [adjective]
[12] a Titan, daughter of Gaia (earth) by Zeus: goddess of justice
[13] straying, wandering
[14] the prayers
[15] having no material being/body
[16] smoked
[17] near
[18] Christ
[19] container in which incense is burned

26   Fruits of more pleasing savor (from Thy seed,
27   Sown with contrition in his heart) than those
28   Which, his own hand manuring,[20] all the trees
29   Of Paradise could have produced, ere fall'n
30   From innocence. Now therefore bend Thine ear
31   To supplication. Hear his sighs, though mute.
32   Unskilful with what words to pray, let me
33   Interpret for him—me, his advocate
34   And propitiation.[21] All his works on me,
35   Good, or not good, engraft.[22] My merit those[23]
36   Shall perfect, and for these[24] my death shall pay.
37   Accept me[25] and, in me, from these receive
38   The smell of peace toward mankind. Let him live
39   Before Thee reconciled, at least his days
40   Numbered, though sad, till death, his doom (which I
41   To mitigate thus plead, not to reverse),
42   To better life shall yield him, where with me
43   All my redeemed may dwell in joy and bliss,
44   Made one with me, as I with Thee am one."
45   To whom the Father, without cloud,[26] serene:
46   "All thy request for man, accepted, Son,
47   Obtain. All thy request was my decree.
48   But longer in that Paradise to dwell
49   The law I gave to Nature him[27] forbids.
50   Those pure immortal elements that know
51   No gross, no unharmonious mixture foul,
52   Eject him, tainted now, and purge him off[28]
53   As a distemper,[29] gross—to air as gross,
54   And mortal food—as may dispose him[30] best
55   For dissolution, wrought by sin, that first
56   Distempered all things, and of incorrupt

---

[20] tilling, cultivating
[21] atonement, expiation, sacrifice
[22] implant, transfer
[23] i.e., the good works of man
[24] i.e., the not good works of man
[25] accept me = receive me with favor
[26] darkening of His countenance
[27] Adam
[28] purge him off = purify him away
[29] disorder, derangement
[30] dispose him = make him fit

57   Corrupted. I, at first, with two fair gifts
58   Created him endowed: with happiness
59   And immortality. That[31] fondly[32] lost,
60   This other[33] served but to eternize[34] woe,
61   Till I provided death. So death becomes
62   His final remedy and, after life
63   Tried[35] in sharp tribulation,[36] and refined
64   By faith and faithful works, to second life,
65   Waked in the renovation[37] of the just,
66   Resigns[38] him up with Heav'n and earth renewed.
67   "But let us call to synod all the Blest
68   Through Heav'n's wide bounds. From them I will not hide
69   My judgments, how with mankind I proceed,
70   As how with peccant[39] Angels late[40] they saw,
71   And in their state,[41] though firm, stood more confirmed."
72   He ended, and the Son gave signal high
73   To the bright minister that watched. He blew
74   His trumpet, heard in Oreb[42] since perhaps
75   When God descended, and perhaps once more
76   To sound at general doom.[43] The Angelic blast
77   Filled all the regions. From their blissful bow'rs
78   Of amarantine[44] shade, fountain or spring,
79   By the waters of life, where'er they sat
80   In fellowships of joy, the sons of light
81   Hasted, resorting[45] to the summons high,
82   And took their seats, till from His throne supreme
83   Th' Almighty thus pronounced His sov'reign will:

---

[31] happiness
[32] foolishly
[33] immortality
[34] make eternal/everlasting
[35] tested
[36] misery, distress, vexation
[37] renewal of the body at the Resurrection
[38] restores (yields up), repays, rewards, produces
[39] sinning
[40] not long ago
[41] rank, position
[42] Horeb/Mt. Sinai
[43] general doom = Judgment Day
[44] mythical flower that never fades
[45] going, proceeding

84   "O Sons, like one of us man is become
85   To know both good and evil, since his taste
86   Of that defended[46] fruit. But let him boast
87   His knowledge of good lost, and evil got,
88   Happier, had it sufficed him to have known
89   Good by itself, and evil not at all.
90   He sorrows now, repents, and prays contrite,
91   My motions[47] in him. Longer[48] than they move,
92   His heart I know,[49] how variable and vain,
93   Self-left.[50] Lest therefore his now bolder hand
94   Reach also of the Tree of Life, and eat,
95   And live forever—dream at least to live
96   Forever—to remove him I decree,
97   And send him from the Garden forth to till
98   The ground whence he was taken: fitter soil.
99   "Michael, this my behest[51] have thou in charge.
100   Take to thee from among the Cherubim
101   Thy choice of flaming warriors, lest the fiend,
102   Or in[52] behalf of man, or to invade
103   Vacant possession,[53] some new trouble raise.
104   Haste thee, and from the Paradise of God
105   Without remorse[54] drive out the sinful pair,
106   From hallowed ground th' unholy, and denounce[55]
107   To them, and to their progeny, from thence
108   Perpetual banishiment. Yet, lest they faint[56]
109   At the sad[57] sentence rigorously urged[58]
110   (For I behold them softened, and with tears
111   Bewailing their excess), all terror hide.
112   If patiently thy bidding they obey,

---

[46] forbidden
[47] inward promptings, workings
[48] but for a longer period
[49] have known
[50] left to itself
[51] command
[52] or in = whether on
[53] i.e., the Garden of Eden, about to become vacant
[54] pity
[55] proclaim, announce
[56] lose heart/courage, droop
[57] mournful
[58] stated, pressed

113   Dismiss them not disconsolate.[59] Reveal
114   To Adam what shall come in future days,
115   As I shall thee enlighten; intermix[60]
116   My cov'nant in the Woman's seed renewed.
117   So send them forth, though sorrowing, yet in peace,
118   And on the east side of the garden place,
119   Where entrance up from Eden easiest climbs,
120   Cherubic watch, and of a sword the flame
121   Wide-waving, all approach far off to fright,
122   And guard all passage to the Tree of Life,
123   Lest Paradise a receptacle[61] prove
124   To Spirits foul, and all my trees their prey,
125   With those stolen fruit man once more to delude."
126   He ceased, and th' Arch-Angelic Power prepared
127   For swift descent, with him the cohort[62] bright
128   Of watchful Cherubim. Four faces each
129   Had, like a double Janus,[63] all their shape
130   Spangled with eyes more numerous than those
131   Of Argus,[64] and more wakeful than to drowse,
132   Charmed with Arcadian pipe, the pastoral reed
133   Of Hermes,[65] or his opiate rod.[66] Meanwhile,
134   To re-salute the world with sacred light,
135   Leucothea[67] waked, and with fresh dews embalmed[68]
136   The earth, when Adam and first matron Eve
137   Had ended now their orisons,[69] and found
138   Strength added from above, new hope to spring
139   Out of despair, joy, but with fear yet linked,
140   Which thus to Eve his[70] welcome words renewed:
141   "Eve, easily may faith admit that all
142   The good which we enjoy from Heav'n descends;

---

[59] miserable
[60] intermingle, blend in
[61] welcoming place [four syllables, first and third accented]
[62] band
[63] double-faced god of gates
[64] hundred-eyed spy for Jove/Jupiter/Zeus
[65] messenger of Jove
[66] opiate rod = sleep-inducing staff
[67] goddess of dawn [trisyllabic, second accented, "-thea" elided]
[68] anointed
[69] prayers
[70] Adam's

143 But that from us aught should ascend to Heav'n
144 So prevalent[71] as to concern the mind
145 Of God high-blest, or to incline His will,
146 Hard to belief may seem, yet this will[72] prayer
147 Or one short sigh of human breath, upborne
148 Ev'n to the seat of God. For since I sought
149 By prayer th' offended[73] Deity to appease,
150 Kneeled and before Him humbled all my heart,
151 Methought I saw him placable[74] and mild,
152 Bending his ear. Persuasion in me grew
153 That I was heard with favor, peace returned
154 Home to my breast, and to my memory
155 His promise, that thy seed shall bruise[75] our foe—
156 Which, then not minded[76] in dismay, yet now
157 Assures me that the bitterness of death
158 Is past, and we shall live. Whence hail to thee,
159 Eve rightly called, mother of all mankind,
160 Mother of all things living, since by thee
161 Man is to live, and all things live for man."
162 To whom thus Eve, with sad[77] demeanor meek:
163   "Ill-worthy I such title should belong,
164 To me transgressor, who for thee ordained
165 A help, became thy snare. To me reproach
166 Rather belongs, distrust, all dispraise.
167 But infinite in pardon was my Judge,
168 That I, who first brought death on all, am graced
169 The source of life, next favorable[78] thou,[79]
170 Who highly[80] thus to entitle[81] me vouchsaf'st,[82]
171 Far other name deserving. But the field

---

[71] efficaciously, powerfully
[72] will do
[73] sinned against
[74] gentle, forgiving
[75] smash, crush, destroy
[76] thought of, remembered
[77] (1) sad, (2) sober
[78] pleasing, gracious
[79] to thou
[80] so high, thus high.
[81] title
[82] granted, deigned, condescended

172 To labor calls us, now[83] with sweat imposed,
173 Though after sleepless night, for see! the morn,
174 All unconcerned with our unrest, begins
175 Her rosy progress smiling. Let us forth,
176 I never from thy side henceforth to stray,
177 Where'er our day's work lies, though now enjoined[84]
178 Laborious, till day droop. While here we dwell,
179 What can be toilsome[85] in these pleasant walks?
180 Here let us live, though in fall'n state, content."
181   So spoke, so wished much humbled Eve, but Fate
182 Subscribed[86] not. Nature first gave signs, impressed[87]
183 On bird, beast, air—air suddenly eclipsed, [88]
184 After short blush[89] of morn. Nigh in her sight
185 The bird of Jove,[90] stooped[91] from his airy tour,[92]
186 Two birds of gayest plume before him drove.
187 Down from a hill the beast that reigns in woods,[93]
188 First hunter then, pursued a gentle brace,[94]
189 Goodliest of all the forest, hart and hind.[95]
190 Direct to the eastern gate was bent their flight.
191 Adam observed, and with his eye the chase
192 Pursuing, not unmoved, to Eve thus spoke:
193   "O Eve, some further change awaits us nigh,
194 Which Heav'n, by these mute signs in Nature, shows
195 Forerunners of His purpose, or to warn
196 Us, haply[96] too secure[97] of[98] our discharge[99]

---

[83] "now the labor is . . ."
[84] imposed
[85] tired, laborious
[86] assented, agreed
[87] produce on, communicated through
[88] darkened, obscured
[89] rosy gleam
[90] the eagle
[91] swiftly descended
[92] circuit
[93] the lion
[94] pair
[95] hart and hind = stag and doe (male and female deer)
[96] perhaps
[97] confident
[98] because of
[99] liberation

197	From penalty, because from death released
198	Some days. How long, and what till then our life,
199	Who knows? Or more than this, that we are dust,
200	And thither must return, and be no more?
201	Why else this double object in our sight
202	Of flight pursued in th' air, and o'er the ground,
203	One way the self-same hour? Why in the east
204	Darkness ere day's mid-course, and morning-light
205	More orient[100] in yon western cloud, that draws
206	O'er the blue firmament a radiant white,
207	And slow descends with something Heavenly fraught?"[101]
208	He erred not, for by this[102] the Heav'nly bands
209	Down from a sky of jasper[103] lighted now
210	In Paradise, and on a hill made halt—
211	A glorious apparition,[104] had not doubt
212	And carnal[105] fear that day dimmed Adam's eye.
213	Not that more glorious[106] when the Angels met
214	Jacob in Mahanaim,[107] where he saw
215	The field pavilioned[108] with His[109] guardians bright,
216	Nor that, which on the flaming mount appeared
217	In Dothan,[110] covered with a camp of fire,
218	Against the Syrian king, who to surprise
219	One man,[111] assassin-like,[112] had levied[113] war,
220	War unproclaimed. The princely Hierarch[114]
221	In their bright stand[115] there left his Powers, to seize
222	Possession of the Garden. He alone,

---

[100] more bright = brighter
[101] filled
[102] this time
[103] jasper is a highly variegated colored form of quartz
[104] manifestation, appearance
[105] bodily
[106] "that 'apparition' was not more glorious when . . ."
[107] "tents of angels"
[108] pavilioned = covered with the tents of
[109] "And Jacob went on his way, and the angels of God met him. And when Jacob saw them, he said, This is God's host"—Genesis 32:1-2
[110] see 2 Kings 6
[111] the prophet Elisha
[112] treacherously
[113] made, commenced
[114] Michael
[115] the formation in which the Cherubim had halted

223   To find where Adam sheltered, took his way,

224   Not unperceived of Adam, who to Eve,

225   While the great visitant approached, thus spoke:

226   "Eve, now expect great tidings, which perhaps

227   Of us will soon determine,[116] or impose

228   New laws to be observed, for I descry,

229   From yonder blazing cloud that veils the hill,

230   One of the Heav'nly host and, by his gait,

231   None of the meanest,[117] some great Potentate

232   Or of the Thrones above, such majesty

233   Invests[118] him coming, yet not terrible

234   (That I should fear) nor sociably[119] mild

235   As Raphael (that I should much confide)[120]

236   But solemn and sublime,[121] whom not t' offend

237   With reverence I must meet, and thou retire."

238   He ended, and the Arch-Angel soon drew nigh,

239   Not in his shape celestial, but as man

240   Clad to meet man. Over his lucid[122] arms[123]

241   A military vest[124] of purple flowed,

242   Livelier[125] than Meliboean[126] or the grain[127]

243   Of Sarra,[128] worn by kings and heroes old

244   In time of truce. Iris[129] had dipped the woof.[130]

245   His starry helm,[131] unbuckled, showed him prime

246   In manhood where youth ended; by his side,

247   As in a glistering zodiac,[132] hung the sword,

---

[116] decide, resolve, end

[117] lowest rank

[118] clothes

[119] [four syllables, first and third accented]

[120] trust, have confidence in

[121] lofty, exalted

[122] luminous, bright

[123] armor

[124] loose robe

[125] more brilliant/vivid

[126] Thessalian town famous for its bright purple dye

[127] dyed cloth

[128] Tyre, Phoenician seaport, now in Lebanon

[129] goddess of the rainbow

[130] thread

[131] helmet

[132] belt of stars

248   Satan's dire dread,[133] and in his hand the spear.
249   Adam bowed low; he,[134] kingly, from his state[135]
250   Inclined not, but his coming thus declared:
251   "Adam, Heav'n's high behest[136] no preface needs.
252   Sufficient that thy prayers are heard, and Death,
253   Then due by sentence when thou didst transgress,
254   Defeated of his seizure many days
255   Giv'n thee of grace, wherein thou may'st repent,
256   And one bad act with many deeds well done
257   May'st cover.[137] Well may then thy Lord, appeased,
258   Redeem thee quite[138] from Death's rapacious[139] claim.
259   But longer in this Paradise to dwell
260   Permits not: to remove thee I am come,
261   And send thee from the garden forth to till[140]
262   The ground whence thou wast taken, fitter soil."
263   He added not, for Adam at the news
264   Heart-struck with chilling grip of sorrow stood,
265   That all his senses bound.[141] Eve, who unseen
266   Yet all had heard, with audible lament
267   Discovered[142] soon[143] the place of her retire:[144]
268   "O unexpected stroke, worse than of Death!
269   Must I thus leave thee, Paradise? Thus leave
270   Thee, native soil, these happy walks and shades,
271   Fit haunt of Gods? Where I had hope to spend,
272   Quiet though sad, the respite[145] of that day
273   That must be mortal[146] to us both. O flow'rs
274   That never will in other climate grow,
275   My early visitation,[147] and my last

---

[133] see Book 6, lines 320–27, above
[134] i.e., the archangel Michael
[135] high rank, dignity
[136] command
[137] compensate for
[138] completely
[139] greedy, grasping
[140] cultivate
[141] held fast, tied up
[142] disclosed, revealed
[143] quickly
[144] withdrawal
[145] delay, temporary extension of time
[146] fatal
[147] stop, visit

276   At ev'n, which I bred up with tender[148] hand
277   From the first op'ning bud, and gave ye names,
278   Who now shall rear ye to the sun? or rank[149]
279   Your tribes, and water[150] from th' ambrosial fount?
280   Thee lastly, nuptial bow'r, by me adorned
281   With what to sight or smell was sweet: from thee
282   How shall I part? and whither wander down
283   Into a lower world, to[151] this obscure[152]
284   And wild? How shall we breathe in other air
285   Less pure, accustomed[153] to immortal fruits?"
286   Whom thus the Angel interrupted mild:
287   "Lament not, Eve, but patiently resign
288   What justly thou hast lost, nor set thy heart,
289   Thus over-fond,[154] on that which is not thine.
290   Thy going is not lonely; with thee goes
291   Thy husband, whom to follow thou art bound.
292   Where he abides, think there thy native soil."
293   Adam, by this from the cold sudden damp[155]
294   Recovering, and his scattered spirits returned,
295   To Michael thus his humble words addressed:
296   "Celestial, whether among the Thrones, or
                 named
297   Of them the highest, for such of shape may seem
298   Prince above Princes, gently hast thou told
299   Thy message, which might else in telling wound,
300   And in performing[156] end us. What besides
301   Of sorrow, and dejection, and despair,
302   Our frailty can sustain, thy tidings bring,
303   Departure from this happy place, our sweet
304   Recess,[157] and only consolation left
305   Familiar to our eyes. All places else
306   Inhospitable appear, and desolate,

---

[148] gentle
[149] arrange
[150] water you
[151] compared to
[152] dark
[153] accustomed as we are
[154] over-fond = over-affectionate
[155] daze, stupor, depression
[156] carrying out, executing
[157] secluded place

307   Nor knowing us, nor known. And if by prayer
308   Incessant I could hope to change the will
309   Of Him who all things can, I would not cease
310   To weary Him with my assiduous[158] cries.
311   But prayer against His absolute decree
312   No more avails than breath against the wind,
313   Blown stifling[159] back on him that breathes it forth.
314   Therefore to His great bidding I submit.
315   "This most afflicts me that, departing hence,
316   As from His face I shall be hid, deprived
317   His blessèd count'nance. Here I could frequent[160]
318   With worship place by place where He vouchsafed
319   Presence Divine, and to my sons relate
320   On this mount He appeared, under this tree
321   Stood visible, among these pines His voice
322   I heard, here with Him at this fountain talked.
323   So many grateful[161] altars I would rear
324   Of grassy turf, and pile up every stone
325   Of luster from the brook, in memory,
326   Or monument to ages, and theron
327   Offer sweet-smelling gums, and fruits, and flow'rs.
328   In yonder nether[162] world where shall I seek
329   His bright appearances, or foot-step trace?
330   For though I fled Him angry, yet recalled
331   To life, prolonged and promised race,[163] I now
332   Gladly behold though but His utmost[164] skirts[165]
333   Of glory, and far off His steps adore."
334   To whom thus Michael, with regard benign:
335   "Adam, thou know'st Heav'n His, and all the
                                                earth,
336   Not this rock only. His omnipresence fills
337   Land, sea, and air, and every kind[166] that lives,

---

[158] persistent
[159] smothering
[160] visit often [verb, second syllable accented]
[161] (1) pleasing, (2) feeling gratitude
[162] lower
[163] offspring, descendants
[164] outermost
[165] (1) bottom part of God's robe, (2) outlying boundaries of His kingdom
[166] species

338   Fomented[167] by His virtual[168] power and warmed.
339   All th' earth He gave thee to possess and rule:
340   No despicable[169] gift. Surmise not then
341   His presence to these narrow bounds confined
342   Of Paradise, or Eden. This had been
343   Perhaps thy capital seat, from whence had spread
344   All generations, and had hither come
345   From all the ends of th' earth, to celebrate
346   And reverence thee, their great progenitor.
347   But this pre-eminence thou hast lost, brought down
348   To dwell on even[170] ground now with thy sons.
349   Yet doubt not but in valley, and in plain,
350   God is as here, and will be found alike
351   Present, and of His presence many a sign
352   Still following thee, still compassing thee round
353   With goodness and paternal love, His face
354   Express,[171] and of His steps the track divine.
355   Which that thou may'st believe, and be confirmed
356   Ere thou from hence depart, know I am sent
357   To show thee what shall come in future days
358   To thee, and to thy offspring. Good with bad
359   Expect to hear, supernal[172] grace contending[173]
360   With sinfulness of men, thereby to learn
361   True patience, and to temper[174] joy with fear
362   And pious sorrow, equally inured
363   By moderation either state to bear,
364   Prosperous or adverse. So shalt thou lead
365   Safest thy life, and best prepared endure
366   Thy mortal[175] passage when it comes.

                                   "Ascend

367   This hill. Let Eve (for I have drenched[176] her eyes)

---

[167] bathed with warm lotions, cherished/roused/stirred up
[168] nourishing
[169] [four syllables, first and third accented]
[170] flat, level
[171] exact, unmistakable
[172] lofty, exalted
[173] disputing, struggling, fighting
[174] alloy
[175] fatal
[176] steeped (drugged)

368   Here sleep below, while thou to foresight[177] wak'st,
369   As once thou slept'st, while she to life was formed."
370   To whom thus Adam gratefully replied:
371   "Ascend, I follow thee, safe guide, the path
372   Thou lead'st me, and to th' hand of Heav'n submit,
373   However chast'ning. To the evil turn[178]
374   My obvious[179] breast, arming to overcome
375   By suffering, and earn rest from labor won,
376   If so I may attain."
                                    So both ascend
377   In the visions of God.[180] It was a hill,
378   Of Paradise the highest, from whose top
379   The hemisphere of earth, in clearest ken,[181]
380   Stretched out[182] to amplest reach of prospect[183] lay.
381   Not higher that hill, nor wider looking round,
382   Whereon, for different cause, the Tempter set
383   Our second Adam,[184] in the wilderness,
384   To show him all earth's kingdoms, and their glory.
385   His[185] eye might there command wherever stood
386   City of old or modern fame, the seat
387   Of mightiest empire, from the destined walls
388   Of Cambalu,[186] seat of Cathaian Can,[187]
389   And Samarchand[188] by Oxus,[189] Temir's throne,
390   To Paquin[190] of Sinaean[191] kings, and thence
391   To Agra[192] and Lahor[193] of great Mogul,

---

[177] sight of the future
[178] [verb]
[179] open, visible
[180] ". . . the hand of the Lord was upon me, and brought me thither. In the visions of God brought He me into the land of Israel, and set me upon a very high mountain . . ."—Ezekiel 40:1–2
[181] range of vision
[182] [the full verb is "lay stretched out"]
[183] view
[184] Christ
[185] Adam's
[186] Peiping (Beijing), capital of Cathay/China
[187] khan, emperor
[188] capital of Temir/Tamerlane's Tatar empire
[189] Asian river, flowing from Turkey/Afghanistan to the Aral Sea in Siberia
[190] Peiping (Beijing)
[191] Chinese
[192] a Mogul capital in southern India
[193] a Mogul capital in northern India

392   Down to the golden Chersonese,[194] or where
393   The Persian in Ecbatan[195] sat, or since
394   In Hispahan,[196] or where the Russian Tsar
395   In Moscow, or the Sultan in Bizance,[197]
396   Turkestan-born,[198] nor could his eye not ken[199]
397   The empire of Negus[200] to his utmost port
398   Ercoco,[201] and the less maritime kings
399   Mombaza,[202] and Quiloa,[203] and Melind,[204]
400   And Sofala,[205] thought[206] Ophir,[207] to the realm
401   Of Congo, and Angola farthest south,
402   Or thence, from Niger flood[208] to Atlas[209] mount,
403   The kingdoms of Almansor,[210] Fez and Sus,[211]
404   Morocco, and Algiers, and Tremisen,[212]
405   On Europe thence, and where Rome was to sway
406   The world. In spirit perhaps he also saw
407   Rich Mexico, the seat of Montezume,[213]
408   And Cusco[214] in Peru, the richer seat
409   Of Atabalipa,[215] and yet unspoiled
410   Guiana, whose great city Geryon's[216] sons
411   Call El Dorado. But to nobler sights
412   Michael from Adam's eyes the film removed,

---

[194] Malacca
[195] Hamadan, ancient summer capital of Persian kings
[196] Isfahan, city in what is now Malaysia
[197] Byzantium/Istanbul
[198] Turkestan is a country in central Asia
[199] see
[200] name of Abyssinian king
[201] now Archico, port city on the Red Sea
[202] Mombasa, in modern Kenya
[203] Kilwa, in modern Tanzania
[204] Malindi, in modern Kenya
[205] port city in what is now Mozambique
[206] thought to be
[207] biblical land from which King Solomon obtained gold for the building of the Temple
[208] river
[209] in modern Mauritania
[210] d. 1002, Muslim ruler in Spain and northern Africa
[211] Fez and Sus are both in Morocco
[212] modern Tlemcen, in Algeria
[213] Montezuma, Aztec emperor of Mexico
[214] capital of the Inca empire; now Cuzco, in modern Peru
[215] Atahuallpa, Inca ruler [five syllables, first, third, and fifth accented]
[216] the Spanish: Geryon = monster, native to Cadiz, in Spain, who was killed by Hercules

413 Which that false fruit that promised clearer sight
414 Had bred, then purged with euphrasy[217] and rue[218]
415 The visual nerve, for he had much to see,
416 And from the well of life three drops instilled.
417 So deep the power of these ingredients pierced,
418 Ev'n to the inmost seat of mental sight,
419 That Adam, now enforced[219] to close his eyes,
420 Sunk down, and all his spirits became entranced.
421 But him the gentle Angel by the hand
422 Soon raised, and his attention thus recalled:
423   "Adam, now ope thine eyes, and first behold
424 Th' effects, which thy original crime hath wrought
425 In some to spring from thee, who never touched
426 Th' excepted[220] tree, nor with the snake conspired,
427 Nor sinned thy sin, yet from that sin derive[221]
428 Corruption to bring forth more violent deeds."
429   His eyes he opened, and beheld a field,
430 Part arable[222] and tilth,[223] whereon were sheaves
431 New reaped, the other part sheep-walks and folds.
432 In th' midst an altar as the landmark stood,
433 Rustic, of grassy sord.[224] Thither[225] anon[226]
434 A sweaty reaper[227] from his tillage brought
435 First fruits, the green ear, and the yellow sheaf,
436 Unculled,[228] as[229] came to hand. A shepherd next,
437 More meek,[230] came with the firstlings of his flock,
438 Choicest and best, then sacrificing, laid
439 The inwards[231] and their fat, with incense strewn,
440 On the cleft wood, and all due rites performed.

---

[217] herb used for treatment of eye diseases
[218] medicinal herb
[219] obliged, forced
[220] forbidden
[221] obtain by descent
[222] ploughland
[223] under cultivation
[224] sward, turf
[225] to the altar
[226] at once
[227] Cain
[228] unselected, a random choice
[229] such as first "came to hand"
[230] courteous
[231] internal organs, entrails

441 His offering soon propitious[232] fire from Heav'n
442 Consumed with nimble[233] glance[234] and grateful steam;
443 The other's[235] not, for his was not sincere,
444 Whereat he inly raged and, as they talked,
445 Smote him[236] into the midriff with a stone
446 That beat out life. He fell, and deadly pale
447 Groaned out his soul with gushing blood effused.[237]
448 Much at that sight was Adam in his heart
449 Dismayed, and thus in haste to th' Angel cried:
450   "O Teacher, some great mischief[238] hath befall'n
451 To that meek man, who well had sacrificed.
452 Is piety thus and pure devotion paid?"
453 T' whom Michael thus, he also moved, replied:
454   "These two are brethren, Adam, and to come
455 Out of thy loins. Th' unjust the just hath slain,
456 For envy that his brother's offering found
457 From Heav'n acceptance. But the bloody fact[239]
458 Will be avenged, and th' other's faith, approved,[240]
459 Lose no reward, though here thou see him die,
460 Rolling in dust and gore."[241]
                                   To which our sire:
461   "Alas! both for the deed, and for the cause!
462 But have I now seen Death? Is this the way
463 I must return to native[242] dust? O sight
464 Of terror, foul and ugly to behold,
465 Horrid to think, how horrible to feel!"
466 To whom thus Michael:[243]
                                   "Death thou hast seen
467 In his first shape on man, but many shapes[244]

---

[232] favorable, gracious
[233] quick, sudden
[234] flash/movement
[235] other's (Cain's) = other's offering
[236] Abel
[237] poured out freely
[238] harm, evil, misfortune
[239] (1) action, deed, (2) crime
[240] attested, confirmed
[241] thickened blood
[242] (1) natural, (2) of his birthplace
[243] [here, though usually bisyllabic, trisyllabic, first and third accented]
[244] "but there are many shapes"

468   Of Death, and many are the ways that lead
469   To his grim cave, all dismal, yet to sense
470   More terrible at th' entrance, than within.
471   Some, as thou saw'st, by violent stroke shall die,
472   By fire, flood, famine, by intemperance more
473   In meats and drinks, which on the earth shall bring
474   Diseases dire, of which a monstrous crew
475   Before thee shall appear, that thou may'st know
476   What misery th' inabstinence[245] of Eve
477   Shall bring on men."
                                        Immediately a place
478   Before his eyes appeared, sad, noisome,[246] dark,
479   A lazar[247]-house it seemed, wherein were laid
480   Numbers of all diseased, all maladies
481   Of ghastly spasm, or racking[248] torture, qualms[249]
482   Of heart-sick agony, all feverous kinds,
483   Convulsions, epilepsies, fierce catarrhs,[250]
484   Intestine stone and ulcer, colic[251] pangs,
485   Daemoniac frenzy, moping melancholy,
486   And moon-struck[252] madness, pining[253] atrophy,[254]
487   Marasmus,[255] and wide-wasting pestilence,[256]
488   Dropsies,[257] and asthmas, and joint-racking rheums.
489   Dire was the tossing, deep the groans. Despair
490   Tended the sick, busiest from couch to couch,
491   And over them triumphant Death his dart
492   Shook, but delayed to strike, though oft invoked
493   With vows, as their chief good and final hope.
494   Sight so deform[258] what heart of rock could long
495   Dry-eyed behold? Adam could not, but wept,

---

[245] failure to abstain
[246] noxious, ill-smelling, offensive
[247] leper
[248] violent stretching/straining
[249] fits
[250] nasal discharge
[251] belly
[252] deranged, lunatic
[253] languishing, wasting
[254] wasting, emaciation
[255] a wasting disease
[256] bubonic plague
[257] swelling up of body parts
[258] hideous

496   Though not of woman born. Compassion quelled[259]
497   His best of man, and gave him up to tears
498   A space, till firmer thoughts restrained excess
499   And, scarce recovering words, his plaint renewed:
500   "O miserable mankind, to what fall
501   Degraded, to what wretched state reserved!
502   Better end here unborn. Why is life giv'n
503   To be thus wrested[260] from us? Rather, why
504   Obtruded[261] on us thus? Who, if we knew
505   What we receive, would either not accept
506   Life offered, or soon beg to lay it down,
507   Glad to be so dismissed in peace. Can thus
508   The image of God in man, created once
509   So goodly[262] and erect, though faulty since,
510   To such unsightly sufferings be debased
511   Under inhuman pains? Why should not man,
512   Retaining still divine similitude[263]
513   In part, from such deformities be free
514   And, for his Maker's image sake, exempt?"
515   "Their Maker's image," answered Michael, "then
516   Forsook them, when themselves they vilified[264]
517   To serve ungoverned appetite, and took
518   His image whom they served, a brutish[265] vice,
519   Inductive[266] mainly to the sin of Eve.
520   Therefore so abject is their punishment,
521   Disfiguring not God's likeness, but their own,
522   Or if His likeness, by themselves defaced,
523   While they pervert pure Nature's healthful rules
524   To loathsome sickness—worthily, since they
525   God's image did not reverence in themselves."
526   "I yield it just," said Adam, "and submit.
527   But is there yet no other way, besides

---

[259] overcame
[260] dragged, wrenched
[261] thrust
[262] beautiful, graceful
[263] likeness
[264] degraded
[265] animal-like
[266] due

528   These painful passages,[267] how we may come
529   To Death, and mix with our connatural[268] dust?"
530   "There is," said Michael, "if thou well observe
531   The rule of not too much, by temperance taught,
532   In what thou eat'st and drink'st, seeking from thence
533   Due nourishment, not gluttonous delight,
534   Till many years over thy head return.[269]
535   So may'st thou live till, like ripe fruit, thou drop
536   Into thy mother's lap, or be with ease
537   Gathered, nor harshly plucked, for Death mature:
538   This is old age. But then thou must outlive
539   Thy youth, thy strength, thy beauty, which will change
540   To withered, weak, and gray. Thy senses, then
541   Obtuse,[270] all taste of pleasure must forego,[271]
542   To what thou hast[272] and, for the air of youth,
543   Hopeful and cheerful, in thy blood will reign
544   A melancholy damp[273] of cold and dry
545   To weigh thy spirits down, and last[274] consume
546   The balm of life." To whom our ancestor:
547   "Henceforth I fly not Death, nor would prolong
548   Life much, bent[275] rather how I may be quit,[276]
549   Fairest and easiest, of this cumbrous[277] charge,[278]
550   Which I must keep till my appointed day
551   Of rend'ring up,[279] and patiently attend[280]
552   My dissolution." Michael[281] replied:
553   "Nor[282] love thy life, nor hate, but what thou
                                   liv'st

---

[267] transitions, journeys
[268] natural, congenital
[269] come, go
[270] blunted
[271] go/leave first
[272] now has (in old age)
[273] depression, stupor
[274] finally
[275] concerned, intending
[276] released, freed
[277] oppressive
[278] duty, responsibility
[279] rendering up = giving back
[280] wait for
[281] [trisyllabic]
[282] neither

554   Live well. How long, or short, permit[283] to Heav'n.
555   And now prepare thee for another sight."
556   He looked, and saw a spacious plain whereon
557   Were tents of various hue. By some,[284] were herds
558   Of cattle grazing; others, whence the sound
559   Of instruments, that made melodious chime,[285]
560   Was heard, of harp and organ, and who[286] moved
561   Their stops and chords was seen, his volant[287] touch,
562   Instinct[288] through all proportions, low and high,
563   Fled and pursued transverse the resonant fugue.
564   In other part stood one who, at the forge
565   Laboring, two massy clods of iron and brass
566   Had melted (whether found where casual[289] fire
567   Had wasted woods on mountain or in vale,
568   Down to the veins of earth, thence gliding hot
569   To some cave's mouth, or whether washed by stream
570   From underground). The liquid ore he drained
571   Into fit moulds prepared, from which he formed
572   First his own tools, then what might else be wrought,[290]
573   Fusil[291] or graven[292] in metal. After these,
574   But on the hither[293] side, a different sort
575   From the high neighboring hills, which was their seat,
576   Down to the plain descended. By their guise[294]
577   Just[295] men they seemed, and all their study bent
578   To worship God aright, and know His works
579   Not hid, nor those things last[296] which might preserve
580   Freedom and peace to men. They on the plain
581   Long had not walked when, from the tents, behold!

─────────────────────────

[283] submit, allow
[284] "near some of the tents"
[285] harmony, accord
[286] he who
[287] rapid, flying
[288] imbued
[289] accidental
[290] worked
[291] fused, cast
[292] carved
[293] other
[294] appearance
[295] upright, righteous
[296] final

582   A bevy[297] of fair women, richly gay
583   In gems and wanton[298] dress! To th' harp they sung
584   Soft amorous ditties,[299] and in dance came on.[300]
585   The men, though grave,[301] eyed them, and let their eyes
586   Rove without rein till, in the amorous net
587   Fast caught, they liked, and each his liking chose,
588   And now of love they treat,[302] till the ev'ning-star,[303]
589   Love's harbinger,[304] appeared. Then all in heat
590   They light the nuptial torch, and bid[305] invoke[306]
591   Hymen,[307] then first[308] to marriage rites invoked:
592   With feast and music all the tents resound.
593   Such happy[309] interview[310] and fair event[311]
594   Of love and youth not lost, songs, garlands, flow'rs,
595   And charming symphonies,[312] attached[313] the heart
596   Of Adam, soon inclined t' admit[314] delight,
597   The bent[315] of Nature, which he thus expressed:
598   "True opener of mine eyes, prime Angel blest,
599   Much better seems this vision, and more hope
600   Of peaceful days portends,[316] than those two past.
601   Those were of hate and Death, or pain much worse.
602   Here Nature seems fulfilled in all her ends."[317]
603   To whom thus Michael:
                              "Judge not what is best

---

[297] company
[298] frivolous, lewd, unchaste
[299] songs
[300] came on = advanced, came forward
[301] serious, weighty, somber
[302] negotiate, deal
[303] Venus
[304] forerunner
[305] offered to
[306] summon
[307] god of marriage
[308] before anything else?
[309] fortunate
[310] meeting
[311] outcome
[312] pieces of music
[313] seized sympathetically
[314] confess, acknowledge
[315] propensity
[316] foreshadows
[317] goals, purposes

604 By pleasure, though to Nature seeming meet,[318]
605 Created, as thou art, to nobler end
606 Holy and pure, conformity[319] divine.
607 Those tents thou saw'st so pleasant were the tents
608 Of wickedness, wherein shall dwell his race
609 Who slew his brother. Studious they appear
610 Of arts that polish[320] life, inventors rare,[321]
611 Unmindful of their Maker, though His Spirit
612 Taught them, but they His gifts acknowledged none.
613 Yet they a beauteous offspring shall beget,
614 For that fair female troop thou saw'st, that seemed
615 Of goddesses, so blithe,[322] so smooth, so gay,
616 Yet empty of all good wherein consists
617 Woman's domestic honor and chief praise,
618 Bred only and completed[323] to the taste
619 Of lustful appetence, to sing, to dance,
620 To dress, and troll[324] the tongue, and roll the eye.
621 To these that sober race of men, whose lives
622 Religious titled them the sons of God,
623 Shall yield up all their virtue, all their fame
624 Ignobly, to the trains[325] and to the smiles
625 Of these fair atheists, and now swim in joy
626 (Erelong to swim at large),[326] and laugh, for which
627 The world erelong a world of tears must weep."
628 To whom thus Adam, of short joy bereft:[327]
629   "O pity and shame, that they who to live well
630 Entered[328] so fair, should turn aside to tread
631 Paths indirect,[329] or in the mid way faint![330]

---

[318] proper, fitting
[319] compliance
[320] smoothen
[321] unusual, uncommon
[322] merry
[323] perfected
[324] wag
[325] snares, tricks
[326] at large = fully, when God sends down the Flood
[327] robbed, deprived
[328] began
[329] crooked, devious
[330] spiritless, oppressive

632   But still I see the tenor[331] of man's woe
633   Holds on the same, from woman[332] to begin."
634   "From man's effeminate slackness it begins,"
635   Said th' Angel, "who should better hold his place
636   By wisdom, and superior gifts received.
637   But now prepare thee for another scene."
638   He looked, and saw wide territory spread
639   Before him, towns, and rural[333] works between,
640   Cities of men with lofty gates and tow'rs,
641   Concourse[334] in arms, fierce faces threat'ning war,
642   Giants of mighty bone and bold emprise.[335]
643   Part wield their arms, part curb the foaming steed,
644   Single or in array of battle ranged
645   Both horse and foot, nor idly must'ring[336] stood.
646   One way a band select[337] from forage drives
647   A herd of beeves,[338] fair oxen and fair kine,[339]
648   From a fat meadow ground, or fleecy flock,
649   Ewes and their bleating lambs over the plain,
650   Their booty. Scarce with life[340] the shepherds fly,
651   But call in aid, which makes a bloody fray;
652   With cruel[341] tournament[342] the squadrons join.
653   Where cattle pastured late,[343] now scattered lies
654   With carcasses and arms th' ensanguined[344] field,
655   Deserted. Others to a city strong
656   Lay siege, encamped, by battery,[345] scale,[346] and mine,[347]

---

[331] course
[332] man's woe = wo-man
[333] country, rustic
[334] assembled
[335] prowess, fame
[336] assembling
[337] choice [adjective]
[338] oxen
[339] cattle
[340] with life = alive
[341] [bisyllabic]
[342] fighting
[343] recently
[344] bloody
[345] battering rams
[346] ladders
[347] underground passages filled with gunpowder, which is then set off

657   Assaulting; others from the wall defend
658   With dart[348] and javelin,[349] stones, and sulphurous fire;
659   On each hand slaughter, and gigantic deeds.
660   In other part the sceptered heralds call
661   To council, in the city-gates. Anon[350]
662   Gray-headed men and grave, with warriors mixed,
663   Assemble, and harangues[351] are heard, but soon
664   In factious[352] opposition, till at last
665   Of middle age one[353] rising, eminent
666   In wise deport,[354] spoke much of right and wrong,
667   Of justice, or religion, truth, and peace,
668   And judgment from above. Him old and young
669   Exploded,[355] and had seized with violent hands,
670   Had not a cloud descending snatched him thence
671   Unseen amid the throng. So violence
672   Proceeded, and oppression, and sword-law,
673   Through all the plain, and refuge none was found.
674   Adam was all in tears, and to his guide
675   Lamenting turned full sad:
                        "O what are these,
676   Death's ministers, not men, who thus deal death
677   Inhumanly to men, and multiply
678   Ten thousandfold the sin of him who slew
679   His brother, for of whom such massacre
680   Make they, but of their brethren, men of men?
681   But who was that just man, whom had not Heav'n
682   Rescued, had in his righteousness been lost?"[356]
683   To whom thus Michael:[357]
                        "These are the product
684   Of those ill-mated marriages thou saw'st,
685   Where good with bad were matched, who of themselves

---

[348] spear
[349] [bisyllabic]
[350] at once
[351] speeches
[352] i.e., split into parties
[353] Enoch: see Genesis 5:21–24
[354] behavior, deportment
[355] hooted at
[356] perished, been destroyed
[357] [trisyllabic]

686   Abhor[358] to join[359] and, by imprudence mixed,[360]
687   Produce prodigious births of body or mind.
688   Such were these giants, men of high renown,
689   For in those days might[361] only shall be admired,
690   And valor and heroic virtue called.[362]
691   To overcome in battle, and subdue
692   Nations, and bring home spoils with infinite
693   Man-slaughter, shall be held the highest pitch
694   Of human glory, and for glory done
695   Of triumph, to be styled great conquerors,
696   Patrons of mankind, gods, and sons of gods—
697   Destroyers rightlier called, and plagues of men.
698   Thus fame shall be achieved, renown on earth,
699   And what most merits fame, in silence hid.
700   But he[363] the seventh from thee, whom thou beheld'st
701   The only righteous in a world perverse,
702   And therefore hated,[364] therefore so beset[365]
703   With foes, for daring single[366] to be just
704   And utter odious truth: that God would come
705   To judge them with His Saints. Him the Most High,
706   Rapt[367] in a balmy[368] cloud with wingèd steeds
707   Did, as thou saw'st, receive[369] to walk with God,
708   High in salvation[370] and the climes of bliss,
709   Exempt from death. To show thee what reward
710   Awaits the good, the rest what punishment,
711   Which now direct thine eyes and soon behold."
712   He looked, and saw the face of things quite
                                    changed.
713   The brazen throat of war had ceased to roar,

---

[358] shrink
[359] join in marriage
[360] muddled
[361] strength, power
[362] proclaimed
[363] Enoch
[364] therefore hated = who was therefore hated
[365] assailed, invested, surrounded
[366] alone
[367] enveloped
[368] fragrant
[369] was given
[370] eternal bliss

714 All now was turned to jollity and game,
715 To luxury and riot, feast and dance,
716 Marrying or prostituting, as befel,[371]
717 Rape or adultery, where passing[372] fair
718 Allured them, thence from cups to civil broils.[373]
719 At length a reverend sire[374] among them came,
720 And of their doings great dislike declared,
721 And testified against their ways. He oft
722 Frequented their assemblies, whereso[375] met,
723 Triumphs or festivals, and to them preached
724 Conversion and repentance, as to souls
725 In prison, under judgments imminent
726 But all in vain. Which when he saw, he ceased
727 Contending,[376] and removed his tents far off.
728 Then from the mountain hewing timber tall,
729 Began to build a vessel of huge bulk,
730 Measured by cubit, length, and breadth, and height,
731 Smeared round with pitch, and in the side a door
732 Contrived, and of provisions laid in large[377]
733 For man and beast, when lo, a wonder strange!
734 Of every beast, and bird, and insect small,
735 Came sevens, and pairs, and entered in as[378] taught
736 Their order. Last the sire and his three sons,
737 With their four wives. And God made fast the door.
738 Meanwhile the south-wind rose, and with black wings
739 Wide-hovering all the clouds together drove
740 From under Heav'n. The hills, to their[379] supply,
741 Vapor and exhalation, dusk and moist,
742 Sent up amain,[380] and now the thickened sky
743 Like a dark ceiling stood, down rushed the rain
744 Impetuous,[381] and continued till the earth
745 No more was seen. The floating vessel swum

---

[371] it came about, happened, occurred
[372] surpassing
[373] quarrels
[374] Noah
[375] wherever they
[376] struggling
[377] in large = a great deal
[378] as if
[379] i.e., the clouds'
[380] violently, with full force
[381] with great force [trisyllabic, second accented, "-uous" elided]

746   Uplifted, and secure with beakèd prow
747   Rode tilting o'er the waves. All dwellings else
748   Flood overwhelmed, and them with all their pomp
749   Deep under water rolled. Sea covered sea,
750   Sea without shore, and in their palaces,
751   Where luxury late reigned, sea-monsters whelped[382]
752   And stabled.[383] Of mankind, so numerous late,[384]
753   All left, in one small bottom[385] swum embarked.
754   How didst thou grieve then, Adam, to behold
755   The end of all thy offspring, end so sad,
756   Depopulation? Thee another flood,
757   Of tears and sorrow a flood, thee also drowned,
758   And sunk thee as thy sons, till gently reared
759   By th' Angel, on thy feet thou stood'st at last,
760   Though comfortless, as when a father mourns
761   His children, all in view destroyed at once,
762   And scarce[386] to th' Angel utter'dst thus thy plaint:
763   "O visions ill foreseen! Better had I
764   Lived ignorant of future, so had borne
765   My part of evil only, each day's lot
766   Enough to bear. Those now, that were dispensed[387]
767   The burden of many ages, on me light[388]
768   At once, by my foreknowledge gaining birth
769   Abortive, to torment me ere their being,
770   With thought that they must be. Let no man seek
771   Henceforth to be foretold what shall befall
772   Him or his children—evil, he may be sure,
773   Which neither his foreknowing can prevent,
774   And he the future evil shall no less
775   In apprehension than in substance feel,
776   Grievous to bear. But that care now is past:
777   Man is not whom to warn.[389] Those few escaped
778   Famine and anguish will at last consume,[390]
779   Wand'ring that wat'ry desert. I had hope,

---

[382] brought forth young
[383] dwelled
[384] not long before
[385] boat
[386] barely, with difficulty
[387] dealt out, given
[388] descend, fall
[389] whom to warn = able to be warned
[390] be destroyed

780 When violence was ceased, and war on earth,
781 All would have then gone well, peace would have
             crowned
782 With length of happy days the race of man.
783 But I was far deceived, for now I see
784 Peace to corrupt no less than war to waste.
785 How comes it thus? Unfold, celestial guide,
786 And whether here the race of man will end."
787 To whom thus Michael:
                              "Those, whom last thou saw'st
788 In triumph and luxurious wealth, are they
789 First seen in acts of prowess eminent
790 And great exploits, but of true virtue void,
791 Who having spilled much blood, and done much waste,
792 Subduing nations, and achieved thereby
793 Fame in the world, high titles, and rich prey,[391]
794 Shall change their course to pleasure, ease, and sloth,
795 Surfeit,[392] and lust, till wantonness[393] and pride
796 Raise out of friendship hostile deeds in peace.
797 The conquered also, and enslaved by war,
798 Shall with their freedom lost all virtue lose
799 And fear of God, from whom their piety feigned
800 In sharp contest[394] of battle found no aid
801 Against invaders. Therefore cooled in zeal,
802 Thenceforth shall practice how to live secure,[395]
803 Worldly or dissolute, on what their lords
804 Shall leave them to enjoy, for th' earth shall bear
805 More than enough that temperance[396] may be tried.[397]
806 So all shall turn degenerate,[398] all depraved,[399]
807 Justice and temperance, truth and faith, forgot—
808 One man[400] except, the only son of light
809 In a dark age, against example good,[401]

---

[391] booty, spoil, plunder
[392] gluttony
[393] self-indulgence, capriciousness
[394] [con*test*]
[395] safely
[396] moderation
[397] tested
[398] debased, degraded
[399] corrupt
[400] Noah
[401] "good against that which is being done"

810	Against allurement,[402] custom,[403] and a world
811	Offended.[404] Fearless of reproach and scorn,
812	Or violence, he of their wicked ways
813	Shall them admonish, and before them set
814	The paths of righteousness, how much more safe
815	And full of peace, denouncing[405] wrath to come
816	Of their impenitence,[406] and shall return
817	Of them derided, but of God observed
818	The one just man alive. By His command
819	Shall build a wondrous ark, as thou beheld'st,
820	To save himself, and household, from amidst
821	A world devote to universal wrack.[407]
822	No sooner he, with them of man and beast
823	Select[408] for life shall in the ark be lodged,
824	And sheltered round, but all the cataracts[409]
825	Of Heav'n set open on the earth shall pour
826	Rain, day and night. All fountains of the deep,
827	Broke up, shall heave the ocean to usurp
828	Beyond all bounds, till inundation rise
829	Above the highest hills. Then shall this mount
830	Of Paradise by might of waves be moved
831	Out of his place, pushed by the hornèd[410] flood,
832	With all his verdure spoiled,[411] and trees adrift,
833	Down the great river[412] to the op'ning gulf,[413]
834	And there take root an island salt and bare,
835	The haunt of seals, and orcs,[414] and sea-mews'[415] clang,[416]
836	To teach thee that God attributes[417] to place

---

[402] enticement
[403] fashion
[404] sinful
[405] proclaiming
[406] stubbornness
[407] wreck, ruin
[408] chosen
[409] waterfalls
[410] producing hornlike branches, as it divides and each branch flows on
[411] destroyed
[412] the Euphrates?
[413] (1) the Perisan Gulf, in particular, *or* (2) the deep, in general
[414] whales
[415] seagulls
[416] harsh screams [noun]
[417] [trisyllabic, first and third accented]

837   No sanctity, if none[418] be thither brought
838   By men who there frequent, or therein dwell.
839   And now, what further shall ensue, behold."
840   He looked, and saw the ark hull[419] on the flood,
841   Which now abated, for the clouds were fled,
842   Driven by a keen north-wind that, blowing dry,
843   Wrinkled the face of deluge, as[420] decayed,[421]
844   And the clear sun on his wide wat'ry glass
845   Gazed hot, and of[422] the fresh wave largely[423] drew,
846   As after thirst, which made their flowing shrink
847   From standing lake to tripping[424] ebb, that stole
848   With soft foot towards the deep, who now had stopped[425]
849   His sluices,[426] as the Heav'n his windows shut.
850   The ark no more now floats, but seems on ground,
851   Fast on the top of some high mountain fixed.
852   And now the tops of hills as rocks appear.
853   With clamor[427] thence the rapid currents drive
854   Towards the retreating sea their furious[428] tide.[429]
855   Forthwith[430] from out the ark a raven flies,
856   And after him the surer[431] messenger,
857   A dove sent forth once and again[432] to spy
858   Green tree or ground, whereon his foot may light.[433]
859   The second time returning, in his bill
860   An olive leaf he brings, pacific[434] sign.
861   Anón[435] dry ground appears, and from his ark

---

[418] no sanctity
[419] floating
[420] as if
[421] declined, dwindled
[422] from
[423] copiously
[424] quick-moving
[425] closed
[426] channels
[427] loud noise
[428] aging
[429] flowing water, here ebbing
[430] at once
[431] more trustworthy/steadfast/reliable
[432] then again
[433] fall, descend
[434] calm, tranquil
[435] quickly

862   The ancient sire descends, with all his train,
863   Then with uplifted hands and eyes devout,
864   Grateful to Heav'n, over his head beholds
865   A dewy cloud, and in the cloud a bow[436]
866   Conspicuous[437] with three lifted[438] colors gay,
867   Betok'ning[439] peace from God, and cov'nant new.
868   Whereat the heart of Adam, erst[440] so sad,
869   Greatly rejoiced, and thus his joy broke forth:
870   "O thou, who future things canst represent
871   As present, Heav'nly instructor, I revive
872   At this last sight, assured that man shall live,
873   With all the creatures and their seed preserve.[441]
874   Far less I now lament for one whole world
875   Of wicked sons destroyed, than I rejoice
876   For one man found so perfect, and so just,
877   That God vouchsafes to raise another world
878   From him, and all His anger to forget.
879   But say, what mean those colored streaks in Heav'n
880   Distended,[442] as[443] the brow of God appeased?
881   Or serve they, as a flow'ry verge,[444] to bind
882   The fluid skirts of that same wat'ry cloud,
883   Lest it again dissolve and show'r the earth?"
884   To whom the Arch-Angel:
                              "Dextrously[445] thou aim'st.
885   So willingly doth God remit[446] His ire,
886   Though late[447] repenting[448] Him of man[449] depraved,[450]
887   Grieved at His heart, when looking down He saw
888   The whole earth filled with violence, and all flesh

---

[436] rainbow
[437] visible
[438] banded, striped
[439] signaling
[440] at first
[441] kept alive
[442] extended, spread out
[443] like
[444] border, edge
[445] cleverly
[446] give up, resign, surrender
[447] not long before
[448] regretting
[449] i.e., of having created man in the first place
[450] corrupted

889 Corrupting each their way. Yet, those removed,
890 Such grace shall one just man find in His sight,
891 That He relents,[451] not to blot[452] out mankind,
892 And makes a covenant never to destroy
893 The earth again by flood, nor let the sea
894 Surpass his bounds, nor rain to drown the world,
895 With man therein or beast. But when He brings
896 Over the earth a cloud, will therein set
897 His triple-colored bow, whereon to look,
898 And call to mind His cov'nant. Day and night,
899 Seed-time and harvest, heat and hoary[453] frost,
900 Shall hold their course, till fire purge all things new,
901 Both Heav'n and earth, wherein the just shall dwell."

The End of the Eleventh Book

---

[451] softens
[452] obliterate
[453] gray

BOOK XII

THE ARGUMENT

THE ANGEL MICHAEL continues from the Flood, to relate what shall succeed; then, in the mention of Abraham, comes by degrees to explain who that seed of the woman shall be, which was promised Adam and Eve in the Fall; his Incarnation, Death, Resurrection, and Ascension; the state of the Church till his Second Coming.

Adam, greatly satisfied and recomforted by these relations and promises, descends the hill with Michael; wakens Eve, who all this while had slept, but with gentle dreams composed to quietness of mind and submission. Michael in either hand leads them out of Paradise, the fiery sword waving behind them, and the Cherubim taking their stations to guard the place.

1   As one who in his journey bates[1] at noon,
2 Though bent[2] on speed, so here the Arch-Angel paused
3 Betwixt the world destroyed and world restored,
4 If Adam aught perhaps might interpose.[3]
5 Then with transition sweet,[4] new speech resumes:
6   "Thus thou hast seen one world begin, and end,
7 And man, as from a second stock, proceed.
8 Much thou hast yet to see, but I perceive
9 Thy mortal sight to fail; objects divine
10 Must needs impair[5] and weary human sense.
11 Henceforth what is to come I will relate.
12 Thou therefore give due audience, and attend.
13   "This second source[6] of men, while yet but few,
14 And while the dread of judgment past remains
15 Fresh in their minds, fearing the Deity,
16 With some[7] regard to what is just and right
17 Shall lead their lives, and multiply apace,[8]
18 Laboring the soil, and reaping plenteous crop,
19 Corn, wine, and oil, and from the herd or flock
20 Oft sacrificing bullock,[9] lamb, or kid,
21 With large wine-offerings poured, and sacred feast,
22 Shall spend their days in joy unblamed,[10] and dwell
23 Long time in peace, by families and tribes,
24 Under paternal rule. Till one[11] shall rise
25 Of proud ambitious heart, who not content
26 With fair equality, fraternal state,
27 Will arrogate dominion undeserved
28 Over his brethren, and quite dispossess[12]
29 Concord[13] and law of nature from the earth,

---

[1] leaves off, breaks away
[2] determined, set
[3] put forward
[4] pleasing
[5] weaken
[6] origin, fountainhead
[7] a certain (substantial)
[8] swiftly
[9] young bull, bull calf
[10] unreproved
[11] Nimrod ("hunter"): see Genesis 10:8–10
[12] cast out, get rid of
[13] peace, harmony

30   Hunting (and men not beasts shall be his game)
31   With war, and hostile snare, such as refuse
32   Subjection to his empire tyrannous.
33   A mighty hunter thence he shall be styled
34   Before the Lord, as in despite[14] of Heav'n,
35   Or from Heav'n claiming second sov'reignty,
36   And from rebellion shall derive his name,
37   Though of rebellion others he accuse.
38   "He with a crew, whom like ambition joins
39   With him or under him to tyrannize,
40   Marching from Eden towards the west, shall find
41   The plain,[15] wherein a black bituminous[16] gurge[17]
42   Boils out from under ground, the mouth of Hell.
43   Of brick, and of that stuff, they cast[18] to build
44   A city and tow'r,[19] whose top may reach to Heav'n,
45   And get themselves a name, lest far dispersed
46   In foreign lands, their memory be lost,
47   Regardless whether good or evil fame.
48   But God, who oft descends to visit men
49   Unseen, and through their habitations walks
50   To mark their doings, them beholding soon,
51   Comes down to see their city, ere the tower
52   Obstruct Heav'n-tow'rs, and in derision sets
53   Upon their tongues a various[20] spirit, to raze[21]
54   Quite out their native language and, instead,
55   To sow[22] a jangling[23] noise of words unknown.
56   Forthwith a hideous gabble rises loud
57   Among the builders; each to other calls
58   Not understood; till hoarse, and all in rage,
59   As mocked they storm.[24] Great laughter was in Heav'n
60   And looking down, to see the hubbub strange

---

[14] contempt, scorn
[15] Shinar
[16] pitchy
[17] whirlpool
[18] determine, decide
[19] the Tower of Babel: see Genesis 10:10 and 11:1–9
[20] differing, unstable
[21] erase, obliterate, sweep away, destroy
[22] scatter
[23] discordant, babbling
[24] rage, complain

61   And hear the din. Thus was the building²⁵ left
62   Ridiculous, and the work Confusion²⁶ named."
63   Whereto thus Adam, fatherly displeased:
64   "O execrable son! so to aspire
65   Above his brethren, to himself assuming
66   Authority usurped, from God not giv'n.
67   He gave us only over beast, fish, fowl,
68   Dominion absolute; that right we hold
69   By His donation.²⁷ But man over men
70   He made not lord, such title to Himself
71   Reserving, human left from human free.
72   But this usurper his encroachment²⁸ proud
73   Stays²⁹ not on man! To God his tower intends
74   Siege³⁰ and defiance. Wretched man! What food
75   Will he convey up thither, to sustain
76   Himself and his rash army, where thin air
77   Above the clouds will pine³¹ his entrails gross,
78   And famish³² him of breath, if not of bread?"
79   To whom thus Michael:
                             "Justly thou abhorr'st
80   That son, who on the quiet state of men
81   Such trouble brought, affecting³³ to subdue
82   Rational liberty. Yet know withal,³⁴
83   Since thy original lapse true liberty
84   Is lost, which always with right reason dwells
85   Twinned, and from her hath no dividual being.
86   Reason in man obscured, or not obeyed,
87   Immediately inordinate desires,
88   And upstart passions, catch³⁵ the government³⁶
89   From reason, and to servitude reduce

---

²⁵ i.e., the act of building, *not* the structure being built
²⁶ "babble" (Babel)
²⁷ gift
²⁸ intrusion
²⁹ stops, remains
³⁰ assault
³¹ waste, pain
³² starve to death
³³ seeking
³⁴ notwithstanding
³⁵ capture, seize, snatch
³⁶ authority, direction

90   Man, till then free. Therefore, since he permits
91   Within himself unworthy powers to reign
92   Over free reason, God, in judgment just,
93   Subjects him from without to violent lords,
94   Who oft as undeservedly enthrall[37]
95   His outward freedom. Tyranny must be—
96   Though to the tyrant thereby no excuse.
97   Yet sometimes nations will decline so low
98   From virtue, which is reason, that no wrong,
99   But justice, and some fatal curse annexed,
100   Deprives them of their outward liberty,
101   Their inward lost. Witness th' irreverent son[38]
102   Of him who built the ark, who for the shame
103   Done to his father,[39] heard this heavy curse,
104   'Servant of servants,' on his vicious[40] race.
105   Thus will this latter, as the former world,
106   Still tend from bad to worse, till God at last,
107   Wearied with their iniquities, withdraw
108   His presence from among them, and avert
109   His holy eyes, resolving from thenceforth
110   To leave them to their own polluted ways,
111   And one peculiar[41] nation[42] to select
112   From all the rest, of whom to be invoked,
113   A nation from one faithful man[43] to spring,
114   Him on this side Euphrates yet residing,
115   Bred up in idol-worship. O that men
116   (Canst thou believe?) should be so stupid grown,
117   While yet the patriarch lived who 'scaped the Flood,
118   As to forsake the living God, and fall
119   To worship their own work in wood and stone
120   For gods! Yet him God the Most High vouchsafes[44]
121   To call by vision from his father's house,
122   His kindred and false gods, into a land

---

[37] enslave
[38] Ham, father of Canaan
[39] see Genesis 9:22–27
[40] depraved, corrupt, malignant
[41] special, singular
[42] the Jews
[43] Abraham
[44] deigns, condescends

123   Which He will show him, and from him will raise
124   A mighty nation, and upon him show'r
125   His benediction so that in his seed
126   All nations shall be blest. He straight[45] obeys,
127   Not knowing to what land, yet firm believes.
128   "I see him, but thou canst not, with what faith
129   He leaves his gods, his friends, and native soil,
130   Ur[46] of Chaldaea, passing now the ford
131   To Haran,[47] after him a cumbrous train
132   Of herds and flocks, and numerous servitude,[48]
133   Not wand'ring poor, but trusting all his wealth
134   With God, who called him, in a land unknown.
135   Canaan he now attains; I see his tents
136   Pitched about Sechem,[49] and the neighbouring plain
137   Of Moreh. There by promise he receives
138   Gift to his progeny of all that land,
139   From Hamath[50] northward to the desert south
140   (Things by their names I call, though yet unnamed),
141   From Hermon[51] east to the great western sea.[52]
142   Mount Hermon—yonder sea—each place behold
143   In prospect, as I point them. On the shore,
144   Mount Carmel.[53] Here, the double-founted[54] stream,
145   Jordan, true limit[55] eastward, but his[56] sons
146   Shall dwell to Senir,[57] that long ridge of hills.
147   "This ponder, that all nations of the earth
148   Shall in his seed be blessèd. By that seed
149   Is meant thy great Deliverer,[58] who shall bruise[59]

---

[45] immediately
[46] west of the Euphrates and south of Babylon; the Chaldeans, a Semitic tribe, had migrated to southern Babylonia
[47] east of the Euphrates, in northwestern Mesopotamia
[48] those in servitude: servants
[49] Shechem, a city in central Palestine, north of Jerusalem
[50] in Syria, on the River Orontes
[51] Mt. Hermon, to the north: the highest peak in Palestine
[52] the Mediterranean
[53] in Haifa, now in Israel
[54] double-sourced
[55] landmark, boundary, border
[56] Abraham's
[57] see 1 Chronicles 5:23
[58] Christ
[59] crush, smash, break

150	The serpent's head, whereof to thee anon[60]
151	Plainlier shall be revealed. This patriarch blest,
152	Whom 'faithful Abraham' due time[61] shall call,
153	A son[62] and of his son a grand-child[63] leaves,
154	Like him in faith, in wisdom, and renown.
155	The grandchild, with twelve sons increased, departs
156	From Canaan to a land hereafter called
157	Egypt, divided by the river Nile.
158	See where it flows, disgorging[64] at seven mouths
159	Into the sea. To sojourn[65] in that land
160	He comes, invited by a younger son[66]
161	In time of dearth,[67] a son whose worthy deeds
162	Raise him to be the second in that realm
163	Of Pharaoh. There he dies, and leaves his race
164	Growing into a nation, and now grown
165	Suspected to a sequent[68] king, who seeks
166	To stop their overgrowth, as inmate[69] guests
167	Too numerous,[70] whence of[71] guests he makes them slaves,
168	Inhospitably, and kills their infant males.
169	Till by two brethren (these two brethren call
170	Moses and Aaron) sent from God to claim
171	His people from enthralment,[72] they return,
172	With glory and spoil, back to their promised land.
173	"But first, the lawless tyrant, who denies[73]
174	To know their God, or message to regard,
175	Must be compelled by signs and judgments dire.
176	To blood unshed[74] the rivers must be turned.

---

[60] soon
[61] due time = in the time that, properly, it should take
[62] Isaac
[63] Jacob
[64] emptying
[65] to lodge, to dwell temporarily
[66] Joseph
[67] scarcity, famine
[68] subsequent, following
[69] (1) occupant, (2) stranger, foreign
[70] [bisyllabic]
[71] from
[72] enslavement
[73] refuses
[74] not poured out from bodies

177   Frogs, lice, and flies, must all his palace fill

178   With loath'd intrusion,[75] and fill all the land.

179   His cattle must of rot and murren[76] die,

180   Botches[77] and blains[78] must all his flesh emboss,[79]

181   And all[80] his people. Thunder mixed with hail,

182   Hail mixed with fire, must rend th' Egyptian sky,

183   And wheel[81] on th' earth, devouring where it rolls.

184   What it devours not, herb, or fruit, or grain,

185   A darksome cloud of locusts swarming down

186   Must eat, and on the ground leave nothing green.

187   Darkness must overshadow all his[82] bounds,

188   Palpable[83] darkness, and blot out three days.

189   Last, with one midnight stroke all the first-born

190   Of Egypt must lie dead. Thus with ten wounds

191   The river-dragon[84] tamed at length submits

192   To let his sojourners depart, and oft

193   Humbles his stubborn heart, but still as ice

194   More hardened after thaw, till in his rage

195   Pursuing whom he late[85] dismissed,[86] the sea

196   Swallows him with his host,[87] but them[88] lets pass

197   As[89] on dry land, between two crystal walls,

198   Awed[90] by the rod of Moses so to stand

199   Divided, till his rescued gain their shore.

200   "Such wondrous power God to His saint will lend,

201   Though present in His Angel, who shall go

---

[75] thrusting/forcing in
[76] plague
[77] boils
[78] blisters
[79] cover, bulge with
[80] also all
[81] turn, sweep
[82] darkness'
[83] potent, obvious
[84] Pharaoh
[85] not long before
[86] sent away
[87] army
[88] his former guests, the Jews
[89] as if
[90] controlled

202 Before them in a cloud and pillar[91] of fire,
203 By day a cloud, by night a pillar of fire,
204 To guide them in their journey, and remove[92]
205 Behind them, while the obdurate[93] king pursues.
206 All night he will pursue, but his approach
207 Darkness defends[94] between[95] till morning watch.
208 Then through the fiery pillar, and the cloud,
209 God looking forth will trouble[96] all his[97] host,
210 And craze[98] their chariot-wheels, when by command
211 Moses once more his potent rod extends
212 Over the sea. The sea his rod obeys;
213 On their embattled[99] ranks the waves return,
214 And overwhelm their war.[100] The race elect[101]
215 Safe toward Canaan from the shore[102] advance
216 Through the wild desert, not the readiest[103] way,
217 Lest ent'ring[104] on the Canaanite alarmed[105]
218 War terrify them[106] inexpert,[107] and fear
219 Return them[108] back to Egypt, choosing rather
220 Inglorious life with servitude, for life
221 To noble (and ignoble) is more sweet
222 Untrained in arms, where rashness leads not on.[109]
223   "This also shall they gain by their delay
224 In the wide wilderness. There they shall found[110]

---

[91] column
[92] take away, clear off, disappear (make disappear)
[93] unyielding, hardened in evil, insensible to moral influence
[94] prevents, wards off, prohibits
[95] in the space between the two groups, Egyptians and Jews
[96] derange
[97] Pharaoh's
[98] shatter, smash, break
[99] in battle formation
[100] troops, soldiers
[101] [adjective]
[102] of the Red Sea
[103] quickest, shortest, most direct
[104] penetrating
[105] thus called to arms
[106] the Jews
[107] not experienced (as the Canaanites definitely were) in war
[108] lead/send them
[109] "not trained (or, by implication, not having anything to do with) weapons and armor (warfare), unless people are drawn on (led on) by reckless impetuosity"
[110] create, initiate, begin building

225   Their government, and their great senate[111] choose
226   Through the twelve tribes,[112] to rule by laws ordained.
227   God from the mount of Sinai, whose gray top
228   Shall tremble, He descending, will Himself
229   In thunder, lightning, and loud trumpets' sound
230   Ordain them laws, part such as appertain[113]
231   To civil justice, part religious rites
232   Of sacrifice, informing them, by types[114]
233   And shadows,[115] of that destined seed[116] to bruise[117]
234   The serpent, by what means he shall achieve
235   Mankind's deliverance. But the voice of God
236   To mortal ear is dreadful. They beseech
237   That Moses might report[118] to them His will,
238   And terror cease. He grants what they besought,
239   Instructed that to God is no access
240   Without mediator, whose high office now
241   Moses in figure[119] bears, to introduce
242   One greater, of whose day he shall foretell,
243   And all the prophets in their age the times
244   Of great Messiah shall sing.
                              "Thus, laws and rites
245   Established, such delight hath God in men
246   Obedient to His will, that He vouchsafes
247   Among them to set up His tabernacle,
248   The Holy One with mortal men to dwell.
249   By His prescript[120] a sanctuary is framed
250   Of cedar, overlaid with gold, therein
251   An ark,[121] and in the ark His testimony,[122]
252   The records of His cov'nant. Over these

---

[111] council of seventy elders, chosen by Moses: see Exodus 24:1–9
[112] derived from the twelve sons of Jacob
[113] belong
[114] symbols
[115] images
[116] Christ
[117] smash, crush
[118] narrate, tell, speak
[119] image, emblem
[120] command
[121] coffer, chest
[122] divine law

253   A mercy-seat of gold,[123] between the wings
254   Of two bright Cherubim. Before him[124] burn
255   Seven lamps as in a zodiac[125] representing
256   The Heav'nly fires. Over the tent a cloud
257   Shall rest by day, a fiery gleam by night,
258   Save when they journey. And at length they come,
259   Conducted by His Angel, to the land
260   Promised to Abraham and his seed.

                                        "The rest

261   Were long to tell, how many battles fought,
262   How many kings destroyed, and kingdoms won,
263   Or how the sun shall in mid Heav'n stand still
264   A day entire, and night's due course adjourn,
265   Man's voice commanding, 'Sun, in Gibeon stand,
266   And thou moon in the vale of Aialon,
267   Till Israel overcome!'[126] So call[127] the third
268   From Abraham, son of Isaac, and from him
269   His whole descent, who thus shall Canaan win."
270   Here Adam interposed:

                           "O sent from Heav'n,

271   Enlight'ner of my darkness, gracious things
272   Thou hast revealed, those chiefly which concern
273   Just Abraham and his seed. Now first I find
274   Mine eyes true-op'ning, and my heart much eased,
275   Erewhile perplexed with thoughts what would become
276   Of me and all mankind. But now I see
277   His day, in whom all nations shall be blest—
278   Favor unmerited by me, who sought
279   Forbidden knowledge by forbidden means.
280   This yet I apprehend not: why to those
281   Among whom God will deign to dwell on earth
282   So many and so various laws are giv'n?
283   So many laws argue so many sins
284   Among them. How can God with such reside?"
285   To whom thus Michael:

---

[123] mercy-seat of gold = golden covering
[124] the ark? God Himself?
[125] i.e., one lamp for each of the seven known planets
[126] see Joshua 10:12
[127] Israel

                        "Doubt not but that sin

286   Will reign among them, as of thee begot,
287   And therefore was law giv'n them, to evince[128]
288   Their natural pravity,[129] by stirring up
289   Sin against law to fight, that when they see
290   Law can discover[130] sin, but not remove
291   (Save by those shadowy[131] expiations[132] weak,
292   The blood of bulls and goats), they may conclude
293   Some blood more precious must be paid for man,
294   Just for unjust, that[133] in such righteousness
295   To them by faith imputed they may find
296   Justification[134] towards God, and peace
297   Of conscience, which the law by ceremonies[135]
298   Cannot appease, nor man the moral part
299   Perform[136] and, not performing, cannot live.
300   So law appears[137] imperfect, and but[138] giv'n
301   With purpose to resign[139] them, in full time,
302   Up to a better cov'nant, disciplined[140]
303   From shadowy types[141] to truth, from flesh to spirit,
304   From imposition of strict laws to free
305   Acceptance of large grace, from servile fear
306   To filial, works of law to works of faith.
307   And therefore shall not Moses, though of God
308   Highly belov'd, being but the minister
309   Of law, his people into Canaan lead,
310   But Joshua, whom the gentiles Jesus call,
311   His name and office bearing, who[142] shall quell

---

[128] subdue, overcome
[129] depravity
[130] expose, reveal, show
[131] (1) insubstantial, (2) foreshadowing (Christ)
[132] atonements
[133] so that
[134] verification, i.e., freeing (justifying) man from the penalty of (original) sin, man being thus made righteous
[135] outward rites
[136] carry out, execute, accomplish
[137] (1) can be plainly seen, shown, (2) is declared
[138] only
[139] confidently yield themselves up to
[140] trained, educated
[141] images
[142] Christ

312   The adversary-serpent, and bring back
313   Through the world's wilderness long-wand'red man
314   Safe to eternal Paradise of rest.
315   Meanwhile, they in their earthly Canaan placed,
316   Long time shall dwell and prosper, but[143] when sins
317   National interrupt their public peace,
318   Provoking God to raise them enemies,
319   From whom as oft He saves them penitent
320   By Judges first, then under Kings. Of whom
321   The second,[144] both for piety renowned
322   And puissant deeds, a promise shall receive
323   Irrevocable, that his regal throne
324   Forever shall endure. The like[145] shall sing[146]
325   All prophecy, that of the royal stock
326   Of David (so I name this king) shall rise
327   A son, the woman's seed to thee foretold,
328   Foretold to Abraham, as in whom shall trust
329   All nations, and to kings foretold, of kings
330   The last, for of his reign shall be no end.
331   But first a long succession must ensue,
332   And his[147] next son,[148] for wealth and wisdom famed,
333   The clouded ark of God, till then in tents
334   Wand'ring, shall in a glorious temple enshrine.
335   Such follow him as shall be registered[149]
336   Part good, part bad—of bad the longer scroll,
337   Whose foul idolatries and other faults
338   Heaped to the popular sum,[150] will so incense
339   God, as to[151] leave them, and expose their land,
340   Their city, His temple, and His holy ark,
341   With all His sacred things, a[152] scorn and prey
342   To that proud city, whose high walls thou saw'st
343   Left in confusion, Babylon thence called.

---

[143] except
[144] David
[145] same
[146] tell, declare, relate
[147] David's
[148] Solomon
[149] recorded
[150] "added (heaped) to the sum (total: large) of the people's (the popular) faults"
[151] as to = so as to make Him
[152] to be a

344 There in captivity He lets them dwell
345 The space of seventy years,[153] then brings them back,
346 Rememb'ring[154] mercy and His cov'nant sworn
347 To David, stablished[155] as the days of Heav'n.
348 Returned from Babylon by leave of kings[156]
349 Their lords, whom God disposed,[157] the house of God
350 They first re-edify,[158] and for a while
351 In mean[159] estate[160] live moderate. Till grown
352 In wealth and multitude, factious they grow.
353 But first among the priests dissention springs,
354 Men who attend[161] the altar, and should most
355 Endeavor[162] peace. Their strife pollution brings
356 Upon the temple itself. At last they[163] seize
357 The scepter, and regard not David's sons,
358 Then lose it to a stranger,[164] that the true
359 Anointed King Messiah might be born
360 Barred[165] of his right. Yet at his birth a star,
361 Unseen before in Heav'n, proclaims him come,
362 And guides the eastern sages, who inquire
363 His place, to offer incense, myrrh, and gold.
364 His place of birth a solemn[166] Angel tells
365 To simple shepherds, keeping watch by night.
366 They gladly thither[167] haste, and by a choir
367 Of squadroned[168] Angels hear his carol sung.
368 A virgin is his mother, but his sire
369 The power of the Most High. He shall ascend
370 The throne hereditary, and bound his reign

---

[153] the Babylonian Captivity, 606–536 B.C.
[154] bearing in mind
[155] established: as fixed as
[156] Cyrus, Darius, Artaxerxes
[157] made ready, so inclined
[158] rebuild
[159] poor/low
[160] condition, degree of prosperity
[161] watch over, look after
[162] strive for
[163] priests
[164] Antipater (a Roman appointee), father of Herod
[165] obstructed, hindered, excluded
[166] majestic
[167] Bethlehem
[168] in military formation

371   With earth's wide bounds, his glory with the Heav'ns."
372   He ceased, discerning Adam with such joy
373   Surcharged[169] as had, like grief, been dewed in tears,
374   Without the vent[170] of words, which these he breathed:
375   "O prophet of glad tidings, finisher[171]
376   Of utmost hope! Now clear I understand
377   What oft my steadiest thoughts have searched in vain,
378   Why our great expectation should be called
379   The seed of woman. Virgin Mother, hail,
380   High in the love of Heav'n! Yet from my loins
381   Thou shalt proceed, and from thy womb the son
382   Of God Most High: so God with man unites!
383   Needs must the serpent now his capital bruise[172]
384   Expect with mortal[173] pain. Say where and when
385   Their fight, what stroke shall bruise the victor's heel."
386   To whom thus Michael:
                    "Dream not of their fight
387   As of a duel,[174] or the local[175] wounds
388   Of head or heel. Not therefore joins the Son
389   Manhood to Godhead, with more strength to foil[176]
390   Thy enemy, nor so is overcome
391   Satan, whose fall from Heav'n, a deadlier bruise,
392   Disabled not to give thee thy death's wound,
393   Which he,[177] who comes thy Savior, shall recure,[178]
394   Not by destroying Satan but his[179] works
395   In thee, and in thy seed. Nor can this be
396   But by fulfilling that which thou did'st want,[180]
397   Obedience to the law of God, imposed
398   On penalty of death, and suffering death,
399   The penalty to thy transgression due,

---

[169] overburdened
[170] outlet
[171] perfector
[172] capital bruise = injury to his head
[173] fatal ("capital" also = "fatal, mortal")
[174] [bisyllabic]
[175] having spatial position
[176] defeat, trample
[177] Christ
[178] remedy
[179] Satan's
[180] lack

400 And due to theirs which out of thine will grow.
401 So only can high Justice rest appaid.[181]
402 The law of God exact he[182] shall fulfill
403 Both by obedience and by love, though love
404 Alone fulfill the law. Thy punishment
405 He shall endure, by coming in the flesh
406 To a reproachful[183] life and cursèd death,
407 Proclaiming life to all who shall believe
408 In his redemption, and that his obedience,
409 Imputed,[184] becomes theirs by faith, his merits
410 To save them, not their own, though[185] legal[186] works.[187]
411 For this he shall live hated, be blasphemed,[188]
412 Seized on by force, judged and to death condemned,
413 A shameful and accursed, nailed to the cross
414 By his own nation, slain for bringing life.
415 But to the cross he nails thy enemies,
416 The law that is against thee, and the sins
417 Of all mankind, with him there crucified,
418 Never to hurt them more who rightly trust
419 In this his satisfaction.[189] So he dies,
420 But soon revives: Death over him no power
421 Shall long usurp.[190] Ere the third dawning light
422 Return, the stars of morn shall see him rise
423 Out of his grave, fresh as the dawning light,
424 Thy ransom paid, which man from death redeems,
425 His death for man, as many as offered[191] life
426 Neglect not, and the benefit[192] embrace[193]
427 By faith not void of works. This God-like act
428 Annuls thy doom, the death thou should'st have died,

---

[181] satisfied, repaid
[182] Christ
[183] shameful
[184] credited (to them)
[185] though their merits are based on
[186] lawful
[187] actions, deeds
[188] reviled
[189] full payment of a debt
[190] seize wrongfully
[191] [adjective]
[192] profit, good thing, favor, kind deed
[193] (1) accept, (2) submit to

429 In sin forever lost from life. This act
430 Shall bruise[194] the head of Satan, crush his strength,
431 Defeating Sin and Death, his two main arms,
432 And fix far deeper in his head their stings
433 Than temporal[195] death shall bruise the victor's heel,
434 Or theirs[196] whom he redeems—a death like sleep,
435 A gentle wafting[197] to immortal life.
436 Nor after resurrection shall he stay
437 Longer on earth than certain[198] times to appear
438 To his disciples, men who in his life
439 Still[199] followed him. To them shall leave in charge
440 To teach all nations what of him they learned
441 And his salvation,[200] them who shall believe
442 Baptizing in the profluent[201] stream, the sign
443 Of washing them from guilt of sin to life
444 Pure, and in mind prepared, if so befall,
445 For death, like that which the Redeemer died.
446 All nations they shall teach. For from that day,
447 Not only to the sons of Abraham's loins
448 Salvation shall be preached, but to the sons
449 Of Abraham's faith wherever through the world.
450 So in his seed all nations shall be blest.
451 Then to the Heav'n of Heav'ns he[202] shall ascend
452 With victory, triumphing[203] through the air
453 Over his foes and thine. There shall surprise
454 The serpent, prince of air, and drag in chains
455 Through all his[204] realm, and there[205] confounded[206]
                         leave,
456 Then enter into glory, and resume

---

[194] crush, smash, break, destroy
[195] temporary, in merely human time
[196] their death
[197] lifting/floating/carrying through the air
[198] definite, fixed
[199] always
[200] his salvation = the saving of the soul which Christ brings to men
[201] fully flowing
[202] Christ
[203] (1) celebrating, (2) being victorious
[204] Satan's
[205] in Hell
[206] defeated, overthrown, brought to nought

457   His seat at God's right hand, exalted high
458   Above all names[207] in Heav'n, and thence shall come,
459   When this world's dissolution shall be ripe,
460   With glory and power to judge both quick[208] and dead—
461   To judge the unfaithful dead, but to reward
462   His faithful, and receive them into bliss,
463   Whether in Heav'n or earth, for then the earth
464   Shall all be Paradise, far happier place
465   Than this of Eden, and far happier days."
466   So spoke the Arch-Angel Michael, then paused,
467   As at the world's great period;[209] and our sire,
468   Replete[210] with joy and wonder, thus replied:
469   "O goodness infinite, goodness immense!
470   That all this good of[211] evil shall produce,[212]
471   And evil turn to good, more wonderful
472   Than that which by creation first brought forth
473   Light out of darkness! Full of doubt I stand,
474   Whether I should repent me now of sin
475   By me done and occasioned,[213] or rejoice
476   Much more, that much more good thereof shall spring,
477   To God more glory, more good-will to men
478   From God, and over wrath grace shall abound.[214]
479   But say, if our Deliverer up to Heav'n
480   Must re-ascend, what will betide[215] the few
481   His faithful, left among the unfaithful herd,
482   The enemies of truth? Who then shall guide
483   His people, who defend? Will they not deal
484   Worse with his followers than with him they dealt?"
485   "Be sure they will," said the Angel, "but from
                                                        Heav'n
486   He to his own a comforter[216] will send,
487   The promise of the Father, who shall dwell

---

[207] those with distinguished reputations
[208] the living
[209] finish, final stage
[210] filled with, full of
[211] from
[212] be brought forth/produced
[213] induced (in others)
[214] be plentiful, overflow
[215] become of, happen to
[216] the Holy Spirit

488   His Spirit within them, and the law of faith,
489   Working through love, upon their hearts shall write,
490   To guide them in all truth, and also arm
491   With spiritual armor, able to resist
492   Satan's assaults, and quench²¹⁷ his fiery darts—
493   What man can do against them, not afraid,
494   Though to the death, against such cruelties
495   With inward consolations recompensed,
496   And oft supported²¹⁸ so as shall amaze
497   Their proudest persecutors. For the Spirit,
498   Poured first on his Apostles, whom he sends
499   T' evangelize the nations, then on all
500   Baptized, shall them with wond'rous gifts endue²¹⁹
501   To speak all tongues,²²⁰ and do all miracles,
502   As did their Lord before them. Thus they win
503   Great numbers of each nation to receive
504   With joy the tidings brought from Heav'n.

                                             "At length

505   Their ministry performed, and race well run,
506   Their doctrine and their story written left,
507   They die, but in their room,²²¹ as they forewarn,
508   Wolves shall succeed for teachers, grievous wolves,
509   Who all the sacred mysteries of Heav'n
510   To their own vile advantages shall turn
511   Of lucre²²² and ambition, and the truth
512   With superstitions and traditions taint,
513   Left only in those written records pure,
514   Though not but²²³ by the Spirit understood.
515   Then shall they²²⁴ seek to avail themselves of names,
516   Places, and titles, and with these to join
517   Secular power, though feigning still to act
518   By spiritual, to themselves appropriating
519   The Spirit of God, promised alike and giv'n

---

²¹⁷ destroy
²¹⁸ endured, sustained, maintained
²¹⁹ endow, invest, supply
²²⁰ languages
²²¹ place
²²² profit, gain
²²³ except
²²⁴ the "wolves" of the Roman Catholic Church

520   To all believers, and from that pretence,
521   Spiritual laws by carnal[225] power shall force
522   On every conscience, laws which none shall find
523   Left them enrolled[226] or what the Spirit within
524   Shall on the heart engrave. What will they then
525   But force the spirit of grace itself, and bind
526   His consort liberty? What but unbuild
527   His living temples, built by faith to stand,
528   Their own faith, not another's—for on earth
529   Who against faith and conscience can be heard
530   Infallible?
           "Yet many will presume.[227]
531   Whence heavy persecution shall arise
532   On all who in the worship persevere
533   Of spirit and truth. The rest, far greater part,
534   Will deem[228] in outward rites and specious[229] forms[230]
535   Religion satisfied.[231] Truth shall retire,[232]
536   Bestuck with sland'rous darts, and works of faith
537   Rarely be found.
           "So shall the world go on,
538   To good malignant, to bad men benign,
539   Under her own weight groaning, till the day
540   Appear of respiration[233] to the just
541   And vengeance to the wicked, at return
542   Of him so lately promised to thy aid,
543   The woman's seed, obscurely then foretold,
544   Now ampler known thy Savior and thy Lord,
545   Last[234] in the clouds from Heav'n to be revealed
546   In glory of the Father, to dissolve
547   Satan with his perverted world, then raise
548   From the conflagrant[235] mass, purged and refined,

---

[225] bodily, fleshly, corporeal
[226] left them enrolled = were (had been) left them in written form (recorded)
[227] venture, dare
[228] consider, judge
[229] fallacious, outwardly respectable
[230] formalities, ceremonies
[231] fulfilled
[232] withdraw
[233] respite
[234] at last, finally
[235] flaming, burning

549   New Heav'ns, new earth, ages of endless date,[236]
550   Founded in righteousness, and peace, and love—
551   To bring forth fruits, joy and eternal bliss."
552   He ended, and thus Adam last[237] replied:
553   "How soon hath thy prediction, seer[238] blest,
554   Measured[239] this transient world, the race[240] of time,
555   Till time stand fixed! Beyond is all abyss,
556   Eternity, whose end no eye can reach.
557   Greatly-instructed I shall hence depart,
558   Greatly in peace of thought, and have my fill
559   Of knowledge, what this vessel can contain,
560   Beyond which was my folly to aspire.
561   Henceforth I learn that to obey is best,
562   And love with fear the only God; to walk
563   As in His presence, ever to observe
564   His providence, and on Him sole depend,
565   Merciful over[241] all His works, with good
566   Still[242] overcoming evil, and by small
567   Accomplishing great things, by things deemed weak
568   Subverting[243] worldly strong, and worldly wise
569   By simply meek; that suffering for truth's sake
570   Is fortitude to highest victory
571   And, to the faithful, death the gate of life,
572   Taught this by his example, whom I now
573   Acknowledge my Redeemer ever blest."
574   To whom thus also th' Angel last[244] replied:
575   "This having learned, thou hast attained the sum
576   Of wisdom. Hope no higher, though all the stars
577   Thou knew'st by name, and all the ethereal powers,
578   All secrets of the deep, all Nature's works,
579   Or works of God in Heav'n, air, earth, or sea,
580   And all the riches of this world enjoy'st,

---

[236] duration
[237] in conclusion
[238] [bisyllabic? (the etymology being "see" + "er," and Michael being, by God's specific direction, here a seer into the future)]
[239] traversed
[240] course, movement
[241] (1) through all, (2) even more than
[242] always
[243] overthrowing
[244] in conclusion

581 And all the rule, one empire. Only add
582 Deeds to thy knowledge answerable,[245] add faith,
583 Add virtue, patience, temperance, add love,
584 By name to come called charity, the soul
585 Of all the rest. Then wilt thou not be loath
586 To leave this Paradise, but shalt possess
587 A Paradise within thee, happier far.
588   "Let us descend now therefore from this top[246]
589 Of speculation,[247] for the hour precise[248]
590 Exacts[249] our parting hence. And see the guards,
591 By me encamped on yonder hill! Expect[250]
592 Their motion, at whose front[251] a flaming sword,
593 In signal of remove,[252] waves fiercely[253] round.
594 We may no longer stay. Go, waken Eve.
595 Her also I with gentle dreams have calmed,
596 Portending[254] good, and all her spirits composed[255]
597 To meek[256] submission. Thou, at season fit,[257]
598 Let her with thee partake[258] what thou hast heard,
599 Chiefly what may concern her faith to know,
600 The great deliverance by her seed to come
601 (For by the woman's seed) on all mankind,
602 That ye may live, which will be many days,
603 Both in one faith unanimous,[259] though sad,
604 With cause, for evils past, yet much more cheered
605 With meditation[260] on the happy end."
606   He ended, and they both descend the hill.
607 Descended Adam to the bow'r where Eve

---

[245] suitable, corresponding [adjective]
[246] highest place, peak
[247] vision
[248] strictly defined/expressed
[249] demands, requires, insists on
[250] look at
[251] at whose front = in front of whom
[252] the act of departure
[253] actively
[254] foretelling
[255] arranged, adjusted, ordered
[256] humble, submissive
[257] season fit = appropriate time
[258] share
[259] agreed, of one mind
[260] serious and sustained reflection

608 Lay sleeping, ran before, but found her waked,
609 And thus with words not sad she him received:
610   "Whence thou return'st, and whither went'st, I
                              know,
611 For God is also in sleep, and dreams advise,[261]
612 Which He hath sent propitious,[262] some great good
613 Presaging, since with sorrow and heart's distress
614 Wearied I fell asleep. But now lead on:
615 In me is no delay. With thee to go
616 Is to stay here. Without thee here to stay
617 Is to go hence unwilling. Thou to me
618 Art all things under Heav'n, all places thou,
619 Who for my wilful crime art banished hence.
620 This further consolation yet secure
621 I carry hence, though all by me is lost,
622 Such favor I unworthy am vouchsafed,[263]
623 By me the promised seed shall all restore."
624   So spoke our mother Eve, and Adam heard
625 Well pleased, but answered not. For now, too nigh
626 The Arch-Angel stood and, from the other hill
627 To their fixed station, all in bright array
628 The Cherubim descended, on the ground
629 Gliding meteorous,[264] as ev'ning-mist
630 Ris'n from a river o'er the marish[265] glides,
631 And gathers ground fast at the laborer's heel
632 Homeward returning. High in front advanced,[266]
633 The brandished sword of God before them blazed,
634 Fierce[267] as a comet, which with torrid heat,
635 And vapor[268] as[269] the Libyan air adust,[270]
636 Began to parch[271] that[272] temperate[273] clime. Whereat

---

[261] inform, give counsel
[262] favorable, gracious
[263] granted
[264] brilliant, flashing, swift [four syllables, first and third accented]
[265] marsh
[266] raised [adjective]
[267] vehement, intense, merciless
[268] waves (of heat)
[269] like
[270] scorched
[271] scorch
[272] (of Eden)
[273] moderate

637   In either hand the hast'ning Angel caught
638   Our ling'ring[274] parents, and to the eastern gate
639   Led them direct, and down the cliff as fast
640   To the subjected[275] plain, then disappeared.[276]
641   They looking back, all th' eastern side beheld
642   Of Paradise, so late their happy seat,
643   Waved over by that flaming brand, the gate
644   With dreadful faces thronged and fiery arms.
645   Some natural tears they dropped, but wiped them soon.
646   The world was all before them, where to choose
647   Their place of rest, and Providence their guide.
648   They hand in hand, with wand'ring steps and slow,
649   Through Eden took their solitary way.

The End

---

[274] reluctant, tardy, dawdling
[275] lying below
[276] i.e., then the angel (and his troop) disappeared

PARADISE REGAINED

BOOK I

        I, who erewhile[1] the happy Garden sung
By one man's disobedience lost, now sing
Recovered Paradise to all mankind,
By one man's firm obedience fully tried[2]
Through all temptation, and the Tempter foiled
In all his wiles, defeated and repulsed,
And Eden raised in the waste wilderness.
        Thou Spirit, who led'st this glorious Eremite[3]
Into the desert, his victorious field
Against the spiritual foe, and brought'st him thence   10
By proof th' undoubted Son of God, inspire,
As thou art wont,[4] my prompted[5] song, else mute,
And bear through height or depth of Nature's bounds,
With prosperous[6] wing full summed,[7] to tell of deeds
Above[8] heroic, though in secret done,
And unrecorded left through many an age—
Worthy t' have not remained so long unsung.
        Now had the great Proclaimer,[9] with a voice
More awful[10] than the sound of trumpet, cried
"Repentance, and Heav'n's kingdom nigh at hand   20
To all baptized!" To his great baptism flocked
With awe[11] the regions round, and with them came
From Nazareth, the son of Joseph deemed,[12]
To the flood Jordan—came as then obscure,
Unmarked,[13] unknown. But him the Baptist soon
Descried,[14] divinely warned, and witness bore
As to his worthier,[15] and would have resigned

---

[1] some time ago
[2] tested
[3] hermit
[4] accustomed to, in the habit of
[5] ready
[6] favored, fortunate
[7] full summed = feathers fully formed/grown, i.e., poetic capacity fully matured
[8] beyond
[9] John the Baptist
[10] sublimely majestic, commanding reverence
[11] reverent wonder
[12] considered
[13] unnoticed
[14] discovered
[15] his worthier = (1) Christ being worthier than John, or (2) one who is his (John's) worthier; the meaning is unchanged either way

To him his Heav'nly office. Nor was long
His witness unconfirmed: on him[16] baptized
Heav'n opened, and in likeness of a dove   30
The Spirit descended, while the Father's voice
From Heav'n pronounced him His belovèd Son.
That heard the Adversary,[17] who roving still
About the world, at that assembly famed[18]
Would not be last, and with the voice divine
Nigh thunder-struck,[19] th' exalted man to whom
Such high attest was giv'n a while surveyed[20]
With wonder. Then with envy fraught,[21] and rage,
Flies to his place,[22] nor rests, but in mid air
To council summons all his mighty Peers,[23]   40
Within thick clouds and dark tenfold involved,[24]
A gloomy consistory,[25] and them amidst,
With looks aghast[26] and sad,[27] he thus bespoke:
        "O ancient Powers of air and this wide world
(For much more willingly I mention air,
This our old conquest, than remember Hell,
Our hated habitation), well ye know
How many ages, as[28] the years of men,
This universe[29] we have possessed, and ruled
In manner at our will th' affairs of earth,   50
Since Adam and his facile[30] consort Eve
Lost Paradise, deceived by me, though since
With dread attending[31] when that fatal wound

---

[16] Christ
[17] Satan
[18] celebrated [adjective]—but does it mean that the assembly is "famed" or that Satan did not want to be ("would not be") less famed?
[19] Satan is "nigh thunder-struck" by God's voice
[20] Satan "surveys" (looks carefully at, examines) Christ, who is "the exalted man"
[21] filled
[22] residence, dwelling, citadel
[23] of the highest rank (*not* "equals")
[24] wreathed
[25] council
[26] frightened
[27] serious, morose
[28] as are counted
[29] world, earth
[30] easily led
[31] awaiting

Shall[32] be inflicted by the seed of Eve
Upon my head. Long the decrees of Heav'n
Delay, for longest time to Him is short.
And now, too soon for us, the circling hours
This dreaded time have compassed,[33] wherein we
Must bide[34] the stroke of that long-threat'ned wound
(At least, if so we can, and by the head   60
Broken[35] be not intended all our power
To be infringed,[36] our freedom and our being
In this fair empire won of earth and air),
For this ill news I bring: the woman's seed,
Destined to this, is late of woman born.
His birth to our just fear gave no small cause,
But his growth now to youth's full flow'r, displaying
All virtue, grace and wisdom to achieve
Things highest, greatest, multiplies my fear.
Before him a great prophet, to proclaim   70
His coming, is sent harbinger,[37] who all
Invites, and in the consecrated stream
Pretends[38] to wash off sin, and fit them so
Purified to receive him pure, or rather
To do him honor as their King. All come,
And he[39] himself among them was baptized—
Not thence to be more pure, but to receive
The testimony of Heav'n, that who he is
Thenceforth the nations may not doubt. I saw
The prophet do him reverence. On him, rising   80
Out of the water, Heav'n above the clouds
Unfold her crystal doors, thence on his head
A perfect dove descend (whate'er it meant),
And out of Heav'n the sov'reign voice I heard,
'This is my Son beloved—in him am pleased.'
His mother, then, is mortal, but his sire

---

[32] in Milton's time, "shall" still carried the sense of "will have to, must"
[33] attained, accomplished
[34] endure, undergo
[35] "bruised"
[36] shattered, broken
[37] as a forerunner
[38] claims, aspires
[39] Christ

He[40] who obtains[41] the monarchy of Heav'n,
And what will He not do t' advance His Son?
His first-begot we know,[42] and sore have felt,
When his fierce thunder drove us to the deep.   90
Who this is we must learn, for man he seems
In all his lineaments,[43] though in his face
The glimpses of his Father's glory shine.
Ye see our danger on the utmost edge
Of hazard,[44] which admits[45] no long debate,
But must with something sudden be opposed
(Not force, but well-couched[46] fraud, well-woven snares),
Ere in the head[47] of nations he appear,
Their king, their leader, and supreme on earth.
I, when no other durst, sole undertook   100
The dismal[48] expedition[49] to find out
And ruin Adam, and the exploit performed
Successfully. A calmer voyage now
Will waft[50] me, and the way found prosperous once
Induces best to hope of like success."
          He ended, and his words impression left
Of much amazement to th' infernal crew,
Distracted and surprised with deep dismay
At these sad tidings. But no time was then[51]
For long indulgence to their fears or grief: 110
Unanimous they all commit the care
And management of this main enterprise
To him, their great dictator,[52] whose attempt
At first against mankind so well had thrived[53]

---

[40] is He
[41] holds
[42] Satan does not yet identify *this* Son of God with Christ
[43] features, characteristics
[44] peril
[45] allows, permits
[46] well put together/hidden
[47] position of leadership/chief importance
[48] somber, malign
[49] warlike enterprise
[50] convey, carry
[51] no time was then = at that moment there was no time
[52] absolute ruler
[53] prospered, been successful

In Adam's overthrow, and led their march
From Hell's deep-vaulted den to dwell in light,
Regents, and potentates, and kings, yea gods,
Of many a pleasant realm and province wide.
      So to the coast of Jordan he directs
His easy[54] steps, girded[55] with snaky wiles,   120
Where he might likeliest find this new-declared,
This man of men, attested Son of God,
Temptation and all guile on him to try—
So to subvert[56] whom[57] he suspected raised
To end his[58] reign on earth so long enjoyed.
But contrary unweeting,[59] he fulfilled
The purposed counsel, pre-ordained and fixed,
Of the Most High, who in full frequence[60] bright
Of Angels, thus to Gabriel smiling spoke:
      "Gabriel, this day, by proof, thou shalt behold,   130
Thou and all Angels conversant[61] on earth
With man or men's affairs, how I begin
To verify that solemn message late,
On which I sent thee to the virgin pure
In Galilee, that she should bear a son,
Great in renown, and called the Son of God.
Then told'st her (doubting[62] how these things could be
To her a virgin) that on her should come
The Holy Ghost, and the power of the Highest
O'ershadow[63] her. This man, born and now upgrown,   140
To show him worthy of his birth divine
And high prediction, henceforth I expose[64]
To Satan. Let him tempt, and now assay[65]
His utmost subtlety, because he boasts

---

[54] smooth
[55] equipped
[56] corrupt, undermine
[57] he whom
[58] Satan's
[59] contrary unweeting = not knowing to the contrary
[60] assembly
[61] occupied, familiar with [trisyllabic, first and third accented]
[62] she doubting
[63] cover
[64] exhibit, set forth
[65] try, attempt

And vaunts of his great cunning to the throng
Of his apostasy. He might have learned
Less overweening,[66] since he failed in Job,
Whose constant perseverance overcame
Whate'er his[67] cruel malice could invent.
He now shall know I can produce a man   150
Of female seed, far abler[68] to resist
All his solicitations, and at length
All his vast force, and drive him back to Hell,
Winning by conquest what the first man lost
By fallacy[69] surprised.
                    "But first I mean
To exercise[70] him[71] in the wilderness.
There he shall first lay down the rudiments[72]
Of his great warfare, ere I send him forth
To conquer Sin and Death, the two grand foes.
By humiliation[73] and strong sufferance[74]   160
His weakness shall o'ercome Satanic strength,
And all the world, and mass[75] of sinful flesh,
That[76] all the Angels and aethereal Powers—
They now, and men hereafter—may discern
From what consummate virtue I have chose
This perfect man, by merit called my Son,
To earn salvation for the sons of men."
                    So spoke th' Eternal Father, and all Heav'n
Admiring[77] stood a space, then into hymns
Burst forth, and in celestial measures[78] moved,   170
Circling the throne and singing while the hand

---

[66] to be less arrogant/prideful
[67] Satan's
[68] than Job
[69] trickery, deceit
[70] employ
[71] Christ
[72] beginnings
[73] [four syllables, first and third accented, third elided]
[74] patient/long-suffering endurance
[75] body, bulk
[76] so that
[77] marveling
[78] rhythms

Sung with the voice, and this the argument:[79]
     "Victory and triumph to the Son of God,
Now ent'ring his great duel,[80] not of arms,
But to vanquish by wisdom hellish wiles!
The Father knows the Son, therefore secure
Ventures his filial virtue, though untried,
Against whate'er may tempt, whate'er seduce,[81]
Allure, or terrify, or undermine.
Be frustrate, all ye stratagems of Hell,   180
And devilish machinations come to nought!"
So they in Heav'n their odes[82] and vigils[83] tuned.[84]
     Meanwhile the Son of God, who yet some days
Lodged in Bethabara,[85] where John baptized,
Musing and much revolving in his breast
How best the mighty work he might begin
Of Savior to mankind, and which way first
Publish[86] his godlike office now mature,[87]
One day forth walked alone, the Spirit leading,
And his deep thoughts, the better to converse   190
With[88] solitude, till far from track[89] of men,
Thought following thought, and step by step led on,
He entered now the bord'ring desert wild,
And with dark shades and rocks environed round
His holy meditations thus pursued:
     "O what a multitude of thoughts at once
Awakened in me swarm, while I consider
What from within I feel myself, and hear
What from without comes often to my ears,
Ill sorting[90] with my present state compared!   200

---

[79] theme, subject
[80] combat
[81] lead astray
[82] hymns
[83] prayers
[84] sang
[85] Bet ha-Arabah, biblical site near north shore of the Dead Sea [four syllables, second and fourth accented]
[86] proclaim, make public
[87] ripe, full-grown
[88] keep company/live with
[89] the paths
[90] consorting, fitting, harmonizing

When I was yet a child, no childish play
To me was pleasing. All my mind was set
Serious to learn and know, and thence to do,
What might be public good. Myself I thought[91]
Born to that end, born to promote all truth,
All righteous things. Therefore, above my years,
The Law of God I read, and found it sweet,
Made it my whole delight, and in it grew
To such perfection that, ere yet my age
Had measured twice six years, at our[92] great feast   210
I went into the Temple, there to hear
The teachers of our Law, and to propose
What might improve my knowledge or their own,
And was admired[93] by all.
                    "Yet this not all
To which my spirit aspired. Victorious deeds
Flamed in my heart, heroic acts—one while[94]
To rescue Israel from the Roman yoke,
Then to subdue and quell,[95] o'er all the earth,
Brute violence and proud tyrannic power,
Till truth were freed, and equity[96] restored—   220
Yet held it more humane, more Heav'nly,[97] first
By winning words to conquer willing hearts,
And make persuasion do the work of fear,
At least to try, and teach the erring soul,
Not wilfully misdoing, but unaware
Misled. The stubborn only to subdue.
          "These growing thoughts my mother soon perceiving,
By words at times cast forth, inly rejoiced,
And said to me apart,[98] 'High are thy thoughts,
O Son! But nourish them, and let them soar   230
To what height sacred virtue and true worth

---

[91] Christ too seems unsure of his prior existence
[92] the Jews'
[93] wondered at
[94] time, period
[95] extinguish, destroy
[96] justice
[97] divine, celestial
[98] privately

Can raise them, though above example[99] high.
By matchless deeds express thy matchless sire.
For know, thou art no son of mortal man,
Though men esteem thee low of parentage.
Thy Father is th' Eternal King who rules
All Heav'n and earth, Angels and sons of men.
A messenger from God foretold thy birth
Conceived in me a virgin. He foretold
Thou should'st be great, and sit on David's throne,   240
And of thy kingdom there should be no end.
At thy nativity a glorious choir
Of Angels, in the fields of Bethlehem, sung
To shepherds, watching at their folds[100] by night,
And told them the Messiah now was born,
Where they might see him, and to thee they came,
Directed to the manger[101] where thou lay'st,
For in the inn was left no better room.[102]
A star, not seen before, in Heav'n appearing,
Guided the Wise Men thither from the East,   250
To honor thee with incense, myrrh, and gold,
By whose[103] bright course led on they found the place,
Affirming it thy star, new-graven[104] in Heav'n,
By which they knew thee King of Israel born.
Just Simeon[105] and prophetic Anna,[106] warned
By vision, found thee in the Temple, and spoke
Before the altar and the vested priest
Like[107] things of thee to all that present stood.'
          "This having heard, straight I again revolved[108]
The Law and prophets, searching what was writ   260
Concerning the Messiah, to our scribes
Known partly, and soon found of whom they spoke

---

[99] above example = unprecedented
[100] sheep pens
[101] feeding trough in a stable
[102] place
[103] the star's
[104] formed, carved, set
[105] see Luke 2:25–35
[106] see Luke 2:36–38
[107] similar
[108] considered, studied, meditated upon

I am—this chiefly, that my way must lie
Through many a hard assay,[109] ev'n to the death,
Ere I the promised kingdom can attain
Or work redemption for mankind, whose sins'
Full weight must be transferred upon my head.
Yet neither thus disheart'ned or dismayed,
The time prefixed[110] I waited, when behold
The Baptist (of whose birth I oft had heard,   270
Not knew by sight) now come, who was to come
Before Messiah, and his way prepare.
I, as all others, to his baptism came,
Which I believed was from above, but he
Straight knew me, and with loudest voice proclaimed
Me him (for it was shewn him so from Heav'n)—
Me him whose harbinger[111] he was, and first
Refused on me his baptism to confer,
As much his greater, and was hardly[112] won.[113]
But as I rose out of the laving[114] stream   280
Heav'n op'ned her eternal doors, from whence
The Spirit descended on me like a dove,
And last—the sum[115] of all—my Father's voice,
Audibly heard from Heav'n, pronounced me His,
Me His belovèd Son, in whom alone
He was well pleased. By which I knew the time
Now full,[116] that I no more should live obscure,[117]
But openly begin, as best becomes
Th' authority which I derived from Heav'n.
            "And now by some strong motion I am led   290
Into this wilderness, to what intent
I learn not yet. Perhaps I need not know,
For what concerns my knowledge God reveals."
            So spoke our morning star, then in his rise,

---

[109] learning experience, endeavor, affliction, temptation
[110] established previously
[111] forerunner
[112] not easily, with difficulty, barely
[113] prevailed upon
[114] pouring, washing
[115] highest point
[116] complete
[117] hidden, retired, unknown

And looking round on every side beheld
A pathless desert, dusk[118] with horrid shades.[119]
The way he came, not having marked return,
Was difficult, by human steps untrod,
And he still on was led, but with such thoughts
Accompanied of things past and to come   300
Lodged in his breast as well might recommend[120]
Such solitude before choicest[121] society.
Full forty days he passed—whether on hill
Sometimes, anon[122] in shady vale, each night
Under the covert[123] of some ancient oak
Or cedar to defend[124] him from the dew,
Or harbored[125] in one cave, is not revealed.
Nor[126] tasted human food, nor hunger felt,
Till those days ended. Hungered then at last
Among wild beasts. They at his sight grew mild,[127]   310
Nor sleeping him nor waking harmed. His walk
The fiery serpent fled and noxious[128] worm,
The lion and fierce tiger glared[129] aloof.[130]
      But now an agèd man in rural weeds,
Following, as seemed, the quest of some stray ewe,
Or withered sticks to gather, which might serve
Against a winter's day when winds blow keen
To warm him, wet returned from field at eve,
He[131] saw approach, who first with curious eye
Perused him, then with words thus uttered spoke: 320
      "Sir, what ill chance hath brought thee to this place,
So far from path or road of men, who pass

---

[118] dark, gloomy
[119] (1) shadows, (2) dark figures, ghosts, specters
[120] commend, advise
[121] the best
[122] soon, in a little while
[123] covering, shelter
[124] keep, protect
[125] lodged, sheltered
[126] he neither
[127] tame, gentle
[128] hurtful, harmful
[129] looked fixedly/fiercely
[130] at a distance
[131] Christ

In troop or caravan? For single[132] none
Durst ever, who returned, and dropped not here
His carcass, pined[133] with hunger and with drought?
I ask the rather, and the more admire,
For that[134] to me thou seem'st the man whom late
Our new baptizing prophet at the ford
Of Jordan honored so, and called thee Son
Of God. I saw and heard, for we sometimes   330
Who dwell this wild,[135] constrained[136] by want, come forth
To town or village nigh (nighest is far),
Where aught we hear, and curious are to hear,
What happens new. Fame[137] also finds us out."
To whom the Son of God:
                                        "Who brought me hither
Will bring me hence. No other guide I seek."
        "By miracle he may," replied the swain.[138]
"What other way I see not, for we here
Live on tough roots and stubs,[139] to thirst inured
More than the camel, and to drink go far—   340
Men to much misery and hardship born.
But if thou be the Son of God, command
That out of these hard stones be made thee bread,
So shalt thou save thyself, and us relieve
With food, whereof we wretched seldom taste."
He ended, and the Son of God replied:
        "Think'st thou such force in bread? Is it not written
(For I discern thee other than thou seem'st),
Man lives not by bread only, but each word
Proceeding from the mouth of God, who fed   350
Our fathers here with manna? In the mount
Moses was forty days, nor ate nor drank,
And forty days Elijah without food
Wandered this barren waste. The same I now.

---

[132] alone
[133] consumed, exhausted
[134] for that = because
[135] desert, wilderness
[136] forced, compelled
[137] public report, rumor
[138] rustic
[139] stubble, stumps

Why dost thou, then, suggest to me distrust,[140]
Knowing who I am, as I know who thou art?"
    Whom thus answered th' arch-fiend, now undisguised:
" 'Tis true, I am that Spirit unfortunate
Who, leagued with millions more in rash revolt,
Kept not my happy station, but was driv'n   360
With them from bliss to the bottomless deep.
Yet to that hideous place not so confined
By rigor[141] unconniving[142] but that oft,
Leaving my dolorous[143] prison, I enjoy
Large liberty to round[144] this globe of earth,
Or range[145] in the air, nor from the Heav'n of Heav'ns
Hath He excluded my resort[146] sometimes.
I came among the Sons of God when He
Gave up into my hands Uzzean[147] Job,
To prove[148] him, and illustrate[149] his high worth.   370
And when to all His Angels He proposed
To draw the proud King Ahab[150] into fraud,
That he might fall in Ramoth,[151] they demurring,[152]
I undertook that office, and the tongues
Of all his[153] flattering prophets glibbed[154] with lies
To his destruction, as I had in charge.[155]
For what He bids I do. Though I have lost
Much luster of my native brightness, lost
To be beloved of God, I have not lost

---

[140] doubt
[141] strict discipline, harshness
[142] not permissive
[143] dismal
[144] travel around
[145] roam
[146] recourse
[147] of Uz, in eastern Palestine
[148] test
[149] make clear [trisyllabic, second accented]
[150] king of Israel, who meets his death after a weltering confusion of prophecies: see 1 Kings 22
[151] Ramoth-Gilead, fortified position east of Jordan
[152] hesitating, balking
[153] Ahab's
[154] caused to chatter
[155] had in charge = was supposed to do

To love, at least contemplate[156] and admire, 380
What I see excellent in good, or fair,
Or virtuous.[157] I should so have lost all sense.
    "What can be then less in me than desire[158]
To see thee and approach thee, whom I know
Declared the Son of God, to hear attent[159]
Thy wisdom, and behold thy godlike deeds?
Men generally think me much a foe
To all mankind. Why should I? They to me
Never did wrong or violence. By them
I lost not what I lost. Rather by them 390
I gained what I have gained, and with them dwell
Copartner in these regions of the world,
If not disposer[160] —lend them oft my aid,
Oft my advice by presages[161] and signs,
And answers, oracles, portents, and dreams,
Whereby they may direct their future life.
    "Envy, they say, excites me, thus to gain
Companions of my misery and woe!
At first it may be but, long since with woe
Nearer acquainted, now I feel by proof 400
That fellowship in pain divides[162] not smart,[163]
Nor lightens aught each man's peculiar[164] load.
Small consolation, then, were man adjoined.[165]
This wounds me most (what can it less?) that man,
Man fall'n, shall be restored, I never more."
    To whom our Savior sternly thus replied:
"Deservedly thou griev'st, composed[166] of lies
From the beginning, and in lies wilt end,

---

[156] [trisyllabic, accent on second]
[157] [bisyllabic, second elided]
[158] "What can I feel less than desire . . ."? (reading "less" as an adverb) or "How could anything make me do less than desire . . ."? (reading "less" not as an adverb but as a verb, said by the *O.E.D.* to have become obsolete when Milton was twenty-five years old)
[159] attentively
[160] i.e., copartner if not "disposer" (one who controls)
[161] predictions, omens
[162] shares
[163] grief
[164] private, individual
[165] united with me
[166] constituted

Who boast'st release from Hell, and leave to come
Into the Heav'n of Heav'ns! Thou com'st indeed,   410
As a poor miserable[167] captive thrall[168]
Comes to the place where he before had sat
Among the prime in splendor, now deposed,
Ejected, emptied, gazed,[169] unpitied, shunned,
A spectacle of ruin, or of scorn,
To all the host of Heav'n. The happy place
Imparts to thee no happiness, no joy,
Rather inflames thy torment, representing
Lost bliss, to thee no more communicable—
So never more in Hell than when in Heav'n.   420
        "But thou art serviceable to Heav'n's King!
Wilt thou impute t' obedience what thy fear
Extorts, or pleasure to do ill excites?
What but thy malice moved thee to misdeem[170]
Of righteous Job, then cruelly to afflict him
With all inflictions? But his patience won.
The other service was thy chosen task,
To be a liar in four hundred mouths,
For lying is thy sustenance, thy food.
Yet thou pretend'st to truth! All oracles   430
By thee are giv'n, and what confessed more true
Among the nations? That hath been thy craft,
By mixing somewhat true to vent more lies.
But what have been thy answers? What but dark,
Ambiguous, and with double sense deluding,
Which they who asked have seldom understood,
And not well understood, as good not known?[171]
Who ever, by consulting at thy shrine,
Returned the wiser, or the more instruct
To fly[172] or follow what concerned him most,   440
And run not sooner to his fatal snare?
For God hath justly giv'n the nations up
To thy delusions—justly, since they fell

---

[167] [four syllables, first and third accented?]
[168] slave
[169] stared at
[170] think evil of
[171] as good = they might/just as well not have known at all
[172] flee

Idolatrous.
          "But when His purpose is
Among them to declare His providence,
To thee not known, whence hast thou then thy truth,
But from Him, or his Angels president[173]
In every province, who themselves disdaining
T' approach thy temples, give thee in command
What, to the smallest tittle,[174] thou shalt say   450
To thy adorers? Thou, with trembling fear,
Or like a fawning[175] parasite, obey'st,
Then to thyself ascrib'st the truth foretold.
But this thy glory shall be soon retrenched.[176]
No more shalt thou by oracling abuse[177]
The gentiles:[178] henceforth oracles are ceased,
And thou no more with pomp and sacrifice
Shalt be inquired at Delphos or elsewhere—
At least[179] in vain, for they shall find thee mute.
God hath now sent His living oracle   460
Into the world to teach His final will,
And sends His Spirit of truth henceforth to dwell
In pious hearts, an inward oracle
To all truth requisite for men to know."
        So spoke our Savior. But the subtle fiend,
Though inly stung with anger and disdain,[180]
Dissembled, and this answer smooth returned:
        "Sharply thou hast insisted on rebuke,
And urged me hard with doings which not will[181]
But misery hath wrested[182] from me. Where   470
Easily canst thou find one[183] miserable,
And not enforced oft-times to part from truth,

---

[173] superintending
[174] tiny point
[175] whining
[176] cut short
[177] [verb]
[178] heathen
[179] "at least, if you are inquired for, it shall be"
[180] indignation
[181] volition [noun]
[182] wrung, extorted
[183] someone who is

If it may stand him more in stead[184] to lie,
Say and unsay, feign, flatter, or abjure?[185]
But thou art placed above me, thou art Lord.
From thee I can, and must, submiss, endure
Check[186] or reproof, and glad to scape so quit.[187]
Hard are the ways of truth, and rough to walk,
Smooth on the tongue discoursed,[188] pleasing to th' ear,
And tunable[189] as sylvan[190] pipe[191] or song.   480
What wonder, then, if I delight to hear
Her dictates[192] from thy mouth? Most men admire[193]
Virtue who follow not her lore. Permit me
To hear thee when I come (since no man comes),
And talk at least, though I despair t' attain.
Thy Father, who is holy, wise, and pure,
Suffers the hypocrite or atheous priest
To tread His sacred courts,[194] and minister[195]
About His altar, handling holy things,
Praying or vowing, and vouchsafed His voice   490
To Balaam,[196] reprobate,[197] a prophet yet[198]
Inspired. Disdain[199] not such access to me."

    To whom our Savior, with unaltered brow:
"Thy coming hither, though I know thy scope,[200]
I bid not, or forbid. Do as thou find'st
Permission from above. Thou canst not more."

    He added not, and Satan, bowing low

---

[184] profit, advantage
[185] renounce, recant, disclaim
[186] (1) restraint, (2) rebuff
[187] free
[188] spoken, uttered
[189] sweet-sounding
[190] characteristic of/belonging to forests or woods
[191] flute
[192] authoritative direction/admonition
[193] marvel at
[194] courtyards, grounds
[195] help, serve
[196] see Numbers 22:5 through 24:25
[197] corrupt
[198] still
[199] scorn
[200] purpose

His gray dissimulation,[201] disappeared,
Into thin air diffused. For now began
Night with her sullen wing to double-shade   500
The desert. Fowls in their clay[202] nests were couched,[203]
And now wild beasts came forth, the woods to roam.

[201] feigned semblance
[202] earthy
[203] lying down, resting

BOOK II

Meanwhile the new-baptized, who yet remained
At Jordan with the Baptist, and had seen
Him whom they heard so late[1] expressly[2] called
Jesus Messiah, Son of God declared,
And on that high authority had believed,
And with him talked, and with him lodged[3]—I mean
Andrew[4] and Simon,[5] famous after[6] known,
With others, though in Holy Writ not named—
Now missing him, their joy so lately found,
So lately found and so abruptly gone,   10
Began to doubt, and doubted many days,
And as the days increased, increased their doubt.
Sometimes they thought he might be only shown[7]
And for a time caught up[8] to God, as once
Moses was in the mount and missing long,
And the great Thisbite,[9] who on fiery wheels
Rode up to Heav'n, yet once again to come.
        Therefore, as those young prophets then with care
Sought lost Elijah, so in each place these
Nigh to Bethabara[10]—in Jericho[11]   20
The city of palms, Aenon,[12] and Salem[13] old,
Machaerus,[14] and each town or city walled
On this side the broad lake Genezaret,[15]
Or in Peraea[16]—but returned in vain.
Then on the bank of Jordan, by a creek,
Where winds with reeds and osiers[17] whispering play,

---

[1] recently
[2] clearly, distinctly
[3] lived in lodgings
[4] see John 1:40
[5] see John 1:41
[6] afterward
[7] displayed, exhibited
[8] caught up = taken
[9] Elijah: see 2 Kings 2:1–12
[10] Bet ha-Arabah, north of the Dead Sea: see John 1:28
[11] north of the Dead Sea: see Deuteronomy 34:3
[12] in Samaria: see John 3:23
[13] Salim, in Samaria: see John 3:23
[14] stronghold east of the Dead Sea, earlier destroyed but rebuilt by Herod
[15] the Sea of Galilee
[16] region east of the Jordan River, between the Sea of Galilee and the Dead Sea
[17] willows

Plain fishermen (no greater, men them call),
Close in a cottage low together got,
Their unexpected loss and plaints[18] outbreathed:
      "Alas, from what high hope to what relapse   30
Unlooked for are we fall'n! Our eyes beheld
Messiah certainly now come, so long
Expected of our fathers. We have heard
His words, his wisdom full of grace and truth.
'Now, now, for sure, deliverance is at hand!
The kingdom shall to Israel be restored!'
Thus we rejoiced, but soon our joy is turned
Into perplexity and new amaze.
For whither is he gone? What accident
Hath rapt[19] him from us? Will he now retire[20]   40
After appearance, and again prolong
Our expectation? God of Israel,
Send Thy Messiah forth. The time is come.
Behold the kings of the earth, how they oppress
Thy chosen, to what height their pow'r unjust
They have exalted, and behind them cast
All fear of Thee. Arise, and vindicate[21]
Thy glory, free Thy people from their yoke!
      "But let us wait. Thus far He hath performed,[22]
Sent His anointed,[23] and to us revealed him   50
By His great prophet pointed at and shown
In public, and with him we have conversed.
Let us be glad of this, and all our fears
Lay on His providence.[24] He will not fail,
Nor will withdraw him[25] now, nor will recall—
Mock us with his blest sight, then snatch him hence.
Soon we shall see our hope, our joy, return."
      Thus they out of their plaints new hope resume
To find whom at the first they found unsought.

---

[18] laments, complaints
[19] carried/swept away
[20] withdraw, disappear
[21] uphold, maintain, justify
[22] completed, brought about, done
[23] consecrated
[24] (1) foreknowledge, beneficent care, (2) divine intervention
[25] Christ

But to his mother Mary, when she saw   60
Others returned from baptism, not her son,
Nor left at Jordan tidings of him none,
Within her breast though calm, her breast though pure,
Motherly cares and fears got head,[26] and raised
Some troubled thoughts, which she in sighs thus clad:
    "Oh what avails me now, that honor high,
To have conceived of God, or that salute,[27]
'Hail, highly favored, among women blest'?
While I to sorrows am no less advanced,[28]
And fears as eminent[29] above the lot   70
Of other women, by the birth I bore—
In such a season born, when scarce a shed
Could be obtained to shelter him or me
From the bleak[30] air. A stable was our warmth,
A manger his, yet soon enforced to fly
Thence into Egypt, till the murd'rous king[31]
Were dead, who sought his life and, missing,[32] filled
With infant blood the streets of Bethlehem.
From Egypt home returned, in Nazareth
Hath been our dwelling many years, his life   80
Private, unactive, calm, contemplative,
Little suspicious to any king. But now,
Full grown to man, acknowledged, as I hear,
By John the Baptist, and in public shown,
Son owned[33] from Heav'n by his Father's voice,
I looked for some great change. To honor? No,
But trouble, as old Simeon[34] plain foretold,
That to the fall and rising he should be
Of many in Israel, and to a sign
Spoken against—that through my very soul   90
A sword shall pierce, this my favored lot,

---

[26] strength
[27] greeting
[28] raised
[29] remarkable
[30] cold
[31] Herod
[32] not found
[33] acknowledged
[34] see Luke 2:34

My exaltation to afflictions high!
Afflicted I may be, it seems, and blest!
I will not argue that, nor will repine.[35]
     "But where delays he now? Some great intent
Conceals him. When twelve years he scarce had seen,
I lost him, but so found as well I saw
He could not lose himself, but went about
His Father's business. What he meant I mused,[36]
Since understand: much more his absence now   100
Thus long to some great purpose he obscures.[37]
But I to wait with patience am inured,
My heart hath been a storehouse long of things
And sayings laid up, portending strange events."
     Thus Mary, pondering oft, and oft to mind
Recalling what remarkably[38] had passed
Since first her salutation[39] heard, with thoughts
Meekly composed awaited the fulfilling,[40]
The while her son, tracing[41] the desert wild,
Sole,[42] but with holiest meditations fed,   110
Into himself descended, and at once
All his great work to come before him set—
How to begin, how to accomplish best
His end[43] of being on earth, and mission high.
For Satan, with sly preface[44] to return,
Had left him vacant,[45] and with speed was gone
Up to the middle region of thick air,
Where all his Potentates in council sat.
There, without sign of boast, or sign of joy,
Solicitous and blank,[46] he thus began: 120
     "Princes, Heav'n's ancient Sons, Ethereal Thrones—

---

[35] murmur, complain
[36] pondered
[37] hides, keeps dark
[38] extraordinarily
[39] heavenly greeting
[40] completion
[41] traversing, traveling, treading
[42] alone
[43] purpose, aim
[44] statement made in a preliminary way, hint
[45] undisturbed
[46] resourceless

Daemonian Spirits now, from the element
Each of his reign allotted, rightlier called,
Powers of fire, air, water, and earth beneath
(So may we hold our place and these mild seats
Without new trouble!)—such an enemy
Is ris'n to invade us, who no less
Threat'ns than our expulsion down to Hell.
I, as I undertook, and with the vote
Consenting in full frequence[47] was empowered,   130
Have found him, viewed him, tasted[48] him, but find
Far other labor to be undergone
Than when I dealt with Adam, first of men,
Though Adam by his wife's allurement[49] fell,
However to this man inferior far—
If he be man by mother's side, at least,
With more than human gifts from Heav'n adorned,
Perfections absolute, graces divine,
And amplitude of mind to greatest deeds.
Therefore I am returned, lest confidence   140
Of my success with Eve in Paradise
Deceive ye to persuasion over-sure
Of like[50] succeeding here. I summon all
Rather to be in readiness with hand
Or counsel to assist, lest I, who erst
Thought none my equal, now be overmatched."
            So spoke the old serpent, doubting, and from all
With clamor was assured their utmost aid
At his command, when from amidst them rose
Belial, the dissolutest Spirit that fell,   150
The sensualest, and after Asmodai[51]
The fleshliest incubus,[52] and thus advised:
            "Set women in his eye and in his walk,
Among daughters of men the fairest found.

---

[47] assembly
[48] examined, tested
[49] enticement
[50] similar
[51] a "womanizing" demon: Asmodeus in *Paradise Lost*, Book 4, line 146, and Asmodai in *Paradise Lost*, Book 6, line 365
[52] demonic womanizer/seducer, who usually descended upon sleeping women

Many are in each region passing[53] fair
As the noon sky, more like to goddesses
Than mortal creatures, graceful and discreet,[54]
Expert in amorous arts, enchanting tongues
Persuasive, virgin majesty with mild
And sweet allayed,[55] yet terrible[56] to approach,   160
Skilled to retire, and in retiring draw
Hearts after them tangled in amorous nets.
Such object hath the power to soft'n and tame
Severest temper,[57] smooth the rugged'st brow,
Enerve[58] and with voluptuous hope dissolve,[59]
Draw out with credulous desire, and lead
At will the manliest, resolutest breast,
As the magnetic[60] hardest iron draws.
Women, when nothing else, beguiled the heart
Of wisest Solomon, and made him build   170
And made him bow to the gods of his wives."
          To whom quick answer Satan thus returned:
"Belial, in much uneven[61] scale thou weigh'st
All others by thyself. Because of old
Thou thyself doat'st on[62] womankind, admiring
Their shape, their color,[63] and attractive grace,
None are, thou think'st, but taken with such toys.[64]
Before the Flood, thou with thy lusty crew,
False titled sons of God, roaming the earth,
Cast wanton eyes on the daughters of men,   180
And coupled with them, and begot a race.
Have we not seen, or by relation[65] heard,
In courts and regal chambers how thou lurk'st,

---

[53] surpassing
[54] well-spoken
[55] mixed
[56] dreadful, frightful
[57] temperament
[58] enervate, weaken
[59] bring to nought, destroy
[60] magnet
[61] irregular
[62] dote on = be infatuated with
[63] complexion
[64] dalliance
[65] narration

In wood or grove, by mossy fountain-side,
In valley or green meadow, to waylay
Some beauty rare? Callisto,[66] Glymene,[67]
Daphne,[68] or Semele,[69] Antiopa,[70]
Or Amymone,[71] Syrinx[72]—many more
Too long. Then lay'st thy scapes[73] on names adored,
Apollo, Neptune, Jupiter, or Pan,   190
Satyr, or Faun, or Silvan![74] But these haunts[75]
Delight not all. Among the sons of men
How many have with a smile made small account
Of beauty and her lures, easily scorned
All her assaults, on worthier things intent?
    "Remember that Pellean[76] conqueror,
A youth, how all the beauties of the East
He slightly[77] viewed, and slightly overpassed.
    "How he surnamed of Africa[78] dismissed,[79]
In his prime youth, the fair Iberian maid.[80]   200
    "For Solomon he lived at ease, and full
Of honor, wealth, high fare,[81] aimed not beyond
Higher design[82] than to enjoy his state,[83]
Thence to the bait of women lay exposed.
    "But he whom we attempt is wiser far

---

[66] nymph, attendant on Artemis, twin sister of Apollo [trisyllabic, second accented]
[67] daughter of Oceanus, mother of Atlas [trisyllabic, first and third accented]
[68] nymph-huntress who fled from all would-be lovers [bisyllabic, first accented]
[69] mother of Dionysus, by Zeus [trisyllabic, first and third accented] .
[70] Antiopé, seduced and impregnated by Zeus [four syllables, second and fourth accented]
[71] rescued from a satyr by Poseidon, who then seduced her [four syllables, first and third accented]
[72] nymph pursued by Pan and transformed into a reed to escape him [bisyllabic, first accented]
[73] transgressions, escapades
[74] god of the wild woods
[75] habits, practices
[76] Alexander the Great [trisyllabic, second accented]
[77] carelessly
[78] Scipio Africanus, 236–183 B.C., who triumphed in Spain and in the Second Punic War
[79] sent away
[80] a young Spanish captive to whom, it was said, he had been attracted; she loved someone else
[81] food
[82] intention, plan
[83] (1) condition, (2) greatness, power

Than Solomon, of more exalted mind,
Made and set wholly on the accomplishment
Of greatest things. What woman will you find,
Though of this age the wonder and the fame,
On whom his leisure[84] will vouchsafe an eye   210
Of fond[85] desire? Or should she, confident
As sitting queen adored on beauty's throne,
Descend with all her winning charms begirt[86]
To enamor, as the zone[87] of Venus once
Wrought that effect on Jove (so fables tell),[88]
How would one look from his majestic brow[89]
(Seated as on the top of virtue's hill)
Discount'nance[90] her despised, and put to rout
All her array, her female pride deject,[91]
Or turn to reverent awe? For beauty stands   - 220
In th' admiration only of weak minds
Led captive. Cease to admire, and all her plumes[92]
Fall flat and shrink into a trivial toy,[93]
At every sudden slighting[94] quite abashed.[95]
        "Therefore with manlier objects we must try
His constancy—with such as have more show
Of worth, of honor, glory, and popular praise
(Rocks whereon greatest men have oftest wrecked),
Or that which only seems to satisfy
Lawful desires of nature, not beyond.   230
And now I know he hungers,[96] where no food
Is to be found, in the wide wilderness.
The rest commit to me. I shall let pass
No advantage, and his strength as oft assay."

---

[84] deliberation
[85] foolish, insipid
[86] encompassed
[87] girdle/belt
[88] see Homer's *Iliad*, 14:214–18
[89] i.e., "how one look from his majestic brow (seated as on the top of virtue's hill)
would . . ."
[90] shame, disapprove
[91] dejected
[92] ostentatious ornament not necessarily composed of, but resembling, feathers
[93] whim, caprice
[94] display of disregard
[95] confused, destroyed
[96] is starving

He ceased, and heard their grant[97] in loud acclaim,
Then forthwith to him takes a chosen band
Of Spirits likest to himself in guile,
To be at hand and at his beck[98] appear
If cause were[99] to unfold some active[100] scene
Of various persons, each to know his part,   240
Then to the desert takes with these his flight,
Where still, from shade to shade, the Son of God,
After forty days' fasting, had remained,
Now hung'ring first,[101] and to himself thus said:
    "Where will this end? Four times ten days I have
        passed,
Wand'ring this woody maze, and human food
Nor tasted, nor had appetite. That fast
To virtue I impute[102] not, or count part
Of what I suffer here. If Nature need not,
Or God support Nature without repast,   250
Though needing, what praise is it to endure?
But now I feel I hunger, which declares
Nature hath need of what she asks. Yet God
Can satisfy that need some other way,
Though hunger still remain. So[103] it remain
Without this body's wasting, I content me,
And from the sting of famine[104] fear no harm,
Nor mind it, fed with better thoughts, that feed
Me hung'ring more to do my Father's will."
    It was the hour of night, when thus the Son   260
Communed[105] in silent walk, then laid him down
Under the hospitable covert nigh
Of trees thick interwoven. There he slept,
And dreamed, as appetite is wont to dream,
Of meats and drinks, Nature's refreshment sweet.

---

[97] consent
[98] signal
[99] "if there were reason (cause)"
[100] energetic
[101] for the first time
[102] ascribe/attribute to
[103] as long as
[104] extreme hunger, starvation
[105] held intimate mental intercourse

Him thought he by the brook of Cherith[106] stood,
And saw the ravens with their horny beaks
Food to Elijah bringing, even and morn,
Though ravenous, taught t' abstain from what they brought.
He saw the prophet also, how he fled					270
Into the desert, and how there he slept
Under a juniper, then how, awaked,
He found his supper on the coals prepared,
And by the Angel was bid rise and eat,
And ate the second time after repose,
The strength whereof sufficed him forty days.
Sometimes that with Elijah he partook,[107]
Or as a guest with Daniel at his pulse.[108]
		Thus wore out night; and now the herald lark
Left his ground-nest, high tow'ring to descry					280
The morn's approach, and greet her with his song.
As lightly from his grassy couch up rose
Our Savior, and found all was but a dream:
Fasting he went to sleep, and fasting waked.
Up to a hill anon[109] his steps he reared,[110]
From whose high top to ken[111] the prospect[112] round,
If cottage were in view, sheep-cote,[113] or herd.
But cottage, herd, or sheep-cote none he saw,
Only in a bottom[114] saw a pleasant grove,
With chant[115] of tuneful birds resounding loud.					290
Thither he bent his way, determined there
To rest at noon, and entered soon the shade
High-roofed, and walks beneath, and alleys[116] brown,
That opened[117] in the midst a[118] woody scene.

---

[106] where God directed Elijah to hide from King Ahab: see 1 Kings 17:2–3
[107] i.e., in his dream
[108] lentils, peas, beans ("plain/simple food")
[109] at once
[110] lifted (went up)
[111] have knowledge of
[112] view, landscape
[113] shed, stall
[114] hollow, valley
[115] singing
[116] walks, passageways
[117] spread out
[118] of a

Nature's own work it seemed (Nature taught[119] art),
And, to a superstitious eye, the haunt
Of wood-gods and wood-nymphs. He viewed it round—
When suddenly a man before him stood,
Not rustic as before, but seemlier[120] clad,
As one in city or court or palace bred,   300
And with fair speech these words to him addressed:
          "With granted leave officious[121] I return,
But much more wonder that the Son of God
In this wild solitude so long should bide,[122]
Of all things destitute and, well I know,
Not without hunger. Others of some note,
As story tells, have trod this wilderness:
The fugitive bond-woman,[123] with her son,
Outcast Nebaioth,[124] yet found here relief
By a providing Angel. All the race   310
Of Israel here had[125] famished, had not God
Rained from Heav'n manna. And that prophet bold,
Native of Thebez,[126] wand'ring here, was fed
Twice by a voice inviting him to eat.
Of thee those forty days none hath regard,
Forty and more deserted here indeed."
          To whom thus Jesus:

                              "What conclud'st thou
          hence?
They all had need. I, as thou see'st, have none."
          "How hast thou hunger then?" Satan replied.
"Tell me, if food were now before thee set,   320
Would'st thou not eat?"

                              "Thereafter as[127] I like[128]
The giver," answered Jesus.

                              "Why should that

---

[119] having been taught
[120] more decorously
[121] dutifully
[122] remain, wait, continue
[123] Hagar: see Genesis 21:14–19
[124] her son was Ishmael, whose son was Nebaioth: see Genesis 25:12–13
[125] would have
[126] Elijah
[127] thereafter as = according to how
[128] approve of

Cause thy refusal?" said the subtle fiend.
"Hast thou not right to all created things?
Owe not all creatures, by just right, to thee
Duty and service, nor to stay till bid,
But tender[129] all their power?[130] Nor mention I
Meats by the law unclean, or offered first
To idols—those young Daniel[131] could refuse.
Nor proffered by an enemy—though who   330
Would scruple[132] that, with want[133] oppressed? Behold!
Nature ashamed (or, better to express,
Troubled) that thou shouldst hunger, hath purveyed[134]
From all the elements her choicest store,
To treat thee as beseems, and as her Lord
With honor. Only deign to sit and eat."

      He spoke no dream, for as his words had end
Our Savior, lifting up his eyes, beheld
In ample space under the broadest shade
A table richly spread in regal mode,   340
With dishes piled and meats of noblest sort
And savor,[135] beasts of chase, or fowl of game,
In pastry built,[136] or from the spit, or boiled,
Grisamber[137]-steamed—all fish, from sea or shore,
Freshet[138] or purling[139] brook, of shell or fin,
And exquisitest name,[140] for which was drained
Pontus,[141] and Lucrine Bay,[142] and Afric coast.
Alas! how simple,[143] to these cates[144] compared,

---

129 offer, present
130 vigor, energy, capacity
131 see Daniel 1:8–16
132 hesitate, be reluctant
133 need
134 supplied, furnished
135 taste, quality
136 framed (contained)
137 ambergris, at one time used in cooking
138 small freshwater stream
139 flowing
140 reputation
141 the Black Sea
142 near Naples
143 plain, low
144 dainties

Was that crude apple that diverted[145] Eve!
And at a stately[146] sideboard,[147] by the wine   350
That fragrant smell diffused,[148] in order stood
Tall stripling[149] youths rich-clad, of fairer hue
Than Ganymede[150] or Hylas.[151] Distant more,
Under the trees now[152] tripped,[153] now solemn stood[154]
Nymphs of Diana's train, and Naiades
With fruits and flowers from Amalthea's horn,[155]
And ladies of the Hesperides,[156] that seemed
Fairer than feigned[157] of old, or fabled since
Of fairy damsels met in forest wide
By knights of Logres,[158] or of Lyonesse,[159]   360
Lancelot, or Pelléas, or Pellenore.[160]
And all the while harmonious airs were heard
Of chiming[161] strings or charming pipes, and winds
Of gentlest gale[162] Arabian odors fanned
From their soft wings, and Flora's[163] earliest smells.
Such was the splendor. And the Tempter now
His invitation earnestly renewed:
          "What doubts[164] the Son of God to sit and eat?
These are not fruits forbidd'n. No interdict[165]

---

[145] deflected, turned aside
[146] splendid, magnificent
[147] tablelike board
[148] spread abroad, poured out
[149] slender
[150] Trojan youth taken by Zeus as his cupbearer
[151] handsome prince carried off by Hercules
[152] now . . . now = first this, then that
[153] danced
[154] stood as if they were
[155] horn of plenty *(corum copiae)*: Amalthea was the all-bountiful goat that suckled infant Zeus
[156] daughters of Night and guardians of the tree that bore golden apples
[157] told, related
[158] middle region of Britain: see Chrétien de Troyes, *Lancelot*
[159] mythical region west of Cornwall, in Britain
[160] knights of King Arthur's court
[161] concordant, harmonizing
[162] a gentle wind, but not so soft as a breeze
[163] goddess of flowers
[164] hesitates, fears [verb]
[165] act of prohibition

Defends[166] the touching of these viands[167] pure.   370
Their taste no knowledge works (at least of evil)
But life preserves, destroys life's enemy,
Hunger, with sweet restorative delight.
All these are Spirits of air, and woods, and springs,
Thy gentle[168] ministers,[169] who come to pay
Thee homage, and acknowledge thee their Lord.
What doubt'st thou, Son of God? Sit down and eat."
                To whom thus Jesus temperately[170] replied:
"Said'st thou not that to all things I had right?
And who withholds my pow'r that right to use?   380
Shall I receive by gift what of my own,
When and where likes me best, I can command?
I can at will, doubt not, as soon as thou,
Command a table in this wilderness,
And call swift flights of Angels ministrant,
Arrayed in glory, on my cup t' attend.
Why should'st thou, then, obtrude[171] this diligence[172]
In vain, where no acceptance it can find?
And with my hunger what hast thou to do?
Thy pompous[173] delicacies[174] I contemn,[175]   390
And count thy specious[176] gifts no gifts, but guiles."
                To whom thus answered Satan, malcontent:[177]
"That I have also power to give thou see'st.
If of that pow'r I bring thee voluntary
What I might have bestowed on whom I pleased,
And, rather,[178] opportunely[179] in this place
Chose to impart to thy apparent[180] need,

---

[166] prohibits (under Jewish law)
[167] food, sustenance, victuals
[168] courteous, excellent, noble
[169] attendants, servants
[170] moderately, restrainedly
[171] push forward
[172] careful attention
[173] splendid, pretentious
[174] [four syllables, first and third accented]
[175] scorn, disdain
[176] showy
[177] dissatisfied
[178] instead
[179] appropriately
[180] obvious

Why should'st thou not accept it? But I see
What I can do or offer is suspect.
Of these things others quickly will dispose,   400
Whose pains have earned the far-fet[181] spoil."

                                        With that

Both table and provision vanished quite,[182]
With sound of harpies' wings and talons heard.
Only the importune[183] Tempter still remained,
And with these words his temptation pursued:
        "By hunger, that each other creature tames,
Thou art not to be harmed, therefore not moved.
Thy temperance,[184] invincible besides,
For no allurement yields to appetite,
And all thy heart is set on high designs,   410
High actions. But wherewith to be achieved?
Great acts require great means of enterprise.[185]
Thou art unknown, unfriended, low of birth,
A carpenter thy father known, thyself
Bred up in poverty and straits[186] at home,
Lost in a desert here and hunger-bit.
Which way, or from what hope, dost thou aspire
To greatness? Whence authority deriv'st?[187]
What followers, what retinue[188] canst thou gain,
Or[189] at thy heels the dizzy[190] multitude,   420
Longer than thou canst feed them on[191] thy cost?
Money brings honor, friends, conquest, and realms.
What raised Antipater[192] the Edomite,[193]
And his son Herod, placed on Judah's throne

---

[181] fetched-from-afar
[182] completely, entirely
[183] troublesome, persistent
[184] (1) temperament, (2) moderation
[185] management
[186] poor circumstances
[187] draw, obtain
[188] suite, train, company of servants
[189] or keep
[190] foolish, stupid, giddy
[191] at
[192] ruler of Judea, 63–43 B.C., and Herod's father [four syllables, second and fourth accented?]
[193] Semitic tribe located south of the Dead Sea; traditionally, descendants of Esau, son of Isaac and elder twin of Jacob

(Thy throne), but gold, that got him puissant friends?
Therefore, if at great things thou would'st arrive,
Get riches first, get wealth, and treasure heap[194] —
Not difficult, if thou hearken to me.
Riches are mine, fortune is in my hand.
They whom I favor thrive in wealth amain,[195]   430
While virtue, valor, wisdom, sit in want."
          To whom thus Jesus patiently replied:
"Yet wealth without these three[196] is impotent
To gain dominion, or to keep it, gained.[197]
Witness those ancient empires of the earth,
In height of all their flowing wealth dissolved,
But men endued with these[198] have oft attained,
In lowest poverty, to highest deeds:
Gideon,[199] and Jephtha,[200] and the shepherd lad[201]
Whose offspring on the throne of Judah sat   440
So many ages, and shall yet regain
That seat, and reign in Israel without end.
Among the heathen (for throughout the world
To me is not unknown what hath been done,
Worthy of memorial) canst thou not remember
Quintius,[202] Fabricius,[203] Curius,[204] Regulus?[205]
For I esteem those names of men so poor
Who could do mighty things, and could contemn

---

[194] heap up [verb]
[195] exceedingly
[196] virtue, valor, wisdom
[197] once gained
[198] virtue, valor, wisdom
[199] see Judges 6–8
[200] see Judges 11–12
[201] David
[202] Lucius Quinctius Cincinnatus, legendary hero, called from farming in 458 and, for urgent military reasons, made dictator; sixteen days later, having won the war, he resigned as dictator and went back to his farm
[203] Gaius Fabricius Luscinus, consul in the early third century B.C., who refused all bribes, gifts, and favors; after his death, since he left nothing for his daughter's dowry, it was provided by the Senate
[204] Manius Curius Dentatus, also early third century B.C., was a successful general who gave all booty to the Roman republic and then, like Cincinnatus, retired to his farm
[205] Marcus Atilius Regulus, captured in the First Punic War (with Carthage) was paroled on condition he present Carthage's demands to Rome and then return; he advised rejection of Carthage's terms, then returned as he had agreed, and was tortured to death: see Horace, *Odes* 3:5

Riches, though offered from the hand of kings.
And what in me seems wanting[206] but that I   450
May also, in this poverty, as soon
Accomplish what they did, perhaps, and more?
Extol not riches, then, the toil[207] of fools,
The wise man's cumbrance, if not snare, more apt
To slacken virtue and abate[208] her edge[209]
Than prompt her to do aught[210] may merit praise.
What if with like[211] aversion I reject
Riches and realms! Yet not for that[212] a crown,
Golden in show, is but a wreath of thorns—
Brings dangers, troubles, cares, and sleepless nights   460
To him who wears the regal diadem,[213]
When on his shoulders each[214] man's burden lies.
For therein stands[215] the office of a king,
His honor, virtue, merit, and chief praise
That for the public all this weight he bears.
        "Yet he who reigns within himself, and rules[216]
Passions, desires, and fears, is more a king—
Which every wise and virtuous man attains.
And who attains not, ill aspires to rule
Cities of men, or headstrong multitudes,   470
Subject[217] himself to anarchy within,
Or lawless passions in him, which he serves.
But to guide nations in the way of truth
By saving[218] doctrine, and from error lead
To know and, knowing, worship God aright,
Is yet more kingly. This attracts the soul,
Governs the inner man, the nobler part;

---

[206] lacking, missing
[207] snare, trap
[208] diminish
[209] sharpness
[210] anything that
[211] similar
[212] "yet not for that reason is"
[213] crown
[214] every
[215] shows, remains
[216] governs, controls
[217] [adjective, accent on first syllable]
[218] protecting, guarding

That other o'er the body only reigns,
And oft by force, which to a generous[219] mind
So reigning can be no sincere delight.   480
     "Besides, to give a kingdom hath been thought
Greater and nobler done, and to lay down[220]
Far more magnanimous,[221] than to assume.[222]
Riches are needless, then, both for themselves
And for thy reason why they should be sought,
To gain a scepter, oftest better missed."[223]

---

[219] noble
[220] i.e., to give up a kingdom
[221] high-souled, nobly valiant
[222] receive, lay claim to: i.e., nobler to give or refuse than to take a kingdom
[223] to be without, omitted

BOOK III

So spoke the Son of God, and Satan stood
A while as mute, confounded[1] what to say,
What to reply, confuted[2] and convinced[3]
Of his weak arguing and fallacious[4] drift.[5]
At length, collecting[6] all his serpent wiles,
With soothing words renewed, him[7] thus accosts:
    "I see thou know'st what is of use to know,
What best to say canst say, to do canst do.
Thy actions to thy words accord, thy words
To thy large heart give utterance due: thy heart   10
Contains of good, wise, just, the perfect shape.
Should kings and nations from thy mouth consult[8]
Thy counsel would be as the oracle
Urim and Thummim,[9] those oraculous gems
On Aaron's breast, or tongue of seers[10] old
Infallible. Or wert thou sought to deeds
That might require the array[11] of war, thy skill
Of conduct would be such that all the world
Could not sustain thy prowess, or subsist[12]
In battle, though against thy few in arms.[12A]   20
    "These godlike virtues wherefore dost thou hide?
Affecting[13] private life, or more obscure
In savage wilderness, wherefore deprive
All earth her wonder at thy acts, thyself
The fame and glory—glory, the reward
That sole excites to high attempts the flame

---

[1] confused, perplexed
[2] (1) proven wrong, (2) futile
[3] (1) convicted, (2) vanquished, overcome
[4] flawed, unsound
[5] direction
[6] summoning up, regaining control of
[7] Christ
[8] ask advice/counsel of
[9] see Leviticus 8:8: sacred means of divination attached to (not necessarily set into) the high priest's breastplate, though exactly what the Urim and Thummim were (both words = grammatically plural) is not known
[10] [bisyllabic]
[11] special preparation/readiness
[12] stand firm, hold out
[12A] i.e., though there are many fighting "against thy few in arms"
[13] professing

Of most erected[14] spirits, most tempered[15] pure
Ethereal, who all pleasures else despise,
All treasures and all gain esteem as dross,
And dignities and powers, all but the highest?   30
Thy years are ripe, and over-ripe. The son
Of Macedonian Philip[16] had ere these
Won Asia, and the throne of Cyrus[17] held
At his dispose. Young Scipio had brought down
The Carthaginian pride;[18] young Pompey quelled
The Pontic king,[19] and in triumph had rode.
Yet years, and to ripe years judgment mature,
Quench not the thirst of glory, but augment.
Great Julius,[20] whom now all the world admires,
The more he grew in years, the more inflamed   40
With glory, wept that he had lived so long
Inglorious. But thou yet art not too late."
      To whom our Savior calmly thus replied:
"Thou neither dost persuade me to seek wealth
For empire's sake, nor empire to affect[21]
For glory's sake, by all thy argument.
For what is glory but the blaze[22] of fame,
The people's praise—if always praise unmixed?
And what[23] the people but a herd confused,
A miscellaneous rabble,[24] who extol   50
Things vulgar and, well weighed,[25] scarce worth the praise?
They praise and they admire they know not what,
And know not whom, but as one leads the other.
And what delight to be by such extolled,
To live upon their tongues, and be their talk?

---

[14] upright, uplifted, exalted
[15] having been brought to the temperament/state of mind
[16] Alexander the Great
[17] kingdom of Persia, founded by Cyrus and overthrown by Alexander at Arbela in 331 B.C.
[18] in Spain, when Scipio was probably less than thirty years old
[19] Mithradates—though by then (66 B.C.) Pompey had reached the age of forty
[20] Julius Caesar
[21] seek
[22] splendid display
[23] what are
[24] swarm
[25] valued

Of whom to be dispraised were no small praise—
His lot who dares be singularly[26] good.
Th' intelligent among them and the wise
Are few, and glory scarce of few is raised.[27]
This is true glory and renown—when God,   60
Looking on the earth, with approbation marks
The just man, and divulges[28] him through Heav'n
To all His Angels, who with true applause
Recount his praises. Thus He did to Job,
When to extend his fame through Heav'n and earth
(As thou to thy reproach may'st well remember)
He asked thee, 'Hast thou seen my servant Job?'
Famous he was in Heav'n; on earth less known,
Where glory is false glory, attributed
To things not glorious, men not worthy of fame.   70
      "They err who count it glorious to subdue
By conquest far and wide, to overrun
Large countries, and in field great battles win,
Great cities by assault. What do these worthies
But rob and spoil, burn, slaughter, and enslave
Peaceable nations, neighboring or remote?
Made captive, yet deserving freedom more
Than those their conquerors, who leave behind
Nothing but ruin wheresoe'er they rove,
And all the flourishing works of peace destroy,   80
Then swell with pride, and must be titled gods,
Great benefactors of mankind, deliverers,
Worshipped with temple, priest, and sacrifice!
One is the son of Jove,[29] of Mars[30] the other,
Till conqueror Death discover[31] them scarce men,
Rolling in brutish vices, and deformed,[32]
Violent or shameful Death their due reward.
      "But if there be in glory aught of good,
It may by means far different be attained,

---

[26] separately, individually
[27] produced
[28] declares
[29] Alexander the Great was so identified
[30] Romulus was so identified
[31] reveal, show
[32] morally ugly/perverted

Without ambition, war, or violence—   90
By deeds of peace, by wisdom eminent,
By patience, temperance. I mention still
Him whom thy wrongs with saintly patience borne,
Made famous in a land and times obscure:
Who names not now with honor patient Job?
Poor Socrates (who next more memorable?)
By what he taught and suffered for so doing,
For truth's sake suffering death unjust, lives now
Equal in fame to proudest conquerors.
Yet if for fame and glory aught be done,   100
Aught suffered—if young African[33] for fame
His wasted country freed from Punic[34] rage—
The deed becomes unpraised, the man at least,
And loses, though but verbal, his reward.
Shall I seek glory, then, as vain men seek,
Oft not deserved? I seek not mine, but His
Who sent me, and thereby witness[35] whence I am."[36]
         To whom the Tempter, murmuring, thus replied:
"Think not so slight of glory, therein least
Resembling thy great Father. He seeks glory,   110
And for His glory all things made, all things
Orders and governs, nor content in Heav'n,
By all His Angels glorified, requires
Glory from men, from all men, good or bad,
Wise or unwise, no difference, no exemption.
Above all sacrifice, or hallowed gift,
Glory He requires, and glory He receives,
Promiscuous[37] from all nations, Jew, or Greek,
Or barbarous, nor exception hath declared.
From us, His foes pronounced, glory He exacts."   120
         To whom our Savior fervently replied:
"And reason,[38] since His Word all things produced,
Though chiefly not for glory as prime end,
But to show forth His goodness, and impart

---

[33] Scipio Africanus
[34] Carthaginian
[35] prove
[36] am from, came
[37] en masse, without distinction
[38] i.e., and with reason

His good communicable to every soul
Freely. Of whom what could He less expect
Than glory and benediction[39]—that is, thanks—
The slightest, easiest, readiest recompense
From them who could return Him nothing else?
And not returning that, would likeliest render   130
Contempt instead, dishonour, obloquy?
Hard recompense, unsuitable return
For so much good, so much beneficence!

  "But why should man seek glory, who of his own
Hath nothing, and to whom nothing belongs
But condemnation, ignominy, and shame?
Who for so many benefits received
Turned recreant[40] to God, ingrate and false,
And so of all true good himself despoiled,[41]
Yet sacrilegious, to himself would take   140
That which to God alone of right belongs?
Yet so much bounty[42] is in God, such grace,
That who advances His glory, not their own,
Them He Himself to glory will advance."

  So spoke the Son of God, and here again
Satan had not to answer, but stood struck
With guilt of his own sin—for he himself,
Insatiable of glory, had lost all.
Yet of another plea bethought him soon:

  "Of glory, as thou wilt," said he, "so deem,   150
Worth or not worth the seeking. Let it pass.
But to a kingdom thou art born—ordained
To sit upon thy father David's throne,
By mother's side thy father, though thy right
Be now in powerful hands that will not part
Easily from possession won with arms.
Judaea now, and all the promised land
Reduced a province under Roman yoke,
Obeys Tiberius,[43] nor is always ruled

---

[39] thankful blessing
[40] false
[41] stripped
[42] goodness, kindness
[43] Roman emperor, A.D. 14–37

With temperate sway. Oft have they violated   160
The Temple, oft the Law, with foul affronts,
Abominations rather, as did once
Antiochus.[44] And think'st thou to regain
Thy right by sitting still, or thus retiring?
So did not Machabeus.[45] He indeed
Retired unto the desert, but with arms,
And o'er a mighty king so oft prevailed
That by strong hand his family obtained,
Though priests, the crown, and David's throne usurped,
With Modin and her suburbs once content.   170
    "If kingdom move thee not, let move thee zeal
And duty. Zeal and duty are not slow,
But on occasion's[46] forelock watchful wait.
They themselves, rather, are occasion best,
Zeal of thy Father's house, duty to free
Thy country from her heathen servitude.
So shalt thou best fulfill, best verify,
The prophets old, who sung thy endless reign—
The happier reign the sooner it begins.
Reign then. What canst thou better do the while?"   180
    To whom our Savior answer thus returned:
"All things are best fulfilled in their due time,
And time there is for all things, truth hath said.
If of my reign prophetic writ hath told
That it shall never end, so when begin
The Father in His purpose hath decreed,
He in whose hand all times and seasons roll.
What if He hath decreed that I shall first
Be tried in humble state, and things adverse,
By tribulations, injuries, insults,   190
Contempts, and scorns, and snares, and violence,
Suffering, abstaining, quietly expecting
Without distrust or doubt, that He may know
What I can suffer, how obey? Who best
Can suffer, best can do, best reign who first

---

[44] He caused the Hasmonean uprising by plundering Temple treasures, desecrating the altar, and more
[45] Judah Maccabeus, who led the Hasmonean uprising; he was born in Modin
[46] opportunity's

Well hath obeyed—just trial ere I merit
My exaltation without change or end.
　　　　"But what concerns it thee when I begin
My everlasting kingdom? Why art thou
Solicitous? What moves thy inquisition?　　　　　　　　　200
Know'st thou not that my rising is thy fall,
And my promotion will be thy destruction?"
　　　　To whom the Tempter, inly racked,[47] replied:
"Let that come when it comes. All hope is lost
Of my reception into grace. What worse?
For where no hope is left, is left no fear.
If there be worse, the expectation more
Of worse torments me than the feeling can.
I would be at the worst. Worst is my port,
My harbor, and my ultimate repose,　　　　　　　　　210
The end I would attain, my final good.
My error was my error, and my crime
My crime, whatever for itself condemned,
And will alike be punished whether thou
Reign or reign not—though to that gentle brow
Willingly I could fly, and hope thy reign,
From that placid[48] aspect and meek regard,
Rather than aggravate my evil state
Would stand between me and thy Father's ire
(Whose ire I dread more than the fire of Hell),　　　　220
A shelter and a kind of shading cool
Interposition,[49] as a summer's cloud.
　　　　"If I, then, to the worst that can be haste,
Why move thy feet so slow to what is best?
Happiest, both to thyself and all the world
That thou, who worthiest art, should'st be their king!
Perhaps thou linger'st in deep thoughts detained
Of the enterprise so hazardous and high!
No wonder, for though in thee be united
What of perfection can in man be found,　　　　　　　230
Or human nature can receive, consider
Thy life hath yet been private, most part spent

---

[47] tortured
[48] peaceful
[49] intervention, mediation

At home, scarce viewed the Galilean towns,
And once a year Jerusalem, few days'
Short sojourn—and what thence could'st thou observe?
The world thou hast not seen, much less her glory,
Empires, and monarchs, and their radiant courts,
Best school of best experience, quickest in sight
In all things that to greatest actions lead.
The wisest, unexperienced, will be ever   240
Timorous, and loath, with novice modesty
(As he who, seeking asses, found a kingdom),[50]
Irresolute, unhardy, unadvent'rous.
But I will bring thee where thou soon shalt quit[51]
Those rudiments,[52] and see before thine eyes
The monarchies of th' earth, their pomp and state,
Sufficient introduction to inform
Thee, of thyself so apt, in regal arts
And regal mysteries, that thou may'st know
How best their opposition to withstand."   250
         With that (such power was giv'n him then), he took
The Son of God up to a mountain high.
It was a mountain at whose verdant feet
A spacious plain, outstretched in circuit wide,
Lay pleasant. From his[53] side two rivers[54] flowed,
The one winding, th' other straight, and left between
Fair champaign,[55] with less[56] rivers interveined,
Then meeting joined their tribute to the sea.
Fertile of corn[57] the glebe,[58] of oil, and wine;
With herds the pasture thronged, with flocks the hills;   260
Huge cities and high-tower'd, that well might seem
The seats of mightiest monarchs; and so large
The prospect[59] was that here and there was room

---

[50] Saul: see 1 Samuel 9ff.
[51] leave, give up
[52] beginnings
[53] i.e., the mountain's
[54] the Tigris and the Euphrates
[55] open, level country
[56] lesser, smaller
[57] grain
[58] soil
[59] view

For barren desert, fountainless[60] and dry.
To this high mountain-top the Tempter brought
Our Savior, and new train of words began:
            "Well have we speeded,[61] and o'er hill and dale,
Forest, and field and flood, temples and towers,
Cut shorter many a league. Here thou behold'st
Assyria, and her empire's ancient bounds,   270
Araxes[62] and the Caspian lake. Thence on
As far as Indus east, Euphrates west,
And oft beyond. To south the Persian Bay,
And, inaccessible,[63] th' Arabian drought.[64]
Here Nineveh,[65] of length within her walls
Several days' journey, built by Ninus[66] old,
Of that first golden monarchy the seat,
And seat of Salmanassar,[67] whose success[68]
Israel in long captivity still mourns.
There Babylon,[69] the wonder of all tongues,   280
As[70] ancient, but rebuilt by him[71] who twice
Judah and all thy father David's house
Led captive, and Jerusalem laid waste,
Till Cyrus[72] set them free. Persepolis,[73]
His city, there thou see'st, and Bactra[74] there.
Ecbatana[75] her structure vast there shows,
And Hecatompylos[76] her hundred gates.

---

[60] without springs or headsprings (sources of rivers)
[61] (1) hastened, (2) gotten where we wanted to go
[62] Armenian river, flowing into the Caspian Sea
[63] unapproachable
[64] desert
[65] capital city of Assyrian empire after about 1100 B.C.
[66] king of Assyria, husband of Semiramis
[67] king of Assyria, d. 722 B.C.
[68] in 726 B.C.
[69] immense city on the Euphrates
[70] just as
[71] Nebuchadnezzar, king of Babylonia, 605–562 B.C.
[72] king of Persia: Cyrus captured Babylon in 538 B.C. and released the captive Jews
[73] in southern Persia: residence and burial place of Cyrus, Darius, Xerxes, etc.
[74] northeast of Persepolis, ancient capital of Bactria, now in Afghanistan
[75] summer residence of Darius
[76] Parthian capital, southeast of the Caspian Sea [five syllables, first, third, and fifth accented]

There Susa[77] by Choaspes,[78] amber stream,
The drink of none but kings. Of later fame,
Built by Emathian[79] or by Parthian[80] hands,   290
The great Seleucia,[81] Nisibis,[82] and there
Artaxata,[83] Teredon,[84] Ctesiphon,[85]
Turning with easy eye, thou may'st behold.
    "All these the Parthian (now some ages past
By great Arsaces[86] led, who founded first
That empire) under his dominion holds,
From the luxurious[87] kings of Antioch[88] won.
And just in time thou com'st to have a view
Of his great power, for now the Parthian king
In Ctesiphon hath gathered all his host   300
Against the Scythian,[89] whose incursions wild
Have wasted Sogdiana.[90] To her aid
He marches now in haste. See, though from far,
His thousands, in what martial equipage
They issue forth, steel bows and shafts their arms,
Of equal dread[91] in flight or in pursuit—
All horsemen, in which fight they most excel.
See how in warlike muster they appear,
In rhombs,[92] and wedges,[93] and half-moons[94] and wings."
      He[95] looked, and saw what numbers numberless   310

---

[77] Shushan, city at northwestern tip of Persian Gulf, capital of Susiana/Elam and later of Persia

[78] river east of Tigris, flowing through Susa/Shushan

[79] Macedonian

[80] seminomadic culture in western Asia, famous for bow-wielding cavalry

[81] capital of Selucid empire, founded by Seleucus I Nicator; located on the Tigris

[82] city in northwestern Mesopotamia, south of the Tigris

[83] city in Armenia, southeast of the Black Sea; located on the Araxes River

[84] town at northeastern end of Persian Gulf, near the juncture of the Tigris and the Euphrates

[85] city on the Tigris, near Seleucia [trisyllabic, first and third accented; first letter silent]

[86] founder of Parthian empire, ca. 248 B.C.

[87] (1) extravagant, (2) unchaste, lewd

[88] city on the Orontes River, capital of Syria

[89] fierce "barbarian" people living north and east of the Black and Caspian Seas

[90] region northeast of Parthia

[91] fearsomeness

[92] lozenge/diamond-shaped military formation

[93] half-rhomb military formation

[94] i.e., with most of the army concentrated in the center

[95] Christ

The city gates outpoured, light-armèd troops
In coats of mail and military pride.[96]
In mail their horses clad, yet fleet[97] and strong,
Prancing their riders bore, the flower and choice
Of many provinces from bound[98] to bound,
From Arachosia,[99] from Candaor[100] east,
And Margiana,[101] to the Hyrcanian[102] cliffs
Of Caucasus, and dark Iberian[103] dales—
From Atropatia,[104] and the neighboring plains
Of Adiabeen,[105] Media,[106] and the south   320
Of Susiana[107] to Balsara's[108] hav'n.[109]
He saw them in their forms of battle ranged,
How quick they wheeled, and flying behind them shot
Sharp sleet of arrowy showers against the face
Of their pursuers, and overcame by flight.
The field all iron cast a gleaming brown,
Nor wanted[110] clouds of foot,[111] nor on each horn[112]
Cuirassiers[113] all in steel for standing fight,
Chariots, or elephants endorsed[114] with towers
Of archers, nor of laboring pioneers[115]   330
A multitude, with spades and axes armed,
To lay hills plain,[116] fell woods, or valleys fill,
Or where plain was, raise hill, or overlay

---

[96] splendor, pomp, display
[97] swift
[98] border
[99] eastern Parthia, a region west of the Indus River
[100] Kandahar, in modern Afghanistan
[101] northern Parthia, between Bactria and Parthia
[102] Hyrcania: province of ancient Persian empire, southeast of the Caspian Sea
[103] region in the Caucasus, *not* Spain
[104] Media-Atropatenia, west of Parthia, between the Caspian Sea and Armenia
[105] near Nineveh, south of Armenia, on the Tigris: part of Assyria
[106] see footnote 104, above
[107] southeastern Persia: Susa was its capital
[108] Basra, north of Persian Gulf, south of Suṣa
[109] port, harbor
[110] lacked
[111] foot soldiers
[112] an army had two horns/wings
[113] soldiers in armor
[114] loaded
[115] soldier-diggers
[116] flat, level, smooth, even

With bridges rivers proud, as with a yoke.
Mules after these, camels and dromedaries,[117]
And wagons fraught[118] with utensils of war.
Such forces met not, nor so wide a camp,
When Agrican[119] with all his northern powers
Besieged Albracca,[120] as romances tell,
The city of Gallaphrone, from thence to win   340
The fairest of her sex, Angelica,
His daughter, sought by many prowest[121] knights,
Both paynim[122] and the peers[123] of Charlemagne.
Such and so numerous was their chivalry,
At sight whereof the fiend yet more presumed,[124]
And to our Savior thus his words renewed:
        "That thou may'st know I seek not to engage[125]
Thy virtue, and not every way secure[126]
On no slight[127] grounds thy safety, hear and mark[128]
To what end I have brought thee hither, and show   350
All this fair sight. Thy kingdom, though foretold
By prophet or by Angel, unless thou
Endeavor, as thy father[129] David did,
Thou never shalt obtain. Prediction still
In all things, and all men, supposes means;
Without means used, what it predicts revokes.
But say thou wert possessed of David's throne
By free consent of all, none opposite,
Samaritan[130] or Jew, how could'st thou hope
Long to enjoy it quiet and secure   360
Between two such enclosing enemies,

---

[117] one-humped swift camels
[118] filled
[119] Tatar king in Boiardo's romance *Orlando Innamorato* ("Roland in Love")
[120] fortress of King Gallophrone, Angelica's father
[121] bravest, most chivalric
[122] pagan
[123] high nobles
[124] pressed forward
[125] win over
[126] make secure/safe [verb]
[127] contemptible, small
[128] note
[129] progenitor, ancestor
[130] descendants of the tribes of Ephraim and Manasseh, religiously and politically at odds with the Jews

Roman and Parthian? Therefore one of these
Thou must make sure thy own. The Parthian first,
By my advice, as nearer, and of late
Found able by invasion to annoy[131]
Thy country, and captive lead away her kings,
Antigonus,[132] and old Hyracanus—bound,
Maugre[133] the Roman. It shall be my task
To render thee the Parthian at dispose,
Choose which thou wilt, by conquest or by league.[134]   370
By him thou shalt regain, without him not,
That which alone can truly reinstall thee
In David's royal seat, his true successor—
Deliverance of thy brethren, those Ten Tribes
Whose offspring in his territory yet serve
In Habor,[135] and among the Medes[136] dispersed:
Ten sons of Jacob, two of Joseph,[137] lost
Thus long from Israel, serving as of old
Their fathers in the land of Egypt served,
This offer sets before thee to deliver.   380
These if from servitude thou shalt restore
To their inheritance, then, nor till then,
Thou on the throne of David in full glory,
From Egypt to Euphrates and beyond,
Shalt reign, and Rome or Caesar not need fear."
       To whom our Savior answered thus, unmoved:
"Much ostentation vain of fleshly arm
And fragile arms, much instrument of war,
Long in preparing, soon to nothing brought,
Before mine eyes thou hast set, and in my ear   390
Vented much policy,[138] and projects deep
Of enemies, of aids, battles, and leagues,
Plausible[139] to the world, to me worth naught.

---

[131] molest, injure
[132] Hyrcanus II, made king of Judah by Rome; he was attacked by Antigonus; both were abducted by Parthians
[133] in spite of
[134] alliance, treaty
[135] modern Khabar, near the Euphrates: see 2 Kings 17:6, 18:11
[136] inhabitants of Media, in Parthia
[137] i.e., those of Joseph's sons, Ephraim and Manasseh: see note 130, above
[138] political cunning
[139] praiseworthy, fair-seeming

Means I must use, thou say'st. Prediction else
Will unpredict, and fail me of the throne!
My time, I told thee (and that time for thee
Were better farthest off), is not yet come.
When that comes, think not thou to find me slack[140]
On my part aught endeavoring, or to need
Thy politic[141] maxims, or that cumbersome   400
Luggage of war there shown me, argument[142]
Of human weakness rather than of strength.
My brethren, as thou call'st them, those Ten Tribes,
I must deliver, if I mean to reign
David's true heir, and his full scepter sway[143]
To just extent over all Israel's sons!
But whence to thee this zeal? Where was it then
For Israel, or for David, or his throne,
When thou stood'st up[144] his tempter[145] to the pride
Of numbering[146] Israel, which cost the lives   410
Of threescore and ten thousand Israelites
By three days' pestilence? Such was thy zeal
To Israel then, the same that now to me.
          "As for those captive tribes, themselves were they
Who wrought their own captivity, fell off
From God to worship calves, the deities
Of Egypt, Baal next and Ashtaroth,
And all th' idolatries of heathen round,
Besides their other worse than heathenish crimes.
Nor in the land of their captivity   420
Humbled themselves, or penitent besought
The God of their forefathers, but so died
Impenitent, and left a race behind
Like to themselves, distinguishable scarce
From gentiles but[147] by circumcision vain,[148]

---

[140] remiss, negelectful
[141] scheming, crafty
[142] evidence
[143] wield
[144] confronted (him) as
[145] see 1 Chronicles 21:1 ff.
[146] counting, making a census of
[147] except
[148] idle, useless, of no significance/value

And God with idols in their worship joined.
Should I of these the liberty regard[149]
Who, freed, as to their ancient patrimony
Unhumbled, unrepentant, unreformed,
Headlong[150] would follow,[151] and to their gods perhaps   430
Of Bethel and of Dan? No, let them serve
Their enemies who serve idols with God.
Yet He at length, time to Himself best known,
Remembering Abraham, by some wondrous call
May bring them back, repentant and sincere,
And at their passing cleave th' Assyrian flood,
While to their native land with joy they haste,
As the Red Sea and Jordan once He cleft
When to the promised land their fathers passed.
To His due time and providence I leave them."   440
          So spoke Israel's true king, and to the fiend
Made answer meet,[152] that made void all his wiles.
So fares it when with truth falsehood contends.

---

[149] look to, have a care for
[150] with blind speed
[151] go after, pursue
[152] fit, suitable

BOOK IV

    Perplexed and troubled at his bad success
The Tempter stood, nor had what to reply,
Discovered in his fraud, thrown from his hope
So oft, and the persuasive rhetoric
That sleeked[1] his tongue, and won so much on Eve,
So little[2] here—nay lost! But Eve was Eve.
This far his over-match, who self-deceived
And rash, beforehand had no better weighed
The strength he was to cope with, or his own.
But as a man who had been matchless held   10
In cunning, over-reached where least he thought,
To salve[3] his credit, and for very spite,
Still will be tempting him who foils[4] him still,
And never cease, though to his shame the more—
Or as a swarm of flies in vintage-time,
About the wine-press where sweet must[5] is poured,
Beat off, returns as oft with humming sound—
Or surging waves against a solid rock,
Though all to shivers[6] dashed, th' assault renew
(Vain battery![7]) and in froth or bubbles end—   20
So Satan, whom repulse upon repulse
Met ever, and to shameful silence brought,
Yet gives not o'er, though desperate[8] of success,
And his vain importunity pursues.
    He brought our Savior to the western side
Of that high mountain, whence he might behold
Another plain,[9] long, but in breadth not wide,
Washed by the southern sea, and on the north
To equal length backed with a ridge of hills
That screened the fruits of th' earth and seats of men   30
From cold Septentrion[10] blasts, thence in the midst

---

[1] polished
[2] little won
[3] heal, make good
[4] defeats, frustrates
[5] new wine in process
[6] splinters, chips
[7] battering
[8] despairing
[9] central Italy: Tyrrhenian Sea to the south, Apennine Range to the northwest, the plain split by the River Tiber
[10] northern

Divided by a river, off whose banks
On each side an imperial city[11] stood,
With towers and temples proudly elevate
On seven small hills, with palaces adorned,
Porches[12] and theaters,[13] baths, aqueducts,
Statues and trophies,[14] and triumphal arcs,[15]
Gardens and groves, presented to his eyes
Above the height of mountains interposed
(By what strange parallax, or optic skill   40
Of vision, multiplied through air, or glass
Of telescope, were curious[16] to enquire).
And now the Tempter thus his silence broke:
        "The city which thou see'st no other deem
Than great and glorious Rome, queen of the earth
So far renowned, and with the spoils enriched
Of nations. There the capitol[17] thou see'st,
Above the rest lifting his stately[18] head
On the Tarpeian rock,[19] her citadel
Impregnable, and there Mount Palatine,   50
Th' imperial palace, compass[20] huge, and high
The structure, skill of noblest architects,
With gilded battlements, conspicuous[21] far,
Turrets and terraces, and glittering spires.
Many a fair edifice besides, more like
Houses of gods (so well I have disposed[22]
My airy microscope[23]) thou may'st behold,
Outside and inside both, pillars and roofs
Carved work, the hand of famed artificers[24]
In cedar, marble, ivory, or gold.   60

---

[11] Rome
[12] galleries, colonnades
[13] [trisyllabic, first and third accented]
[14] memorial structures, commemorating military success
[15] arches
[16] noteworthy (interesting)
[17] citadel (fortress) built on top of a hill
[18] majestic, dignified
[19] part of the Capitoline Hill
[20] of limits/bounds
[21] visible
[22] adjusted, placed
[23] optical instrument
[24] craftsmen [four syllables, second and fourth accented]

      "Thence to the gates cast round thine eye, and see
What conflux[25] issuing forth, or entering in:
Praetors,[26] proconsuls[27] to their provinces
Hasting, or on return, in robes of state,
Lictors[28] and rods, the ensigns[29] of their power;
Legions and cohorts,[30] turms[31] of horse and wings,
Or embassies from regions far remote,
In various habits,[32] on the Appian road,[33]
Or on the Emilian,[34] some from farthest south,
Syene,[35] and where the shadow both way falls,   70
Meroë,[36] Nilotic isle, and more to west
The realm of Bocchus[37] to the Blackmoor sea.[38]
From th' Asian kings (and Parthian among these),
From India and the golden Chersoness,[39]
And utmost Indian isle, Taprobane,[40]
Dusk faces with white silken turbants[41] wreathed.
From Gallia,[42] Gades,[43] and the British west,
Germans, and Scythians, and Sarmatians[44] north
Beyond Danubius to the Tauric pool.[45]
All nations now to Rome obedience pay,   80
To Rome's great Emperor, whose wide domain,
In ample territory, wealth and power,

---

[25] stream, flowing
[26] magistrates
[27] governors of provinces
[28] attendants carrying bundles of rods with an ax wrapped inside, the blade projecting
[29] symbols
[30] one-tenth of a legion
[31] cavalry: one-tenth of a wing (flank)
[32] garments, dress, clothing
[33] from Rome to Brindisi, seaport in southern Italy
[34] from Rome north to the Adriatic Sea
[35] Aswan, in southern Egypt on the Upper Nile
[36] region in the Upper Nile, considered (but in fact not) an island
[37] North African king, ca. 105 B.C.
[38] i.e., the Mediterranean Sea off the northwest African coast
[39] Chersonese: the Malay Peninsula
[40] Ceylon or Sumatra
[41] turbans
[42] Gaul (now France)
[43] Cadiz
[44] people east of Germany, between the Vistula and the Volga
[45] the Sea of Azov, northeast of and connected to the Black Sea

Civility[46] of manners, arts and arms,
And long renown, thou justly may'st prefer
Before the Parthian. These two thrones except,
The rest are barbarous, and scarce worth the sight,
Shared among petty kings too far removed.[47]
These having shown thee, I have shown thee all
The kingdoms of the world, and all their glory.

      "This Emperor[48] hath no son, and now is old,   90
Old and lascivious, and from Rome retired
To Capri,[49] an island small but strong
On the Campanian[50] shore, with purpose there
His horrid lusts in private to enjoy,
Committing to a wicked favorite[51]
All public cares, and yet of him suspicious—
Hated of all, and hating. With what ease,
Endued with regal virtues as thou art,
Appearing, and beginning noble deeds,
Might'st thou expel this monster from his throne,   100
Now made a sty, and in his place ascending,
A victor-people free[52] from servile yoke!

      "And with my help thou may'st. To me the power
Is giv'n, and by that right I give it thee.
Aim, therefore, at no less than all the world.
Aim at the highest: without the highest attained
Will be for thee no sitting, or not long,
On David's throne, be prophesied what will."

      To whom the Son of God, unmoved, replied:
"Nor doth this grandeur and majestic show   110
Of luxury, though called magnificence,
More than of arms, before, allure mine eye,
Much less my mind, though thou should'st add to tell
Their sumptuous gluttonies, and gorgeous[53] feasts

---

[46] politeness
[47] distant, remote, secluded
[48] Tiberius
[49] island south of Naples
[50] Roman province (Naples, Pompeii, etc.)
[51] Sejanus, finally executed in A.D. 29
[52] [verb]
[53] showy

On citron[54] tables or Atlantic stone[55]
(For I have also heard, perhaps have read),
Their wines of Setia, Cales, and Falerne,[56]
Chios and Crete,[57] and how they quaff in gold,
Crystal, and myrrhine cups embossed with gems
And studs[58] of pearl—to me should'st tell, who thirst   120
And hunger still. Then embassies thou show'st
From nations far and nigh! What honor that?
But tedious waste of time, to sit and hear
So many hollow compliments and lies,
Outlandish[59] flatteries. Then proceed'st to talk
Of the Emperor, how easily subdued,
How gloriously. I shall, thou say'st, expel
A brutish monster. What if I withal
Expel a Devil who first made him such?
Let his tormentor, conscience, find him out.   130
For him I was not sent, nor yet to free
That people, victor once, now vile and base,
Deservedly made vassal—who, once just,
Frugal, and mild, and temperate, conquered well,
But govern ill the nations under yoke,
Peeling[60] their provinces, exhausted all
By lust and rapine—first ambitious grown
Of triumph, that insulting[61] vanity,
Then cruel, by their sports to blood inured
Of fighting beasts, and men to beasts exposed,   140
Luxurious[62] by[63] their wealth, and greedier still,
And from[64] the daily scene[65] effeminate.[66]
What wise and valiant man would seek to free

---

[54] of citrus wood
[55] marble from the Atlas mountains in North Africa
[56] three then-famous Italian wines, from Sezza, near Rome, and Cales and Falernia, near Mt. Vesuvius
[57] two then-famous Greek wines: see Horace, _Odes_ 3:19
[58] ornaments
[59] foreign, bizarre, uncouth
[60] pillaging
[61] (1) arrogant, (2) outrageous
[62] unchaste
[63] because of
[64] because of
[65] (1) theatrical performances, (2) their daily existence
[66] overly refined, soft

These, thus degenerate, by themselves enslaved,
Or could of inward slaves make outward free?
    "Know, therefore, when my season comes to sit
On David's throne, it shall be like a tree
Spreading and overshadowing all the earth,
Or as a stone that shall to pieces dash
All monarchies besides[67] throughout the world,   150
And of my kingdom there shall be no end.
Means there shall be to this, but what the means
Is not for thee to know, nor me to tell."
    To whom the Tempter, impudent,[68] replied:
"I see all offers made by me how slight
Thou valu'st, because offered and reject'st.
Nothing will please the difficult and nice,[69]
Or nothing more than still[70] to contradict.
On th' other side, know also thou that I
On what I offer set as high esteem,   160
Nor what I part with mean to give for naught.
All these, which in a moment thou behold'st,
The kingdoms of the world, to thee I give
(For, giv'n to me, I give to whom I please),
No trifle; yet with this reserve, not else—
On this condition, if thou wilt fall down
And worship me as thy superior Lord
(Easily done), and hold them all of me.
For what can less so great a gift deserve?"
    Whom thus our Savior answered with disdain: 170
"I never liked thy talk, thy offers less,
Now both abhor, since thou hast dared to utter
Th' abominable terms, impious condition.
But I endure[71] the time, till which expired
Thou hast permission[72] on me. It is written,
The first of all commandments, 'Thou shalt worship
The Lord thy God, and only Him shalt serve.'[73]

---

[67] "besides my own"
[68] shameless
[69] fussy, fastidious
[70] always
[71] submit to
[72] liberty, licence
[73] see Exodus 20:2–3, Deuteronomy 6:12–15, and Matthew 4:8–10

And dar'st thou to the Son of God propound[74]
To worship thee, accursed? Now more accursed
For this attempt, bolder than that on Eve,   180
And more blasphemous, which expect to rue.
The kingdoms of the world to thee were giv'n!
Permitted, rather, and by thee usurped.
Other donation[75] none thou canst produce.
If given, by whom but by the King of kings,
God over all supreme? If giv'n to thee,
By thee how fairly is the giver now
Repaid? But gratitude in thee is lost
Long since. Wert thou so void of fear or shame
As offer them to me, the Son of God—   190
To me my own, on such abhorrèd pact,
That I fall down and worship thee as God?
Get thee behind me! Plain thou now appear'st
That Evil One, Satan, forever damned."

    To whom the fiend, with fear abashed, replied:
"Be not so sore offended, Son of God—
Though Sons of God both Angels are and men—
If I, to try[76] whether in higher sort[77]
Than these thou bear'st that title, have proposed
What both from men and Angels I receive,   200
Tetrarchs[78] of fire, air, flood, and on the earth
Nations besides, from all the quartered winds—[79]
God of this world invoked,[80] and world beneath.
Who then thou art, whose coming is foretold
To me so fatal, me it most concerns.
The trial[81] hath endamaged thee no way—
Rather more honor left, and more esteem—
Me naught advantaged, missing what I aimed.
Therefore let pass, as they are transitory,
The kingdoms of this world. I shall no more   210

---

[74] propose
[75] grant, gift
[76] test
[77] state
[78] the lesser rulers
[79] i.e., blowing from the four quarters of the earth
[80] called: that is, Satan is currently called god both of earth and of Hell
[81] test

Advise thee. Gain them as thou canst, or not.
      "And thou thyself seem'st otherwise inclined
Than to a worldly crown, addicted[82] more
To contemplation and profound dispute,
As by that early action may be judged,
When slipping from thy mother's eye, thou went'st
Alone into the Temple. There wast found
Among the gravest[83] rabbis disputant
On points and questions fitting Moses' chair,[84]
Teaching, not taught.[85] The childhood shows the man,   220
As morning shows the day. Be famous, then,
By wisdom. As thy empire must extend,
So let extend thy mind o'er all the world
In knowledge, all things in it comprehend.
All knowledge is not couched[86] in Moses' law,
The Pentateuch,[87] or what the prophets wrote.
The gentiles[88] also know, and write, and teach
To admiration,[89] led by Nature's light,
And with the gentiles much thou must converse,
Ruling them by persuasion, as thou mean'st.   230
Without their learning, how wilt thou with them,
Or they with thee, hold conversation meet?[90]
How wilt thou reason with them, how refute
Their idolisms, traditions, paradoxes?
Error by his own arms[91] is best evinced.[92]
      "Look once more, ere we leave this specular[93] mount,
Westward, much nearer by south-west. Behold
Where on th' Aegean shore a city stands,
Built nobly, pure the air and light the soil—

---

[82] devoted
[83] most authoritative
[84] "Then spake Jesus . . . , saying, The scribes and the Pharisees sit in Moses' seat . . ." Matthew 23:1–2
[85] see Luke 2:42–49
[86] contained
[87] the first five books of the Old Testament
[88] heathen, pagans
[89] to admiration: wonderfully
[90] appropriate [adjective]
[91] weapons
[92] convinced
[93] affording a wide view

Athens, the eye of Greece, mother of arts   240
And eloquence, native to famous wits
Or hospitable,[94] in her sweet recess,[95]
City or suburban, studious walks and shades.
See there the olive-grove of Academe,[96]
Plato's retirement,[97] where the Attic bird[98]
Trills her thick-warbled notes the summer long.
There flow'ry hill, Hymettus,[99] with the sound
Of bees' industrious murmur, oft invites
To studious musing; there Ilissus[100] rolls
His whispering stream. Within the walls then view   250
The schools of ancient sages—his[101] who bred[102]
Great Alexander to subdue the world,
Lyceum[103] there, and painted Stoa[104] next.
There thou shalt hear and learn the secret power
Of harmony, in tones and numbers[105] hit[106]
By voice or hand, and various-measured verse,
Aeolian[107] charms[108] and Dorian[109] lyric odes,
And his who gave them breath, but higher sung,
Blind Melesigenes,[110] thence Homer called,
Whose poem Phoebus[111] challenged[112] for his own.   260
Thence what the lofty grave tragedians taught

---

[94] i.e., either "native" or "hospitable" to those not native
[95] (1) niche, coastal indentation, (2) privacy
[96] public park northwest of Athens
[97] secluded place
[98] nightingale
[99] mountain near Athens
[100] river running from Mt. Hymettus south into the sea
[101] Aristotle
[102] developed, produced (as Alexander's tutor)
[103] park east of Athens
[104] Athenian colonnade, with painted frescoes, where Zeno the Stoic taught
[105] measures, rhythms: the term was used both in music and in poetry
[106] attained
[107] Aeolic: Greek dialect used by Sappho, Alcaeus, and others
[108] songs
[109] (1) the Doric dialect of Greek, (2) the choral lyric poetry written in that dialect (as, e.g., by Pindar, who was himself a speaker of the Boeotian dialect)
[110] "born in/of Meles": the River Meles, in Asia Minor, was one of Homer's supposed birthplaces [five syllables, first, third, and fifth accented]
[111] Apollo
[112] claimed

In chorus or iambic,[113] teachers best
Of moral prudence,[114] with delight received
In brief sententious[115] precepts, while they treat
Of fate, and chance, and change in human life,
High actions and high passions best describing.
Thence to the famous orators repair,[116]
Those ancient whose resistless eloquence
Wielded[117] at will that fierce democraty,
Shook the Arsenal,[118] and fulmined[119] over Greece   270
To Macedon[120] and Artaxerxes'[121] throne.
To sage philosophy next lend thine ear,
From Heav'n descended to the low-roofed house
Of Socrates—see there his tenement,[122]
Whom well inspired the oracle pronounced
Wisest of men, from whose mouth issued forth
Mellifluous[123] streams, that watered all the schools
Of Academics old and new, with those
Surnamed[124] Peripatetics,[125] and the sect
Epicurean,[126] and the Stoic severe.   280
      "These here revolve[127] or, as thou lik'st, at home,
Till time mature thee to a kingdom's weight.
These rules will render thee a king complete
Within thyself, much more with empire joined."
      To whom our Savior sagely thus replied:
"Think not but that I know these things, or think

---

[113] iambic trimeter, used in dramatic scenes
[114] wisdom
[115] full of wisdom
[116] make one's way, go, resort
[117] ruled, commanded, controlled, directed
[118] Athenian harbor building, construction of which was suspended in 339 B.C. because of Demosthenes, 384–322, famous Athenian orator
[119] thundered
[120] region between Balkans and Greece: famous for Philip II and his son, Alexander the Great
[121] Persian king; on Sparta's side in the war against Athens
[122] dwelling
[123] sweetly flowing
[124] given an additional name, title, or epithetic description
[125] Aristotle and his pupils were peripatetic ("walking about")
[126] Epicurus and his followers
[127] consider, meditate upon

I know them not. Not therefore am I short[128]
Of knowing what I ought. He who receives
Light from above, from the Fountain of Light,
No other doctrine needs, though[129] granted[130] true.   290
But these are false, or little else but dreams,
Conjectures, fancies, built on nothing firm.
The first and wisest[131] of them all professed
To know this only, that he nothing knew.
The next[132] to fabling fell and smooth conceits.
A third sort[133] doubted all things, though plain sense.
Others in virtue placed felicity,
But virtue joined with riches and long life.
In corporal pleasure he,[134] and careless ease.
The Stoic last, in philosophic pride   300
(By him called virtue) and his virtuous man,
Wise, perfect in himself, and all possessing
Equal to God, oft shames not to prefer,
As fearing God nor man, contemning[135] all
Wealth, pleasure, pain or torment, death and life—
Which, when he lists,[136] he leaves, or boasts he can,
For all his tedious talk is but vain boast,
Or subtle shifts,[137] conviction to evade.

    "Alas! what can they teach, and not mislead,
Ignorant of themselves, of God much more,   310
And how the world began, and how man fell,
Degraded by himself, on grace depending?
Much of the soul they talk, but all awry,
And in themselves seek virtue, and to themselves
All glory arrogate,[138] to God give none,
Rather accuse Him under usual names,
Fortune and Fate, as one regardless quite

---

[128] inadequate
[129] even if
[130] acknowledged, admitted
[131] Socrates
[132] Plato
[133] Pyrrho, Sceptic founder
[134] Epicurus
[135] disdaining
[136] wishes, desires
[137] stratagems, contrivances
[138] claim, assume

Of mortal things. Who, therefore, seeks in these
True wisdom finds her not, or by delusion
Far worse, her false resemblance only meets,   320
An empty cloud. However many books,
Wise men have said, are wearisome. Who[139] reads
Incessantly, and to his reading brings not
A spirit and judgment equal or superior
(And what he brings what needs he elsewhere seek?),
Uncertain and unsettled still remains,
Deep-versed in books and shallow in himself,
Crude or intoxicate, collecting toys
And trifles for[140] choice[141] matters, worth a sponge,[142]
As[143] children gathering pebbles on the shore.   330
Or if I would delight my private hours
With music or with poem, where so soon
As in our native language[144] can I find
That solace? All our Law and story strewn[145]
With hymns, our Psalms with artful terms inscribed,
Our Hebrew songs and harps, in Babylon
That pleased so well our victor's ear, declare
That rather Greece from us these arts derived—
Ill imitated while they loudest sing
The vices of their deities, and their own,   340
In fable, hymn, or song, so personating[146]
Their gods ridiculous, and themselves past shame.
Remove their swelling epithets, thick-laid
As varnish[147] on a harlot's cheek, the rest,
Thin-sown with aught of profit or delight,
Will far be found unworthy to compare
With Sion's songs, to all true tastes excelling,
Where God is praised aright and godlike men,
The Holiest of Holies and His Saints.

---

[139] whoever
[140] as if they were
[141] select, of special excellence
[142] eraser
[143] like
[144] Hebrew
[145] sprinkled, spread
[146] impersonating, playing the part of
[147] means of adornment/embellishment, veneer, paint

Such are from God inspired, not such from thee,[148] 350
Unless where[149] moral virtue is expressed
By light of Nature, not in all quite lost.
Their orators thou then extoll'st as those
The top of eloquence—statists[150] indeed,
And lovers of their country, as may seem.
But herein to our prophets far beneath,
As men divinely taught, and better teaching
The solid rules of civil government,
In their majestic, unaffected style,
Than all the oratory of Greece and Rome. 360
In them is plainest taught, and easiest learnt,
What makes a nation happy, and keeps it so,
What ruins kingdoms, and lays cities flat.
These only, with our Law, best form a king."
    So spoke the Son of God. But Satan, now
Quite at a loss (for all his darts were spent),[151]
Thus to our Savior, with stern brow, replied:
    "Since neither wealth nor honor, arms nor arts,
Kingdom nor empire, pleases thee, nor aught
By me proposed in life contemplative 370
Or active, tended on by glory or fame,
What dost thou in this world? The wilderness
For thee is fittest place! I found thee there,
And thither will return thee. Yet remember
What I foretell thee. Soon thou shalt have cause
To wish thou never had'st rejected, thus
Nicely[152] or cautiously, my offered aid,
Which would have set thee in short time with ease
On David's throne, or throne of all the world,
Now at full age, fulness of time, thy season, 380
When prophecies of thee are best fulfilled.
Now, contrary, if I read aught in Heav'n,
Or Heav'n write aught of Fate, by what the stars
Voluminous,[153] or single characters

---

[148] Satan
[149] in those cases where
[150] politicians
[151] used up, exhausted
[152] fussily
[153] massive, copious

In their conjunction met, give me to spell,[154]
Sorrows and labors, opposition, hate,
Attends thee, scorns, reproaches, injuries,
Violence and stripes[155] and, lastly, cruel death.
A kingdom they portend[156] thee, but what kingdom,
Real or allegoric, I discern[157] not,   390
Nor when: Eternal sure—as without end,
Without beginning, for no date prefixed
Directs[158] me in the starry rubric[159] set."
    So saying, he took (for still he knew his power
Not yet expired), and to the wilderness
Brought back the Son of God, and left him there,
Feigning to disappear. Darkness now rose,
As daylight sunk, and brought in louring[160] night,
Her shadowy offspring, unsubstantial both,
Privation mere[161] of light and absent day.   400
Our Savior, meek,[162] and with untroubled mind
After his airy jaunt,[163] though hurried sore,[164]
Hungry and cold betook him to his rest,
Wherever, under some concourse[165] of shades
Whose branching arms thick intertwined might shield
From dews and damps of night his sheltered head,
But sheltered, slept in vain, for at his head
The Tempter watched, and soon with ugly dreams
Disturbed his sleep. And either Tropic[166] now
'Gan thunder, and both ends of Heav'n. The clouds   410
From many a horrid rift abortive[167] poured
Fierce rain with lightning mixed, water with fire,

---

[154] utter, discourse
[155] whip lashes
[156] foretell
[157] perceive distinctly
[158] guides, gives directions
[159] instructive red-lettered text printed in prayer book margins
[160] sullen, dark
[161] absolute, entire
[162] calm, patient
[163] excursion, journey
[164] severely, very much
[165] flowing together, meeting
[166] either Tropic: both circles of the celestial sphere
[167] premature

In ruin[168] reconciled,[169] nor slept the winds
Within their stony caves, but rushed abroad
From the four hinges of the world and fell
On the vexed[170] wilderness, whose tallest pines,
Though rooted deep as high,[171] and sturdiest oaks,
Bowed their stiff necks, loaden with stormy blasts,
Or torn up sheer.[172] Ill wast thou shrouded[173] then,
O patient Son of God, yet only stood'st   420
Unshaken! Nor yet stayed[174] the terror there.
Infernal ghosts and hellish furies round
Environed thee: some howled, some yelled, some shrieked,
Some bent at thee their fiery darts, while thou
Sat'st unappalled[175] in calm and sinless peace.
Thus passed the night so foul, till morning fair
Came forth with pilgrim steps, in amice[176] gray,
Who with her radiant finger stilled the roar
Of thunder, chased the clouds, and laid[177] the winds
And grisly[178] specters, which the fiend had raised   430
To tempt[179] the Son of God with terrors dire.
          And now the sun with more effectual[180] beams
Had cheered the face of earth, and dried the wet
From drooping plant, or dropping tree. The birds,
Who all things now behold more fresh and green,
After a night of storm so ruinous,
Cleared up[181] their choicest notes in bush and spray,[182]
To gratulate[183] the sweet return of morn.
          Nor yet, amidst this joy and brightest morn,

---

[168] falling
[169] equivalent
[170] agitated
[171] roots extending as far into the earth as the tree extends into the air
[172] completely
[173] covered
[174] stopped
[175] undismayed
[176] hood with gray fur, worn by clerics
[177] caused to subside
[178] horrible, ugly
[179] make trial of
[180] effective
[181] i.e., clearly sounded/uttered/brought forth
[182] twig, shoot, slender branches
[183] welcome, greet, give thanks for

Was absent, after all his mischief done,   440
The Prince of darkness—glad would also seem
Of this fair change, and to our Savior came,
Yet with no new device[184] (they all were spent),
Rather by this his last affront[185] resolved,[186]
Desperate of better course, to vent his rage
And mad despite[187] to be so oft repelled.
          Him walking on a sunny hill he found,
Backed on the north and west by a thick wood.
Out of the wood he starts in wonted[188] shape,
And in a careless[189] mood thus to him said: 450
          "Fair morning yet betides[190] thee, Son of God,
After a dismal night. I heard the wrack,[191]
As earth and sky would mingle, but myself
Was distant, and these flaws,[192] though mortals fear them
As dangerous to the pillared frame of Heav'n,
Or to the earth's dark basis underneath,
Are to the main[193] as inconsiderable
And harmless, if not wholesome, as a sneeze
To man's lesser universe,[194] and soon are gone.
Yet, as being oft-times noxious[195] where they light   460
On man, beast, plant, wasteful and turbulent,
Like turbulencies in the affairs of men
(Over whose heads they roar, and seem to point),[196]
They oft fore-signify and threaten ill.
          "This tempest at this desert most was bent,[197]
Of men at thee, for only thou here dwell'st.
Did I not tell thee, if thou didst reject

---

[184] plan, trick, strategem
[185] encounter, meeting
[186] (1) relaxed, calmed, (2) determined
[187] outrage [noun]
[188] his usual
[189] unconcerned, artless
[190] befalls
[191] storming
[192] gusts, blasts
[193] the larger universe
[194] i.e., the human body
[195] harmful, injurious
[196] point to, mark
[197] directed

The perfect season[198] offered with my aid
To win thy destined seat, but wilt prolong
All to the push[199] of Fate, pursue thy way   470
Of gaining David's throne no man knows when
(For both the when and how is nowhere told):
Thou shalt be what thou art ordained, no doubt,
For Angels have proclaimed it, but concealing
The time and means. Each act is rightliest done
Not when it must, but when it may be best.
If thou observe not this, be sure to find
What I foretold thee, many a hard assay[200]
Of dangers, and adversities, and pains,
Ere thou of Israel's scepter get fast hold,   480
Whereof this ominous[201] night that closed thee round,
So many terrors, voices, prodigies,[202]
May warn thee, as a sure foregoing sign."
   So talked he, while the Son of God went on,
And stayed not, but in brief him answered thus:
   "Me worse than wet thou find'st not. Other harm
Those terrors which thou speak'st of did me none.
I never feared they could, though noising loud
And threat'ning nigh. What they can do as signs
Betokening or ill-boding I contemn   490
As false portents, not sent from God, but thee,
Who knowing I shall reign past thy preventing,
Obtrud'st thy offered aid, that I, accepting,
At least might seem to hold all power of thee,
Ambitious Spirit, and would'st be thought my God,
And storm'st,[203] refused, thinking to terrify
Me to thy will! Desist (thou art discerned,
And toil'st in vain), nor me in vain molest."
   To whom the fiend, now swoll'n with rage, replied:
"Then hear, O Son of David, virgin-born!   500
For Son of God to me is yet in doubt.
Of the Messiah I have heard foretold

---

[198] time, period, occasion
[199] exerted influence
[200] assault
[201] ill-omened
[202] portents, omens
[203] rage

By all the prophets; of thy birth, at length
Announced by Gabriel, with the first I knew,
And of th' Angelic song in Bethlehem field
On thy birth-night, that sung thee Savior born.
    "From that time seldom have I ceased to eye
Thy infancy, thy childhood, and thy youth,
Thy manhood last, though yet in private bred,
Till at the ford of Jordan, whither all   510
Flocked to the Baptist, I among the rest
(Though not to be baptized), by voice from Heav'n
Heard thee pronounced the Son of God beloved.
Thenceforth I thought thee worth my nearer view
And narrower scrutiny, that I might learn
In what degree[204] or meaning thou art called
The Son of God, which bears no single sense.
The Son of God I also am, or was,
And if I was, I am. Relation stands:
All men are Sons of God. Yet thee I thought   520
In some respect far higher so declared.
    "Therefore I watched thy footsteps from that hour,
And followed thee still on to this waste wild,
Where by all best conjectures I collect
Thou art to be my fatal enemy.
Good reason, then, if I beforehand seek
To understand my adversary, who
And what he is, his wisdom, power, intent,
By parle[205] or composition,[206] truce or league,
To win him, or win from him what I can.   530
    "And opportunity I here have had
To try thee, sift[207] thee, and confess have found thee
Proof against all temptation, as a rock
Of adamant and as a center, firm
To th' utmost of mere man both wise and good,
Not more, for honors, riches, kingdoms, glory,
Have been before contemned,[208] and may again.

---

[204] in what degree = at what level/rank
[205] parley
[206] agreement, treaty
[207] examine
[208] disdained

Therefore, to know what more thou art than man,
Worth naming the Son of God by voice from Heav'n,
Another method I must now begin."   540
　　　　So saying, he caught him up and, without wing
Of hippogrif,[209] bore through the air sublime,[210]
Over the wilderness and o'er the plain,
Till underneath them fair Jerusalem,
The Holy City, lifted high her towers,
And higher yet the glorious Temple reared
Her pile,[211] far off appearing like a mount
Of alabaster, topped with golden spires.
There on the highest pinnacle, he set
The Son of God, and added thus in scorn: 550
　　　　"There stand, if thou wilt stand. To stand upright
Will ask[212] thee skill. I to thy Father's house
Have brought thee, and highest placed: highest is best.
Now show thy progeny![213] If not to stand,
Cast thyself down—safely, if Son of God,
For it is written, 'He will give command
Concerning thee to His Angels; in their hands
They shall uplift thee, lest at any time
Thou chance to dash[214] thy foot against a stone.' "[215]
　　　　To whom thus Jesus: "Also it is written,   560
'Tempt not the Lord thy God.' " He said, and stood,
But Satan, smitten with amazement, fell.
As when Earth's son, Antaeus[216] (to compare
Small things with greatest), in Irassa[217] strove
With Jove's Alcides[218] and, oft foiled,[219] still rose,
Receiving from his mother Earth new strength,
Fresh from his fall, and fiercer grapple joined,
Throttled at length in th' air, expired and fell,

---

[209] winged beast, half horse, half griffin (head and wings of an eagle)
[210] lofty
[211] a large building
[212] need, demand, call upon
[213] lineage
[214] knock, strike
[215] see Psalms 91:11–12 and Matthew 4:5–7
[216] son of Poseidon and Gaia (earth)
[217] in North Africa
[218] Hercules
[219] defeated

So after many a foil, the Tempter proud,
Renewing fresh assaults, amidst his pride   570
Fell whence he stood to see[220] his victor fall.
And as that Theban monster[221] that proposed
Her riddle and, him who solved it not, devoured,
That[222] once found out and solved, for grief and spite
Cast herself headlong from the Ismenian[223] steep,
So strook[224] with dread and anguish fell the fiend,
And to his crew, that sat consulting, brought
Joyless triumphals[225] of his hoped success,
Ruin, and desperation, and dismay,
Who durst so proudly tempt the Son of God.   580
    So Satan fell, and straight a fiery globe[226]
Of Angels on full sail of wing flew nigh,
Who on their plumey vans[227] received him[228] soft
From his uneasy[229] station,[230] and upbore,
As on a floating couch, through the blithe[231] air,
Then, in a flow'ry valley, set him down
On a green bank, and set before him spread
A table of celestial food, divine
Ambrosial fruits fetched from the Tree of Life,
And from the fount of life ambrosial drink,   590
That soon refreshed him, wearied, and repaired[232]
What hunger, if aught hunger, had impaired,[233]
Or thirst. And, as he fed, Angelic choirs
Sung Heavenly anthems[234] of his victory
Over temptation and the Tempter proud:
    "True Image of the Father, whether throned

---

[220] stood to see = stood intending/hoping to see
[221] sphinx
[222] i.e., the riddle
[223] a river
[224] struck
[225] celebrations
[226] a compact body of persons
[227] wings
[228] Jesus
[229] difficult, uncomfortable
[230] standing place, position
[231] joyous, well-pleased
[232] restored, renewed, mended
[233] weakened, injured
[234] hymns

In the bosom of bliss, and light of light
Conceiving, or remote from Heav'n, enshrined
In fleshly tabernacle[235] and human form,
Wand'ring the wilderness—whatever place,   600
Habit, or state, or motion, still expressing
The Son of God, with Godlike force endued[236]
Against th' attempter of thy Father's throne
And thief of Paradise! Him long of old
Thou didst debel,[237] and down from Heav'n cast
With all his army. Now thou hast avenged
Supplanted[238] Adam and, by vanquishing
Temptation, hast regained lost Paradise,
And frustrated the conquest fraudulent.
He never more henceforth will dare set foot   610
In Paradise to tempt. His snares are broke.
For though that seat of earthly bliss be failed,
A fairer Paradise is founded now
For Adam and his chosen sons, whom thou,
A Savior, art come down to reinstall,
Where they shall dwell secure, when time shall be,
Of Tempter and temptation without fear.
        "But thou, Infernal Serpent! shalt not long
Rule in the clouds. Like an autumnal star,
Or lightning, thou shalt fall from Heav'n, trod down   620
Under his feet. For proof, ere this thou feel'st
Thy wound (yet not thy last and deadliest wound)
By this repulse received, and hold'st in Hell
No triumph. In all her gates[239] Abaddon[240] rues
Thy bold attempt. Hereafter learn with awe
To dread the Son of God. He, all unarmed,
Shall chase thee, with the terror of his voice,
From thy demoniac holds, possession foul—
Thee and thy legions. Yelling they shall fly,
And beg to hide them in a herd of swine,   630
Lest he command them down into the deep,

---

[235] temporary dwelling
[236] endowed, supplied
[237] expel, vanquish
[238] dispossessed
[239] streets, roads
[240] hell

Bound, and to torment[241] sent before their time.
    "Hail, Son of the Most High, heir of both worlds,
Queller[242] of Satan! On thy glorious work
Now enter, and begin to save mankind."
    Thus they the Son of God, our Savior meek,
Sung victor and, from Heav'nly feast refreshed,
Brought on his way with joy. He, unobserved,
Home to his mother's house private[243] returned.

---

[241] [noun]
[242] destroyer, slayer, conqueror
[243] alone, unseen

SAMSON AGONISTES[1]

[*date uncertain: everything from 1646 to 1670 has been proposed*]

OF THAT SORT OF DRAMATIC POEM WHICH IS CALLED TRAGEDY

TRAGEDY, AS IT was anciently composed, hath been ever held the gravest,[2] moralest, and most profitable of all other poems—therefore said by Aristotle to be of power by raising pity and fear, or terror, to purge the mind of those and such like passions. That is, to temper[3] and reduce[4] them to just,[5] with a kind of delight, stirred up by reading or seeing those passions well imitated.

Nor is Nature wanting[6] in her own effects[7] to make good his assertion, for so, in physic,[8] things of melancholic hue and quality are used against melancholy, sour against sour, salt to remove salt humors.[9] Hence philosophers and other gravest writers, as Cicero, Plutarch and others, frequently cite out of[10] tragic poets, both to adorn and illustrate their discourse. The Apostle Paul himself thought it not unworthy to insert a verse of Euripides[11]

---

[1] contestant, actor, champion (of God)
[2] authoritative, important
[3] modify, moderate [verb]
[4] bring to, change, restore
[5] right, proper, correct
[6] lacking
[7] operative influences, accomplishments
[8] medical science/art/practice
[9] physical/mental states
[10] from
[11] now considered to be by Menander rather than Euripides

into the text of Holy Scripture (I Cor. 15:33), and Paraeus,[12] commenting on the Revelation, divides the whole book as a tragedy, into acts distinguished each by a chorus of Heavenly harpings and song between.[13]

Heretofore men in highest dignity have labored not a little to be thought able to compose a tragedy. Of that honour Dionysius the elder was no less ambitious, then[14] before of his attaining to the Tyranny.[15] Augustus Caesar also had begun his Ajax, but unable to please his own judgment with what he had begun, left it unfinished. Seneca the philosopher is by some thought the author of those tragedies (at least the best of them) that go under that name. Gregory Nazianzen,[16] a Father of the Church, thought it not unbeseeming the sanctity of his person to write a tragedy, which he entitled, *Christ Suffering*.

This is mentioned to vindicate tragedy from the small esteem, or rather infamy, which in the account of many it undergoes at this day, with other common interludes[17] — happening through the poets' error of intermixing comic stuff with tragic sadness[18] and gravity, or introducing trivial and vulgar persons, which by all judicious[19] hath been counted absurd, and brought in without discretion, corruptly to gratify the people. And though ancient tragedy use no prologue (yet using sometimes, in case of self defense or explanation, that which Martial calls an "epistle"), in behalf of this tragedy coming forth after the ancient manner, much different from what among us passes for best, thus much beforehand may be "epistled."

The chorus is here introduced after the Greek manner, not ancient only but modern, and still in use among the Italians. In the modelling therefore of this poem, with good reason, the ancients and Italians are rather followed, as of much more authority and fame. The measure[20] of verse used in the chorus is of all sorts, called by the Greeks monostrophic, or rather apolelymenon,[21]

---

[12] David Pareus, 1548–1622, German Protestant theologian
[13] i.e., (1) act, (2) chorus, (3) act, (4) chorus, etc.
[14] in the time
[15] a state governed by an absolute ruler/dictator
[16] d. ca. A.D. 389; he probably was not the author of *Christ Suffering*
[17] stage plays, usually comic
[18] seriousness
[19] [noun]
[20] meter
[21] having no stanzaic patterning

without regard had to strophe, antistrophe or epode (which were a kind of stanza framed only for the music, then[22] used with the chorus that sung; not essential to the poem, and therefore not material)[23] or being divided into stanzas or pauses, they may be call'd allaeostropha.[24] Division into act and scene, referring chiefly to the stage (to which this work never was intended), is here omitted.

It suffices if the whole drama be found[25] not produced[26] beyond the fifth act, of the style and uniformity, and that[27] commonly called the plot, whether intricate or explicit, which is nothing indeed but such economy[28] or disposition[29] of the fable[30] as may stand best with verisimilitude and decorum. They only will best judge who are not unacquainted with Aeschulus, Sophocles, and Euripides, the three tragic poets unequalled yet by any, and the best rule to all who endeavor to write tragedy. The circumscription[31] of time wherein the whole drama begins and ends is, according to ancient rule and best example, within the space of 24 hours.

THE ARGUMENT

SAMSON (MADE CAPTIVE, blind, and now in the prison at Gaza, there to labor as in a common work-house), on a festival day, in the general cessation from labor, comes forth into the open air, to a place nigh,[32] somewhat retired,[33] there to sit a while and bemoan his condition. Where he happens at length to be visited by

---

[22] at that time
[23] important
[24] having stanzas (strophes) of varying form
[25] created?
[26] extended
[27] i.e., that which is
[28] organization, management
[29] arrangement, ordering
[30] narrative, story
[31] boundary, limit
[32] nearby
[33] withdrawn

certain friends and equals of his tribe, which make[34] the chorus, who seek to comfort him what[35] they can, then[36] by his old father, Manoa, who endeavors the like, and withal[37] tells him his purpose to procure his liberty by ransom, [and] lastly, that this feast was proclaimed by the Philistines as a day of thanksgiving for their deliverance from the hands of Samson, which yet more troubles him.

Manoa then departs to prosecute[38] his endeavor[39] with the Philistian lords for Samson's redemption, who in the meanwhile is visited by other persons, and lastly by a public officer to require his coming to the feast, before[40] the lords and people, to play[41] or show his strength in their presence. He at first refuses, dismissing the public officer with absolute denial to come. At length, persuaded inwardly that this was from God, he yields to go along with him, who came now, the second time, with great threatenings, to fetch him.

The chorus yet remaining on the place, Manoa returns full of joyful hope to procure, ere long, his son's deliverance, in the midst of which discourse an Hebrew comes in haste, confusedly at first, and afterward more distinctly, relating the catastrophe: what Samson had done to the Philistines, and by accident to himself, wherewith the tragedy ends.

---

[34] form, compose
[35] as much as
[36] i.e., then visited
[37] in addition
[38] follow up on, pursue
[39] attempt
[40] in front of
[41] exercise

The Persons

Samson.
Harapha of Gath.
Manoa, the father of Samson.
Public officer.
Messenger.
Dalila, his wife.
Chorus of Danites.[42]

The scene: before the prison in Gaza.

      Sams. A little onward lend thy guiding hand
To these dark steps, a little further on,
For yonder bank[43] hath choice of sun or shade.
There I am wont[44] to sit, when any chance
Relieves me from my task of servile[45] toil,
Daily in the common prison else enjoined[46] me,
Where I, a prisoner chained, scarce freely draw[47]
The air—imprisoned also, close and damp,
Unwholesome[48] draught.[49] But here I feel amends,[50]
The breath of Heav'n fresh-blowing, pure and sweet,   10
With day-spring born. Here leave me to respire.[51]
This day a solemn feast the people hold
To Dagon[52] their sea-Idol, and forbid
Laborious[53] works. Unwillingly this rest
Their superstition[54] yields me. Hence with leave[55]
Retiring from the popular[56] noise, I seek

---

[42] tribe of Dan (Manoa and Samson's tribe), northwest of Judah
[43] ridge, elevation
[44] accustomed, in the habit of
[45] enslaved
[46] imposed on
[47] breathe
[48] unhealthy
[49] flow, current of air
[50] improvement
[51] (1) draw breath, (2) recover
[52] Philistine national god
[53] hard-work-requiring
[54] ignorant/irrational/false belief
[55] permission
[56] plebeian, common, general

This unfrequented[57] place to find some ease,
Ease to the body some, none to the mind
From restless thoughts, that like a deadly swarm
Of hornets armed, no sooner found alone   20
But rush upon me thronging,[58] and present[59]
Times past, what once I was, and what am now.
       O wherefore was my birth from Heav'n foretold
Twice, by an Angel, who at last in sight
Of both my parents all in flames ascended
From off the altar, where an off'ring burned,
As in a fiery column charioting
His godlike presence, and from some great act
Or benefit revealed to Abraham's race?
Why was my breeding[60] ordered and prescribed   30
As of a person separate[61] to God,
Designed for great exploits, if I must die
Betrayed, captived, and both my eyes put out,
Made of my enemies the scorn and gaze?
To grind[62] in brazen[63] fetters[64] under task[65]
With this Heav'n-gifted strength? O glorious strength
Put to the labor of a beast, debased
Lower than bondslave! Promise was that I
Should Israel from Philistian yoke deliver.
Ask for this great deliverer now, and find him   40
Eyeless in Gaza at the mill[66] with slaves,
Himself in bonds under Philistian yoke.
       Yet stay, let me not rashly call in doubt
Divine prediction. What if all foretold
Had been fulfilled but[67] through mine own default,[68]
Whom have I to complain of but myself?

---

57 unvisited, uncrowded
58 crowding, pressing
59 [verb]
60 development, training, education
61 special
62 work laboriously
63 brass, brasslike, as strong as brass
64 chains, shackles
65 assigned compulsion
66 building containing machinery (here water-driven) for processing, manufacturing, etc.
67 except
68 defect, failure, guilt

Who this high gift of strength, committed to me,
In what part lodged, how easily bereft[69] me,
Under the seal of silence could not keep
But weakly to a woman must reveal it,   50
O'ercome with importunity and tears.
O impotence of mind, in body strong!
But what is strength without a double share
Of wisdom, vast, unwieldy,[70] burdensome,
Proudly secure,[71] yet liable to fall
By weakest subtleties, not made to rule
But to subserve[72] where wisdom bears[73] command.
God, when He gave me strength, to show withal
How slight the gift was, hung it in my hair.
But peace! I must not quarrel with the will   60
Of highest dispensation,[74] which herein
Happ'ly[75] had ends[76] above my reach to know.
Suffices that to me strength is my bane,[77]
And proves the source of all my miseries,
So many, and so huge, that each apart
Would ask[78] a life to wail—but of all,
O loss of sight, of thee I most complain!
Blind among enemies, O worse than chains,
Dungeon, or beggary, or decrepit age!
Light, the prime work of God, to me is extinct,   70
And all her various objects of delight
Annulled,[79] which might in part my grief have eased,
Inferior to the vilest now become
Of man or worm. The vilest here excel me,
They creep, yet see, I dark in light exposed
To daily fraud, contempt, abuse and wrong,

---

[69] robbed, stripped
[70] clumsy, awkward
[71] confident
[72] be subordinated
[73] wields
[74] ordering, management
[75] (1) probably, (2) appropriately
[76] goals, purposes
[77] curse, poison, slayer, ruin
[78] demand, call for
[79] ended, destroyed

Within doors, or without, still[80] as a fool,
In power of others, never in my own.
Scarce half I seem to live, dead more than half.
O dark, dark, dark, dark, dark, amid the blaze of noon,   80
Irrecoverably dark, total eclipse
Without all[81] hope of day!
          O first created beam, and thou great Word,
"Let there be light, and light was over all,"[82]
Why am I thus bereaved thy prime[83] decree?
The sun to me is dark
And silent as the moon
When she deserts the night,
Hid in her vacant[84] interlunar cave.[85]
Since light so necessary is to life,   90
And almost life itself, if it be true
That light is in the soul,
She all in every part, why was the sight
To such a tender ball as th' eye confined?[86]
So obvious[87] and so easy to be quenched,[88]
And not, as feeling, through all parts diffused
That she might look at will[89] through every pore?
Then had I not been thus exiled from light,
As in the land of darkness, yet in light,
To live a life half dead, a living death,   100
And buried, but O yet more miserable!
Myself my sepulcher,[90] a moving grave,
Buried, yet not exempt
By privilege of death and burial
From worst of other evils, pains and wrongs,
But made hereby obnoxious[91] more

---

[80] (1) silent, (2) always
[81] every, any, all
[82] see Genesis 1:3
[83] (1) first, beginning, (2) primary
[84] empty, destitute of life/activity
[85] in which the moon was thought to hide between its old and new phases
[86] relegated, fastened
[87] visible
[88] extinguished, destroyed
[89] at will = at pleasure/choice
[90] tomb, burial place
[91] susceptible, amenable, exposed

To all the miseries of life,
Life in captivity
Among inhuman foes.
        But who are these? For with joint[92] pace[93] I hear   110
The tread of many feet steering this way—
Perhaps my enemies who come to stare
At my affliction, and perhaps to insult,
Their daily practice to afflict me more.
        Chor. This, this is he. Softly a while,
Let us not break in upon him.
O change beyond report, thought, or belief!
See how he lies at random, carelessly diffused,[94]
With languished[95] head unpropped,
As one past hope, abandoned   120
And by himself given over,
In slavish habit,[96] ill-fitted weeds[97]
O'er worn and soiled.
        Or do my eyes misrepresent? Can this be he,
That heroic, that renowned,
Irresistible Samson? Whom unarmed
No strength of man or fiercest wild beast could withstand?
Who tore the lion, as the lion tears the kid?
Ran on embattled[98] armies clad in iron,
And weaponless himself   130
Made arms ridiculous, useless the forgery[99]
Of brazen[100] shield and spear, the hammered cuirass,[101]
Chalybean[102] tempered steel, and frock[103] of mail
Adamantean proof?
But safest he who stood aloof,

---

[92] two or more
[93] steps
[94] sprawled, spread out
[95] slack, feeble
[96] clothes
[97] garments
[98] in battle formation
[99] (1) forging, (2) invention
[100] brass
[101] upper-body armor
[102] from the Black Sea region, famous for their metalworking [four syllables, second and fourth accented]
[103] tunic, upper garment

When insupportably[104] his foot advanced
In scorn of their proud arms and warlike tools,
Spurned[105] them to death—by troops! The bold Ascalonite[106]
Fled from his lion ramp,[107] old warriors turned[108]
Their plated[109] backs under his heel   140
Or, grov'ling, soiled[110] their crested helmets in the dust.
Then with what[111] trivial[112] weapon came to hand—
The jaw of a dead ass, his sword of bone—
A thousand fore-skins[113] fell, the flower of Palestine,
In Ramath-lechi,[114] famous to this day.
Then by main[115] force pulled up, and on his shoulders bore
The Gates of Azza[116]—post[117] and massy bar—[118]
Up to the hill by Hebron,[119] seat of giants old,[120]
No journey of a sabbath day,[121] and[122] loaded so:
Like[123] whom[124] the gentiles feign[125] to bear up Heav'n.[126]   150
          Which shall I first bewail,
Thy bondage or lost sight,
Prison within prison
Inseparably dark?
Thou art become (O worst imprisonment!)
The dungeon of thyself! Thy soul
(Which men enjoying sight oft without cause complain)

---

[104] too strongly to be resisted/endured ("supported")
[105] thrust, struck, trampled
[106] Ascalon: ancient Philistine port city
[107] rearing and raging
[108] twisted, writhed, bent, reversed
[109] covered with layer(s) of metal
[110] dirtied, fouled, polluted
[111] whatever
[112] common
[113] unlike the Jews, the Philistines were not circumcised
[114] the suffix "-lechi" = lifting up/casting away of the jawbone: see Judges 15:14–17
[115] mighty
[116] Gaza
[117] gatepost/stake
[118] used to lock the gates
[119] south of Jerusalem, more than thirty miles from Gaza
[120] see Numbers 13:22 ("anak" = "giant," in Hebrew)
[121] on which day only very short journeys were permitted
[122] and in addition
[123] i.e., loaded like
[124] he whom
[125] tell in myths/fables
[126] the giant Atlas

Imprisoned now indeed,
In real darkness of the body dwells,
Shut up from outward light   160
T' incorporate[127] with gloomy night,
For inward light alas
Puts forth no visual beam.
      O mirror of our fickle[128] state,
Since man[129] on earth unparalleled!
The rarer[130] thy example stands
By how much from the top of wondrous glory,
Strongest of mortal men,
To lowest pitch of abject fortune thou art fall'n.
For him I reckon not in high estate   170
Whom long descent of birth
Or the sphere of fortune raises,
But thee whose strength, while virtue was her mate,
Might have subdued the earth,
Universally crowned with highest praises.
      Sam. I hear the sound of words; their sense the air
Dissolves unjointed[131] ere it reach my ear.
      Chor. He speaks: let us draw nigh.

                           Matchless in might,
The glory late of Israel, now the grief!
We come thy friends and neighbours not unknown   180
From Eshtaol and Zora's fruitful vale[132]
To visit or bewail thee or, if better,
Counsel or consolation we may bring,
Salve to thy sores. Apt words have power to suage
The tumors[133] of a troubled mind,
And are as balm to festered wounds.
      Sam. Your coming, friends, revives me, for I learn
Now of my own experience, not by talk,
How counterfeit a coin they are who friends

---

[127] unite, combine
[128] uncertain, changeable
[129] man has been
[130] more unusual
[131] incoherent
[132] Eshtaol and Zora: west of Jerusalem, in the valley of Sorec (Sorek) (see line 229, below)
[133] swellings

Bear in their superscription[134] (of the most,[135]   190
I would be understood): in prosperous days
They swarm, but in adverse withdraw their head,
Not to be found, though sought. Ye see, O friends,
How many evils have enclosed me round.
Yet that which was the worst now least afflicts me,
Blindness, for had I sight, confused with shame,
How could I once look up, or heave[136] the head,
Who like a foolish pilot have shipwracked
My vessel, trusted to me from above,
Gloriously rigged, and for a word, a tear   200
—Fool!—have divulged the secret gift of God
To a deceitful woman? Tell me, friends,
Am I not sung and proverbed for a fool
In every street? Do they not say how well
Are come upon him his deserts? Yet why?
Immeasurable strength they might behold
In me, of wisdom nothing more than mean.[137]
This with the other should, at least, have paired;[138]
These two, proportioned ill, drove me transverse.[139]

      Chor. Tax[140] not divine disposal.[141] Wisest men   210
Have erred, and by bad women been deceived,
And shall again, pretend they ne're so wise.
Deject not then so overmuch thyself,
Who hast of sorrow thy full load besides.
Yet truth to say, I oft have heard men wonder
Why thou should'st wed Philistian women rather
Than of thine own tribe—fairer, or as fair,
At least of thy own nation, and as noble.

      Sam. The first I saw at Timna,[142] and she pleased
Me (not my parents), that[143] I sought to wed,   220

---

[134] name, inscription on coins
[135] i.e., most of them
[136] raise, uplift
[137] poor, inferior
[138] have paired = been equal
[139] crosswise, sideways
[140] blame, accuse, challenge
[141] ordering, arranging
[142] Timnath, Philistine city
[143] so that

The daughter of an infidel. They[144] knew not
That what I motioned[145] was of God; I knew
From intimate[146] impulse,[147] and therefore urged[148]
The marriage on, that by occasion[149] hence[150]
I might begin Israel's deliverance,
The work to which I was divinely called.
She proving false, the next I took to wife
(O that I never had! fond[151] wish, too late)
Was in the Vale of Sorec, Dalila,[152]
That specious[153] monster, my accomplished[154] snare.   230
I thought it lawful, from[155] my former act
And the same end, still watching to oppress
Israel's oppressors. Of what now I suffer
She was not the prime cause, but I myself
Who, vanquished with a peal[156] of words (O weakness!),
Gave up[157] my fort of silence to a woman.
          Chor. In seeking just occasion to provoke[158]
The Philistine, thy country's enemy,
Thou never wast remiss:[159] I bear thee witness.
Yet Israel still serves,[160] with all his sons.   240
          Sam. That fault I take not on me, but transfer
On Israel's governors and heads of tribes,
Who seeing those great acts which God had done
Singly[161] by me against their conquerors
Acknowledged not, or not at all considered

---

[144] Samson's parents
[145] proposed, planned
[146] inmost
[147] influence, incitement
[148] pressed, pushed
[149] opportunity, the course of events
[150] stemming from (the marriage)
[151] foolish
[152] [three syllables, second stressed]
[153] showily beautiful
[154] accomplished, completed, perfected
[155] because of
[156] outburst
[157] gave up = surrendered
[158] challenge, fight
[159] negligent
[160] is in servitude
[161] all alone

Deliverance offered. I on th' other side
Used[162] no ambition[163] to commend[164] my deeds:
The deeds themselves, though mute, spoke loud the doer.
But they[165] persisted deaf, and would not seem
To count them things worth notice, till at length   250
Their lords the Philistines with gathered[166] powers
Entered Judea, seeking me, who then
Safe to the rock of Etham[167] was retired,
Not flying,[168] but fore-casting[169] in what place
To set upon them, what advantaged[170] best.
Meanwhile the men of Judah, to prevent
The harass of their land, beset[171] me round.
I willingly (on some[172] conditions) came
Into their hands, and they as gladly yield me
To the uncircumcised, a welcome prey,[173]   260
Bound with two cords[174]—but cords to me were threads
Touched with the flame. On their whole host I flew,
Unarmed, and with a trivial[175] weapon felled
Their choicest youth; they only lived who fled.
Had Judah that day joined, or one whole tribe,
They had by this possessed the towers of Gath,[176]
And lorded over them whom now they serve.
But what more oft, in nations grown corrupt
And by their vices brought to servitude,
Than to love bondage more than liberty,   270
Bondage with ease than[177] strenuous liberty,
And to despise, or envy, or suspect

---

[162] engaged in
[163] canvassing: soliciting (as for votes, in an election)
[164] praise, adorn
[165] "Israel's governors and heads of tribes"
[166] assembled
[167] see Judges 15:8
[168] fleeing
[169] planning, considering, estimating
[170] benefited, profited
[171] besieged
[172] certain
[173] victim, quarry
[174] small ropes, braided for strength
[175] common
[176] a principal Philistine city
[177] rather than

Whom God hath of his special favor raised
As their deliverer? If he aught begin,
How frequent to desert him, and at last
To heap ingratitude on worthiest deeds?
      Chor. Thy words to my remembrance bring
How Succoth and the fort of Penuel[178]
Their great deliverer contemned,
The matchless Gideon, in pursuit   280
Of Madian and her vanquished kings.
And how ungrateful Ephraim[179]
Had dealt with Jephtha,[180] who by argument
Not worse than by his shield and spear,
Defended Israel from the Ammonite,[181]
Had not his prowess quelled their pride
In that sore battle when so many died,
Without reprieve adjudged to death
For want of well-pronouncing "shibboleth."[182]
      Sam. Of such examples add me to the roll.   290
Me easily indeed mine may neglect,[183]
But God's proposed deliverance not so.
      Chor. Just are the ways of God,
And justifiable to men,
Unless there be who think not God at all.[184]
If any be, they walk obscure,[185]
For of such doctrine never was there school,
But the heart of the fool,
And no man therein doctor[186] but himself.
      Yet more there be who doubt[187] His ways not just,   300
As to His own edicts found contradicting,
Then give the reins to wand'ring[188] thought,

---

[178] Succoth and Penuel: Israelite cities (see Judges 8:4–9)
[179] the tribe of Ephraim, in the hill region north of Bethel
[180] see Judges 12:1–4
[181] Semitic tribe frequently hostile to Israel
[182] the Ephraimites were identified by their inability to pronounce the "sh" in "shibboleth": see Judges 12:5–6
[183] "my nation/people ('mine') may easily neglect me"
[184] "unless there be those who think God does not exist"
[185] hidden, unknown
[186] teacher, learned man
[187] suspect
[188] disordered

Regardless of His glory's diminution,
Till by their own perplexities involved[189]
They ravel[190] more, still less resolved,
But never find self-satisfying solution.
        As if they would confine th' interminable,[191]
And tie Him to His own prescript,[192]
Who made our Laws to bind us, not Himself,
And hath full right t' exempt   310
Whom so it pleases Him by choice
From national obstriction,[193] without taint
Of sin, or legal debt,
For with His own Laws He can best dispense.
        He would not else (who never wanted[194] means,
Nor in respect of th' enemy just cause
To set His people free)
Have prompted this heroic Nazarite,[195]
Against his vow of strictest purity,
To seek in marriage that fallacious[196] bride,   320
Unclean, unchaste.
        Down[197] reason, then—at least, vain reasonings down,
Though reason here aver[198]
That moral verdict quits[199] her[200] of unclean:
Unchaste was subsequent, her stain not his.
        But see, here comes thy reverend sire
With careful[201] step, locks white as down,
Old Manoa. Advise[202]
Forthwith how thou ought'st to receive him.
        Sam. Aye me, another inward grief awaked: 330
With mention of that name, renews th' assault.

---

[189] enwrapped
[190] are confused/perplexed/entangled
[191] endless, everlasting
[192] commands, laws
[193] obligation (see Deuteronomy 7:2–5)
[194] lacked
[195] a person who had vowed to abstain from sex: see Numbers 6:2ff.
[196] deceitful
[197] put/go down
[198] plead, claim
[199] frees, releases, acquits
[200] Dalila
[201] heavy, full of care
[202] consider

Man. Brethren and men of Dan, for such ye seem,
Though in this uncouth[203] place: if old respect,
As I suppose, towards your once gloried friend,
My son now captive, hither hath informed[204]
Your younger feet, while mine, cast[205] back with age,
Came lagging after, say if he be here.

    Chor. As signal[206] now, in low dejected state,
As erst in highest, behold him where he lies.

    Man. O miserable change! Is this the man,   304
That invincible Samson, far renowned,
The dread of Israel's foes, who with a strength
Equivalent to Angels walked their streets,
None offering fight? who single combatant
Duelled their armies, ranked in proud array,
Himself an army, now unequal match
To save himself against a coward, armed,
At one spear's length? O ever failing trust
In mortal strength! and oh what not in man
Deceivable and vain! Nay, what thing good   350
Prayed for, but often proves our woe, our bane?[207]
I prayed for children, and thought barrenness
In wedlock a reproach. I gained a son,
And such a son as all men hailed me happy.
Who would be now a father in my stead?
O wherefore did God grant me my request,
And as a blessing with such pomp[208] adorned?
Why are His gifts desirable,[209] to tempt
Our earnest prayers, then giv'n with solemn hand
As graces, draw a scorpion's tail behind?   360
For this did th' Angel twice descend? for this
Ordained thy nurture holy, as of a plant
Select and sacred, glorious for a while,
The miracle of men, then in an hour
Ensnared, assaulted, overcome, led bound,

---

[203] strange, unfamiliar
[204] guided, led
[205] bent
[206] notable
[207] destroyer, poison
[208] splendor
[209] wished for

Thy foes' derision, captive, poor, and blind,
Into a dungeon thrust, to work with slaves?
Alas, methinks whom God hath chosen once
To worthiest deeds, if he through frailty err
He[210] should not so oerwhelm, and as a thrall[211]   370
Subject him to so foul indignities,
Be it but for honor's sake, of former deeds.

     Sam. Appoint[212] not Heav'nly disposition, father.
Nothing of all these evils hath befall'n me
But justly. I myself have brought them on,
Sole author I, sole cause. If aught seem vile,
As[213] vile hath been my folly, who have profaned
The mystery of God giv'n me under pledge
Of vow, and have betrayed it to a woman,
A Canaanite, my faithless enemy.   380
This well I knew, nor was at all surprised,
But warned by oft experience. Did not she
Of Timna[214] first betray me, and reveal
The secret wrested from me in her height
Of nuptial love professed, carrying it straight
To them who had corrupted her, my spies
And rivals? In this other was there found
More faith? who also in her prime of love,
Spousal embraces, vitiated[215] with gold,
Though offered only, by the scent[216] conceived   390
Her spurious[217] first-born, treason against me?
Thrice she assayed, with flattering prayers and sighs,
And amorous reproaches, to win from me
My capital[218] secret, in what part my strength
Lay stored, in what part summed, that she might know.
Thrice I deluded[219] her, and turned to sport[220]

---

[210] God
[211] slave
[212] decide, declare
[213] equally
[214] biblical Timnath: see Judges 14:1–20
[215] corrupted
[216] i.e., of gold
[217] false
[218] major
[219] eluded
[220] a jest/joke

Her importunity, each time perceiving
How openly and with what impudence
She purposed to betray me, and (which was worse
Than undissembled hate) with what contempt   400
She sought to make me traitor to myself.
Yet the fourth time, when must'ring all her wiles,
With blandished[221] parleys,[222] feminine assaults,
Tongue-batteries,[223] she surceased not day nor night
To storm[224] me, over-watched[225] and wearied out.
At times when men seek most repose and rest
I yielded, and unlocked her all my heart,
Who with a grain of manhood well resolved[226]
Might easily have shook off all her snares.
But foul effeminacy[227] held me yoked   410
Her bondslave. O indignity, O blot
To honor and religion! Servile mind
Rewarded well with servile punishment!
The base degree to which I now am fall'n,
These rags, this grinding,[228] is not yet so base
As was my former servitude, ignoble,
Unmanly, ignominious, infamous,
True slavery, and that blindness worse than this,
That saw not how degenerately I served.
    Man. I cannot praise thy marriage choices, son—   420
Rather approved them not. But thou didst plead
Divine impulsion[229] prompting how thou might'st
Find some occasion to infest[230] our foes.
I state not that. This I am sure: our foes
Found soon occasion thereby to make thee
Their captive, and their triumph. Thou the sooner
Temptation found'st, or over-potent charms
To violate the sacred trust of silence

---

[221] flattering
[222] speech
[223] batteries = (1) battering rams, (2) artillery
[224] to make a military assault
[225] exhausted (from "watching" too long/much)
[226] firm, steadfast
[227] addiction to women
[228] working laboriously
[229] instigation, incitement
[230] attack

Deposited within thee, which t' have kept
Tacit[231] was in thy power. True: and thou bear'st   430
Enough, and more, the burden of that fault.
Bitterly hast thou paid, and still art paying
That rigid[232] score.[233] A worse thing yet remains.
This day the Philistines a popular feast
Here celebrate in Gaza, and proclaim
Great pomp, and sacrifice, and praises loud
To Dagon, as their god who hath delivered
Thee, Samson, bound and blind into their hands,
Them out of thine, who slew'st them many a slain.
So Dagon shall be magnified, and God,   440
Besides whom is no God, compared with idols,
Disglorified, blasphemed, and had in scorn
By th' idolatrous rout[234] amidst their wine,
Which to have come to pass by means of thee,
Samson, of all thy sufferings think the heaviest,
Of all reproach the most with shame that ever
Could have befall'n thee and thy father's house.[235]

      Sam. Father, I do acknowledge and confess
That I this honor, I this pomp have brought
To Dagon, and advanced his praises high   450
Among the heathen round[236] —to God have brought
Dishonor, obloquy,[237] and op't[238] the mouths
Of idolists, and atheists, have brought scandal
To Israel, diffidence[239] of God, and doubt
In feeble hearts, propense[240] enough before
To waver, or fall off and join with idols.
Which is my chief affliction, shame and sorrow,
The anguish of my soul, that suffers not
Mine eye to harbor[241] sleep, or thoughts to rest.

---

[231] unspoken
[232] harsh, unyielding
[233] account
[234] mob, crowd
[235] lineage
[236] assemblage [noun]
[237] reproach
[238] opened
[239] mistrust, distrust
[240] ready, willing
[241] find room for, hold, shelter

This only hope relieves me, that the strife   460
With me hath end: all the contest is now
'Twixt God and Dagon. Dagon hath presumed
(Me overthrown) to enter lists[242] with God,
His deity comparing and preferring
Before the God of Abraham. He,[243] be sure,
Will not connive,[244] or linger, thus provoked,
But will arise and His great name assert.
Dagon must stoop,[245] and shall ere long receive
Such a discomfit[246] as shall quite despoil[247] him
Of all these boasted trophies won on me,   470
And with confusion blank[248] his worshippers.
    Man. With cause[249] this hope relieves thee, and these
                words
I as a prophecy receive, for God—
Nothing more certain—will not long defer
To vindicate the glory of His name
Against all competition, nor will long
Endure it, doubtful[250] whether God be Lord
Or Dagon. But for thee what shall be done?
Thou must not in the meanwhile here forgot
Lie, in this miserable, loathsome plight   480
Neglected. I already have made way[251]
To some Philistian lords, with whom to treat[252]
About thy ransom. Well they may by this[253]
Have satisfied their utmost of revenge
By pains and slaveries worse than death inflicted
On thee, who now no more canst do them harm.
    Sam. Spare[254] that proposal, father, spare the trouble

---

[242] literally, the enclosed space where jousting took place; metaphorically, "enter lists" = to fight/challenge
[243] God
[244] shut His eyes
[245] bow
[246] defeat
[247] deprive, strip
[248] frustrate, confound
[249] reason
[250] that it be unsettled/uncertain
[251] connection, opportunity
[252] deal, negotiate
[253] this time
[254] leave, abstain, refrain

Of that solicitation. Let me here,
As I deserve, pay on my punishment,
And expiate, if possible, my crime,   490
Shameful garrulity. To have revealed
Secrets of men, the secrets of a friend,
How heinous had the fact been, how deserving
Contempt, and scorn of all, to be excluded
All friendship, and avoided as a blab,
The mark of fool set on his front?[255] But I
God's counsel have not kept, His holy secret
Presumptuously have published,[256] impiously,
Weakly at least, and shamefully, a sin
That gentiles in their parables[257] condemn[258]   500
To their abyss and horrid pains confined.[259]

     Man. Be penitent and for thy fault contrite,
But act not in thy own affliction, son.
Repent the sin, but if the punishment
Thou canst avoid, self-preservation bids,
Or th' execution leav̄e to high disposal,[260]
And let another hand, not thine, exact
Thy penal forfeit[261] from thyself. Perhaps
God will relent, and quit[262] thee all His debt,
Who evermore approves and more accepts   510
(Best pleased with humble and filial submission)
Him who imploring mercy sues[263] for life,
Than who, self-rigorous, chooses death as due,
Which argues over-just, and self-displeased
For self-offence, more than for God offended.
Reject not then what offered means[264] (who knows
But God hath set before us) to return thee
Home to thy country and His sacred house,
Where thou may'st bring thy off'rings, to avert

---

[255] forehead
[256] made public
[257] fictitious narratives
[258] Tantalus, Zeus' son, was thus punished for telling the gods' secrets to his friends
[259] [adjective]
[260] ordering, arranging
[261] a fine/penalty
[262] free, release
[263] pleads, petitions
[264] instrumentality [noun]

His further ire with prayers and vows renewed. 520
      Sam. His pardon I implore. But as for life,
To what end should I seek it? When in strength
All mortals I excelled, and great in hopes
With youthful courage and magnanimous[265] thoughts
Of birth from Heav'n foretold and high exploits,
Full of divine instinct,[266] after some proof
Of acts indeed heroic, far beyond
The sons of Anac,[267] famous now and blazed,[268]
Fearless of danger, like a petty god
I walked about, admired of all and dreaded 530
On hostile ground, none daring my affront.[269]
Then swoll'n with pride into the snare I fell
Of fair fallacious[270] looks, venereal trains,[271]
Softn'd with pleasure and voluptuous life,
At length to lay my head and hallowed pledge[272]
Of all my strength in the lascivious lap
Of a deceitful concubine, who shore me
Like a tame wether, all my precious fleece,
Then turned me out ridiculous, despoiled,
Shav'n, and disarmed among my enemies. 540
      Chor. Desire of wine and all delicious drinks,
Which many a famous warrior overturns,
Thou could'st repress, nor did the dancing ruby[273]
Sparkling, out-poured, the flavor, or the smell,
Or taste that cheers the heart of gods and men,
Allure thee from[274] the cool crystalline stream.
      Sam. Wherever fountain or fresh current flowed
Against the eastern ray, translucent, pure
With touch aetherial of Heav'ns fiery rod,[275]

---

[265] lofty, high-souled
[266] impulse
[267] sons of Anak: the race of giants
[268] celebrated, proclaimed
[269] confrontation
[270] false
[271] venereal trains = love's tricks/snares
[272] sign of favor
[273] i.e., red wine
[274] away from
[275] the sun's beams?

I drank, from the clear milky[276] juice[277] allaying   550
Thirst, and refreshed, nor envied them the grape
Whose heads that turbulent liquor fills with fumes.
    Chor. O madness, to think use of strongest wines
And strongest drinks our chief support of health,
When God with these forbidd'n made choice to rear
His mighty champion, strong above compare,
Whose drink was only from the liquid brook.
    Sam. But what availed this temperance, not complete
Against another object more enticing?
What boots it at one gate to make defence   560
And at another to let in the foe,
Effeminately vanquished? By which means,
Now blind, disheart'ned, shamed, dishonored, quelled,[278]
To what can I be useful? wherein serve
My nation, and the work from Heav'n imposed,
But to sit idle on the household hearth,
A burdenous drone? to visitants a gaze,[279]
Or pitied object, these redundant[280] locks
Robustious[281] to no purpose clust'ring down,
Vain monument of strength, till length of years   570
And sedentary numbness craze[282] my limbs
To a contemptible old age obscure.
Here rather let me drudge and earn my bread,
Till vermin or the draff[283] of servile food
Consume me, and oft-invocated death
Hast'n the welcome end of all my pains.
    Man. Wilt thou then serve the Philistines with that gift
Which was expressly giv'n thee to annoy[284] them?
Better at home lie bed-rid, not only idle —
Inglorious, unemployed,[285] with age out-worn.   580
But God who caused a fountain at thy prayer

---

[276] soft?
[277] fluid
[278] ruined, destroyed
[279] something to stare at
[280] plentiful, flowing, excessive
[281] healthy-looking, strong
[282] break down, destroy
[283] garbage, refuse, offal
[284] to trouble, molest, injure
[285] unoccupied

From the dry ground to spring, thy thirst to allay
After the brunt[286] of battle,[287] can as easy
Cause light again within thy eyes to spring,
Wherewith to serve Him better than thou hast.
And I persuade me so. Why else this strength
Miraculous yet remaining in those locks?
His might continues in thee, not for naught,
Nor shall His wondrous gifts be frustrate thus.

      Sam. All otherwise to me my thoughts portend,[288]   590
That these dark orbs no more shall treat[289] with light,
Nor th' other light of life continue long,
But yield to double darkness nigh at hand.
So much I feel my genial[290] spirits droop,
My hopes all flat. Nature within me seems
In all her functions weary of herself,
My race of glory run, and race of shame,
And I shall shortly be with them that rest.

      Man. Believe not these suggestions, which proceed
From anguish of the mind and humors[291] black,   600
That mingle with thy fancy.[292] I however
Must not omit a father's timely care
To prosecute[293] the means of thy deliverance,
By ransom or how else. Meanwhile be calm,
And healing words from these thy friends admit.[294]

      Sam. O that torment[295] should not be confined[296]
To the body's wounds and sores,
With maladies innumerable
In heart, head, breast, and reins,[297]
But must secret passage find   610
To th' inmost mind,

---

[286] violence, shock
[287] see Judges 15:18–19
[288] point to, indicate, foretell
[289] entertain, deal with
[290] natural
[291] state of mind, disposition
[292] fantasy, whim, inclination
[293] pursue, perform
[294] receive
[295] that which produces pain/suffering
[296] limited
[297] kidneys

There exercise[298] all his fierce accidents,[299]
And on her purest spirits prey,
As on entrails, joints, and limbs,
With answerable[300] pains, but more intense,
Though void of corporal sense.[301]
     My griefs not only pain me
As a ling'ring disease,
But finding no redress, ferment[302] and rage,
Nor less than wounds immedicable[303]   620
Rankle,[304] and fester, and gangrene[305]
To black mortification.[306]
Thoughts (my tormentors) armed with deadly stings
Mangle my apprehensive[307] tenderest parts,
Exasperate,[308] exulcerate, and raise
Dire inflammation which no cooling herb
Or med'cinal liquor can assuage,[309]
Nor breath of vernal air from snowy Alp.
Sleep hath forsook and giv'n me o'er
To death's benumbing opium as my only cure.   630
Thence faintings, swoonings of despair,
And sense of Heav'n's desertion.
     I was His nursling once, and choice delight,
His destined[310] from the womb,
Promised by Heav'nly message twice descending.
Under His special[311] eye
Abstemious[312] I grew up and thrived amain.[313]
He led me on to mightiest deeds

---

[298] employ, perform
[299] appearances, symptoms
[300] corresponding
[301] sensation, feeling
[302] excite, stir up
[303] incurable
[304] continue to cause pain, fester
[305] [verb]
[306] necrosis, destruction
[307] conscious
[308] irritate
[309] abate
[310] [adjective]
[311] particular, intimate
[312] temperate, abstinent
[313] exceedingly

(Above the nerve[314] of mortal arm)
Against th' uncircumcised, our enemies, 640
But now hath cast me off as[315] never known,
And to those cruel enemies,
Whom I by His appointment[316] had provoked,[317]
Left me all helpless with th' irreparable loss
Of sight, reserved alive to be repeated[318]
The subject of their cruelty, or scorn.
Nor am I in the list[319] of them that hope.
Hopeless are all my evils, all remediless.
This one prayer yet remains, might I be heard:
No long petition, speedy death, 650
The close of all my miseries, and the balm.
    Chor. Many are the sayings of the wise,
In ancient and in modern books enrolled,[320]
Extolling patience as the truest fortitude,[321]
And to the bearing well of all calamities,
All chances incident to man's frail life,
Consolatories writ
With studied[322] argument, and much persuasion[323] sought,[324]
Lenient[325] of grief and anxious thought.
But with th' afflicted in his pangs their sound 660
Little prevails, or rather seems a tune
Harsh, and of dissonant mood from his complaint,
Unless he feel within
Some source of consolation from above,
Secret refreshings, that repair[326] his strength,
And fainting spirits uphold.
      God of our fathers, what is man!

---

[314] strength
[315] as if
[316] assignment
[317] defied, incited
[318] repeatedly [adverb]
[319] roll, catalogue
[320] written, placed, entered
[321] strength
[322] learned, carefully thought out, practiced
[323] belief, conviction
[324] searched for, obtained
[325] mild, soothing
[326] restore

That Thou towards him with hand so various,[327]
Or might I say contrarious,
Temper'st Thy providence through his short course[328]   670
Not evenly, as thou rul'st
The Angelic orders and inferior creatures mute,
Irrational and brute.
Nor do I name of men the common rout,[329]
That wand'ring loose[330] about
Grow up and perish, as[331] the summer fly,
Heads without name no more remembered!
But such as Thou hast solemnly[332] elected,[333]
With gifts and graces eminently adorned
To some great work, Thy glory   680
And people's safety,[334] which in part they effect.
Yet toward these thus dignified,[335] Thou oft
Amidst their height of noon
Changest Thy countenance and Thy hand, with no regard
Of highest favors past
From Thee on them, or them to Thee of service.
          Nor only dost degrade them, or remit[336]
To life obscured, which were a fair dismission,
But throw'st them lower than Thou did'st exalt them high,
Unseemly falls,[337] in human eye,   690
Too grievous for the trespass or omission—
Oft leav'st them to the hostile sword
Of heathen and profane,[338] their carcasses
To dogs and fowls a prey, or else captived,
Or to the unjust tribunals, under change of times,
And condemnation of the ungrateful multitude.
If these they scape, perhaps in poverty

---

[327] (1) changing, (2) unstable, fickle
[328] path
[329] crowd, mob
[330] lax, stray, random
[331] like
[332] formally, seriously
[333] chosen, picked
[334] protection, safeguard
[335] honored
[336] abandon
[337] [noun]
[338] unclean, polluted

With sickness and disease Thou bow'st them down,
Painful diseases and deformed,
In crude[339] old age,　　　　　　　　　　　　　　700
Though not disordinate,[340] yet causeless suff'ring
The punishment of dissolute days. In fine,[341]
Just or unjust alike seem miserable,
For oft alike both come to evil end.
　　　　So[342] deal not, with this once Thy glorious champion,
The image of Thy strength, and mighty minister.[343]
What do I beg? How hast Thou dealt[344] already?
Behold him in this state calamitous, and turn
His labors—for Thou canst—to peaceful end.
　　　　But who is this, what thing of sea or land?　　710
Female of sex it seems,
That so bedecked, ornate, and gay,
Comes this way sailing
Like a stately ship
Of Tarsus,[345] bound for th' Isles
Of Javan[346] or Gadier,[347]
With all her bravery[348] on, and tackle[349] trim,[350]
Sails filled, and streamers[351] waving
(Courted by all the winds that hold them play),[352]
An amber scent of odorous perfume　　　　　　720
Her harbinger,[353] a damsel train[354] behind.
Some rich Philistian matron she may seem,
And now at nearer view, no other, certain,

---

[339] rough
[340] excessive
[341] conclusion
[342] in that way
[343] servant, officer
[344] acted
[345] biblical Tarshish: see 2 Chronicles 9:21 ("the ships of Tarshish bringing gold, and silver, ivory, and apes, and peacocks")
[346] Javan, son of Japhet, was the founder of Ionia: the islands of Greece
[347] Cadiz
[348] show, display, finery
[349] apparatus, rigging, implements of war
[350] beautiful, smartly made
[351] flags, banners
[352] strut, flutter
[353] forerunner
[354] retinue, suite: i.e., maids, female attendants

Than Dalila, thy wife.

       Sam. My wife, my traitress, let her not come near me.

       Cho. Yet on she moves, now stands and eyes thee

                fixed,[355]

About t' have spoke, but now, with head declined

Like a fair flower surcharged[356] with dew, she weeps

And words addressed[357] seem into tears dissolved,

Wetting the borders of her silken veil.   730

But now again she makes address[358] to speak.

       Dal. With doubtful feet and wavering resolution

I came, still dreading thy displeasure, Samson,

Which to have merited, without excuse,

I cannot but acknowledge. Yet if tears

May expiate (though the fact more evil drew[359]

In the perverse[360] event than I foresaw)

My penance hath not slack'ned, though my pardon

No way assured. But conjugal affection

Prevailing over fear and timorous doubt,   740

Hath led me on, desirous to behold

Once more thy face, and know of thy estate.[361]

If aught in my ability may serve

To lighten what thou suffer'st, and appease

Thy mind with what amends is in my power,

Though late, yet in some part to recompense

My rash but more unfortunate misdeed.

       Sam. Out, out hyena! These are thy wonted[362] arts,

And arts of every woman false like thee,

To break all faith, all vows, deceive, betray,   750

Then as[363] repentant to submit, beseech

And reconcilement move[364] with feigned remorse,

Confess, and promise wonders in her change,

---

[355] unchanging, firmly resolved
[356] overloaded
[357] prepared
[358] preparation
[359] pulled after it, led to
[360] wicked, evil
[361] condition
[362] accustomed
[363] as if
[364] propose, urge

Not truly penitent, but chief[365] to try[366]
Her husband, how far urged[367] his patience bears,
His virtue or weakness which way t' assail,
Then with more cautious and instructed[368] skill
Again transgresses, and again submits,
That[369] wisest and best men full oft beguiled
With goodness, principled[370] not to reject   760
The penitent, but ever to forgive,
Are drawn to wear out miserable days,
Entangled with a pois'nous bosom[371] snake,
If not by quick destruction soon cut off,
As I by thee, to ages an example.
    Dal. Yet hear me Samson. Not that I endeavor
To lessen or extenuate my offence,
But that on th' other side if it be weighed
By itself, with aggravations[372] not surcharged,[373]
Or else with just allowance counterpoised,[374]   770
I may, if possible, thy pardon find
The easier towards me, or thy hatred less.
First granting, as I do, it was a weakness
In me, but incident[375] to all our sex,
Curiosity, inquisitive, importune[376]
Of secrets, then with like infirmity
To publish[377] them, both common female faults.
Was it not weakness also to make known,
For[378] importunity (that is, for naught),
Wherein consisted all thy strength and safety?   780
To what I did thou showd'st me first the way.
But I to enemies revealed, and should not.

---

[365] chiefly, principally
[366] test
[367] pushed, driven
[368] skillful
[369] so that
[370] trained, habituated
[371] interior, inward
[372] exaggerations
[373] overloaded
[374] counterbalanced
[375] likely, natural
[376] pressing, persistent
[377] make public, proclaim
[378] because of

Nor should'st thou have trusted that to woman's frailty:
Ere I to thee, thou to thyself wast cruel.
Let weakness then with weakness come to parle,[379]
So near related, or the same of kind,
Thine forgive mine, that men may censure thine
The gentler, if severely thou exact not
More strength from me than in thyself was found.
And what if love, which thou interpret'st[380] hate,   790
The jealousy of love, powerful of sway
In human hearts, nor less in mine towards thee,
Caused what I did? I saw thee mutable[381]
Of fancy,[382] feared lest one day thou would'st leave me
As her at Timna,[383] sought by all means therefore
How to endear, and hold thee to me firmest.
No better way I saw than by importuning
To learn thy secrets, get into my power
Thy key of strength and safety. Thou wilt say,
Why then revealed? I was assured by those   800
Who tempted me that nothing was designed[384]
Against thee but safe custody, and hold.[385]
That made for me.[386] I knew that liberty
Would draw thee forth to perilous enterprises,
While I at home sat full of cares and fears,
Wailing thy absence in my widowed bed.
Here[387] I should still enjoy thee day and night,
Mine and love's prisoner, not the Philistines',
Whole[388] to myself, unhazarded[389] abroad,
Fearless[390] at home of partners[391] in my love.   810
These reasons in love's law have passed for good,

---

[379] discussion
[380] interpret as
[381] unsettled, variable, fickle
[382] (1) mind, (2) affection, love
[383] his first wife: see lines 219–27, above
[384] intended, planned
[385] confinement
[386] "that was sufficient/did it for me"
[387] this way
[388] wholly, entirely
[389] not risked
[390] not afraid
[391] sharers

Though fond[392] and reasonless to some, perhaps.
And love hath oft, well meaning, wrought much woe,
Yet always pity or pardon hath obtained.
Be not unlike all others, not austere[393]
As thou art strong, inflexible as steel.
If thou in strength all mortals dost exceed,
In uncompassionate anger do not so.

    Sam. How cunningly the sorceress displays
Her own transgressions, to upbraid me mine!   820
That malice, not repentance, brought thee hither,
By this appears. I gave, thou say'st, th' example,
I led the way. Bitter reproach, but true.
I to myself was false ere thou to me.
Such pardon therefore as I give my folly,
Take to thy wicked deed, which when thou see'st
Impartial, self-severe, inexorable,
Thou wilt renounce thy seeking, and much rather
Confess it feigned. Weakness is thy excuse,
And I believe it—weakness to resist   830
Philistian gold! If weakness may excuse,
What murderer, what traitor, parricide,
Incestuous, sacrilegious, but may plead it?
All wickedness is weakness: that plea therefore
With God or man will gain thee no remission.
But love constrain'd[394] thee! Call it furious[395] rage[396]
To satisfy thy lust. Love seeks to have love.
My love how could'st thou hope, who took'st the way
To raise in me inexpiable[397] hate,
Knowing,[398] as needs I must, by thee betrayed?   840
In vain thou striv'st to cover shame with shame,
Or by evasions thy crime uncover'st more.

    Dal. Since thou determin'st[399] weakness for no plea
In man or woman, though to thy own condemning,

---

[392] foolish
[393] harsh, grim, bitter
[394] forced, compelled
[395] frantic
[396] passion, appetite
[397] irreconcilable
[398] knowing that I had been
[399] decides, ordains

Hear what assaults I had, what snares besides,
What sieges girt me round, ere I consented,
Which might have awed the best resolved of men,
The constantest t' have yielded without blame.
It was not gold, as to my charge thou lay'st,
That wrought[400] with me. Thou know'st the magistrates[401]   850
And princes of my country came in person,
Solicited, commanded, threatened, urged,
Adjured[402] by all the bonds of civil duty
And of religion, pressed[403] how just it was,
How honorable, how glorious to entrap
A common[404] enemy, who had destroyed
Such numbers of our nation. And the priest
Was not behind,[405] but ever at my ear,
Preaching how meritorious with the gods
It would be to ensnare an irreligious   860
Dishonorer of Dagon. What had I
T' oppose against such powerful arguments?
Only my love of thee held long debate,
And combated in silence all these reasons
With hard contest.[406] At length that grounded[407] maxim,
So rife[408] and celebrated in the mouths
Of wisest men, that to the public good
Private respects[409] must yield, with grave authority
Took full possession of me, and prevailed,
Virtue, as I thought—truth—duty so enjoining.[410]   870
        Sam. I thought where all thy circling wiles would end!
In feigned religion, smooth hypocrisy.
But had thy love, still odiously[411] pretended,
Been, as it ought, sincere, it would have taught thee

---

[400] worked, prevailed
[401] officers of the executive government
[402] swore, solemnly entreated
[403] insisted, urged
[404] communal, general
[405] backward
[406] struggle
[407] well-founded
[408] common, widespread
[409] considerations
[410] prescribing, imposing
[411] offensively

Far other reasonings, brought forth other deeds.
I before[412] all the daughters of my tribe
And of my nation chose thee from among
My enemies, loved thee, as too well thou knew'st—
Too well—unbosomed all my secrets to thee,
Not out of levity,[413] but over-pow'red   880
By thy request, who[414] could deny thee nothing,
Yet now am judged an enemy. Why then
Didst thou at first receive me for thy husband,
Then, as since then, thy country's foe professed?[415]
Being once a wife, for me thou wast to leave
Parents and country, nor was I their[416] subject,[417]
Nor under their protection, but my own,
Thou mine,[418] not theirs. If aught against my life
Thy country sought of thee, it sought unjustly,
Against the law of Nature, law of nations,   890
No more thy country, but an impious crew
Of men conspiring to uphold their state
By worse than hostile deeds, violating the ends
For which our country is a name so dear,
Not therefore to be obeyed. But zeal moved thee!
To please thy gods thou didst it—gods unable
To acquit[419] themselves and prosecute their foes.
But by ungodly deeds, the contradiction
Of their own deity, gods cannot be—
Less therefore to be pleased, obeyed, or feared.   900
These false pretexts and varnished colors failing,
Bare in thy guilt how foul must thou appear!
     Dal. In argument with men a woman ever
Goes by the worse,[420] whatever be her cause.
     Sam. For want of words no doubt, or lack of breath!

---

[412] over, in preference to
[413] frivolity, lack of serious thought
[414] I who
[415] acknowledged, openly declared
[416] the Philistines'
[417] subject of a realm, citizen
[418] thou mine = thou under my protection
[419] free
[420] goes by the worse = gets the worst of it

Witness when I was worried with[421] thy peals.[422]
     Dal. I was a fool, too rash, and quite mistaken
In what I thought would have succeeded best.
Let me obtain forgiveness of thee, Samson!
Afford[423] me place[424] to show what recompense   910
Towards thee I intend for what I have misdone,
Misguided. Only what remains past cure
Bear not too sensibly,[425] nor still insist
T' afflict thyself in vain. Though sight be lost,
Life yet hath many solaces, enjoyed
Where other senses want[426] not their delights,
At home in leisure and domestic ease,
Exempt from many a care and chance[427] to which
Eye-sight exposes, daily, men abroad.[428]
I to the lords will intercede, not doubting   920
Their favorable ear,[429] that I may fetch thee
From forth this loathsome prison-house, t' abide
With me, where my redoubled love and care,
With nursing diligence (to me glad office),[430]
May ever tend about thee to[431] old age
With all things grateful[432] cheered, and so supplied
That what by me thou hast lost thou least shalt miss.
     Sam. No, no, of my condition take no care!
It fits not.[433] Thou and I long since are twain,[434]
Nor think me so unwary or accurst   930
To bring my feet again into the snare
Where once I have been caught. I know thy trains,[435]

---

[421] by
[422] outbursts/volleys of sound (words)
[423] spare, give, yield
[424] occasion, opportunity
[425] acutely
[426] lack
[427] accident
[428] out of their houses
[429] attention
[430] duty, function
[431] up to, until
[432] pleasant
[433] fits not = is not suitable
[434] separated, disunited, estranged
[435] tricks

Though dearly to my cost! Thy ginns,[436] and toils.[437]
Thy fair enchanted cup, and warbling charms
No more on me have power, their force is nulled.[438]
So much of adders' wisdom[439] I have learned
To fence my ear against thy sorceries.
If in my flower of youth and strength, when all men
Loved, honored, feared me, thou alone could hate me,
Thy husband, slight[440] me, sell[441] me, and forego[442] me,   940
How would'st thou use me now, blind, and thereby
Deceiveable, in most things as a child
Helpless, thence easily contemned,[443] and scorned,
And last[444] neglected? How would'st thou insult[445]
When I must live uxorious[446] to thy will
In perfect[447] thraldom?[448] How again betray me,
Bearing my words and doings to the lords
To gloss[449] upon, and censuring,[450] frown or smile?
This jail I count[451] the house of liberty
To thine, whose doors my feet shall never enter!   950
   Dal. Let me approach, at least, and touch thy hand.
   Sam. Not for thy life, lest fierce remembrance wake
My sudden rage to tear thee joint by joint.
At distance I forgive thee, go with that.
Bewail thy falsehood, and the pious works
It hath brought forth to make thee memorable
Among illustrious women, faithful wives.
Cherish thy hast'ned widowhood with the gold

---

[436] devices, contrivances
[437] nets and snares
[438] annulled
[439] "they are like the deaf adder that stoppeth her ear, which will not hearken to the voice of charmers" (Psalm 58:4–5)
[440] disdain
[441] betray
[442] leave
[443] despised
[444] finally, at last
[445] affront, exult
[446] displaying excessive affection/regard for one's wife
[447] complete, unqualified
[448] slavery
[449] explain, interpret
[450] judging, criticizing
[451] hold, reckon

Of matrimonial treason. So farewell.
      Dal. I see thou art implacable,[452] more deaf   960
To prayers than winds and seas. Yet winds to seas
Are reconciled at length, and sea to shore.
Thy anger, unappeasable, still rages,
Eternal tempest never to be calmed.
Why do I humble thus myself, and suing[453]
For peace, reap nothing but repulse and hate—
Bid go,[454] with evil omen and the brand
Of infamy upon my name denounced?
To mix with thy concernments[455] I desist
Henceforth, nor too much disapprove my own.   970
Fame if not double-faced is double-mouthed,
And with contrary blast proclaims most deeds.
On both his wings, one black, th' other white,
Bears greatest names in his wild airy flight.
My name perhaps among the circumcised[456]
In Dan, in Judah, and the bordering tribes,
To all posterity may stand defamed,
With malediction mentioned, and the blot
Of falsehood most unconjugal traduced.[457]
But in my country, where I most desire,   980
In Ecron, Gaza, Asdod, and in Gath
I shall be named among the famousest
Of women, sung at solemn festivals,
Living and dead recorded,[458] who to save
Her country from a fierce destroyer chose
Above[459] the faith of wedlock-bands[460]—my tomb
With odors[461] visited and annual flowers.
Not less renowned than in Mount Ephraim
Jael, who with inhospitable guile

---

[452] inexorable, irreconcilable
[453] pursuing, petitioning
[454] bid (directed) to go (to leave)
[455] affairs
[456] the Jews
[457] slandered
[458] recited, sung, narrated
[459] higher than
[460] ties, agreements
[461] incense, perfume

Smote Sisera sleeping through the temples nailed.[462]   990
Nor shall I count it heinous[463] to enjoy
The public marks of honor and reward
Conferred upon me, for the piety
Which to my country I was judged t' have shown.
At this whoever envies or repines[464]
I leave him to his lot, and like my own.
     Chor. She's gone, a manifest[465] serpent by her sting
Discovered in the end, till now concealed.
     Sam. So let her go. God sent her to debase me
And aggravate my folly, who committed   1000
To such a viper his most sacred trust
Of secrecy, my safety, and my life.
     Chor. Yet beauty, though injurious, hath strange power,
After offence returning, to regain
Love once possessed, nor can be easily
Repulsed, without much inward passion felt
And secret sting of amorous remorse.
     Sam. Love-quarrels oft in pleasing concord end.
Not wedlock-treachery, endangering life.
     Chor. It is not virtue, wisdom, valor, wit,   1010
Strength, comeliness of shape, or amplest merit
That woman's love can win or long inherit,[466]
But what it is, hard is to say,
Harder to hit[467]
(Which way soever men refer[468] it),
Much like thy riddle, Samson,[469] in one day
Or seven, though one should musing sit.
     If any of these or all, the Timnian bride
Had not so soon preferred
Thy paranymph,[470] worthless to thee compared,   1020

---

[462] Sisera, a Canaanite hostile to the Jews, fled their pursuit; Jael, wife of Sisera's host, drove a nail through his head as he lay sleeping: see Judges 4, 5
[463] criminal
[464] is discontented
[465] evident, obvious
[466] receive, hold
[467] find, light upon
[468] consult upon
[469] the "secret" referred to in line 384, above
[470] best man at a wedding: Samson's first wife was subsequently married to this former best man

Successor in thy bed,
Nor both[471] so loosely disallied
Their nuptials, nor this last so treacherously
Had shorn the fatal[472] harvest of thy head.
Is it for that[473] such outward ornament
Was lavished on their sex, that inward gifts
Were left for haste unfinished, judgment scant,[474]
Capacity not raised[475] to apprehend
Or value what is best
In choice, but oftest to affect[476] the wrong?   1030
Or was too much of self-love mixed,
Of constancy no root[477] infixed,[478]
That either they love nothing, or not long?
    What e'er it be, to wisest men and best
Seeming at first all Heav'nly under virgin veil,
Soft, modest, meek, demure,[479]
Once joined the contrary she proves, a thorn
Intestine, far within defensive[480] arms
A cleaving[481] mischief, in[482] his way to virtue
Adverse and turbulent,[483] or by her charms   1040
Draws him awry,[484] enslaved
With dotage,[485] and his sense depraved[486]
To folly and shameful deeds which ruin ends.
What pilot so expert but needs must wreck,
Embarked with such a steer-mate at the helm?
    Favored of Heav'n who finds

---

[471] neither would both wives have
[472] destined, ruinous, deadly
[473] for that = because
[474] limited, very little
[475] formed, created, produced
[476] prefer
[477] basis, inner/essential part
[478] implanted
[479] serious, calm
[480] defending
[481] (1) sundering, separating, (2) clinging, adhering
[482] on, along
[483] disorderly, troubling
[484] out of the right path
[485] excessive fondness
[486] corrupted

One[487] virtuous (rarely found),
That in domestic good combines.[488]
Happy that house! His way to peace is smooth.
But virtue which breaks through all opposition, 1050
And all temptation can remove,
Most shines and most is acceptable above.
   Therefore God's universal Law
Gave to the man despotic[489] power
Over his female in due[490] awe,[491]
Nor from that right to part[492] an hour,
Smile she[493] or lour.[494]
So shall he least confusion draw
On his whole life, not swayed
By female usurpation, nor dismayed. 1060
   But had we best retire, I see a storm?
  Sam. Fair days have oft contracted[495] wind and rain.
  Chor. But this another kind of tempest brings.
  Sam. Be less abstruse,[496] my riddling days are past.
  Chor. Look now for no enchanting voice, nor fear
The bait of honeyed words. A rougher tongue
Draws hitherward. I know him by his stride,
The giant Harapha[497] of Gath, his look
Haughty as is his pile[498] high-built and proud.
Comes he in peace? What wind hath blown him hither 1070
I less conjecture[499] than when first I saw
The sumptuous[500] Dalila floating this way.
His habit[501] carries peace, his brow defiance.

---

[487] a woman
[488] joins/unites (with her virtue)
[489] arbitrarily/absolutely authoritative
[490] proper
[491] dread mixed with veneration
[492] sever, quit
[493] smile she = whether she smiles
[494] frown, scowl
[495] been involved in
[496] hidden, secret, recondite
[497] "the giant"
[498] home
[499] can guess/predict
[500] magnificent, splendid
[501] dress

  Sam. Or[502] peace or not, alike to me he comes.
  Chor. His fraught[503] we soon shall know. He now
   arrives.
  Har. I come not, Samson, to condole thy chance,[504]
As these perhaps, yet wish it had not been,
Though for no friendly intent. I am of Gath.
Men call me Harapha, of stock renowned
As Og[505] or Anak[506] and the Emims[507] old   1080
That Kiriathaim[508] held: thou knowst me now,
If thou at all art known. Much I have heard
Of thy prodigious[509] might and feats performed,
Incredible to me, in this displeased,
That I was never present on the place
Of those encounters, where we might have tried[510]
Each other's force in camp[511] or listed field:[512]
And now am come to see of whom such noise
Hath walked about, and each limb to survey,
If thy appearance answer loud report.[513]   1090
   Sam. The way to know were not to see but taste.
   Har. Dost thou already single[514] me? I thought
Gyves[515] and the mill had tamed thee. O that fortune
Had brought me to the field where thou art famed
T' have wrought such wonders with an ass's jaw!
I should have forced thee soon wish other arms,
Or left thy carcass where the ass lay thrown.
So had the glory of prowess been recovered
To Palestine, won by a Philistine

---

[502] whether
[503] freight
[504] mischance, luck
[505] see Deuteronomy 3:1–11
[506] see Numbers 13:33
[507] a race of giants dwelling east of the River Jordan: see Deuteronomy 2:10–11
[508] see Genesis 14:5
[509] unnatural, amazing, vast, monstrous
[510] tested
[511] in camp: on a campaign
[512] listed field: battlefield divided into lists (areas for jousting tournaments)
[513] rumor, common talk
[514] challenge to single combat
[515] shackles, fetters

From[516] the unforeskinned race,[517] of whom thou bear'st   1100
The highest name for valiant acts. That honor
Certain t' have won by mortal[518] duel from thee,
I lose, prevented by thy eyes put out.
> *Sam.* Boast not of what thou would'st have done, but
> do
What then thou would'st. Thou see'st it in thy hand.
> *Har.* To combat with a blind man I disdain.
And thou hast need much washing to be[519] touched.
> *Sam.* Such usage as your honorable lords
Afford me, assassinated[520] and betrayed,
Who durst not with their whole united powers   1110
In fight withstand me single and unarmed,
Nor in the house with chamber[521] ambushes
Close-banded[522] durst attack me—no, not sleeping—
Till they had hired a woman with their gold,
Breaking her marriage faith to circumvent[523] me.
Therefore without feigned shifts[524] let be assigned
Some narrow place enclosed, where sight may give thee
(Or rather flight) no great advantage on me.
Then put on all thy gorgeous[525] arms,[526] thy helmet
And brigandine[527] of brass, thy broad habergeon,[528]   1120
Vant-brass[529] and greves,[530] and gauntlet,[531] add thy spear,
A weaver's beam,[532] and seven-times-folded[533] shield.
I only with an oaken staff will meet thee,

---

[516] away from
[517] the circumcised, the Jews
[518] deadly
[519] in order to be
[520] destroyed by treachery
[521] room (in a house)
[522] close-banded = closely joined
[523] get the better of
[524] expedients, stratagems
[525] showy
[526] armor
[527] body armor: rings (or plates) of metal covered with canvas, linen, or leather
[528] upper-body armor
[529] vant-brace: armor for forearms
[530] leg armor
[531] glove of leather, covered with metal plates
[532] weaver's beam: wooden cylinder in a loom, on which, before weaving, the warp is wound (see 1 Samuel 7:7)
[533] i.e., seven laminations (layers) of leather

'And raise such out-cries on thy clattered[534] iron
Which long shall not with-hold me from thy head,
That in a little time, while breath remains thee,
Thou oft shalt wish thyself at Gath to boast
Again in safety what thou would'st have done
To Samson, but shalt never see Gath more.

    Har. Thou durst not thus disparage glorious
               arms,   1130
Which greatest heroes have in battle worn,
Their ornament and safety, had not spells
And black enchantments, some magician's art
Armed thee or charmed thee strong, which thou from Heav'n
Feign'dst at thy birth was giv'n thee in thy hair,
Where strength can least abide, though all thy hairs
Were bristles ranged like those that ridge the back
Of chafed[535] wild boars or ruffled[536] porcupines.

    Sam. I know no spells, use no forbidden arts.
My trust is in the living God who gave me   1140
At my nativity this strength, diffused
No less through all my sinews, joints and bones,
Than thine, while[537] I preserved these locks unshorn,
The pledge of my unviolated vow.
For proof hereof, if Dagon be thy god,
Go to his temple, invocate[538] his aid
With solemnest devotion, spread before him
How highly it concerns his glory now
To frustrate and dissolve these magic spells,
Which I to be the power of Israel's God   1150
Avow, and challenge Dagon to the test,
Offering to combat thee, his champion bold,
With th' utmost of his godhead seconded:[539]
Then thou shalt see, or rather to thy sorrow
Soon feel, whose God is strongest, thine or mine.

    Har. Presume not on thy God, what e'er He be.

---

[534] rattling, noisy
[535] raging
[536] stiff-spined
[537] as long as
[538] invoke
[539] supported

Thee He regards[540] not, owns[541] not, hath cut off
Quite from his[542] people and delivered up
Into thy enemies' hand, permitted them
To put out both thine eyes, and fettered send thee   1160
Into the common prison, there to grind[543]
Among the slaves and asses, thy comrades,
As good for nothing else, no better service
With those thy boist'rous[544] locks. No worthy match
For valor to assail, nor by the sword
Of noble warrior, so to stain his honor,
But by the barber's razor best subdued.[545]

    Sam. All these indignities, for such they are
From thine,[546] these evils I deserve and more,
Acknowledge them from God inflicted on me   1170
Justly, yet despair not of His final pardon
Whose ear is ever open, and His eye
Gracious[547] to re-admit the suppliant.
In confidence whereof I once again
Defy[548] thee to the trial of mortal fight,
By combat to decide whose god is God,
Thine or whom I with Israel's sons adore.

    Har. Fair honor that thou dost thy God, in trusting
He will accept thee to defend his cause —
A murderer, a revolter,[549] and a robber.   1180

    Sam. Tongue-doughty[550] giant, how dost thou prove me
these?

    Har. Is not thy nation subject to our lords?
Their magistrates confessed it, when they took thee
As a league[551]-breaker and delivered, bound,
Into our hands—for hadst thou not committed

---

[540] notices, cares about
[541] acknowledges
[542] Samson's
[543] labor
[544] coarse-growing, rank, rough
[545] conquered, overcome
[546] thine (your) people
[547] indulgent, beneficent
[548] challenge
[549] rebel
[550] tongue-valiant
[551] treaty

Notorious[552] murder on those thirty men
At Askalon, who never did thee harm,
Then like a robber strip'dst them of their robes?[553]
The Philistines, when thou hadst broke the league,
Went up with armèd powers, thee only seeking,   1190
To others did no violence nor spoil.[554]

      Sam. Among the daughters of the Philistines
I chose a wife, which argued[555] me no foe,
And in your city held my nuptial feast.
But your ill-meaning politician[556] lords,
Under pretence of bridal friends and guests,
Appointed to await me thirty spies,
Who threat'ning cruel death constrained[557] the bride
To wring from me and tell to them my secret
That solved the riddle which I had proposed.   1200
When I perceived all set on enmity,
As[558] on my enemies, wherever chanced,
I used[559] hostility, and took their spoil
To pay my underminers[560] in their coin.
My nation was subjected to your lords.
It was the force of conquest; force with force
Is well ejected when the conquered can.
But I a private[561] person, whom my country
As a league[562]-breaker gave up,[563] bound, presumed[564]
Single[565] rebellion and did hostile acts?   1210
I was no private but a person raised
With strength sufficient, and command from Heav'n,
To free my country. If their servile minds
Me their deliverer sent would not receive,

---

[552] well-known (and bad)
[553] see Judges 14:10–19
[554] booty, loot
[555] indicated, proved
[556] crafty intriguers
[557] forced, compelled
[558] so
[559] engaged in, employed
[560] secret enemies
[561] holding no official position
[562] treaty
[563] gave up = surrendered
[564] undertook, ventured, dared
[565] solitary

But to their masters gave me up for nought,
Th' unworthier they. Whence to this day they serve.
I was to do my part from Heav'n assigned,
And had performed it if my known[566] offense
Had not disabled me[567]—not all your force.
These shifts[568] refuted, answer thy appellant[569]   1220
(Though by his blindness maimed for high attempts)
Who now defies[570] thee thrice[571] to single fight,
As a petty[572] enterprise[573] of small[574] enforce.[575]

    Har. With thee, a man condemned, a slave enrolled,
Due by the law to capital punishment?
To fight with thee no man of arms will deign.

    Sam. Cam'st thou for this, vain boaster, to survey[576]
            me,
To descant[577] on my strength, and give thy verdict?
Come nearer, part not hence so slight informed—
But take good heed my hand survey not thee.   1230

    Har. O Baal-zebub![578] Can my ears, unused,[579]
Hear these dishonors and not render[580] death?

    Sam. No man withholds thee, nothing from thy hand
Fear I incurable: bring up thy van![581]
My heels are fettered, but my fist is free.

    Har. This insolence[582] other kind of answer fits.[583]

    Sam. Go, baffled[584] coward, lest I run upon thee,

---

[566] familiar, well-known
[567] i.e., revealing the secret of his strength to Dalila, who then cut off his hair
[568] tricks, sophistries, evasions
[569] challenger
[570] challenges
[571] for the third time, three times in succession
[572] trivial, minor, unimportant
[573] undertaking, business
[574] little, slight, no great
[575] exercise
[576] examine, inspect, evaluate
[577] comment on, carp about
[578] Philistine god
[579] unaccustomed
[580] give in return, cause
[581] front line of battle formations
[582] offensive arrogance
[583] is appropriate for
[584] bewildered

Though in these chains—bulk[585] without spirit vast!—[586]
And with one buffet[587] lay thy structure[588] low,
Or swing thee in the air, then dash thee down   1240
To th' hazard[589] of thy brains and shattered sides.
    Har. By Astaroth, ere long thou shalt lament
These braveries,[590] in irons loaden on thee.
    Chor. His giantship is gone, somewhat crestfall'n,
Stalking[591] with less unconscionable[592] strides
And lower looks, but in a sultry[593] chafe.[594]
    Sam. I dread him not, nor all his giant-brood,
Though fame[595] divulge[596] him father of five sons,
All of gigantic size, Goliath chief.[597]
    Chor. He will directly to the lords, I fear,   1250
And with malicious counsel stir them up
Some way or other yet further to afflict thee.
    Sam. He must allege some cause, and offered fight
Will not dare mention, lest a question rise
Whether he durst accept the offer or not,
And that he durst not plain enough appeared.
Much more affliction than already felt
They cannot well impose, nor I sustain,
If they intend advantage[598] of my labors,
The work of many hands, which earns my keeping   1260
With no small profit daily to my owners.
    But come what will, my deadliest foe will prove
My speediest friend, by death to rid me hence:
The worst that he can give, to me the best.
Yet so it may fall out, because their end

---

[585] huge/massy frame
[586] large
[587] blow (of the hand)
[588] frame, body
[589] peril
[590] acts of bravado/defiance
[591] marching
[592] unconcerned, indifferent, uncaring
[593] passionate
[594] temper
[595] common talk
[596] publicly declare
[597] the greatest
[598] benefit, profit

Is hate, not help to me, it may—with mine—[599]
Draw their own ruin who attempt the deed.
   Chor. Oh how comely[600] it is, and how reviving
To the spirits of just men long oppressed,
When God into the hands of their deliverer   1270
Puts invincible might
To quell[601] the mighty of the earth, th' oppressor,
The brute and boist'rous[602] force of violent men,
Hardy[603] and industrious[604] to support
Tyrannic power, but raging[605] to pursue
The righteous and all such as honor truth!
He[606] all their ammunition[607]
And feats of war defeats
With plain heroic magnitude of mind
And celestial vigor armed,   1280
Their armories and magazines contemns,[608]
Renders them useless, while
With wingèd expedition,[609]
Swift as the lightning glance,[610] he executes[611]
His errand on the wicked, who surprised
Lose their defence, distracted[612] and amazed.[613]
   But patience is more oft the exercise[614]
Of Saints, the trial of their fortitude,[615]
Making them each his own deliverer,
And victor over all[616]   1290

---

[599] my death
[600] pleasing, proper
[601] overcome, vanquish
[602] violent, truculent
[603] bold
[604] zealous, assiduous
[605] frenzied, furious
[606] their deliverer
[607] military stores/equipment
[608] disdains
[609] speed
[610] flash
[611] performs, fulfills, discharges
[612] perplexed, confused, disordered
[613] panicked, overwhelmed, astonished
[614] act of worship, religious observance
[615] moral strength/courage
[616] everything

That tyranny or fortune can inflict.
Either of these is in thy lot,
Samson, with might endued[617]
Above the sons of men. But sight bereaved[618]
May chance to number thee with those
Whom patience finally must crown.
This idol's day hath been to thee no day of rest,
      Laboring thy mind
More than the working day thy hands.
And yet perhaps more trouble is behind.[619]   1300
For I descry this way
Some other tending.[620] In his hand
A scepter or quaint[621] staff he bears,
Comes on amain,[622] speed in his look.
By his habit I discern him now
A public officer, and now at hand.
His message will be short and voluble.[623]

      Off. Hebrews, the pris'ner Samson here I seek.
      Chor. His manacles remark[624] him. There he sits.
      Off. Samson, to thee our lords thus bid me say: 1310
This day to Dagon is a solemn feast,
With sacrifices, triumph, pomp,[625] and games.
Thy strength they know surpassing human rate,[626]
And now some public proof[627] thereof require
To honor this great feast and great assembly.
Rise therefore with all speed and come along,
Where I will see thee heartn'd[628] and fresh clad
To appear as fits before th' illustrious lords.
      Sam. Thou know'st I am an Hebrew. Therefore tell
                     them

---

[617] endowed
[618] deprived, stripped
[619] in reserve, still to come
[620] making his way
[621] skillfully worked
[622] at full speed
[623] fluent
[624] distinguish, mark out
[625] pageants, parades, displays
[626] standard, degree
[627] evidence
[628] strengthened, cheered (often by alcohol)

Our Law forbids at their religious rites   1320
My presence. For that cause I cannot come.
      Off. This answer, be assured, will not content them.
      Sam. Have they not sword-players, and every sort
Of gymnic artists, wrestlers, riders, runners,
Jugglers and dancers, antics,[629] mummers,[630] mimics,[631]
But they must pick me out, with shackles tired
And over-labored at their public mill,
To make[632] them sport[633] with blind activity?
Do they not seek occasion of new quarrels
On my refusal to distress[634] me more,   1330
Or make a game of my calamities?
Return the way thou cam'st. I will not come.
      Off. Regard[635] thyself: this will offend them highly.
      Sam. Myself? My conscience and internal peace!
Can they think me so broken, so debased
With corporal servitude, that my mind ever
Will condescend to such absurd commands?
Although their drudge,[636] to be their fool or jester,
And in my midst of sorrow and heart-grief
To show them feats, and play[637] before their god,   1340
The worst of all indignities, yet on me
Joined[638] with extreme contempt? I will not come.
      Off. My message was imposed on me with speed,
Brooks no delay: is this thy resolution?[639]
      Sam. So take it, with what speed thy message needs.
      Off. I am sorry[640] what this stoutness[641] will produce.
      Sam. Perhaps thou shalt have cause to sorrow indeed.
      Chor. Consider, Samson. Matters now are strained

---

[629] clowns
[630] actors
[631] mimes, burlesque actors
[632] furnish
[633] diversion
[634] afflict, strain, make miserable
[635] look to
[636] worker at low/servile/hard/distasteful tasks
[637] frolic, exercise
[638] enjoined, commanded
[639] formal decision
[640] pained
[641] defiance

Up to the height, whether to hold or break.
He's gone, and who knows how he may report   135(
Thy words by adding fuel to the flame?
Expect another message more imperious,
More lordly thund'ring than thou well wilt bear.

    Sam. Shall I abuse this consecrated gift
Of strength, again returning with my hair
After my great transgression? So requite[642]
Favor[643] renewed, and add a greater sin
By prostituting holy things to idols?
A Nazarite[644] in place abominable
Vaunting[645] my strength in honor to their Dagon?   136(
Besides, how vile, contemptible, ridiculous,
What act more execrably unclean, profane?

    Chor. Yet with this strength thou serv'st the Philistines,
Idolatrous, uncircumcised, unclean.

    Sam. Not in their idol-worship, but by labor
Honest and lawful to deserve my food
Of those who have me in their civil[646] power.

    Chor. Where the heart joins not, outward acts defile
                 not.

    Sam. Where outward force constrains,[647] the
                 sentence[648] holds.
But who constrains me to the temple of Dagon,   137(
Not dragging? The Philistian lords command!
Commands are no constraints. If I obey them,
I do it freely, venturing to displease
God for the fear of man, and man prefer,
Set God behind—which in His jealously[649]
Shall never, unrepented, find forgiveness.
Yet that He may dispense[650] with me or thee,
Present in temples at idolatrous rites

---

[642] pay back
[643] God's favor
[644] one pledged to abstinence
[645] glorifying
[646] legal
[647] compels
[648] saying, maxim
[649] anger
[650] relax rules, grant dispensations/permission

For some important cause, thou need'st not doubt.
      Chor. How thou wilt here come off surmounts my
             reach.   1380
      Sam. Be of good courage. I begin to feel
Some rousing[651] motions in me which dispose[652]
To something extraordinary my thoughts.
I with this messenger will go along—
Nothing to do, be sure, that may dishonor
Our Law, or stain my vow of Nazarite.
If there be aught of presage[653] in the mind,
This day will be remarkable in my life
By some great act, or of my days the last.
      Chor. In time thou hast resolved: the man
             returns.   1390
      Off. Samson, this second message from our lords
To thee I am bid say. Art thou our slave,
Our captive, at the public mill our drudge,
And dar'st thou at our sending and command
Dispute thy coming? Come without delay,
Or we shall find[654] such engines[655] to assail[656]
And hamper[657] thee, as thou shalt come of force,
Though thou wert firmlier fast'ned than a rock.
      Sam. I could be well content to try[658] their art,[659]
Which to no few of them would prove pernicious.[660]   1400
Yet knowing their advantages too many,
Because they shall[661] not trail[662] me through their streets
Like a wild beast, I am content to go.
Masters' commands come with a power resistless
To such as owe them absolute subjection,
And for a life who will not change his purpose?

---

[651] waking, stirring
[652] incline toward, prepare
[653] prognostication, prediction
[654] obtain, invent, provide for
[655] devices, usually but not necessarily mechanical
[656] assault, attack
[657] confine
[658] test
[659] technical skill
[660] fatal
[661] must
[662] drag

(So mutable are all the ways of men)
Yet this be sure, in nothing to comply
Scandalous or forbidden in our Law.

    Off. I praise thy resolution. Doff[663] these links:[664]   1410
By this compliance thou wilt win the lords
To favor, and perhaps to set thee free.

    Sam. Brethren, farewell. Your company along
I will not wish, lest it perhaps offend them
To see me girt[665] with friends. And how the sight
Of me as of a common enemy,
So dreaded once, may now exasperate[666] them
I know not. Lords are lordliest in their wine,
And the well-feasted priest then soonest fired
With zeal, if aught religion seem concerned.   1420
No less the people on their holy-days
Impetuous,[667] insolent,[668] unquenchable.
Happ'n what may, of me expect to hear
Nothing dishonorable, impure, unworthy
Our God, our Law, my nation, or myself.
The last of me or no, I cannot warrant.[669]

    Chor. Go, and the Holy One
Of Israel be thy guide
To what may serve
His glory best, and spread His name
Great among the heathen round—[670]   1430
Send thee the Angel of thy birth, to stand
Fast by thy side, who from thy father's field
Rode up in flames after his message told
Of thy conception, and be now a shield
Of fire—that Spirit that first rushed on thee
In the camp of Dan
Be efficacious in thee, now at need.
For never was from Heav'n imparted

---

663 take off, lay aside
664 chains
665 surrounded
666 irritate
667 violent
668 arrogant, immoderate
669 guarantee, promise
670 round about, all around

Measure[671] of strength so great to mortal seed,
As in thy wond'rous actions hath been seen.   1440
       But wherefore comes old Manoa in such haste,
With youthful steps? Much livelier than erewhile
He seems: supposing here to find his son,
Or of him bringing to us some glad news?
       Man. Peace with you, brethren. My inducement[672]
                hither
Was not at present here to find my son,
By order of the lords new parted hence
To come and play[673] before them at their feast.
I heard all as I came, the city rings
And numbers thither flock. I had no will,[674]   1450
Lest I should see him forced to things unseemly.
But that which moved my coming, now, was chiefly
To give ye part[675] with me what hope I have
With good success to work his liberty.
       Chor. That hope would much rejoice us to partake[676]
With thee. Say reverend Sire, we thirst to hear.
       Man. I have attempted[677] one by one the lords,
Either at home, or through the high street passing,
With supplication prone and father's tears,
T' accept of ransom for my son, their pris'ner.   1460
Some much averse[678] I found, and wondrous harsh,
Contemptuous, proud, set on revenge and spite;
That part most reverenc'd Dagon and his priests.
Others more moderate seeming, but their aim
Private reward, for which both god and state
They easily would set to sale. A third
More generous[679] far and civil,[680] who confessed
They had enough revenged, having reduced
Their foe to misery beneath their fears.

---

[671] quantity, degree
[672] my inducement = what has led/brought me
[673] frolic, exercise
[674] desire
[675] share
[676] share, participate in
[677] tried to make use of
[678] disinclined, opposed
[679] liberal, magnanimous
[680] courteous

The rest[681] was[682] magnanimity[683] to remit,[684]   1470
If some convenient[685] ransom were proposed.
    What noise or shout was that? It tore the sky.
    Chor. Doubtless the people shouting, to behold
Their once great dread, captive and blind before them,
Or at some proof of strength before them shown.
    Man. His ransom, if my whole inheritance[686]
May compass[687] it, shall willingly be paid
And numbered down.[688] Much rather I shall choose
To live the poorest in my tribe, than richest,
And he in that calamitous[689] prison left.   1480
No, I am fixed[690] not to part hence without him.
For his redemption all my patrimony,
If need be, I am ready to forego
And quit: not wanting[691] him, I shall want nothing.
    Chor. Fathers are wont[692] to lay up[693] for their sons:
Thou for thy son art bent to lay out all.
Sons wont to nurse their parents in old age:
Thou in old age car'st how to nurse thy son,
Made older than thy age, through eye-sight lost.
    Man. It shall be my delight to tend his eyes, 1490
And view him sitting in the house, enobled[694]
With all those high exploits by him achieved,
And on his shoulders waving down those locks,
That of a nation armed[695] the strength contained.
And I persuade me God had not permitted
His strength again to grow up, with his hair

---

[681] of his sentence/punishment
[682] would be
[683] high-souled kindness
[684] pardon, forgive, release
[685] agreeable
[686] property, estate
[687] accomplish
[688] numbered down = counted out, paid down
[689] miserable
[690] firm, settled, determined
[691] lacking, missing
[692] accustomed
[693] lay up = save
[694] elevated, dignified
[695] [adjective]

Garrisoned[696] round about him like a camp[697]
Of faithful soldiery, were not His purpose
To use him further yet in some great service,
Not to sit idle with so great a gift   1500
Useless, and thence ridiculous[698] about him.
And since his strength with eye-sight was not lost,
God will restore him eye-sight to his strength.

    Chor. Thy hopes are not ill founded nor seem vain[699]
Of His delivery,[700] and thy joy thereon
Conceived,[701] agreeable[702] to a father's love,
In both which we, as next,[703] participate.

    Man. I know your friendly minds and—O what noise!
Mercy of Heav'n, what hideous noise was that!
Horribly loud, unlike the former shout.   1510

    Chor. Noise call you it? or universal groan,
As if the whole inhabitation[704] perished.
Blood, death, and deathful deeds are in that noise,
Ruin, destruction at the utmost point.

    Man. Of ruin indeed methought I heard the noise.
Oh it continues, they have slain my son!

    Chor. Thy son is rather slaying them: that outcry
From slaughter of one foe could not ascend.

    Man. Some dismal[705] accident[706] it needs must be.
What shall we do, stay here or run and see?   1520

    Chor. Best keep together here, lest running thither
We unawares run into danger's mouth.
This evil on the Philistines is fall'n:
From whom could else a general cry be heard?
The sufferers then will scarce molest us here;
From other hands we need not much to fear.
What if his eye-sight (for to Israel's God

---

[696] on garrison (protection, defense) duty
[697] body of troops
[698] laughable, absurd
[699] empty, unavailing
[700] action, accomplishing
[701] formed
[702] consistent/harmonious with
[703] of the same tribe, they are in a sense next of kin
[704] place, population
[705] disastrous, evil
[706] happening

Nothing is hard) by miracle restored,
He now be dealing dole[707] among his foes,
And over heaps of slaughtered walk his way? 1530
      Man. That were a joy presumptuous to be thought.
      Chor. Yet God hath wrought things as incredible
For His people of old. What hinders now?
      Man. He can, I know, but doubt to think He will,
Yet hope would fain subscribe,[708] and tempts belief.
A little stay[709] will bring some notice hither.
      Chor. Of good or bad so great, of bad the sooner,
For evil news rides post,[710] while good news baits.[711]
And to our wish I see one hither speeding,
An Hebrew, as I guess, and of our tribe. 1540
      Mess. O whither shall I run, or which way fly[712]
The sight of this so horrid spectacle
Which erst my eyes beheld and yet behold,
For dire[713] imagination still pursues me?
But providence or instinct of nature seems,
Or reason (though disturbed, and scarce consulted)
To have guided me aright, I know not how,
To thee first, reverend Manoa, and to these
My countrymen, whom here I knew remaining,
As at some distance from the place of horror, 1550
So in the sad event too much concerned.
      Man. The accident[714] was loud, and here before thee,
With rueful cry, yet what it was we hear not.
No preface needs: thou see'st we long to know.
      Mess. It would burst forth, but I recover breath
And sense distract,[715] to know well what I utter.
      Man. Tell us the sum,[716] the circumstance[717] defer.
      Mess. Gaza yet stands, but all her sons are fall'n,

---

[707] sorrow, grief
[708] assent
[709] wait, delay
[710] express (fast)
[711] abates, stops for a while
[712] flee
[713] dreadful, terrible
[714] event
[715] confused, disordered, deranged
[716] upshot, conclusion
[717] details, particulars

All in a moment overwhelmed and fall'n.
      Man. Sad, but thou know'st to Israelites not
                                      saddest,   1560
The desolation of a hostile city.
      Mess. Feed on that first, there may in grief be surfeit.[718]
      Man. Relate by whom.
                  Mess. By Samson.
                              Man. That still
                                      lessens
The sorrow, and converts it nigh to joy.
      Mess. Ah Manoa, I refrain too suddenly[719]
To utter what will come at last too soon,[720]
Lest evil tidings with too rude eruption[721]
Hitting thy agèd ear should pierce too deep.
      Man. Suspense in news is torture: speak them out.
      Mess. Then take the worst in brief: Samson is
                                    dead.   1570
      Man. The worst indeed. O all my hope's defeated
To free him hence! But death who sets all free
Hath paid his ransom now and full discharge.
What windy[722] joy this day had I conceived,
Hopeful of his delivery, which now proves
Abortive as the first-born bloom of spring
Nipped with the lagging rear of winter's frost.
Yet ere I give the reins to grief, say first,
How died he? Death to life is crown or shame.
All by him fell, thou say'st. By whom fell he?   1580
What glorious hand gave Samson his death's wound?
      Mess. Unwounded of his enemies he fell.
      Man. Wearied with slaughter, then, or how? Explain.
      Mess. By his own hands.
                        Man. Self-violence? What
                                    cause
Brought him so soon at variance[723] with himself,
Among his foes?

---

[718] excess, more than enough
[719] promptly, hastily
[720] quickly
[721] bursting out
[722] worthless, vain
[723] discord, quarrel

> > *Mess.* Inevitable cause
> At once both to destroy and be destroyed.
> The edifice where all were met to see him
> Upon their heads and on his own he pulled.

> > *Man.* O lastly[724] over-strong against thyself!   1590
> A dreadful way thou took'st to thy revenge.
> More than enough we know, but while things yet
> Are in confusion, give us, if thou canst,
> Eye-witness of what first or last was done,
> Relation[725] more particular and distinct.

> > *Mess.* Occasions[726] drew me early to this city,
> And as the gates I entered with sun-rise,
> The morning trumpets festival proclaimed
> Through each high street.[727] Little I had dispatched[728]
> When all abroad[729] was rumored that this day   1600
> Samson should be brought forth to show the people
> Proof of his mighty strength in feats and games.
> I sorrowed at his captive state, but minded[730]
> Not to be absent at that spectacle.
> The building was a spacious theater[731]
> Half round on two main pillars vaulted high,
> With seats where all the lords and each degree
> Of sort[732] might sit in order to behold.
> The other side was open, where the throng
> On banks[733] and scaffolds under sky might stand.   1610
> I among these aloof[734] obscurely[735] stood.
> The feast and noon grew high, and sacrifice
> Had filled their hearts with mirth, high cheer, and wine,
> When to their sports[736] they turned. Immediately

---

[724] finally, in the end
[725] narration
[726] business
[727] high street = main road
[728] gotten done
[729] all abroad = widely
[730] thought, decided
[731] hall, amphitheater
[732] quality, rank
[733] benches
[734] at a distance
[735] inconspicuous, unnoticed
[736] diversions

Was Samson as a public servant brought,
In their state livery[737] clad. Before him pipes[738]
And timbrels,[739] on each side went armèd guards,
Both horse and foot before him, and behind
Archers, and slingers, cataphracts[740] and spears.
At sight of him the people with a shout   1620
Rifted[741] the air, clamoring[742] their god with praise,
Who had made their dreadful[743] enemy their thrall.[744]
He patient but undaunted where they led him
Came to the place, and what was set before him
Which without help of eye, might be assayed,
To heave, pull, draw, or break, he still performed
All with incredible, stupendous force,
None daring to appear antagonist.[745]
At length for intermission sake they led him
Between the pillars. He his guide requested   1630
(For so from such as nearer stood we heard)
As over-tired to let him lean a while
With both his arms on those two massy pillars
That to the archèd roof gave main support.
He[746] unsuspicious led him, which when Samson
Felt in his arms, with head a while inclined[747]
And eyes fast fixed he stood, as one who prayed,
Or some great matter in his mind revolved.
At last with head erect thus cried aloud,
"Hitherto, lords, what your commands imposed   1640
I have performed, as reason was, obeying,
Not without wonder or delight beheld.
Now of my own accord such other trial[748]
I mean to show you of my strength, yet greater,

---

[737] distinctive clothing, uniform
[738] flutes
[739] tambourines
[740] soldiers in full armor
[741] split
[742] raising an outcry for
[743] fearful, terrible
[744] slave
[745] as opponent/adversary
[746] the guard
[747] bowed
[748] test

As with amaze shall strike all who behold."
This uttered, straining all his nerves[749] he bowed.
As with the force of winds and waters pent[750]
When mountains tremble, those two massy pillars
With horrible convulsion[751] to and fro
He tugged, he shook, till down they came and drew   1650
The whole roof after them, with burst of thunder
Upon the heads of all who sat beneath,
Lords, ladies, captains, councillors, or priests,
Their choice nobility and flower, not only
Of this but each Philistian city round,
Met from all parts to solemnize this feast.
Samson with these immixed,[752] inevitably
Pulled down the same destruction on himself.
The vulgar[753] only scaped, who stood without.[754]

   Chor. O dearly-bought revenge, yet glorious!   1660
Living or dying thou hast fulfilled
The work for which thou wast foretold
To Israel, and now ly'st victorious
Among thy slain, self-killed
Not willingly, but tangled in the fold[755]
Of dire necessity, whose law in death conjoined
Thee with thy slaughtered foes, in number more
Then all thy life had slain before.

   Semichor. While their hearts were jocund[756] and
            sublime,[757]

Drunk with idolatry, drunk with wine   1670
And fat regorged[758] of bulls and goats,
Chanting their idol, and preferring[759]
Before our living Dread who dwells

---

[749] sinews
[750] confined, shut in
[751] wrenching
[752] commingled
[753] common/ordinary people
[754] outside
[755] (1) coils, wrappings, (2) pen, enclosure
[756] happy
[757] proud, lofty
[758] swallowed
[759] preferring him (their idol)

In Silo[760] His bright sanctuary:
Among them He a Spirit of frenzy[761] sent,
Who[762] hurt[763] their minds,
And urged them on with mad desire
To call in haste for their destroyer.
They only set on sport[764] and play
Unweetingly[765] importuned   1680
Their own destruction to come speedy upon them.
So fond[766] are mortal men
Fallen into[767] wrath divine,
As their own ruin on themselves t' invite,
Insensate left, or to sense reprobate,[768]
And with blindness internal struck.
      Semichor. But he though blind of sight,
Despised and thought extinguished quite,
With inward eyes illuminated,
His fiery virtue[769] roused   1690
From under ashes into sudden flame,
And as an ev'ning dragon[770] came,
Assailant on the perchèd roosts
And nests, in order ranged
Of tame villatic[771] fowl, but as an eagle
His cloudless thunder bolted[772] on their heads.
So virtue giv'n for lost,
Depressed,[773] and overthrown (as seemed),
Like that self-begotten bird[774]
In th' Arabian woods embossed,[775]   1700

---

[760] Shiloh
[761] derangement, madness
[762] i.e., the spirit of frenzy
[763] injured
[764] diversion
[765] unknowingly
[766] foolish, stupid
[767] onto
[768] corrupt
[769] powers
[770] serpent
[771] rural, farmhouse
[772] discharged
[773] rendered weak
[774] the phoenix
[775] wrapped

That no second knows nor third,
And lay erewhile a holocaust,[776]
From out her ashy womb now teemed—[777]
Revives, reflourishes, then[778] vigorous most
When most unactive deemed.
And though her body die, her fame survives
(A secular[779] bird) ages of lives.

      Man. Come, come, no time for lamentation now,
Nor much more cause. Samson hath quit[780] himself
Like Samson, and heroically hath finished   1710
A life heroic, on his enemies
Fully revenged, hath left them years of mourning,
And lamentation to the sons of Caphtor[781]
Through all Philistian bounds.[782] To Israel
Honor hath left, and freedom. Let but them
Find courage to lay hold[783] on this occasion—
To himself and father's house[784] eternal fame.
And which is best and happiest yet, all this
With God not parted from him, as was feared,
But favoring and assisting to the end.   1720
Nothing is here for tears, nothing to wail
Or knock the breast, no weakness, no contempt,
Dispraise, or blame, nothing but well and fair,
And what may quiet us in a death so noble.

      Let us go find the body where it lies
Soaked in his enemies' blood, and from the stream
With lavers[785] pure, and cleansing herbs, wash off
The clotted gore.[786] I with what speed the while
(Gaza is not in plight[787] to say us nay)
Will send for all my kindred, all my friends   1730

---

[776] sacrificial fire, complete destruction
[777] brought forth, generated
[778] at the time
[779] long-lived (for centuries)
[780] (1) redeemed, acquitted, (2) ended
[781] original location of the Philistines
[782] (1) boundaries, (2) lands
[783] lay hold = grasp
[784] lineage
[785] vessels of water
[786] dried blood
[787] condition, state

To fetch him hence and solemnly attend
With silent obsequy[788] and funeral train[789]
Home to his father's house. There will I build him
A monument, and plant it round with shade
Of laurel ever green, and branching palm,
With all his trophies hung, and acts enrolled[790]
In copious legend[791] or sweet lyric song.
Thither shall all the valiant youth resort,[792]
And from his memory inflame their breasts
To matchless valor, and adventures high.   1740
The virgins also shall on feastful days
Visit his tomb with flowers, only bewailing
His lot unfortunate in nuptial choice,
From whence captivity and loss of eyes.
    Chor. All is best, though we oft doubt,
What th' unsearchable[793] dispose[794]
Of highest wisdom brings about,
And ever best found in the close.
Oft He seems to hide His face,
But unexpectedly returns—   1750
And to His faithful champion hath in place
Bore witness gloriously. Whence Gaza mourns
And all that band[795] them to resist
His uncontrollable[796] intent,[797]
His servants He with new acquist[798]
Of true experience from this great event
With peace and consolation hath dismissed,[799]
And calm of mind, all passion spent.

---

[788] rites (funereal)
[789] procession
[790] recorded, written
[791] story
[792] come, proceed
[793] inscrutable
[794] disposition
[795] organize [verb]
[796] absolute
[797] will, purpose, pleasure
[798] acquisition
[799] sent away

SUGGESTIONS FOR FURTHER READING

This cannot be more than a brief, more or less representative glimpse of what Carrithers and Hardy (below, at p. 15) call "the prodigious landscape of relevant scholarship." All of the listed books contain useful citations to a much wider portion of the landscape.

EDITIONS OF MILTON

Bush, Douglas, ed. *The Complete Poetical Works of John Milton*. Cambridge: Harvard University Press, 1965 [poetically the most sensitive edition].

Flannagan, Roy, ed. *The Riverside Milton*. Boston: Houghton Mifflin, 1998 [the most capacious edition—1,213 pages, many double-columned—bristling with information: early biographies; poems English and Latin; much prose].

Shawcross, John T., ed. *The Complete English Poetry of John Milton*. New York: Doubleday Anchor, 1963 [handy, inexpensive, far-ranging].

HISTORICAL BACKGROUND

Fallon, Robert Thomas. *Milton in Government*. University Park: Pennsylvania State University Press, 1993.

Hill, Christopher. *The Century of Revolution, 1603–1714*. London: Nelson, 1961. 2nd ed., Sphere paperback, 1972.

————. *Milton and the English Revolution.* New York: Viking, 1977.

————. *The Experience of Defeat: Milton and Some Contemporaries.* New York: Viking, 1984.

————. *The English Bible and the Seventeenth-Century Revolution.* London: Allan Lane, 1993. Penguin, 1994.

LANGUAGE

The Oxford English Dictionary on Historical Principles. 10 vols. Oxford: Oxford University Press, 1933.

LITERARY CRITICISM

Collections

Barker, Arthur E., ed. *Milton: Modern Essays in Criticism.* Oxford: Oxford University Press, 1965.

Danielson, Dennis, ed. *The Cambridge Companion to Milton.* Cambridge: Cambridge University Press, 1989.

Patrides, C. A., and Joseph Wittreich. *The Apocalypse in English Renaissance Thought and Literature.* Ithaca: Cornell University Press, 1984.

Individual Studies

Carrithers, Gale H., and James D. Hardy Jr. *Milton and the Hermeneutic Journey.* Baton Rouge: Louisiana State University Press, 1994.

Ferry, Anne D. *Milton's Epic Voice: The Narrator in Paradise Lost.* Cambridge: Harvard University Press, 1963.

Lewis, C. S. "A Note on *Comus*." In C. S. Lewis, *Studies in Medieval and Renaissance Literature.* Cambridge: Cambridge University Press, 1966.

————. *A Preface to* Paradise Lost. Oxford, Oxford University Press, 1942. Rev. ed., 1960.

Marotti, Arthur F. *Manuscript, Print, and the English Renaissance Lyric*. Ithaca: Cornell University Press, 1995.

Martz, Louis I. *Poet of Exile: A Study of Milton's Poetry*. New Haven: Yale University Press, 1980.

Nicolson, Marjorie Hope. *John Milton: A Reader's Guide to His Poetry*. New York: Farrar, 1963.

Rumrich, John Peter. *Matter of Glory: A New Preface to* Paradise Lost. Pittsburgh: University of Pittsburgh Press, 1987.

Steadman, John M. *The Wall of Paradise: Essays on Milton's Poetics*. Baton Rouge: Louisiana State University Press, 1985.

Stein, Arnold. *The Art of Presence: The Poet and* Paradise Lost. Berkeley: University of California Press, 1977.